BLAC

THE OMNIBUS

Pistolier Reiner Hetzau is in prison for a crime he definitely did commit, it's just that his superiors don't believe his wild claims that the woman he killed was a servant of Chaos. Under threat of death, and with the hangman's noose swinging, Reiner and his fellow prisoners are given one last chance. Unless they agree to work for Count Manfred Valdenheim, doing the Empire's dirty work, they will be executed as common criminals. And so it is that Reiner and the Blackhearts are forced to carry out the most desperate and suicidal secret missions: missions that take them to the wildest parts of the Empire, and pit them against Chaos cultists, ratmen, dark elves, rogue army commanders and more. They fight to preserve their lives, but what they want most is the one thing they can never have: their freedom.

Also by Nathan Long

ORCSLAYER
A Gotrek & Felix novel

More Warhammer omnibuses from the Black Library

GOTREK & FELIX: THE FIRST OMNIBUS
by William King

(Contains the novels
Trollslayer, Skavenslayer and *Daemonslayer*)

GOTREK & FELIX: THE SECOND OMNIBUS
by William King

(Contains the novels
Dragonslayer, Beastslayer and *Vampireslayer*)

GENEVIEVE
by Jack Yeovil

(Contains the novels
Drachenfels, Genevieve Undead, Beasts in Velvet and *Silver Nails*)

THE AMBASSADOR CHRONICLES
by Graham McNeill

(Contains the novels
The Ambassador and *Ursun's Teeth*)

THE KONRAD SAGA
by David Ferring

(Contains the novels
Konrad, Shadowbreed and *Warblade*)

A WARHAMMER OMNIBUS

BLACKHEARTS
THE OMNIBUS

Nathan Long

A Black Library Publication

This omnibus edition published in Great Britain in 2007 by
BL Publishing,
Games Workshop Ltd.,
Willow Road, Nottingham,
NG7 2WS, UK.

10 9 8 7 6 5 4 3 2 1

Cover illustration by Christer Sveen.
Map by Nuala Kinrade.

A CIP record for this book is available from the British Library.

ISBN 13: 978 1 84416 510 0
ISBN 10: 1 84416 510 8

Distributed in the US by Simon & Schuster
1230 Avenue of the Americas, New York, NY 10020, US.

THIS IS A DARK age, a bloody age, an age of daemons and of sorcery. It is an age of battle and death, and of the world's ending. Amidst all of the fire, flame and fury it is a time, too, of mighty heroes, of bold deeds and great courage.

AT THE HEART of the Old World sprawls the Empire, the largest and most powerful of the human realms. Known for its engineers, sorcerers, traders and soldiers, it is a land of great mountains, mighty rivers, dark forests and vast cities. And from his throne in Altdorf reigns the Emperor Karl Franz, sacred descendant of the founder of these lands, Sigmar, and wielder of his magical warhammer.

BUT THESE ARE far from civilised times. Across the length and breadth of the Old World, from the knightly palaces of Bretonnia to ice-bound Kislev in the far north, come rumblings of war. In the towering World's Edge Mountains, the orc tribes are gathering for another assault. Bandits and renegades harry the wild southern lands of the Border Princes. There are rumours of rat-things, the skaven, emerging from the sewers and swamps across the land. And from the northern wildernesses there is the ever-present threat of Chaos, of daemons and beastmen corrupted by the foul powers of the Dark Gods. As the time of battle draws ever near, the Empire needs heroes like never before.

Norsca
Sea of Chaos...
L'Anguille.
Couronne.
The Wasteland.
Marienburg.
Arden forest.
Gisoreux.
Bordeleaux.
Bretonnia
Brionne.
Quenelles.
Loren forest

North of Here Lie The
Dreaded Chaos Wastes.

f Claus

Erengrad.

Here Be Trolls...

Praag.

middle mountains.

lenheim.

Kislev

Kislev.

Wolfenburg.

Talabheim.

The Empire

Altdorf.

Karak Kad

Nuln.

The
Moot.

Sylvania.

Dracken
-hof.

Zhufbar.

ains.

Averheim.

Black
Water.

Black fire Pass.

Karak
Norn.

CONTENTS

AUTHOR'S INTRODUCTION
A Finger In The Eye

WHEN I MOVED out to Hollywood twenty years ago, my 'big idea' was to write traditional action movies with non-traditional heroes. I loved action movies – still do – but I got tired of the heroes. Too many of them were big, square-jawed white guys who ran around like they owned the place and solved all their problems with their fists or their guns – James Bond, Dirty Harry, Commando, Rambo, Batman, Robo-Cop. They were always the biggest, toughest – and here's the important one – the *least human* characters in the movie.

True, there were exceptions, and it was the exceptions that I loved the best. *Aliens, Indiana Jones, Die Hard, The Road Warrior, Southern Comfort* – all starred heroes that had at least some flaws and a few scraps of humanity.

I wanted to take that notion further. I wanted my heroes to be people of average ability but above-average heart – working men, house wives, punk rockers, beat cops, common soldiers, small-time hoods – who were swept up in an extraordinary situation and, because they weren't the best fighters or athletes, and because they didn't have the biggest guns or biceps, had to use their guts and their brains to stay alive and save the day.

Needless to say, I didn't sell too many scripts, but when Black Library asked me to write a novel for them... well, I thought I'd give my 'big idea' another shot.

In his introduction to *The Founding*, the first Gaunt's Ghosts omnibus, Dan Abnett talks about choosing to write about the Imperial Guard because he found them easier to relate to than Space Marines. I had the same problem with Warhammer Fantasy. I loved the grim horror and grimy patina of the Old World, but I didn't want to write about the noble knights of the Empire. I couldn't get inside their heads. To me, they were the same big, square-jawed white guys who bored me to tears in the movies.

How can anyone care about men so brave, and so certain in their beliefs that they never have a moment of fear or doubt. I don't believe these people exist, and if they do, I don't want to know them. They're dangerous to be around, and they're boring to talk to at parties. If you have no fear of the enemy and don't think twice about running into burning buildings to save dewy-eyed children you're not a hero, you're an idiot. A hero, at least in my mind, is the guy who pees his pants when he thinks about the enemy, and is terrified of burning, yet, when faced with the choice of fleeing or doing the right thing, overcomes his fears and runs into the fire.

So I asked Lindsey Priestley, my sainted editor, if the Black Library would let me write about that kind of hero and that kind of heroism – about the Old World equivalents of my working men, house wives, punk rockers, beat cops, common soldiers and small-time hoods, and tell a story about how they conquered their fears and their natural self-centred cowardice to battle and beat the bullies on both sides of the never-ending war. Wonder of wonders, she said yes.

Valnir's Bane, the book that resulted from this meeting of minds, starts off with the oldest cliché in the writer's handy guide to plots – a group of convicts are let out of prison to go on a suicide mission, with the promise of freedom if they succeed. As quite a few people have pointed out to me, it's 'The Dirty Dozen' Warhammer-style. Yes, I did know. Thank you.

So what?

It was the perfect structure on which to hang my kind of story, and feature my kind of people.

Who are the Blackhearts? Over the course of the three books contained in this omnibus edition we meet a noble second son turned failed student and professional gambler, a pair of sly farm boys, a field surgeon with nasty habits, a larcenous mercenary, a construction engineer, a fencing instructor, a quartermaster, a student of botany, and a handful of low-ranking professional soldiers, and many others. There's not a square-jawed hero among them. Of course they have the occasional heroic impulse, but these are surrounded by episodes of villainy, cowardice, self-doubt, self-loathing, self-interest, and plain old stupidity. And they rarely win with their swords. They win with guts, determination and brains – crapping themselves all the while.

There is a precedent for this sort of hero. There was a time in popular culture when the big guy with the big muscles and the big gun who beat everybody up was the bad guy, and the little guy who stood up to him and fought back with brains and heart and guts was the good guy. Those little guys are my idols – Charlie Chaplin outwitting the Keystone Cops, Robin Hood tricking the Sheriff of Nottingham, Bugs Bunny getting the better of Elmer Fudd, Jackie Chan running circles around an army of gangsters, the Marx Brothers talking circles around an army of bureaucrats, David knocking out Goliath with nothing but a rock and a leather strap.

The Blackhearts are the scrappy descendants of these little guys – a band of hard-luck losers caught in a war between monolithic armor-clad behemoths that care not one whit for the survival of the mere mortals scrambling desperately to stay alive beneath their enormous, iron-shod feet. I wanted their stories to be a reminder that, no matter what insignia the behemoths may wear, or what philosophy they may spout, a bully is a bully, and no matter how much they beat you down, as long as you've got one finger left, you can still poke the bastards in the eye.

Nathan Long
Hollywood
2007

PS. Rotten Fruit, the second short story in the collection, which appeared for the first time in *Tales of the Old World*, has been fleshed out with almost two thousand more words, making it a fifth longer and juicier. Enjoy the extra rottenness!

HETZAU'S FOLLIES

Reiner Hetzau watched through the barred window of the camp brig as the hangman tested the trap of the gallows on the parade ground. With the pull of a lever, the trap fell open and a sack of dirt hung from the noose dropped and jerked in a way that made Reiner swallow – then laugh.

He swallowed because he was due for that drop tomorrow morning at dawn before the assembled troops of Count Jurgen's army. He laughed because, after all the foolish things he'd done in his misspent young life, he was to be hung for crimes he had not committed.

Certainly he wasn't entirely blameless in the affair. But when he had recognized his errors and seen the coming horror he had done his best to rectify the situation. In fact, it wouldn't be going too far to say that he had saved the camp, and by extension the whole army, from a plague of Chaos that might have brought down the Empire.

But had they rewarded him? Showered him with titles and lands? No. They had thrown him in the brig with the dregs of the Empire's armies: murderers, deserters, thieves, rapists, profiteers and smugglers, and fitted him for a noose.

He laughed again. To think that three days ago he had been complaining to Hennig – poor Hennig – of boredom. By Ranald, he would give all the gold in the world to be that bored again.

REINER AND HENNIG stood with their feet in the door of Madam Tolshnaya's house of joy, trying to keep her from closing it in their faces. Their breath hung in the air and fat snowflakes pin-wheeled down from the grey sky and clung to their cloaks.

'I assure you, my dear procuress,' said Reiner, 'the paywagon is due tomorrow. We will be able to pay you twice what we owe.'

'You say that last week,' said Madam Tolshnaya, a proud Kislevite beauty of middle years with a nose like a hawk and the curves of an Araby harem dancer.

'But this week it's true,' said Hennig.

'Have a heart,' begged Reiner. 'We are stranded far from home, deprived of all gentle company.' He put an arm around Hennig's shoulder. 'Look at this lonely lad.' Karl was a beardless boy of seventeen, three years Reiner's junior. 'Won't you do your part to raise the spirits of a noble warrior who defends your land from the depredations of Chaos?'

Madam Tolshnaya curled her lip. 'You want spirits raised, raise you some money.' She slammed the door.

Hennig jerked his foot back in time, but Reiner wasn't so quick. The door caught his toe and he hopped around on his bad leg, hissing and cursing in the muddy street. He flung himself onto a wooden bench outside the tavern next door to Madam Tolshnaya's, groaning. 'Any more of that Samogon, Hennig?' he asked.

Hennig joined him and handed him his flask. 'Just a swallow.'

Reiner gulped down the potent Kislevite liquor, wincing as it burned its way to his empty stomach. 'Good lad. I'll fill this again tomorrow, when...'

'When the paywagon comes,' finished Hennig dryly.

They sat for a while in the lazily falling snow, watching the endless river of shabby refugees who were crowding into the town, fleeing the devastation in the north, from Praag, Erengrad and little hamlets too numerous to name, all razed to the ground by the unstoppable hordes of Chaos.

That was why Reiner and Hennig were here on the Empire's border with Kislev. Noble sons, like most pistoliers, they had come up with Von Stolmen's Pistols from Whitgart only two weeks ago, attached to Count Jurgen's army. Upon arrival, they had been sent instantly to the front without a chance to recover from the long march, and thrown into a fierce action against mounted marauders at Kirstaad. What a mess that had been. No briefing. No orders. Just in at a gallop and every man for himself. The pistols, light cavalry meant to wheel, fire and retire, had been forced to stand and fight like armoured knights when a troop of halberdiers broke before a Chaos charge and blundered willy-nilly into their line of retreat.

Reiner and Hennig had both been wounded in the hard-fought withdrawal; Reiner with a gash in his thigh – and hadn't that bled like a river – Karl with a handful of broken fingers. After the battle they had been declared unfit to fight, and sent back to Vulsk with the other wounded, where the army was quartered, to recover from their wounds.

Now, two weeks later, with his wound only a throbbing annoyance, Reiner was going stir crazy. Vulsk, like border towns the world over, had its share of diversions: brothels, taverns and bear pits, even a crude little inn-yard theatre where broad slap-sticks were performed, but nearly all had been commandeered by the army for officers' quarters, stock rooms and stables. Every space with four walls and a roof was packed with counts and their retinues, knightly orders with their grooms, cooks and servants, companies of greatswords, crossbowmen and pistoliers and engineers with barrels of volatile substances, as well as assorted priests of Sigmar and Morr, and their acolytes. And what space the army disdained was crawling with refugees: starving peasants huddled in the lees of buildings, desperate merchants standing guard over mud-spattered wagons, thread-bare Kislevite cavalry tented with their horses on frozen stubble fields. There wasn't room in town to swing a cat, not that there were cats to swing, for food was scarce, and many was the peasant Reiner had seen eating cat, rat or his own shoe leather and calling it dinner.

But even if the army and the refugees hadn't been in residence, and all the town's entertainments open for business, Reiner and

Hennig still wouldn't have been able to partake, for they were flat broke. Reiner had not lied to Madam Tolshnaya. The pay-wagon was due the next day, just as it had been due a week previous, when a party of raiders had ambushed it and made off with everything. The army hadn't been paid in a fortnight, and the meagre allowance Reiner's miserly father had reluctantly doled out to him before he left home was long gone.

'By Sigmar, Hennig,' said Reiner. 'I am damned tired of this poverty.'

'As am I,' agreed Hennig. 'I wonder how the poor stand it.'

'I'm a man of the world,' said Reiner, gesturing grandly. 'I need sophisticated diversion. Music, poetry, stimulating company, food worthy of the name.'

'Eh?' said Hennig, affronted. 'You don't find me stimulating company?'

'Not below the waist, lad. Terribly sorry.'

Hennig guffawed. 'You cut me to the quick.'

Reiner rested his chin on his palm. 'How to make some money? There's no looting to be done.' He waved at the shambling river of refugees. 'These poor wretches have nothing, and the campaign will be over before we're allowed back to the front. No chance at battlefield trophies or Chaos curios to sell to "men of learning." Even selling my armour wouldn't buy enough for a night's drinking. Sigmar curse my father's skinflint heart. He wouldn't pay for new kit. Hand-me-downs he gives me. A bunch of dented tin an orc wouldn't go to battle in.'

'What about dice?' asked Hennig. 'Didn't you tell me you once made your living at the tables?'

'One needs a stake to enter a game,' said Reiner defensively. He didn't care to mention that he'd lost his taste for gaming during the hurried retreat from Kirstaad, when he'd also lost his 'special' dice.

There was a commotion across the street. Reiner and Hennig looked up. An Empire foot patrol had stopped three carts crowded with prostrate forms – sick soldiers by their moans and shivers. The drivers didn't look much better than their passengers, slack jawed, rheumy-eyed fellows. The only member of the party who seemed at all alert was a woman on the lead cart. She was a slim waif in the robes of a Sister of Shallya, goddess of mercy and healing.

The captain of the patrol was Deiter Ulstaadt, a pompous fool whom Reiner knew well. He was an 'unbribable' who had broken up some of Reiner's recent money-making schemes: the card parlour in the powder magazine, the conscript prize fights, the sale in charms for protection against Chaos. Reiner leaned forward to listen.

'It is out of the question,' Deiter was saying. 'You'll have to take them elsewhere.'

'But, my lord,' said the priestess, 'they can go no further. They are very ill.'

'Precisely the point, sister,' said Deiter. 'With the town so full and our hospitals overflowing, disease spreads like wildfire. We need no more fuel for the blaze.'

The sister looked about to weep. Reiner's heart went out to her. The poor thing seemed crushed by her responsibilities.

'Sir knight,' she said, 'will you truly turn away noble heroes of the Empire, struck down in the fight of Chaos?'

'I have my orders, miss.'

'Could you not relax them for pity's sake? Our convent was not wealthy, but in the wake of its burning, I have been entrusted with its treasury. I know the lot of a soldier far from home is a hard one...' She moved the skirts of her habit aside to reveal a silver chased casket under her seat.

Deiter held up a hand, his face reddening. 'In light of your desperation, sister, I will forget this if you turn about now and leave here peaceably.'

The priestess of Shallya hung her head, and Reiner thought he saw a not very Shallyan snarl twitch her lips as she motioned her drivers to turn the carts around. Deiter marched away with his squad, no doubt to find some poor innocent to harass.

Reiner sat up, mashed toes forgotten. 'Hennig, my lad,' he said. 'If that wasn't the hand of Ranald dropping golden opportunity in our laps, I'm a ratman.'

'You mean to steal that box of swag?'

'Don't be crude. Of course not. She's going to give it to us.'

Reiner and Hennig stepped into the crowded street where the priestess's caravan of casualties was still manoeuvring.

'Reverend sister,' called Reiner. 'I couldn't help overhearing your poor treatment at the hands of that oaf, and I think I may have a solution that could benefit us both.'

The priestess, who was quite attractive, in a pale, drawn sort of way, looked nervously over her shoulder. 'I have no wish to break the law, my lord.'

'Oh, pish,' said Reiner smoothly. 'Is it a just law that turns out the sick? If you can pay a little for rent, and... ah, the efforts of your humble servant, the law won't enter into it.'

The woman sighed, relieved. 'The blessings of Shallya upon you, my lord.'

A warm glow filled Reiner's heart. 'My thanks, sister. Wait but a moment, and I will arrange all.'

'ABSOLUTE NO!' SAID Madam Tolshnaya, crossing her arms over her ample chest. 'This clean house. I want no sickness here. Bad for business.'

'But madam,' said Reiner, 'there is no need to put them in the house. Are not your stables vacant? Kuryev and his Eagles certainly don't need them anymore.'

'You speak so of the dead?'

'I meant no disrespect. The tale of their valiant sacrifice will be sung in the halls of the boyars for generations, but they have left a vacancy, have they not?'

'Not for sick peoples.'

'Madam.' Reiner lowered his voice conspiratorially. 'The sister carries the treasury of her convent with her. You could charge her double, perhaps triple.'

Madam Tolshnaya's eyes narrowed. 'Triple?'

'And I would ask only a fifth, for bringing the business your way.'

'Only a fifth,' said Madam Tolshnaya dryly. But Reiner could see her calculating. At last she nodded. 'Yes. Is good. Bring around back, so nobody see. And they no come in house, ever!'

'Of course not, madam,' said Reiner, bowing. 'You won't regret this.'

He strode back to the street, grinning. Money at last!

IT WASN'T EASY money. The invalids were more diseased than Reiner could have imagined. In fact, he had a hard time believing men so ill could still be alive. Most were carried into the stables on planks, and even those who could walk shambled like sleepwalkers and were covered in purple pustules. One little fellow, a Kislevite with long moustaches and an enormous hat of snow leopard fur decorated with a gold and red cockade, had an open wound in his arm that crawled with maggots. They were laid down one to a stall on either side of the stable's central aisle.

Reiner stood well upwind of them as he accepted from the priestess, who introduced herself as Sister Anyaka, a small purse of reikmarks and jewels. He palmed it quickly. It wouldn't do to let Madam Tolshnaya see the transaction. Not when she had already paid him.

THAT NIGHT, AT one of Vulsk's better taverns – which meant only that the floor was stone and not dirt, and that they burned wood and not yak dung in the fireplace – Reiner and Hennig toasted their good fortune with mugs of samogon bought with the sister's gold.

'It gives one a warm feeling, Hennig, doing good,' said Reiner.

'Absholutely,' said Hennig, well on his way to inebriation. 'Burns all the way down.'

Reiner wiped his mouth. 'There's nothing more gratifying than charity. Particularly when it pays so well.'

'Poor li'l sister,' said Hennig. 'Tendin' all those sickies. How does she stand the shmell?'

'That's what religion is for, lad.'

'It takes away the shmell?'

'No. Just makes you feel noble for bearing it. To your health.'

'And to yers.'

THE NEXT MORNING, with heads that felt full of burning rocks, Reiner and Hennig returned to Madam Tolshnaya's to see if there was anymore milking to be done. By Reiner's estimation, the jewelled casket Sister Anyaka was carrying was still two-thirds full. But as the two friends walked around the brothel to the stables, Madam Tolshnaya stormed out to intercept them.

'She not keep them in stables!' she cried.

Reiner clutched his aching head. 'Say again, madam? Quietly, if you please.'

'The sick men. They walk around in middle of night. Scare my girls.'

'Ridiculous,' said Reiner. 'Those lads can barely crawl.'

'Svetya say she see sick man limp out back gate.'

'Most likely a drunk soldier,' said Hennig. 'Off to make yellow snow.'

'You're jumping at shadows,' added Reiner.

'Well,' said the madam sulkily, 'you tell shadows I want more money.'

They left her and knocked on the stable door. After a moment the sister opened it.

Reiner bowed. 'Good morning, sister. I trust the accommodations are adequate?'

'Most satisfactory, my lord.'

'I am gratified to hear it. We came to ask if there was anything else you required.'

The priestess frowned. 'Er, there are two things, but I hesitate to ask. One is less than pleasant.'

'We are yours to command,' said Reiner.

The woman bit her lip. 'Well, the first thing is easy enough.' She pulled a piece of parchment from her robe. 'Only take this to a wise woman and purchase these medicines. It is the second that may tax you. One of my patients is beyond my abilities to cure. He has a problem of the liver and needs the care of a surgeon. If you could get him to the infirmary of your camp, all would be well. The trouble is that he is a Kislevite.'

Reiner sucked air through his teeth. 'Mmm, yes. That is difficult. The doctors are a bit strict about who they let in. I'd have to ask a few people to look the other way, which might require further applications of cash.'

'Oh, certainly,' said the priestess. She opened the purse at her belt and pulled out a handful of coins, rings and brooches. 'Will this be enough?'

Reiner elbowed Hennig in the ribs, for the lad was gaping. 'Oh yes, this should do,' he said nonchalantly.

HALF AN HOUR later, Reiner and Hennig were laughing and slapping one another on the back as they rode from the

Empire camp on the cart with which they had delivered the sick man to the infirmary.

'A bit difficult, he says,' giggled Hennig. 'It was all I could do to keep a straight face.'

'Well you did, lad. There's more to be had from that fountain. We wouldn't want to spoil things. The girl's the easiest mark I've ever laid eyes upon.'

It had cost Reiner and Hennig exactly four silver pfennigs to purchase a uniform of the Talabheim Pike from a black marketeer, and while dressing the sick man in it and shaving his Kislevite moustaches had been less than pleasant experiences – he smelled awful and complained constantly that he was infested with daemons – the effort was worth it, for the rest had been easy. They had delivered him to the infirmary, left him and a description of his symptoms with an orderly, and rode away again with no questions asked and the golden contents of Reiner's purse untouched.

'Now,' said Reiner cheerily, 'let's go get the shopping done, and retire to Madam Tolshnaya's for a much-deserved reward.'

But the second task proved more difficult. Even finding a wise woman was a chore. The villagers they asked wouldn't even admit that the town had a wise woman, insisting that they were modern people just like their Empire neighbours.

Reiner was confused by this attitude, attributing it first to anxiety over being thought inferior, but the words weren't said defensively, but with a sullen furtiveness. At last Reiner realised that the townsfolk were afraid he was a Sigmarite witch finder, looking to hang their local dispenser of love charms for witchcraft.

The response changed instantly when he asked instead, in the hesitant and embarrassed voice of a schoolboy, if there was someone who sold talismans for protection against lover's pox. Then he was told, with smirks and elbow nudges, to go see old Mother Yagna. She would put everything right.

Reiner and Hennig found the wise woman in a thatch-roofed shack outside a small fishing village just a few leagues down the river road. She was a short, frog-faced old crone in colourful rags who scuttled between towering jar-lined shelves, a clay stove and her mortar and pestle with the activity of a spider. She was less suspicious than the villagers. It was obvious she was used to soldiers seeking her out for protections against hangovers, pox and unfriendly arrows, but her demeanour changed abruptly when she glanced at Anyaka's list.

She looked up at them sharply. 'You be murder somebody?'

'I beg your pardon?' said Reiner.

She waved a gnarled hand at the paper. 'These very dangerous. Make you sick. This one poison. This one...' She hesitated. 'Bad magic.'

'Ridiculous,' said Reiner. 'These were ordered by a Sister of Shallya, sworn to preserve life, not take it.'

The wise woman grunted. 'Huh. She got rats, this sister?'

'Undoubtedly. She's staying in a stables. Would this kill rats?'

The crone chuckled. 'Oh sure. Plenty rats.' But she made no move toward her jars and bottles, only continued looking at Anyaka's list.

'I don't mean to rush you, woman,' said Reiner impatiently. 'But we have many things to do today.'

Mother Yagna pursed her lips and held out the list. 'Am sorry. I have not these things. I cannot help you.'

'Foolish old crone,' said Reiner, losing patience. 'Do you dare defy me?'

Reiner loomed over the woman menacingly. She smelled of turnips and bitter herbs. 'Listen, witch. You exist here at the mercy of the Empire, which has so far turned a blind eye to your heathen hedge magics. But it could just as easily go hard on you if you were accused of consorting with daemons, if someone were to say you'd been kissing the enemy's fundament by the light of the full moon. Do you understand me?'

Mother Yagna met his eye with an unblinking glare. She said nothing.

'Now, I am a fair man,' Reiner continued, 'I care not what two pfennig wart charms you fob off on ignorant peasants. I only want what I know you have, and I am willing to pay for it. Look!' He shook his purse. It jingled impressively. 'I will give you ten times what your leaves and twigs are worth. Only fill the order and let me be on my way.'

The old woman's expression hardened to stone. She turned without a word and began filling packets of dry leaves with powders and herbs. By the time she had finished, a hard knot of remorse had formed in Reiner's chest. He had no compunctions about getting what he wanted through guile, but intimidation of the weak wasn't his way. It had no finesse. Consequently, when he dipped into his purse to pay her, he took out more than he intended, letting fall on her table a handful of coins and jewels.

'Here, mother,' he said. 'May this soothe your pride.'

The old woman sneered. 'I no want your...' She stopped, staring. With trembling hands she picked up a ring. 'Where you get this?' she demanded.

'Curse your insolence,' snarled Reiner. 'Why should I...'

'Graverobber!' The old woman advanced on Reiner, eyes wild. 'This ring of boyar of village. Give him by Queen Katarin herself. He die fighting at Praag. You dig him up! You steal his ring!'

'Madam,' said Reiner, 'I assure you...'

'I know you now!' she interrupted. 'You no Imperial. You Chaos! Beast of Chaos!'

'Madam, please. Contain yourself.'

The old woman scooped up the coins and jewels and hurled them at Reiner and Hennig. The two pistoliers ran, ducking out of the door.

HALFWAY BACK TO Vulsk, Hennig turned to Reiner, who sat lost in thought next to him on the buckboard of the cart.

'She didn't say it was for rats.'

'Hmmm?' Reiner lifted his chin off his palm.

'The sister. She didn't say the stuff was for rats. She said it was medicine.'

'I know that, lad,' said Reiner.

'But then why did you say...'

'I was only trying to ease things along.' He laughed harshly at that.

Hennig frowned. 'So then, do you think the witch was right?'

'Of course not! The witch is an ignorant peasant. She is doubtless unaware of the higher curative properties of her so-called poisons.' But Reiner was less than sanguine. If the business with the boyar's ring had been an isolated incident, he might have laughed it off as the crazed imaginings of a demented crone, but the ring, on top of the revelation of the poisons, and Madam Tolshnaya's grumblings about the priestess's patients going bump in the night, it was all beginning to gnaw on him.

Reiner stole alone into the stables. Hennig was buying samogon for the both of them in the tavern next door.

'Sister Anyaka?' Reiner called. 'Sister, I would speak with you!' He glared around in the dim interior, looking for the priestess. He wished instantly that he hadn't entered. The smell was horrific, and the moans of the sick men fell unpleasantly on the ear. He could only barely make out their forms in the stalls, and was glad of it, but found that he was oddly distressed that he didn't see the little fellow with the snow leopard hat.

Sister Anyaka hurried out of the tack room at the back of the stable. 'Master Hetzau, is all well?'

'That you shall have to tell me, lady,' said Reiner stiffly. 'I have just... Er, could we talk outside. It's a bit, er...'

'Certainly,' said the priestess. 'I am used to the smell, but I understand completely.'

She led him into the yard. The afternoon sun had melted the morning's snow and there was a dry bench against the stable wall. They sat.

'Tell me, my lord,' said Anyaka, turning to Reiner. 'What is troubling you?'

Now that he came to it, Reiner was suddenly less certain about things. The young woman looked so innocent that he found his suspicions melting away. 'Er, well, er... I say, where's the little fellow with the big hat? The snow leopard hat.'

Anyaka looked confused a moment. 'Oh, you must mean Ulenko. He's getting some air.'

'Is he now? You surprise me. I wouldn't have thought he could even sit up.'

The priestess frowned. 'My lord, I can't believe you've called on me to ask after the health of one of my patients. What is wrong?'

Reiner's face fell. 'Forgive me. It's just a bit... Well, you see, I had a most awkward encounter with the wise woman you asked me to find. She recognized a ring you gave me and accused me of robbing her boyar's grave to get it. Most disturbing. And I was wondering...'

Anyaka put a soft hand on his arm. 'You poor man,' she said. 'To be harangued so on a mission of mercy. I only wish I had been there to explain to the woman.' She looked at him sadly. Her eyes were green, with the depth of the ocean. 'She was indeed correct. The ring's owner was a boyar from near here. I curse myself for not thinking of the distress it might cause.'

She touched a hand to her chest. 'You see, our mission was just outside of Praag. We took in many of the dying during the battle, and many, being devout men, bequeathed to us their possessions as thanks for the comfort we gave them in their final hours. When...' She paused, and a shiver passed though her. 'When the raiders overran the convent, I brought the treasury and those I could save south to continue Shallya's work here.' She looked up at him again, eyes moist. 'Have I explained things to your satisfaction, my lord?'

'Oh, yes. Absolutely,' said Reiner, blushing. He felt horrible, having asked such a question of so virtuous a woman. 'I crave your forgiveness.'

'You require none.' She put her hand on his. A warm thrill shot through him. 'Anyone might have thought the same.'

'Nonetheless...'

'And I wish,' she said, leaning forward so that the fabric of her habit tightened against the swell of her breasts, 'that since you are obviously a man who cares little for gold, there were some other way I might repay you for your trouble.'

Reiner's heart thudded audibly in his chest and perspiration sprung out on his brow. The priestess traced the veins of his hand with a delicate finger. 'The sisterhood of Shallya is dedicated to relieving suffering in all its forms,' she said softly. 'And I sense, Master Hetzau, that you are suffering from loneliness, that you are ill from want.'

'Sister,' said Reiner hoarsely, and took her by the shoulders. She stopped him with a hand on his chest.

'Forgive me, my lord. It would be an honour – nay a pleasure – to tend to your needs, but the needs of my patients are greater, and there are things I must do before I can give you the attention you deserve.'

'How soon will you be done?' asked Reiner curtly. He couldn't remember when he had been so filled with desire.

The priestess smiled. 'Well, I'll be done the sooner, if you will once again assist me.'

'Anything,' said Reiner, licking his lips. 'Anything.'

'THE LENGTHS YOU will go to get your wick waxed will be the death of me,' growled Hennig as they again manoeuvred the cart through the teaming town. 'Sigmar's oxter, what a stench.'

'Don't blaspheme, Hennig,' said Reiner. 'We do holy work.'

'But you're the only one who'll be getting a reward.'

'Now, lad. It isn't as if you've lost on the deal. I convinced the sister to give us more gold, as well as, er, intangibles.'

'I'm not sure if it's worth it.'

This time the cart's cargo was two corpses, reeking of death and disease, and covered in lesions and festering boils. Anyaka had tried her best, she said, but the two men – a handgunner from Nuln and a Kislevite lancer – had slipped through her fingers. She had asked Reiner to dispose of the corpses: the handgunner to the army's priest of Morr, who operated the camp mortuary on the west side of town, and the Kislevite to the village's cemetery on the east, where the priests incorporated local customs into the ceremonies.

It was not a pleasant task. Even in the cold, the smell was overwhelming, and Hennig, stomach still delicate after the previous night's revels, had had to jump off the cart and vomit before they'd travelled half a league. But eventually they reached their first stop, the camp mortuary. Erected a discreet distance from the camp itself, it consisted of a few low black tents, one of which was a consecrated temple of Morr. A small, wood-framed shack sat behind it, which housed the furnace that cremated the dead. Tall stacks of firewood were piled next to this, and stacks of bodies, almost as high, were piled in front of the temple. The smell that drifted from them was the first thing to drown out the stench of the bodies Reiner and Hennig carried. Black-robed acolytes of Morr crawled over the mounds like flies over carrion, preparing the corpses and taking them into the black canvas temple.

A burly acolyte with his sleeves folded back approached them as they trundled up.

'What have you there, my lords?' he asked.

'A citizen of Nuln,' said Reiner. 'Name unknown. And a Kislevite who we take to the local temple.'

'Very good, my lord,' said the man, turning to whistle at two acolytes who wore heavy gloves and kerchiefs over their faces. 'Though there'll be a wait until we can see to him properly.'

Reiner surveyed the mounds as the masked acolytes lifted the body off the cart, 'Does the war truly go so poorly?'

'T'aint the war, my lord. It's sickness. Last day or so they been dropping like flies. Don't know why.'

'Most disturbing.'

'Yes, sir.'

IT WAS DUSK. Shopkeeps were boarding up their storefronts and taverns were hanging out lanterns. As they rode through town to drop off the second body Reiner and Hennig noticed a commotion in the town square. Villagers were using ropes to haul something out of the well, and just as Reiner pulled abreast, the men succeeded in getting it over the lip. It flopped to the street with a wet smack. It was a body, so bloated as to be unrecognizable. What was readily apparent however, was that the fellow had been terribly sick before he fell in. Though his waterlogged skin was the colour and consistency of gruel, Reiner could see black gangrenous wounds all over it.

'That accounts for the wave of illness,' he said.

'Good thing we only drink samogon,' said Hennig.

Reiner was urging the carthorse forward again when a villager fished something else out of the well. At first Reiner thought it was a drowned cat, but then he saw it was a large Kislevite hat of snow leopard fur, pinned with a red and gold cockade.

'Damn and blast!'

'What's the matter?' asked Hennig.

Reiner geed the cart horse into a trot. 'That hat! Getting some air, was he? Ranald curse the woman!' he cried.

'Who?' asked Hennig. 'The sister? Why are you angry at her?'

'Because if she's up to what I think she's up to, I won't be getting my "heavenly reward" this evening.'

Reiner drove the cart as fast as he could, which wasn't very fast. The streets were as crowded as ever with refugees, and Reiner spent as much time bawling at lollygaggers to get out of his way as he did moving forward. They were just three blocks from Madam Tolshnaya's and moving well at last when Reiner heard Hennig gasp.

'Reiner!' he said. 'Reiner, look! The corpse!'

Reiner glanced behind him and froze at the sight that met his eyes.

The Kislevite had been a trim, well muscled warrior in life. Now his abdomen was more bloated than that of the fellow who had drowned in the well. He looked like he'd swallowed a hogshead of Marienburg Ale whole. His belly was taut as a drum head; so tight that the skin was splitting. But that wasn't the worst of it. The balloon of flesh bulged and squirmed like a sack full of rats.

Reiner pulled on the reins and brought the cart to a juddering stop, then turned, staring.

'What is it?' asked Hennig. 'I've heard corpses fill with gas when they–'

His sentence went unfinished, for with a horrible wet pop, the body's stomach erupted in a shower of rotting flesh and putrid viscera. Reiner and Hennig recoiled, instinctively covering their faces as they were spattered with clots of stinking flesh. Choking and blinded, they didn't at first notice that, mixed in with the reeking ejecta, were small snot-coloured creatures that skittered over the cart on tiny, malformed legs.

The first Reiner knew of them was when one sank needle-like teeth through his boot into the flesh of his calf. He yelped and knocked it to the ground. His hand came away smeared with slime. Another bit his left toe. More climbed Hennig's legs. He plucked them off, gagging.

The street, a narrow way lined with tanneries and low taverns, was crowded with idle soldiers, street-hawkers and sisters of joy. The slimy vermin leapt off the cart into that river of humanity like fleas, biting and clawing, and the normal street chatter was replaced by bellows of pain and surprise. A roiling knot of victims twisted and swatted at the miniature horrors, looking for all the world as if they performed some strenuous dance. It would have been ludicrous were it not for the unfortunate soul, who fell, screaming, with eyes plucked out and veins chewed open to the muddy ground.

'What are they?' wailed Hennig, trying to knock one loose with his sabre.

'Nurglings!' said Reiner, snatching one off his shoulder and hurling it away. 'Revolting little beasts, aren't they? Ow!' He stomped on one that was biting his ankle.

Recovering from their initial shock, soldiers lounging outside nearby taverns rushed forward, swinging swords and stabbing with daggers. Reiner and Hennig jumped down and joined them.

'Second time today,' said a crossbowman. 'Things just like this attacked the camp hospital not two hours ago. Killed a score of wounded before we put 'em down.'

Reiner frowned at this news, but a nurgling jumped on his leg and he had to attend to it.

The tide was turning when a young guardsman, riding past at a gallop, reined up sharply. 'What happens here?' he demanded, breathless.

'Nurglings,' said Hennig, still swatting. 'Corpse was full of them.'

'Sigmar preserve us,' said the guard, making the sign of the Hammer. 'It's an infestation. The same thing happened at the mortuary. I ride to inform Captain Ulstaadt. Now I shall have two tales to tell.'

'The mortuary?' said Reiner, but the boy had already spurred away. Reiner's stomach sank like he had swallowed lead shot. 'Hennig!' he called, climbing onto the cart. 'Mount up.' He pushed the exploded corpse off the cart with his boot, then grabbed the reins as Hennig swung up to the buck board beside him. Reiner slapped the reins across the horse's rump and they were off at a trot.

It was full dark when they reached Madam Tolshnaya's, and the evening's festivities were already in full swing. Drunk troopers staggering in and out, arm in arm, singing bawdy songs. Knights intent on breaking their knightly vows ducked in discreetly, the badges of their orders hidden under plain cloaks. Fiddles and flutes mixed with feminine laughter behind the glowing mullioned windows. But though those sights and sounds would normally have made Reiner green with envy, tonight he was too angry to pay them any mind. He disliked being beaten at his own game. He was nobody's dupe. Nobody's.

He slewed the cart into the yard behind the brothel, scattering protesting soldiers as he went, and reined up with a skidding of hooves and a skittering of wheels. Drawing their sabres, he and Hennig leapt off the cart before it had come to a full stop and kicked in the stable door.

The long room was dark and silent, but smelled like a charnel house. Reiner and Hennig clapped hands over their faces, retching. At first they could see nothing, but soon their eyes adjusted. Anyaka's patients lay in their stalls as before, but seemed now very still – too still. Reiner and Hennig could hear no breathing or movement. All sound was lost in a constant low buzzing.

'What's that?' whispered Hennig through his fingers.

Reiner swallowed thickly. 'Flies, lad.'

The patients were dead, all of them. Reiner wondered with a prickle of dread if he had ever seen them alive, if they had all along been corpses, animated by some foul magic.

A faint orange glow emanated from the tack room. He put a finger to his lips and they tiptoed down the aisle, trying unsuccessfully to breathe without smelling. As they reached the tack room door the death stench mixed with another scent: a sweet, cloying mildew odour over a thick fecal reek that burned the eyes. They looked in the door.

Kneeling with her eyes closed behind a brazier of coals was Anyaka, but not the sweet Anyaka Reiner and Hennig knew. She had thrown open her priestess's habit, revealing her small but sinewy body, which glistened in the heat of the coals. At first Reiner thought that the swirling designs and eldritch symbols that covered her body – and which were echoed by others painted upon the tack room's wooden walls – were tattoos, but looking again, he realised, with a heaving of nausea, that they were deep cuts sliced into her skin, black with necrosis.

Over the brazier's coals sat a frying pan in which bubbled a viscous green stew. Prehensile tendrils of steam rose from it to caress Anyaka's nakedness obscenely.

As Reiner and Hennig watched, the priestess added to the stew from the packets Reiner had purchased for her, then ran her finger inside the cuts in her breast and abdomen and flicked into the pan the pus she gathered there. Fetid steam billowed up from the soup.

Hennig choked as the noxious cloud overwhelmed them. Anyaka's eyes flashed open. 'Defilers!' she cried. 'The ritual must not be interrupted!'

'Oh, but it must, lass,' said Reiner, advancing. 'Now back away from that fire.'

Anyaka did just that, but rather quicker than Reiner expected. She leapt up, snatched a dagger from her robe, and pulled a whip from a peg on the wall.

'Charge her!' cried Reiner. He and Hennig ran around the brazier. But as they did, Anyaka leapt over it and dashed out of the door. Reiner turned and ran after her, but Hennig paused.

'Wait, Hetz.' He kicked the frying pan. It slid off the brazier and splashed to the ground. Hennig jumped to avoid the spray and joined Reiner at the door.

'Good thinking, boyo,' said Reiner. 'Now quick, before she gets too far.'

But as they ran into the stables they saw Anyaka was standing near the door, hands raised. 'Servants of Nurgle, come forth and slay these unbelievers!' she called.

Reiner and Hennig slowed, looking around uneasily, half expecting daemons to materialise out of thin air. Reiner smirked when nothing happened. 'You seem to have an exaggerated opinion of your powers, lass.'

He and Hennig advanced on her again, but faint sounds to their left and right made them pause. It was a creaking, stretching noise, like leather being pulled taut. Their eyes settled on the body in the stall nearest them. Its stomach was swelling like a bladder filling with air. Reiner glanced at the stall opposite. That body too was swelling.

'Oh gods,' he groaned.

A wet pop sounded from the darkness, and another, followed by a horrible chittering and rustling. The body on their left exploded, showering them with rotten flesh as mucus-covered nurglings spewed from its stomach. The body on the right followed like an echo.

'Sigmar save us,' quavered Hennig. 'So many.'

'Forget 'em, lad.' said Reiner, starting forward. 'Get their mistress.'

He and Hennig ran at the sorceress, while corpses exploded left and right. But before they'd closed half the distance, Hennig cried out and fell.

Reiner stopped. Hennig was clutching his boot and screaming. Reiner looked down. Hennig's boot was falling apart. Where splashings of Anyaka's brew had touched it, the leather was eaten away, and the flesh beneath it boiled with blisters that split and popped as if Hennig's foot was on fire.

Hennig's shrieks grew louder. His hands, having touched his boots, were blistering as well. 'Stop it, Reiner! Make it stop!'

'Lad, I…'

Anyaka laughed. Reiner looked up. The sorceress was stepping into the yard and closing the door behind her.

'Foul witch!' he cried, but there was no time for curses. Out of the darkness a seething carpet of nurglings was converging on them.

'Hang on, lad.' Reiner grabbed Hennig under the arms and dragged him as fast as he could toward the closed door. It wasn't fast enough. A nurgling leapt on Reiner's back. Three climbed up his legs. Another bit into his arm. They were crawling over Hennig like roaches. The boy swatted at them weakly, but they only bit his hands.

A nurgling clawed Reiner's neck. He dropped Hennig involuntarily and flung the little beast away. Hennig instantly disappeared under the wave of vermin. Reiner tried to pull him out, but nurglings swarmed around him, biting and scratching him to the bone. He roared with rage and pain and was forced to leap onto a parked draycart, stamping his feet and scraping with dagger and sabre to dislodge the beasts that clung to him. He was bleeding all over.

'Reiner!' shrieked Hennig, his voice unrecognizable in his terror. 'Reiner, save me!'

Hennig was but a thrashing mound under the madly squirming forms. An arm shot up out of the mass, clawing the air. It was stripped, only a few pink scraps hanging from wet bones. Then the arm sank again, falling apart as it dropped. The little daemons had even eaten the cartilage.

Reiner's throat constricted. His friend was gone, who had moments before been a laughing, skirt-chasing lad with a contagious smile. 'Hennig... Karl. I... Gods, what am I to tell your mother?'

A nurgling bit his foot. Reiner yelped and danced back. No time for grief. The little daemons were swarming up the cart's wheels. Reiner looked around desperately. He was too far from the door to run for it. The nurglings would bring him down before he got halfway there. He couldn't kill them all. He was no Sigmar, and nurglings were much smaller targets than orcs. If only he had wings.

The thought made him glance up, and his heart flooded with new hope. The hayloft had a small door, directly over the main door. Reiner leapt up, caught a crossbeam, and clambered up to the loft. A few nurglings came with him, clinging to his boots, and he rolled and kicked, twitching and biting back screams, until he had crushed the tenacious vermin into red paste.

The others didn't give up. Hearing a scrabbling, he looked down. The nurglings were climbing the posts, digging their needle-sharp claws into the wood. Reiner hurried to the loft door and pushed it open. In the yard below, Anyaka listened at the stable door, belting her robe. Reiner smiled. Here was an opportunity not to be missed.

He leapt down, slashing with his sabre.

It was not quite the devastating attack he envisaged. First, he misjudged his leap, and jarred his sword arm against the wall as he dropped, so that while he knocked Anyaka flat, he missed her utterly with his sword. Second, he had forgotten his wounded leg. He grunted in pain as he landed on it and fell flat on his back.

Anyaka was up instantly, advancing with dagger and whip.

Reiner raised his sabre. 'Sorry, lass. Your ceremony will remain unfinished while I live.'

She smiled, her eyes focusing behind him. 'That won't be long.'

Reiner glanced back. The stable doors were swinging out, pushed open by a mass of nurglings spilling into the yard like a river breaking through a dam.

'Your doom is upon you,' laughed Anyaka.

Reiner cursed and scrambled painfully to his feet. 'At least you won't live to rejoice in it.' He lunged at her and cut her shoulder.

She yelped and ran, trying to angle toward to the street, but Reiner blocked her way, slashing again. The nurglings swarmed toward them, their little eyes glinting in the lamp light like jewels.

Anyaka wheeled for the brothel's back door and disappeared into the kitchen. Reiner was behind her, limping madly.

The nurglings were right behind him.

ANYAKA AND REINER crashed through the narrow kitchen, frightening the Kislevite cook and the half-naked serving maids, and burst into the brothel's front room, a candle-lit salon crowded with rowdy, red-faced knights and laughing, languorous harlots.

'Save me!' cried Anyaka. 'Save me, gentles! He means to slay me!'

'Stop her!' bellowed Reiner. 'She's a sorceress! She's loosed a plague upon us!'

But both appeals were lost in a rising chorus of shrieks and curses as the nurglings erupted from the kitchen and fell upon the revellers. Harlots screamed and climbed the furniture, drunken knights roared and bashed at the nurglings with daggers, bottles and candlesticks, shouting for their swords. In their inebriated state, the men did as much damage to each other as to the nurglings: wild swings cut fingers, mashed toes and bloodied noses. Fights broke out among friends.

In this carnage the nurglings flourished; raking eyes, biting hands and feet, opening veins in leg, neck and arm. All over the room harlots and soldiers alike shrieked as blood pumped from shredded arteries. Others fell to the floor with severed tendons to drown in a chittering swell of teeth and claws.

Caught in this mad whirlpool, Reiner and Anyaka continued their chase. Reiner felt like he was in a dream, where no matter how swiftly he ran, he moved only inches, but at last he cornered the sorceress in a romantic nook, complete with a love seat and plaster cherubs.

'Spare me!' cried Anyaka, piteously.

'As you spared Hennig?' Reiner pulled back for the killing thrust, but strong hands pinned his arms.

'How now, sir?' said a black-bearded knight. 'Do you violence to the good lady?'

'For shame,' said another, a blond giant with cavalry braids.

'She's not a good lady,' panted Reiner. 'She's a priestess of Nurgle!'

'Protect me, noble knights!' Anyaka begged. 'It is he who is a servant of Nurgle. It is he who has summoned these foul vermin.'

'A sorcerer, hey?' said the first knight. 'He has the look.'

'Don't believe her!' said Reiner desperately. 'She wears marks of Chaos carved into her very flesh. Open her robe and look for yourself.'

The blond knight punched him in the face. 'Swine! Dare you ask us to abuse a Sister of Shallya thus?'

Reiner spat blood. 'But she's–'

He was interrupted as a pack of nurglings discovered the party and attacked. Anyaka bolted from the alcove. Roaring in pain, the knights dropped Reiner and slashed at the nurglings with wild abandon.

Reiner wormed between the two giants, chopping at clinging nurglings as he went, and ran back into the salon. He spied Anyaka through the surging crowd, making for the kitchen. He ploughed after her, and after a frantic push reached the kitchen and rushed through it. A serving maid sobbed, eyeless, in a corner. The cook lay sizzling in his cooking fire, dead from a thousand bites.

Reiner ran into the yard. Anyaka wasn't there. He limped quickly to the stable and listened. A murmur of chanting reached him.

Picking up a wooden bucket, he crept down the aisle past poor Hennig's bones to the tack room door, and listened again. The chanting continued unabated. He looked in. Anyaka had righted the frying pan and was once again filling it with poisonous ingredients, muttering over it all the while.

Reiner drew back. He hefted the bucket, took a deep breath, then spun into the door and hurled it. The bucket crashed into the brazier, overturning it, scattering hot coals and sending the frying pan flying.

Anyaka shrieked and fell back as boiling liquid splashed her. Reiner limped forward, sabre high, but the sorceress rolled away from him, around the fire. Reiner attempted to turn, but had to leap awkwardly over the spreading pool of poison and jarred his bad leg. Anyaka scrambled out of the door.

Reiner staggered after her, kicking through the fire that was spreading across the straw-covered floor. The stable aisle was empty, but he could hear the sorceress moaning from one of the stalls. He approached it cautiously. Anyaka was crooning as if enjoying the most sensuous pleasures imaginable. 'Lord Nurgle, I thank you for this glorious pain, for the poison that wracks my body so deliciously, for the gift of plague that I shall spread to all who feel my touch.'

Reiner looked into the stall. Anyaka huddled beside an exploded corpse, but as Reiner's flame-cast shadow crossed her, she looked up. He stepped back, aghast. The boiling poison had splashed her face, raising flame-red blisters from her left temple to her chin. Her lips on that side had shrivelled away from her teeth, and her left eye was a bulging white orb with no pupil, too big for its socket.

With an animal snarl the sorceress leapt at him, the corpse's curved Kislevite sword in her hand. Reiner parried, but her blow was so powerful it knocked his blade against his brow, stunning him. He fell back, Anyaka raining blows on him like twenty women. She was frighteningly strong, striking sparks with every slash. His sabre was soon so pitted it looked like a saw blade.

At last he bound her high, but she kicked him in the chest and he flew back, crashing against a stall. She advanced slowly, smiling, the fire from the tack room billowing into the aisle behind her.

'I congratulate you, my lord,' she said. 'You have stopped my plans from reaching fruition.' She raised her sword to her face and drew the honed edge down her scalded flesh, slicing open angry blisters. Thick yellow pus oozed out, coating the blade and eating into its steel. 'But there will be other camps, and other greedy fools ready to help a poor, Sister of Shallya in need.'

'You won't win many hearts with that face, lass,' said Reiner, struggling to get up.

'Grandfather will heal me, as he has before. He will hide my wounds and corruption within, so that I may walk among the populace undetected and spread his blessings to all.'

Reiner grimaced. 'I begin to be glad we didn't kiss.'

She lunged with the poison blade. Reiner blocked it an inch from his face. Its foul ichor choked him. He staggered back, and she pressed her attack, forcing him toward a mound of burning hay. The fire was spreading quickly. The posts that held the hayloft were trees of flame. Hot smoke burned Reiner's eyes, but he couldn't blink, couldn't let Anyaka past his guard, for the merest scratch from her blade would mean death. His lungs ached. His strength was waning, while hers seemed only to increase. He dodged a slash and fell backward over Hennig's bones. She knocked his sabre away into a flaming stall, then stepped over him, triumphant, raising her sword for the killing blow.

Reiner scrabbled for something, anything, to throw, and grabbed Hennig's skull. He hurled it. It caught her on her blistered face. She barked in pain and stumbled back.

Reiner rolled to his feet and kicked her before she could recover. He looked frantically for a weapon. His sword was behind a wall of flame. A length of rope hung coiled on a peg. He grabbed it.

Anyaka lunged again. Reiner dodged and stepped behind her, looping the rope around her neck like a garrotte. She flailed wildly. Her sword bit into his boot. Had she cut him? He couldn't tell.

He kicked her legs out from under her. She choked and thrashed again with her sword. He needed to get away from that poisoned steel. He threw two more loops of rope around her neck and knotted it, then jumped back.

Hissing like a cat, Anyaka scrabbled at the rope, but before she could free herself, Reiner tossed the coil over a beam and hauled on it. Anyaka jerked into the air, kicking and retching. Reiner heaved again until she swung a yard off the ground. She dropped her sword and clawed at the makeshift noose.

Reiner laughed. 'Where's your grandfather now, witch?'

Anyaka turned flame-reflecting eyes on him, so filled with hate that, impossible as it was for her to reach him, Reiner still stepped back. She ceased struggling and began instead to spit out a rasping incantation while calmly moving her hands in sinuous patterns. A green glow began trailing from them. Fear gripped Reiner's heart as he felt invisible forces squeezing his windpipe, shutting off his breath like the rope shut off Anyaka's. He'd hung her, and she was still killing him.

Choking, eyes streaming from pain and smoke, Reiner darted forward and snatched Anyaka's poisoned blade from below her feet. She kicked feebly at him, still chanting.

Reiner's throat closed entirely. The world turned black and red and spun past his eyes. He swung the blade blindly and was rewarded with the satisfying bite of steel into flesh. Anyaka cried out. Her incantation stopped, and the pressure in Reiner's neck eased. He swung again and again, until the sorceress's screams stopped at last.

Reiner collapsed to the ground, sucking air as his throat opening fully. Hennig's skull looked at him, tilted at a jaunty angle. Reiner nodded to it. 'Thank you, lad. Well struck.'

The flames encroached from all sides. Reiner was just heaving himself up and make for the door when a group of men hurried through it.

'What's all this?' asked a familiar voice.

Reiner squinted through the smoke. It was Captain Deiter Ulstaadt and the watch.

'Hetzau,' cried Deiter. 'I might have known. What in Sigmar's name have you done?'

'Saved the Empire,' coughed Reiner, staggering up. 'Or at least this little bit of it.'

'You call murdering a Sister of Shallya saving the Empire?'

'But she wasn't. She was a priestess of Nurgle. She meant to spread disease and confusion though the camp.'

Deiter scowled sceptically. 'This little thing? I don't believe it.'

Reiner waved behind him. 'Look in the tack room. She covered it with unholy symbols. She was brewing...'

The tack room collapsed in an explosion of falling beams and roaring flames. Reiner and Deiter and his men jumped back.

'Most convenient,' drawled Deiter.

'But, but... look at her. Look under her robes. She's carved marks of Chaos in her flesh!'

Deiter wrinkled his nose. 'You ask a Knight of the Banner to look upon a woman's nakedness?'

'No, you pompous ass!' cried Reiner, losing patience, 'I ask you to use your head for once in your miserable life!'

Deiter sniffed. 'I think we have had more than enough of that.' He motioned to his men. 'Bring him.'

The guardsmen marched Reiner out, still protesting, just seconds before the roof beam cracked and the stable collapsed.

In the yard, soldiers, knights and harlots had formed a bucket brigade to try and quench the fire, while the brothel's neighbours were draping their roofs and walls with wet blankets. Others were tending to those who had been maimed and killed by the nurgling invasion.

'He's the one!' shouted a pikeman, pointing at Reiner. 'He's the villain who lead those little horrors into the brothel.'

'And he the one who talk me into putting up sick people in first place,' said Madam Tolshnaya, bustling up importantly.

Deiter glared at Reiner. 'After I turned them away?'

'And I saw him earlier today,' said a handgunner. 'He kicked a body off a cart and it exploded with nurglings.'

'Actually, it exploded, then I kicked it off,' said Reiner weakly, but nobody was listening.

The burly acolyte of Morr pushed through the crowd. 'And he left a corpse at the mortuary that birthed a swarm of monsters!'

Deiter looked at Reiner in disgust. 'It becomes clear that it was you, not the sister, who meant to spread disease and confusion, that it is you who is the servant of Chaos.' He raised his voice. 'Reiner Hetzau, in the name of our benevolent Emperor, Karl Franz, I arrest you for the crimes of murder, treason, sorcery, and consorting with the enemy.' He turned to his men. 'Gentlemen, take him away.'

Reiner sighed as the guardsmen marched him to the street. It was just as Ranald taught. No good deed goes unpunished.

THE HANGMAN CHECKED the lever again. The trap dropped and the sack of earth twitched at the end of the noose. It was late afternoon. The long shadow of the gallows touched Reiner's face. He turned away from the brig window. There was no laughter in him now. The sunset behind the gallows would be his last. No more dice. No more cards. No more women. No more fine food and drink. He hung his head. It wasn't fair. His life couldn't end like this. He had to escape. There must be a way!

If he could get out of the camp – out of the cell – he could make his way to the Sea of Claws. Then he might sail south to... anywhere really, anywhere the Empire's shadow didn't fall: Tilea, Estalia, the Border Princes. There were always opportunities for men of adventurous nature to be had there. All he had to do was get out of here.

He looked around with eyes refreshed by desperation: thick walls, iron bars, narrow windows. He couldn't break though all that, not by tomorrow morning, certainly. He stepped to the cell's heavy oak door. The lock looked simple enough, but picking locks was not a skill he'd learned, and smashing the door down was a foolish fantasy. It was as thick as the walls.

He looked through the door's tiny barred window. The turnkey sat on a stool just outside, picking his nose. Reiner brightened. He knew the man: a dull, stolid trooper he had diced with on many occasions – and taken many a reikmark from. It had been like stealing alms from a blind man. There was hope after all.

'Vassendorf, my lad,' he whispered through the bars. 'A word in your ear.'

VALNIR'S BANE

ONE
Victims Of Circumstance

REINER HETZAU HAD not had a good war. When he had ridden north with von Stolmen's Pistoliers to join in the last push to drive the heathen horde back north of Kislev where they belonged, he'd hoped to return home to Altdorf with a few battle-scars to impress his various sweethearts and bedmates, a few trunks full of plunder and battlefield souvenirs to sell on the black market, and a few saddlebags full of gold crowns, won from his fellow soldiers in games of chance played behind the cavalry stables. Instead, what had happened? He had been wounded in his first battle and forced to sit out the rest of the offensive in Vulsk, a Kislev border town that fell further and further behind the front as the Grand Alliance forced the raiders deeper into the Chaos Wastes.

Then, while recuperating, he had single-handedly flushed out an evil sorceress disguised as a sister of Shallya and had slain her before she had succeeded in spreading disease and confusion throughout the army. But had they heaped praise and promotions upon him for this heroic act? No. Through the blind stupidity of his superiors, he was charged with murdering a clergywoman and perpetrating the very crimes he had stopped the false sister from committing.

Fortunately – or unfortunately – depending on how one looked at it, his arrest had coincided with the final offensive of the war, and the outcome had been so uncertain that little things like court martials and executions had been postponed while the conflict came to its blood-soaked climax. Reiner had cooled his heels in various cells for months, being moved from brig to brig as the vagaries of war demanded. At last, with the war half a year over, he sat in the garrison brig at Smallhof Castle, an Empire outpost just west of the Kislev border, awaiting execution by hanging at dawn in a cell full of the lowest sort of gallows trash.

No, it had not been a good war. Not a good war at all.

Reiner, however, was not the sort of fellow to give up hope. He was a gambler, a follower of Ranald. He knew that luck could be twisted in one's favour by an astute player with an eye for the main chance. Already he had succeeded in bribing the thick-witted turnkey with tales of treasure he had hidden before his arrest. The man was going to sneak him out of the brig at midnight in return for a cut of that fictitious cache. Now all he needed was one further accomplice. It would be a long, dangerous road to freedom: out of the camp, out of the Empire, into the unknown, and he would need someone to keep watch while he slept, to boost him over walls, to stand lookout while he liberated horses, food or clothes from their rightful owners. Particularly, he needed someone to push in the way of the authorities so that he could make his escape if they were trapped.

As the sun set outside the barred brig window, Reiner turned and surveyed his fellow prisoners, trying to determine which of them might be the most desirable travelling companion. He was looking for the right combination of competence, steadiness and gullibility – not qualities to be found in great abundance inside a prison. The others were all trading stories of how they came to be imprisoned. Reiner curled a lip as he listened. Every one of them proclaimed his innocence. The fools. In their eyes, not one of them deserved to be there.

The engineer in the corner, a brooding, black-browed giant with hands the size of Wissenberg cheeses, was shaking his head like a baffled bull. 'I didn't mean to kill anyone. But they wouldn't stop. They just kept pushing and pushing.

Jokes and names and...' His hands flexed. 'I didn't swing to kill. But we were framing a siege tower and I held a maul and...'

'And yer a bloody great orc what don't know his own strength, that's what,' said a burly pikeman with a bald head and a jutting chin beard.

The engineer's head jerked up. 'I am not an orc!'

'Easy now, man,' said a second pikeman, as thin and wiry as his companion was sturdy. 'We none of us need another helping of trouble. Hals meant no harm. He just lets his mouth run away with him now and again.'

'Is that why you're here?' asked Reiner, for he liked the look of the pair – sturdy sons of toil with an alert air – and wanted to know more about them. 'Did your mouths dig a hole your fists couldn't fill?'

'No, my lord,' said the thin pikeman. 'Entirely innocent we are. Victims of circumstance. Our captain...'

'Blundering half-wit who couldn't fall out of bed without a map,' interjected Hals.

'Our captain,' repeated his friend, 'was found with a pair of pikes stuck in his back, and somehow the brass came to blame us for it. But as the coward was running from a charge at the time, we reckon it was Kurgan done for him.'

Hals laughed darkly. 'Aye. The Kurgan.'

There was a giggle from the shadows near the door. A fellow with white teeth and a curling black moustache grinned at them. 'Is no need to make stories, boys,' he said in a Tilean accent. 'We all in boats the same, hey?'

'What do you know about it, garlic-eater?' growled Hals. 'I suppose you're as pure as snow. What are you in for?'

'A mis-standing-under,' said the Tilean. 'I sell some guns I find to some Kossar boys. How I know the Empire so stingy? How I know they don't share with allies?'

'The Empire has no allies, you thieving mercenary,' said a knight who sat near the door. 'Only grateful neighbours who flock to it in times of need like sheep to the shepherd.'

Reiner eyed the man warily. He was the only other man of noble blood in the brig, but Reiner felt no kinship for him. He was tall and powerfully built, with a fierce blond beard and piercing blue eyes, a hero of the Empire from head to toe. Reiner was certain the fellow saluted in his sleep.

'You seem awfully keen for a man whose Empire has locked him up,' he said dryly.

'A mistake, certain to be rectified,' said the knight. 'I killed a man in an affair of honour. There's no crime in that.'

'Somebody must have thought so.'

The knight waved a dismissive hand. 'They said he was a boy.'

'And how did he run afoul of you?'

'We were tent-pegging. The fool blundered across my line and cost me a win.'

'A killing offence indeed,' said Reiner.

'Do you mock me, sir?'

'Not at all, my lord. I wouldn't dare.'

Reiner looked beyond the knight to a beardless archer, a dark-haired boy more pretty than handsome. 'And you, lad. How comes one so young to such dire straits?'

'Aye,' said Hals. 'Did y'bite yer nursie's tit?'

The boy looked up, eyes flashing. 'I killed a man! My tent mate. He...' The boy swallowed. 'He tried to put his hands on me. And I'll do for any of you as I did for him, if you try the like.'

Hals barked a laugh. 'Lovers' tiff was it?'

The boy leapt to his feet. 'You'll take that back.'

Reiner sighed. Another hothead. Too bad. He liked the boy's spirit. A sparrow undaunted in an eyrie of hawks.

'Peace, lad,' said the thin pikeman. ''Twas only a jest. You leave him be, Hals.'

A tall, thin figure stood up from the wall, a nervous looking artilleryman with a trim beard and wild eyes. 'I ran from my gun. Fire fell from the sky. Fire that moved like a man. It reached for me. I...' He shivered and hung his head, then sat back down abruptly.

For a moment no one spoke, or met anyone else's eye. He's honest, at least, thought Reiner, poor fellow.

There was one last man in the room, who had not spoken or seemed to take any interest in the conversation: a plump, tidy fellow dressed in the white canvas jerkin of a field surgeon. He sat with his face to the wall.

'And you, bone-cutter,' Reiner called to him. 'What's your folly?'

The others looked at the man, relieved to turn to a new subject after the artilleryman's embarrassing admission.

The surgeon didn't raise his head or look around. 'Never you mind what ain't your business.'

'Oh, come sir,' said Reiner. 'We're all dead men here. No one will betray your secrets.'

But the man said nothing, only hunched his shoulders further and continued to stare at the wall.

Reiner shrugged and leaned back, looking over his cellmates again, contemplating his choices. Not the knight: too hot-headed. Nor the engineer: too moody. The pikemen perhaps, though they were a right pair of villains.

The sound of footsteps outside the cell door interrupted his thoughts. Everyone looked up. A key turned in the lock, the door squealed open, and two guards entered followed by a sergeant. 'On your feet, scum,' he said.

'Taking us to our last meal?' asked Hals.

'Yer last meal'll be my boot if y'don't move. Now file out.'

The prisoners shuffled out of the cell. Two more guards waited outside. They led the way with the sergeant into the chilly evening, and across the muddy grounds of the castle in which the garrison was housed.

Thick flakes of wet snow were falling. The hackles rose on Reiner's neck as he passed the gallows in the centre of the courtyard.

They entered the castle keep through a small door, and after descending many a twisting stair, were ordered into a low-ceilinged chamber that smelled of wood smoke and hot iron. Reiner swallowed nervously as he looked around. Manacles and cages lined the walls, as well as instruments of torture – racks, gridirons, metal boots. In a corner, a man in a leather apron tended brands that glowed in beds of hot coals.

'Eyes front!' bawled the sergeant. 'Dress ranks! Attention!'

The prisoners came to attention in the centre of the room with varying degrees of alacrity, and then stood rigid for what seemed like an hour while the sergeant glared at them. At last, just as Reiner felt his knees couldn't take it any longer, a door opened behind them.

'Eyes front, curse you!' shouted the sergeant. He snapped to attention himself as two men stepped into Reiner's line of vision.

The first man Reiner didn't know: a scarred old soldier with iron grey hair and a hitch in his walk. His face was grim and heavily lined, with eyes like slits hidden under shaggy brows. He wore the black-slashed-with-red doublet and breeks of an Ostland captain of pike.

The second man Reiner had once or twice seen at a distance – Baron Albrecht Valdenheim, younger brother to Count Manfred Valdenheim of Nordbergbruche, and second-in-command of his army. He was tall and barrel-chested, with a powerful frame running a little to fat, and he had a lantern jaw. His reputation for ruthlessness showed in his face, which was as cold and closed as an iron door. He wore dark blue velvet under a fur coat that swept the floor.

The sergeant saluted. 'The prisoners, my lord.'

Albrecht nodded absently, his ice-blue eyes surveying them from under a fringe of short, dark hair.

'Ulf Urquart, my lord,' said the sergeant as Albrecht and the scarred captain stopped in front of the brooding giant. 'Engineer. Charged with the murder of a fellow sapper. Killed him with a maul.'

They moved to Hals and his skinny friend. 'Hals Kiir and Pavel Voss. Pikemen. Murdered their captain while in battle.'

'We didn't, though,' said Hals.

'Silence, scum!' shouted the sergeant and backhanded him with a gloved hand.

'That's all right, sergeant,' said Albrecht. 'Who's this?' He indicated the pretty youth.

'Franz Shoentag, archer. Killed his tentmate, claims self-defence.'

Albrecht and the captain grunted and moved on to the angular artilleryman.

'Oskar Lichtmar, cannon. Cowardice in front of the enemy. He left his gun.'

The grizzled captain pursed his lips. Albrecht shrugged and stepped to the blond knight, who stared straight ahead, perfectly at attention.

'Erich von Eisenberg, Novitiate Knight in the Order of the Sceptre,' said the sergeant. 'Killed Viscount Olin Marburg in a duel.'

Albrecht raised an eyebrow. 'A capital offence?'

'The viscount had only fifteen summers.'

'Ah.'

They next came to the Tilean.

'Giano Ostini,' said the brig captain. 'Mercenary crossbowman. Stole Empire handguns and sold 'em to foreigners.'

Albrecht nodded and stepped to the plump man who had refused to name his crime. The sergeant eyed him with distaste. 'Gustaf Schlecht, surgeon. Charged with doing violence to a person bringing provisions to the forces.'

Albrecht looked up. 'Not familiar with that one.'

The sergeant looked uneasy. 'He, er, molested and killed the daughter of the farmer his unit was billeted with.'

'Charming.'

The men stepped in front of Reiner. Albrecht and the captain of pike looked him up and down coolly. The sergeant glared at him. 'Reiner Hetzau, pistolier. The worst of the lot. A sorcerer who murdered a holy woman and summoned foul creatures to attack his camp. Don't know as I recommend him, my lord. The others are wicked men, but this one, he's the enemy.'

'Nonsense,' said the captain of pike, speaking for the first time. He had a voice like gravel under iron wheels. 'He ain't Chaos. I'd smell it.'

'Of course he isn't,' agreed Albrecht.

Reiner's jaw dropped. He was stunned. 'But... but then, my lord, surely the charges against me must be false. If you know I am no sorcerer, then it is impossible that I summoned those creatures, and...'

The sergeant kicked him in the stomach. 'Silence! You horrible man!'

Reiner bent double, retching and clutching his belly.

'I read your account, sir,' said Albrecht, as if nothing had happened. 'And I believe it.'

'Then... you'll let me go?'

'I think not. For it proves that you are something infinitely more dangerous than a sorcerer. You are a greedy fool who would allow the land of his birth to burn if he thought he could make a gold crown from it.'

'My lord, I beseech you. I may have made a few lapses in judgement, but if you know I am innocent...'

Albrecht sniffed and turned away from him. 'Well, captain?' he asked.

The old captain curled his lip. 'I wouldn't pay a penny for the lot of them.'

'I'm afraid they're all we have at the moment.'

'Then I'll have to make do, won't I?'

'Indeed.' Albrecht turned to the sergeant. 'Sergeant, prepare them.'

'Aye sir.' The man signalled the guards. 'Into the cell with them. All but Orc-heart here.'

'I am not an orc!' said Ulf as two guards stuffed Reiner and the rest into a tiny steel cage on the left wall. The other two led Ulf to the far side of the room where the man in the leather apron stirred his coals. The guards kicked Ulf's legs until he kneeled, then flattened his hand on a wooden tabletop.

'What are you doing?' asked the big man uneasily.

One of the guards put a spear to his neck. 'Just hold still.'

The man in the apron picked a brand out of the fire. The glowing tip was in the shape of a hammer.

Ulf's eyes went wide. 'No! You can't! This isn't right!' He struggled. The other guards hurried over and held him down.

The guard with the spear pricked his skin. 'Easy now.'

The torturer pressed the brand into the flesh of Ulf's hand. It sizzled. Ulf screamed and slumped in a dead faint.

Reiner swallowed queasily as he smelled the unpleasantly pleasant odour of cooking meat.

'Right,' said the sergeant. 'Next.'

Reiner suppressed a shudder. Next to him, Oskar, the artilleryman, was weeping like a child.

REINER WOKE WITH a sensation of cold on his cheek and searing agony on the back of his hand. He opened his eyes and found that he was lying on the flagstones of the torture chamber. Apparently he too had passed out when they had branded him.

Someone kicked his legs. The sergeant. 'On your feet, sorcerer.'

It was hard to understand the order. His mind was far away – detached from his body like a kite at the end of a string. The world seemed to revolve around him behind a wall of thick glass. He tried to stand – thought he had, in fact – but when he focused again, he found he was still on the floor, the pain in his hand rolling up his arm in waves like heavy surf.

'Stand at attention, curse you!' roared the sergeant, and kicked him again.

This time he managed it, though not without mishap, and joined the others who formed a ragged line before Albrecht and the captain. Each prisoner had an ugly, blistering, hammer-shaped burn on his hand. Reiner resisted the urge to look at his. He didn't want to see it.

'Sergeant,' Albrecht barked. 'Give the surgeon fellow some bandages and have him dress those wounds.'

The torturer in the leather apron produced some unguents and dressings which he gave to Schlecht. The plump surgeon salved and bound first his own burn, then started on the others.

'Now then,' said Albrecht, as Schlecht worked. 'Now that we have you leashed, we can proceed.'

Reiner snarled under his breath. They had leashed him indeed. They had scarred him for life. The hammer brand told all who saw it that the man who wore it was a deserter and could be killed on sight.

'I am here to offer you something you did not have an hour ago,' said Albrecht. 'A choice. You can serve your Emperor on a mission of great importance, or you can be hanged from the gallows this very evening and go to the fate that awaits you.'

Reiner cursed. Hanged this evening? He was to escape at midnight. Now the fiends had stolen even that from him.

'The chances of surviving the mission are slim, I warrant you,' continued Albrecht. 'But the rewards will be great. You will receive a full pardon for your crimes and be given your weight in gold crowns.'

'What good is all that when you also gave us this?' growled Hals, holding up the back of his ruined hand.

'The Emperor values your service in this matter so highly that he will command a sage of the Order of Light to remove the brands when you return successful.'

This sounded too good to be true, thought Reiner. The sort of thing he himself would say if he was trying to con a mark into some foolish course of action.

'What's the job?' asked Pavel, sullen.

Albrecht smirked. 'You mean to haggle? You will learn the nature of the mission once you have volunteered for it. Now, sirs, give me your answers.'

There was much hesitation, but one by one the others voiced or nodded their assent. Reiner damned Albrecht under his breath. A choice, he called it. What choice was there? Wearing the hammer brand, Reiner could never again travel easily within the Empire. It was early spring now. He might still wear gloves for a while, but come summer he would stick out like a sheep in a wolf pack. Never would he be able to go back to his beloved Altdorf, to the card rooms and cafes, the theatres and dog pits and brothels that he thought of as home. Even if he could somehow escape the brig, he would have to leave the Empire for foreign lands and never come back. And now that Albrecht had moved his execution to this evening instead of tomorrow at dawn, and thus foiling his only plan, even that unappetising option was closed to him.

Only by accepting the mission did he gain any chance of escape. Somewhere along the road he could perhaps slip away: west to Marienburg, or south to Tilea or the Border Princes or some other foul hole. Or perhaps the mission wouldn't be as dangerous as Albrecht made out. Perhaps he would see it through to the finish and take his reward – if Albrecht truly meant to give him one.

All that was certain was that if he declined the mission, he would die tonight, and there would be no more perhapses.

'Aye,' he said at last. 'Aye, my lord. I'm your man.'

TWO
A Task Simple In The Telling

'VERY GOOD,' SAID Albrecht, when all the prisoners had volunteered. 'Now you shall hear your mission.' He indicated the grizzled veteran at his side. 'Under the command of Captain Veirt here, you shall escort Lady Magda Bandauer, an abbess of Shallya, to a Shallyan convent in the foothills of the Middle Mountains. A holy relic lies there in a hidden crypt. Lady Magda shall open the crypt, then you will escort her and the relic back here to me with all possible speed. Time is of the essence.' He smiled. 'It is a task simple in the telling, but I have no need to remind soldiers of the Empire, no matter how debased, that the lands 'twixt here and the mountains are not yet entirely reclaimed, and that the mountains have become the refuge of Chaos marauders – Kurgan, Norse and worse things. We have word that the convent was recently pillaged by Kurgan. They may still be in the area. You will be sorely pressed, but for those who survive, and return the relic and the abbess to me, the Empire's munificence will know no bounds.'

Reiner heard little of Albrecht's speech. He had stopped listening after 'abbess of Shallya.' Another sister of Shallya? He had barely survived his last encounter with one such. Granted, that one had been a sorceress in disguise, but once bitten twice shy, as he always said. He wanted no more to do with that order. They weren't to be trusted.

Erich, the blond knight, seemed to have some objections to the plan as well. 'Do you mean to tell me,' he burst out indignantly, 'that we are to be led by this... this foot soldier? I am a Knight of the Sceptre. My horse and armour cost more than he has made in his whole career.'

'Bloody jagger,' muttered Hals. 'My spear's killed more northers than his horse and armour ever will.'

'Captain Veirt also outranks you,' said Albrecht. 'He has thirty years of battles under his belt, while you are, what? Vexillary? Bugle? Have you even blooded your lance yet?'

'I am a nobleman. I cannot take orders from a common peasant. My father is Frederich von Eisenberg, Baron of...'

I know your father, boy,' said Albrecht. 'Would you like me to tell him how many young knights you have slain and maimed in "affairs of honour?" You deprive the Empire of good men and call it sport.'

Erich's fists clenched, but he hung his head. 'No, my lord.'

'Very good. You will obey Captain Veirt in all things, is that clear?'

'Yes, my lord.'

'Good.' Albrecht surveyed the whole group. 'Horses are waiting for you at the postern gate. You leave at once. But before you go, your commanding officer has a few words. Captain?'

Captain Veirt stepped forward and looked them all in the eye, one by one. His glance shot through Reiner like an arrow from a longbow. 'You have been chosen for a great honour tonight, and offered a clemency which none of you deserve. So if any of you attempts to abuse this kindness, by trying to escape, by betraying our company to the enemy, by killing each other or sabotaging the mission, I give you my personal guarantee that I will make the rest of your very short life a living hell the likes of which would make the depredations of the daemons of Chaos look like a country dance.' He turned toward the door and limped toward it. 'That is all.'

Reiner shivered, then joined the rest as the guards began herding them out.

IF NOTHING ELSE, Albrecht made sure they were well kitted out. They were led through the castle and out through the postern gate, where a narrow wooden drawbridge spanned the moat. On the far side, on a strip of cleared land flanked by a fallow field, a pack mule and ten horses were waiting for them – their breath white steam in the chill night air. The horses were saddled, bridled and loaded with regulation packs, complete with bed roll, rations, skillet, flint, canteen, and the like. Reiner's sabre was returned to him – a beautiful weapon, made to his measure, and the only gift his skinflint father had ever given him that was worth a damn. There was also a padded leather jerkin and sturdy boots to replace the ones taken from him in the brig, as well as a dagger, a boot knife, saddlebags full of powder and shot, and two pistols in saddle holsters – though not loaded or primed. Albrecht was no fool. A cloak, steel lobster-tail bassinet, and back-and-breastplate strapped over the pack completed the inventory.

Almost everybody seemed satisfied with their gear. Only Ulf and Erich complained.

'What's this?' asked Ulf angrily, holding up a huge iron-bound wooden maul that looked bigger than Sigmar's hammer. 'Is this a joke?'

Veirt smirked. ''Tis the only weapon we know you're competent with.'

'Do you ask a knight to ride a pack horse?' interrupted Erich. 'This beast is barely fourteen hands.'

'We go into the mountains, your grace,' said Veirt dryly. 'Yer charger might find the going a bit rough.'

'Looks tall enough to me,' said Hals, eyeing his horse uneasily.

'Aye,' said Pavel. 'Can you make 'em kneel so we can get on?'

'Sigmar, save us!' said Erich. 'Will we have to teach these peasants to ride?'

'Oh, they'll pick it up quick enough,' said Reiner. 'Just learn from his lordship, lads. If you ride like you've got a pike up your fundament, you're on the mark.'

Pavel and Hals guffawed. Erich shot Reiner a venomous glance and turned toward him as if he meant to pursue the matter. Fortunately, at that moment Albrecht came through the gate, leading a chestnut palfrey on which sat a woman dressed in the robes of an abbess of Shallya. Reiner's fears were somewhat allayed when he saw her, for Lady Magda was a stern, sober-looking woman of middle years – attractive enough in a cold, haughty way, but by no means the sort of dewy-eyed, waif-like temptress that had so recently been his ruin.

This woman looked like she measured out the charity of Shallya with an assayer's scale, and healed the sick by shaming them into health. She seemed as unhappy to be travelling in their company as they were to be in Veirt's. She looked them over with barely concealed disdain.

Only when Albrecht led her to her place beside Veirt did Reiner see her show anything like human feeling. As the baron handed her her bridle he took her hand and kissed it. She smiled down at him in return and stroked his cheek fondly. Reiner smirked. There was some fire in the cold sister after all. Still, the moment of affection gave Reiner pause. Why would Albrecht leave a woman he cared for in such disreputable company? It was curious.

When they were all mounted, Albrecht faced them. 'Ride swiftly and return quickly. Remember that riches await you if you succeed, and that I will kill you like dogs if you betray me. Now go, and may the eye of Sigmar watch over your journey.'

He saluted as Veirt spurred his horse and signalled them forward. Only Veirt, Erich and Reiner returned the salute.

As they started down the rutted dirt road between tilled fields toward the dark band of forest in the distance, it began to drizzle. Reiner and the rest all reached behind them to unstrap their hooded cloaks from their packs and pull them on.

Hals grumbled under his breath as the rain spattered his forehead. 'There's a good omen for you, and no mistake.'

It rained all night, turning the road to mud. Spring was coming to Ostland as it did every year, cold and wet. The party rode through the moonless night huddled in their cloaks, teeth chattering and noses running. The throbbing pain of his brand was now only the first in a long list of miseries that Reiner mentally added to with each passing mile. They could see little of the countryside. The woods were pitch black. Only when they passed open fields, where the previous week's blanket of snow was melting into grey slush, was there enough light for them to see any distance at all.

This was wild land. Smallhof was on the Empire's easternmost marches and there was much forest and few towns. It was relatively safe, however. The tide of Chaos had crested, then receded back east and north leaving the land desolate, even of the bandits and beasts that normally terrorised the local farms and towns. The few crude huts they passed were mere blackened shells.

Just before dawn, as Reiner was nodding and swaying in the saddle, Veirt called a halt by a river. A patch of tall pines clustered near it, and into this he led them. It was black as a cave within the spinney, but the ground was almost dry.

Veirt dismounted briskly. 'We'll rest here until dawn. No tents. And sleep in your gear.'

'What?' said Reiner. 'But dawn's only an hour away.'

'His lordship said time is of the essence,' said Veirt. 'You'll get a full night's sleep when we make camp tonight.'

'Another day of riding?' moaned Hals. 'My arse won't stand it.'

'Would you rather your arse was swinging by a rope?' asked Veirt darkly. 'Now get your heads down. Urquart, help me.'

While the company saw to their horses and made pillows of their bedrolls, Ulf and Veirt put up a tidy little tent for Lady Magda that included a folding cot. When it was finished and Lady Magda installed within it, Veirt laid down in front of it, blocking the entrance.

'Don't worry, captain,' said Hals under his breath. 'We don't want none.' He laughed and nudged Pavel. 'Ha! Get it? We don't want nun!'

'Aye,' said Pavel wearily. 'I get it. Now go to sleep, y'pillock. Blood of Sigmar, I don't know which hurts worse, my hand or my arse.'

REINER WOKE WITH a start. He had been having a vivid nightmare that Kronhof, Altdorf's most notorious moneylender, was drilling though his left hand with a carpenter's auger as punishment for unpaid debts, when someone in the dream had begun banging on an iron door. He opened his eyes and found himself in the pine spinney, but the pain in his hand and the banging continued. It took a moment to remember that he was a now a branded man, and another moment to realise that the horrible noise was Veirt, banging his skillet against a rock and shouting, 'Rise and shine, my beauties! We've a long day ahead of us.'

'I'll make him eat that skillet in a minute,' growled Hals, clutching his head.

Reiner climbed painfully to his feet. He wasn't sore from riding. He was a pistolier – born in the saddle. But lack of sleep made his bones feel like they were made of lead. They dragged at his flesh. The pain in his hand seemed to have spread to his head; while the rest of him was frozen, his head felt on fire. His eyes ached. His teeth ached. Even his hair seemed to ache.

Worse than Veirt's banging and shouting was his clear-eyed alertness. To Reiner's annoyance, the man seemed utterly unaffected by lack of sleep. Lady Magda was the same. She waited calmly outside her tent, hands folded, as clean and pressed as if she had just led morning prayers. Veirt chivvied them through a rushed breakfast of bread, cheese and some ale and then onto their horses. Last to mount up were Pavel and Hals, who lowered themselves into their saddles with much hissing and groaning, like men settling bare-arsed into thorn bushes. Less than half an hour after waking, they were on the road again.

The rain had stopped, but there was no sun. The sky was a featureless and uninterrupted grey from horizon to horizon, like a dull pewter tray hung upside down over the world. The party pulled their cloaks tight around them and leaned into a wet spring wind as they rode toward the Middle Mountains, which rose out of the seemingly endless forest like islands in a green sea.

As the day went on and they left the scrubby wastelands of the east behind, the forest grew denser and they came across a few villages, tiny communities carved out of the wilderness and surrounded by winter fields. But while these so typically Imperial sights should have cheered men so long from home, instead the convicts' faces grew longer and longer, for the villages were empty shells – sacked and burned to the ground, with rotting skeletons strewn about like children's playthings. Some still smoked, for though the war was officially over months ago, Chaos Warlord Archaon and his hordes having at last been pushed back beyond Kislev, fighting continued, and doubtless would for some time. The endless forest of Ostland could swallow armies whole, with scattered bands of marauders, lost or left behind by their fleeing compatriots, still wandered it, looking for food and easy plunder. Other northmen had reportedly fled into the Middle Mountains and stayed, finding the frozen heights to their liking.

Still reeling from its all-or-nothing fight, the Empire was too busy regrouping and rebuilding to send armies out to vanquish these scavengers, and so it was left to the beleaguered local lords to defend their people with the ragged remnants of their household guard. But here, in these forsaken hinterlands, no lord but Karl Franz held sway, and the villagers must fend for themselves or die. Most often they died.

In one village, decapitated heads rotted on spikes mounted on the palisade. Bodies decomposed where they had fallen because there was no one left alive to bury them. The stench of death rose from wells and barns and cottages.

At noon they passed a temple of Sigmar. The old priest had been crucified before it, his ribs pried back and his deflated lungs flapping in the wind like wings. Pavel and Hals cursed under their breath and spat to avert bad luck. Erich rode straighter in the saddle, his jaw muscles twitching. Franz shivered and looked away. Reiner found himself torn between hiding his eyes and staring. He'd never had much use for priests, but no man of the Empire could see such a thing and be unaffected.

AFTER A LUNCH eaten in the saddle, a watery sun came out and the mood lifted a little. The forest receded away from the road and for a while they rode through a marshy area of rushes and clumps of snow that dripped into meandering streams. The men began to talk amongst themselves and Reiner found it interesting to see how the group sorted out. He was mildly surprised to see Pavel and Hals, a pair of Ostland farmers who had never left their homeland before being called to war, getting on well with the Tilean mercenary Giano. The typical insularity of the peasant, to whom even Altdorf was a foreign country, and who viewed all outsiders with mistrust, seemed to have been trumped by the commonality of all foot soldiers, and soon the three were laughing and exchanging tales of rotten provisions, terrible billets and worse commanders.

Behind them, little Franz and giant Ulf talked in low tones – a confederacy of the teased, thought Reiner. While bringing up the rear were Gustaf and Oskar, riding in glum silence and staring straight ahead – a confederacy of the shunned.

Veirt rode at the head of the party with Lady Magda. They were silent as well: Veirt constantly on the lookout for danger and Lady Magda, with her nose in a leather-bound volume, pointedly ignoring all that surrounded her. Reiner rode behind them, and much to his annoyance, so did Erich. It was inevitable, of course. Other than Lady Magda, Reiner was the only person of Erich's class in the party. He was the only prisoner Erich could acknowledge as an equal, the only one he would deign to talk to. Reiner would have been much happier swapping bawdy songs and barracks insults with Hals, Pavel and Giano, but Erich had attached himself like glue and babbled incessantly at his shoulder.

'If you were in Altdorf you must know my cousin Viscount Norrich Oberholt. He was trying to become a Knight Panther. Damned fine rider. Spent a lot of time at the Plume and Pennant.'

'I'm afraid I didn't mix much with the orders. I was at university.'

Erich made a face. 'University? Gads! I had enough learning from my tutor. Were you studying to be a priest?'

'Literature, when I studied at all. Mostly I was just there to escape Draeholt.'

'Eh? What's wrong with Draeholt? Excellent hunting there. Bagged a boar there once.'

'Did you?'

'Yes. Damned fine animal. I say, your name is Hetzau? I believe I met your father on a Draeholt hunt once. Jolly old fellow.'

Reiner winced. 'Oh yes, he's always at his jolliest killing the lesser orders.'

There was a rustle in the dead grass beside the road. Giano instantly unslung his crossbow and fired. A rabbit bolted out of hiding and sprinted across their march. Before Giano could do more than cry out in disgust, Franz raised his bow from his shoulders and an arrow from his quiver and fired in a single smooth motion. The rabbit turned a cartwheel and flopped dead in the melting snow, a clothyard shaft between his shoulder blades.

The entire party turned and looked at the boy with newfound respect. Even Erich nodded curtly. 'Neat shooting, that. Lad would make a good beater.'

Franz hopped lightly off his horse, removed the arrow and handed the rabbit to Giano, who had three more hanging from his pommel that he had shot earlier. 'One more for the stew,' he said with a smirk.

'Grazie, boy,' said Giano. 'Much thank yous.' He added the coney to his brace.

As Franz climbed back on his horse again, Reiner leaned in to Erich. 'Care to bet on who pots the next one?'

Erich pursed his lips. 'I never wager, except on horses. I say, have you seen the racers Count Schlaeger is breeding down at Helmgart? Damned fine runners.'

And on and on it went. Reiner groaned. Here he was, out in the world, freed from prison, his neck spared – at least temporarily – from the noose. But was he allowed to enjoy it? No. Apparently Sigmar had a nasty sense of humour. Erich was talking about his father's annual hunt ball now. It was going to be a long trip.

Veirt finally called a halt in the lee of a low cliff just before sunset and the men fell to making camp. Reiner found it curious that the men all found roles for themselves without any apparent communication. Pavel and Hals groaned about how sore they were from riding while they fetched water from a nearby stream and hunted for wild carrots and dandelion leaves to add to the stew. Reiner saw to the horses. Ulf erected Magda's tent and then assisted the others with theirs. Franz and Oskar collected wood and started the fire. Gustaf flayed and deboned the rabbits with an intensity Reiner found disturbing, while Giano seasoned the stew and talked endlessly about how much better the food was in Tilea.

The stew was delicious, if a bit garlicky for Imperial tastes, and they slurped it down eagerly as they hunched close around the fire.

'Draw lots for tents,' said Veirt between mouthfuls. 'I'll not have anyone pulling rank or any fighting over who tents with who. Yer all scum to me.'

The men made their marks on leaves and put them in a helmet. There were five tents: a fancy one for Lady Magda, a small one for Captain Veirt, and three standard-issue cavalry tents, which slept four uncomfortably, as the old barracks joke went, so the nine men could sleep three to a tent. Luxury. But when the helmet passed to Franz, he passed it on without adding a lot.

'Can't write your name, lad?' asked Veirt.

'I'll sleep alone,' said Franz.

Heads came up all around the fire.

Veirt scowled. 'You'll sleep with the others. There's no spare tent.'

'I'll tent under my cloak.' He looked straight into the fire.

Reiner smirked. 'The army ain't *all* inverts, boyo.'

'It only takes one.'

'Soldier,' said Veirt, with soft menace. 'Men who sleep alone tend to be found missing in the morning. Sometimes they run. Sometimes something takes them. I will allow neither. I need all the men I have for this goose chase. You…'

'Captain, please,' said Hals. 'Let him sleep alone. The last thing any of us needs is some excitable lad with a hair trigger cutting our throats for rolling over.'

A chorus of 'ayes' echoed from around the fire. Veirt shrugged. It seemed that Franz's stock with the company, which had risen after his display of bowmanship, had fallen precipitously once again.

When the lots were drawn – with a blank leaf holding Franz's place – Reiner shared a tent with Pavel and Ulf. Hals, Giano and Oskar had another, and Erich and Gustaf had the third tent to themselves. Veirt took first watch, and the rest bedded down immediately, near dropping from their night and day in the saddle. Still, it took Reiner a while to get to sleep. He couldn't stop thinking about what an odd lot of madmen and malcontents the company was. He couldn't understand why Valdenheim had entrusted them with such an important mission, and with the life of a woman he obviously held dear. Why hadn't he dispatched a squadron of knights to be her escort?

Reiner at last drifted off into fitful dreams without having found a satisfactory answer to his questions.

THREE
In The Doghouse

IN THE MIDDLE of the third day of their journey, with the ground rising beneath them and the Middle Mountains looming above, Pavel and Hals began to look about them with increased interest.

'This is the road to Ferlangen, or I'm a goblin,' said Hals.

'And there's the Three Hags,' said Pavel, pointing to a trio of mountains in the distance that looked from this angle like three hunched old women. 'My dad's farm ain't half a day south.'

Hals sniffed the air. 'I knew we was home, just by breathing. Lady of Peace, I could swear I smell my mother's pork and cabbage cooking in the pot right now.'

Gustaf chuckled unpleasantly and spoke for the first time that day. 'Don't get your hopes up, yokel. It's more likely your mother cooking in the pot.'

'Y'filthy clot!' cried Hals, trying clumsily to turn his horse toward Gustaf. 'You'll take that back or I'll have yer guts for garters!'

Captain Veirt interposed his horse between the men before Reiner even noticed him moving. 'Stand down, pikeman,' he barked at Hals, then wheeled to face Gustaf. 'And you, leech. If you open yer trap only for that sort of garbage, yer better off leaving it shut.' He stood up in his stirrups and glowered around at the whole troop. 'You'll not lack for fighting before we're done, I guarantee it. But if any man wants more than what's coming to him, come see me. I'll show you yer own spine. Am I clear?'

'Perfectly, captain,' said Gustaf, turning his horse away.

Hals nodded, head lowered. 'Aye, captain.'

'Right then,' said Veirt. 'Ride on. We've twenty more miles to make today.'

AT DUSK THEY rode through a ruined town. The houses, taverns and shops were nothing but blackened sticks. Drifts of ash-blackened snow clung to crumbled stone walls. Pavel and Hals stared around in blank dismay.

'This is Draetau,' said Pavel. 'My cousin lives in Draetau.'

'Lived,' said Gustaf.

'We sell our pigs in the market down there,' said Hals, pointing down a cross street. There was no longer any market.

Pavel trembled with rage and wiped at his eyes. 'The heathen bastards. Filthy, daemon worshipping swine.'

Beyond the edge of the town they saw an orange glow through a stand of trees and heard faint cries and the clash of arms.

'Weapons out!' barked Veirt, and drew his sword. The men followed suit. Giano wound his crossbow and Franz nocked an arrow on his string. Reiner checked that his pistols were primed and cocked.

'Von Eisenberg, Hetzau,' called Veirt. 'With the lady.'

Erich and Reiner jogged up so that they flanked Lady Magda. Veirt rode directly before her. Through a gap in the trees they could see that a small cluster of farmhouses were burning. The silhouettes of huge men with horns – whether sprouting from their helmets or growing from their heads it was impossible to tell – ran through the flames, chasing smaller silhouettes. Others drove off sheep and cattle. A few carried human prizes. Reiner and the others could hear the thin shrieks of women over the crackle of fire.

Pavel and Hals kicked their horses awkwardly forward. 'Captain,' said Hals. 'Those are our people. We can't just…'

'No,' said Veirt grimly. 'We've a job to do. Ride on.' But he didn't look happy about it.

Erich coughed. 'Captain, for once I agree with the pike. The village isn't much out of our line of march, and we might…'

'I said no!' bellowed Veirt, so they rode on. But before they had gone another quarter mile, Veirt struck his leg with his gloved fist. 'This is all the fault of those mealy-mouthed fools who surround the Emperor and fill his ears with cowardice disguised as caution. We are too extended, they say. The treasury is depleted, they say. We cannot afford to prolong the war. The fools! They can't afford not to!'

The squad looked at him, surprised. From their short association with him, they knew Veirt as a taciturn man, who kept his emotions to himself, but here he was raging like tap-room orator.

'It wasn't enough to push the hordes beyond our borders and into the mountains, and then return as if the mission were accomplished. It is as Baron Albrecht says. We must destroy them utterly. Otherwise it will be as you see – a little raid here, a little raid there, with our mothers and sisters never truly safe, the Empire never truly sovereign. Unless we want to endlessly fight for land we have called our own for centuries, we must seek out the barbarians in their own lairs and kill them to the last man, woman and child.'

'Hear hear,' said Erich. 'Well said. But then...'

'No,' said Veirt. 'The relic Baron Albrecht has commanded us to recover is more important. It could turn the tide at last. It could mean the end of the northern curse for all time. Once m'lord Albrecht has it, he and his brother Manfred will be able to retake Nordbergbruche, their ancestral home, from the Chaos filth that stole it while m'lords were fighting in the east. Then it will become a bastion against the scum that hide in the mountains, and Valnir's Bane will be the spear with which the Empire will at last drive out...'

'Captain,' said Lady Magda, sharply. 'This is a *secret* mission.'

Veirt looked up at her and visibly composed himself. 'Forgive me, lady. I let my tongue get away from me.'

Veirt returned his horse to her side and they got under way once more.

'Quite a speech,' muttered Reiner, dropping back a bit.

'Oh yes,' said Hals, grinning. 'Old Veirt's a firebreather all right.'

'You served under him?'

Pavel shook his head. 'Would that we had. There's one who wouldn't run in battle.'

Hals laughed. 'Not him. That's why he's here, trying to win his way back into Albrecht's good graces.'

'Veirt's in the doghouse too?' asked Reiner, surprised.

'Worse than the doghouse. His neck's on the block. Direct disobedience of orders,' said Pavel.

'He was under the command of Albrecht's brother, Manfred, at the battle of Vandengart. Manfred told him to hold his position,' continued Hals, 'but Veirt saw a troop of gunners being destroyed by some horrible norther beasties and couldn't stand it. He charged. Cost Manfred the battle.'

'Lost him nearly a hundred men,' added Pavel.

'But Veirt's pikes never broke,' said Hals proudly. 'Slaughtered every last one of those nightmares. There's a captain.'

'Aye,' said Pavel.

Reiner chuckled. 'A squadron of the condemned led by the condemned.'

'It's nothing to laugh at,' sniffed Erich. 'I had no idea. The man's cashiered.'

Reiner spotted more torches moving through the fields just north of the road. 'Captain. On your right.'

Veirt looked where he pointed and cursed under his breath. 'Right. We turn west. Von Eisenberg, on point.'

The company reluctantly turned off the road. With a last, longing look over his shoulder at the marauders, Erich nudged his horse forward until he was fifty paces ahead. They rode through fields and sparse woods in a large half-circle until the Kurgan torches were out of sight and all they could see of the burning farms was a faint orange glow on the underside of the low-hanging clouds.

At last Veirt turned them north again. A long finger of wood lay between them and the road. Veirt called Erich back until he rode only a few yards ahead, gave him a slotted lantern which emitted a narrow wedge of light but hid its flame from prying eyes, and they began to pick their way through the wood.

Though narrow, the centre of the strip of woods became thick and tangled with undergrowth, and their progress was reduced to a walk. The horses pushed through the brush as if breasting through a stream, and it was necessary to hack at the branches that dangled overhead to avoid being dragged off their mounts.

'Captain,' said Erich. 'May I suggest we go about and circle this briar patch?'

Veirt nodded. 'Turn around. Back the way we...'

'Captain,' said Lady Magda. 'I believe my horse's hoof is caught. I cannot turn.'

Veirt grunted and sheathed his sword in his saddle-mounted scabbard. 'A moment, lady.' He dismounted, took Erich's lantern, and squatted by Lady Magda's horse. After a moment he stood. 'Urquart. Her hoof's wedged between two roots. I need your strength.'

The big engineer dismounted and joined Veirt. As they hauled at the roots, Oskar's head snapped up. 'Do you hear something?' he asked tremulously.

The others fell still and listened. There was something, almost lost in the creaking of leather and shifting of horses – a rhythmic murmering like a tide over a pebble beach, like... breathing. They looked into the blackness of the woods. On all sides of them, glowing yellow eyes reflected their lantern light.

Veirt cursed and waded for his horse, trying to get to his sword. The men drew their weapons and tugged on their reins, attempting to settle their horses, which were shying into each other nervously as they scented the hidden threat.

'Protect the lady!' called Veirt.

A horse whinneyed.

Reiner looked back. A black shape, the size of a wild boar, but leaner, was pulling down Franz's horse, its teeth and claws deep in the poor beast's haunches. The horse crashed on its side in the undergrowth and Franz was thrown clear. Before Reiner could even call the boy's name, more of the black shapes attacked, roaring and howling.

Reiner and Erich pulled their pistols from their holsters. Oskar reached for his handgun.

'No guns!' called Veirt as he retrieved his sword. 'Their masters might hear!'

'Masters?' thought Reiner. Boars had no masters. Then he saw that one of the charging monsters wore a studded collar. They were hounds! But such hounds he had never seen: huge, deformed things with twisted, overmuscled limbs and fat, fleshy goitres bulging from their distorted faces. Their fanged jaws dripped with yellow mucus.

Erich spurred his horse forward and took a hound's charge on his spear. The impact wasn't strong enough to kill the beast, for both hound and horse were slowed by the tangle of undergrowth. The hound twisted and fought, clawing and biting at the spear. Reiner rode up beside it and jabbed down at its back with his sword. It was like trying to pierce a saddle. The muscle was nearly as dense as wood. Even its matted fur was hard to penetrate. Reiner raised his sword again and stabbed down with both hands.

Behind him, Pavel and Hals jumped off their horses and faced a charging hound on foot like the pikemen they were. They planted their spear-butts and took the leaping brute in the chest.

Giano fired his crossbow at another. It caught the hound in the eye. The beast howled and whipped its head around, trying to dislodge the annoyance. The bolt stayed put. The hound stopped and attempted to wipe the bolt away on the ground and instead drove it further into its skull. It vomited blood and died. Giano cranked his crossbow for another shot.

Ulf swung his huge maul at a slavering hound. He hit it square in the shoulder, knocking the thing flat, but overbalanced and fell himself.

Another beast leapt at Oskar's horse. Oskar flailed at it with his sword, but his horse, rearing and kicking, did more damage.

Captain Veirt shouldered through the brush toward the bedevilled artilleryman.

Reiner finally forced his blade through his hound's ribs and found its heart. The thing shuddered and slumped beneath him. He pulled his sword free and surveyed the battle, looking for Franz. There was a swirl of movement beyond the boy's horse. A hound leaping and bucking. There was something on its back. Franz! The boy was riding the beast, one hand on its collar, the other stabbing it over and over again with a dagger while the beast snapped at him over its shoulder. Reiner had never seen anyone look so frightened. The boy's expression might have seemed comical had his situation not been so desperate.

Gustaf was closest to the boy, but though he had his sword out and watched alertly, he made no move to help. Reiner cursed and kicked his horse toward the boy, but the animal was entangled in the brush and was having difficulty turning. Damn this wood! He jumped from the saddle and pushed toward the boy on foot, taking briar scratches with every step.

Erich withdrew his spear from the beast Reiner had killed, but sought no new target, instead holding his place at Lady Magda's side.

Pavel's spear snapped under the weight of the beast he and Hals had stopped, and he went down beneath it. Hals bellowed and stabbed the hound in the side, trying to drive it off his friend. Pavel threw his arms up to protect his face. The beast clawed his arm.

The hound attacking Oskar got its teeth into the artilleryman's boot and dragged him, screaming, from the saddle. Giano fired at it, but missed. Veirt surged forward and hacked at the beast, cutting deep into its shoulder. The hound turned and leapt on him. Veirt stuffed his mail-clad fist in its maw and stabbed it through the neck.

Nearby, Ulf swung his maul again and this time crushed his creature's skull. The brute dropped at his feet, oozing grey matter and noxious purple fluids.

Reiner charged Franz's beast, roaring, but missed as he checked his swing for fear of hitting the boy. At least he'd got the hound's attention. The hound leapt at him, shaking off Franz at last. Reiner barely got his blade up in time. He caught the thing on the breastbone with a jarring impact. It bowled him over and slammed him to the ground, knocking the wind out of him. Fortunately, it was caught on the point of Reiner's sword, and couldn't reach him with its teeth or claws. It would likely kill him anyway. Its entire weight was on the sword, and the pommel was pressing into Reiner's ribs. Reiner could hear them creaking. He couldn't draw a breath. The creature's foetid drool dripped onto his face.

Something leapt out of the darkness – Franz! The boy hit the beast in the shoulder and toppled it to one side, stabbing at it in a frenzy. The beast snapped at him, and rolled on top of him. The boy shrieked like a girl as the beast's teeth clashed an inch from his face.

Reiner struggled up, sucking air. He swung wildly at the creature's head. His blade whanged off its skull, stinging his hand, but doing little damage.

'Come on, you mangy beast!' He stabbed it in the shoulder, again doing nothing. The hound looked up at him, snarling, and crouched to spring, but as it did, Franz stabbed it in the neck, directly below the jaw. The hound yelped, and a river of blood drenched the boy's arm. The beast collapsed on top of him, crushing him.

'Get it off,' he gasped. 'I can't breathe!'

'Stay there a moment,' said Reiner, looking around. 'Safest place for you.'

The melee seemed over at last. Veirt stood over a dead beast. Oskar was getting unsteadily to his feet. His boot was shredded, but the flesh beneath it thankfully only scratched. Behind them, Hals was helping Pavel up.

Pavel clutched his face. The left side was red and slick. The hound the two pikemen had fought lay with a foreleg in the air, their spears sticking from its ribs.

'All right,' said Reiner to Franz. 'All clear.' He rolled the hound off the boy and helped him to his feet. His arm was crimson to the shoulder.

'Any of that yours?' asked Reiner.

'Mostly the hound's, I think,' said Franz.

Reiner chuckled. 'Game little scrapper, ain't you?'

Franz looked embarrassed. 'You came to help me. I couldn't just stand by while...'

Reiner was embarrassed in turn. 'Aye aye, enough of that.' He shot glances at Erich, still on his horse by Lady Magda, and Gustaf, who was untouched. 'I could wish all our fellows felt the same. Didn't swing once, did you?' he snarled at Gustaf.

'I'm a surgeon. Who would patch you up if I got hurt?'

'Leech!' called Veirt. 'See to the wounded.'

Gustaf sneered smugly at Reiner and hurried to Pavel, his field kit over his shoulder.

Reiner watched him go. 'There's a fellow I wouldn't mind finding dead in a ditch.'

Franz grinned. They looked up at the sound of raised voices.

'And where were you, then?' Hals was shouting at Erich. 'Standing right there with yer spear at the ready and not doing nothing while we was getting slaughtered. Pavel's lost an eye, y'snot-nosed jagger!'

'Don't you dare take that tone with me, you insolent peasant.' Erich raised his spear as if to strike the pikeman.

Veirt stepped in the way. 'Don't you try it, my lord.'

'Insolent or not,' said Reiner joining them, 'he isn't wrong. You hung back almost as much as the surgeon here.'

'I killed my one.'

'*I* killed your one,' Reiner countered. 'You could have at least tried for another.'

'We were ordered to protect the lady.'

'Ha! I wonder do you obey all orders so literally?'

'Do you question my courage, sir?'

'Less of it!' growled Veirt. 'All of you. These hounds don't travel far from their masters. Do you want raiders breathing down our necks?'

He spoke too late, for as the men grew silent, harsh voices and the sound of tramping boots reached them. They looked toward the road. Flickering torches and hulking shapes were pushing swiftly through the woods.

'Blood of Sigmar!' swore Captain Veirt. 'Tie off your wounds and mount up, on the double.'

Gustaf finished wrapping a bandage around Pavel's head and closed up his kit.

'What about me?' asked Oskar, plaintively pointing at his leg. 'Look at all this blood.'

'What blood?' asked Gustaf as he packed up his kit. 'I've had fleabites that bled more.'

The men hurriedly mounted their horses, but Franz's was dead, its throat ripped out by the monstrous beast, and the mule carried too much to take a rider. No one looked eager to share a saddle with him.

'I don't need a knife in the ribs if he gets the wrong idea,' said Hals.

Reiner sighed and offered Franz a hand up. 'Come on, lad.'

Franz grabbed his kit from the dead horse and swung up behind Reiner, but sat far back on the saddle.

'Hold tight,' said Reiner. 'It might be a wild ride.'

'I... I'll be fine.'

There was no time to argue. Before they had all turned their horses, huge almost-human figures crashed out of the darkness, roaring and swinging enormous weapons.

FOUR
A Breath Of Fresh Air

THERE WERE A few moments of nightmarish confusion as the men savagely spurred their horses away from their pursuers and the company plunged into the darkness of the tangled woods. Trees seemed to spring out before them and roots rise up to trip them, and Reiner swore he felt the raiders' hot breath on his neck, but at last they burst out into the open fields and the horses stretched into a headlong gallop. Pavel and Hals, who had never ridden faster than a trot before, didn't like this at all, and clung to their horses' necks with death-grip terror, but by Sigmar's grace they didn't fall, and the company soon left the raiders behind.

Veirt took no chances. He kept up a punishing pace for a good hour until they had left the environs of the farming village far behind and reached an area of low hills and deep, wooded ravines. They filed into one of these, walking the horses down the centre of an ice-rimed stream for nearly a mile, until Veirt found a flat, pebbly stretch of riverbank and told them to put up their tents.

It was a sorry camp. Veirt allowed no fire, so they dined on cold rations while Gustaf cleaned and bound their wounds and a light snow melted on their horses' sweating flanks. Pavel's sobs and his cries of, 'It can't be gone! I can still feel it!' as he held his hand over his missing eye were not an aid to digestion.

Reiner's newfound friendship with Franz didn't change the boy's mind about tenting alone, and while the others bundled into their sturdy tents, he curled up best he could under his cloak, propped up at one end with his short sword and at the other with his scabbard.

For the next two days it got colder and colder as Lady Magda led them higher into the foothills of the Middle Mountains and the rain of the flatlands became wet, clinging snow. It was as if each gain in elevation turned back time, as if spring were becoming winter instead of summer. Gustaf had them smear their hands and faces with bear fat to prevent frostbite, a disgusting but effective trick.

Veirt, a native of Ostland, seemed to blossom in the cold, growing cheerier and more voluble the more bitter it got, telling stories of forced marches and desperate last stands, but Giano, from sun-baked Tilea, hated it. His usual cheery disposition soon became replaced with angry snappishness and long, whining reminiscences about the beauty of his homeland and the warmth of its sun.

Pavel's empty eye socket grew red and choked with pus. He developed a fever that had him screaming and gibbering in the night and waking the others up, which did nothing to lighten the general disposition of the group. During the day he couldn't sit astride his saddle, so Ulf knocked together a simple stretcher out of saplings and twine that dragged behind his horse. Gustaf bound him into it and packed him in snow to keep him from burning up. Though it pained him, Reiner begrudgingly allowed that Gustaf did his job well, even changing the dressing on Pavel's eye at every meal stop. Hals was unusually quiet during his friend's sickness, his normal flow of insult and wit frozen with worry.

The tiny mountain villages they passed through were all deserted, and most destroyed. Axe-scarred skeletons lay between the houses, picked clean by crows, and it was obvious by the many tracks of unshod hooves that Kurgan raiders passed back and forth through the area constantly. Reiner expected the villages to be picked as clean as the skeletons, but Hals, who, being a peasant, knew the tricks of peasants, showed them how to find hidden caches of food and liquor under dirt floors and at the bottoms of wells.

They made camp outside one such village two nights after the fight with the beasts and, armed with Hals's knowledge, went searching for hidden food to supplement their meagre rations.

Reiner, Franz and Hals were prying up the flagstones in a cottage kitchen when they heard a woman's scream. Fearing that Lady Magda was being attacked, they dropped the stone and ran out to the steep, twisting track that served the little settlement as a high street. The scream came again, from a shack further up the hill. They ran to it.

Hals was about to kick the door in, but Reiner stopped him, and motioned for him and Franz to circle around the tiny, tumbledown place. 'Block the back door,' he whispered. 'If it has one.'

Reiner waited at the front door as the others crept through the muddy yard. The cry came again, but muffled this time, and then a male voice. 'Hold still, curse you!'

The voice sounded familiar. Reiner stepped silently to an unglassed window and looked in. It was dim inside, and hard to see, but Reiner could just make out a pair of legs in torn woollen hose lying on the floor, and another pair in breeks lying on top of them. A male hand fumbled at a belt buckle. He couldn't make out the man's face, but he recognised the body. He'd been looking at it for days.

'Schlecht!' he roared. He ran to the door and kicked it in.

Gustaf looked up from where he lay on top of a wild-eyed peasant girl on the dusty wood floor. Her skirts were rucked up around her waist and he had his knife under her jaw. Splotches and smears of blood surrounded her.

'You filthy swine,' growled Reiner. 'Get off of her.'

'I... I thought she was a raider,' said Schlecht, pushing hurriedly to his knees. 'I was... I was...'

The back door burst in and Franz and Hals entered.

'What's all the...' Hals broke off as he took in the tableau. Franz went pale.

'You rotten little...' Hals stepped forward and kicked Gustaf in the face.

The surgeon fell off the girl, and Hals pulled her to her feet. There were bloody cuts on her chest. It looked as if Schlecht had carved his initials there. Reiner shuddered.

'Here now, lass,' Hals said softly. 'He can't hurt you now. Are you…?'

The girl wasn't listening. She screamed and lashed out, striping Hals across the cheek with her nails, and dashed for the door. Reiner didn't get in her way.

Hals turned back to Gustaf, who was sitting up groggily. 'You filth,' he growled. 'I knew what you were the minute I laid eyes on you, and I'm ashamed of myself that I didn't kill you then.' He kicked Gustaf in the face again and raised his sword.

'No!' cried Gustaf, crabbing backward. 'You daren't! You daren't! I'm your surgeon. Do you want your friend to die?'

Hals checked his swing, knuckles turning white on the hilt.

'He's right,' said Reiner, though he hated to say it. 'We need him. All of us. We've the whole trip to do again, with who knows how many raiders in the way. We'll need someone to patch us up.'

Hals's shoulders slumped. 'Aye,' he said. 'Aye, yer right.' He raised his head and glared at Gustaf. 'But when we get back, don't expect to live long enough to spend yer reward.'

Gustaf sneered. 'Do you think it wise to threaten the man who will tend to your wounds, pike?'

Hals rushed the surgeon again, but Reiner held him back. 'Ignore him, lad. Don't give him the satisfaction.'

Hals snarled, but turned toward the door. He motioned to Franz. 'Come on, lad. Let's get a breath of fresh air. It stinks in here.'

The two soldiers walked out. Reiner joined them, turning his back pointedly on Gustaf.

As THE SUN reached noon the next day, they saw the white-washed stone walls of the Convent of Shallya on an outcrop above them. It shone like a pearl.

'Don't look pillaged from here,' said Hals.

Pavel, whose fever had broken that morning, and who sat swaying and fragile on his horse, grinned. 'Pillaged or not, we're here at last,' he said. 'Now we can get this whatsit and go home.

I just hope the trip back don't cost me my other eye. I won't be able to see all me gold.'

'It is an hour's ride from here,' said Lady Magda. 'The path is narrow and winding.'

Oskar shielded his eyes against the noon-day glare. 'There is smoke. Coming from the convent.'

Veirt squinted where Oskar pointed. 'Are you certain?'

'Aye captain,' said the artilleryman. 'Campfire or chimney it might be.'

'Could be the nuns,' said Hals.

Veirt gave him a withering look.

The revelation of the smoke lengthened their trip up the mountain to two hours, for they went at a walk, with Giano and Franz spying ahead on foot, scouting each bend in the path for enemies. There were none, though they found evidence of recent passage: gnawed bones, prints in the snow, a discarded jar of wine shattered on a rock.

Reiner caught Hals looking uneasily at these traces, and smirked. 'A messy lot, these nuns.'

About three-quarters of the way up, the trail was joined by a much wider path winding around the mountains from the south, and on this wider path were countless snow-filled foot and hoofprints going in both directions, indicating that large groups of men and horses travelled it with some regularity.

Veirt eyed these signs with grim interest. 'Must be a nest of them further up.'

'Not in the convent?' quavered Oskar.

'You only saw one column of smoke?'

'Oh yes, of course.' Oskar looked relieved.

At last they reached the narrow shelf of rock upon which the convent was built, a sort of landing before the wide path continued up the stepped hills into the mountains. There was evidence that the forces that travelled up and down the path often made camp on the ledge – scorched circles of old campfires, bones, rubbish.

The convent's white walls extended from the cliff edge, which looked east toward Smallhof and Kislev, to the face of the mountain, cutting off the tapering end of the shelf. But the appearance of gleaming perfection that the walls had given at the base of the hill proved an illusion up close. They had been shattered and blackened in many places, and the great wooden gates hung off their hinges in a jumble of charred timber. The convent buildings rose in three steps behind the gates, with the spire of a chapel of Shallya highest and furthest back. Even from a distance Veirt's men could see that entire place had been gutted, walls burned, roofs caved in, garbage scattered about. The thin column of smoke still rose, seeming to come from the third step.

Giano made the sign of Shallya as he looked at the wreckage and muttered under his breath.

'It appears that Baron Albrecht's information was correct,' said Erich.

'Aye,' said Veirt.

Reiner looked to Lady Magda, expecting a reaction, but the sister seemed made of iron. She gazed at the wreckage with tight-lipped stoicism. 'The crypt we must enter is beneath the chapel,' she said. 'So we must get beyond whoever has lit that fire.'

'Very good, my lady,' said Veirt, and turned to the men. 'Dismount, you lot. Ostini, Shoentag, have a look and report back.'

As the men dismounted – much to the relief of Pavel and Hals, who rubbed their aching backsides vigorously – the mercenary and the boy tip-toed through the gate and disappeared. While they were gone, the party found a hidden corner in which to tie up the horses and then refreshed themselves with a drink of nearly frozen water from their canteens. Reiner could hear the ice sloshing around in his. Veirt ordered Ulf to set up Lady Magda's tent, and suggested to her that she wait while they saw to any difficulties, but she refused. She seemed as eager as the rest of them to get this whatever-it-was and return to civilisation. She declared that she would come with them.

Franz and Giano returned shortly.

'Six,' said Giano. 'Big boys, and with the big swords, hey? Northers?'

'Kurgan,' corrected Franz. 'Same as we faced at Kirstaad. They look to be foot troops. No horses I could see. No fresh droppings.'

'Two walking around,' continued Giano, making a circling motion with his fingers. 'Four in garden, eating.'

'You sure that's all of them?' asked Veirt.

Franz and Giano nodded.

'Right, then.' Veirt hunched forward. 'We take out the two on patrol as quiet as shadows, got it? Then everyone with a bow or gun will find good vantage on the four in the garden and put as much iron into them as we can. These lads are tough as your boot. If we have to come to grips with 'em I want 'em well peppered, you mark me?'

A chorus of 'Ayes' answered him.

'Right then; commend your souls to Sigmar and let's be at it.'

FIVE
Heroes Don't Win By Trickery

THEY ADVANCED CAUTIOUSLY through the forecourt, weapons at the ready, Lady Magda and Pavel, still too weak from his fever to fight, at the rear. There were burned stables to the left and the remains of a dry storage to the right, shattered oil jars and empty sacks of grain lying among jumbled timbers. The main convent building faced them, a two-storey structure clad in white marble where the nuns had once taken their meals, and where the library and offices of the abbess and her staff were housed. Its walls still stood, but black smears of soot above each smashed-in window gave evidence of the destruction within. The walls were daubed with vile symbols that Reiner was glad he didn't understand. Decaying corpses in nuns' robes were scattered around the yard like rotting fruit fallen from some macabre tree. Oskar shivered at the sight.

They crept up wide curved steps that led to the level of the convent dormitory, where the nuns and novitiates had slept. The building was fronted by a small plaza. Neither had fared well. The dormitory, a wide, half-timbered, three-storey building, had lost its left wing to fire, and the right was sagging badly. The plaza seemed to have been used as a latrine and dump by the raiders, and was filled with rotting food, broken and burnt furniture, rusting weapons and excrement. It smelled like a charnel house that had caved into a sewer.

Giano stopped them on the last step before the plaza and they crouched down. He pointed up to the next level: a ruined garden, reached by another set of curving steps, and surrounded by a balustrade that looked over the plaza. Over a row of high burnt hedges, they could see pikes pointing up to the sky, with long-haired skulls spiked on top like totems. 'They making the camp there,' he said. 'Behind hedgings. Patrol walk around edge.'

Veirt nodded. 'Right. Ostini – no – Lichtmar and Shoentag, I want you up in the dormitory. There should be windows in the third floor that overlook the garden. If not, get on the roof. You cover the boys at the fire. Ostini, you join 'em once we've finished off the patrols.'

'Surely it won't take seven of us to kill two men?' said Erich.

'They are hardly men,' said Veirt. 'And I hope seven of us are enough to take them out one at a time. Now here is what I want to see.'

As Veirt laid out his strategy they saw the first of the raiders pass. He was an intimidating sight, a shaggy-haired giant in leather and furs, a head taller than Ulf, and unnaturally thick with muscle. Fetishes and charms dangled from braids in his beard, and the scabbarded sword that hung from his belt looked taller than Franz – and probably outweighed him too.

After waiting for the second raider to pass they hurried to their positions – Oskar and Franz running low for the dormitory door, and the rest heading for the steps that led up to the garden. Pavel, armed with one of Reiner's pistols, stayed behind with Lady Magda.

There was a smashed statue of Shallya directly below the balustrade that edged the garden. A blow from above had sheared it off from shoulder to hip, so that what remained was a sharp shard that pointed at the sky, while Shallya's serene face looked up from the rubble at the base of her pedestal. Giano touched his heart with his palm when he saw it.

'Heathens,' he muttered. 'Desecrate the lady. Blasphemy.'

Reiner smirked. 'A mercenary who venerates Shallya?'

'Always I fight for peace,' said Giano proudly.

'Ah.'

While the others pressed against the wall on either side of the steps where they wouldn't be seen, Reiner and Giano tip-toed up to the garden level. On its east side, it overlooked the cliff, and here the balustrade was lined with tall columns. These had once been topped with statues of Shallyan martyrs looking off toward the heathen wastelands, but the raiders had pulled them down, and the columns were empty.

Reiner eyed them uneasily. Veirt had asked him and Giano to climb the first two, and he didn't like the idea. It wasn't that they were hard to climb: they were wreathed with sturdy, if thorny, rose vines, which made for easy hand and foot holds. It was that they sat on the very edge of the cliff, and though Reiner wasn't terribly afraid of heights, clinging to a column by one's fingers and toes above a four hundred foot drop to jagged rocks would give any sane man qualms. It might have been his imagination, but the wind seemed to pick up just as he began his climb.

At last, well after Giano was already perched on his, Reiner pulled himself on top of the pillar. He swallowed. The top had looked wide enough when he was on the ground, but now seemed to have shrunk to the diameter of a dinner plate. He crouched down, knees trembling. Fortunately the briars were thick around the capital, so unless someone was actually looking for them, they were hidden from the ground. What was going to make them conspicuous was the blanket.

With a look to make sure the raider guards were out of sight, Reiner pulled his blanket from his pack, unrolled it and – holding firmly to a twist of vine – flipped one end over to Giano. The mercenary seemed to have no fear of heights. He reached out over the chasm and caught the blanket without a quiver. He gave Reiner a grin and the circled thumb and forefinger.

Reiner's pulse beat against his throat. If the raiders spotted anything, it would be the blanket, drooping between the two pillars like festive bunting. At least the sun was at such an angle that the thing cast no shadow over the walk.

He had little time to agonise. Just as he and Giano set themselves, the first of the raiders came around the high hedge and started toward them. Reiner crouched lower in the briars and gripped the blanket with both hands. He watched as the raider walked along, gazing idly out over the cliff at the endless forest below, then reached the steps and turned to walk along the balustrade that looked over the plaza, oblivious to the men above and below him.

Now was the moment. Reiner and Giano exchanged a look, then jumped off the pillars as one, holding the blanket out wide between them. They landed perfectly, catching the raider's head in the blanket while he was in mid-step and pulling back hard. The giant slammed flat on his back, gasping as the air was knocked from him, and before he had time to recover and cry out, the rest of Veirt's men had raced up the steps and leapt on him: Ulf sitting on his chest and pinning his arms, Gustaf and Hals holding his legs, and Veirt grabbing his head through the blanket and cramming the butt of his pistol into the man's mouth as he fought for air.

Erich raised his sword, but hesitated, for, though pinned, the Kurgan was so strong he jerked the three men that held him down this way and that and nearly threw them off. 'Hold him still, curse you,' he hissed.

Reiner pulled the bag of pistol shot from his belt and cracked the giant over the head with all his strength. The fight went out of his massive limbs, and Erich brought his blade down like an executioner's axe. The blow severed the raider's head from his body. Veirt wrapped it up in the blanket and pressed it against the giant's spouting neck. 'Now get him out of here before he bleeds all over the place.'

This was easier said than done. Ulf caught the warrior under the arms, and Gustaf and Hals lifted his legs, but he seemed twice as heavy as he should be, and they could barely inch him along. Beyond that, there was no stopping the blood. Though Giano tucked a second blanket under the raider's neck as they moved him, the flagstones of the walk were still spattered with bright red drops.

'Clean that up,' whispered Veirt, but it was too late. They could hear the second guard coming. Reiner and Giano ran to their columns again and started climbing while Veirt mopped at the bloody pavers with his cloak. Ulf, Gustaf and Hals, grunting with effort, tried to muscle the headless corpse down the steps, but Ulf lost his footing and went over backwards, tumbling down to the plaza with the body crashing on top of him as the rest ducked out of sight.

Reiner heard the second Kurgan call a question. He came around the hedge with his massive sword drawn and looked around suspiciously. He was as big as his companion, but bald, and with eyebrows so shaggy that he had braided the ends. He wore a mail shirt and a bearskin cloak. Reiner and Giano froze halfway up their pillars and edged around out of his line of sight like squirrels. The raider crept forward, wary. Reiner held his breath.

The raider barked another question, then stopped as he spotted the smeared blood on the flagstones. He backed up, shouting a warning to his comrades over his shoulder.

Raised voices answered him from behind the hedge.

'Kill him!' cried Veirt, and raced up the steps with Erich, Hals and Gustaf behind him.

The Kurgan turned to face them, which opened his back to Giano and Reiner. They leapt at him, daggers drawn, as he met Veirt and Erich's charge sword to sword. Reiner's dagger turned on his mail, but Giano's struck home and the raider roared in pain. He backhanded Giano and Reiner with his free hand while slashing at the others with his blade.

Giano was knocked to the ground, but Reiner hit the balustrade and came within an inch of tumbling over it into the void. Only a painful grab at a thorny vine stopped him. Pulling himself back to safety, Reiner heard the sound of running feet, and over it, the thrum of a bow and the crack of a gun, as Franz and Oskar fired from the dormitory windows at their suddenly moving targets.

Reiner helped Giano to his feet and they ran forward to help. The bald raider was surrounded by Veirt and the others, roaring like a cornered bull. Hals had his spear in his guts, and Veirt and Erich were laying into him like woodsmen felling a tree, but still the northman fought on. As he looked for an opening, Reiner saw Ulf, still dazed from his tumble, struggling back up the stairs, and behind him Pavel, hurrying across the plaza, pistol in hand, puffing like he'd run ten miles instead of ten yards.

The raider caught Erich a glancing blow on the shoulder and knocked him flat, then chopped through the haft of Hals's spear and pulled the head out of his innards. He used it to block Veirt's sword and returned the blow with a slash that sent Veirt's helmet clattering down the steps and dropped the grizzled captain to his hands and knees.

Reiner, Giano and Ulf rushed in to fill up the gaps. Reiner parried the raider's blade with his sabre. It was like trying to stop a battering ram with a fly whisk. His whole arm went numb with the force of the blow.

Giano too was knocked back, but not before he jabbed his sword into the crook of the giant's arm and cut something vital. Blood soaked the northman's leather wrist guard and his sword drooped to the ground. Ulf grabbed his other arm, shouting, 'I've got him! Kill him!'

Reiner drove his sword deep into the raider's chest. The man roared in pain and swung Ulf like he was a child. He crashed into Reiner and they went down in a heap.

'Hoy,' said a quiet voice.

Reiner looked up. The raider was turning to find the speaker, and came face to face with the barrel of the pistol in Pavel's shaking hand.

Pavel fired. The back of the raider's head exploded in an eruption of brains and gore. He dropped like a felled ox.

'Nice one,' said Hals.

Their relief was short-lived. Before Reiner and Ulf could do more than stand, four more raiders rounded the hedge at a run, axes and swords in hand. One had an arrow in his shoulder, evidence that Franz could hit more than rabbits.

Veirt stood and drew his pistol. 'Fire!'

Reiner and Erich drew as well and all fired in unison. Only two of the shots hit and only one was telling, ripping a raider's throat out. He fell to his knees, hands to his neck, guzzling his own blood. The others kept coming, and there was no time for another volley. Reiner tossed away his spent piece and mumbled a prayer to Ranald that the dice would roll his way.

Hals snatched Pavel's spear from him and pushed his friend down the stairs, crying, 'Get out of the way, y'old fool.'

Erich, Veirt, Giano and Ulf squared up to meet the charge, while Gustaf, as Reiner expected, hung back.

Just before the two sides met, a shot rang out and one of the raiders stumbled. Reiner saw Oskar and Franz running from the door of the dormitory. Oskar's gun was smoking.

Then there was no more time for looking around. With an impact like ships colliding, the two sides came together. Erich and Ulf, the biggest of the men, took the charge full on, and held, while Veirt, canny old warrior that he was, ducked low and slashed at the shins of his man. Reiner and Giano dodged left and right and swung at the raiders' backs as they ran by.

The three raiders took these attacks without flinching. Even wounded and outnumbered two to one, they looked to Reiner to be the winning side. They slashed at the circling men with a fearless ferocity that was frightening to behold. Reiner wondered how the Empire had ever prevailed against monsters such as these.

Ulf quickly found himself in trouble, forced away from the others by a raider with tattoos winding around his bare arms. He was overmatched, and gave ground with every exchange, the haft of his wooden maul splintering under repeated hacks from the norther's sword. But just as he was about to break through the engineer's defences, the Kurgan slipped on Reiner's discarded pistol and his leg skidded out from under him. Ulf took advantage, shattering the northman's shin with a scooping swing. The raider fell to one knee and Ulf darted in, aiming for his skull. But even unable to move, the raider was a danger. He parried the blow with his sword and gashed Ulf across the chest.

'Ulf!' cried Franz. 'Fall back! Back away!'

Ulf jumped back, bleeding, and Franz and Oskar, who had been hanging fire, shot the kneeling Kurgan point blank. Franz's arrow caught him in the throat. Oskar's ball smashed through his groin. He collapsed sideways, clutching himself, crimson to the knees in seconds.

There were two left, and one of them, the one with Franz's arrow in his shoulder, went down almost immediately, Veirt's long sword slipping neatly through his ribs, but the last – the leader by his size and power – fought on, roaring like a mountain cat. Though he bled from a hundred cuts, he only seemed to get stronger – and to Reiner's disbelieving eyes – bigger.

Reiner blinked and shook his head, ducking a wild slash from the man's axe, but when he looked again, the illusion remained. The raider seemed to be bursting out of his armour. The leather bands around his biceps snapped as he backhanded Veirt to the ground. The links of his chain mail shirt strained and popped. A weird glyph on his powerful chest seemed to glow as if lit from within. His pupils enlarged to fill his whole eye.

'What happens to him?' asked Giano, uneasily, as the raider's armour dropped from him like a shed skin.

'He is touched by his god,' said Veirt, recovering. 'His battle rage is upon him.'

'Well, I'm a mite peeved myself,' said Hals, and jabbed the monstrous warrior in the ribs. The spearhead snapped off as if he had jammed it into a stone wall. The raider kicked the pikeman back so hard he crashed into a pillar and collapsed. Giano swung his sword at the warrior's now naked back. It glanced off as if he wore field plate. Erich and Veirt hacked at him with similar results. Erich parried an axe blow on his sword and was knocked to the flagstones, a finger-deep notch in the edge of his blade.

This was ridiculous, thought Reiner. They outnumbered the raider ten to one and still they couldn't finish him? There had to be something sharp enough to pierce the inhuman warrior's skin. He frowned, thinking hard. The change had made the raider bigger and stronger, but he didn't seem any smarter – in fact he grew more bestial by the moment. 'Back toward the plaza!' Reiner shouted. 'I've an idea!'

The men looked to Veirt.

'Do it,' he rasped. 'We're not winning this way.'

He and the others backed toward the steps, following Reiner. The raider pressed after them, slashing mindlessly.

'Hals, Ulf,' called Reiner. 'Kneel at the balustrade with Hals's spear between you.'

'But the head's broken off,' said Hals.

''Tisn't the point I want,' said Reiner. He scooped up a handful of loose rocks, and as Hals and Ulf knelt, holding the broken spear between them, he hopped up on the balustrade, looking down into the plaza to make sure he had positioned himself correctly.

'All right,' he cried. 'Scatter!'

Giano and Veirt jumped back, but Erich hesitated.

'You heard him,' bellowed Veirt. 'Get away!'

Erich leapt to the side, and before the transformed northman could go after any of them, Reiner shied a rock at him. It hit him in the chest. He looked up.

'Come on, you dirt-eating heathen!' shouted Reiner. He hurled another rock. It caught the Kurgan on the bridge of the nose. He howled.

'You overgrown ox!' shouted Reiner. He bounced another rock off the warrior's forehead. 'You motherless son of a goatherd! I've stepped in things that smelled better than you.'

With an ear-splitting roar, the mutated marauder charged Reiner, axe swinging. At the last possible second, Reiner dived to the side and crashed to the flags. The raider hit the balustrade at thigh level and toppled forward. Hals and Ulf helped him along, raising his legs with the broken spear and flipping him over the rail to the plaza below.

There was a horrible wet crunch and an animal cry of agony cut short. Reiner stood, holding his mouth. He'd bitten his tongue when he landed and it was bleeding. He looked over the balustrade with the rest. They gasped. He smirked. His plan had worked. The Chaos marauder was impaled on the sheared-off statue of Shallya, the sharp wedge of marble jutting up through his shattered ribs like a white island rising from a red swamp.

'Sigmar's hammer,' said Hals, rubbing his chest where the raider had kicked him. 'He didn't half deserve that.'

'Bravo,' said Giano. 'But he might have missed. Why not just…?' He pointed to the cliff-edge balustrade.

'Because, unlike you,' Reiner said, rubbing his jaw, 'I have some regard for my own skin. A slip here and I bite my tongue. A slip there and…' Reiner swallowed at the very thought.

'Ah, yes.'

Veirt clapped Reiner on the back. 'Smart work, lad. Very smart.'

Erich sniffed. 'Hardly one for the bards, though. Heroes don't win by trickery.'

'That's why there are so many dead heroes,' Reiner retorted.

'Well, I thought it was fine,' said Pavel coming up the stairs. 'Never would have thought of something like that in a hundred years.'

The others nodded in agreement. Franz grinned and gave him the circled thumb and forefinger. Erich glowered and turned away.

Lady Magda appeared at the top of the stairs. 'If the danger has passed, it is time to enter the chamber.'

SIX
You Will Obey Me

THEY MOVED THROUGH the garden that fronted the Chapel of Shallya with wary vigilance. Franz and Giano had only seen six marauders, but there might well be more. In the centre of the garden they found a cooking fire burning inside a circle of planted spears and pikes, each with a grisly trophy affixed on top. Lady Magda's face was set as she surveyed the whitening skulls of those who had once been her sisters. The smell of roasting meat rose from the fire. Nobody looked too closely at what was cooking.

It was evident that a much larger force had camped here in the recent past. The remains of other fires were dotted around the garden, and heaps of rotting garbage were piled in the corners. The rose bushes and decorative borders had been trampled, the statues smashed and the fountains used as latrines. At one side a crude forge had been built, and broken and half-repaired weapons and pieces of armour were strewn about it.

But none of the vandalism the party had seen prepared them for the horrors wreaked upon the chapel. The white marble walls were blackened with smoke and the tile roof had caved in, leaving the interior open to the sky. And there were worse things than mere destruction. The raiders seemed to have reserved their most imaginative blasphemies for this shining symbol of charity and mercy. The statues in the alcoves around the white marble walls had been pulled down and replaced with naked nuns tied to stakes and left to die. Eldritch runes, so evil that it was difficult even to look at them, had been smeared on all the walls in blood, and the simple wooden dove-wings carving, the symbol of the Shallyan faith which was mounted over the door, had been hung upside down and covered with the most obscene blasphemies.

Inside, among the charred ruins of the roof beams, were the bound bodies of more nuns, who had been abused most cruelly before they died. The beautiful tapestries illustrating the miracles of Shallya had been torn down and burned, and worst of all, upon the sacred altar some perverse ceremony had been performed. Strange symbols and arrows had been burnt into the stone floor in a circle around the dais, pointing toward all the compass points. Blood had been dribbled in unsettling designs, and on the altar itself, inside a thicket of melted candles and piled skulls, the body of the abbess, in life a plump, middle-aged woman, lay splayed, bound and naked, with runes carved into her flesh with a knife, and a huge sword driven down through her abdomen and into the stone table beneath her – a feat of strength Reiner could hardly credit. Shadows seemed to move around her. It took Reiner a moment to realise that these were rats, eating her extremities.

A sob exploded from Giano's throat and he rushed forward. 'Lady of peace, no! It no can be allow! We must clean! We must fix!'

'Ostini!' shouted Veirt. 'Leave off. We've other business!'

But the Tilean had jumped up on the altar and was knocking away the candles and rats and cutting at the ropes that held the abbess. 'Cursed rats! Defilers!'

Veirt marched to Giano and yanked him off the altar by his belt. 'I said, leave off!'

Lady Magda's face was grim and pale. She made the sign of Shallya over the abbess, then turned toward an arch in the right wall without a backward glance. 'This way,' she said.

The archway led to a stone stair which spiralled down into darkness. While torches were kindled, Veirt ordered Oskar to stand guard outside the chapel, then the rest started down the stairs. Veirt led the way, followed by Lady Magda. Erich brought up the rear.

At the bottom of the stairs they stepped out into an intersection of three short hallways. It was obvious that the raiders had found their way here as well. The bodies of a few nuns who looked as though they had died defending the catacombs lay butchered on the stone floor, and the large and intricately decorated bronze doors which glinted orange in the torchlight at the end of each hallway had been smashed open and hung from their hinges, revealing shadowed rooms beyond. The rats were feasting. Giano shuddered.

'The convent's mausoleums,' said Lady Magda. 'Where are buried all the abbesses who have led us down through the ages.'

Hals shivered and made the sign of the hammer. 'Graves?'

Lady Magda shot him a look. 'After the horrors through which we have just passed you are frightened of the long dead?'

Hals stuck his chin out. 'Course not. Just don't like it, is all.'

Magda started down the middle hallway to the desecrated mausoleum at the end. The men followed, weapons at the ready.

Veirt chewed his lip. 'Do y'think they found the Bane?'

'Impossible,' said Magda. 'The door to the chamber is cunningly hidden and impenetrable unless the correct incantation is spoken.'

They entered the mausoleum, a cramped, narrow room. The side walls had been lined with marble memorial plaques engraved with the names and dates of birth and death of generations of abbesses. The Kurgan vandals had pried most of the plaques off, then pulled the bones out of the holes they covered and scattered them, looking for loot. Hals stepped fastidiously around the remains, mumbling prayers under his breath.

The back wall was a finely painted frieze of Shallya holding a golden chalice to the lips of a dying hero as a host of Shallyan nuns looked on. Though age had dulled it, and the Kurgans had defaced it with axe and fire, it was still beautiful, with much gold leaf and intricate detail. Reiner could see every hair of Shallya's tresses.

Veirt looked around, confused. 'Is this it?'

'Stand well back,' said Lady Magda, 'and I will show you.'

Veirt backed to the door, motioning his men behind him. Lady Magda faced the painting and began to speak in a language Reiner half-recognised from his studies at university as an archaic ancestor of his own. Her hands moved constantly as she chanted, describing precise patterns in the air. At last she spread her arms wide, and with a grating of stone on stone, the entire back wall swung slowly out on a hidden hinge, crushing the scattered bones and shards of marble on the floor to powder until it touched the left wall.

As the torchlight found its way through billowing bone dust to the area behind the secret door, Reiner could see that it was larger that the mausoleum, much larger. Wide stairs led down to a vaulted central chamber that seemed almost as big as the chapel upstairs, and dark archways opened into further rooms all along the perimeter.

A weak voice came from inside. 'Abbess? Is… is that you?'

'Who's there?' Lady Magda peered through the dust.

Small forms in Shallyan robes lay like drifts of grey snow around the door. More nuns, skeletal, with gaunt faces and black lips.

One still lived. A gangrenous wound had blackened her left arm up to the shoulder and it smelled of death. Pink pus bubbled from her lips. It looked as if she had tried to eat the leather of her slippers and belt to stay alive. She raised her head as if it weighed as much as the chapel. Her dull, sunken eyes blinked. 'Praise Shallya, we thought they had killed…' She paused as she saw Magda approaching, and her eyes widened. 'Magda…' she croaked. 'You…'

Lady Magda knelt and covered the holy woman's mouth with her hand. 'Don't speak, sister. There is no need. I know what you desire.'

Magda drew her eating knife from her belt, and before any of the men even knew what she was doing, sunk it into the sister's neck just below the jaw, piercing the artery, then did the same on the other side. The woman's blood flowed out of her like water.

'Lady!' cried Veirt, shocked. The others murmured under their breath, confused.

Magda ignored him, whispering a prayer over the dying sister and moving her hands in ritual patterns. When she was finished, and the sister had breathed her last, she turned to the captain. 'I apologise. Her wound was too far gone. It was the only mercy I could give her.'

Veirt looked at her levelly for a long moment, then bowed his head. 'I understand, m'lady. Sorry to have spoken.'

'It matters not. Come, let us finish our business here and leave this unhappy place.'

Veirt and Lady Magda entered first, kicking up puffs of dust with each step as they walked down the stairs to the central chamber. The others followed, quieted by the sister's actions. Reiner heard Hals mutter to Pavel under his breath. 'That's a cold one, and no mistake, mercy or no.'

Pavel nodded and Reiner had to agree as well.

Magda stopped in the centre of the main chamber. 'These are the convent's holiest treasures, acquired over the centuries. Gifts and relics and tomes of forgotten wisdom. Here also lie many heroes and martyrs who gave their lives in the defence of Shallya and the Empire.'

Giano, Hals and Pavel looked around with greedy eyes, but were quickly disappointed.

'It's just a lot of old books,' said Hals.

Reiner smirked. Though he was as fond of coin as any man who made the dice his life, he had been a student as well, and the 'old books' Hals scoffed at were greater treasures in his eyes than jewel-encrusted swords and chalices of gold ever could be. Reiner longed to be able to flip through them all and feast on the old knowledge, the stories out of the mists of time, the strange histories that were contained there. What a treat. The books were stacked all over, surrounding a few legitimate treasures: statues, paintings, suits of armour, the finger-bones of Shallyan saints displayed in reliquaries, iron-bound chests that could have held anything from manuscripts to gold crowns.

'Which is Kelgoth's crypt?' asked Veirt.

For the first time since he had met her, Reiner saw uncertainty in Lady Magda's eyes. She pursed her lips. 'It has been many years since I entered this place. I believe it is one of the three along the far wall, but I cannot be sure.'

Veirt sighed and looked around at the men. 'All right, you gallows birds, if we want to get out of these mountains before sundown we need to find this relic quick. You will help the lady search, but you will not slip any bits and pieces into your pockets, or I will pull off your fingers one by one, do I make myself clear?'

The men nodded.

'Right then, listen first,' said Veirt. 'What you're looking for is a battle standard.' The captain's voice suddenly trembled with emotion. 'The Griffin's Wing. The Heart of Kelgoth, known since the battle of Morntau Crag as...'

'Valnir's Bane!' said Erich in a reverent whisper. 'By the hammer!'

'Never heard of it,' grumbled Hals.

Erich sneered. 'Ignorant villain, it is one of the great lost relics of the Empire. A banner so pure and powerful that the mere sight of it could give an entire army the courage of a griffin.'

'Legend has it,' continued Veirt, 'that at Morntau, the daemon Valnir shattered the hammer of Lord Daegen Kelgoth and pierced his heart with a sword of flame. But with his dying breath, Kelgoth snatched up the Griffin's Wing, his family's sacred banner, and plunged the halberd on which it was mounted into the daemon's mouth, slaying it. Kelgoth died as well, but the day was saved and his name has inspired generations to valour.'

'Never heard of him either,' said Hals.

'I don't remember hearing that the banner was lost,' said Reiner, who vaguely recalled the legend from his tutor's lessons. 'I thought it was destroyed.'

'It was neither lost nor destroyed,' said Lady Magda brusquely. 'It was hidden away. Returned to the tomb of the hero who wielded it. For its power was too strong a temptation to ambitious men, who used it against their fellows rather than evil.'

Reiner raised an eyebrow. 'And you've noticed a change for the better in man's nature of late?'

'Hardly,' said Lady Magda. 'But desperate times require desperate measures. When we bring it to him, Baron Albrecht will use the Bane to instil in his troops the courage to turn back the Chaos tide and save these mountains from the foul clutches of Chaos.' She glared around at them all. 'Now may we begin the search?'

The men nodded and turned toward the crypts.

'The banner is described as pure white,' called Veirt as they spread out. 'With a griffin rampant emblazoned upon it in gold and silver thread, flanked by the hammer and the chalice and crowned with the jewelled circlet of the Lords of Kelgoth.'

'If you find it,' added Lady Magda, 'do not touch it, but call to me. It is too powerful and dangerous for the uninitiated to hold.'

The men began peeking into the crypts. Those of Shallyan martyrs were plain, with simple coffins and pious verse engraved on the walls. The crypts of heroes were more elaborate, with sarcophagi carved into the likenesses of their occupants and frescos of battle scenes painted on the walls.

Reiner and Franz investigated an arch in the back wall. Reiner raised his torch. A crowned 'K' was carved over the lintel.

He smirked. 'Promising.'

They stepped inside. The dust was so thick that it was difficult to make out the episodes of heroism depicted on the walls. A sarcophagus sat on a granite pedestal in the centre of the narrow room, but an old pike was propped against it, and it was draped with a filthy, dust-covered blanket, so it was hard to see what the hero beneath looked like.

'Pull that mess off and let's have a look at him,' said Reiner.

Franz pushed the pike aside and the blanket came with it, flopping to the floor in an eruption of dust. The boy yelped and jumped back, shaking his hand.

'What's the matter, lad?' asked Reiner.

'Something stuck me.' Franz sucked his palm. 'A splinter or something.' He looked at the stone casket, shaped like a knight in full plate armour, bare-headed, with long hair that flowed over the pedestal upon which he lay. 'Is it him, do you think?'

Reiner circled the stone knight. 'I see no banner.'

'You fools!' cried Lady Magda from the archway. 'You are stepping on it!'

Reiner looked down. His boots were on the dirty blanket. Magda hurried forward and pushed him off it. 'Step away! Step away, you imbeciles!' She stooped and snatched up the pike. A wince of pain twisted her face for an eyeblink as she raised it. The blanket came up too, and now Reiner could see that it was attached to the pike by a cross bar. He raised an eyebrow. It *was* a banner, but it couldn't possibly be *the* banner. In the shadowy crypt it was impossible to tell what colour it was, but it was certainly not white.

With shaking arms and clenched jaw, Lady Magda backed out of the crypt with the pike. Reiner and Franz followed her into the central chamber. Veirt and the others gathered around her as she shook the dust from the cloth, raising their torches to shine light on it.

'That can't be it,' said Veirt, frowning. 'It's all wrong.'

Reiner had to agree. The banner was dull red, emblazoned with a manticore rampant in black and dark green, flanked by a twisted sword and a skull, and crowned with a circlet of thorns. It made Reiner uneasy to look at it. He felt as if he needed to wash.

'It is,' insisted Magda. 'Look again.'

Veirt held his torch closer and the men leaned in. Reiner forced himself to examine it. Close up, he could see that the brown-red of the banner was dried blood, and that the black and green of the manticore, as well as the skull, sword and thorns, were clumps of crusted blood and mould and hairy mildew. Buried beneath this filth and gore Reiner could make out the faint raised outlines of the original design: the embroidered griffin, flanked by the hammer and chalice, and crowned by the circlet Veirt had described. The broken blade of the halberd was caked in dried blood which had run halfway down the haft.

Veirt recoiled in disgust. 'It has been tainted. The blood of the daemon has corrupted it. We should burn it.'

'Nonsense,' said Lady Magda. 'It only needs cleaning. Come, we must return to Baron Albrecht. There is no time to be lost.'

'But, lady, 'tis profane,' protested Veirt. 'Sigmar knows what would happen if an army marched under this... this foulness.'

'What does a common foot soldier know of such things?' Lady Magda retorted. 'You may have won a commission, captain, but you are still an unlearned peasant. Now do as Baron Albrecht commanded you to and accompany me back to Smallhof.'

Veirt's jaw set. His fists clenched at his sides. Reiner could see that there was a war raging within him between his duty and his instinct. At last his shoulders slumped. He hung his head. 'Forgive me, lady. But I cannot. I am indeed the peasant you name me, but I have fought the hordes and their evil sorceries for nearly as many years as you have lived, and I've learned that once touched by Chaos, a thing can never be truly cleaned.' He shifted uncomfortably. 'Now please give me the banner. We will burn it in the garden.'

'Dare you order me?' said Lady Magda, haughtily. 'Without the banner, the battle for Nordbergbruche may be lost. Will you face Baron Albrecht and tell him that, because of a feeling, you destroyed that which would have assured him victory?'

Reiner stared at her. Though no physical transformation had occurred, Lady Magda had changed. Gone was the quiet, stern holy woman. In her place stood some high priestess of old, eyes blazing with righteous wrath. She looked wild, powerful and dangerous, and as unsettled as he was by her sudden sinister metamorphosis, he also found her uncomfortably attractive. Her body, under her habit, which he had thought a touch overstuffed, suddenly looked voluptuous and wanton. She looked like she was used to getting her way and taking what she wanted, and Reiner had always had a weakness for that sort of woman.

'Lady,' said Veirt quietly. 'I am well aware of Baron Albrecht's plans, having helped form them, but no good could come from any venture undertaken under this debased banner. I will destroy it and accept what punishment he sees fit to mete out.'

'You dirty ranker,' burst out Erich. 'What about us? We face death if we fail in this mission. You condemn us to die for your backward superstitions.'

Veirt glared at him. 'Would you rather hundreds, maybe thousands, of your comrades died if we succeed?'

'We only have your word for it that anything would happen. Your word against the lady's.'

Reiner raised an eyebrow at this. If Erich couldn't feel the blood-soaked banner's evil influence he must have a head of solid granite.

Veirt ignored the novice knight and held out a hand to the sister. 'Give me the banner, lady. I beg you.'

'I will not,' she said, drawing back.

'Then I'm afraid I must take it from you.'

'Touch her at your peril!' shouted Erich.

As the lancer struggled to draw his sword, Veirt grabbed the haft of the banner and tried to tug it from Lady Magda's grasp, but with an angry cry, she shoved at his chest with her fingers.

Veirt stood a head and a half taller than the woman and must have been double her weight, but at her touch he stumbled back, gasping, and sat down heavily on the stone floor. To Reiner it appeared that the old warrior had tripped over something. Lady Magda had hardly touched him, and even with all her strength he doubted she could have budged him an inch.

Reiner and the others gaped at Veirt, who sat on the floor, clutching his chest and sucking air.

Hals knelt. 'Captain, are you hurt? Has the witch hexed you?'

Lady Magda raised the banner. Reiner could feel it behind him like a great eye watching over his shoulder. It felt as if it was pulling at him, forcing him to turn and face it.

'Leave him be,' said the woman. 'He has disobeyed the command of his lord. He is a traitor to Baron Albrecht and the entire Empire. From now on you will take your orders from me.' She pointed to Veirt. 'Now slay this traitor and escort me back to Smallhof.'

Reiner moaned. He had come to like the grizzled old bear and knew he was in the right, but orders were orders. Lady Magda was in command now. And it was for the good of the Empire. He drew his sword as the others were doing and turned to face Veirt.

'Just... just a minute... lassie,' said Pavel. It sounded as if he was pushing each word out through his teeth with his tongue. 'Baron Albrecht... put us under... command of Captain... Veirt. And until... he says otherwise... I take my orders... from him.'

Reiner paused in raising his sword and looked at the one-eyed pikeman. The ranker's brow was beaded in sweat and his arm shook as he forced his dagger to stay at his side.

'You will obey me!' cried Lady Magda. 'I am your leader now.'

Now Hals shook his head, less like he was disagreeing, and more like a bull trying to shake off flies. 'Sorry lass,' he said, straining to speak. 'I... don't think y've... got a... commission.'

Reiner frowned, trying to focus on what Pavel and Hals were saying. It was what he felt himself, so why was he still raising his sword to kill Veirt? Why was he, who had never followed an order in his life without making sure it was in his own best interest, blindly obeying a woman who had no official authority over him at all? He might have a weakness for commanding women, but he was no love-struck pup either. He hadn't let his little head rule his big head for years. What was causing him to act like a flagellant following a firebrand priest?

The banner. It had to be. Though the daemon's blood had corrupted it, it still gave its bearer a supernatural aura of authority, a presence so commanding that it could bend men's will and make them do whatever he – or in this case she – ordered, no matter how much it went against their natural inclinations.

Reiner tried to lower his sword, but to his chagrin, even knowing that he was being manipulated, he found it hard to fight the banner's power. It took every iota of will to force his arm down. The feelings of pride and patriotism that so rarely moved him, that he sneered at in the stiff-necked knights and mindless boobs who thought the Empire wasn't just the centre of the world, but the world entire, were welling up in him and making him want to kill. He wanted to strike down Veirt for the glory of the Empire. He wanted to slay all that questioned Lady Magda or doubted her motives. He wanted to...

'No!' Reiner slapped his own face, hard. The pain broke the banner's spell, only for a moment, but it was enough. He made eye contact with Hals and Pavel and was strengthened by their rage. Beyond them, the others were frozen in tortured poses, all fighting the urge to kill Veirt. Little Franz stood shaking, his short sword frozen over his head. There were tears in his eyes. Reiner shook the boy's shoulder.

'Fight it, lad.'

But Franz remained frozen.

'I won't!'

The bellow made Reiner turn. Ulf, his face twisted with rage, flung his upraised maul across the room. It knocked a suit of armour to the floor with a clanging clatter. Franz jerked at the noise like a waking sleeper.

Feeling stronger now, Reiner turned to Lady Magda. 'We won't follow you. You aren't our captain.'

'Then you are traitors,' said Erich, drawing his sword and stepping in front of the holy woman.

'You're the traitor,' growled Hals, unsheathing his short sword. Pavel pulled a dagger.

'The captain,' said Franz. 'He's bleeding.'

'What?' Reiner turned.

Veirt lay flat on his back. Blood was seeping from under his breastplate.

'Captain?' said Reiner, stepping forward.

He heard running feet behind him and spun back around. Lady Magda was racing, with very un-nunlike haste, for the secret door, the banner in her hands.

'Stop her!' called Reiner.

Only Franz, Hals and Pavel had recovered enough to respond. They started forward with Reiner, but Erich jumped in front of them, brandishing his sword.

'You'll go through me first,' he said.

Franz tried to dart around him, but Erich kicked the boy in the hip and sent him sprawling into the clutter of treasures. Pavel and Hals shifted left and right, feinting with their daggers. Reiner grunted, annoyed. Was there ever a more thick-headed knight? He picked up a book from a chest and threw it at Erich's head. The knight blocked it easily, but the century of dust that covered it exploded in his face and he doubled up, choking and cursing. Reiner shouldered him to the floor and ran with Pavel and Hals for the steps.

Lady Magda stood just outside the chamber, mumbling and motioning with her free hand.

Dread dragged at Reiner's guts. She was closing the crypt door. She meant to trap them in there forever, like the poor dead nuns. He bellowed over his shoulder. 'Franz! Ostini! Cut her down.'

It was too late. Before the boy or the mercenary could ready their weapons, the door began to grind closed and Lady Magda ran away toward the spiral stair.

Reiner cursed and redoubled his speed, bounding up the stairs three at a time. Hals and Pavel were right behind him. They put their shoulders to the closing door and pushed, but their combined weight had no effect. Their boots skidded back through a gravel of crushed bone and marble.

'Urquart!' called Reiner. 'Bring a chest! Something big and bound in iron.'

Gustaf, Franz and Giano reached the door and pushed as well. The six of them slowed it a little, but it continued to close. Reiner looked over his shoulder. Ulf was waddling forward carrying a heavy oaken chest, his face beet red with strain.

'Hurry, you great ox!' Reiner looked to Franz, who was pushing mightily, but pointlessly. 'Leave off, lad. Go after her. Warn Oskar. Tell him to gun her down.'

'Aye,' said the boy, and dashed through the narrowing gap. But almost instantly Erich ran out after him, sword in hand.

'Deserter!' shouted Reiner after the lancer. 'Will you leave us to die?' He cursed. 'He'll kill the boy.'

'Go on. Catch him up,' said Pavel. 'We'll hold this. Don't you worry.'

Reiner looked back. Ulf was humping the chest up the broad stairs, one agonising step at a time. He bit his lip. 'You'd better.'

Reiner ran through the closing door and down the passage to the spiral stair, expecting at any moment to trip over Franz's body. He stumbled up the uneven, wedge-shaped steps and burst out into the ruined chapel.

Lady Magda, surprisingly, was still in sight. She had only just reached the great arched door that led to the garden. Must have had some trouble getting the unwieldy standard up the twisting stairs, thought Reiner.

In the centre of the chapel Erich had caught up to Franz, who was dodging and ducking to avoid the knight's slashing sword, and shouting at the top of his voice. 'Oskar! Stop her! Stop the lady!'

Reiner ran for Erich, drawing his sabre. 'Coward!' he cried. 'Picking on boys again? Face me if you want a fight.'

Erich looked up, but unfortunately so did Franz, and Erich, trained in close combat, took advantage. His blade caught the boy a glancing blow on the top of the head and he hit the floor in a jumble of limbs.

Reiner cursed and slashed at the blond knight, but kept running for the door, yelling as Franz had. 'Oskar! Stop her!'

Erich caught up to him in the huge open doorway, stabbing at his back. Reiner squirmed to the side and fell across one of the massive bronze doors that lay twisted on the ground. He rolled aside as Erich's greatsword slashed down at him, then hacked at the knight's knees.

Erich leapt back and Reiner jumped up. They squared off, each too wary of the other to run after the sister.

Oskar was trotting across the garden from his post at the plaza stairs, long gun in his hands. Lady Magda was running right for him.

'Oskar!' Reiner called. 'Stop her! Gun her down!'

'Hey?' said the artilleryman, confused.

'Stop her! She's betrayed us all.'

Oskar looked at the oncoming woman, a puzzled frown on his face. 'Lady?'

The holy woman raised the banner and he stepped back, confusion becoming fear as he stared at it.

'Back away!' she cried. 'Bow down!'

Oskar shied away, throwing up his arms to shield his face from the banner. She swung it at him, knocking him flat, then disappeared down the steps.

Reiner cursed and moved to go after her, but Erich stepped in his way. 'No, traitor,' he said. 'You will not pass me again.'

Reiner grunted angrily. Even if he could beat the knight, which was an open question, it would take too long. Lady Magda would be on horseback and away long before the fight was over. With a sigh, Reiner shrugged and backed away. 'Very well. You win.'

He turned and ran back into the chapel. Franz was picking himself off the floor, clutching his bleeding head. 'Did she get away?' he asked.

'We'll get her later,' muttered Reiner, helping the boy stand. 'No woman can outpace me on horseback. Come on. Down to the vault.'

Erich came through the door. 'Where are you going? Are you afraid to face me?'

Reiner sheathed his sword. 'I am going to try to save my companions. The men you left to die.'

'They are traitors.'

'*They* didn't turn on their captain.'

Reiner and Franz hurried down the stairs.

'You all right?' asked Reiner, looking at the gash in Franz's scalp.

'It'll heal.'

A loud metallic groaning echoed around them as they exited the stairs. They raced for the crypt. Ulf had placed the iron-bound chest between the massive door and the wall, stopping it from closing, but it was slowly being crushed, the iron bands bending and the wood cracking.

Ulf and Gustaf stood outside the door, taking Veirt in their arms as Pavel and Hals, still inside, handed the stricken captain out to them. 'Bring him upstairs,' said Gustaf. 'I'll need more light.'

Pavel, Hals and Giano climbed out over the splintering chest and joined them. Reiner heard footsteps coming down the hall and looked back.

Erich approached, sheathing his sword. 'Does he live?'

'As if you care,' said Reiner.

'I do care,' said the knight. 'He is a good man. Just confused in his thinking.' He seemed calmer, almost contrite.

'Stand aside,' said Gustaf, and he started for the spiral stair with Ulf behind him, carrying Captain Veirt. The rest followed.

Erich brought up the rear, behind Reiner. 'I have no wish to fight fellow soldiers of the Empire, but you must see that you are in the wrong.'

Reiner rolled his eyes. Halfway up the stairs there was a horrendous crack from below and a deep echoing boom as the crypt door at last crushed the chest and slammed shut. It gave Reiner the shivers.

As the party entered the chapel they heard a faint high screaming, inhuman and frightened.

'Lady Magda,' said Erich, alarmed. He drew his sword and hurried for the door.

'If that's the lady,' said Reiner. 'I'm a Kossar.'

He followed Erich out of the chapel and ran with him through the garden, then across the plaza to the forecourt. The screaming, which had trailed away into whistling sighs of pain, was further on. Erich and Reiner paused at the broken gates, then stepped out of the convent cautiously, looking all around. The horrible sound was coming from the hidden ravine where they had tethered the horses. They crept forward.

As they edged around the entrance to the ravine, Reiner jerked back, shocked. There was a lot of blood. The mule and the horses had been ripped to pieces, as if by some giant beast. Limbs and torsos were strewn about. One or two horses were still alive, lying on their sides with their entrails spilling out, weakly lifting their heads and wailing in animal agony.

'The lady,' gasped Erich. 'Some horror has slain her and all the horses.'

'Don't bet on it,' said Reiner. 'Her palfrey's missing.'

He turned and ran for the cliff face. Erich followed. 'Where are you going? We must find her.'

'That's what I'm doing.'

Reiner looked out over the cliff. The winding path that had brought them up to the convent zig-zagged away below him. Rounding one of its switchbacks was a figure on a palfrey, hair flying in the wind, and deep red banner fluttering above her.

Reiner groaned. 'Sigmar curse all sisters of Shallya.'

SEVEN
The Right Thing To Do

WHEN REINER AND Erich returned to the convent garden, they found the others clustered around Veirt, whom Ulf had laid upon a stone bench. Gustaf had taken the captain's breast-and-back off and was kneeling over him, unbuckling his leather jerkin, which was soaked in blood.

'What was it?' asked Franz, looking up at Reiner.

'Some terrible beast has slain all the horses,' said Erich. 'Fortunately, Lady Magda has escaped unharmed with the banner.'

'Or,' said Reiner dryly, 'Lady Magda has slaughtered all the horses so we can't follow her, and escaped with the banner.'

Erich glared at him. 'Are you mad? Whatever killed the horses ripped them limb from limb. Lady Magda could never do that.'

'Don't be so sure,' said Gustaf. 'Look here.' He pulled open Veirt's jerkin to reveal his chest. The men hissed in surprise. A tremor of superstitious fear shivered through Reiner for, though Veirt's back-and-breast was without a dent or scratch, and his jerkin unmarked, deep gashes had opened his chest to the bone and shattered his ribs. It looked like some monstrous animal with enormous claws had mauled him. The wound bubbled with each of Veirt's shallow trembling breaths. Franz choked and looked away.

'Surely you can't be suggesting that Lady Magda did this?' said Erich as Gustaf began determining the extent of the damage.

'She barely touched him. This looks like the work of a... mountain lion, or a...'

'A manticore!' said Hals with superstitious awe. 'Like the one on the banner.'

'Yes,' said Erich. 'A manticore.' Then, 'No! If you are suggesting...'

Reiner raised an eyebrow at Hals. 'That she killed the horses and cut down the captain with unnatural strength given her by the banner? I'd believe that before a mountain lion.'

Erich's face was turning red. 'And... and if she did, can you blame her? Veirt turned against her. You all did. You were sworn to bring her here, protect her, and return with her and the banner to Baron Valdenheim, and instead, the moment she finds what we came for, you, a motley collection of peasants and gallows trash, decide you know more of the lore of Shallya and the Empire than a noble lady of learning. You doubt her word, and when Veirt lays hands on her, do you jump to her defence? No. You...'

A wet gasp returned their attention to Veirt. With a hacking cough that sprayed blood across Gustaf's knees, the captain's eyes opened. He looked around at them all without any sign of recognition, then saw his chest. His eyes focused. 'Damn the woman. And damn Albrecht too, for listening...'

Reiner knelt beside him. 'What are you trying to say, captain?'

Veirt turned glazed eyes to him. He seemed to be looking at him from a far shore. 'Count... Manfred. Tell him his brother...' He coughed again, spraying Reiner with red spittle, then forced another word out. 'Tre... tre... treachery!' Blood welled up from his mouth like a spring. His head sank back until it touched the marble bench, but his eyes never closed.

The men stared down at him for a long moment, as if unable to comprehend what they were seeing. Pavel and Hals made the sign of the hammer and touched their hearts. Only Gustaf seemed unmoved, cleaning and putting away his knives and supplies like a scribe tidying his desk at the end of his day.

At last Ulf broke the silence. 'So, what now?' he asked.

They all exchanged wary glances. It was a simple question, but a dangerous one. What *did* they do?

More importantly, Reiner wondered, what did *he* do. Where did self-interest lie? What course of action was most likely to keep his skin intact? Did he go back to Albrecht? Did he follow Veirt's last order and look for Albrecht's brother, the count? Did he try to hunt down Lady Magda and stop her? Did he go it alone? Or did he stick with his newfound companions?

'We must follow our duty, of course,' said Erich. 'We must do our best to catch up with Lady Magda and escort her back to Baron Valdenheim as we were ordered to do.'

'Yer off your head, jagger,' said Hals. 'She'd do for us in an eye-blink. The captain's dead. She got her precious banner. I say our job's done, and there ain't nothing waiting for us but the hang-man's noose when we get back. I say we go our separate ways and every man for himself.'

There were many nods and grunts of assent from the others.

'Suits me,' said Gustaf.

But Erich was having none of it. 'Do you abandon your duty so easily? You pledged to see this mission through. You cannot just walk away with it half done.'

Hals pulled off his right glove and showed Erich the brand – still red – on the back of his hand. 'I made no pledge. I submitted to blackmail is all. I'm off.' He turned to Pavel. 'What you think, boyo? Marienburg? I hear they pay honest gold for steady pikes.'

'Sounds as good a place as any,' said Pavel.

'In Tilea is summer now,' Giano said wistfully.

'They'd never find me in Nuln,' Gustaf muttered under his breath.

'I've relatives in Kislev,' said Ulf. 'Somewhere.'

Reiner shook his head, coming to a decision at last. 'You're making a mistake, lads. I think we're better off sticking together.' Or rather, he thought to himself, I'm better off if all of you protect me.

The others turned to him.

Erich smiled, smug. 'Come to your senses, have you, Hetzau?'

'This is wild country,' said Reiner, ignoring him. 'Raiders everywhere, wild beasts, unnatural things. I don't fancy going it alone. I don't know about you, but I wouldn't last a night. Until we're back in civilised lands, I think we need each other.'

'Makes sense,' said Hals.

'As to where we go,' continued Reiner, 'that's another question. I am inclined to believe Captain Veirt was right in thinking that the banner is tainted. I think...'

'You have no proof of that,' said Erich.

Reiner paid him no mind. 'Whether or not Lady Magda knew so before we found it, she certainly didn't think twice about using it once she knew its true nature.' He scratched his head. 'The real question is, what will Baron Valdenheim do with it once she brings it to him? Will he burn it as any sane man would, or will he let her convince him to use it to further his ambitions?'

'What makes you think she'll bring the banner to Valdenheim at all?' asked Franz. 'She might head straight north and deliver it into the hands of some daemon-worshipping chieftain.'

Reiner shook his head. 'That woman owes fealty to no one. She worships none but herself. I saw it in her eyes. She wants power in the realms of men, not in some deathless otherworld. Did you not see Albrecht with her when we started this journey? The way he looked at her. He may rule his army with an iron fist, but she has him wrapped around her little finger. Whatever his ambitions are, you can be sure they were hers first, and my guess is that Lady Magda's ambition is to be the wife of Baron Albrecht Valdenheim, and for Baron Albrecht Valdenheim to become *Count* Albrecht Valdenheim, and that she means to use the banner to accomplish these things.'

Ulf frowned. 'But Albrecht's older brother is already Count Vald... Oh. Oh, I see.'

'This is the merest conjecture,' complained Erich. 'You build castles out of air. Even if Lady Magda intends to use the banner for some unjust purpose, which I don't for a second suggest is the truth, you have no evidence that Baron Albrecht has any malicious intent.'

'Don't I?' asked Reiner. 'Then tell me this. If this banner is so important, and is meant to be used in the defence of the Empire, why didn't Albrecht send a battalion of pike and a squadron of lancers to accompany Lady Magda here? Why didn't he send handgunners and greatswords instead of a tiny band of condemned men?' Reiner smirked. 'Because he didn't want anyone to know what he was about. Because he intends to murder us all when we complete the mission in order to ensure our silence.'

'You speak treason, sir,' said Erich.

'Fluently,' said Reiner. He sighed and rubbed his eyes. 'My fear is, that if Baron Albrecht and Lady Magda suspect we live, and that we know what they intend, it will not matter how far we run, or where we hide. They will hunt us down and kill us wherever we go. And with the hammer brands on our hands, we will be that much easier to find. We will never be safe.'

'There's still Marienburg,' said Hals. 'Like I said before. And Tilea, and the Border Princes. The hammer brand means nothing there.'

'Aye,' said Reiner. 'That's true. But how long would it be before you were longing for home? Before you were homesick for Hochland ale and Carolsburg sausages? How long before you wanted to hear your mother's voice?'

'That's all lost to us, y'torturer,' said Hals bitterly. 'We're branded men.'

'Perhaps not,' said Reiner. 'There is one way I can see that we might get out of this with our skins and maybe even win the reward that was promised us.'

Giano's ears perked up at that. 'And how is this?'

Reiner shrugged. 'Follow Veirt's last order and warn Count Valdenheim of his brother's intrigue.'

There was a murmur of approval at this, but Hals laughed. 'And what makes you think Count Manfred is going to take the word of a bunch of murderers and deserters – for you know that's what they'll name us – over that of his brother and a reverend priestess of Shallya? What if he has us killed? Or throws us back into the brig?'

The others nodded, and turned to Reiner.

'Aye,' he sighed. 'There is that. And I've no answer for you. But there must be one honourable count in the Empire?'

'You'd know better than us, my lord,' sneered Pavel.

'It's a risk, I'll warrant you, but what's the alternative? Do you want to spend the rest of your life in foreign lands? Or living the life of an outlaw here, hiding your hands and skulking from place to place, with the law of the Empire always sniffing at your heels like a wolfhound? Do you want to never go home again? I say Manfred is the best of a lot of bad choices.'

'Not to mention that it's the right thing to do,' said Franz.

Reiner smirked. Hals and Pavel burst out laughing. Giano giggled.

Hals wiped his eyes, 'Oh laddie, you shame us all.'

Reiner looked around. 'So are we decided? Do we seek out Manfred?'

The men answered with 'Ayes' and grunts of approval, but Erich, who had been standing with his arms crossed at the edge of the circle at last spoke up.

'No, we are not decided,' he said. 'You've a smooth tongue, Hetzau, but I remain unconvinced. The *right* thing to do...' He shot a withering glance at Franz, 'Is to follow the orders we were given by Baron Albrecht and complete the mission. And as the ranking officer now that Veirt is dead, that is exactly what I command you to do.'

Pavel and Hals laughed again, and the rest glared at the lancer mutinously. Reiner groaned. Things would move much more smoothly without this parade-ground popinjay gumming up the works, but he was the best sword among them, and if Reiner wanted to get back to civilisation he would need around him all the swords they had. 'The Empire's authority doesn't mean much this far from Altdorf, von Eisenberg. We could kill you where you stand and no one would ever know, but if you want to play at rank, I'm not entirely sure you outrank me.'

'I am a novitiate knight of the Order of the Sceptre!' said Erich, drawing himself up.

'Aye,' drawled Reiner. 'Doesn't that mean that you polish the boots and fetch the beer?'

The men laughed.

Erich was turning red. 'I was to win my commission after my first battle!'

Reiner gaped in mock surprise. 'So you've yet to blood your lance? And you want to lead us? Laddie, my father may not have had the coin to buy me a position in an order, but at least I've seen battle. I was wounded at Kiirstad.'

Erich sputtered, but it was a charge he couldn't answer.

Reiner shrugged. 'My preference is that we have no leader. We're all worldly men – most of us anyway. Why don't we put the decision to a vote? All who want to return to Baron Valdenheim, step left, all who want to seek out and warn his brother the count, step right.'

'Vote?' bellowed Erich before anyone could move. 'There is no voting in the army. One does as one's commander orders. This is not the council of elector counts.' He glared at Reiner. 'If you mean to flout my authority in this way, then we will decide who commands here in the proper way. We will settle the matter on the field of honour.'

And with that he pulled off his left glove and threw it at Reiner's feet.

EIGHT
They Still Come

REINER STARED AT the glove with his stomach sinking. The last thing he wanted to do was fight Erich. Reiner had always been an indifferent blade, his strong suits in the area of martial endeavours being riding and shooting. He knew Erich was the better man by far. And yet fight him he must.

Though the temptation to just kill the knight when his back was turned was almost overwhelming, he would be a fool to do it. In the first place, he needed Erich's sword for the dangerous journey ahead. In the second, for all his talk of not wanting to be leader, Reiner thought himself the coolest, wisest head among the motley band, and wanted the others to listen to him and do as he suggested. Though some of them might at first applaud him for shooting Erich in the back, he knew that the more they thought about it, the less they would trust him, and the more they would be worried that they might be next.

No, if he wanted to get home in one piece he needed all the men he had, and if he wanted them to guard his back he needed their trust. He would have to fight Erich and, sadly, fight him cleanly. Reiner was certain that the traditions of honour were so deeply entrenched in Erich that if Reiner won the duel fairly Erich would reluctantly obey its stipulations and agree to be led by him. But if Reiner cheated, Erich would refuse to be bound by the outcome. The only difficulty was that the odds of Reiner winning the fight without cheating were slim to none.

Of course if Reiner lost, and Erich commanded them to return to Albrecht, then something else might be done, but he would worry about that if it happened.

He looked up at Erich. 'To first blood?'

Erich sneered. 'If that is all you are prepared to risk.'

'I will need your blade when I win. If you had any sense you would realise that you will need mine if you become leader.'

Erich flushed, embarrassed not to have thought of it on his own. 'And if I win you will submit to my command?'

Reiner nodded. 'I will. As will you if I win, yes?'

Erich hesitated unhappily, then nodded. 'You have my word.'

'Very well.' Reiner pulled his cavalry sabre and scabbard from his belt. 'I'm afraid I cannot match the length of your longsword, so you will have to match mine. Would you care to select the ground?'

'Fine.'

After a hasty colloquy they determined that Oskar's sword matched Reiner's in length, and Erich took a few practice lunges with it to get the feel. The novitiate knight felt it would be unseemly to conduct an affair of honour in a convent, so they marked out the lists just outside the convent's gates. Here also they laid to rest the body of Veirt, for it didn't feel right to leave him unburied among the horrors and desecrations of the convent garden. The ground was rocky and they had nothing to dig with so instead they covered him with loose rocks – though not before Reiner had emptied his pockets of all that was useful: gold crowns, a whetstone, a compass, charms and fetishes to ward off harm and bring luck. Finally, much to Pavel's disappointment, Reiner posted him as lookout, telling him to keep his one eye on the paths leading to and away from the convent.

At last they were ready. Reiner swallowed queasily as the scent of the blood of the butchered horses in the hidden canyon reached his nose. It was too reminiscent of a slaughterhouse for his peace of mind at this particular moment. He rolled his shoulders and circled his arms to warm up, all the while watching Erich doing the same on the opposite side of the ground. Gustaf waited to one side with his field kit at the ready, and

Giano, whose people were credited with making the practice of duelling into the ceremony it had become, stood in the centre ready to act as master of the lists. The rest of the men, Pavel, Hals, Oskar, Ulf and Franz, stood around the edges of the ground, their faces a mixture of anxiety and eagerness.

'Gentlemen, please to come to centre?' asked Giano.

Erich strode forward confidently, sword in hand and stripped to the waist despite the freezing wind. A look at the blond knight's broad chest and chiselled midsection made Reiner glad he'd kept his shirt on. The comparison would have done nothing for his morale. He stepped to Giano with a tremor in his knees he hoped no one else could detect.

Giano bowed formally to both of them. 'Weapons and ground alright by both gentlemen? Then we beginning. To the first bleeding, hey? If one gentleman can no continue, the contest go to the man who still stand. If no can see who strike first blood, then fight one more, hey?'

'Fine,' said Erich, sneering down his nose at Reiner.

'Yes,' said Reiner, looking at his boots.

'Excellent. Gentlemen please to stand at ends of blades.'

Reiner and Erich stepped back and extended their arms and swords. Giano held them until their sword tips touched. 'Gentlemen are ready?'

Erich and Reiner nodded.

'Very good.' Giano let go of the tips of the sabres and leapt back. 'Then begin!'

Reiner and Erich dropped into guard and began to circle, eyeing each other alertly. Reiner tried desperately to remember all the lessons he had ignored on those interminable afternoons with his father's master of the fence, when he would rather have been in the hayloft, learning a different sort of lunge and thrust from his second cousin Marina. Was he supposed to look into Erich's eyes to watch for what he intended next, or was it best to focus on his chest? He couldn't recall. He was so out of practice. All his life he had been able to talk his way out of fights, and when he hadn't, when some angry rustic had caught him with weighted dice or an extra ace in his hand, he had fought dirty, throwing furniture, beer, sand, whatever came to hand. He had no experience fighting within a set of rules.

Erich lunged forward, executing a lightning thrust. Reiner parried, but much too wide. Erich's blade dipped easily under his and slid directly for his heart. Only an undignified backwards hop saved Reiner from being cut to the bone.

'Easy, sir,' gasped Reiner. 'Do you mean to mark me or kill me?'

'My apologies,' said Erich, looking not one whit apologetic. 'I expected more resistance.'

Reiner danced back, sweating, as Erich advanced gracefully, pressing his advantage. Reiner parried and blocked like mad, stopping Erich's blade mere inches from his face and chest time and again. There was no question of him riposting. He was too busy defending. If he tried an attack, Erich would slip past his guard and it would be over. He had to hope Erich would make some error, or lose his balance. It didn't seem likely.

As he dodged this way and that, the faces of the men who surrounded them flashed by: Hals, leaning on his spear and watching with grim intensity, Ulf, his brow furrowed, Giano, eyes shining, Franz with his fingers over his mouth. The boy seemed almost more worried than Reiner himself.

Erich slashed again. Reiner stopped the blow, but it was so strong it drove his own blade back into his shoulder. As he jumped back Reiner felt his arm. No blood.

'Nearly had you there,' said Erich, grinning.

'Nearly.'

Curse the man, thought Reiner. The lancer was so calm, so sure of himself. He had yet to break a sweat, while Reiner was perspiring so much the hilt of his sabre was twisting in his hand.

Erich came in again, jabbing and slashing. His blade seemed to be everywhere at once. Reiner could see it as little more than a blur. He backed away in a panic and his boot heel caught on a lip of rock. He started to fall and threw out his sword arm to try to regain his footing.

Even a lesser swordsman than Erich might have taken advantage of such an opening. Erich lunged like a striking cat, blade arrowing straight toward Reiner's chest. There was no way Reiner could bring his sword to guard in time to stop it.

But then suddenly Erich was tripping himself, his sword arm flailing. Reiner watched amazed, while time seemed to slow to a crawl and his sword swung forward just as Erich's arm fell into its path. It was the slightest touch. A scratch from a rose thorn, and yet there was blood – a line on Erich's arm, a smear on Reiner's blade.

Erich caught himself and jerked back again instantly, but not to press his attack. He spun to point his sabre accusingly at Hals. 'You tripped me, you vermin! You stuck out your spear and tripped me.'

'I didn't, my lord!' said Hals, his face as innocent as a newborn's. 'You tripped over it, certain. But I never moved it.'

'Liar!' Erich turned back to Reiner. 'It doesn't count. He tripped me. You saw him.'

'I'm afraid I didn't,' said Reiner truthfully. 'I was too busy tripping myself.'

Erich's eyes narrowed. 'Wait a moment. I see what it is. You're in collusion, the two of you. You knew you couldn't beat me fairly, so you conspired to cheat.'

'Not at all,' said Reiner. 'At least I didn't. Whether Hals tripped you on purpose you'll have to take up with him.'

'I swear, my lord,' said Hals. 'By Sigmar, I swear. I was leaning on my spear. I didn't move it.'

Erich snorted derisively. 'We'll have to go again.' He motioned to Giano brusquely. 'Come, Tilean. Do the necessary.'

'Sir,' said Reiner. 'You *are* bleeding.'

'It wasn't a fair touch,' snapped Erich. 'I told you. The man tripped me.'

'I have only your word for it.'

'Over that of a peasant. Surely there can be no question.' Erich snatched up his shirt and pulled it on over his steaming chest.

Reiner turned to the others. 'Did any of you see? Did Hals trip him?'

They all shook their heads.

He turned to Giano. 'Master of the lists?'

Giano shrugged. 'I see nothing. The contest go to Master Hetzau.'

Erich threw up his hands. 'This is preposterous! You're all in on it! You never intended for it to be a fair contest.' He turned to Reiner. 'You are a cheat, sir. The leader of a band of cheats.'

Reiner clenched his fists, affronted. The one time in his life that he had fought a duel cleanly, and he was accused of cheating anyway. Of course he had little doubt that Hals had tripped Erich, but for once he'd truly had nothing to do with it. He put the blame squarely on Erich's shoulders. If the fellow hadn't made himself so disliked by one and all he would have easily won the day. 'I'm sorry, old man,' he said to Erich, 'But you agreed to abide by the outcome of the fight, and if you didn't trust the impartiality of the master of the lists you should have said something before we began.'

'This is intolerable!' Erich cried. 'I refuse to submit! We must go again! We must...'

'Hoy!' came a shout from the far end of the ledge.

They all turned. Pavel was running toward them, waving. 'Kurgan coming!' he called. 'A whole bloody column!'

Reiner and Erich cursed in unison and ran with the others for the cliff edge, their argument for the moment forgotten.

Pavel pointed down and to the right. 'There. See 'em?'

Reiner squinted into the frosty haze. Coming up the broad southern path, like a gigantic metal snake winding around the curves of the mountain, was a long train of Kurgan, their bronze helmets and steel spearpoints glinting in the late afternoon sun. They were led by a large squadron of barbaric horsemen, resplendent in outlandish armour and huge swords scabbarded over their shoulders. Huge hounds like the ones Reiner and the others had fought in the thorny wood paced alongside their mounted masters. There were also shackled slaves, shuffling in step under the cracking whips of overseers. Wagons loaded with plunder and provisions brought up the rear of the column. They had not yet reached the point where their path joined the narrow path Reiner and the others had climbed, but they were close. Too close.

'We'll never make it down in time,' said Hals.

'We'll have to hide somewhere,' said Erich.

'Yes, but where?' asked Reiner.

Franz frowned. 'In the convent? In the chapel?'

Reiner shook his head. 'What if they make camp there? We'd be trapped.'

'The hidden canyon?' suggested Oskar. 'Where we put the horses?'

'No, lad,' said Hals. 'All that fresh meat? Those hounds'll sniff it out in a second.'

'If their masters don't first,' Pavel said with a shiver.

'We'll have to go further up,' said Reiner. 'Further into the mountains.'

'Are you mad?' asked Erich. 'Run pell mell into unknown territory with an enemy at our back?'

'Have you another suggestion?'

'There would be no need for suggestions if we had gone after Lady Magda an hour ago as we should have.'

'He didn't ask for complaints, jagger,' muttered Hals.

Reiner turned away from the cliff and started for the box canyon. 'We'd best collect what we can from the packs, but don't carry too much. We may have occasion to run.'

The others followed after him. Erich sniffed, disgusted, but followed as well.

STEPPING QUEASILY AMONGST the scattered horse parts, the company salvaged what they could from the saddlebags, tied the contents up inside their back-and-breasts, and slung them over their shoulders. Pavel and Hals hung theirs off spears they took from the garden of horrors to replace the ones they had lost fighting the Kurgan warriors. As quickly as they could, they started up the wide path that rose from the convent's ledge and wound further into the mountains. The Chaos column was less than half a league behind them.

Reiner took some comfort from the fact that, because of the slaves' slow pace, the column was moving at half march. Reiner's companions would outdistance them easily, but he was less than heartened to see that on this path too were signs of heavy traffic. What if they met another force coming down and found themselves trapped in the middle? Speed wouldn't matter then.

It was less than an hour from nightfall. A cold wind bullied them along and blew high clouds across the lowering sun. The path was alternately bathed in red-gold sunshine or plunged into cold, purple shadows as the trail wound along steep cliffs and through tight defiles. Maddeningly, it didn't divide. Through all its twists and turns it remained a single line, with no branches or crossings, and though they found a few places where two men could hide, or even three or four, there was no place large enough to conceal them all, or far enough from the path that the hounds wouldn't scent them.

After they'd gone a few miles Reiner sent Giano back down the path to see if the Chaos troops had made camp at the convent. He returned just as the sun touched the horizon, mopping the sweat from his brow.

'They still come,' he said between breaths. 'Pass the convent. And more fast than we think. They push slaves hard.'

Reiner frowned. 'Are they gaining on us?'

'No, no, but best we keep moving, hey?'

The nine companions marched on into the dwindling twilight. Reiner was becoming nervous. The wind was getting colder, and the clouds thickening. The men were slowing with fatigue. *He* was slowing. It had been a long day, and they had all received some hard knocks in the fight with the Kurgan. Pavel, still not recovered from his fever, was leaning on Hals and sweating like he was in the desert. Ulf was limping. They needed to find a safe place off the path to make camp.

Reiner cursed Veirt for dying. The old bear would have found a way out of this mess in an eyeblink. If he hadn't died, the duel would never have happened. He would have put Erich in his place with a single glare and they would have been off down the mountain long before the Kurgan host came into view.

Though he put on a brave front for the men, Reiner was in a panic. He didn't know what he was doing. The only reason he had taken command was that following Erich would have led to disaster. Of course, he seemed to be leading them to disaster at a brisk trot himself.

Half an hour later, as the purple twilight was thickening into murky blue, the trail finally divided. It had been hugging a steep mountainside, but then widened into a broad, boulder-strewn shoulder that rose at its far end into a razor-backed ridge. The path split around this, the left way swinging wide and angling down the ridge's outer slope, the right rising up into the cleft 'twixt it and the mountain. To Reiner's annoyance, both were wide enough to accommodate a marching column. The men examined the ground of each in the dim half light.

'Plenty of hoofprints up this side,' called Hals.

'Here too,' said Oskar.

Reiner groaned. Why couldn't it be a simple decision? Why couldn't he say boldly, 'This is the one, lads. Clearly this is the path less travelled.' Now he had to guess, take an even-odds gamble. He *never* made a wager at even odds. Gambling was for fools. Though laymen often called Ranald the god of gamblers, in reality, followers of the Trickster gambled as little as possible. Rigging the odds in one's favour was a holy duty, a sacrament. One never entered a game of chance without an edge of some kind: loaded dice, marked cards, an accomplice. Here there was no way to force an advantage. Here there was no mark to gull, no extra ace to palm. He had to roll clean dice with fate like some rustic peasant, and hope.

'What do you think, lads?' he asked. 'Which way looks more promising?'

'Both the same,' said Giano shrugging.

'This one might be a little sparse,' said Hals uncertainly. 'Then again it might not.'

'What if we wait at the fork?' said Franz. 'See which way they mean to go, then go the other.'

The company turned to stare at him. Reiner gaped. It was a good idea.

'But they'll see us.' said Oskar.

'No. No they won't,' said Reiner, heart pounding with newfound hope. 'They'll have torches by now. We'll stay dark, invisible. And the path splits early enough that we'll know which way they're heading long before they're upon us.' He patted Franz on the shoulder. 'Good thinking, lad.'

The boy beamed.

Reiner looked back down the trail. It was so dark now he could hardly see five yards. 'We'll sit right here. Wear your cloaks over your packs, and wrap your swords. We don't want any steel reflecting their torchlight. Might as well have a bite to eat while we wait.'

They huddled together at the blunt tip of the ridge, gnawing on nearly frozen bread and sipping from canteens they had to bang against rocks in order to break the skins of ice that stoppered them. Fast-moving clouds nearly filled the sky. The rising moons were only rarely visible. Finally, almost an hour after full dark, the Kurgan host arrived. The men heard them before they saw them, a faint rumble like a far-off avalanche that never stopped: the sound of boots and hooves on stone, chains dragging through gravel, the crack of whips and the guttural marching cadences of the raider infantry.

By the time the men put away their food and made ready to move, a dim orange glow began to rim the path where it curved around the mountain. The glow grew brighter and the rumble louder until at last the Kurgan column appeared around the bend. Three slaves on long leashes came first. They held aloft torches on tall poles that cast a baleful light upon the Kurgan horsemen that followed them. Reiner swallowed as he saw them. He heard Franz moan beside him.

Though it was difficult to judge scale at this distance, all of the mounted marauders looked enormous, larger even than the monstrous men they had faced in the convent, but in the centre of the first rank rode a veritable giant. Mounted on a barded warhorse that made the largest destrier Reiner had ever seen look like a pony, was a knight – if a daemon-worshipping northern vandal could be given so noble a title – in full plate armour, lacquered a deep blood red and chased with bronze accents. His head was entirely encased in an elaborate helmet, built to look like a dragon's head. The resemblance was heightened by the two double-headed axes that rose from behind his massive shoulders like steel wings. Each must have been as tall as a man. The very sight of him turned Reiner's blood to water. The knight seemed to radiate fear like a stove radiates heat. Reiner wanted to run and hide, to curl up and weep.

His retinue was only less fearsome by comparison. Had the evil knight not been there, the marauders alone would have been quite enough to make Reiner quake in his boots. They were massive, muscular northmen, most in horned helmets and armour of ringmail, leather and the occasional gorget or breastplate. Some rode bare-chested, their sinewy arms and knotted torsos seemingly impervious to cold. But all had the same fell look. Their eyes were hooded and hidden. Not a glint of light reflected from them, not even those who wore no covering helmet, and they stared dead ahead, looking neither left nor right, though Reiner's skin crawled with the feeling that their awareness was examining every part of him like the beam of some glowing eye. Every fibre of his being told him to run.

'Wait for it, lads,' he whispered, as jauntily as he could manage. 'Wait for it.'

The horsemen continued pouring around the curve five abreast until more than a hundred rode behind the knight, then came foot soldiers, a ragged group who walked rather than marched into the valley.

'Look at 'em,' sneered Hals. 'Not one of 'em in step. No discipline.'

Just as the ranks of slaves began shuffling into view and the head of the column had reached the widening shoulder, one of the fell knight's lieutenants peeled off from the squad of riders and faced about. As the others rode on, he raised his hand and began bellowing orders in a bestial voice.

'Do they set up camp?' asked Erich uneasily.

Reiner hoped that it was true, for it would give the party some time to find a way around them, but he wasn't so lucky. There was movement in the ranks: captains shouting at their companies, overseers roaring at their slaves, wagon masters calling to each other, and for a moment all seemed chaos and confusion.

Hals squinted at the reforming column. 'What are they about? Oskar, you've got the eyes. What are they doing?'

'They are... They are...' said the artilleryman as he tried to make it out.

But by then it was clear to everyone what the Kurgan force was doing. As the mounted lieutenant stood in his saddle, motioning and shouting, the column began to split to his left and right like a river breaking around an island, some going one way, some the other.

Reiner's heart sunk. He groaned. 'The cursed heathen. They're splitting up. They're taking both paths.'

'Myrmidia, protect us,' said Ulf.

Oskar was whimpering, high in his throat.

Reiner wanted to cut and run, but he forced his fear down with both hands and remained where he was.

Erich turned on Franz. 'Foolish boy, we could have been far away by now. Now they are upon us.'

'Lay off him, von Eisenberg,' said Reiner. 'He suggested it. I ordered it.'

'But which way do we go?' asked Gustaf, querulously.

'Whichever way he doesn't,' muttered Hals, and no one had to ask who 'he' was. They could feel the fell knight's presence growing stronger as he neared.

'We go the way the slaves go,' said Reiner, relieved to be able to give an order he had some confidence in. 'They'll slow the train.'

The slaves went right, and the company breathed a simultaneous sigh of relief, for the red knight and most of his retinue had angled left, followed by half of the foot soldiers. A smaller company of horsemen led the slaves and the rest of the infantry.

'Right, lads,' said Reiner, letting the tension out of his shoulders. 'That's decided. Off we go.'

The party stood and hurried up the right-hand path into the dark cleft. No, thought Reiner. Though he hated to admit it, they didn't hurry. They fled.

NINE
Trapped Like Rats

REINER AND THE rest ran up the path in almost total darkness, tripping and cursing, but not daring to light a torch. When the wind-whipped clouds allowed it, the light of Morrslieb and Mannslieb illuminated the mountain tops, but the two moons hadn't yet risen high enough to shine down into the tight crevasse through which the company stumbled. They might have passed any number of branching paths, but they were invisible, blending into the dark basalt of the cliff sides.

All around Reiner came the hoarse breathing of the men. He recognised Franz's light quick breaths, Pavel's thready wheeze, Ulf's deep inhalations. They were exhausted. Waiting for the Chaos army had refreshed them a little, but it had been no replacement for sleep. They must stop soon. Even in the midst of their panicked flight, Reiner felt his eyelids drooping. It was pitch dark anyway. He might as well walk with his eyes closed.

After that Reiner was often unsure whether he was walking or sleeping – whether he was walking in a dream, or dreaming that he was walking. He drifted in and out of consciousness so often that he had no sense of the passage of time. He had no idea how long they had been travelling when, just as they topped a rise in the path, the steep ridges that had hemmed them in for so long opened away from them and they found themselves standing on the lip of a deep valley carpeted with a thousand points of light.

Reiner frowned sleepily. The lights looked like stars, but stars belonged in the sky. Maybe it was a lake.

'Torches,' said Oskar.

Reiner shook his head, clearing the fog from his brain. They *were* torches.

He stepped back into the shadows, heart thudding, and surveyed the valley. The others did the same. As if on cue, the clouds parted again and the two moons shone down on the scene.

The curving walls of the valley were rusty orange stone, and terraced like some giant's staircase. There were holes in the walls on each level, and odd ramshackle structures clinging precariously to the steps: little shacks, wooden sluice runs, scaffolding – except where one of the terraces had collapsed and slid in a heap to the valley floor. The furthest third of the valley was walled off by thick stone battlements, beyond which the party could just make out a confusion of low buildings built around the glowing orange mouth of what looked like a giant cave. But the sight that drew all their eyes was what was in front of the battlements: a sprawling camp of leather tents and blazing campfires, wagons and horses, and laughing, drinking, fighting barbarians.

Kurgan.

'Sigmar preserve us,' whimpered Oskar.

Reiner clamped a hand over the artilleryman's mouth, for he had suddenly noticed, not twenty paces to their left, a stone watch tower carved out of the valley wall. Oskar grunted in protest. The others turned. Reiner pointed to the tower. There were no torches visible, but Reiner was sure he'd seen a hulking figure moving above the crenellations. He motioned the others to retreat. When they were out of sight, Reiner slumped against the rocky wall and closed his eyes. The others gathered around him.

He rubbed his face with his hands. 'Well, we're in a spot, and no mistake.'

'Trapped like rats,' quavered Oskar.

'Kurgan in front of us,' said Ulf.

'Kurgan behind us,' said Pavel.

'Kurgan up our bloody fundaments,' growled Hals.

Reiner chuckled mirthlessly. 'I suppose, Erich, this is where you tell me "I told you so".'

There was no answer. Reiner looked up. He didn't see the blond knight. 'Where's von Eisenberg?'

The others looked around. Erich wasn't with them.

Reiner frowned. 'Any of you hear him drop back?'

Everyone shook their heads.

'Any of you slip a knife in his back?'

Silence.

'I wouldn't blame you if you did, but I want to know.'

More headshaking and 'not I's' answered him.

'Then where's he got to?'

'Maybe he's having a piss,' muttered Gustaf.

'That one don't piss,' said Hals. 'He's perfect.'

'Probably found a little hidey hole back there in the dark,' said Pavel. 'And didn't see fit to tell us. He'll slip around the northers once they've passed.'

'Aye,' said Giano. 'Stupid schoolboy. All he want is to tattle tales to Valdenheim.'

'A lot of good that'll do him,' said Franz.

'Well, never mind about him,' said Reiner. 'He's made his decision. We have to make ours. This place, whatever it is, is obviously the destination of the fellows behind us.'

'It's a mine,' said Ulf. 'An iron mine.'

The others looked up at him.

'Myrmidia's mercy,' said Franz. 'The slaves. They're bringing them here for the mine.'

'And mining iron for weapons and armour,' said Ulf.

'Bad news for the Empire,' said Hals.

'But good news for us,' said Reiner. 'At least I hope so.' He turned to Ulf. 'Urquart, those holes in the walls. They're mineheads, yes?'

'Aye.'

'Then they'll be deep enough to hide in?'

'Oh, certainly.'

'Then here's the plan. We slip past the tower, sneak along one of those ledges, duck into a hole and wait there until tomorrow night. By that time, the enemy troops behind us will have made camp, and we can sneak back out and away from these damned mountains with none the wiser.'

'Hear hear,' said Franz.

'You make it sound so easy,' said Gustaf. 'What if we're seen passing the tower? What if another force comes up the path tomorrow night?'

'I'll take any suggestions,' said Reiner.

Gustaf grunted, but said nothing.

The party edged back to the lip of the valley, standing just within the shadow of the canyon walls, and looked up at the tower. The Kurgan guard appeared and disappeared at regular intervals as he paced the top of the tower.

'Now?' asked Franz as the guard turned away again.

Reiner looked at the sky, another armada of clouds was sailing in from the north east. 'A moment.'

The clouds ate the moons once again and darkness covered the valley.

'Now we go.'

The men tiptoed swiftly to the nearest terrace, each of which connected to the path as it sloped down the hill. There was a collapsed shack near the close end. They crowded in behind it and waited, listening for the guard to call a challenge. None came.

'Come on. Before the clouds pass,' said Reiner.

They crept along the terrace to the first entrance. It was boarded up. Reiner tugged experimentally on the planks. They creaked alarmingly.

'Let's try further on.'

But the next entrance was walled up with brick and mortar.

'Why would anyone go to the trouble?' asked Reiner, annoyed.

'Cave-ins,' said Ulf. 'Or sink holes. You saw the landslide. This wall was probably overmined and became unstable.'

Oskar gulped. 'Unstable?'

The third hole was boarded up as well, but the boards were so weathered and warped that they had pulled away almost entirely from their nails. A trickle of water ran out from under the barricade and had carved a channel in the terrace.

'This looks promising,' said Reiner.

He and Hals and Giano began pulling the boards away as quietly as possible and set them aside. Some were so rotten they crumbled in their hands.

At last they had cleared the opening, and the timber-framed entrance yawned before them. It was easy to see why it had been closed. Water dripped from above, and it was clear that it had eaten away much of the ceiling. An attempt had been made to shore it up with wide boards propped up by posts, beams and bits of scrap lumber – so many that the entrance looked like a forest of thin, limbless trees – but the water had seeped into all of these, and they were bowed and rotting. The floor of the tunnel was muddy and calf-deep in loose rock and earth which had fallen from above. Reiner didn't like the look of it at all, but the clouds were thinning. There was no time to find another.

'Come on, then,' he said. 'In we go. And each of you carry a board. We'll have to close it up again from the inside or they'll notice.'

The others trooped in, each with a board under one arm, picking their way through the thicket of supports, but Oskar hung back, looking at the gaping hole with trepidation.

'Come on, gunner,' said Reiner.

The artilleryman shook his head. 'I don't like holes.'

Reiner rolled his eyes, impatient. 'Nor do I. But in we must go.'

'I cannot,' whimpered Oskar. 'I cannot.'

'You'll have to. There's no help for it.' Reiner stepped toward Oskar, reaching out to him.

The gunner pulled back. 'No.'

Reiner shot a glance over his shoulder and clenched his fists. 'Oskar! Stop messing about!' he hissed. He grabbed for Oskar's elbow.

Oskar flinched away and kicked a discarded beam with his heel. It tottered on the lip of the ledge, then tumbled down to the level below.

Reiner groaned and looked back toward the tower. It was too dark out to see it. But he thought he heard a guttural voice call a question.

Reiner lost his temper. 'Curse you, you craven ninny!' he whispered hoarsely, 'Get in there!' He leapt forward, grabbed Oskar by the arm and flung him into the opening.

He regretted the action instantly, for the artilleryman flew into the first rank of props and knocked them hither and thither. One snapped in half. A shower of dirt and small stones rained down on the fallen Oskar and the ceiling groaned ominously.

'Sigmar blast it!' Reiner ran into the entrance, grabbed Oskar by the collar and dragged him through the supports to where the rest of the men had turned at the noise. The floor was clearer here, and the posts fewer. He stopped and looked back.

There was a crack, loud as a pistol shot, then another. First one post, then two more began to bend and fold, then another three.

'Back!' Reiner shouted. 'Back!'

The men ran into the darkness, Franz helping to drag Oskar further down the tunnel.

With a thunderous crash the ceiling above the entrance collapsed, deafening them. A cloud of dust, invisible in the utter darkness, blew around them, making them choke and cough. Sharp rocks spat at their shins and ankles.

At last, with a few final thuds and plinks, the avalanche ended and the men's coughing and retching dwindled off into silence. It was pitch black.

'Everyone here?' asked Reiner. He called out their names one by one and they answered. All but Oskar.

Reiner sighed. 'Strike a light, someone.'

Hals got a taper going and they looked around for Oskar. He was still on the floor, clutching his knees and looking around him wildly. As the flame grew brighter he looked beyond them to the sloping mound of rock and mud that blocked the entrance. He cried out, an animal sound, and scrambled forward on his hands and knees. As the men watched, non-plussed, he began to scrabble at the rocks with his bare hands. 'Dig! We must dig! We must get out! No air! There is no air!'

The rocks were impossible to shift. Oskar began pounding on them, bloodying his hands and shrieking wordlessly.

The men grimaced and turned their heads, but Reiner had had enough. 'Sigmar's balls!' he blasphemed, stepping forward, 'Will you shut *up*!' He spun Oskar around by the shoulder and punched him as hard as he could in the jaw.

Reiner's knuckles flared with pain at the contact, but the result was extremely gratifying. Oskar flopped bonelessly to the ground and lay there, silent at last – out cold.

Reiner turned to the others, sucking a bleeding knuckle. They beamed appreciatively at him. He tried to think of something witty to say, but he couldn't. Exhaustion suddenly overcame him. His knees nearly gave way.

'Well,' he said wearily. 'I think this day's gone on long enough. Let's make camp.'

CHAPTER TEN
Let The Wind Be Your Guide

WORN TO A frazzle though he was, Reiner still had some difficulty getting to sleep. He might have sneered at Oskar's panic, but he had punched the artilleryman because he'd felt it spreading to his own heart as well. He too had been overcome with an overwhelming sense of doom when the roof collapsed. And of guilt. He had done this. If he hadn't lost his temper and thrown Oskar into the posts it might not have happened. He had trapped them. Anything that happened to them now would be his fault. If they couldn't find another way out? His fault. If something crawled out of the dark, unexplored tunnel and devoured them? His fault. If the air became so sour they couldn't breathe? His fault. If they starved to death? If they went mad and ate each other to stay alive? His fault.

But at last even guilt couldn't keep him awake. Exhaustion dragged him down like a mermaid pulling him beneath the waves, and he slept the sleep of the dead until, sometime later, the scratching and squeaking began. He ignored it for as long as he could, drifting in and out of dreams where it was his old dog scratching at his door, a harlot of his acquaintance combing her hair on the creaking bed in his apartment back in Altdorf, a tree branch rubbing against the roof of his tent on the march up from Wissenberg, but finally images of rats and giant insects and bloodsucking bats forced him to open his eyes and look around.

There was nothing to see, of course. It was still as black as an orc's armpit. He could tell by the snores that the rest were still asleep. With a grunt of annoyance he fished around in his pack until he found his flint and steel, then struck a spark onto his tinder paper and lit a taper.

His moving around woke some of the others and they sat up blinking in the unaccustomed light as Reiner raised the taper and looked for the source of the scratching.

It was Oskar again, whining and clawing dispiritedly at the pile of stone. Reiner winced. The gunner must have been at it for hours. His fingernails were gone, ripped away, and the tips of his fingers were bloody shreds.

'Oskar,' Reiner called.

The gunner didn't respond. Reiner stood and stepped to him. Oskar's lips were moving. Reiner leaned in to hear what he was saying.

'Nearly there. Nearly there. Nearly there. Nearly there. Nearly there. Nearly there. Nearly there.'

Reiner put his hand on Oskar's shoulder and shook him. 'Come on, Oskar. We're going to see what's down the hall. Might be another way out, eh?'

Oskar pulled violently away. 'No! We must dig! We'll all die if we don't dig!' He began digging with renewed vigour, but no better results. The rock he was clawing at was stained a brownish-red from his blood.

Reiner sighed and turned. The others were frowning sleepily at him and Oskar. Reiner found Gustaf among them. 'Gustaf. Have you anything in your kit to quiet him?'

'Oh aye,' said the surgeon dryly. 'I've just the thing.'

Reiner caught his tone and shot him a hard look. 'If he dies of it, you'll follow him.'

Gustaf shrugged, and began unbuckling his kit.

'But, captain,' said Hals, 'why not just put him out of his misery? He has no mind no more, the poor fellow. He's no use to anybody, least of all himself.'

Reiner shook his head. 'With Erich deserting us, we need every man we have. Do you think we should leave Pavel behind just because he's having trouble keeping up?'

Hals stuck out his chin. 'No, sir. No, I wouldn't like that.'

'I'm feeling much better now, sir,' Pavel piped up anxiously.

Gustaf stepped forward and held out a small black bottle and a tin spoon. 'Here. A spoonful will calm him. Juice of the poppy. Nothing poisonous.'

Reiner took the bottle. 'Thank you. I'm familiar with it.'

Gustaf smiled slyly. 'I've no doubt.'

Reiner flushed. He pulled the cork and inhaled. The sweet, cloying scent teased his nose. He fought the urge to have a spoonful himself. It would be so nice to drift away from all this unpleasantness and get some real rest, but that was a bad idea. He had been down that road once before and nearly lost his way.

He filled the spoon and squatted beside Oskar. 'Here, lad. It'll give you strength for your digging.'

The gunner turned his head without stopping and opened his mouth. Reiner spooned some of the liquid into him. He felt like a nurse feeding an infant, which was near enough to the truth.

He stood and turned to the men. He sighed. It was time to face the music. 'Listen, you lot. I want to speak to you.' He paused, hesitant to go on, then cleared his throat and continued. 'It was I who got you into this mess. I led us up into these blasted mountains, I picked this path instead of the other one, and I threw poor Oskar into those posts and brought the roof down on us. I'm about ready to stop playing at captain and let someone else take over. In fact, I'm a little surprised someone didn't murder me in my sleep just now and assume command.'

The others said nothing, only stared at him.

He swallowed. 'So, if anyone else wants the job, speak up. I'll step down, and happily.'

More silence, then finally Pavel coughed.

'Sorry, captain,' he said. 'We're only rankers. Peasants and merchants' sons and the like. Ye be gentry. Yer meant to lead. It's yer job.'

'But I'm making a mess of it! Look where we are! I did this! We are trapped in here because I lost my temper. You ought to be mutinying by now.'

'Naw, captain,' said Hals. 'We don't blame you for all that. You done your best, and none can ask more than that. It's when a captain starts to worry more about his own skin than the skins of his men. That's when... er, well, when things might happen.'

Reiner blushed, embarrassed. They thought so highly of him, and he was such a villain. His own skin was exactly what he was worried about. He'd taken the lead because he wanted the rest of the men around to protect him if things went wrong. It was only because he was endangering himself by doing so terrible a job that he wanted to pass the baton to someone more competent.

He sighed. 'Very well. If no one will take the burden.' He turned and began packing up his bedroll. 'Let's find a way out of this hole.'

By the time the others had collected their gear and choked down a dry breakfast, Oskar was slumped against the boulders with his eyes closed.

'Well done, Gustaf,' said Reiner. 'Now dress his wounds and tend to him. He's your patient now. Keep him moving.'

'A pleasure, sir,' said Gustaf. But he didn't mean it.

Gustaf bound Oskar's fingertips and got him on his feet while Hals lit two of their precious torches and Veirt's slotted lantern. Then they all shouldered their packs and they started into the darkness. Giano took point, creeping down the tunnel twenty paces ahead holding the lantern close-shuttered. Reiner and Franz led the rest. Ulf walked behind them, then came Pavel leaning on Hals, and Oskar leaning on Gustaf. They walked into a steady breeze, which gave Reiner hope. Moving air meant some passage to the outside. What was curious was that the breeze was sometimes cold and sometimes warm.

The tunnel joined another almost immediately, this one with two iron rails running down the centre fixed to wooden ties. Some of the rail was missing, and the ties rotten.

'Which way?' asked Giano, turning back to them.

'Let the wind be your guide,' said Reiner. 'Take whichever passage it blows from.'

Giano turned into the wind and they followed the glow of his lantern further into the mine. The tunnel dipped and turned eccentrically as it followed a seam of ore through the earth, and the longer they paced it the more cross tunnels and branching ways they passed. Sometimes it opened it out into wide columned areas where a particularly rich deposit had been found, only to narrow down again.

After a quarter of an hour Giano came hurrying back flapping his free hand. 'Douse torches!' he hissed. 'Douse torches.'

Reiner and Hals stabbed their torches into the dirt of the tunnel floor as Giano closed the lantern's slot. They were surprised to find that they were not in total darkness. A faint flickering glow reached them from around a bend in the passage, and the tramp of heavy feet echoed in the distance.

'Kurgan,' whispered Giano.

Reiner and the others drew their weapons and held their breath as the light grew brighter and the footsteps got louder. They began to hear gruff voices mumbling in a barbaric tongue. Reiner found himself gripping his sabre so hard that his knuckles ached, but after a long moment when it sounded as if the Kurgan were standing beside them, talking in their ears, the voices and the light faded again, and then disappeared altogether.

The party breathed a collective sigh of relief.

'Well,' said Reiner, trying for jocularity. 'I'm fairly sure there's another way out now.'

'Aye,' said Hals. 'Through them.'

They relit the torches, then rounded the bend and entered an intersection. The wind blew from the direction the Kurgan had taken. The rails went that way too. They took it.

'Just don't catch up with them,' Reiner said to Giano.

The Tilean grinned and returned to point position.

Soon they began to hear great clankings and groanings, and the susurrus of hundreds of voices shouting and talking. Harsh cries rose above the murmur, and crackings and clashings. A steady red glow filtered down the tunnel, and the wind gusted hot and cold. It began to smell of sweat and smoke and death.

As Reiner passed a right-hand tunnel he was buffeted by a blast of oven-hot air. He stopped. A spur of the rails branched into the tunnel. Red light shone on the rocky walls at the far end and the clanking and roaring was louder here.

'Giano,' he called softly. 'Back here.'

Reiner led his companions into the cross tunnel, edging cautiously toward the red light. Thirty paces in, the tunnel came to an abrupt end at a rough arch. Through it they could see underlit clouds of smoke rising from below. There was no floor beyond the arch, just two short lengths of twisted rail and the splintered remains of a wooden trestle jutting out over a precipitous drop.

Reiner slid forward and peered down into an enormous cave, the floor of which was a good forty feet below them. The others crowded in behind him, craning their necks. A hellish panorama spread out before them. Directly below the opening was the source of the smoke – two giant, pyramid-shaped stone furnaces, each as big as an Altdorf row house. The smoke belched from square openings at their apexes. Into these holes two endless lines of slaves were dumping buckets of red-streaked black rocks. The slaves crawled up the sides of the pyramids like ants, dropped their burdens into the smoking chimneys, then filed away again to the far side of the cave to great mountains of the reddish stuff, where they filled their buckets again and repeated the journey, over and over again.

'So much ore,' said Ulf, awestruck. 'This rivals the ironworks of Nuln.'

To the right of the furnaces the cave narrowed down to a yawning black hole into which vanished more iron rails. A long train of slaves was shuffling into the hole, six abreast. They were shackled at the ankles and carried pickaxes over their shoulders. Huge Kurgan overseers herded them forward, bellowing and cracking whips over their heads. At their sides were huge, leashed hounds that lunged and barked at the slaves.

More slaves pushed large wooden carts out of the hole on the iron rails, then pulled them up long ramps supported by a wooden scaffolding that rose over the mounds of ore. They tipped the contents of the carts onto the heaps, then lowered them back down the ramp and into the hole again.

The slaves were men, women and children, but so gaunt and starved, so careworn and covered in filth that it was difficult to determine their sex or age. They all looked like stooped old men, hair lank and patchy, faces lined and slack. Their eyes were as dull as dry clay. Many were horribly maimed, missing fingers or hands or arms or eyes. Some limped around on poorly-fashioned wooden legs. Whip marks criss-crossed their naked backs, and shiny patches of scar tissue from countless burns covered their arms and legs. Their overseers took no pity on them, however, kicking and whipping those who lagged or paused in their labours, and beating mercilessly any that showed even the slightest glimmer of fight.

Franz clenched his fists. 'The animals! I'll kill them all!'

At the backs of the furnaces more slaves fed split logs into roaring fireboxes, while others worked great bellows, as big as rich men's beds. At the front, slaves in heavy aprons and thick gloves dragged stone moulds shaped like keg-sized loaves of bread under endless streams of white-hot molten iron. As each mould was filled, it was dragged aside and replaced by another. Off to one side, iron loaves that had cooled were knocked out of the moulds with wooden mauls and loaded onto carts.

Reiner watched a cart as it rolled into a further chamber. It was hard to see through the smoke, but he thought he could make out the fires of forges and the glistening bodies of smiths making armour and weapons with terrifying industry and piling them into great heaps. And beyond that... He squinted and shielded his eyes from a harsh white light. What fresh horror was this? It looked almost like... His heart lurched as he realised that he was looking outside, and that it was daylight. He hadn't realised how much he'd longed for it. But as his eyes adjusted to the brightness he saw buildings and stables and Chaos troops milling about, and most discouraging of all, the great stone battlements they had seen when they first entered the valley the night before.

Hals sighed. 'We've to get through all that?'

'We'll find a way, lad,' said Reiner. 'Don't worry.' But he wished someone would tell him how. He was about to ask for suggestions, when something else caught his eye. A wide column of Kurgan warriors was marching into the caves from outside. They looked to be the same fellows who had chased them here in the first place, but instead of the ragged leathers and bits and pieces of plundered armour they had worn before, now they wore matching suits of shining armour that encased breast, back, shoulders and arms. Close fitting helms hid their shaggy heads and long skirts of chainmail covered their legs. All was brand new, undented and flawless, and the spears and axes and swords they rested on their shoulders were freshly made as well, the honed edges flashing red in the furnace glow.

The column filed into the cave, eight abreast, with no end in sight. It looked like an army on the march, but where could they be marching to? There wasn't enough room for them all in the furnace cavern. Were they coming to slaughter all the slaves? That made no sense. Were there barracks further into the caves?

The head of the column wound between the furnaces and the mountains of ore, scattering slaves left and right, then marched straight into the minehead tunnel.

'Where are they going?' he muttered.

'Maybe there's been an insurrection in the mines,' said Franz hopefully.

Reiner shook his head. 'Look at those poor fellows. You think they have the energy to revolt? Let alone the will?'

'Captain,' said Pavel. 'Look!'

Reiner looked back toward the cave entrance. The end of the column of troops was at last in sight, and there was a sting in its tail. A phalanx of slaves was pulling a huge cannon on a massive gun carriage.

Ulf sucked in a horrified breath. 'Cannon!' he whispered. 'They have a cannon.'

'Impossible,' said Hals, pushing forward. 'Chaos troops don't have guns. They haven't the know-how.'

'Then someone has given it to them,' said Reiner.

ELEVEN
The End Of The Empire

CAUTIOUSLY, SO AS not to draw attention to their hiding place, Reiner studied the massive cannon the slaves pulled. It was the biggest field piece he had ever seen, twice as long as the Empire's great cannon, with a muzzle as wide as a keg of Marienburg ale. Its mouth was decorated to resemble a screaming daemonic maw, ringed with fangs. The barrel was detailed in silver dragon scales and barbaric designs. The carriage that it rested upon was made in the shape of two crouching legs, also scaled, that gripped the axle in two immense bronze claws. Its wooden wheels were each as tall as a man.

Reiner shivered. 'A few of those would turn the tide of a battle, eh?'

Franz looked around at him, eyes wide. 'Sigmar! Pray there isn't more than one!'

'But where did they get the knowledge?' asked Ulf. 'The secrets of gunnery are the Empire's most closely guarded.'

His question was answered as they saw the figures that followed the gun, berating the slaves who pulled it. They were half the height of the smallest slave, but bulging with muscles, and wore beards braided to their knees.

'Dwarfs!' said Franz, gaping.

'Those are dwarfs?' asked Pavel, uncertainly.

Reiner looked closer. He hadn't seen many dwarfs in his lifetime – they didn't come much to Altdorf – but these fellows looked like no dwarf he'd ever encountered. They seemed almost deformed by their muscles: stumping around on twisted but powerful legs. Their heads were distorted by ridges of bone, and their hands crowded with extra fingers.

'Bent on the forge of Chaos,' said Gustaf under his breath.

Reiner shivered.

'The forces of Chaos with artillery,' groaned Ulf. 'This could mean the end of the Empire. They must be stopped. We must tell someone.'

'Certainly,' said Pavel sourly. 'Right after we get out of here.'

Reiner shook his head as the warriors continued to file into the tunnel. 'I don't understand it. They can't be going to make war underground. No one in their right mind, not even a Chaos-crazed berzerker, fires a cannon in a mine. What do they mean to do?'

'They go south to fight a battle,' said Gustaf. 'There are old tunnels beneath the mine that run the length of the range.'

Everyone turned to stare at him.

'How do you know this?' asked Reiner.

'I overheard the patrol who passed us speaking of it.'

Reiner raised an eyebrow. 'You understand their jabber?'

'Course he does,' said Hals, spitting. 'A servant always learns his master's tongue. I knew there was something wrong about you, y'daemon worshipping filth.'

'If I serve the dark ones, then why am I not betraying you now?'

'And how *do* you come to speak their language?' asked Reiner.

Gustaf looked for a moment as if he wasn't going to speak, then he sighed. 'I don't, but it is similar to the tongue of the Kossars. The company of lancers I served with in Kislev had a detachment of Kossar horse. I learned their speech – particularly their curses – when I treated their wounds.'

The others eyed him coolly, weighing this. They didn't look as if they believed him.

'What else did they say?' asked Reiner. 'Did they give any details?'

Gustaf shrugged. 'As I said, I only speak a few words. They said the word south, and tunnel, and castle. I got the idea that they were going to fight at the castle, though whether they were fighting to take it or defend it, I don't know. They said the name. Norse something? North, perhaps?'

Reiner's heart thudded in his chest. 'Nordbergbruche!'

'It might have been.'

'Ain't that Lord Manfred's castle?' asked Pavel. 'What Captain Veirt was going on about? Didn't he say the northers had taken it?'

'Aye,' said Reiner. He turned on Gustaf. 'Why didn't you tell us this earlier?'

'You didn't ask.'

Reiner curled his lip and turned back to the cave in time to see the cannon vanish into the tunnel. He thought furiously. It would be a terrible blow to the Empire if that cannon was loosed upon it. But did he care? The Empire had jailed and branded him unjustly. He owed it no favours. At the same time, it might be in his best interests to help his homeland. If Manfred could be convinced to reward them for warning him of his brother's treachery, how much bigger might the reward be if Reiner informed him of the coming of the cannon as well?

He gnawed a knuckle. Which was the least dangerous path? Which was the most profitable? How did he decide?

At last he turned. 'Well lads, I've a plan. I doubt any of you will like it much. But I think it's our best chance, so we'll put it to a vote, eh?'

The men waited patiently. Gustaf folded his arms.

Reiner swallowed. 'It's my guess that Count Manfred is waiting for Albrecht to join him before the two of them storm Nordbergbruche together. And as soon as he gets Lady Magda's banner Albrecht will be on his way, but not to help his brother. I think he's marching to fight him, army against army, and with that unholy thing on his side, Albrecht may well win.' Reiner coughed uneasily. 'If we somehow found a way out of here and made it down to the flatlands without running into more northers, it would take us weeks, maybe a month, to circle the mountains and make it to Nordbergbruche – if we're lucky and aren't eaten by Sigmar-knows-what along the way. By that time the battle might already have occurred. Albrecht may have won, and we would be too late to warn Manfred and collect our reward.' He pointed down toward the minehead. 'These fellows have found a short cut, a direct line from here to there. I... I say we take it.'

There were grunts of shock and dismay.

'I know it's a rotten idea,' said Reiner. 'But I think it's the only way we can make it in time. What do you say?'

There was a long silence. Finally Hals chuckled.

'Laddie,' he said. 'That speech you made, back there at the cave-in, about leading us wrong at every turn. Well, most of it was true, I suppose. But y'still have more ideas than the rest of us, and one's bound to come right one of these days, so... I'm with you.'

'And I,' said Pavel.

'And I,' said Franz.

'The Empire must be told of these cannon as soon as possible,' said Ulf. 'Count me in.'

Giano spread his hands. 'One way is as bad as the other, hey?'

'Go into the mine?' asked Oskar numbly.

Gustaf shrugged. 'I wouldn't make it on my own, would I?'

'You might not make it *with* us, daemon worshipper,' snarled Hals.

Gustaf curled his lip. 'That's as may be, but you certainly won't make it without me.'

'And what's the meaning of that?' asked Reiner, looking up.

Gustaf smirked. 'The Kurgan spoke of an obstacle, a choke point near the end of the tunnels, that we will have difficulty circumventing. But there is a way.'

'What is it?' asked Reiner. 'How do we get around it?'

Gustaf shook his head. 'Do you think me a fool? I know what you think of me. I know you'd stick a knife in my guts if you thought I was no longer useful to you. Consider this extra protection against... accidents.'

Reiner and the others glared at him.

'You really are a loathsome little worm,' said Reiner at last. He turned away before Gustaf had a chance to retort, and clapped his hands. 'Right then,' he said. 'It's decided. Now the trick is getting to the minehead undetected.'

'Go into the mines?' asked Oskar again, mournfully.

'Sorry, old man,' said Reiner. 'But Gustaf will take care of you.' He shot the surgeon a look. 'Won't you, Gustaf?'

They returned to the main passage. After fifty paces, the rails sloped down a ramp to the level of the cave floor as the noises of hammering and the roar of fire grew louder and louder. At its base, the ramp bent right into a short corridor. A narrow passage intersected it, and ten paces beyond that, it opened into the giant cavern. Reiner could see ranks of smiths at their anvils, hammering out swords and pieces of armour as slaves scurried around them, holding the work steady, feeding the fires, squeezing the bellows. The cross corridor looked more promising. It was small and dark and smelled of death, decay, and cooking meat.

'Smells like pork,' said Pavel hungrily.

Gustaf snorted. 'Two legged pork.'

'Shut your mouth, y'filthy dog,' snarled Hals.

'Quiet,' said Reiner. 'Now douse torches. Weapons out.'

The men drew their swords and daggers, then slipped around the corner into the dark passage. The stench was almost overwhelming and it only got worse as they continued – as did the noise. Twenty paces along they saw ahead of them on the left wall a tiny, leather-curtained doorway, through which came a ground-shaking hammering and flashes of blinding green light, and under the deafening banging, a chorus of guttural voices chanting in unison. A moment later the curtain flipped open and two slaves pushed through it, dragging a third, who was obviously dead.

Reiner and the others halted and held their breath, but the slaves looked neither left or right, only hauled their burden listlessly down the hall, oblivious. Reiner crept to the curtain and peeked through, then drew back reflexively at the sight that met his eyes. After waiting a moment to quiet his heart, he looked again. The others peered over his shoulders.

Through the tiny door was a pillared, seven-sided room that had been hacked crudely out of the living rock. Towering representations of blood-red daemons were painted on each of the seven walls, though whether they were seven different entities or seven aspects of the same god, Reiner didn't know. Seven pillars surrounded a raised dais. On his first glance Reiner had thought that the pillars were decorated with carvings of skulls, but a second look showed that the skulls were real – with chipped teeth and crushed crowns – and covered every inch of the pillars from floor to ceiling. There were thousands of them.

But what had made Reiner draw back in fear were the occupants of the room. A ring of armoured Kurgan stood along the walls, chanting unceasingly. They were bare-headed, and Reiner could see that their eyes were rolled back in their heads. Lines and sigils had been smeared on their cheeks with blood. The focus of their attention was the dais in the centre of the room. Here, where one would have expected some heathen altar, there stood instead a huge iron anvil, with a glowing furnace beside it, and a wide, shallow basin before it, filled with a red liquid that could only be blood. Behind the altar a hulking, barely-human smith worked a set of enormous bellows. He stood seven feet tall if he was an inch, and his massive, muscled arms each looked as big around as Reiner's ribcage. He was stripped to the waist and covered in a pattern of scars and burns that looked more decorative than accidental. Lank black hair hung over his face, hiding it, but Reiner could see the flash of white tusks jutting up from the corners of his mouth and two blunt horns pushing through the skin of his brow.

A wild-eyed shaman with a dreadlocked beard and hairy robes that seemed to have been stitched from scalps stood at his side, leading the chanting in a hoarse voice. Two Kurgan warriors stood at the edge of the dais holding a sagging slave between them. More slaves stood behind the first.

As Reiner and the others watched, the giant smith pulled a glowing blade from the furnace by the naked tang and set it on the anvil. He raised a mighty hammer over his head and began beating the edge of the blade with it. Though the blade glowed orange-white, the sparks that flew at each hammer-fall were an eerie green that burned Reiner's eyes as if he was looking directly into the sun. The host of Kurgan grunted in unison with each hammer fall.

With a final blow, the smith finished shaping the blade and held it flat on the anvil. As the chanting rose to a fever pitch, the shaman stepped forward, wielding a smaller hammer and an iron implement that looked something like a wine bottle. He set the base of the iron bottle on the blade, just above the tang, and smote it with the hammer as the warriors barked a two syllable word. More green sparks splashed and the smith raised the blade. It had been imprinted with a crude runic symbol that Reiner's eyes shied uneasily away from.

At a signal from the shaman, the Kurgan guards shoved a slave forward. In unison, the smith, the shaman and the assembled Kurgan shouted a short, guttural incantation, then the smith ran the slave through with the still glowing blade. It hissed. The slave screamed and doubled up. The smith, with inhuman strength, lifted the slave off the ground on the point and held him aloft until the blood from his wound ran, spitting and boiling, down the fuller to fill the pattern of the stamped rune.

Reiner flinched back involuntarily again, for as the blood touched the rune, the sword suddenly seemed to have a presence. It felt as if some malevolent entity had entered the temple. The warriors fell to their knees and raised their arms in adulation.

Reiner and the others cringed back from the curtain, grimacing, as the smith gave the blade to the shaman, who held it over his head and showed it to the ring of warriors. They roared their approval.

'Are we tainted just for seeing that?' asked Franz.

'It pains a son of Sigmar,' said Hals, 'to see a hammer used for so evil a purpose.'

Ulf raised a hand. 'The slaves return.'

The company backed into the shadows as the two slaves – a man and a woman, they could now see, both skeleton thin – padded back to the curtained door and passed through it. After a moment, they reappeared, dragging the body of the impaled slave behind them and disappeared once again down the dark hallway.

After waiting a moment, Reiner motioned them forward.

Franz shivered. 'I dread to see what lies at the end of this.'

Reiner patted the boy's shoulder. 'What in death could be worse than the life these poor souls have suffered in bondage?'

As they continued down the hall, the reek of death increased. There was more light ahead as well. Faint torchglow shone from two curtained doorways, one on either side of the hall. They reached the left-hand one first and Reiner cautiously peeked in.

It was an enormous room: not deep, but so long that the two ends were hidden in darkness. A wide doorway on the opposite wall opened directly into the cavern that housed the furnaces, and through it Reiner could see the lines of bucket-toting slaves making their endless rounds. The room itself was filled with rank after rank of poorly-made plank beds, stacked six high and none as wide as Ulf's shoulders.

The beds to the left side of the door were empty. Those to the right were full of bony, huddled forms, their elbows, knees and hips raw and bruised from lying on the naked wood. They moaned and coughed and twitched in their fitful slumbers, or worse, moved not at all.

As Reiner watched, a curious procession came into view between two rows of beds. A Kurgan guard swaggered along, followed by four slaves pushing a flat cart piled with bodies. The Kurgan had a sharp stick, and with it, he prodded the sleeping slaves one by one. Most flinched and cried out. Those that didn't, the Kurgan jabbed again, harder this time. If a slave still failed to respond, the Kurgan dragged him off his plank and threw him on the cart, then moved on.

At the end of the row the cart was full and the Kurgan barked an order. Reiner ducked back as the slaves turned the cart toward him, and waved the others back down the hall into the shadows.

The Kurgan led the slaves out of the barracks and into the door on the opposite side of the hall. After a pause Reiner edged to it, at once compelled by curiosity and terrified at what he might see. The others followed. Reiner looked in, hoping against hope that what he would see would be some kind of embalming chamber or garbage pit. It was not. It was what his nose told him it would be: a kitchen. He pulled back, disgusted, and pushed Franz past the door. 'Don't look, lad. Keep moving.'

Franz made to protest, but Reiner shoved him roughly down the hall. He and the others slipped past in ones and twos as it was safe, and continued down the hall, shuddering with revulsion at the sights within the kitchen. Reiner wished he could get the smell of meat out of his nose.

A little further on, Ulf stopped at another open door. 'Wait,' he whispered. 'In here.'

He entered the room. The others looked in. Ulf was picking though piles of poorly made picks and shovels that were heaped against the walls along with stacks of pitch-smeared torches, coils of rope, wooden buckets, lengths of chain, sections of iron rail, iron wheels, leather aprons and gloves. All were of poorest quality – made by slaves, for slaves.

'If we are to travel long underground,' said Ulf as the others entered, 'we will want torches and rope, and possibly picks and shovels as well. Everyone should take what they can.'

'We're not all built like pack horses, engineer,' said Hals.

Ulf slung a coil of rope over his shoulder. 'We've encountered one cave-in already. We may have to dig our way out of another. Then there are the dangers of pitfalls, uncrossable chasms, unscalable cliffs. We may need to widen a passage to get through. Or block a passage to prevent pursuit. And...'

'All right, Urquart,' said Reiner quickly. 'You've made your point. We don't want to give Oskar the fibertygibbits again. Everyone take torches and rope. For the rest you may do as you please.'

Everyone did as he asked. Hals, though he had complained the loudest, took a pick and gave a shovel to Pavel. When all had been packed away, they moved on.

The passage ended fifty paces later in a doorway through which shone the red glow of the main cavern. Reiner and the others eased forward to peer through. The doorway came out just behind the two massive furnaces. The slaves that fed the fires and their overseers were less than three long strides from the door. Reiner could have spat on them. Instead, he looked toward the minehead, just beyond the furnaces to the right. It was close. A short sprint and they would be within its shadow and away, but that sprint was fraught with dangers.

At least a dozen Kurgan guards stood between them and the mine head, and there were a hundred within easy call. Reiner frowned. If only there was some way to distract them, to draw the attention of the entire room for the few seconds they needed to dart through unnoticed.

And just as he thought it, a great, almost musical, crash sounded through the cavern. Every head looked up, Kurgan and slave alike. The crash came again. Reiner craned his neck and saw to the left, a Kurgan beating a cracked gong, hung from a rope, as out of the wide door that led from the sleeping quarters came a procession of slaves staggering under the weight of huge steaming cauldrons they carried on long poles.

The overseers barked orders to their work parties and motioned them toward the centre of the cavern where the kitchen slaves were setting the cauldrons. There was no need for orders. The slaves downed tools and flocked toward the stew pots like wolves running down a deer, licking their lips and fighting each other to be first in line.

Pavel turned away, shuddering.

'Don't blame them, lad,' said Reiner. 'Blame the fiends who drove them to it. Now pull yourselves together. We daren't miss this chance.'

The furnaces were deserted. Reiner and the rest darted around the right hand one, taking cover behind its great bulk. They were instantly drenched in sweat from the heat that radiated from it. To their left the cave wall narrowed to the blackness of the mine-head. They crept along it, crouching low.

Halfway to the hole they ran out of cover. They would have to make the last thirty feet out in the open. Reiner stood on his toes to see where the Kurgan were. All of them seemed fully occupied at the stew pots, the overseers reaching in and stealing the choicer bits of flesh from the slaves. He turned to the men.

'Ready, lads?'

Everyone except Oskar nodded.

'Keep him pointed in the right direction.' Reiner said to Gustaf, then took one last look toward the centre of the cave. 'Right,' he said. 'Run.'

The men ran fast and low, Gustaf holding Oskar down by the scruff of the neck. The run lasted only a few seconds, but it seemed an eternity to Reiner, who swore he could feel the eyes of every Kurgan in the cave turning towards him. But as they sprinted into the black mouth of the mine no shouts echoed down the cave, no gongs crashed, no arrows rattled off the rocks around them. They reined to a stop twenty paces into the shadow and looked back. No one was coming after them.

'We make it, hey?' said Giano, smiling.

'Aye,' said Pavel dryly. 'The first step in a thousand-league journey.'

'Less of that, pikeman!' growled Reiner, unconsciously mimicking Veirt. 'Now come on. I want to be well away from here.'

'As do I,' said Hals.

They started down the long dark passage, not yet sure enough of their surroundings to light torches. Behind him, Reiner could hear Oskar whimper as the blackness closed in completely around them.

TWELVE
There Is No Good Decision Here

AFTER A HALF hour of utter darkness and silence it seemed safe to light torches, and all breathed sighs of relief. All except Oskar. The soothing effects of Gustaf's draught were wearing off and he began to look around uneasily and mutter about, 'The weight. The stone. There is no air.'

'Why ever did you decide to become a soldier, gunner?' grumbled Hals. 'Is there nothing you ain't afraid of?'

'I never meant to be a soldier,' murmured Oskar, slurring a little. 'I was m'lord Gottenstet's secretary. I wrote his correspondence for him. Read it too. Illiterate, the old fool. But one day...' he sighed and stopped.

The others waited for him to continue, but he seemed to have forgotten he was talking.

'One day, what?' asked Pavel, annoyed.

'Eh?' said Oskar. 'Oh... yes. Well, one day I was with m'lord as he was surveying some land he owned. He wanted to build a, a hunting lodge I think it was. And while the surveyor was using his plumb line and his measuring sticks to calculate distances and heights, I was guessing, and coming right almost to the foot. I picked out far away things that the surveyor needed his spyglass to make out. "Sigmar's lightning, lad," says Gottenstet. "Y've the making of a fine mortar man." And nothing would do but he must send me to the Artillery School at Nuln. Me! A scholar! I tried to tell him that though my eyes might be strong, my insides were weak, but he would have none of it.' He shrugged. 'Of course I didn't help matters by coming out top of my class. I liked the work: making the sightings, calling out the degrees, but on the field...' He shivered and hugged his shoulders. 'Did you ever see the fire from the sky? The thing with the mouths.' He looked around him suddenly as if waking up, his eyes widening as he took in the close stone walls, the low ceiling. 'The weight,' he murmured. 'Sigmar, save us, the weight. Can't breathe.'

Reiner grimaced, uncomfortable. 'Gustaf, give him another sip, will you?'

THE CORRIDOR SANK deeper and deeper into the mountains. Occasionally corridors branched off to the left and right, iron rails gleaming away into the shadows. Some were barricaded off and the party could see evidence of cave-ins behind them, but there was no confusion on which way to go. The deep tracks of the cannon's wheels always pointed the way.

A while later the iron rails began to sing, and soon after came a metallic rumbling. The company doused their torches and ducked into a side tunnel. After a moment a train of carts rolled by, full of ore, each pushed by a team of shackled slaves, their eyes dull. A Kurgan overseer reclined in the first cart, a lantern at his side.

Franz cursed under his breath once they'd passed. 'So many of them, and one of him. Couldn't they strangle him? Dump him down a shaft?'

'And then?' asked Reiner.

The boy grunted with frustration, but couldn't answer.

As the train's rumble faded, it revealed nearer sounds: the thud and chunk of picks biting into rock, the crack of whips, the barking of hounds. They stepped back into the main corridor and looked forward. A faint light picked out distant sections of wall, the glint of rails.

Reiner looked at the cannon's wheel tracks, running straight ahead and sighed. 'It looks as if the warband marched beyond the work party. We will have to take side corridors around them and hope we can find the tracks on the other side. Keep the torches dark. We'll travel by the lantern only.'

They continued forward in the main tunnel until the reflected light became bright enough for them to be able to see each other's faces, then began hunting for cross corridors. The sounds of mining came mostly from the left of the main tunnel, so they edged right, taking thinner tunnels and winding crawlways.

After a time they found a promising corridor that paralleled the main corridor. It was nearly as wide and had rails running down the centre. These seemed both newer and cruder than the rails they had followed from the ironworks. The sounds of mining reached them only as echoes here, and came more from their left than from in front of them. Reiner began to feel almost hopeful. As long as they could find a way back to the main tunnel from here, there was a good chance they would pass the work party without incident.

But just as he thought it, the rails began to ring and rattle. There were carts coming. Reiner groaned. 'Speak of evil…'

There was a small side tunnel up ahead. Reiner pointed to it. 'In there. It has no rails.' They hurried into it. It ended after thirty paces in a round, dug-out area with no other exit – a dead end.

'Right,' said Reiner. 'We'll wait here until they pass.'

The echoing rumble of wheels grew suddenly louder, and the torch glow much brighter, as if the approaching carts had turned a corner. The men faced back to the wide corridor, hands on their weapons. Giano shuttered his lantern and hid it behind him. As they watched, a procession of four heavily loaded carts passed by their hiding place. A Kurgan guard followed the carts, torch in one hand and a huge hound on a leash snuffling along at his side.

The Kurgan walked on, kicking pebbles, but the hound stopped, sniffing at the mouth of the tunnel. The Kurgan tugged on his leash, but the hound refused to move.

Reiner's shoulders tensed. 'Go,' he whispered under his breath. 'Go. Go!'

The Kurgan stopped and cursed the hound, jerking its leash. The hound snarled at him, then began barking down the corridor.

'Sigmar curse you, heathen,' muttered Hals. 'Beat that cur. Make him heel.'

But the Kurgan had decided that the hound was on to something and came forward warily, the hound still barking and straining at his leash.

Reiner and the rest backed out of sight into the round chamber. 'Better kill 'em quick,' whispered Reiner, drawing his sword. 'But no guns, or they'll all be down on us.'

The others armed themselves.

'We should draw 'em in,' said Hals. 'Get 'em from all sides.'

'Good idea,' said Reiner. 'Franz, you're the bait.'

'What?' said Franz, confused.

Reiner shoved the boy hard between the shoulder blades. He stumbled out of cover and froze like a rabbit, staring up the tunnel at the advancing Kurgan in wide-eyed terror. The Kurgan roared a challenge and ran forward, dropping the hound's leash and drawing a hand axe.

The hound bounded forward, baying savagely. Franz scurried for the back wall. 'You bastard!' he shrieked at Reiner. 'You dirty bastard!'

Pavel stuck his spear out across the opening at ankle height as the Kurgan and the hound charged in. The beast leapt it easily, but the norther fell flat on his face and Hals, Giano and Reiner stuck him with their spears and swords. Ulf swung his maul at the hound and knocked it sideways as it lunged at Franz.

The monster landed, snarling, and spun to meet this new threat. Ulf raised his hammer as it leapt, and jammed the haft between its gaping jaws, stopping its fangs from reaching his neck, but the beast was so massive it knocked the big man flat and began raking at him with its claws.

The Kurgan surged up, screaming fury and bleeding from three grievous wounds. Reiner was afraid they had another iron-skinned berserker on their hands, but fortunately, though as big as a bull, the guard was no chosen champion, only a ranker, stuck in the mines guarding slaves while others won glory on the fields of honour. Reiner chopped halfway through his windpipe and he died on his knees, breathing his last through his neck.

The hound was another matter. Franz and Oskar were slashing at it with their swords, but their blows couldn't penetrate the beast's matted coat. Ulf, on his back under the monster, was forcing its head back with the haft of his maul, but his straining arms were being shredded by its claws.

Reiner ran forward with Hals and Pavel. Giano dropped his sword and unslung his crossbow, drawing a bolt from his quiver. Gustaf kept out of the way, as usual.

Reiner slashed at the hound's back legs, severing its left hamstring. It howled and turned, but fell as it put weight on its dead leg. Pavel and Hals gored it in the side with their spears. Still it fought, twisting so savagely that Pavel's spear was wrenched out of his fever-weakened hands and cracked Hals in the forehead. The hound lunged for the dazed pikeman, but Ulf, freed of its weight, clubbed it with all his might, square on its spinal ridge. It dropped flat, its legs splayed. Giano stepped forward and fired his crossbow point blank. The bolt pinned the monster's head to the ground. It died in a spreading pool of blood.

'Nice work, lads,' said Reiner. 'Ulf, are you badly hurt? Hals?'

'Just a little swimmy, captain,' said Hals. 'It'll pass.'

'I've had worse,' said Ulf, grimacing as he examined his lacerated biceps. 'But not by much.'

'Just coming,' said Gustaf. He began opening his kit.

Reiner looked toward the corridor, listening for reinforcements, and froze, heart thudding, as he saw half a dozen faces looking back at him. The slaves were peering anxiously down the tunnel at them. Reiner had forgotten all about them.

'What do we do about that lot?' asked Hals, joining him.

Pavel looked up. 'Poor devils.'

'We must free them!' said Franz. 'Bring them with us.'

'You crazy, boy,' said Giano. 'They slow us down. We no make it.'

'But we can't leave 'em here,' said Pavel. 'The Kurgan'd kill 'em sure.'

Ulf grunted as Gustaf cleaned his wounds. 'The Kurgan will kill them regardless, whether now or later.'

'It's your decision, captain,' said Hals.

Reiner cursed under his breath. 'This is exactly why I don't want to lead. There is no good decision here.'

He chewed his lip, thinking, but whichever way he turned it, it was bad.

'Your best course is to put them out of their misery,' said Gustaf. 'They are no longer men.'

'What does a monster know of men?' spit Hals.

Reiner wanted to punch Gustaf, not for being wrong, but for being right. The surgeon always took the bleakest view of every situation, had the most cynical view of human nature, and so often turned out to be one Reiner should have listened to. Killing them *would* be best. The slaves were too weak to keep up, and would stretch their food supply much too thin, but Reiner could feel Franz's eyes hot upon him, and Pavel's one-eyed gaze as well, and couldn't give the order.

'We... we'll free them, and... and offer them the choice to follow us or not.' He flushed as he said it, for it was a horrible equivocation, a mere sop to common sense. What other choice did the slaves have? He was dooming the men who depended on him because he hadn't the heart to kill men who were virtually dead already.

Franz and Pavel nodded, satisfied, but Gustaf made a disgusted sound and Giano groaned. The rest looked non-committal. Reiner fished the keys from the dead Kurgan's belt and started down the tunnel to the larger corridor.

Franz fell in beside him. 'That was a rotten trick just then, pushing me into danger.'

Reiner's teeth clenched. He was tired of feeling guilty. 'I had faith in you.'

'But I've lost a little in you,' the boy countered, then shrugged. 'Though you do a brave thing here.'

'I do a foolish thing here.'

The slaves edged warily back as Reiner and his men came out of the tunnel. There were sixteen of them, four teams to push the four carts, which were filled with waste rock. Each starveling quartet was shackled together at the ankles.

Reiner held up the keys. 'Don't be afraid. We're going to free you.'

The slaves stared, uncomprehending, and flinched back again as he approached them.

'Hold still.'

The slaves did as they were told. Commands seemed the only speech they understood. Reiner squatted and unlocked the four locks in turn. Franz and Pavel followed behind him, pulling the chain that linked them out through the slaves' shackles until all were free.

Reiner faced them. 'There you are. You are slaves no more. We welcome you to follow us to freedom, or… or to take what path you think best.'

The slaves blinked at him, eyes blank. Reiner coughed. What was wrong with them? Were they deaf? 'Do you understand? You're free. You can travel with us if you wish.'

One of the slaves, a woman with no hair, began to weep, a dry, scratchy sound.

'It's a trick,' said another. 'They mean to trap us again.'

'Stop torturing us!' cried a third.

'It isn't a trick,' said Franz, as the slaves whispered among themselves. 'You are truly free.'

'Don't listen to them!' said the slave who had first spoken. 'They only mean to catch us out. Go back to the work face! Warn the masters!'

He backed away from Reiner and began running back down the corridor. The others ran with him, like sheep running because other sheep were running.

'Curse it!' growled Reiner. 'Stop!' He grabbed at a fleeing slave, but the skeletal man squirmed out of his fingers. 'Stop them!' he called to the others.

'What are they doing?' asked Franz, confounded, as the others tried to corral the slaves. 'Why are they running?'

'They are lost, as I told you,' said Gustaf, sneering.

Pavel, Hals, Oskar and Giano grabbed a handful of the slaves and pushed them to the floor, but more were disappearing into darkness.

'Never mind why,' said Reiner, running down the hall. 'We have to shut them up before they bring their overseers down on us. Giano, bring the lantern!'

Reiner and Franz chased the slaves with Giano, Ulf and Hals running behind them, Giano's slotted lantern throwing dancing bars of light on the uneven walls. Reiner was surprised at how fast the slaves moved. He thought they would be weak from starvation, but it seemed that their constant labour had given them a wiry strength, and Reiner and the others had difficulty keeping up, let alone catching up, for the slaves seemed to know every inch of the tunnels in the dark.

'Come back, curse you!' he called after them, but this order they did not follow.

The slaves reached the main corridor and turned right. As he angled in behind them, Reiner could see the glow of torches up ahead. He put on a burst of speed and caught the last slave around the neck, bringing him down.

The slave cried out. The others leapt ahead, wailing, and scattered. Some continued down the main corridor. Some swerved into side corridors. All started shouting as loud as their rusty voices would allow.

'Masters! Masters! Help!'

'Interlopers, masters! Protect us!'

'They have killed our overseer!'

Franz darted into the first side corridor after two slaves, but Reiner collared him and pulled him back.

'Don't be a fool! We must stick together.'

'Too late anyway,' sighed Giano, as hounds began to bay and harsh Kurgan orders echoed through the tunnels. The thud of heavy boots began to converge on them.

Reiner groaned. 'Back to the others, quick.'

He turned and started running back down the corridor. Franz, Giano, Oskar and Hals following in his wake.

Franz seemed almost on the point of tears. 'Why did they do it? We only wanted to help them.'

'Been underground so long,' said Hals, 'they believe no more in the sun.'

'I don't understand,' Franz wailed.

'I'll explain it to you if we live,' said Reiner. 'Now run.'

They sprinted back toward where they had left the others. The Kurgan were too big to move quickly, and did not gain on them, but the hounds were faster than horses. Reiner could hear their baying coming closer and closer. At last he rounded a bend in the corridor and saw Pavel, Oskar, and Gustaf by the mine carts, standing guard over the slaves they had caught.

'Run!' called Reiner.

'Up, you lot,' growled Pavel to the slaves, prodding them with his spear. 'Get moving.'

But when he and Oskar let them up the slaves ran toward Reiner and his companions. Reiner tried to stop one as she ran by, as did Franz, but the slaves dodged away from them and ran on, toward the hounds.

'The fools,' sobbed Franz.

The company squeezed past the mine carts. Screams of agony and animal snarls echoed from behind. Reiner felt a stab of self-loathing as he found himself hoping that the hounds would stop to eat the slaves that he had gone to such pains to free only moments earlier. This did not appear to be the case, for the baying and shouting continued to grow louder.

They rounded another bend and Giano fell sprawling over some loose rock. The lantern bounced out of his hand and smashed on the rail. The flame went out. Total darkness closed over them. They jumbled to a stop.

'Myrmidia curse me!' cried Giano.

'No one move,' said Reiner as the baying and running boots echoed ever closer. 'All hold hands. If you are not holding a hand, speak up.'

He stretched out and took a rough hand. He had no idea who it was.

'I stand alone,' said Gustaf.

'You certainly do, mate,' said Hals.

Reiner reached toward Gustaf's voice. 'Take my hand.'

Gustaf's soft fleshy hand batted at his, then caught it.

'Hurry!' wailed Oskar. 'They're coming!'

Reiner looked back. Far down the corridor, huge hound shadows bounded and swooped along the walls. Then the hounds themselves came into view, massive black silhouettes running ahead of the Chaos troops' torches.

Reiner turned and ran, forgetting to give an order. There was no need. The rest ran with him, blind as bats, whimpering in their throats. They all knew it was useless to run, but it was impossible not to. Fear drove their legs, not thought – the primal instinct for flight in the face of certain death.

Reiner tripped over the rails, caught himself, and crowded against the wall to avoid the ties. He could hear Gustaf wheezing and stumbling behind him, and not twenty paces behind him, the panting and snarling of the hounds.

So this was it, Reiner thought. He was going to die, lost to all he loved and all who loved him, in a black tunnel under the Middle Mountains, eaten by monstrous hounds. The things he had yet to do crowded into his head, all the money he hadn't yet won or spent, all the women he had yet to bed, books unread, the loves unloved. He found himself weeping with regret. It had all been so damned useless, the whole horrible journey – his whole life.

Franz shrieked from the back of the line. Ulf roared something incoherent and Reiner heard an impact and an animal yelp. He looked back, but there was little to see except leaping shadows and bobbing torches in the distance.

'Franz?'

The boy's answer was lost as, at the head of the line, Giano screamed. His scream was repeated by Pavel and Hals. And there was a sound of rattling pebbles and strange echoes. Reiner tried to halt before he ran into the hidden danger, but Gustaf, Ulf and Franz piled into him from behind, sending him flying forward again.

'Wait!' he cried. 'Something…'

His left foot came down on empty air. He yelled in surprise and threw his hands out, expecting to hit the tunnel floor face first. His hands touched nothing. There was nothing below him.

He was falling into a bottomless void.

THIRTEEN
All Is Not Entirely Lost

THE FALL WAS just long enough to allow Reiner to wonder how far down the bottom was, and to tense for the inevitable fatal bone-shattering, organ-exploding impact. But when it came at last it was less of a slam than a slide.

Not that it wasn't painful.

Reiner's first thought was that he was scraping against the cliff he was falling past, but the surface that was abrading his clothes was loose and crumbly and slid with him. It quickly turned into an almost perpendicular slope, made up of gravel, dirt and large rocks. Reiner caught one of these amidships and curled up in blinding pain. He began rolling and bouncing down the slope at breakneck speed, scraping and bashing his elbows and knees and shoulders. His brain bounced around in his head until he had no idea which way was up, if he was alive or dead, broken or whole. Only half conscious, he buried his head in his arms as the angle of the slope began to grow less acute and the speed of his fall to lessen.

He was just slowing to a stop, sliding down the mound, half buried in an avalanche of gravel, and thinking that he might possibly have survived, when a body dropped on his chest, crushing his ribs, and bounced away again, grunting. Reiner gasped, but couldn't draw a breath. It felt as if his lungs were locked in a vice.

A second body, lighter, but bonier, landed on his face. A knee cracked him in the nose and blood flooded his mouth. He slid at last to a stop, sucking air and spitting blood. All around him weak voices moaned and cried in pain. There were lights dancing in the centre of his vision. At first he thought they were after effects of the fall, but then he realised that they were torches, about as far above him as the top of a castle wall. He would have sworn he had fallen much farther than that. The Kurgan were looking down into the void to see what had become of them. He thought he heard them laughing. He doubted they could see anything.

'N...' He tried to speak and failed. He hadn't enough breath. After a moment he tried again. 'No one... strike... a light. Wait.'

He heard a hacking chuckle from nearby. 'No fear of that, captain,' said Hals. 'Dead men got no use for torches.'

After a moment the torches disappeared and they were left in total darkness.

'Unfortunately,' said Reiner at last, 'we appear to still live. If you've your flint handy, Hals?'

'Aye, captain.'

Reiner heard him shift around, then hiss in sudden pain. 'Ah, Sigmar's blood! I think I've bust my leg.'

'Any more hurt?' asked Reiner, though he was afraid to ask. 'Pavel?'

There was a muffled reply, then a curse. 'I've lost a bloody tooth.'

'Oskar?'

'I... I know not. I don't feel much of anything.'

'Franz? Did that monster get you?'

'I... I'm fine.'

'Ulf?'

There was no reply.

'Ulf?'

Silence.

'Just a moment, sir,' said Hals. 'Light's on its way.'

Reiner resumed the roll call. 'Gustaf?'

'I've lost some skin, that's all.'

'That's a relief. I hope you haven't lost your kit.'

'I have it.'

'Giano?'

'A rock, she cut me. I bleed a lot, I think.'

Light flashed as Hals struck sparks off his flint, followed by a steady glow as his tinder started. He touched it to a taper.

Reiner raised his head. His face felt twice as big as it ought to be, and twice as heavy. He looked around, squinting in the yellow light. The men were strewn like broken dolls at the base of a huge scree of gravel and loose rock that rose up into the darkness above them. This was obviously where the slaves dumped the waste rock they chipped away as they mined the ore. He looked at the men one by one.

Pavel was sitting up, holding his mouth, his fingers dripping blood. Hals was near him, holding aloft the candle. One of his legs was bent at an angle. Franz lay further down the slope, curled up and clutching his side. Reiner couldn't see the boy's face, but he seemed to be trembling. Oskar lay flat on his back staring straight up. He held one of his arms against his chest. Gustaf was hunched over his pack, sorting out his supplies. His canvas jacket was ripped to shreds on his left side, as was the skin under it. He bled from a hundred minor lacerations. Giano sat, naked to the waist, pressing a cut in his thigh with his shirt. His arms, shoulders and chest were mottled with blossoming bruises. Reiner was certain that all of them looked just the same under their clothes. Ulf he found at last, at the edge of the candle light, a motionless mass lying on his side at the base of the mound.

'Gustaf,' said Reiner, lowering his head again. 'Could you see if Master Urquart still lives.'

'Aye.'

Gustaf made his way cautiously down the slope, slipping and sinking into the loose gravel. He bent over Ulf, touching his neck and chest, and peeling back his eyelids. 'He lives,' he said. 'But he has struck his head. I don't know when he will wake. It is possible he won't.'

Reiner groaned. Just what they needed.

''Tis a miracle,' said Pavel unclearly, as Gustaf climbed the slope again to Giano, who was bleeding the most. 'All of us alive. Sigmar must be watching over us.'

'If Sigmar was watching over us,' said Hals dryly as he lit a torch from the taper, 'he wouldn't have let us fall off the cursed cliff in the first place.'

'If your hammer god care one bit of damn for us,' spat Giano, 'he not let us take this fooling mission.'

'I can't work here,' said Gustaf. He had tied off Giano's gash, but his kit was sliding away down the slope, and he was sunk in almost to his knees. 'We must find somewhere flat.'

With a groan Reiner sat up and looked around as Hals's torch flared to life and the others began slowly and painfully to stand. The hole they had fallen into was a natural crevasse, deep and wide, that wandered off into darkness to their left and right. The hill of gravel they lay on spread out in a semi-circle across an uneven mud floor that made Reiner think water ran through the chasm occasionally. He was wondering if one direction was better than the other when he noticed that there was a circular opening in the opposite wall of the crevasse. More decisions. Which way was best?

Then he remembered that he had Veirt's compass, taken from his dead body, in his belt pouch. He took it out and frowned at it. South pointed almost directly at the circular opening. 'Try in there,' he said, pointing to it.

Pavel began helping Hals down the slope, arms over each other's shoulder, both of them hissing and grunting in pain. Reiner felt as bad as they sounded. His ribs ached with every breath, and every joint seemed to have its own separate and particular pain. He and Giano opened a blanket and rolled Ulf's supine body onto it, then, with Gustaf's help, they pulled the blanket and Ulf down to the floor.

Oskar and Franz brought up the rear, Oskar holding his left arm with his right, Franz clutching his ribs and crabbing along, almost bent double. His jacket was torn at the back, and his breeks, below it, were turning black with blood.

'Lad,' said Reiner. 'Are you certain you're well?'

'It's nothing,' the boy grunted between clenched teeth. 'Nothing.'

Dragging Ulf across the dried mud floor took quite an effort and Reiner's ribs and muscles complained mightily, but it got easier once they entered the tunnel. Though crudely worked, it was almost perfectly circular, and the floor was worn smooth from what must have been centuries of traffic. Adding to the slickness was a hard, oily coating that covered everything like a glaze. It was as if the whole tunnel had been varnished. Reiner was repulsed by the feel of it, yet it made pulling Ulf almost effortless.

Giano sniffed suspiciously. 'Smell of rat-men.'

Reiner chuckled. 'Don't be a fool, man. Rat-men are a myth.'

'Is not true. They live.'

Pavel smirked back over his shoulder. 'Giant rats that talk? Come on, Tilean. What do y'take us for?'

Giano pulled himself up, insulted. 'They live, I tell you. My whole village they kill. My mama and papa. Come out of ground and kill everybodies. I have swear vengeance upon them.'

'Bit difficult, seeing as they don't exist.'

Giano sniffed. 'Men of Empire think they know everythings.'

'Captain,' called Hals. 'Found a room of sorts. Might do for a surgery.'

He was sticking his torch into a round opening in the tunnel wall. Letting go of Ulf's makeshift stretcher, Reiner joined him and looked in. The hole opened into a round, curve-walled chamber with eight smaller chambers branching off it like the fingers of a glove. Reiner took the torch from Hals and stepped in. A chill ran up his spine. At some time in the past the chamber had been occupied, though by who or what he couldn't say. The walls were carved with jagged, geometric reliefs that Reiner could make neither head nor tail of. A few warped wooden shelves leaned against them, with a scattering of cracked clay jugs and bowls upon them. Reiner poked the torch into each of the eight chambers. They were small and nearly circular, the floors calf deep in scraps of cloth and straw. Reiner wrinkled his nose. They smelled of dust and animal musk. The whole place gave him an uneasy feeling, but it was dry and flat and there appeared to be no danger.

'Excellent,' he said with more enthusiasm than he felt. He waved the others forward. 'Come on, in we go.'

Pavel and Hals limped in first, followed by Gustaf and Giano, dragging Ulf. Giano grimaced. 'You see. Rat-men. We find nest.'

'You don't know that,' said Reiner. 'Anybody could have made these holes.'

'Looks more like orc work,' said Gustaf, toeing aside a broken jug. 'Crude stuff.'

Pavel and Hals exchanged a nervous look.

'Only orcs?' said Hals dryly. 'That's a relief.'

'Can you no see?' asked Giano, pointing at the walls. 'Look. Rat faces. Rat bodies.'

Reiner looked at the reliefs again as Franz and Oskar entered. The designs might have been rat heads with wide-set eyes and sharp fangs, but they were so abstract and poorly carved that they might have been anything.

He waved a dismissive hand. 'Orcs or rat-men, whoever lived here is long gone.' He stuck his torch upright in the mouth of an unbroken urn and turned to Gustaf. 'Surgeon, what do you need of us?' He was trying his best to be bright and efficient like a good captain should, but his head ached abominably and his stomach was churning from all the blood that ran from his nose down the back of his throat.

Gustaf left Ulf on his blanket in the centre of the floor and opened his kit. 'Decide who is most injured. I will work from worst to least. If someone can break down these shelves for splints it would be a help. And if someone can sacrifice a shirt, I am running short of bandages.'

'I think Franz must be seen to first,' said Reiner. 'He is losing blood.'

'No!' said the boy, white-lipped. 'I am fine. I can attend to myself.' He limped hurriedly to one of the little chambers and disappeared inside.

'Come back here, you little brat,' barked Reiner. 'You are in no way fine.' With a grunt of annoyance he followed the boy into the room.

Franz was bracing himself against the wall with one trembling arm, his head bowed to his chest. His breath came in ragged gasps, and he pressed his left elbow against his side. The cloth of his shirt made a wet, squelching sound. 'Get out!' he gasped. 'Leave me be.'

Reiner glared at him. 'Don't be a fool, lad. You're grievously injured. You must let Gustaf have a look at you.'

'No,' whimpered Franz. 'He... he mustn't. No one...'

'But lad, you...'

The boy's knees gave way and he slid down the wall to sprawl on the floor.

'Curse it,' said Reiner. He returned to the main chamber. 'Surgeon, the boy's collapsed.'

Gustaf rose from examining Oskar's wrist. 'I'll see to him.' As he passed Reiner, he raised an eyebrow. 'Your nose is on sideways, captain. I believe you've broken it.'

Reiner raised his hand to his face. 'Ah. That would explain why my head feels as big as a melon.'

'I'll set it momentarily,' said the surgeon. 'In the meantime, if you could rip your shirt into strips.' He ducked into the small chamber with his kit.

Reiner joined the others on the floor and took off his jerkin and shirt. The air in the chamber was stuffy, but much warmer than that in the mine. It was almost comfortable. Hals was sawing at his spear with his dagger, trying to fashion it into a crutch. Giano was breaking the shelves into usable lengths. Oskar rocked back and forth, holding his arm. Pavel was pressing a rag of shirt against his mouth. His upper lip was split to his nose and bleeding freely.

He grinned at Reiner, showing red teeth. 'And I didn't think I could get any uglier.'

'Maybe y'll lose the other eye,' said Hals. 'So y'won't have to look at yerself.'

Pavel chuckled. 'I can only hope.'

After a short time Gustaf returned. Reiner thought there was something odd about his expression, a suppressed smirk possibly, but the surgeon always looked like he was stifling an evil thought, so he couldn't be sure.

'How's the boy,' Reiner asked.

Gustaf's smirk broadened for a moment, then disappeared. 'He sleeps. I gave him a draught. He was clawed along the ribs by the hound, then a sharp stone became lodged in the wound during the fall. Very painful. I removed the stone and bound the wound. He will be weak for a while, but he will live.' He snorted. 'If any of us do.'

'Brave little fool,' said Reiner with grudging respect. 'He tries too hard to be hard.'

'Yes,' said Gustaf, then crossed to Pavel and took out a needle and thread.

Just as he crouched down, Ulf suddenly jack-knifed into a sitting position, flailing and roaring. 'The beasts! The beasts!' He clubbed

Gustaf and Oskar with his wild swings. The others edged away from him.

Reiner stood. 'Ulf! Urquart! Calm yourself. The hounds are gone.'

Ulf's fists slowed and he blinked around him. 'What...?'

'We fell. You don't remember?'

'I... I thought... '

'You've hit your head,' said Gustaf, as he recovered himself. 'How do you feel?'

Ulf rubbed his eyes. He swayed where he sat, as if drunk. 'My head hurts. Eyes blurry. We fell?'

'Down a tailings pit,' said Reiner. 'We're all hurt.'

'But at least we escaped the hounds!' laughed Hals.

Gustaf looked in Ulf's eyes. 'You are concussed. Let me know if your vision fails to improve.' He returned to stitching up Pavel's lip.

'But where are we?' asked Ulf, suddenly anxious. 'Where is the Kurgan warband? Have we lost them? Can we get back to where we were? Are we lost in here?'

'Shut up, fool!' shouted Reiner. 'I don't need two Oskars on my hands. Gustaf will run out of elixir.'

He groaned. The engineer had said too much. He could see anxiety spreading from face to face.

'Calm yourselves,' he said. 'All of you. Yes we're in a tight spot, but as Hals just said, we have escaped the hounds, so we're better off than we were, right? Now, I don't know where the warband is from here, or where here is for that matter, but someone made these tunnels. They must lead somewhere.' he fished out Veirt's compass again. 'And for the moment they lead south, which is the way we want to go, so all is not entirely lost.'

He closed his eyes for a second and almost forgot to open them again, he was so weary. 'I say we rest here,' he said at last. 'There are rooms for all of us. When our surgeon has finished doctoring us we will turn in, and decide a course of action when we wake and can think straight, fair enough?'

He sighed with relief as he saw the men nodding and calming themselves. 'Good. We'll set two watches. I'll take the second if someone feels up to taking the first.'

'I will,' said Gustaf quickly. 'I am the least wounded of all of us.'

Reiner nodded his thanks, though he was slightly puzzled. The surgeon had never volunteered for watch before.

They made a curious discovery after Gustaf had bound and set all their wounds and breaks and they had settled into the eight little rooms. The darkness was no longer absolute. They had expected to be plunged into blackness once Gustaf stationed himself in the main room and snuffed the torch, but a faint light, so dim they were at first not sure it was there, illuminated the chambers. The greenish luminescence seemed to come from the walls, or more accurately, from the slick glaze that covered the walls.

'That's a small blessing,' said Pavel from his and Hals's chamber.

Yes, thought Reiner, as he lowered his head carefully into his nest of smelly rags. At least we will be able to see what ever cyclopean horror slithers out of the tunnels and kills us.

An agonised scream jerked Reiner from a dream of dicing with a mysterious opponent. He knew the fellow was using loaded dice, and yet he kept playing, kept betting, though he lost every time.

He blinked around in the green murk, for a moment at a loss as to where he was. The scream came again. He recognised it as Gustaf's voice this time. Gustaf! Gustaf was on watch. They were under attack! He jumped up and grabbed his sword, and almost fell again, his body ached so much in so many places. It felt like he was bound in iron ropes that tightened with each movement.

He forced himself to move through the pain and stumbled out into the main chamber. The others were peeking out of their rooms as well, weapons in hand. Oskar wasn't there.

Reiner limped to the tunnel, but a horrible rattling groan echoing from Franz's chamber stopped him. Reiner turned, and he and the others crowded into it, ready to fight.

A confusing tableau met their eyes. Franz was pressed against the wall, eyes wild, one hand holding his jerkin closed, the other gripping a bloody dagger. Gustaf lay at his feet in a pool of red, clutching at a wound in his throat that would never close. As Reiner watched, his arms relaxed and flopped loosely to the ground. The room filled with the smell of urine.

'Sigmar's holy hammer, boy!' said Reiner, aghast. 'What have you done?'

'He…' said Franz. He seemed not quite awake.

'He's killed our only hope of getting out of here, is what he's done,' growled Hals angrily. 'Stupid little fool! I ought to ring your neck!'

Franz hugged himself. 'He tried to… to put his hands on me.'

'That again?' said Hals. 'Well it won't fly, lad. You were with us when Gustaf went after that poor girl. He don't care for boys, no matter how unmanly they are.'

'Who care what the fellow do!' cried Giano. 'If he want to eat you, you give him you arm. We need him. How we be now if he not fix us up, eh?' He spat on Franz's boots.

'Gustaf knew the way out,' said a voice behind them. It was Oskar, clinging to the wall, looking too alert for his own good. 'You remember. There was some obstacle further on. He wouldn't tell us.'

'He wouldn't tell us, so we wouldn't kill him,' said Hals. 'And now this fool has gone and killed him!' He balled his fists. 'I think it's time we show this mewling baby what it means to be a man. I say we give him a few hard lessons, hey?'

'No!' said Reiner. 'We're all hurt enough as it is. It's a bad thing he's done, I admit. But we need all the hands we have, and…'

'Shhhh!' said Ulf, from the door. 'Do you hear something?'

They all fell silent and listened. There was something, more a vibration in the rock than a heard sound.

'Into the tunnel,' said Reiner.

They tiptoed into the hall, leaving Franz with Gustaf's corpse, and stood, ears cocked.

The sound was louder here, a rumbling murmur. The vibrations seemed to be coming from above them and far forward. There was a song over the murmur, a harsh, angry chant.

'The warband!' said Oskar. 'It must be!'

Pavel grinned. 'Never thought I'd be glad to hear Kurgan marching.'

Reiner smiled. 'Right then, get your gear together. We leave immediately.'

They re-entered the round room. 'Go when you're packed,' said Reiner, stepping to Franz's chamber. 'I'll be along shortly. I want a word alone with young Master Shoentag.'

'Aye, captain,' said Hals.

Reiner entered the chamber as the others began collecting their things. The boy was inching painfully into his leather doublet, teeth clenched, his feet pulled fastidiously back from the puddle of blood spreading from beneath Gustaf's corpse.

Reiner folded his arms and leaned against the wall. 'All right, laddie. Let's have it.'

Franz glanced up at him, then away. 'I don't know what you mean.'

'Don't play the fool with me, boy. I know there's more to this than there appears. Hals was right. Gustaf fancied girls, not boys, so your excuse won't work this time. What did he want from you? Was he blackmailing you?'

'No,' Franz said, surly. 'Why... why would he?'

'That's for you to tell me. My guess is he found out something about you while he was doctoring you. Some secret you want hidden.'

The boy, clutched his knees and stared at the floor. He didn't answer.

'Come now, lad,' said Reiner kindly, 'I'm no raving Sigmarite. I'll not turn you over to the witch hunters, but if I'm to lead you well, I need to know who I'm leading: your strengths, your weaknesses, the little things from your past that might trip us up in the future?'

Franz just sniffed miserably.

'So what is it?' Reiner asked. 'Do you bear the brand of some heathen god upon you? Are you warp-touched? Have you a second pair of arms? Or a mouth in your belly? Are you a lover of men?'

'I can't tell you,' said Franz. 'I can't.'

'Oh come, it can't be worse than what I've just said. Just tell me and be done with it.'

Franz's shoulders slumped. His head touched his knees. Then, with a sigh, he climbed painfully to his feet. He looked to the door. The others were filing into the tunnel. When they were gone he turned to Reiner. 'Do you promise to tell no one.'

'I make no promises, boy, so I never have to break any. But I can keep a secret, if there's a reason to.'

Franz frowned at this, then sighed again. With reluctant hands he undid the ties that held his shirt together and pulled it open. His chest was bandaged from his armpits to his belly.

Reiner grimaced. 'Were you wounded so badly?'

'The wound is bad,' said Franz, 'but the bandages are only partly for the wound.' And with eyes lowered he tugged the tight bindings down to his ribs.

Reiner gaped. The boy *was* deformed! Two plump pink protuberances rose from his chest. By the gods, Reiner thought, the poor lad truly was warp-touched. It almost looked as if he had...

'Sigmar's balls! You're a girl!'

FOURTEEN
Come Taste Imperial Steel

'SHHH!' WHISPERED THE girl harshly as she tugged her bandages back into place. 'Please don't betray me! I beg you!'

'Betray you?' said Reiner. 'I ought to thrash you!' Reiner was deeply chagrined. How could he, a connoisseur of womanhood in all its forms, have been fooled this way? How could he not have known? Now that the truth was revealed it was so obvious as to be painful. The beardless jaw, the slight frame, the full lips, the large, dark eyes. Why, he had seen girls disguised as boys in plays who were more convincing. It must have been, he decided, the audacity of the thing that had made it possible. A man simply could not accept that a woman would disguise herself as a soldier, or could live a soldier's life, so any faults in the charade, any uncertainties about her sex, were dismissed before they could be considered, because one would never even think to contemplate that a soldier could be a woman.

He shook his head. 'What do you mean by this foolishness, you lunatic child? What possessed you to engage in this pitiful charade?'

The girl raised her chin. 'I do my duty. I protect my homeland.'

'Your duty as a woman is to give birth to more soldiers, not to take up arms yourself.'

The girl sneered. 'Really? And do the harlots you consort with in the brothels of Altdorf perform such a duty?'

The question caught Reiner off guard. He expected the girl to cower before him, not counter his arguments. 'Er, some do, I suppose. I'm certain they do. But that's beside the point. What you have done is a perversion. An outrage!'

'You sound like a fanatical priest. I thought you were a man of the world. A sophisticate.'

Reiner flushed. She was right. In the theatres and brothels he had frequented before being called up he had known women who dressed like men and men who dressed like women and had thought little of it. He was more outraged at being tricked than by what she had done. But he was still troubled. 'But women aren't cut out to be soldiers! They are too weak. They can't do the work required. They haven't the stomach for killing.'

The girl drew herself up. 'Have you found my soldiering lacking? Did I lag behind on the trail? Did I shirk my duties? Did I flinch from danger? I admit I am not strong, and I am nothing with a sword, but what bowman is? Was I less of a soldier for that?'

'You were,' said Reiner, feeling at last on solid ground. 'For look at the trouble you've caused. The nonsense about not sharing a tent, Not allowing a surgeon to heal you. And you have killed fellow soldiers twice to keep them from revealing your secret – the poor fellow you were jailed for murdering, and now Gustaf.'

'I did not kill them to keep my secret,' said the girl sharply. 'I would have been angry at them had they betrayed me, but I wouldn't have killed them.' She looked Reiner in the eye. 'I told the truth in our prison. When my tentmate learned my sex, he attempted to force himself upon me, thinking I would do his will in order to keep him quiet.' She shivered. 'Gustaf tried the same, only worse. He said he would give me another reason for my bandages. He tried to cut me, with his scalpel, as he had that poor girl.'

Reiner winced. 'The monster.' He looked up at the girl. 'But, you realise, if you had been a man, neither of them would have tried anything. The temptation would not have been there.'

The girl clenched her fists. 'No. They would have only assaulted peasant girls and harlots instead, and no one would have stopped them!' She calmed herself and hung her head. 'Forgive me. I forget myself. I know I don't belong in the army – that my presence is a disruption, a crime.' She looked up at Reiner pleadingly. 'But are we all not criminals? Are we not a band of outlaws? Must you cast me out for it? In all other things I am a good soldier. I beg you, don't tell the others. I couldn't bear it if they turned on me, or worse, treated me like a porcelain doll. Let me serve out at least this mission. When we return to the Empire, you may do as you wish. I will make no complaint.'

Reiner stared at the girl for a long time. Revealing the girl's secret would be more of a disruption than keeping it, and yet it went against every instinct he had as a gentleman and a lover of women to allow a girl to fight and come into harm's way. He ground his teeth. He must think as a captain and do the thing that was best for the group, not the individual. It was better for the group to have more fighters and to work smoothly as a unit.

'What's your name, girl?'

'Franka. Franka Mueller.'

Reiner sighed and pinched the bridge of his nose. 'That was foolish of me. It would have been much smarter not to know you by any other name than Franz. That way it would be impossible to make a mistake.' He shrugged. 'Ah well, can't be helped. Get your kit together, the rest are getting far ahead.'

Franka looked at him uncertainly. 'So you won't betray me?'

'No, confound you, I won't. I need you. But I make no promises for when we return to civilisation, I hope that's understood.'

Franka saluted smartly, her lips twitching a smile. 'Perfectly, captain. And my thanks.'

Reiner grunted and began gathering up Gustaf's kit, trying to get the image of Franka's naked breasts out of his head. It was going to be difficult thinking of the girl as a lad again.

THEY CAUGHT UP to the others a short while later.

Hals shot Franka a dirty look. 'I'm surprised he didn't murder you too, captain. You being alone with him and all.'

'Less of it, pikeman,' said Reiner. 'I've listened to the las… to the lad's story and I believe it. He showed me cuts on his chest like those Gustaf carved into that girl. It seems our surgeon had more wide-ranging tastes than we suspected.'

'That's as may be,' said Pavel. 'But don't expect me to bunk with him.'

The men continued following the distant sounds of marching. There were no stairs in the strange round tunnels, just sharply sloping ramps that connected one level to the other. The ramps were cut with toe holds that seemed to have been placed for beasts with four legs, not two, which set Giano raving about ratmen again. The marching continued to echo down from above them, and they climbed through five levels before the sound began coming from ahead of them.

'Let's increase our pace until we find the cannon tracks,' said Reiner. 'I don't want to miss our way.'

They walked faster, though all were exhausted from their interrupted sleep. Hals hopped gamely on his makeshift crutch, while Giano kept a hand on Ulf's elbow, for the big man hadn't fully recovered his balance after his blow to the head. Oskar shuffled somnambulantly in the middle of the pack, at peace now that Reiner had given him another sip from Gustaf's bottle. The journey was made somewhat easier because they no longer needed torches. The pale green glow of the walls was just enough to see by, though it gave them all a sickly cast that was unpleasant to look at.

A few hours into their march Hals found a broken cleaver discarded in a shallow alcove. It was enormous, the handle so big even Ulf had a hard time closing his fingers around it. There was dried blood caked on its snapped blade.

'Orcs,' said Pavel. 'Right enough.'

Hals poked at the crusted blood. It flaked away. 'No way to tell if this was dropped last week or last century.'

Reiner swallowed unhappily. 'Well, we can't be more alert than we already are, can we? Carry on.'

They resumed their march and despite Reiner's words, the men were indeed more alert, looking nervously over their shoulders at every turn and jumping at shadows.

Reiner let the others get a little ahead and walked with Franka. 'I still don't understand how you became a soldier,' he said. 'What possessed you to take up this life?'

Franka sighed. 'Love.'

'Love?'

'I am the daughter of a miller in a town called Hovern. Do you know it?'

'I think so. Just south of Nuln, yes?'

'Aye. My father arranged a marriage for me to the son of a Nuln wheat merchant. He hoped to win a better wholesale price from the boy's father. I, unfortunately, was in love with the son of a farmer who came often to our mill with his wheat – Yarl. I didn't like the merchant's son. He was an ass. But my father didn't listen to my wishes.'

'As fathers so often fail to do,' said Reiner wryly, thinking of his own less than understanding father.

'The merchant's son and I were to be married last spring, and I thought I could bear it if I could slip away and see Yarl now and then, but then the hordes began their advance and Yarl was called by Lord von Goss to string his bow in defence of the Empire.' She chuckled bitterly. 'The merchant's son got a dispensation because he and his father were provisioning the army. It came to me suddenly that I would be alone with that puny braggart while Yarl was away fighting, and that... and that Yarl might not come back.'

'Such is the lot of women since the beginning of time,' said Reiner.

'Chaos take the "lot of women", sneered Franka. 'On the eve of my wedding I could stand it no longer. I cut my hair, stole my father's bow, and ran off to Gossheim where Lord von Goss's army was mustering for the march north. I enlisted as Yarl's younger brother Franz and took his last name. It was...' She blushed. 'It was the best six months of my life. We ate together, tented together. Every happiness I dreamed marriage would bring, we had.'

It was Reiner's turn to blush. 'But how did you pass? How did you learn the bow? The ways of the soldier? A life of embroidery and dresses...'

Franka laughed. 'Do you think me a noblewoman? I was a miller's daughter, and not a rich one. My mother had no sons. I milled. I lifted sacks of grain. I haggled and joked with the farmers and the draysmen.'

'But the bow?'

Franka smiled. 'Yarl taught me. He was my playmate from childhood. We ran in the fields. Hunted squirrels on his father's farm. Played at prince and princess. I wanted to do everything he did, so I learned the bow at his side. When he vouched for me at von Goss's camp no one gave me a second look.'

'So how did you come to kill the fellow who…'

Franka hung her head. 'Yarl died. At Vodny Field. Killed by a diseased arrow. I could have run away then, I suppose. Many did. But the idea of returning to the merchant's son and his big house with the big bed and the cowering servants…' she shivered. 'I couldn't face it. And I had come to like the army. Yarl and I had made good friends there. We were a band of brothers…'

'And one sister,' quipped Reiner.

'A band of brothers,' continued Franka, ignoring him. 'United against a great enemy. I felt I had a purpose in life. And with Yarl gone, I needed something to make me want to keep living.' She shook her head. 'I was a fool. I thought I could keep my secret, but of course my captain assigned me a new tent-mate, and it wasn't long before the dog caught me out and… well, you know the rest.'

They walked in silence for a moment.

'You are a singular woman,' Reiner said at last.

Franka snorted. 'Aye, that's a word for it.' She stopped and turned suddenly, ear cocked. 'Do you hear…'

Reiner listened behind them and heard it as well. What he had thought of as a faint echo of the Kurgan marching, was growing louder. 'Curse it,' he growled. 'Have we got ahead of them? Or is it a second force on the heels of the first? Are we trapped again?'

They ran to catch up with the others.

'Marchers coming up behind us,' Reiner announced. 'Are you positive the warband is still before us?'

'Can't you hear 'em singing, captain?' asked Hals.

Reiner listened. The dull, two-toned chant was clear. 'Then who in Sigmar's name is behind us?'

'I'll go back, captain,' said Franka.

'No,' said Reiner. 'I forbid it. You aren't…'

'Captain!' Franka interrupted quickly. 'I am recovered from Gustaf's assault. There is no need to treat me with kid gloves.'

'No,' said Reiner, cursing her inwardly. The foolish girl was deliberately trying to force him to put her into danger. 'But you lost more blood than any of us. You are still weak. Giano will scout back. We will continue forward at march pace and leave way marks at any turnings we make.'

Franka stuck her lip out. Giano sighed. 'The thanking I get for be quick on my foots.'

He hurried back down the tunnel as Reiner and the rest continued forward. Franka glared straight ahead as they marched and said not a word. Reiner sighed.

After another quarter hour, they began closing on the Chaos column. The different sounds were becoming distinct from one another. The creak and groan of the cannon's wheels, the monotonous chant of the soldiers, the ragged rumble of hundreds of marching feet. They entered a larger but still perfectly cylindrical tunnel with many branching side tunnels, and found at last the tracks of the great gun carriage, so heavy that it cracked the floor's greenish glaze and turned it to a resinous powder. Reiner used his dagger to scrape an arrow in the tunnel wall to indicate to Giano the direction they were taking and they continued on.

'Cautiously now, men,' he said. 'They're just a few bends ahead.' He shot a look at Franka. 'Er, I'll take the lead. Give me thirty paces.'

Franka sniffed as he crept ahead. They proceeded forward in that fashion until at last Reiner could see the tail of the Kurgan train ahead of him – shambling horned silhouettes against the yellow glow of torches in the distance. He stopped and raised a hand to the others, at once fearful and relieved. It was like following a bear through the woods to find a stream. He didn't want to lose the bear, but letting it know of his presence was suicide.

The others caught up with him.

'Move at this pace,' he said, 'and we should just keep them in...'

Running footsteps interrupted him. The men turned, weapons at the ready. Giano came out of the darkness, wheezing and wild-eyed.

'Greenskins!' he said between gasps. 'Half league back. Almost they see me.'

'Quiet!' whispered Reiner, pointing down the tunnel. 'The Kurgan are just there.'

'They coming fast,' Giano continued more quietly. 'Hunting. Little bands, spreading out, every way?'

'Hunting for us?' asked Reiner.

'Does it matter?' asked Franka.

Hals groaned. 'Trapped again. Sigmar curse this whole enterprise!'

'He has, mate,' said Pavel. 'Trust me.'

'Not trapped yet,' said Reiner. 'We've more tunnels to manoeuvre in here. If we can...'

A rumbling voice called a challenge from down the tunnel.

Reiner jumped. He and the rest turned toward the enemy troops' line of march in time to see Kurgan-shaped shadows step out of a side tunnel fifty paces away. It was hard to tell in the murky green light, but they seemed to be looking their way. Reiner groaned. 'Right. Now we're trapped. Back away, and if they start toward us, run.'

The party backed down the corridor as more Kurgan came out of the side tunnel.

The challenge came again.

'What's the point, captain?' asked Hals. 'We can't outrun 'em, banged up like this. We might as well die gloriously.'

'I'd rather live ingloriously,' said Reiner. 'If it's all the same to you. Come now, speed it up. I have a plan.'

Hals muttered something Reiner couldn't quite hear about 'too many cursed plans' but he hobbled along gamely with the rest of them as they hurried further down the hall.

Their challenge unanswered, the Kurgan came forward cautiously, unslinging axes that glinted green in the eerie glow of the walls. One of them went trotting down the tunnel toward the main force. It seemed to Reiner that the axe-men were being more circumspect than Kurgan had a reputation for, and he wondered if they too knew that there were orcs in the area. He cursed himself for not expecting the Kurgan to have outriders patrolling the line of march. It was something a real captain would have known instinctively.

The men had just reached the side tunnel they'd originally entered from, when a lone Kurgan poked his head out of another tunnel directly behind them. He laughed and called back to the squad derisively. Reiner couldn't understand the words, but the meaning was clear – 'It's only men.'

An answering laugh echoed from the axe squad and Reiner heard them start forward at a trot.

'Run!' cried Reiner, motioning them into the side tunnel. Oskar, Franka and Ulf ran in first, followed by Giano, still winded from his reconnaissance. Pavel and Hals came last, Hals skipping with his crutch and wincing at each step. It was clear to Reiner that Hals would soon fall behind, and that Pavel wouldn't leave his side.

'Ulf! Carry Hals! Pavel, keep Ulf steady!'

'No sir,' protested Hals. 'No man carries me.'

'I have him, sir,' said Pavel. 'We'll keep up.'

'Damn your pride, the both of you,' said Reiner. 'I'll not have you die of it. Ulf!'

The engineer fell back and hoisted Hals onto his back and they ran on, Pavel keeping a hand on the concussed engineer's arm to guide him.

Reiner could hear the axe men turning into the tunnel behind them. They were already gaining. 'Shout, lads!' he bellowed. 'Shout as loud as you can!'

'Hey?' cried Giano, confused. 'You want they find us?'

'Not just them,' said Reiner, then raised his voice to a piercing cry. 'Hoy! Greenies! Fresh meat here! Come and get us!'

'Ah,' said Franka, grinning in spite of herself. 'I see.' She too raised her voice. 'Coo-ee! Pig snouts! Where are you? Come taste Imperial steel!'

Bouncing on Ulf's back, Hals laughed. 'You *are* mad, captain! But 'tis my kind of madness.' He began to roar. 'Come on, y'green bastards! Show us what y've got! I'll paint the walls with yer green blood, y'great lumbering cowards!'

Reiner heard an angry roar behind him and the Kurgans' loping gait quickened to a run. It seemed they had guessed Reiner's strategy as well, and were less than happy about it. They were getting closer by the second.

But an answering roar came from before them, and the floor shook with heavy footsteps.

Reiner sent up a silent thanks to Sigmar. 'Eyes out for a side tunnel, lads. We don't want to be pinched between when the hammer hits the anvil.'

'This way, greenskins!' shouted Franka. 'Dinner's on the table!'

'Aie!' cried Giano suddenly. 'They come! Hide!'

Reiner got a quick flash of huge, blurred forms holding enormous black-iron cleavers, before he and the rest ducked into a side corridor.

The Kurgan behind them cried out, but their voices were drowned out almost instantly by a roar of hideous animal triumph from the other direction. Voices that were more like the squealing of angry boars than anything human rose in fury as the orcs charged forward.

The impact as the orcs and the Chaos marauders came together sounded like two iron wagons full of meat slamming into each other at unimaginable speed. It was followed instantly by the clash of cleavers and axes and screams of frenzy and agony. Reiner couldn't resist a look back. All he could see in the uncertain green light were giant, indistinct shapes in violent movement and the slashing gleam of cutting edges rising and falling.

'On, boys, on!' he called. 'Look for a way back to the main...'

But Giano was suddenly skidding to a stop. Ulf crashed into him.

'What's the matter?' asked Reiner.

'Yer plan worked too well, laddie,' said Hals, from Ulf's shoulders. 'There's another lot coming.'

Reiner cursed as he saw more lumbering shadows approaching in the distance. Fortunately the area was honeycombed with tunnels and they were able to slip down another passage before the orcs saw them. But now the sound of heavy feet echoed from every direction. There seemed no way to go that wasn't clogged with orcs.

'My genius continues to astound me,' said Reiner through clenched teeth, as they edged down a curving tunnel.

'Oh, you do all right,' said Pavel. 'You always get us out of our tight spots.'

'And into tighter ones,' muttered Hals.

At last they wormed their way through the maze, dodging hurrying squads of orcs and Kurgan as they went, and reached the main tunnel safely. They started after the Kurgan column again, but hadn't taken twenty steps before they saw a detachment of fifty or so Kurgan marauders running toward them, torches bobbing. They were led by a giant in black chainmail skirts, an axeman trotting beside him, pointing out the way. But before the northers could turn into the side tunnel, orcs burst from other tunnels all along their flanks, roaring and squealing, and tore into them, cleavers swinging.

Reiner and the others took refuge in a side corridor and watched awestruck the murderous melee that unfolded before them. It was a swirling chaos of flailing limbs, slashing blades, and flying bodies. The orcs attacked with animal fury, making up for an utter lack of discipline by the brute mass of their charge. The Kurgan, by human standards almost impossibly muscular, were puny in comparison to the orcs, whose mere skeletons probably weighed more than most men. They knocked the Kurgan flat from both sides, and chopped those who fell to pieces with cleavers the size of shields.

The Chaos marauders were marginally more disciplined. After the initial shock of the orc ambush, their captains roared rallying cries and the marauders crowded around them, facing out to make primitive squares. In this posture of defence they formed a whirling wall of steel, huge axes slashing in figure-eights, and severing the hands and arms of any orc who tried to pierce it.

Stymied by this simple manoeuvre, the orcs began hurling things at the Kurgan from a distance. There were very few rocks in the smooth tunnels, so they threw severed heads and limbs and entire bodies, both marauder and orc, then followed up this bombardment with charges. But though flying orc carcasses flattened more than a few Kurgan, the northers were prepared for the charges now, and their skill and the reach of their axes began to turn the tide.

A few more squads of orcs spilled out of the side tunnels and joined the fray, but the Kurgan held their own until a further detachment of marauders came howling down the tunnel. They plowed into the fray like a battering ram, and the orcs quickly lost any stomach for the fight. They scattered into side tunnels like rats fleeing a terrier, leaving their wounded to the tender mercies of the marauders.

Reiner and his men shrunk back, prepared to flee if any of the orcs came their way. None did. Nor did the Kurgan, who didn't bother to pursue their attackers. Instead, they slaughtered the wounded orcs, stripped the bodies of weapons and armour, and marched back toward the main column.

'Men,' said Reiner, letting out a long held breath, 'I think we're back on track.'

The men started forward at an easy pace, following the sounds of the receding Kurgan.

THEY TAILED THE warband at a cautious distance until they stopped to make camp. Reiner backed up the tunnel for more than half a league before he felt it safe enough to bed down. He wanted to be well clear of any pickets the marauders might set around their perimeter. The night – if it was night, for there was no telling in the sunless tunnels – passed without incident, and when they woke to the sound of the Kurgan preparing to march again, they did the same, more refreshed than they had been since they entered the endless underworld.

Reiner spooned another dose of poppy into Oskar as they got under way. He hoped that they were nearing the end of the tunnels, for the supply was running low.

As they travelled, side tunnels and doors began to become more numerous, until the underworld felt less like a system of tunnels and more like the halls and rooms of a castle, or the streets and avenues of a city, the chambers between them houses and tenements. More frequent, as well, were the steep ramps that led to higher levels.

'Whoever built these tunnels,' said Reiner, as they looked around them in wonder, 'this was their Altdorf.'

'Maybe this *is* Altdorf,' said Oskar dreamily. 'Maybe we are under Karl Franz Strasse and nearly home.'

Hals snorted. 'Don't be daft, lad. We haven't travelled near that far.'

'It feels like we've half crossed the world,' said Franka with feeling.

'Shhhh, all you,' said Giano, flapping a hand. 'I think they stopping again.'

The company stopped and listened, trying to determine by sound alone what was happening. At this distance it was difficult. They could hear orders being shouted and the sound of great bustle and activity, but a new sound, a deep booming howl that sounded like wind in a canyon, drowned out all the details.

'We'll have to reconnoitre,' said Reiner. 'Maybe we can use the upper levels to spy down on them. Giano, come with me. 'Franka gave him another dirty look, but there was nothing she could say.

Reiner and Giano climbed a nearby ramp and began to weave their way through a warren of tunnels, galleries and chambers. They passed rooms, and suites of rooms, that had at one time had low wooden doors, but these had long ago been smashed in, and the contents, whatever they might have been, stolen away. At each turning they listened to be sure that the sound of the Kurgan was coming from ahead of them, then crept on.

At last, after climbing to a third level, they turned a corner and torchlight and noise welled out of a round opening before them. Giano motioned for Reiner to drop to his hands and knees and they crawled to the entrance. It opened out onto a wide tier that ringed an enormous circular chamber. There were tiers above and below them, set back like seats in an amphitheatre, with the same steep ramps connecting them at regular intervals. The walls of the tiers were riddled with round holes, most of which led into small rooms, though whether they had been storerooms or dwellings Reiner could not begin to guess.

The floor of the chamber was entirely filled by the Chaos warband, who were crowded together so tightly they hardly had room to turn around. Most were sitting on their packs, or eating quick meals. The cannon squatted in the middle of them like some bird of prey surrounded by her brood. Reiner edged to the lip of the tier and looked right and left. To the right was the entrance to the chamber, a large black arch into which the tail of the Kurgan column disappeared. These men too sat where they had stopped, waiting with the resignation of soldiers everywhere. To the left was the reason for the wait and the source of the booming sound Reiner and his companions had been hearing since the halt.

It was a wide, swift river, its channel slicing through the left wall of the huge chamber at a shallow angle like a sword cutting through the top of a skull. The rushing current roared like a dragon, crashing against the broken piers of a ruined stone bridge with such force that permanent bow waves rose up around them in great white ruffles. A heavy but clumsily built wooden bridge had been constructed upon these ruins, and it was this that had brought the march to a halt. It was only wide enough to allow three men to march abreast.

A massively armoured warrior was calling the various captains and chieftains forward to lead their squads over the bridge one at a time, while bawling overseers directed slaves as they began pushing and turning the cannon in order to bring it into line.

Reiner groaned as he eyed the narrow crossing. He could see no other way across the river. 'I believe we have at last found Gustaf's "obstacle".'

FIFTEEN
Breastplates Won't Be Enough To Save Us

'We have two options, as I see it,' said Reiner when he and Giano returned to the others and gave them the news. 'We can look for other ways to cross the river, or we can wait at the back of the queue and follow the Kurgan over once they've gone.'

'I ain't keen on waiting,' said Hals. 'What's to stop another column coming up behind us and catching us in the middle again?'

'We mustn't wait,' said Ulf. 'If we are to reach Count Manfred in time to warm him of the Kurgans' coming, we must get out before they do.'

'I don't know if that's entirely possible,' said Reiner. 'Seeing as they are crossing already, but the sooner the better, as you say.'

'Did not Gustaf say he knew a way around?' asked Oskar, worriedly.

'Aye,' said Hals, giving Franka a significant look. 'But Gustaf is dead.'

'We can only hope we come across it as we search,' said Reiner hurriedly. 'We'll split into two squads and search east and west of the bridge for another way across, then meet back here when we're done. Giano, take Pavel and Oskar west. I'll take Franz and Ulf. Hals, you stay here. If any more Chaos troops come through move one level up. We'll find you there.'

'Aye, captain,' said Hals.

The others split off into left and right passages, leaving him alone.

REINER, FRANKA AND Ulf gave the river chamber a wide berth, travelling east as far as the warren of tunnels would allow, then moving south to find the river. It was easy to find. Its roaring filled the tunnels, and they used the noise and the wet wind that accompanied it as a compass. After a short while they found a tunnel that seemed to parallel it. They could feel the current vibrating the left wall. The tunnel began to descend gradually and soon they were splashing through shallow water.

About thirty paces ahead a hole had been worn through the wall by the constant abrasion of the water. Reiner could see the river through it, and a brackish backwater filled the tunnel to knee height just inside it. More water lapped in and out constantly with each cresting swell.

Reiner and the others waded down to the hole and looked through. Reiner winced as the fiercely cold water topped his boots and trickled down his calves. There was little to see. The river rushed out of darkness on the left and into darkness on the right. There was no sign of a bridge.

They moved on, winding though tunnels and galleries, tall chambers, and passages through which they had to crawl on hands and knees. There were many openings to the river, some intentional, some, like the first they had encountered, mere erosion, but no bridge. They found once the remains of one – a spur of rock that jutted out only a few steps over the river. There was another spur on the opposite side, and a tunnel mouth, beckoning invitingly.

'Can we bridge it?' Reiner asked Ulf. 'If we found some timber?'

Ulf shook his head. 'No, captain. The river is too wide and too fast. We would need two tall trees and a pier in the centre to span it.'

'All right. Let's try further on.'

But there was nothing. Closer to the main chamber, they found the first of a series of narrow landings – built out into the water at the bottom of stone ramps – but these didn't reach far enough to be of any use. There were a few on the opposite side as well. Some of them had stone pilings that jutted up like crocodile teeth along the water's edge.

At last they could go no further. The last landing they discovered was so close to the main chamber that they could see part of the bridge from it, and hear the bellowing of the Kurgan over the rush of the water.

Ulf squinted at the rebuilt bridge with a critical eye. 'Orc work,' he said with a sniff. 'Shoddy construction. The biggest bits of timber they can find, and string to hold it together. Surprised it's still standing.'

Reiner shrugged. 'Maybe they'll all fall in.' He turned back the way they had come. 'Let's get back and see if the others have found anything.'

Ulf followed, but Franka continued to stare at the bridge. 'I don't suppose we could float down to it from here, then cross underneath it through all those beams.'

'What?' said Reiner, turning back. He smirked. 'Well, you could, I suppose, if you didn't get swept away by the current, but then where would you be? Trapped under the bridge on the far side with the Kurgan marching over your head. And soaking wet to boot.'

'Aye,' agreed Franka. 'But what if there was another landing on the other side, downstream from the bridge?'

'You would still be swept away,' said Reiner.

'Not if you used ropes,' said Ulf, rubbing his chin thoughtfully. 'Yes. If we did it in stages, it might work.'

Reiner scowled, thinking of the cold water in his boots and imagining immersing himself entirely in it. He sighed. 'Let's see if the others have found a more civilized crossing.'

THEY HADN'T. ALL paths stopped at the river.

'But,' said Pavel, when Franka had mentioned her floating-down-the-river plan, 'there was a landing on the far side of the river, now that you mention it. About thirty paces below it.'

'Fifty-five feet,' said Oskar sleepily. 'Give or take a foot.'

Everybody turned to stare at him.

'Can you truly be so precise?' asked Reiner.

Oskar shrugged. 'It is my curse.'

'The landing above the bridge is roughly the same distance,' said Ulf. 'Perhaps a little closer.'

They moved away from the main tunnel into the criss-cross of side passages and measured out all the rope they had. Some of them had lost theirs in all the running and falling and hiding, but among them they had more than a hundred and fifty feet.

Ulf nodded, satisfied. 'This may work.'

Reiner though it was the first time he had seen the big man happy.

Once they had worked out who would do what and how, they made their way through the twists and turns of the city of tunnels until they reached the river again.

Reiner and the others eyed the water with trepidation. Talking about jumping into it was one thing, the reality was quite another. It was terrifyingly swift and sure to be colder than glacier ice. Visions of smashing into the granite piers at full speed filled Reiner's head, and from the shivers and swallows of the others they were having similar thoughts.

'I can't swim,' said Hals, anxiously.

'Nor can I,' said Pavel.

'There will be no swimming involved,' said Ulf, tying the longest length of rope around a stone piling. 'The current will carry you faster than you could swim anyway.'

'What you must do,' said Reiner, dreading it himself even as he did his best to make it sound easy, 'is hold your breath and try to stay underwater until you are beneath the bridge. We don't want some dirt-eater looking over and seeing us floundering about.'

'We shall have to leave our breastplates behind,' said Ulf, 'or we will sink like stones.'

'Leave our breastplates!' cried Hals. 'Are you mad? What if we have to fight the Kurgan?'

'If we find ourselves fighting the Kurgan,' said Reiner, 'breastplates won't be enough to save us.'

Ulf looked toward the bridge again, paying out rope, then turned to Oskar. 'Gunner, how far to the bridge?'

Oskar was examining a hole in his jerkin with an all-consuming interest.

'Oskar,' said Reiner. 'Oskar, wake up, lad. How far is it to the bridge?'

Oskar looked up, blinking, then squinted at the bridge. 'Forty-seven feet. I'd like another sip from the bottle, please.'

'When we reach the far shore,' said Reiner.

Ulf paid out forty-seven feet of rope, using his enormous boot as a measure. 'Too little and we won't reach the bridge,' he said. 'Too much and we'll bash our heads in.'

Reiner swallowed thickly, 'Then I better go first, as I have the thickest head.' He wanted to go last, but it was expected of the leader that he lead.

Ulf tied the rope around Reiner's waist. 'Don't gasp as you come up,' he said. 'They may hear.'

'Why not tie a stone to my feet and knock me senseless,' snarled Reiner. 'They'd never see me then.'

Ulf looked as if he was considering it.

Reiner turned and sat on the edge of the stone pier. He took a deep breath, and then another. He realised that no amount of deep breaths was going to prepare him, so with a sigh he began to lower himself into the river.

The shock of the cold water almost made him scream, and the strength of the current pulled at his legs so fiercely that what he had meant to be a silent graceful slide became a clumsy plop as he was yanked away from the landing by the rushing water. There was no difficulty in staying underwater. The river pulled him down like a lover. He could see nothing – feel nothing but cold and the pummelling power of the current. But almost as soon as the journey had begun it was over. He jolted to a stop, face down, the rope pulling tight around his waist, and the river knocking him back and forth like a kite in a high wind. He stretched out his arms, feeling for the pier.

It was almost impossible to push against the current, to hold his arm out to his side. If he relaxed at all his arms snapped above his head. His lungs were burning, exploding, desperate to take a breath. At last his left hand touched stone and he pulled himself toward the pier.

His head broke water and he remembered at the last moment not to gasp, inhaling slowly instead, though he longed to suck in air in great gulps. The granite pier rose only a few feet out of the water. He climbed onto its crumbling top and clung, shivering and weak, to the wooden understructure of the orc bridge.

He looked up, listening for some sign that he had been spotted, but heard nothing except the endless tread of Kurgan boots passing overhead. He was so cold he could barely feel his fingers. When he had recovered himself somewhat he untied the rope, gave it a sharp tug, and let it slip back into the water. He watched it slither away into the shadows like a snake on the rolling surface of the water.

After what seemed to him to be an endless wait, in which he became convinced that the rest of the party had been discovered and slaughtered and that he was stuck on this pier alone, surrounded by Kurgan in an endless underworld, Oskar broke the water an arm's length from the pier. He was remarkably calm, and Reiner pulled him in with no trouble.

'All right, Oskar?' he whispered.

'Oh yes,' said Oskar, wiping water from his eyes. 'I have no fear of water. I was raised near a lake. It is remarkably cold, though. I might just have a little sip, to keep the chill away.'

'This is not yet the other side.'

They sent the rope back and were joined in turn by Franka, Pavel, Hals and Giano and lastly Ulf. Everyone made their landing quietly except Hals, who cried out in pain because the rope had twisted around his broken leg and wrenched it when he stopped short. Pavel clapped a hand over his friend's mouth until he had recovered himself and everyone looked up, waiting for a horned helmet to peer down at them. Fortunately the roar of the rushing water was loud enough to cover incidental noises.

When at last Ulf arrived and had untied himself, he pried a piece of crumbling rock from the pier and fixed it to the end of the rope so that it would sink and not betray their presence by floating on the surface.

'First part accomplished,' said Reiner, relieved. 'Now for the far wall.'

In a drier environment, those of the party who had a full complement of working limbs would have had little trouble navigating the understructure of the bridge, for the logs were wide and numerous. Unfortunately, the wood had not been seasoned or treated in any way – and was in fact just fresh-cut trees, with sap still oozing from the cut ends – and was slimy with moss and algae, so each step had to be carefully made. In places the logs were so poorly joined – tied together with rope rather than pinned with nails or dowels – that they shifted when weight was put on them. It reminded Reiner of a time when he had been fooling about in the apple trees of his father's orchard after a spring rain and sprained his wrist when he lost his footing. For Hals, with his broken leg, and Oskar with his broken arm, the journey was impossible unassisted. They had to be helped every step of the way. Pavel looked after Hals as usual, and Reiner stayed at Oskar's side, bracing him and taking his hand when he needed it. There were a few near disastrous slips, but at last they all reached the far wall and sat or leaned on the slick logs, catching their breath.

Ulf was shaking his head in dismay. 'Shocking. A child could have built a sturdier bridge. Look.' He poked a thick finger at the ropes that held the logs together. 'They have used the poorest quality rope. It has loosened and rotted in the damp. Why a few strokes with a knife here and there and the whole structure would…' He trailed off, his eyes glazing over.

'Not on your life, you madman,' said Reiner, catching on.

'But we must!' whispered Ulf, suddenly alive with urgency. 'We must! We can stop them in their tracks. More than half of their force would be trapped behind the river. The cannon as well. It would take them days, maybe weeks to rebuild it.'

'What's this now?' asked Hals. 'What does he mean to do?'

'He wants to knock down the bridge,' said Reiner. 'With us on it.' He shook his head at Ulf. 'You'll kill us all.'

'I won't!' said Ulf. There was a catch of desperate hope in his voice. 'If I loosen it just enough, I can tie a rope to a key support and pull it out once we are all clear.'

'And if you loosen it too much, it all falls on our heads before you get a chance,' countered Reiner.

Ulf clenched his fists, controlling his temper. 'Captain, I am an engineer. This is what I know. Will you not trust me in my field as I have trusted you in yours?'

'I do trust you, as an engineer. My fear is that you are allowing your eagerness to stop the Kurgan to drown your engineering knowledge in wishful dreams.'

They all looked up as they became aware that there was silence above them. No troops were crossing the bridge.

'Have they all gone?' asked Franka.

'They can't have,' said Hals.

The silence ended with a fresh roaring and cracking of whips, followed after a long moment by a creaking of wood, a groaning of slaves, and a grinding of iron on stone.

'The cannon,' said Pavel. 'They're moving the cannon.'

Ulf turned to Reiner, eyes pleading. 'Captain, this is an opportunity not to be missed. If we can drop the cannon in the river, we will not only slow them, we will... *castrate* them! They will be half the threat they are now. They may even give up and go home.'

Reiner bit his lip. They didn't have long to act. 'All right,' he said at last. 'What do we need to do?'

Ulf grinned, and began tying what was left of their rope to the support closest to the wall. 'Hals and Oskar. You will tie yourselves to this rope and wait here. The rest of us will spread out along this side of the bridge and cut the ropes that join the supports together. Once you unwind the rope, bring it here and tie one end to this pillar, the other around your waist. We do not want to leap into the river untethered, but if the bridge begins to go, jump, tethered or not. You understand me?'

'I understand yer a madman, and yer going to kill us all,' said Hals, but began to tie the rope around his waist.

Reiner, Ulf, Franka, Pavel and Giano started working their way quickly back through the timbers. The cannon was rolling closer. There wasn't much time. Reiner braced himself in a V and began sawing at a knotted mass of rope that lashed two logs together. For all of Ulf's talk of rotten rope, the fibres were tough and fought his blade. He longed to chop at them, but didn't want to risk the noise. To his left Franka was cutting feverishly. Giano was on his right, cursing under his breath as he worked and looking up constantly.

The cannon was picking up speed, and despite being wet and half frozen, Reiner started to sweat. There was a good chance the great gun would bring the bridge down without their help. Visions of being pinned to the river bottom flashed before his eyes.

Shouts of alarm came from above and the bridge shook with a jarring impact. Reiner clung to the supports as they shivered and swayed. He held his breath. Amazingly, the bridge remained intact. He exhaled. He could hear the Kurgan screaming and a fresh flurry of whip cracking. It sounded as if the slaves had steered the cannon into one of the railings.

A reprieve. Reiner began cutting again as the slaves moaned out a weary chant and began pulling the cannon back for another try. At last he parted the heavy hemp and started unwinding it, reaching around the trunk again and again like a tailor measuring the waist of a fat priest.

He had the binding unwound and had sawn halfway through the fixed end when the cannon rumbled forward again, and this time the slaves' aim was true. The heavy, iron-shod wheels boomed onto the wooden planks and the entire bridge groaned in pain. Reiner could feel the timbers compressing and shifting around him.

When the bridge didn't collapse immediately, he returned to cutting. Franka spidered past him, a coil of rope over one shoulder. Giano was nearly finished as well. They'd done it!

A sudden cry and a splash from the far end of the bridge snapped Reiner's head around. Pavel was clinging to a support beam, his legs dangling over the water. A length of tree trunk was bobbing away down the river, followed by a tangle of rope.

'Sigmar's balls!' cursed Reiner, glancing up fearfully. Had the Chaos troops heard? He chopped through the last few strands of his rope, slung it over his shoulder, and monkeyed toward Pavel as fast as he could. The pikeman's hands were slipping as he tried to get purchase on the slimy log.

A harsh voice barked down from above. Reiner looked up, and locked eyes with a Kurgan overseer, his helmet glinting in the torchlight. For a moment, both of them froze, then the overseer disappeared and Reiner heard him shouting a warning. The cannon stopped.

'Ulf!' Reiner cried as he reached Pavel. 'We have been discovered! Rope off and into the water.'

'But I must still remove the centre joist!' came Ulf's reply.

'It's too late!' Reiner braced himself, grabbed Pavel's arm and pulled.

'Shouldn't we just drop in?' the pikeman asked as he struggled to get on top of the log.

'Without tying off?' asked Reiner. 'We'd never stop.'

Pavel was fortunately wiry and light. With Reiner's help he got a fresh grip on the log and swung his legs up to brace against another. 'Sorry, captain,' he said as he scrambled to his feet. 'It fell away as I stepped on it.'

'Forget it. Just move. We need to tie off by the wall or we'll miss the landing.'

But as they turned toward the south bank, Kurgan began climbing over the side of the bridge.

'Hurry!' said Reiner, drawing his sword.

As he and Pavel clambered through the beams, the cannon began moving again, but this time it was moving back toward the north side of the bridge. The slaves were pulling it back, out of danger.

'No!' wailed Ulf. He started forward, maul in hand, ducking recklessly though the supports. 'The cannon must fall!'

'Urquart! Fall back!' Reiner bellowed. 'I order you...!'

A Kurgan dropped on the beam before him, roaring and swinging his axe – and immediately slipped and fell into the rushing water. He disappeared instantly. Reiner laughed, but a second, a hulking heathen with a flaming red beard, was more cautious, bracing with one hand while menacing Reiner with his sword. More were climbing down behind him.

'We'll never get through that lot,' said Pavel.

Reiner pulled the coiled rope off his shoulder and handed it back to the pikeman, his eyes never leaving the advancing Kurgan. 'Tie off. We'll go together.'

Pavel hesitated. 'But did you not say...'

'We'll have to risk it. It may be death, but it's not certain death.'

The redbearded Kurgan lashed out. Reiner ducked and the heavy sword bit into a support trunk. Reiner had a clear shot. He thrust at the man's chest, but his sword glanced off the norther's mail shirt.

Reiner retreated back behind the pillar as red beard's blade splintered it again. Behind the giant another Kurgan screamed and tumbled into the water. The others turned. Ulf was behind them, wading into them, maul swinging. Reiner gasped, amazed at the big man's agility on the treacherous framework. He seemed more at home there than on solid ground. All those years clambering up and down scaffolding, building fortifications, Reiner decided.

For a foolish moment, as another Kurgan fell victim to Ulf's maul, Reiner thought the engineer might win, but more and more Kurgan were climbing over the rail. There was an endless supply of them. The battle could not be won.

'Tied off, captain,' said Pavel, behind him.

'Tie my waist.' Reiner dodged another cautious blow from red beard and backed up. He felt Pavel's hands go around his waist. 'Ulf!' he bellowed. 'Fall back! Abandon the bridge!'

'No!' shouted the engineer. 'I must strike just one blow!' He dodged back from two Kurgan, then slipped around the far side of a pillar, ending up behind them. 'Jump!' he called. 'Everyone jump! I will join you.'

Red-beard leapt forward and lunged at Reiner. Reiner jumped back desperately and evaded the blade by a finger's-width, but lost his balance. His feet flew out from under him and he fell backward. He had a brief flash of Pavel flailing, and then icy black water closed over him. The current yanked him down river like a giant hand.

The answer to whether Pavel had finished tying him off came almost immediately. He jerked to a brutal stop, the thin rope biting painfully into his waist. Something slammed into his left side. Pavel. The current stretched them out in the water like men side by side on a rack. The cold was unbearable. Reiner fought to bring his arms down and grab the rope. He tried to raise his head out of the river. The water split at his chin like the prow of a ship. It filled his mouth.

Reiner at last caught the rope. He pulled, and rose a little from the water. He sucked air. Pavel was struggling to do the same at his side. Reiner let go with one hand and grabbed him behind the neck. He nearly fell back again for this kindness, but Pavel at last found the rope and they both got their shoulders above the waves, though the strain was considerable.

To his right, Reiner could see that Oskar, Franka, Hals and Giano were in the water as well, all together in a knot at the end of their ropes. They were tantalisingly close to the landing and were straining to reach it. A Kurgan splashed by between them, trying to swim, and Reiner looked back at the bridge.

The cannon had nearly reached the north bank again, with slaves pushing and pulling at it fore and aft. Below them, Ulf was swinging at a support post in the centre of the bridge as Kurgan climbed toward him from all directions. He struck a mighty blow that Reiner heard above even the noise of the water, but the post remained in place. He swung again, but a Kurgan leapt at him and spoiled his aim. Then they were all around him, slashing and thrusting. Ulf took a cut in the shoulder, another in the leg. He roared and swung in a circle, knocking three Kurgan into the drink. Five took their place.

Pavel began pulling at the rope, trying to climb toward the bridge, against the current. 'Curse the lummox!' he cried. 'Pull, captain! We have to help him!'

'Ulf!' screamed Reiner. 'Jump, you fool.'

Ulf laid about him like Sigmar-in-the-pass and amazingly, for a moment, the Kurgan fell back before him, uncertain on the precarious struts. With a desperate, all or nothing swing, Ulf bashed the post again, a terrific smash that jarred it loose at last. It spun out of place and bounced down through the joists and beams to splash into the water.

The Kurgan under the bridge froze, looking around uneasily. At first it seemed that nothing would happen, then the bridge groaned like a dyspeptic giant. Another post fell out of place and dropped into the river, then another.

With a roar of rage, one of the Kurgan leapt at Ulf, bringing his sword down like a headsman's axe. Reiner watched in horror as the stroke chopped down through the engineer's collarbone all the way to his heart, causing an eruption of blood.

Ulf was dead, but it seemed that, by slaying him, the Kurgan had slain the bridge as well, for as Ulf fell, so did the span, twisting and collapsing with a slow grace.

'The damned fool,' said Reiner, swallowing hard. 'I told him...'

The bridge sagged first in the centre, and then disintegrated all along its length. On the north side the overseers were screeching at the cannon slaves to pull faster, but the great gun was still on the planks, and began rolling back down the swiftly steepening incline, dragging slaves and Chaos marauders with it, until at last its weight proved too much for the remaining supports, and it crashed through into the drooping understructure. The cannon crushed Ulf and the Kurgan warriors and took them and the bridge with it as it plunged into the river with an enormous splash.

A huge swell of water rose and began rolling down the river as the cannon's daemon mouth sank below the waves like some sea monster in its death throes. Reiner felt the tension on the rope around his waist slacken as the bridge became free-floating debris, all of which was heading their way.

'Brace yourself!' Reiner cried to Pavel, and risked a glance toward Hals, Franka, Oskar and Giano. They were just pulling themselves onto the landing. Franka lay gasping on the flagstones. Giano was trying desperately to get a leg up. Then the wave hit, covering the landing in a waist deep blanket of water. As he was lifted and tossed about on the swell, Reiner saw Franka and Giano swept off the landing and back into the river with Oskar and Hals as if by a broom.

Their only piece of fortune – if it could be called that – was that the wave pushed the four toward Reiner and Pavel; almost drove them into them in fact. Reiner had to raise his hands to fend off Oskar's knees as he whirled past him.

'Catch them!' Reiner called to Pavel. 'Hold 'em fast!'

He and Pavel grabbed at the spinning mass of limbs and torsos. Through the splash and foam, Reiner locked eyes with Franka. He grabbed her arm and pulled her close. Pavel had Hals by the collar.

'At least,' choked Giano, spitting water, 'we all die together, eh?'

'Watch out!' shouted Franka.

Reiner looked back, and almost had his head caved in by a huge log rising and turning on the swell. He kicked it away and another struck him in the back. The remains of the bridge were bounding past them, tumbling and knocking together with great hollow thuds, ropes like spiderwebs tangling them together.

A rope caught Oskar across the chest, jerking him forward, which in turn dragged his companions. Hals pulled the rope up and over Oskar's head. The artilleryman was barely conscious. Hals and Pavel tried to hold him out of the water, but they were sinking as well.

Reiner caught a rope-draped log and clung to it. 'Climb on! All of you.'

The light, which had been dimming quickly as they sped away from the Kurgan's torches, went out entirely as the river took them around a bend. Reiner pulled Franka to the log by feel and she threw an arm over it. Reiner heard the others doing the same as the current swept them further into the darkness at a terrifying speed.

SIXTEEN
Fellows Of The Brand

THEY CLUNG SILENTLY to the log as it hurtled through the deafening black, the sound of their gasping breaths lost in the rushing roar of the river. All of them were too cold, too battered and too frightened to speak. There was no room in Reiner's head for wondering what might happen next, for making plans. He was a rat, clutching at flotsam, trying to keep his head above water, fighting for one more breath, all higher thoughts gone, surrendered to the unconquerable animal instinct to hold on to life while there was yet strength in his limbs.

Other pieces of debris glanced off them, causing fresh cries of pain and fear, and they careered bruisingly into the walls as the river whipped them around corners, each time making Reiner think that they had crashed into the invisible obstacle that would at last break their bodies and crack their skulls.

His brain was so numb that he failed to wonder what the steadily growing roaring in his ears might mean until he and the log and his companions flew helter skelter down smooth, stairstepped rapids and plunged into a roiling boil of leaping water.

After a frightening liquid battering, the log resurfaced and Reiner found that they were floating in relatively calm water. When he had caught his breath, he raised his voice. 'Are we all here?'

'Aye, captain,' said Pavel.

'Here,' said Franka.

'And where might here be?' grumbled Hals.

'We are swallowed by the dragon,' said Oskar. 'He will use us as fuel for his fire.'

'Shut you mouth, crazy man,' said Giano angrily.

From the echoes they seemed to be in a large cavern. There was still a current, pulling them insistently along, but there were no waves. A hollow knocking – almost musical – came from their left. It sounded to Reiner like enormous wooden wind chimes banging together.

Reiner had been in the cold water for so long he hardly felt it anymore, but he had a dangerous urge to sleep, to let go of the log and drift away. He shook himself.

'I don't suppose anyone's tinder is dry enough to...' He paused as the roar of the rapids, which had been growing gradually quieter, got louder once again. 'Are we coming to a second set of rapids?' he asked.

'I don't believe so,' said Franka, her teeth chattering. 'For the other sound is still to our left.'

The rapids roared in their ears and they were splashed with spray, then after a moment the rumble once again diminished, while the wood-on-wood sound remained a constant.

'We are travelling in a circle,' said Reiner, his stomach sinking. 'We are caught in a vortex, a whirlpool.'

There was a short silence as this sunk in, then Pavel spoke.

'So what's to be done? What d'we do?'

'Do?' Reiner laughed mirthlessly. 'My dear pikeman, we are doing it.'

'But captain,' said Hals uneasily. 'You must have a plan. Y'haven't failed us yet.'

Reiner cursed inwardly. Damn them and their confidence in him. In his mind he had failed them at every turn. Why couldn't they see it? 'I'm sorry, lad. I'm fresh out.'

The sound of the rapids came and went again, but this time not so loudly, while the hollow wooden knocking grew slowly but steadily louder. The current was getting stronger as well, pulling them around the vortex more and more quickly, while at the same time tugging them down as well. Their tired arms were finding it harder and harder to hold onto the log.

'Is no shore to swim?' asked Giano querulously.

'I know not,' said Reiner. 'But feel free to explore,'

The Tilean didn't seem so inclined.

As they passed the sound of the rapids for the sixth or seventh time Reiner noted a strange phenomenon. The surface of the water was not level. It sloped away on their left like the side of a soup bowl, and now the wooden knocking was drowning out everything else.

'The bridge,' said Reiner, understanding at last. 'All the timbers have gathered here, but wood doesn't sink.'

'Oh!' Franka cried. 'It's pulling me down!'

'By Sigmar,' said Hals. 'It has me too!'

'Hold fast!' Reiner cried, though he knew now it was hopeless.

The current pulled almost straight down now. Their log slid down the side of the soup bowl and smashed end-on into the others as they spun in a violent circle, held forever in agitated equilibrium in the centre of the vortex by the current that pulled them down and their buoyancy that forced them up. The impact jarred Reiner so hard his teeth snapped. He lost his grip and was instantly sucked down the whirlpool's maw. The swirling logs bludgeoned him as he sank, but he was soon below them, pulled inexorably down, as if some sea-serpent had him by the legs and dragged him to its underwater lair.

Once again animal instinct overcame him, and though he knew that struggle was useless, he clawed at the water, trying desperately to swim to the surface, to reach air again, while his lungs screamed in fiery agony.

The current angled suddenly sideways and his shoulder struck a rocky surface hard enough that he almost gasped. He was dragged into an airless tunnel, scraping along the rough roof at a furious pace. He could feel his clothes, and then his skin shredding. All became a jumble of pain and speed and disorientation. He knew not if he was alive or dead, cold or hot, in pain or unable to feel anything at all. Red lines wormed across the blackness of his vision. A rapid thumping pounded in his ears. His chest felt as if it were being crushed in a vice.

And then, suddenly, there was air.

And he was falling.

Into water.

Again.

THE FIRST THING Reiner thought when he broke the surface was, 'What is that Sigmar-cursed light?' For a unbearable brightness seared through his eyelids. Then he began coughing violently, retching out great quantities of water as he paddled his arms to stay afloat. He could hear others around him doing the same. His eyes watered. His nose ran. His throat felt like he had swallowed broken glass, but at last he cleared his lungs and looked around.

He and his companions were bobbing in a small mountain lake, surrounded by tall pines. A high waterfall dropped to the lake from a cleft in a crag. A pair of ducks skimmed into a landing on the water. He was outside. The bright light was the sun, setting over a carpet of evergreens. They were out of the tunnels at last!

Pavel gurgled beside him. 'Captain, I… Hals is… I can't…'

Reiner looked at him. The pikeman was thrashing around, trying unsuccessfully to keep his head above water. Hals floated face down beside him, not moving. Beyond them, Oskar was calmly paddling one-handed for the shore, while Franka and Giano recovered themselves.

'Giano, Franz,' called Reiner. 'Can you swim?'

'Aye,' they said in unison.

'Then help Pavel to shore.'

Reiner caught Hals around the shoulders and turned him face up, then swam him to the nearest landfall, a muddy bank, thick with rushes.

As they reached the shallows Pavel crawled out under his own power and Franka and Giano helped Reiner drag Hals out and lay him on his side. Reiner pounded him on the back.

For a moment Hals didn't move, and Pavel sat watching anxiously. But at last, with a violent convulsion, the pikeman began coughing and spewed an alarming amount of water out onto the mud. Reiner held his head until he was through.

'All right, pikeman?' asked Reiner.

Hals looked at him with bloodshot eyes. 'I'm… never bathing… again.'

Pavel grinned with relief. 'And why should ye start now anyway, y'old goat?'

Reiner patted Hals's shoulder and stood, looking at them all. He shook his head. 'A sorrier lot of wretches I have never seen.'

Hals laughed. 'Yer no beauty yerself, captain.' He sneezed and shivered.

They were all shivering. Franka's teeth were chattering uncontrollably and Reiner realised that his were doing the same. Tremors racked his body. His fingers were blue. Though there were buds sprouting on the nearby dogwoods it was only early spring yet, and they were still high in the mountains. 'Any missing fingers? Any bones broken?'

They all shook their heads, but it was clear that they had all been badly battered by the river and the vortex. Hals has lost his crutch. Pavel's eye-patch was missing and his eye socket gaped like a red cave. Oskar had a fresh wound on his brow. Giano's forearm was badly scraped and Franka's shirt was newly red, as if the gashes she had received from the warhound had reopened.

Reiner squinted at the nearby mountain tops, looking for familiar landmarks. 'Have we any idea where we are?' he asked.

Hals sat up and looked around. 'It don't look familiar,' he said. 'But by the sun we must be on the southern face of the Middle Mountains.'

Reiner nodded. 'Wherever we are, we must find shelter. We need to dry off in front of a fire before we all catch our deaths.'

'There's chimney smoke down the hill, captain,' said Oskar. 'And do you still have the bottle?'

Reiner was loath to give Oskar any more of the juice. It already seemed to have him in its clutches, but he'd been most helpful of late. He put his hand in his jerkin. The vial was gone. 'Sorry, old son. I've lost the bottle.'

Oskar swallowed, and nodded. 'I see. Very well.' He hugged his arms and shivered.

Reiner coughed and sniffed. 'Right. Come on, you lot. Let us go take advantage of their hospitality, whoever they are.'

The party got to their feet and began limping and staggering down the piney slope.

Reiner looked back at the waterfall. It was as high as three houses. He shook his head. It seemed incredible they had survived.

'Water is a softer landing than rock,' said Franka, reading his thoughts.

Reiner grimaced. 'Not by much.' They started after the others.

Reiner stole a sidelong look at the girl, who walked contentedly beside him. Curse her for being so companionable, he thought. It was unnerving for a woman to be so easy to get along with, so much like a friend, and yet so...

He shook his head, trying to dislodge the image of her standing before him, naked to the waist.

It was only a short walk to the village – a good thing, for none of them were capable of a long walk, and they were ill-equipped to face any danger they might come across. In addition to being lame and sore, they were almost entirely unarmed. Though Reiner had his pistols – but no powder or shot – and he and Giano still had swords, the river had taken almost everything they hadn't lost earlier. Giano's crossbow was gone. Oskar's long gun, Franka's bow, Pavel's spear, Hals's crutch-that-was-once-a-spear, all lost in the darkness of the underworld, leaving them with only their daggers.

They reached the village just as the sun disappeared behind the mountains and the landscape shaded to purple. At first, as they came upon it through the trees, it seemed a quaint place, strangely untouched by the war – a few small stone and shingle cottages tucked in a fold of hills by the stream that wound away from the lake. Smoke rose from a few chimneys.

Reiner heard Franka choke back a sob beside him.

'It's so much like home,' she said, recovering herself.

Reiner knew just how she felt. After so long in such an alien place, these little huts, which he wouldn't have given a second look a fortnight ago, looked more welcoming to him now than the finest inn in Altdorf.

But as they got closer, the hair began to rise on Reiner's neck. Though he couldn't put a finger on it, something didn't feel quite right. Despite the smoke coming from the chimneys, the place had a neglected, deserted air. Weeds grew unrestrained around the houses and windows gaped open, their shutters hanging off their hinges. There was a disconcerting look of vacancy about the whole place.

The companions walked warily up the muddy street to the well at the centre. Not a sound of human occupation did they hear: not a voice or movement, not the crying of a child or the hammering of a smith. They looked around them, hands on the pommels of their swords and daggers. The empty windows stared back at them.

'Ahoy, the village!' called Reiner.

His voice echoed between the houses and away into the woods.

'Where are they?' asked Franka in a hushed voice. 'Where have they gone?'

'And whose smoke is that coming from the chimneys?' grunted Hals.

'Maybe they went for a walk,' said Oskar.

'And maybe you'll die finding out,' said a rough voice behind them.

The companions whipped around. A gaunt man with lank hair that hung over his forehead stood at the corner of a house. He was dressed in patched and filthy clothes and carried a bow, an arrow nocked and ready. He raised a hand and more ragged men stepped out behind him, and from behind every house that faced the square. All levelled bows at Reiner's men. They were surrounded.

The gaunt man stepped into the square with two lieutenants, a short, pug-nosed fellow with a tuft of sandy beard on his chin, and a grim, powerfully built warrior with long braids that hung to his chest. They gave the companions a once over. The leader grinned, revealing teeth like a horse's.

'Yer a sorry lot,' he said. 'What chewed you up?'

'Almost not worth jumping,' said pug-nose with a sneer.

Braids pointed at the Reiner's leather jerkin, then Hals's and Pavel's. 'Their kit's regulation, what's left of it. They're soldiers.'

The smirk died on horse-face's lips. His eyes turned cold. 'You hunting us?' he asked Reiner. 'You scouts?'

'Best to kill 'em, Horst,' said pug-nose. 'Just t'be safe.'

'Aye,' said horse-face, pushing his hair aside to rub his brow. 'Aye, I suppose we must.' As his hair fell back, Reiner thought he saw a familiar scar on his forehead. The bandit signalled his men and Reiner heard the creak of two-dozen bowstrings being pulled back.

'Wait!' cried Pavel.

'What we do?' gabbled Giano, anxiously. 'What we do?'

'Take off your gloves, quick!' said Reiner.

'Take off...?' echoed Giano, puzzled.

Reiner yanked off his still-damp glove with his teeth and held up his hand, showing the scar on the back. 'Brothers!' he shouted, smiling as wide as he could. 'How glad we are to see fellows of the brand.'

The men paused. Horse-face and his lieutenants squinted at his hand in the dying twilight as Reiner's companions tore off their gloves and showed their brands as well. The ring of archers relaxed their strings, but did not yet lower their bows.

'We... we are recently escaped from a convict column,' said Reiner, making it up as he said it. 'On the way to Middenheim to slave in the rebuilding of the walls. We were closely hounded by wolf swords, and nearly...'

Braids stepped forward, menacing. 'You have brought Knights of Ulric into our hills?'

'No, no,' said Reiner quickly, holding up his hands. 'No, no. We lost them a day ago, but then, alas, became lost ourselves. And many a misadventure have we had since. There was the bear...'

'And the waterfall,' added Franka, picking it up.

Reiner nodded. 'And the tumble down the cliff.'

Braids grabbed Reiner's hand in an iron grip and examined the brand closely. He rubbed it with his thumb, as if he expected it to smear. When it didn't, he grunted and turned away.

Horse-face grinned. 'You really are a sad bunch, ain't you? Tenderfoot flatlanders stumbling about in the hills like little lost babes.'

Reiner drew himself up. 'We are not yet hard-bitten brigands like yourselves. Our brands are still fresh. But we have all our lives to learn.'

Horse-face and pug-nose laughed and their men joined in.

'Well then, my young sprouts,' said horse-face. 'Let us start you off on the right foot. Let us show you the joys of the life of the outlaw.' He bowed. 'Welcome to our humble home.'

And as he said it, a few gaunt women and dirty children stepped out of hiding and peered from the windows and doors of the rundown huts to stare at the newcomers.

Reiner frowned, confused, as Horse-face led him and the others to the largest house. It was fully dark now. '*Are* you bandits? Or is this your village?'

Horse-face grimaced. 'Well, both, really. A lot of us lived here before the war. Or here abouts. But then we went off to fight for Karl Franz – and much thanks we got for it I can tell ye. Cut down in our thousands while the knights made fine speeches.' He waved a hand. 'But y'know all about that, yes? At any rate, when we returned, they're all dead, our mothers and fathers, sisters and sons...' He sighed and looked around. 'We'd love to live here again, but with them northern devils nesting up in the hills, we've to be on our guard. Can't set up anything permanent.'

'You do a good job of disappearing,' said Reiner.

'Aye,' said Horse-face. 'Plenty of practice.' He shrugged. 'If we could ask m'lord Hulshelft for protection he'd root the heathen out and make this land safe again, but, well, we're marked men, most of us, like you. He'd string us up sooner than help us.'

They entered the house. Reiner's visions of venison and boar roasting on spits and wine flowing from casks of stolen monastery wine were dashed as Horse-face offered him and his companions a place at the small fireplace and called for food. There was no furniture. They sat on the floor. The wind whistled through the missing windows and leaves and dirt gathered in drifts in the corners. The fire was barely large enough to warm Reiner's hands, let alone dry his clothes.

Though they had little, the bandits weren't stingy. They filled bowls and cups for them and refilled them when they were empty. There was no venison. No boar. Only stringy rabbits and squirrels crisping on sticks, and a thin gruel of oats and wild carrots that was mostly water. At least it filled their bellies and warmed their bones.

As he gnawed the last bits from the bones of a rabbit, Hals leaned in and murmured in Reiner's ear. 'Why don't we throw in our lot with these lads?' said the pikeman. 'They seem a likely bunch.'

Reiner made a face. In the light of the fire it was easy to see how malnourished the bandits were, their faces hollow and sickly. These were not merry outlaws living a life free from care. They were wanted men, hard hunted and longing to return to their former lives – a dream as impossible for them as flying to Mannslieb on the back of a griffin.

'Why not?' Reiner asked. 'Because I'd be at home here as you would be in the court of the king of Bretonnia.'

'Ah,' said Hals. ''Tain't so bad.'

'You think not? Look at them. They're starving.'

'That's winter,' said Pavel, joining in. 'Things get a touch lean in the winter, certain. But it's spring now. There'll be food aplenty soon.'

'And another winter next year.'

Hals shrugged.

Reiner lowered his voice and hunched closer to them. He didn't want the bandits to hear. 'You're more than welcome to stay. I'll not stop you.' He held up his scarred hand. 'But there's a chance at the end of this journey to erase this mark and return to a normal life – for me to go back to my card rooms and taverns, for you to go back to your farms. That sounds better to me than mucking about in the woods eating coneys for the rest of our lives.'

Hals and Pavel frowned and sat back to whisper between themselves. After a moment Hals leaned forward again, looking sheepish. 'We're with ye, captain.' He shrugged. 'We... well, sometimes it's a mite hard to believe in going home, after everything what's happened.'

'Aye,' said Reiner. 'I know.'

A hand slapped his back and Horse-face sat down next to him with Pug-nose and Braids at his sides. 'Well, how do you like our homely fare?' he asked with a grin.

'The best we've had in days,' said Reiner truthfully. 'And we thank you for your hospitality.'

The bandit waved a dismissive hand. ''Tisn't hospitality. Y'll pay for it, one way or the other. If you stay with us y'll pull yer weight. If you leave us, yer purses will be lighter.' He grinned. 'Have y'decided which it's to be?'

Reiner sighed. He had expected something like this. The men were bandits after all. 'I believe we will be moving on. You have been more than generous, but I can see that you have little to share. You have no need of six more mouths to feed.'

'Where will you go?' asked braids.

Reiner frowned and rubbed his hand. 'The man who gave us these brands rides with Count Manfred, who means to win back Nordbergbruche from the northers. We have unfinished business with that man, if we can find Nordbergbruche.' He grinned wryly. 'We're sorely lost.'

Pug-nose made a face. 'You would run back to the arms of your executioners? Are you mad?'

'We are willing to die, so long as our nemesis does as well.'

'They go to betray us,' said Braids. 'They hope to win clemency by turning us in.'

Reiner glared at him. 'Do you think I am such a fool, sir? I know the Empire's justice as well as any. There is no clemency for one who wears the hammer brand. They may spare me the axe, but only to give me a pick and shovel. I will die in chains one way or the other.'

Braids snorted, but Horse-face waved an annoyed hand at him. 'Leave off, Gherholt. You would suspect Sigmar himself.' He smiled at Reiner. 'You've picked a busy destination. We spied Manfred marching toward Nordbergbruche this morning, and Chaos troops have been coming down out of the crags to defend it. We mean to go there after the battle, to pick the bones of the dead.'

A thrill of fear ran up Reiner's spine. 'Do you think battle has already been joined, then? Did you see the troops of the count's brother, Baron Albrecht?'

'Afraid your nemesis might die without your help?' asked Pug-nose.

'Precisely. I don't want some filthy norther cheating me of my vengeance.'

Horse-face shook his head. 'Manfred wouldn't have reached Nordbergbruche before dark. They won't form up until daybreak. We didn't see his brother.'

Reiner made a noise halfway between a sigh of relief and a moan. He was relieved that they hadn't come too late, but almost undone by the realisation of what they must now do. 'And how far is Nordbergbruche from here? Can we reach it by morning?'

Pug-nose laughed. 'In your condition? I doubt you'll make it at all.'

'Ye'll walk all night,' said Horse-face. 'But you'll be there before dawn.'

Reiner's companions groaned.

'Can y'tell us the way?' asked Hals.

'Aye, we can,' said Pug-nose.

They waited for him to continue, but he didn't.

'*Will* y'tell us the way?' asked Pavel.

Horse-face shrugged. 'Well, friends, that depends on the contents of your purses.'

Reiner smirked. He had known it would eventually come to this. Fortunately, unlike the cut and thrust of duelling, hard bargaining was a kind of melee he was comfortable engaging in. Here he could lead with confidence.

'Well, we don't have much to barter with, do we? For if you don't like our offer you can just kill us and take what you want. Therefore I must call upon your honour as brothers of the brand to deal squarely with us, and to remind you that cornered rats bite. You will get a fair price for your help if we make a bargain. You will get more than you bargained for if you fight us.'

Horse-face exchanged a look with his companions, then nodded. 'Fair enough. Tell us what you want, and make your offer.'

In the end, they got away with their lives, but it cost Reiner all Veirt's gold crowns, one of his pistols, and the sword his father had given him to do it. He hadn't minded giving away the gold. Gold always came and went. That was its purpose. And if Count Manfred rewarded them as he hoped, they would all soon be knee-deep in gold. The sword however was a painful parting. Certainly he could buy a better sword with Manfred's gold, but it wouldn't be *his* sword, would it?

In addition to not killing them, the bandits had patched their wounds – though not as expertly as Gustaf would have – given them directions and provided them all with weapons: a lesser sword for Reiner, spears for Pavel and Hals – as well as a crutch – bows for Franka and Giano, and an enormous old blunderbuss for Oskar, but only enough powder or shot for a handful of charges.

As per the bandits' directions, they followed the stream down the mountain until it reached a rutted track, took that east until it crossed a main road, and then travelled north and east as fast as their bruised, exhausted bodies would carry them.

Franka grinned as she walked beside Reiner. 'Never have I heard someone lie like that. So fluently, so credibly. Hurrying to kill the man who branded us. Ha!'

'Well, isn't it the truth?' asked Reiner. 'We may not have the pleasure of killing Albrecht with our own swords, but if we succeed, we will certainly cause his downfall.'

'But that is not what you implied. You made us out to be the most bloodthirsty of villains, out for terrible vengeance. Never have I known such a master of deceit.'

Reiner smirked. 'Have you glanced in a looking glass lately?'

Franka punched him and looked around anxiously to see if anyone else had heard.

They followed the road all night, shambling like sleepwalkers for mile upon endless mile. Soon all conversations ceased. All pretences of vigilance fell by the wayside. Reiner felt in a dream. Sometimes it seemed he walked in place and the world rolled beneath him. Sometimes he seemed to float above himself, watching from the clouds the line of ragged, limping figures as they wound through the dark woods and moonlit wastelands. It grew colder as they marched into the early morning and the warmth of the fire became a distant memory. They huddled in their torn and threadbare jerkins, longing for the heavy cloaks they had been issued at the beginning of this mad journey.

Long after the moons had set, they reached the turning the bandits had mentioned and began to climb back into the hills. Their pace became even slower. More than once Reiner caught himself just before his knees buckled. He wanted more than anything in the world to curl up and sleep, right in the middle of the road, if need be. His chin sank to his chest at regular intervals, and there were a few times when he opened his eyes and couldn't be sure when he had closed them.

At last, just as a faint pink light was touching the snowy peaks of the mountains, they crested a pass and saw in the distance a massive stone castle looming like a vulture over a shadowed valley. The valley opened before Reiner and his companions like a Y, with the castle perched on a high crag at the intersection of the two arms. At the base of the Y, just below where they stood, was a village. No lights shone there, but further up the valley, a cautious distance from the castle, the morning campfires of a great army shone in the darkness.

'Come on, lads,' said Reiner. 'Journey's end.'

'One way or the other,' grumbled Hals, but he was too tired to put much feeling into it.

They marched wearily down the hill to the valley floor. As they reached the village they saw that it had been destroyed. Not a building had its roof, or all four of its walls. Most had been burned to the ground. The yawning holes of the burned-out windows stared at them reproachfully, like betrayed comrades come back from the dead. The silence was utter. Though dawn was breaking, not a bird sang. No wind stirred the blackened, leafless trees. It felt as if the world had died, had uttered its last breath, and lay cold and motionless at their feet.

As they trudged up the dirt road that ran up the middle of the valley, the camp began to appear over the intervening trees and hedgerows – the white tents in their ordered ranks, the banners of the knights or companies housed within hanging limp above them, Manfred's banner of a lion in white and gold rising over them all, and to Reiner's relief, no sign what so ever of the manticore banner.

Noise returned to the world as they got closer – pots and pans clanked, ropes and harnesses creaked, hooves thudded, grindstones whirred, sleepy soldiers coughed and grumbled. Smells followed the sounds: porridge and bacon, horse, man, leather and canvas, wood smoke and gunpowder. Reiner and his companions inhaled deeply. Though Reiner had enlisted with reluctance, and would have sworn that he'd hated every minute of his time in the army, the sounds and smells of the camp filled him with such homesick joy that there were tears in his eyes.

He had to swallow a few times before he could speak. 'Cover your brands. We don't want to be thrown in the brig *before* we see Manfred.'

At the perimeter of the camp a picket stopped them. 'Who goes there!' cried a sentry.

'Couriers, with news for Count Manfred,' said Reiner, with as much military brusqueness as he could muster.

The picket stepped out of the shadows, eight men led by a sergeant – a square-shouldered, square-jawed swordsman. He wrinkled his nose and gave Reiner's company a suspicious once over. 'You look more like tinkers. Where is your seal?'

'We have been set upon, as you can see,' said Reiner. 'And have lost almost everything, but we have urgent news of Baron Albrecht's advance that the count must hear.'

'I'll decide that. What's the news?'

'It isn't for your ears, damn your eyes!' said Reiner drawing himself up. 'Do you think I'd tell a mere sergeant what torture couldn't get out of me? My name is Captain Reiner Hetzau and I demand to see Count Manfred!'

The sergeant gave Reiner a dirty look for pulling rank, and turned to one of his men. 'Hergig. Take his lordship and his men to see Captain Shaffer. I've had enough of him.'

This comedy was repeated four times in front of various captains, lieutenants and knights – before Reiner and his companions were at last led to the majestic white tent with the gold and white pennons in the centre of the camp.

'Your men will wait out here,' said the captain of the count's guard. 'And you will hand over your sword and daggers.'

Reiner did as he was told and the knight ushered him through the canvas flap.

In the tent, Count Manfred Valdenheim was at his breakfast. He sat at a big table, wolfing down ham and eggs and ale while his generals stood around him, splendid in their brightly polished armour and colourful capes, debating positions and strategies on the map spread out under the count's plates and cups. Manfred was still in his small clothes and shirt, his hair rumpled from sleep. A soldier's camp bed heaped with furs sat unmade in one corner, the count's suit of gold-chased steel armour standing like a sentinel on a rack at its foot.

The count was much like his younger brother in size and build, a large, barrel-chested man with the general aspect of an all-in wrestler, but where Albrecht's face had a cruel, shrewd cast, Manfred, with silver touching his temples and streaking his beard, had a kindly, bemused look. He seemed, in fact, almost too gentle to be the leader of a great army. But when the captain who had ushered Reiner into the tent whispered in his ear and he looked up, the ice blue gaze he turned on Reiner showed the steel beneath his fatherly exterior. He wasn't a wolf in sheep's clothing, thought Reiner, for he sensed that the count's easy nature was not a pretence, but rather a sheep who ate wolves for dinner – a man to be wary of, a man it would not be wise to lie to.

'What news, courier?' he asked briskly.

Reiner dropped to one knee, as much from exhaustion as deference. 'My lord, I have news of your brother which I am afraid you will not want to hear or wish to believe.'

The generals paused in their muttering and looked up at him.

Manfred lowered his knife and fork. 'Go on, my son.'

Reiner swallowed. Now that it came time to speak, he was afraid to tell his tale. It seemed so damned implausible. 'My lord, a fortnight ago, I and my companions were ordered by your brother to escort the Lady Magda Bandauer, an abbess of Shallya, to a Shallyan convent in the foothills of the Middle Mountains, where she was to open a sealed vault and retrieve from it a battle standard of great power.'

'Valnir's Bane,' said Manfred. 'I know of it, though the nuns always denied they had it.'

'And well they might, my lord,' said Reiner. 'For it is no longer the mighty weapon for good it once was. The blood of Valnir has soaked into the very fibre of the banner and corrupted it, making it into a thing of great evil. But when we discovered this, Lady Magda was not dissuaded from taking it. Instead she attacked us with its malevolent power and escaped, killing our captain and leaving us to die.'

Manfred raised an eyebrow.

Reiner hurried on. 'My lord, at the beginning of the journey we were led to believe that your brother hoped to use the banner to aid you in retaking Nordbergbruche, but I believe now that this is not the case.'

The generals muttered in consternation. Manfred waved them silent.

'I do not wish to speak ill of your brother,' continued Reiner. 'But Lady Magda is an ambitious woman who longs for power, and I believe that under her influence, Albrecht has come to share her ambitions. It is my fear that he marches south under

Valnir's Bane not to help you win back Nordbergbruche, but to take it for his own.'

'Lies!' cried a voice as the generals erupted in angry babbling. 'It's all lies!'

Reiner turned with the others.

Standing in the tent's opening were Lady Magda, once again the stiff, stern sister of Shallya, and Erich von Eisenberg, resplendent in beautiful blued steel armour, a plumed helmet tucked under his arm. It was he who had spoken.

SEVENTEEN
The Banner Has Enslaved Them

'THIS MAN IS a traitor and a murderer,' said Lady Magda, pointing at Reiner. 'Arrest him immediately.'

'It is he, not the reverend abbess,' chimed in Erich, 'who tried to take the banner for his own. It is he who murdered the valiant Captain Veirt and nearly slew me when I came to Lady Magda's aid.'

'My lord,' said Reiner, turning to Manfred. 'I beseech you. Do not believe them. They mean you ill...'

'Enough!' cried Manfred. 'All of you.' He turned on Erich and Lady Magda. 'What is this intrusion? What is your business here?'

Erich saluted. 'My lord, we come from your brother. He bids you a good morning and wishes to inform you that he is an hour away with a force of two thousand men. They are well rested and will be at your disposal upon their arrival.'

The generals met these words with glad cries, but Manfred looked from Erich to Reiner and back with a scowl of uncertainty upon his brow. 'Until a moment ago I would have welcomed this news, for two thousand men will almost double our army, but now...'

'My lord,' said Erich, 'you mustn't believe him. This man is a traitor, a convicted sorcerer, charged with a hundred murders by witchcraft.'

'That isn't true, my lord,' countered Reiner. 'Your brother himself acknowledged that the charges against me were false.'

'If that is so,' said Erich, 'then ask him to remove his left glove and explain the brand he wears there.'

'You wear the hammer brand?' asked Manfred.

Reiner pulled off his glove and raised his hand for Manfred to see. 'We all do,' he said. 'Baron Albrecht chose all the men for the mission in secret from the brig at Smallhof – more proof that his intentions were less than above board. He branded us all to make it more difficult for us to desert. Master von Eisenberg wears it as well.'

Erich smiled. 'He convicts himself out of his own mouth, my lord.' He drew off his mailed gauntlet and held up his hand. 'I have no brand, as you can see.'

Reiner stared. The back of Erich's hand was smooth and unblemished. The scar was gone. Reiner thought he saw a cruel smirk flash across Lady Magda's haughty face.

'My lord,' Reiner cried. 'It was part of the bargain! Baron Albrecht promised us that he would have a sage of the Order of Light remove the brands when we returned with Lady Magda and the banner! Von Eisenberg is as much a criminal as any of us. He was to be hanged for murdering a child.'

'He piles lie upon lie, my lord,' said Erich. 'He knows not when to stop.'

'Nor do you, sir,' said Manfred, hotly. 'Now be silent both of you and let me think.'

Reiner closed his mouth on further protests and watched as Manfred eyed them both appraisingly. Reiner groaned. Though he hoped against hope, he knew he had lost. Erich's last thrust had struck home, and even if it hadn't, he looked the hero of the piece, with his shining armour and handsome face, his golden beard and noble bearing, he was every inch a champion of the Empire. While Reiner, though he was loath to admit it, looked like a villain, with his half-starved, unshaven face, his unwashed black hair and gambler's moustache, his filthy, shredded clothes, his ancient, rusty sword. Even freshly scrubbed and impeccably dressed he had always looked a bit of a rogue. In his present condition, he looked the worst sort of guttersnipe, an alley-basher and ne'er-do-well.

A knight burst through the tent flap. 'My lords! The Chaos troops are moving! They form up in front of the castle!'

'What?' cried a general. 'They leave the protection of the castle? Are they mad?'

'Mad indeed,' said Manfred, standing and wiping his mouth. 'They are warptouched. But there is method here.' He crossed to his armour, snapping his fingers for his valets to begin dressing him. 'If their look outs have told them of Albrecht's approach then they may mean to destroy us before we double our strength.' He looked at his generals. 'Call your men to arms. I will have all units in position within a half hour.'

The generals saluted and filed out of the tent.

The knight who had brought Reiner in stepped forward. 'My lord, what would you have me do with this one?'

Manfred glanced up at Reiner as if he had already forgotten who he was. He waved a hand. 'Hold him and his companions until the battle is over. I will decide what to do with them later.' He turned to Erich and Lady Magda. 'Return to my brother. Tell him to advance with all possible speed.'

Erich saluted. 'At once, my lord.'

As he and Lady Magda turned to leave, Erich caught Reiner's eye. He curled his lip in a triumphant sneer. Reiner tried to give him a rude gesture in response, but the knight grabbed his arm in a crushing grip and marched him out before he could get his fingers up.

THERE WAS NO brig in the camp, so after they had been fed and their wounds seen to by a hurried field surgeon, they were placed under guard in a dry-goods tent behind the camp kitchen. They could see nothing but the sacks of flour they sat on and the jars of cooking oil and lard and the dried peas and lentils that were stacked around them, but through the thin canvas they could hear the cries and horn blasts of captains calling their companies to order, the thudding thunder of cavalry galloping by, the trot of infantry quick-marching into position to the sharp tattoo of regimental drums.

Pavel and Hals fidgeted at the sounds like the old warhorses they were, turning at every new sound, longing to be part of the action. Oskar sat huddled in a corner, shivering. He had asked

Reiner twenty times for a sip from Gustaf's bottle, forgetting each time that Reiner had lost it in the tunnels. In another corner Giano cursed and muttered to himself in his native tongue.

Reiner was too angry to sit. He paced back and forth between the hessian sacks.

'Damn Manfred,' he growled. 'Damn Karl Franz. Damn the whole bloody Empire! Here we are, a bunch of villians and ne'er-do-wells, going against our nature and our self interest to do them a good turn, to save them from not one, but two grave dangers and do they thank us? Do they heap riches at our feet, feed us oranges and ambrosia? No! They ignore our warnings and fit us for the noose again.' He kicked a pickle barrel. 'Well, I for one have finished playing at heroes. Chaos can take Karl Franz, Count Manfred and all the other high-born fools. From now on I am no longer a citizen of the Empire. I will be free of its grim pieties and stifling stoicism. From now on, I will be a citizen of the world. Who needs Aldorf when I have Marienburg, Tilea, Estalia, Araby, even far Cathay and all the mysteries of the unknown east? I will drink deep of freedom and call for more.' He turned to his companions, fire in his eyes. 'Who's with me? Who wants to walk a free man in a place where the hammer brand means nothing?'

The others stared at him, blinking.

'That was quite a speech,' said Hals. 'Almost as good as the one y'gave us about being homesick if we left the Empire, when you wanted us to stay with you.'

'Which one's the truth?' asked Pavel.

Reiner frowned. He'd forgotten the other speech. 'Er, why, both. I don't say I won't be homesick. I will. Altdorf is where my heart is, but as the Empire has turned its back on us, I will turn my back on it. And I'll be damned if I'll be miserable doing it. I'll go laughing, and to the depths with them all.'

Hals grinned. 'I hope y'never try to sell me a cow. I bet I'd end up giving ye my farm to buy it.'

'He's right all the same,' said Pavel. 'The jaggers have done us down. We owe 'em no favours. I'm in.'

'Oh, aye,' said Hals. 'Me as well.'

'And me,' chimed in Franka.

'You come to Tilea?' Giano grinned. 'I bring you my home. Cook you Tilean feasting, hey?'

'I certainly don't want to stay here,' said Oskar. 'I think they mean to hang us.'

'Good lads,' said Reiner. 'So where shall it be first? We'll need to make some money before we travel too far.'

'I vote for Marienburg,' said Hals. 'They speak our language. They pay good gold for willing pikes, and...' he nodded knowingly at Reiner. 'I hear their card-rooms rival Altdorf's.'

Reiner smirked. 'Hardly. But it is a port city. From there we can go anywhere. Are we agreed?'

The others nodded.

'Excellent.' Reiner looked around. 'Then we should find a way out of this tent.' He crossed to the tent flap and peeked out. The two guards who were meant to be guarding them stood well away from the opening, craning their necks, trying to see over the intervening tents to the field of battle. The camp seemed otherwise deserted, doused campfires smouldering and pennants flapping limply in a fitful breeze.

Reiner turned to his companions. 'Well, I don't think we'll have much trouble...'

A hair-raising noise interrupted him. It was the sound of five thousand savage throats raised in unison, roaring a barbaric war cry. The ground shook beneath Reiner's feet, and the muffled reports of cannon buffeted the tent.

'They've charged us,' said Franka. 'It's begun.'

Pavel and Hals were rooted to the spot. Giano's eyes darted around, anxious. Oskar flinched.

A second roar answered the first and the ground shook again. The noise rose to a continuous low rumble, pierced with shouts and trumpet blasts.

Reiner peeked through the tent flap again. Their two guards had almost disappeared around the mess tent. Their whole posture said that they longed to be supporting their fellows, not stuck far behind the lines.

Reiner turned back. 'Under the back wall. Our jailers will pay us no mind.' He paused as he saw Pavel and Hals's faces. They were stricken and grim. 'Have you changed your mind so soon?'

The pikemen were tortured with indecision. It was obvious that the idea of leaving their countrymen to fight the Chaos troops alone was odious to them, but at the same time, their sense of honour and justice had been wounded.

At last Hals shrugged. 'After the way they treated us? Let Chaos take them. I care not.'

'Nor do I,' said Pavel, but Reiner could tell he felt uncomfortable saying it.

'Then now is the time,' Reiner crossed to the back wall of the tent and began shifting sacks of flour out of the way. The others joined in. There was little danger of discovery. The air was filled with the sound of cannon fire, screaming horses, and the clash of arms.

When the sacks were cleared they pulled up on the bottom of the canvas wall until they loosened a tent peg, then wormed through the gap. Reiner stood watch behind the tent as the others squirmed out behind him. They were close to the south edge of the camp, in the stem of the Y-shaped valley. The sounds of the battle came from the north.

'Now,' said Reiner. 'Back to the road we came in on and west to Marienburg.'

'Wait,' said Giano, dragging a flour sack out of the tent. 'Prepare this time.' The sack had been emptied of most of its flour and filled with various dry goods. He grinned at them as he slung it over his shoulder and gestured around at the nearby tents. 'Store is open.'

Reiner smirked. 'You haven't a clear idea of the difference 'twixt mine and thine, do you, Tilean?'

He shrugged. 'If they want, they would take with them.'

Hals and Pavel scowled at him, but they joined in the hunt for weapons, clothes, armour, packs and cooking utensils. There was almost no one in the camp, only a few camp-followers and cooks – easily avoided, and though the soldiers had taken their main weapons to the battle, they had left all manner of swords and daggers, bows and spears behind. Reiner found a brace of pistols with powder and shot in a knight's tent. Oskar found a caisson full of handguns and took one, though he found it difficult to load with his left arm in a sling. Within the space of half an hour they were almost as well kitted out as they had been when Albrecht first freed them.

They assembled at the edge of camp, dressed in the colours of half a dozen companies, weapons bristling from belts and scabbards, and bulging packs over their shoulders.

'Now are we ready?' asked Reiner.

His companions nodded, though Pavel, Hals and Franka looked a trifle uncomfortable to be wearing gear stolen from their fellow soldiers.

'Then we march.'

They followed the path that had led them to the camp not two hours before. They were still dead tired, but their confinement had allowed them something resembling rest, and they were at least alert.

They had almost reached the village at the south end of the valley when Oskar pointed over the burned out buildings. 'Look.'

Winding down the hill beyond the town was a column of marching men, spearpoints and helms aglitter in the morning sun. The head of the column was hidden within the town, but there was no question as to whose army they must be.

'Albrecht,' said Pavel.

'Aye,' said Reiner. 'Come, we'll take cover 'til they pass.'

They hurried to a blackened barn on the outskirts of the town and hid inside it. Almost instantly they heard the tramp of marching feet and the clop of hooves. They stepped to the walls and peered through the charred boards as the head of the column emerged from the town. First to appear were Albrecht, Erich and Lady Magda, leading a company of more than a hundred knights. Erich rode between the baron and the abbess on a white charger clad in shining barding, but though Albrecht was splendid in his dark blue armour and a scarlet-plumed helm, and the company of knights was a magnificent sight that should have filled the hearts of men of the Empire with pride, the sight of the blood-red banner that Erich held aloft, couched in his lance socket, killed all emotions except an all pervading dread.

It was awesome and awful to look upon, slapping thickly against its pike, less like heavy cloth than a square of flesh cut from some umber giant, and though Reiner couldn't take his eyes off it, it was at the same time hard to look upon directly, for it radiated gloom and dread like a black sun. He felt at once physically sick, and at the same time compelled to join the column of men that followed it. Its power was a hundredfold greater than it had been in the crypt. Held by a hero at the head of an army, it had acquired at last its full allure. It tugged at Reiner like a magnet, and as he tore his eyes from it and looked around at his companions he could see that it affected them the same way. Pavel and Hals white-knuckled their spears. Franka and Giano stared, grimacing. Oskar was standing, stepping out from cover.

'Get down, you fool,' hissed Reiner, pulling the artilleryman back by his jerkin. He was glad of the distraction. Anything to keep him from looking at the banner again.

'Myrmidia,' breathed Franka. 'Look at them. The poor damned souls.'

Reiner reluctantly peered again through the wall. The knights had emerged entirely from the town and now companies of pike, sword and gun were marching out after them. In a way it was the most ordinary sight in the world, soldiers of the Empire on the march – simple farmers, millers, blacksmiths and merchants taking up arms in a time of war as they had done for centuries. But there was something about them, something almost indefinable, that was repulsive. They marched well enough, almost perfectly in fact, all in step, ranks dressed neat enough to warm a sergeant major's heart, but there was something about their gait, something loose and boneless, that reminded of Reiner of sleepwalkers. They stared straight ahead, jaws slack, eyes glazed. Not one of them looked left or right, or squinted at the sun to judge the time, or talked to his companions, or scratched his backside. Their eyes seemed fixed on the banner before them. They hardly seemed to blink.

'Zombies,' said Giano, making a warding sign.

'The banner has enslaved them,' said Franka, shuddering.

Reiner nodded. 'There is no longer any doubt of Albrecht's intentions. He comes not as his brother's saviour, but as his slayer.' He whistled out a breath. 'I'm glad we will be nowhere near when Manfred gets pinched 'twixt that hammer and the Kurgan anvil.'

The last of the mindless troops trailed out of the town. Reiner shouldered his pack and stood, but the others hesitated, gazing after the receding column.

'Captain,' said Hals, uncertainly. 'We can't just...' He trailed off.

'What do you mean?' asked Reiner.

Hals scratched his neck and made a face. He shifted uncomfortably on his feet. 'Captain. I know what I said before. I care not a fig what happens to Manfred. I hope he and Albrecht tear each other to pieces, but those lads back there in the camp...'

'*And* the ones in the column...' said Franka.

'Aye,' continued Hals. 'Them too. Enslaved or not, they're our mates. It's them who'll be pinched 'twixt hammer and anvil. It's them what will die in their thousands.'

'It ain't right to see Empire men fighting one another,' added Pavel. 'Brother against brother. It's wrong.'

'This is no war to protect Empire lands,' said Franka. 'Those men go to die so that Lady Magda can be a countess. So that Albrecht can take from his brother what he was not given at birth.'

Reiner swallowed a curse. He didn't like where this was going. 'So, do you say that we go and die as well? What side do you suggest we fight on?'

'I say that we do what Captain Veirt was trying to do when he died,' said Franka. 'Destroy the banner.'

Pavel and Hals nodded emphatically.

'Maybe we get our rewards then, hey?' said Giano.

'But what about freedom?' asked Reiner. 'What about Marienburg and Tilea and all the rest? What about drinking the world dry?'

The others shrugged uncomfortably. Even Giano wouldn't meet his eye.

'Sorry, captain,' said Hals at last.

Reiner groaned and looked longingly toward the path that rose up out of the valley. On the far side of that hill was the road to freedom. He had only to climb it and Albrecht, Manfred and Lady Magda would be mere unpleasant memories. What did he care about the fates of a few thousand peasants? It wasn't he who was leading them to their doom. All he wanted was a quiet life, free from evil banners, power-hungry nuns and mad barons. All he wanted was to be back in Altdorf or, if he must, Marienburg or Tilea, parting fools from their money by day and dallying with delicious doxies by night.

And yet...

And yet, though he was reluctant to admit it, the banner and the mindless marchers who followed it had sickened him as well. He had always had a problem with authority. That, more than any faintness of heart was the reason he had done his best to avoid serving in the army. He valued his individuality too much to obey orders without questioning them. He knew too many noble idiots – his beloved father came to mind, not to mention Erich von Eisenberg – to think that a lord was always right just because he was a lord. The idea of some eldritch relic that could remove one's ability to question an order, that took away one's individuality entirely and made of one a mindless drone, enslaved to the will of one's leader, filled him with outrage.

The banner was an abomination. He could imagine the whole Empire falling under its sway. A whole nation blindly following the whims of its leader, taking over its neighbours until there were no more Marienburgs or Tileas to escape to, until at last Reiner too marched along with all the others, just one more sheep happily following the butcher to the slaughterhouse.

'Right,' he said suddenly. 'On your feet. We'll need to cut wide to avoid their line of march, then hurry back on the double to beat them there.'

Pavel and Hals let out great sighs of relief. Franka smiled. Giano nodded. Oskar looked upset, but fell in line with the others as they started across the muddy stubblefields north of the village.

EIGHTEEN
The Claws Of The Manticore

THE JOURNEY CROSS-COUNTRY was harder than they expected. Climbing fieldstone walls and hunting for openings in high hedges slowed them down, and they were still as sore as they had been the evening before. Hals winced with each step, not just from the pain of his broken leg, but from the raw skin under his arm from the rubbing of his makeshift crutch.

Reiner shook his head as he surveyed them. What chance had the likes of them to destroy the banner? They would most likely have to fight Albrecht to do it, not to mention Erich and a host of knights. It was ridiculous. They were like beggars planning to storm Middenheim.

They lost sight of Albrecht's column as they stole back through Manfred's deserted camp and came at last upon the battlefield. From their position far behind Manfred's lines it was difficult to see anything, just a confusion of men and horses and horned helmets appearing and disappearing through drifting streamers of smoke. Reiner couldn't tell which, if any, were Albrecht's men or if they had even arrived yet.

'We need a better view,' he said. The steep hills to the right of the camp seemed a good vantage point. 'Up there.'

Hals groaned, but with Pavel assisting him he gamely limped up the slope behind the others. After a while, they found a goat path that made the climb easier and led them along the side of the hill to a spot where the battle was laid out before them like a painting.

They stood facing west above the branching of the Y-shaped valley. Nordbergbruche castle was a little to their north, rising from the promontory between the angled arms of the Y. Manfred's camp was to the south, well within the stem of the Y. From the armies' current positions, it was easy for Reiner to picture how the battle had begun. The Chaos troops had spilled out of the castle's gate and formed a long line that spanned the valley just below the branching arms. Manfred had lined up to face them in the mouth of the stem. He was outnumbered two to one, and was downhill from the Kurgan force, but he had two minor advantages: the steep hills on either side of the valley made it difficult for the Kurgan to flank him, and a rocky hill with a small wooden shrine of Sigmar at its top jutted up out of a thicket of bare-branched trees just inside the mouth of the stem, further narrowing the front that the Kurgan could attack him on, as well as providing a perfect platform for his mortars and cannon. The hill was virtually a cliff at its northern end, but sloped away gently to the south, and Manfred's army was split, one half on either side of it.

Unsurprisingly, Manfred's army had been giving ground. The Chaos force were forcing them into the stem like a handgunner packing wadding into the barrel of his gun. They had not yet pushed Manfred so far south that he had lost the advantage of the rocky hill, though this looked likely on the east side of the hill, where Manfred's forces were stretched thinner and the Kurgan forces were heaviest. If this happened it would be disaster for Manfred, for the Kurgan would then be able to sweep around the little hill from the south and attack the forces on the west side of the hill from the rear.

Hals sucked air through his teeth. 'Looks grim.'

'Aye,' said Reiner. 'But imagine how much worse it would be if we hadn't tipped the northers' cannon into the river. If they were firing that monster from the castle ramparts it might be over by now.'

'Where's Albrecht?' asked Franka.

'There,' said Oskar.

Reiner and the others looked where he was pointing. Through the haze of smoke that wafted over the battlefield, Reiner could just see a troop of knights riding out of patchy woods on a hillside on the far side of the valley. Albrecht was at their head, a vexillary holding aloft his family banner beside him. Several companies of swordsmen and handgunners followed the knights, and four cannon crews began to wheel their pieces into position. Somehow the baron had found a path through the hills and had come out north of the battle line. A charge down the steep hillside and he could take the Chaos force in the rear.

'And there,' said Oskar again, pointing south.

Reiner looked left. Out of Manfred's camp came company after company of spearmen, all marching in the disturbing loose-limbed gait Reiner's companions had seen before. They formed a broad front two hundred paces behind Manfred's lines.

'Does he support Manfred after all?' asked Pavel, confused. 'Have we been wrong all along?'

A great cheer went up as Manfred's beleaguered army noticed Albrecht's forces, and they began to fight with renewed vigour. The Kurgan saw the fresh troops as well, and began frantically trying to manoeuvre men into position to meet Albrecht's knights. But the elation of the men and the terror of the Kurgan were both short-lived, for strangely, though they were in excellent positions to attack and support, Albrecht's troops, both on the hill and behind Manfred's lines, remained where they were, silent watchers to the bloody battle before them.

'What is he waiting for?' asked Hals angrily. 'He could have 'em on the run.'

'Where is the banner?' asked Reiner.

They looked for it, but couldn't see it.

Meanwhile, the few feet of ground Manfred's troops had won back when the Chaos force had become confused by the new threat were rapidly being lost again as the northers fought desperately to beat the foe they faced before the new foe attacked.

Beside Reiner, Franka choked. 'There it is! On the little hill.'

Reiner and the others followed her gaze. Riding up the rocky hill in the centre of Manfred's line was Erich, mounted on his white charger and holding the vile banner in his lance socket.

Reiner could see Manfred's gun crews advancing toward the young knight, weapons drawn, but they didn't attack. Instead, the men fell to their knees before the banner and let him pass.

Erich reached the crest of the hill and raised the banner high over his head. It flapped thickly in the wind. Though there was no change in the weather, a pall seemed to fall across the whole valley, as if the banner sucked up light. Reiner felt a chill shiver through him. Franka moaned. The effect on the troops in the valley was even stronger. Manfred's men faltered and fell back all along his line, stunned into inaction by the banner's dread influence.

The Chaos troops hesitated as well, confused by this strange symbol, but they seemed not to fear it as the men of the Empire did, and took advantage of their foes' numb horror to press their attack. Manfred's army defended itself, but it was clear that their morale was at low ebb, and they fought as if distracted.

'We've got to reach that banner before it's too late,' said Franka.

'Is already too late,' said Giano. 'I want to help, but they dead men. We go, hey?'

Reiner shook his head. It was strange. He could hear the screams of the dying and the bellowing of captains and sergeants trying desperately to rally dispirited troops. He knew the situation was hopeless. He knew riding into that mess was suicide. If he did what was in his best interest, he would be slinking over the hill with his tail between his legs, but he couldn't do it. He couldn't let that stiff-necked clot Erich win the day. He couldn't let Lady Magda and that overstuffed sausage Albrecht have their way either. 'No. We stay. Come on. Straight for the hill.'

He started down the steep hill with his companions limping and grunting behind him. They reached the valley floor just south of Manfred's line, where field surgeons and camp followers were dragging the dead and the wounded away from the fighting, and broken men moaned on the ground. A hundred paces to their left, standing in eerie silence, was Albrecht's infantry: rank after rank of spearmen and archers gazing blankly forward like flesh statues. Reiner's companions began picking their way across the body-littered field. Dressed as they were in Empire colours, none of Manfred's troops paid them any mind.

Halfway across, a movement out of the corner of his eye made Reiner look up. On top of the rocky hill, Erich was standing in his stirrups and waving the evil banner in a circle over his head.

'Sigmar's hammer!' grunted Hals. 'Here they come.'

Reiner looked to his left. Albrecht's infantry were advancing in perfect unison, spears lowered, eyes dead. Behind them, the archers aimed at the sky and loosed their arrows.

'Run!' Reiner cried. 'Run for the hill!'

The company ran as fast as they could, hobbling and stumbling and cursing as a cloud of arrows arched overhead, momentarily blocking out the sun, then fell to earth like black rain. Fortunately, the archers' target was Manfred's line, and only a few that fell short landed near them. It wasn't so fortunate for Manfred's men, who screamed in surprise and terror as the arrows cut them down.

'The traitor!' cried Franka.

Over the shoulder of the rocky hill, Reiner could see that Albrecht and his knights had answered Erich's signal as well. They were charging down into the valley, lances levelled. From Reiner's vantage, it was impossible to see who they were attacking, but the barbaric howl of rage that echoed across the valley gave the answer. Albrecht had lowered the boom on the Kurgan at last.

'He attacks both sides!' barked Hals as he limped on. 'What is the mad fool about.'

'Mad?' gasped Reiner. 'He has more genius than I credited him with. He wants the castle for himself, so he waits until each side has weakened the other, then attacks both.'

They reached the thin woods that surrounded the rocky hill just as Albrecht's spears overran their latitude. Manfred's battle line, already much depleted, had divided into two back-to-back fronts, one line continuing to face the Kurgan, the other turning to face their ensorcelled brothers, who at the last twenty paces broke into a charge.

It was a disturbing sight, for Albrecht's troops showed no emotion as they rushed forward. They raised no battle cry, snarled no challenge, only stared dead ahead as they drove their spears into Manfred's ragged line in perfect unison. And yet for all their lack of emotion, they were savagely bloodthirsty, slashing and hacking like butchers, biting and clawing and gouging eyes as they came to grips with their foes, and all the while gazing blankly into the middle distance.

Adding to the slaughter was the fact that Manfred's troops were hesitant to attack the spearmen. Cries of 'Erhardt, what ails you? Do you not know me?' and 'Beren, brother, I beg you, stop!' rose over the melee, only to end in gurgling screams. Reiner heard a sob beside him and saw that Hals was weeping. The only factor even slightly in Manfred's troops' favour was that Albrecht's spears, though unimaginably fierce and brutal, were also clumsy and awkward – puppets manipulated by a poor master.

'Up the hill,' said Reiner, turning Hals away from the battle and pushing him into the bare woods. 'Hurry.'

But before they got far, they saw that the base of the slope was guarded by a unit of swordsmen, all with the glazed look of the slaves of the banner.

'This way,' said Reiner, and quietly led the others north along the side of the rising hill until the swordsmen were out of sight behind them. The hill angled up like a board pried out of a plank floor and the sides were steep. Reiner pushed through brambles and brush until he reached it.

'Oskar, take my arm.'

He helped the artilleryman mount the slanting strata while Pavel did the same for Hals. Franka and Giano spidered up around them. They pulled themselves over the edge a third of the way up the slope and crouched in a clump of bushes, looking down to see if the swords had noticed them. The men continued to stare blankly into the woods. Further up the hill Manfred's gun crews were back at work at their cannons, and it was with a sick lurch of the heart that Reiner realised that they were firing on their own troops. The banner had turned them against their own. Beyond the gun crews, at the crest of the hill, Erich stood, facing out over the battle field, banner held high. His back was protected by six more swordsmen. Lady Magda stood beside him, watching the battle intensely.

A grunt came from the nearest cannon. One of the crew was shambling toward them, eyes dull, his ram-rod raised like a weapon. Reiner looked down the hill. The swords hadn't yet noticed him.

'Shoot him,' he whispered.

Franka hesitated. 'He isn't our enemy. He is one of Manfred's men.'

The man's grunts were getting louder as he tried to warn his fellows. He waved the ram-rod around his head.

'No longer. Shoot him.'

'But his mind is not his own.'

A dull thwack sounded beside them and the crewman dropped with a crossbow bolt in his chest.

Giano shrugged and reloaded. 'Any man try to kill me is enemy.'

But he had silenced the man too late. The swordsmen had heard him, and were lumbering up the hill, while more cannoneers were turning their way.

'That's torn it,' said Reiner. 'We'll be surrounded in a minute.'

'Just a moment,' said Oskar suddenly. 'I have an idea.' He hurried toward the approaching cannon crew.

'Oskar!' Reiner groaned, then started after him. 'Come on you lot,' he said over his shoulder. 'It's now or never.'

'Since when does that one have ideas?' growled Hals, as he and the others followed.

Oskar dodged around the gunners' clumsy swings and ran for their gun. Pavel clubbed one of the gunners aside with the haft of his spear and Reiner kicked the other to the ground, reluctant despite his orders to Franka to kill the befuddled soldiers.

At the cannon, Oskar uncorked a keg of black powder, stuffed a length of lit match-cord in the hole, and kicked it down the hill. It rolled and bounced down the slope toward the advancing swords, fuse fizzing, as he primed a second keg.

Reiner grinned. It *was* a good idea. He hadn't thought the gunner had it in him.

As Oskar started the second keg rolling, the first hit one of the advancing swordsmen in the chest, knocking him flat. The others turned somnambulantly to look at him – and paid the price. The keg exploded amidst them, blowing them all to red ruin.

Oskar gaped. 'They... they didn't run.'

Reiner grimaced. 'You haven't been paying attention.'

The second keg bounded past the troops' maimed bodies and exploded in the woods at the base of the hill. A dozen trees caught fire, and the flames began to spread.

'That'll keep reinforcements at bay,' said Pavel.

'They won't need reinforcements,' said Hals. 'This lot'll do for us.'

Reiner looked behind him. All the men on the hill had turned at the explosion. The gun crews were leaving their cannon and advancing on them, and Lady Magda, Erich, and his swords were staring at them.

'Scum!' cried Erich, stepping toward them. 'Do you still plague me?'

'No,' said Lady Magda, holding him back. 'The banner must stay here.'

'As you wish, lady,' said Erich, shrugging off her hand. 'There is no need to move. Back to your cannon!' he called to the gun crews. 'I'll handle this rabble.'

The artillerymen obeyed like sheep.

'Shoot him!' shouted Reiner, drawing his pistols, as Erich started to turn the banner. 'Kill him!'

Franka and Giano raised their bows as Oskar aimed his handgun by laying the long barrel across the splint of his broken wrist.

'Hold your fire!' Erich commanded, and to Reiner's chagrin, he found it impossible to disobey the order. He could not force his fingers to squeeze the triggers. The others were similarly affected, shaking with the effort to shoot.

Hands shaking, Giano finally fired his crossbow, but the bolt flew off at an angle. 'Curse it!' said the Tilean, frustrated. 'My hands no listen!'

'It's the banner,' said Franka, her arms trembling as she held her bow at full draw.

Erich laughed and raised the banner, pointing at them with his free hand as his six swordsmen advanced. 'Kneel, soldiers! Listen to your leader. I am your rightful captain, You must follow my orders. Kneel and bow your heads.'

To Reiner's left and right Pavel, Hals and Oskar fell to their knees. Their chins dropped to their chests, though he could see them struggling to raise them. Reiner felt an almost unconquerable urge to follow suit. Erich *was* their rightful leader. He was the most senior officer now that Veirt was dead, and he was so strong and brave and had so much more experience than Reiner. It would be such a relief to let the mantle of command slip from his shoulders and let someone else lead again. Reiner's knees bent, but as he looked up to his beloved leader, he paused halfway to the ground.

Erich's face was twisted in a smug sneer, a jarring discontinuity with the noble image of him Reiner held in his head. He froze as his mind fought to reconcile the two pictures. To his left he saw that Giano and Franka were similarly halted in mid-genuflection.

Erich's swordsmen were closing, moving not like soldiers of the Empire, but like apes, hunched and menacing, eyes blank, mouths slack. Reiner tried to move, but his limbs couldn't answer the conflicting commands his mind was sending them.

The first swordsman reached Franka and raised his sword like an executioner. Franka shook with the effort to leap away, but could not. The sword was coming down.

'No!' barked Reiner, and fired his first pistol without thinking, blasting a ball up through the swordsman's jaw and out of the top of his head. The man dropped, gouting blood and spilling brains, and Reiner found that this small disobedience had broken the banner's hold on him. He could move.

The pistol's report had freed Franka and Giano as well. They stumbled back from the attacking swordsmen, gasping and cursing, but Oskar, Pavel and Hals were still frozen, sagging bonelessly to the ground. The swordsmen closed to cut them down.

Franka, Reiner and Giano jumped forward again to defend their comrades. Franka lunged under a swinging blade with her dagger, but was clubbed to the ground by the swordsman's elbow. Reiner blocked a sword that swung for Oskar's head, then shot its owner through the heart with his second pistol. Giano threw his crossbow in a swordsman's face and stabbed him through the heart with his sword.

'Kneel, curse you!' Erich bellowed, but they were too busy to listen.

'Hals! Pavel! Oskar!' cried Reiner as he parried two blades. 'Wake up!'

Franka stumbled up, dazed. A swordsman pulled back his sword to hack at her. She dodged unsteadily to the side and he missed. Reiner chopped through the man's shoulder to the bone. He looked up dully and stabbed at Reiner as if he hadn't felt the blow at all.

Surprised, Reiner forgot to parry, and had to drop desperately to the ground to avoid the thrust. The swordsman raised his sword for the killing blow, but suddenly a spear thrust up into his ribs. Reiner glanced to the side. Pavel clung to the spear like a lifeline.

'Thankee, lad,' said Reiner, rising. He hamstrung the swordsman and turned to face another.

Pavel was still too muddled to answer. Beside him, Hals was slapping himself in the face and cursing, fighting the banner with all his will. Reiner and Giano guarded them. Oskar crawled away from the melee, dragging his gun.

Three swordsmen remained. They fought with crude strength, but little finesse. If Reiner and his companions had been in good health and in full possession of their faculties they would have made short work of them, but dazed and wounded as they were, they were nearly as ungainly as their mesmerized opponents. The swordsmen's attacks smashed into their parries with numbing force, and they shrugged off wounds that would have had normal men screaming.

Franka helped Reiner kill another sword, cutting his throat with her dagger from behind while Reiner kept him busy.

'Go on, captain,' called Hals as the swordsman fell. 'We've these last two. Go teach that brainless jagger a lesson.'

Reiner looked to where Erich and Lady Magda watched the fight with anxious eyes. He didn't want to face von Eisenberg one on one, especially when the knight had the power of the banner giving him strength. But someone had to do it. With a sigh he plucked a pistol from the belt of a fallen swordsman and started up the hill as his companions fought on behind him. Smoke and sparks blew all around him as the woods that surrounded the hill burned like brittle hay. It was almost impossible to see the battlefield through the flames.

Erich thrust the banner at him. 'Kneel, dog! As Baron Albrecht's vexillary, I command you! Do as he ordered! Obey me!'

Lady Magda smirked as Reiner staggered, the force of the order like a yoke on his neck, bearing down on him. The urge to kneel and kiss the ground was nearly overpowering. But having fought it off once, it was easier to disobey a second time. He kept walking, shaking his head in an attempt to clear it.

'Sorry, von Eisenberg,' he said, forcing the words through his lips. 'You've picked the wrong troops to try your sorceries on. Brig scum are terrible at following orders.'

With a squeak of fear, Lady Magda backed away, then turned and ran to the edge of the cliff. She snatched up a yellow flag from the ground and began to wave it vigorously over her head.

Reiner paid her no mind. He raised his pistol and aimed at Erich.

'Put it down, Hetzau,' called Erich. 'I command you.'

Reiner fought the order and kept hold of the gun, but only just. Firing it was out of the question. His fingers would not obey him.

Erich laughed and slashed at him with his free hand. The knight was unarmed, and ten paces away, and yet Reiner flew back as if punched in the chest with a battering ram. He crashed to the ground, gasping, a fiery pain burning his ribs and abdomen. He looked down at himself. His leather jerkin was untouched, but blood was seeping through his shirt. He tore it open. Three deep gashes had opened the flesh of his abdomen. He could see the white of his ribs through one. He winced in agony.

'The claws of the manticore,' he croaked.

'The claws of the *griffin*,' said Erich, smug. 'To rend the enemies of the Empire.'

He slashed again. Reiner rolled to the side and claw marks appeared in the turf where he'd lain.

'If you still think you're fighting for the Empire, you're more of a fool than I thought,' grunted Reiner. 'And griffin or manticore, it's still an unfair advantage.'

'Unfair?' said Erich, offended. 'This is a holy weapon.'

Reiner tied his jerkin as tightly as he could against his wounds. 'And I have only this sword.' He climbed unsteadily to his feet, hissing with pain, and glared up at Erich, who looked like a hero in a painting, his head haloed by the sun. 'I thought you were a man of honour, Erich. A gentleman. What's has become of level ground? Of fair play and a choice of weapons?'

'Why should I play fair when you cheated in our last encounter?'

'I did not cheat. Hals acted on his own. I was perfectly willing to fight another touch with you, only fate intervened.'

'A likely story,' sneered Erich.

'Think what you like,' said Reiner, 'but here I am, ready to go again, to prove who is the better man, and you attack me with invisible claws and muddle my mind with the power of the banner. Dare you call that fair? Dare you call yourself a gentlemen?'

'You question my honour, sir?'

'I do until you put down that banner and fight me man to man.'

'Don't listen to him, you fool!' cried Lady Magda, hurrying back from the cliff-edge. 'You must not put down the banner.'

'Lady, please,' said Erich. 'This is a quarrel between men.' He glared at Reiner. 'How do I know you won't cheat me again?'

Reiner put his hand on his heart. 'You have my word as a gentleman and the son of a Knight of the Bower. I will fight you in accordance with the rules of knightly combat. May Sigmar strike me down if I lie.'

Erich hesitated, frowning.

Lady Magda balled her fists. 'You clothheaded infant, I order you to hold fast to the banner and kill this man instantly.'

This seemed to decide Erich. He raised the banner high over his head, then jammed it savagely into the ground so that it stood on its own. He turned to Reiner, removing his sword belt and drawing his beautiful long sword. 'So,' he said. 'To the death this time?'

'Oh yes,' said Reiner, and shot him in the face. The ball smashed through Erich's nose and exploded out the back of his head with a spray of gore. The knight folded like a house of cards, an expression of surprise frozen on his ruined face. He was dead before he hit the ground.

'You were right after all, Erich,' said Reiner as he threw the pistol aside. 'I *am* a cheat.'

NINETEEN
I Will Not Fail Again

REINER LOOKED FROM Erich's lifeless body to Valnir's Bane, stuck in the ground beside it. The banner was within his grasp, all he had to do was to throw it into the burning trees below and it would be destroyed, yet he hesitated to touch it. He forced his hand to reach for it.

'No!' Lady Magda shrieked and launched herself at him with a stiletto. He cuffed her to the ground and turned on her, raising his sword. 'Fine, I'll finish you first.'

She rolled out of reach, then laughed and pointed behind him. 'You insect. Turn and face your doom!'

Reiner looked over his shoulder. Bursting out of the wall of fire that cut off the base of the hill was Baron Albrecht and ten of his knights, their steeds mad with fear, manes and tails smoking.

Reiner's men, standing over the bodies of the swordsmen they had only just defeated, turned as well and stared at the squadron of knights advancing up the slope toward them. Hals lay on the ground, clutching a wound in his good leg, no longer good. Reiner noticed with superstitious dread that sparks from the burning trees had set the little shrine of Sigmar on fire and it burned like a torch. Not a good omen.

The knights lowered their lances and charged the companions. They stepped back wearily, too dazed to run. There seemed no way to prevent them from being run down. Unless...

Suddenly inspired, Reiner snatched up the cursed banner and ran forward, his slashed ribs screaming in protest at the awkward weight. The haft bit his hands with crackling black energy. It surged up his arms and made his joints throb in agony.

'Stop!' he shouted. 'Albrecht! Knights, I command you! In the name of Valnir, stop and turn back!'

Albrecht and his knights reined up hard, their chargers rearing and plunging, as if suddenly faced with a stone wall. One fell from the saddle.

Albrecht forced his horse down and reached for his sword.

'Fall back!' bellowed Reiner. 'Turn about! Down the hill.'

Albrecht froze, his hand halfway to his hilt, fighting the banner's influence with all his concentration, but his knights obeyed the order without a fight, wheeling their horses and starting down the hill again. At the base, the horses shied from entering the burning woods again, and would not continue. The knights spurred them savagely. The horses wheeled and bucked, throwing off their riders, who, horribly, picked themselves up and walked into the burning trees. Through the flames, Reiner could see their cloaks and tabards catching fire as the flames leapt at them. Reiner winced. It was horrible death.

Albrecht remained where he was, visibly shaking as he tried to ignore Reiner's order.

'Turn about, baron!' called Reiner. 'I am your leader now. I command you to charge down the hill!'

Albrecht began haltingly to turn, cursing and sweating as his hands jerked the horse's reins to the right against his will.

Reiner laughed. Baron Albrecht was obeying his commands! What a delicious joke. A giddy thrill ran up his spine. With the power of the banner coursing through him, he could make anyone do anything. A vision of ordering his father to kiss his own arse flashed across his mind, but that was mere childish vengeance. With power such as this he could do great things. It was a dark power, true, but if a man was strong enough to control it, it could be made to work for good. He could right grievous wrongs, depose cruel despots, force evil men to lay down their arms. Or better yet, he thought with a chuckle, he could turn them against each other, make evil fight evil for once, and slaughter each other to the last man. Wash the world clean with their blood. He would be king! Emperor! He would remake the world in his...

A searing pain erupted in his back. Something sharp ground between his ribs. He shrieked and dropped the banner. The here-and-now snapped back around him. Magda was drawing back her stiletto to stab him again. He backhanded her across the mouth. She fell on top of the banner.

Hissing in pain, Reiner turned, raising his sword, 'You should have cut my throat, sister.'

'Stand, villain!'

Reiner looked over his shoulder. Albrecht had returned to himself, and was dismounting his charger.

'Touch not the lady!' he said, striding forward and drawing his long sword. His blue-hued plate flashed darkly in the sun.

'The lady is a conniving seductress who has turned you against your brother and your homeland,' said Reiner, stepping back. But despite his brave words, he felt like a rabbit in the path of a chariot. Albrecht was stronger, fresher, better armed and armoured – not to mention a head taller. He braced for the baron's swing.

A shot rang out. Albrecht staggered as one of his shoulder pieces spun off, holed and twisted. Behind the baron Reiner could see Oskar, kneeling near the unconscious Hals, lowering his smoking handgun. Franka and Giano fired as well, but their missiles glanced off Albrecht's armour. Pavel was shambling forward, dragging his spear. Reiner's heart swelled. He had forgotten. He was not alone.

Albrecht recovered and closed with Reiner, swinging mightily. Reiner ducked and stepped past the baron to hack at his back. His sword bounced off the shining plate, ineffectual, and he had to twist away as Albrecht lashed out behind him.

'Hold him, captain,' called Pavel. 'We're coming.'

Oskar had dropped his gun and Giano his crossbow and they were limping after Pavel, swords drawn. Franka was circling wide, nocking another arrow.

'Lady Magda,' Albrecht shouted. 'Take cover. I will deal with these traitors.'

'No,' said Lady Magda as she pulled herself to her feet. 'The banner must fly or the battle is lost.' With an effort she lifted the Bane and staggered with it toward the crest of the hill.

'Someone stop her!' called Reiner, dodging a thrust from Albrecht. 'Knock down that banner.'

Pavel and Giano turned, but it was Oskar who ran after the abbess. 'I have failed you too often, captain,' he cried. 'She will not escape me again!'

'Be careful!' called Reiner, but Albrecht's sword was in his face and he could spare Oskar no more of his attention. He parried and, with Pavel and Giano, began circling the baron like dogs baiting a bull... They lunged in with their swords and spears as he spun this way and that.

'Dishonourable knaves,' Albrecht gasped, his face red within his helmet. 'Three on one? Is this how men of the Empire fight?'

Reiner danced in and cut Albrecht across the calf. 'Do men of the Empire enslave their subjects with sorcery and pit them against their brothers? Do men of the Empire slay their own kin to win power?'

'My brother is weak!' said Albrecht. 'He does Karl Franz's bidding like a lap-dog, and refuses to join me in ridding the mountains of Chaos for good and all.'

'And so you bring a new evil to the land to fight the first?'

'You know not of what you speak.'

As he circled, Reiner saw, over Albrecht's shoulder, Oskar catch up to Lady Magda. The abbess turned at his approach, raising her hand to command him, but Oskar shielded his eyes and slashed at her with his sword. It was a weak strike, hardly more than a scratch across the back of Lady Magda's hand, but it was enough to cause her to yelp and drop the banner, which fell against Oskar's chest.

Lady Magda leapt at the artilleryman like a wild cat, stiletto held high. He blocked it with the haft of the banner and bashed her in the face with the pommel of his sword. She dropped like a stone.

'Magda!' cried Albrecht, as the sister sprawled limp on the grass. He started toward her, his own combat suddenly forgotten.

The three companions took advantage and lunged in together, but once again Albrecht's armour defeated them. Giano's sword caromed off his helmet. Pavel's spear pierced his leg guard, but not deep enough to wound him. Reiner's sword skidded off his chest plate.

With a howl of fury, Albrecht lashed out at them. He kicked Giano to the ground, cut a deep gash in Pavel's shoulder, then slashed back at Reiner and caught him a glancing blow to the scalp.

Reiner dropped, eyes unfocused with pain, the world spinning around him. He felt the ground hit his back, but wasn't sure where the rest of his body was. Albrecht was a blurry form above him, raising his sword over his head. Reiner knew this was bad, but couldn't remember why.

Franka's voice echoed in his ears. 'Reiner! No!'

The shaft of an arrow buried itself deep in Albrecht's armpit, sticking out of the gap between his breastplate and his rerebrace. Albrecht roared in agony and dropped his sword. It fell point-first, dangerously close to Reiner's ear. Reiner rolled up, weaving wildly, all balance gone, and stabbed blind at Albrecht with all his might. The tip impaled the baron's left eye. Reiner felt it smash through the back of the socket and enter his brain.

Albrecht dropped to his knees, wrenching the sword from Reiner's grip. He swayed but didn't fall. Reiner grabbed his hilt again, put a foot on the baron's chest and shoved. Albrecht's face slid off the blade and he crashed to the side like a wagon full of scrap metal tipping into a ditch.

'Cursed lunatic,' spat Reiner, and sat down hard, clutching his bloody, buzzing head.

'Reiner! Captain!' cried Franka, running to kneel beside him. 'Are you hurt?'

Reiner looked up. His vision cleared. The girl's face was so full of sweet concern that all at once Reiner wanted to crush her to him. 'I...'

Their eyes locked. There was an instant of perfect communication between them, where Reiner suddenly knew that Franka wanted to hold him as much as he wanted to hold her. This was followed by a second look, in which, still without speaking, they both agreed that this was neither the time nor the place, and that the charade must continue.

With a forced grin, Reiner broke eye contact and clapped Franka heartily on the shoulder. 'Why I'm fine lad, just fine. Nothing a needle and thread won't fix.'

Franka grinned in return. 'I'm happy to hear it.'

It sounded like bad acting in Reiner's ears, but Pavel and Giano were struggling to their feet on either side of them, so he carried on.

'And I am happy with your shooting,' said Reiner. 'You saved my bacon with that shot.'

'Thank you, sir.'

Pavel looked up the hill and groaned. 'Lady of Mercy, what's he done now?'

Reiner turned. At the crest of the hill, Oskar stood hunched, still holding the banner, his face twisted in a grimace of agony.

'Oskar!' called Reiner. 'Oskar! Drop it! Put it down!'

Oskar didn't move. He was frozen to the spot, shaking like a man in a high fever. His face was drenched in sweat, the yellow glow of the burning shrine of Sigmar shining upon it. He spoke through clenched teeth. 'I... cannot.'

Reiner and the others started toward him.

'No!' he cried. 'Come no closer! It makes me want to do terrible things.'

Reiner took another step. 'Come now. You must fight...'

Oskar swiped the banner at him. 'Please, captain! Stay back! I cannot control it!'

Reiner cursed. 'Oskar, you must put it down. While you hold it aloft it continues to control Albrecht's troops. '

'I know,' said Oskar miserably.

'I held it,' said Reiner. 'I know what it whispers to you. But you must fight it. You must...' Reiner trailed off as he realised that he hadn't been able to put the banner down of his own volition either. It was Magda's knife in the back that had saved him.

Tears ran down Oskar's frozen face. 'I cannot fight it, captain. I am weak. You know I am. I...' With an agonised cry he slashed at them again with the banner and staggered forward a few steps, then forced himself to stop. He looked like a man struggling to hold his ground against a giant kite. 'No,' he muttered furiously. 'I will not fail again. I will not.'

Straining as if he had the weight of a mountain on his shoulders, Oskar straightened and turned away from them. He took a step toward the shrine of Sigmar. Then another. He moved like a man in quicksand.

'Very good, Oskar,' said Reiner. 'Throw it in the fire. That's a good man.'

Oskar closed on the shrine at a snail's pace, but at last stood mere feet from the fire. He reached out, and Reiner and the others could see his arms shake with the effort of trying to let go of the banner. It remained in his hands.

'Sigmar help me,' he wailed. 'But I cannot. I cannot!'

Reiner stepped forward again. 'Oskar, be strong!' he called. 'Be strong!'

'Yes,' hissed Oskar, through his teeth. He closed his eyes. 'Yes. I will be strong.'

And as Reiner and the others stared, aghast, he walked slowly, but deliberately, into the roaring flames of the burning shrine.

Franka screamed. Reiner shouted something, but he wasn't sure it was words.

'Oh, laddie,' murmured Pavel.

They could see, through the sheets of flame, Oskar standing in the middle of the shrine, shoulders back, burning like a candle, his clothes and hair charring, his skin crackling and bubbling. The flames raced up the pike and the banner caught, first only at the edges, which burned with a weird purple light, then all at once. There was a sound that was more than the roar of flames, a deep rumbling howl of inhuman fury that made Reiner's hair stand on end, and then, with a deafening crack, the banner exploded.

Reiner and the others were knocked flat by a blast larger than all the battle's cannon shots put together. A huge ball of purple flame erupted above the shrine as its splintered timbers spun past them like straw in a tempest. The last thing Reiner saw – or at least thought he saw – as he lost consciousness was a daemonic face, screaming with rage, boiling out of the fireball. Then it was gone, lost in billows of thick, grey smoke, and the blissful black of concussion.

TWENTY
Your Greatest Service

REINER OPENED HIS eyes. Thick smoke was still rising around him, so he couldn't have been out long. Groaning like an old man, he sat up and looked around. There was no trace of Oskar or the shrine of Sigmar except a patch of burned earth. Franka was getting to her hands and knees beside him. Giano was hissing as he pulled a dagger-long splinter of wood out of the meat of his arm. Pavel sat with his head between his knees, holding his face.

There was an irregular thumping behind them. They turned. Hals was crutching their way, the sleeve of his shirt tied around his head. 'So, we're alive then,' he said. 'Who'da thought, hey?'

'All but Oskar,' said Franka.

'Aye,' said Hals. 'I saw the end of that. Braver than we gave him credit for, I reckon.'

The boom of a cannon made them look up. Manfred's gun crews were at their pieces again, firing down at the battlefield below. Reiner and the others levered themselves to their feet and limped to the cliff edge, and discovered to their great relief that the crews were firing at the Chaos troops again.

'That's the stuff, lads!' cried Hals, waving his crutch. 'Give 'em some pepper!'

The same thing was happening all over the field. Though the battle was such a jumble that it was difficult to see what was happening, at last it became apparent that, Albrecht's troops, finally free of the banner's evil influence, were coming to their senses and joining their brothers in Manfred's army in attacking the Kurgan and driving them back toward the castle. Where before there had been tangled knots of frightened men fighting any who approached them, now the clarion calls of horn and drum were rallying the men of both armies into cohesive units which attacked their common foe with renewed fury. The pall of gloom was lifting from the field with the clearing smoke. The sun shone brightly on the burnished helms and breastplates of the Imperial knights and the ranked spear points of the state troops. The Kurgan, who seconds ago had had the upper hand, now found themselves outnumbered, and fell back in confusion. All over the field, companies of marauders were breaking and fleeing before the newly ordered ranks of the Imperials.

Franka, Pavel and Hals cheered.

Giano gave a satisfied grunt. 'We do our job, hey? They paying us now? Give us reward?'

Reiner nodded. 'Aye, I hope so. We've done the hard work. Killed Erich and Albrecht and…' He stopped, then spun, cursing. 'The witch! Where is she? We've forgotten the evil harridan who was the cause of it all.'

The others turned as well, looking for Lady Magda. She was no longer where Oskar had laid her out. They looked down the slope. She was nowhere to be seen.

'Curse the woman,' said Reiner. 'She's as slippery as an Altdorf barrister. Find her.'

But though they combed the hill all the way down to the smouldering woods, Lady Magda was nowhere to be found.

'She's flown the coop, captain,' said Pavel as they all gathered at the crest again.

Hals spat. 'Wouldn't I have liked to have seen her burn at the stake?'

Franka nodded. 'Better her than poor Oskar.'

They surveyed the field again. While they had searched, the battle had come to an end. There was still some mopping up going on, but for the most part the Kurgan had retired from the field, scrambling into the hills above Nordbergbruche castle and back into their holes. A large force of Empire troops was marching up the causeway to the castle gates and meeting little resistance.

Reiner turned away from the scene with a weary grunt, looking for a place to sit and tend his wounds, when he saw movement at the bottom of the hill. Knights were advancing up toward them at a walk, supported by a company of greatswords. It was Manfred.

Reiner sighed. 'Here comes his nibs. Time to face the music.'

He tried to brush the soot and dirt from his jerkin and tidy up his kit as best he could. The others did the same. It was pointless. They all looked like they'd been dragged through a briar patch backwards.

Manfred reined to a stop before his brother's body, his generals around him. He gave the corpse a long, sad look.

Reiner swallowed, nervous, and saluted. 'My lord. I can explain. It is as I said before. The banner, which you must have seen, gave Albrecht...'

Manfred held up his hand. 'There is no need to explain, you blackhearts. 'Tis obvious what happened here. You have disobeyed me by escaping from the confinement I put you in, and you have killed my noble brother.' He turned to the captain of the greatswords. 'Captain Longrin, fetch a litter for my brother's body and bring him to his rooms in Nordbergbruche once they have been prepared. Be sure to drape the banner of our house over him, that all may know that a hero died today. Then arrest these men and see that their wounds are seen to. It wouldn't do for them to die before I had the pleasure of hanging them. When they are presentable, have them brought to me. I wish to interrogate them personally.' He reined his horse around. 'Now let us hurry. I want to see what those animals have done to my home.'

The greatswords advanced on Reiner and the others, who stood open-mouthed with shock. They had expected angry questions, or an argument over whether they had done right or wrong, but this curt dismissal flabbergasted them.

'Y'ungrateful bastard,' snarled Hals at Manfred's retreating back. 'Y'bleeding boil on Sigmar's arse. Y'don't know when somebody's done ye a favour, do ye? Well I hope y'get the pox and it falls off.' He spit. 'I wish I had it to do all over again. I woulda' took the hanging at the beginning and saved myself the trouble.'

Captain Longrin slapped Hals across the face with a mailed glove, knocking him to the ground. 'That'll be enough of that, gallows bird.' He motioned to his men. 'Bind 'em, lads. They've still some fight in 'em.'

The greatswords tied the wrists of the company and marched them down the hill.

'Curse all counts,' said Reiner bitterly. 'Never will I trust another.'

'Hear hear,' said Franka.

BUT MANFRED WAS as good as his word, at least in one regard. Reiner and his companions received the best care. Their wounds were salved and bound, their broken limbs set and wrapped in plaster casts. They were fed and cleaned and dressed in plain, but well-made clothes, and then placed in an empty barracks tent to wait upon Manfred's pleasure, under a much more alert guard than before.

Pavel, Hals and Giano took advantage of the delay to lie on the cots and get some shut-eye, but Franka sat huddled in a corner, glaring at nothing. The company had been separated in the hospital tent as their various hurts had been seen to, and Reiner suddenly realised that Franka's masquerade might have been discovered.

He sat down next to her and spoke in a whisper. 'Er, has your, er, manhood survived?'

She shook her head. 'I fought them, but they gave me a bath.'

Reiner sighed. She choked out a sob and butted her head against his shoulder. 'I don't want to go back!'

He put an arm around her. 'Shhh, now. Shhh. You'll wake the others.' He chuckled bleakly. 'And there's no fear of you going back. They'll hang you with the rest of us.'

She fought to smile. 'Aye, there's a comfort.'

After another hour, as the sunset turned the walls of the tent a deep glowing orange, a captain of the guard opened the flap. 'File out, scum.'

They stood, hissing and groaning, their wounds stiff, and followed him out. A double file of greatswords flanked them as they marched through the camp and came at last again to

Manfred's magnificent tent. The captain held the canvas aside and they entered one by one.

It was dark in the tent, only a few candles illuminating the rich fabrics and dark woods of Manfred's furniture. Manfred sat in a fur-draped chair. Three more men sat in the shadows behind him. All were dressed in fine clothes and fur cloaks. To Reiner's surprise, there were no guards present, and five empty camp chairs waited for them, facing Manfred.

The companions hesitated in the doorway.

'Forgive me for not seeing you in my home,' said Manfred. 'But the savages have made it unlivable. There is much cleaning to be done. Please sit.'

They sat, looking around suspiciously, afraid it was some new kind of trap.

'Gollenz!' called the count. 'Wine for our guests.'

A servant came out of the shadows with goblets of wine on a silver tray. Reiner and his companions took them as warily as they had taken their seats. Perhaps Manfred meant to watch them die in throes of agony from poisoned wine. Or perhaps he meant to drug them to make them talk.

When the servant had retired, Manfred leaned forward. He coughed, seemingly embarrassed. 'Er, I want to apologise for the deception I employed earlier. There was indeed no need to explain, for when that unholy banner appeared on the hilltop, I knew that you had told the truth, and that my brother did mean to slay me.'

'But then...' said Reiner.

Manfred held up a hand. 'I and the Empire owe you all a debt of gratitude that we can never repay. You, more than any others in my army, have won this day, and the destruction of the Bane has prevented its influence from spreading any further. You have saved the Empire from a long and fratricidal war.'

'So...' said Reiner.

Manfred coughed again. 'Unfortunately, in these troubled times, with the great war over but the cost not yet counted, and the rebuilding still to be done, the morale of the citizenry is low. It would not do for them to believe that their lords were so weak that they could be corrupted as Albrecht was corrupted. They must not learn of his betrayal and the falling out between us. It would shake their faith in the nobility just when they most need us to be strong.'

A cold coil of dread snaked around Reiner's heart. Something bad was coming.

'Therefore,' said Manfred. 'Though it pains me to do it, you will still charged with Albrecht's crimes.'

'What!' barked Hals.

'The public needs a villain, a focus for their hatred. A scape-goat who can be disposed of so that life can return to normal.'

'And we're it,' said Reiner hollowly.

Manfred nodded. 'It will be your greatest service to the Empire.'

Hals pounded the arm of his chair and rose. 'Y'twisty little worm! Y'admit we saved your skin, and the Empire's, and still ye mean to give us the drop? I'm starting to wonder if we're fight-ing on the right side!'

Manfred raised his hand again. 'I haven't finished.' He waited until Hals sank back into his chair. 'I said it will be your greatest service to the Empire, but it will not be your last. You will be hanged with great public spectacle in Middenheim in a week's time.'

Franka tried to hold in a sob, but failed.

'At least,' continued Manfred, 'the crowd will believe it to be you. In reality it will be some other garrison scum: deserters, saboteurs, the like.'

A spark of hope kindled in Reiner's chest. 'So you mean to free us after all?'

'You will be freed, eventually. But first you will have the hon-our of further serving your Empire.'

The spark of hope fizzled out, and the feeling of foreboding began to creep over him again. 'How so?'

Manfred smiled thinly. 'The more I thought about what you accomplished here today, and the lengths you went to achieve it, the more I came to believe that we could make use of you.' He leaned forward again. 'The Empire needs blackhearts like your-selves – men who will do things that would be beyond the pale to the average soldier, men who are not awed by rank or power, who think for themselves and keep their wits in desperate situa-tions.' He took a sip of wine. 'Battles are not the only way the

Empire stays strong. There are less honourable deeds that must be done to keep our homeland safe. Deeds no true-hearted knight could allow himself to undertake. Deeds only knaves, villains and dishonoured men could stomach.'

'Y'high-talking twister!' growled Hals. 'All yer fine manners and all yer asking is for us to do your back-stabbing for ye!'

'Precisely,' said Manfred. 'After your doppelgangers are executed, you will become invisible. No one in the world but myself and the men you see before you will know that you still live. You will be ciphers, able to enter any situation and become who we wish you to be. The perfect spies.'

'And what if your perfect spies decide they don't want to do your dirty work?' asked Reiner. 'What if they decide to slip their leashes? These brands are only a death sentence within the Empire.'

'Aye,' said Giano, crossing his arms. 'I be my own man. No one control me.'

'Do we not?' asked Manfred. 'My brother had the right idea, branding you, but his methods were crude.' He motioned to the man behind him on his left, a white-bearded ancient in the black robes of a scholar. 'Magus Handfort is a member of the royal college of alchemy. He has developed a poison that can be activated from afar, at any time he chooses. While the surgeons were tending to your wounds, they rubbed this poison into your cuts.' He raised his hand as Reiner and his friends began to stand and protest. 'Take your ease, please. The solution is perfectly harmless until the magus reads aloud a particular incantation. Only then will you die a horrible agonising death.' He smiled, as warmly as if he were wishing them a happy and prosperous new year. 'And he will only read the incantation if you fail to report back to me at the end of the assignments I shall give you.'

'You swine,' said Reiner. 'You're worse than your brother. At least he offered a reward if we completed our mission. At least there was to be an end to our bondage.'

'My brother never intended to honour his end of the bargain, as you well know,' said Manfred. 'And he used you for his own interests, whereas now you will be working for the good of the Empire.'

'He said that too,' said Pavel.

'You will be well rewarded,' continued Manfred. 'When duty does not call you, you will live well indeed, within the walls of my castle. And when this time of crisis is over and the terror is at last vanquished, you will be freed from your service and given riches enough to build entire new lives. In addition, as you have all died, all your crimes will die with you.' He gave Franka a significant look. 'Your secrets will remain buried in your past, and you may live as you choose, new men.'

Reiner and his companions looked blankly at Manfred as he sat back and folded his hands in his lap.

'So,' he said. 'What have you to say? Do you take my offer? Will you help the Empire in its hour of need?'

'I'll say what I said to your brother,' sneered Reiner. 'We haven't much choice have we?'

'No,' said Manfred. 'You have not.'

A SHORT WHILE later, riding toward Nordbergbruche castle in a coach with heavily curtained windows, Reiner and his companions looked at each other glumly.

'That some loads of horse mess, hey?' said Giano.

'Aye,' said Pavel. 'Until the terror is vanquished, he says. The Empire has stood for two thousand years and there's always been some terror or other banging on the gates.'

'We're in it for the duration all right,' said Hals.

'Isn't there anything we can do?' asked Franka.

Reiner shook his head. 'Not unless we can find a way to flush the magus's poison from our system. But until then…'

'Until then,' said Pavel, 'they have us.'

'Aye,' growled Hals. 'By the short hairs.'

Reiner laughed and couldn't stop. His life might have become a never-ending nightmare, but at least the company was good.

ROTTEN FRUIT

IT ISN'T OFTEN a man gets to witness his own hanging, but Reiner Hetzau was being given the privilege. He didn't much care for it.

It was a week after the battle of Nordbergbusche, where Reiner and his companions had helped Count Manfred Valdenheim reclaim his family castle from the Kurgan who had occupied it since the Chaos invasion. This despite the fact that Manfred's younger brother Albrecht had turned on him, attacking him with two thousand troops, all under the spell of the cursed banner, Valnir's Bane, which had turned them into bloodthirsty automatons. If Reiner and his companions hadn't slain Albrecht and destroyed the banner, the day would have been lost. And for this great service to Manfred and the Empire, Reiner and his companions were to hang. At least it was to appear so.

'Poor damn butcher lambs,' said Giano, the Tilean mercenary, as he peered through the slats of the louvre-windowed coach Reiner shared with his fellow condemned. 'Bet they sorry now they born with our faces, hey?'

Pavel, the scrawny pikeman, swallowed and blinked his one good eye. 'There but for the grace of Sigmar…'

Reiner nodded, squinting at the scene outside. The coach sat amidst Manfred's retinue of twenty knights in the square before the Middenheim gaol. A great crowd surrounded them, all looking towards the gallows in the centre – a gallows that could hang five at once. The crowd was in a cheerful mood. There was nothing like a hanging to break up the monotony of rubble clearing and rebuilding that had become the daily life of Middenheim, the site of the final battle of Archaon's aborted invasion. Sellers of pinwheels and sweetmeats wound through the crowds, while on the gallows, five frightened men with passing resemblances to Reiner and his companions were about to dance on air.

'Why do I feel guilty it isn't us up there?' asked Franka, a dark-haired archer who only Reiner knew was not the boy she pretended to be.

'Because yer a soft-hearted fool,' said Hals, a bald, jut-bearded pikeman. 'They're villains. They'll be guilty of something.'

'But not guilty of what they're to hang for,' Franka pressed. 'They're being hanged for looking like us.'

'They're being hanged because Manfred doesn't want his family name besmirched by his brother's infamy,' said Reiner. He affected Manfred's statesmanlike tones: 'It would not do for the citizenry to believe their betters could be corrupted as Albrecht was.' Reiner snorted. 'I'm sure if Albrecht were someone else's brother, Manfred wouldn't be so concerned with the morale of the citizenry.'

A drum roll began. The crowd fell silent. Reiner and his companions stared through the narrow louvres.

On the gallows, Middenheim's chief magistrate read the charges as Manfred and a host of dignitaries looked solemnly on. 'Reiner Hetzau, Hals Kiir, Pavel Voss, Giano Ostini, Franz Shoentag, you are charged with the foul murder of Baron Albrecht Valdenheim; of bewitching his troops by means of heathen sorcery; and causing them to attack his brother, Count Manfred Valdenheim, thereby bringing about the deaths of countless innocent men. For these and sundry other bestial crimes you are to be hanged by the neck until dead. May Sigmar have mercy on your souls.'

As the hangman pulled sacks over the condemned men's heads, Reiner looked at the man chosen to be his replacement, a debauched-looking villain with a pencil-thin moustache. Reiner wasn't flattered by the comparison.

Beside him, Franka sobbed. 'He's only a boy.'

Reiner looked at the lad who had been picked to die for her. It was doubtful he'd seen sixteen summers. He wouldn't see seventeen. His face was frozen in a mask of dumb incomprehension as the bag was tugged down over his head.

The drums stopped. The trap banged open and the five men dropped and jerked at the end of their ropes until the hangman's apprentices jumped up and hung from their knees to make certain of the deed. The crowd cheered.

'There's another five deaths on our consciences,' sighed Pavel.

'Speak for yourself,' said Hals. 'I put 'em square on Manfred. He's the one ordered 'em hung.'

But the reason he'd hung the impostors instead of us, thought Reiner, was that we were too damned clever for our own good. Manfred had gone to the trouble of all this subterfuge because he had been impressed by the guile Reiner and his companions had demonstrated in their defeat of Albrecht, and wanted to employ it for himself. As he'd told them, winning battles was not the only way the Empire stayed strong. There were less honourable deeds that had to be done to keep the citizenry safe, deeds no true-hearted knight could undertake, deeds only blackhearts could stomach. Reiner and his companions were those 'Blackhearts'.

Manfred was having them 'executed' so that they would be invisible men – perfect spies who did not exist in the eyes of the world. But because he also feared they might abandon their new duties at their earliest opportunity – a not unreasonable fear – the count had insured their co-operation by magical means.

'We are just as much hanged men as those poor devils,' said Reiner. 'For the cursed poison Manfred put into our blood is a noose around our necks – and he could drop the trap at any time.'

Outside they heard Strieger, the captain of Manfred's retinue, call 'Forward!' and the coach lurched into motion. As they rode out of the square Reiner took a last look at the five hooded bodies swaying in the breeze.

THEY WERE BOUND for Altdorf, where Manfred had a townhouse and where he advised the Emperor on matters of state. The road travelled south from Middenheim through the depths of the Drakwald Forest until it at last crossed the Reik and entered Altdorf. Reiner and the other Blackhearts saw none of it. Locked in the louvred coach, the world passed them by only as light, shadow and sound, the monotonous symphony of creaking wheels, clopping hooves and jingling harnesses lulling them into a state of torpidity. At least they were alone, with no one to overhear them, and this allowed them to plot their escape, however fruitlessly.

'Why not we kill the mage who know the poison spell?' suggested Giano.

'Manfred would get another, and have him unleash the poison,' said Reiner.

'What if we broke the mage's fingers until he removed the poison?' asked Hals.

'And if he said the spell that killed us instead of the spell that freed us, would you know the difference?' countered Reiner.

Pavel folded his arms, 'Alright then, captain. If yer so smart, what do we do? Let us poke holes in your ideas for once.'

'Well,' said Reiner, leaning back, 'perhaps we could pay a hedge witch to remove the poison.'

'If we could find one, and that would require a lot of gold,' said Franka. 'Something we are sorely lacking.'

Reiner nodded. 'True. But fortunes change. While helping Manfred we may find opportunity to help ourselves.'

'But a hedge witch could cheat us as well,' said Hals. 'He could spout any sort of mumbo jumbo and we wouldn't know if he'd removed the poison until we tried to run and fell dead on the spot.'

And on and on it went, an endless circle of argument as monotonous as the sound of the wheels rolling below them. Only occasionally would the monotony be broken when Reiner would look up to find Franka's eyes hot upon him.

She and he had first shared that look after they had killed Albrecht. Since then, each time they locked eyes, visions of Franka's lithe body stripped of her boyish trappings danced through Reiner's head. But even these pleasant dreams led to frustration, for none of the others knew Franka was a woman, so their desire could not be acted upon, and the cycle of lust stirred followed by lust denied became as grinding and dull as everything else.

THE AGONY CONTINUED for three days, with the Blackhearts only let out of the coach when the company made camp. The coach had become thick with the smell of their unwashed bodies and their conversation had been reduced to ill-tempered grunts, when, late on the afternoon of the third day, the sudden booming of the coach wheels rolling over wood woke them from their stupor.

All five crowded to the slatted windows. The narrow view told them little more than they were crossing over a drawbridge into the courtyard of a castle. After a moment the coach came to a stop amid hails and responses from Manfred's retinue and the house guards.

One voice rose above the rest. 'Count Manfred! Well met, my lord.'

'And you, Groff,' came Manfred's voice. 'I see you survived the troubles.'

'Barely, my lord. Only barely.'

The coach door was unlocked and the guard in charge of the Blackhearts' transport, a sour veteran named Klaus, swung it open. 'Fall out, vermin,' he growled. 'And no nonsense. We're staying with quality tonight.'

'We'll be on our best behaviour,' said Reiner stepping out. 'Lay out my finest suit and ruff, won't you?'

'That's just the sort of thing I'm talking about,' snarled Klaus.

He lined them up at attention as Captain Strieger talked over their lodging with the head of Groff's house guard, and Manfred and Groff continued their conversation.

'We were hit very hard, my lord,' Groff was saying. He was a short, dark-haired man with a flabby, careworn face. 'We held supplies for Baron Hegel's cannon, and somehow the devils got wind of it. Tried for three days to force their way in before Boecher's garrison came up and chased them off, by the grace of Sigmar. But by then three-quarters of my men died, and as you can see...'

Groff gestured around at his castle, which was in terrible disrepair. Crews of peasants laboured to close up holes in the outer walls that one could have led a company of lancers through, but they were making little progress. The roof of the stables had burned away, and one of the keep's towers had collapsed, and now lay across the courtyard like the corpse of a dragon.

Groff nodded at the ruined tower. 'Lost my older son when that fell. He was fighting some horror with bones for skin. It called lighting from the sky and...' He swallowed.

Manfred put a hand on his shoulder. 'At least he died as Sigmar commands us to, fighting corruption.'

'Aye, he died well,' said Groff sadly. 'But we seem to have bested one evil only to have another spring up. Indeed, I am glad you have graced us with your presence, m'lord, for something's brewing in the forest that I would have you warn Altdorf about.'

Manfred looked up. 'Remnants of the Chaos horde?'

Groff shrugged. 'Something in there is carrying off the villagers and driving the woodsmen mad. I'd appreciate you asking Altdorf to send reinforcements. We're in no state to face any–'

'Right, you lot,' said Klaus at Reiner's side, drawing his attention away from the lords' conversation. 'We've got your lodgings sorted. This way.'

But before they could follow, there was a clatter of hooves at the gate and everyone turned to face the potential threat. It was a single horseman, a flush-faced youth in black and silver, with fevered excitement in his bright blue eyes.

'Father!' he cried as he reined his horse to a halt. 'Father, I saw a white stag in the woods just now. It was beautiful. You should hunt it with me.'

Manfred's knights relaxed. Their hands dropped from their hilts.

Groff looked embarrassed. 'Udo, pay your respects to Count Valdenheim. My lord, may I introduce my son, Udo.'

Udo dismounted and bowed distractedly to Manfred. 'My lord count. Forgive me. Welcome to our humble house.' He turned back to his father. 'So, may we have a hunt, father?'

As Klaus led the Blackhearts away, Reiner looked back to see Lord Groff bowing Count Manfred towards the main door and shooting angry looks at his son. Udo seemed oblivious. He followed his father into the keep with a far-away smile on his too-red lips. It looked like he had been eating cherries.

THAT EVENING, WHILE Count Manfred and his knights dined with their host in the great hall, Reiner and his companions ate with Klaus and the coachman and Lord Groff's servants in the castle's kitchens. It was a much less formal affair than the dinner upstairs, but undoubtedly warmer. Apparently, during the battle for Groff's castle, the horde's weird lightning had set fire to the great hall's roof, and half of it was open to the cold spring night.

The Blackhearts ate in silence at the long kitchen table, more interested in food than conversation, after their cramped, claustrophobic journey. The servants talked enough for all of them anyway.

'Hans the baker disappeared last night,' said a serving maid. 'Third this month.'

The groom snorted. 'Disappeared? Everyone knows where he's gone. Off to join them in the woods.'

The cook nodded. 'His woman said he woke up from a dead sleep sayin' he heard music, and just ran off.'

'Yestere'en when I was huntin' coney deep in the woods, I seen Laney, the carpenter's daughter what disappeared the other week,' said a young potboy. He giggled. 'She weren't wearin' no clothes.'

The head footman laughed. 'You *dreamed* that, I'm thinking, laddie. As we all have.'

'Even you, husband?' asked the cook sharply.

The servants laughed as the head footman blushed. Some of the Blackhearts smiled.

Reiner was too busy trying to manoeuvre his left foot through the forest of booted legs under the table so that he could lay it beside Franka's. It would be highly embarrassing to lovingly stroke Hal's foot, or Pavel's. Very difficult to explain. At last he was rewarded with a surprised glance from Franka, and then a private smile and a return of pressure from her foot. His heart leapt, then he chuckled. He, who had spent so much of his youth in brothels where the girls stuck their tongues down your throat as a casual greeting, being aroused by such schoolboy flirtation. Ridiculous. Aye, but undeniable as well.

He glanced around the room, suddenly desperate to discover a way to be alone with Franka that night. They would be back in the coach on the morrow and he had no idea how they would be lodged in Altdorf. Tonight could be their only chance at intimacy – their only chance even to speak privately.

'Tain't funny, young Grig,' said a burly huntsman to a grinning young footman. 'Those fools are dangerous as well as mad. They'd eat you as soon as look at you. And the wood ain't the same neither. The trees are changing. Honest Drakwald oaks growing thorns and...' he made a face, 'fat purple plums. It ain't natural.'

'If there's a danger in the forest,' asked Hals, his garrulous nature surfacing, 'why are yer walls still all a jumble?'

'There's not many left to build 'em, friend,' said the footman. 'The war took so many. The village was nearly deserted even before this business in the woods begun. Now–'

'Even the bandits what used to steal our sheep are leaving,' said the cook. 'And there's those who won't work at Castle Groff because they think it an unlucky house. Hard to build walls when nobody will...'

'Less of that, foolish woman,' snapped the head footman. 'There's no need to be airing our dirty linen.'

'I don't say 'tis unlucky,' answered the cook. 'I'm still here, ain't I? It's only what they say in the village. What with the young master dying, and m'lord's lady taken away by fever, and master Udo taking on so queer...'

'There's nothing wrong with master Udo,' barked a long-faced fellow who hadn't spoken before.

Reiner looked up at him. He was a long-faced fellow in the garb of a manservant. A lock of prematurely grey hair hung over one eye.

The man chuckled, trying to smooth over his outburst. 'The boy's moon-eyed over a girl in the village is all.' He winked. 'She wears him out.'

'He don't go to the village, Stier,' said the groom. 'He goes to the woods.'

'Don't talk of what you don't know, boy,' Stier snapped. 'I'm his manservant. I think I should know what he does.' He stood, stiff. 'It will be time to serve the port. Come, Burgo.'

The footman wiped his lips and joined Stier as he unlocked the wine cabinet. They selected a few bottles, and went upstairs.

Reiner stared at the cabinet. They had left it open. He smiled.

'You lot are lucky they ain't got a full complement of servants,' said Klaus as he herded them into a below-stairs dormitory. 'You'd be sleeping in the stables else.' He turned on Reiner. 'And I'll be right outside the door, you, so no sneaking out windows, no sneaking in serving girls, no gambling with the grooms. We're on our best behaviour. Understand?'

Reiner looked suddenly contrite. 'Actually, sergeant, if I might have a word alone, I have a confession to make.'

Klaus sighed and beckoned him into the hall, then closed the door behind them. 'What is it now, Hetzau?'

Reiner slipped a bottle of wine from under his jacket. 'Well...'

'What's this?' asked Klaus suspiciously. 'You trying to bribe me?'

'Bribe you?' said Reiner, astonished. 'Sergeant, bribery was the furthest thing from my mind, I assure you.'

'Then...?'

'I, er, well, I nicked this to share with the lads, but your admonitions have shamed me, and I want you to return it to its rightful place. I don't want to embarrass Manfred with any bad behaviour.'

Klaus looked longingly at the bottle. 'Why, that's damned decent of ye, Hetzau. I'll put in a good word for you with Count Manfred for this.'

Reiner gave Klaus the bottle. 'I was just hoping you wouldn't report me.'

'No fear,' said Klaus, not taking his eyes off the bottle. 'No fear.'

Later, after the other Blackhearts had gone to sleep, Reiner slipped out of his cot and peeked into the hall. He was gratified to see Klaus sprawled in his chair snoring like a lumber mill, the wine bottle empty beside him. Reiner tip-toed to Franka's bed and shook her gently. Like a good soldier, Franka came awake without a murmur, merely opening her eyes and reaching for her dagger – which she didn't have, as Manfred had disarmed them.

Reiner put his finger to his lips and nodded towards the door. Franka looked around, frowning when she saw the other Blackhearts still asleep.

'What's this foolishness?' she mouthed.

He winked and motioned to the door again. Franka hesitated, then, with a shrug, swung out of bed, tugged on her boots and doublet, and joined him. He checked the hall again, then eased out. She followed and closed the door behind her. The latch clicked and they both turned to look at Klaus, ready to fight, but he did nothing but snore.

Reiner led Franka quietly through the dark hallways and twisting stairs of the silent castle until he found the musicians' gallery above the main hall. He pulled her in and sat her down on a long wooden bench. Sheet music was strewn underfoot, and moonlight from the huge hole in the great hall's roof shone through the gallery's lattice work, casting geometric patterns of light and shadow on Franka's sweet face. Reiner was overcome.

'Alone at last,' he breathed, leaning forward to encircle her in his arms.

Something stopped him. He looked down to find Franka's small hand pushing firmly on his sternum. 'You presume much, my lord.'

'Do I?' asked Reiner, genuinely surprised. 'Er, I thought, from your glances, from your coming away with me…'

'I came so that we might speak of… all this.'

'Speak? You want to waste these few precious moments we have speaking? This may be our only opportunity to…'

'My lord, please.' said Franka. 'It's true that I have discovered, er, feelings, for you that I did not expect, and I too desire to, er, be closer to you, but…'

'Then be with me now,' said Reiner reaching for her again. 'There's no telling how things will be when we get to Altdorf.'

Once again her hand held him away. 'Let me finish, my lord. I am not the sort of woman you are used to trafficking with. I am a miller's daughter, not a harlot. The thing you ask I do not give lightly.'

'You aren't exactly a proper Talabheim matron either,' countered Reiner. 'They don't join the army. And I doubt you and your Yarl ever crossed hands under the Hammer.'

Franka looked at the floor. 'We were married in our way. In Sigmar's eyes if not those of the law. And that is one of the reasons I beg you to wait a while.' She looked up at Reiner. 'I made a vow on Yarl's death, in honour of my love for him, that a year would pass before I took a husband, or another lover. I intend to honour that vow.'

Reiner fought to keep the frustration from his face. 'And a year hasn't yet passed?'

'There are five months left before I may love again.'

'Five months!' The words echoed through the great hall and Reiner and Franka froze, listening for a challenge. None came. Reiner lowered his voice to a harsh whisper. 'Five months? We could be dead in five months! Sigmar knows what madness Manfred has in store for us. He could send us to the Chas Wastes, for all we know.'

'Please, m'lord. You are cruel to press me like this.'

Reiner sighed and sat back. 'Very well. I won't make a fool of myself. But could we not at least share a single kiss – as chaste as you like – as acknowledgement of our feelings toward one another?'

Franka chuckled. 'And one kiss won't lead to another?'

'Upon my honour, lady, I...'

Franka held up a hand. 'Don't. It would pain me to be disappointed with you, so I won't give you the opportunity to lie.' She opened her arms. 'Instead, I will grant you your kiss, and be ready to defend myself.'

'You wound me, lady.'

'You will recover, I'm sure.'

They closed each other in an embrace. Franka raised her face to Reiner's. He lowered his lips to hers. It was a chaste kiss, at first, but after a moment the tension went out of their arms and they pressed closer, melting into each other as if the boundaries between them were blurring. Franka moaned in her throat and her hands ran down Reiner's back. Her lips parted. Reiner gripped her hips and pulled her into him.

'No!' Franka was suddenly pushing back, turning her head away. Reiner thought he saw tears in her eyes.

'But why?' asked Reiner urgently. 'Your need is obviously as great as mine. Why do you deny yourself?'

'Because I have made a vow. I would dishonour Yarl's memory if I broke it.'

'Damn all vows,' growled Reiner, reaching for her again. 'You dishonour your true nature by denying–'

'Hist!' said Franka, turning. 'I heard a noise.'

'None of your tricks,' said Reiner, but now he heard it too: a rustling and bumping. He and Franka stepped to the lattice that screened the gallery from the great hall below and looked down.

Shuffling somnolently through the patches of moonlight that illuminated the big room, dressed only in his night shirt, was Groff's son Udo. His eyes were open, but he moved like a blind man pulled forward by some invisible rope.

'He sleepwalks,' murmured Reiner.

'We... er, we should follow him,' whispered Franka. 'And make sure he doesn't do himself a mischief.' She turned towards the door.

Reiner gave her a sly look. 'Are you concerned for his safety or your own?'

Franka smirked. 'You are very perceptive, sir.' And before he could pull her back, she evaded his arms and slipped into the corridor. Reiner sighed and followed.

As they started down the stairs to the hall, they saw Udo coming up. They backed around a corner until he topped the stairs and walked away down the corridor.

Franka started after him. Reiner cursed. He had felt her desire. It would only have been a matter of time before she succumbed. Now who knew when they could come to grips again. Five months? Unthinkable.

Udo turned a corner. When Reiner and Franka reached it, Franka peeked around, then pulled quickly back.

'What is it?' asked Reiner.

'A... a woman,' said Franka, frowning.

'What?' Reiner eased his head around the corner.

At the end of a short hallway, open doors revealed a scene from some old romantic painting – a couple embracing on an ivy-covered balcony, the lovers haloed softly in the moonlight – except in the painting, the man would undoubtedly have worn breeches.

The woman was shockingly beautiful, a voluptuous succubus in a plum velvet dress, with glossy black hair and a full-lipped, heart-shaped face. Udo was fully under her spell, trying to close with her like a lust-crazed schoolboy while she held him off.

'Later, beloved,' she was saying. 'We must speak of other things first.'

The scene felt familiar, but Reiner was so beglamoured by the woman's beauty he couldn't remember why. He only wanted to continue to look at her.

A hand pulled him roughly back. 'Do you want them to see you?' hissed Franka.

'I was, er, well...'

Franka rolled her eyes.

The woman's voice floated around the corner: a throaty contralto. 'No, beloved. First you must tell me what was said at dinner. Why is Valdenheim here? Does he mean to destroy us?'

Reiner and Franka froze at the mention of Manfred's name.

'Dinner be damned,' whined Udo. 'You don't understand how much I need you. I ache for you.'

'I know exactly how much you need me, silly boy. Now tell me or I shall leave.'

Udo yelped. 'No! You mustn't! I will tell! Though they said little enough. Father begged Valdenheim for help fighting the "horror" in the forest, but Valdenheim put him off, saying the Empire hasn't the resources.'

'So he hasn't come to hunt us down?'

'No. He's only passing through. Taking spies to be questioned in Altdorf, he said.'

Reiner and Franka heard the woman's relieved sigh. 'Very good. Now did you tell your father of the white stag as I asked? Has he agreed to the hunt?'

'I told him, but... but, beloved, is it really necessary to kill him? I know he's a fool, but he is my...'

'He will never consent to our union, my sweet. Or to the kingdom of pleasure we hope to found here. It is best...' She stopped suddenly, then murmured something Reiner and Franka couldn't hear.

'What?' said Udo loudly. 'Overheard?'

Reiner and Franka began backing hastily away, but before they could take three steps Udo was around the corner, swinging his fists wildly. 'Assassins!' he cried. 'Spies!'

'Hush, beloved!' hissed the woman, following him. 'You'll wake the house.'

Reiner and Franka dropped Udo with a few well-placed fists and knees, and he rolled away, groaning. The woman was another matter. She flashed towards them like an oiled shadow, a stiletto glinting in her hand. Reiner and Franka dropped their hands to their belts, forgetting again that they had no daggers.

The woman lunged at Reiner, her blade seeking his neck. He grabbed her wrist, trying to force it back. It was like trying to bend iron. He looked in her eyes. They shone with a weird light. His mind began to swim. Franka kicked the woman in the stomach. The beauty snarled and backhanded her, breaking eye-contact with Reiner. Franka flew back, head bouncing off the wall, and she slid to the floor.

Reiner caught the woman's arm as she stabbed again, this time averting his eyes, but even using his whole body to hold the stiletto away, still it inched towards his neck.

Sounds of doors opening echoed down the hall.

'Unhand her, villain!' cried Udo, staggering up. Franka grabbed his legs. He kicked her in the face.

'Idiot child!' hissed the beauty. 'Be silent!'

Udo pummelled Reiner. His blows were weak, but a lucky punch to the kidney made Reiner's knees buckle and the witch's stiletto jerked forward, gashing his collar bone.

With a look of triumph, she ripped her arm free of Reiner's grip and raised the stiletto, but feet were running towards them and they heard the scrape of unsheathing swords. The beauty looked up, cursing, then jumped back, eyes flashing angrily at Udo. 'Fool! I told you to be silent.' With a frustrated hiss, she ran to the balcony and leapt over. Reiner half expected her to fly away like some bird of prey, but she dropped out of sight and was gone.

Udo's fist caught Reiner on the cheekbone. 'Spoilsport! You've chased her away!'

Reiner ducked back and grabbed Udo's arms. Franka lurched up and caught Udo's collar from behind, pulling his shirt down over his shoulders to trap his arms. Reiner was about to head butt the youth when he saw a livid mark on Udo's exposed chest. A small puncture wound, purple-black with infection, rose directly over his heart. It looked like a third nipple.

'Ware,' muttered Franka, looking past Reiner. 'Manfred and our host.'

Reiner looked back. Manfred and Groff were hurrying towards them in robes and nightshirts, swords drawn, leading a handful of knights and house guards.

Udo shoved Reiner back and pulled his shirt closed. 'Father,' he cried. 'These men have assaulted me! Arrest them!'

'What is the meaning of this?' demanded Groff, bustling up. 'Manfred, aren't these your prisoners?'

'They are,' said Manfred. 'And I promise a reckoning when I discover who let them out.'

'My lords,' said Reiner quickly, 'there is greater evil afoot here than our petty truancy. Your house is infiltrated, Lord Groff. There is a witch on your grounds. She came to meet your son and just now leapt over the balcony. If you hurry–'

'What nonsense is this?' barked Groff. 'You try to draw attention from your crimes by accusing my son of witchcraft? Manfred, slay these insolent–'

'But 'tis the truth, my lord,' said Reiner. 'She has marked him. You have only to look at his...'

'Enough,' said Manfred. 'What are you doing out of quarters, and who let you out?'

'My lord,' said Franka, imploring. 'She is getting away.'

'Answer my question, curse you!'

Reiner ground his teeth. 'Here's your answer, y'damned fools.' And before anyone could stop him, he grabbed Udo's collar and ripped his nightshirt clean off.

Groff jumped forward, shouting and swinging his sword as Reiner dodged back. 'He assaults my son before my eyes! Stand, villain, I will...'

But Manfred was staring at Udo, who stood dumbly, with the unclean wound exposed for all to see. Groff followed his gaze and choked as he saw it.

'Groff,' Manfred said quietly. 'Lock up your son. He has been tainted and cannot be trusted.' He turned to one of his knights. 'Strieger, rouse the others and make ready. And lock the prisoners in the carriage. We ride within the hour.'

'You're not leaving?' exclaimed Lord Groff. 'Not now?'

'We must,' said Manfred. 'This was obviously an attempt to corrupt your house from the inside, but now that they know we know of their existence and their intent, they will try to stop us from warning Altdorf. We must be away before they surround us.'

'But they'll slaughter us!' cried Groff.

'Twenty knights would do nothing to change that outcome,' said Manfred, striding down the hall. 'We will pass Boecher's garrison on our way south. I will ask them to send reinforcements.'

Groff trotted after Manfred, mewling his distress, as Manfred's knights took Reiner and Franka in tow while Groff's guards did the same with Udo.

'But my lady doesn't wish to hurt anyone,' whined Udo. 'She wants us all to live only for pleasure.'

A HALF HOUR later, the Blackhearts were back in the cramped coach, bouncing and jolting uncomfortably as they raced down the rough track that led to the main Altdorf road. The thunder of Manfred's knights riding at full gallop drowned out all other sound and made conversation impossible.

A quarter of an hour out, there came a cry of 'Ware, bandits!' and the Blackhearts heard the knights draw steel.

Reiner and the others crowded to the slatted windows. On both sides of the road was a large, hastily-made camp. Bandits caught in the act of raising tents and starting fires were backing towards the woods as they gaped at Manfred's retinue. Others were snatching up weapons and preparing to fight. But when it became clear that the knights didn't intend to stop, some of the bandits waved their arms and called out after them.

'What they say?' asked Giano.

Pavel swallowed, nervous. 'They said, "Turn back".'

ONLY A FEW minutes later there was another cry from the knights, and the coach reined to a sudden, slewing stop. Reiner and his companions again pressed to the windows. It was impossible for them to see forward, but they heard anxious muttering from the knights, and on both sides of the coach the forest crowded too close to the road.

'It's blocked,' said a knight.

The forest was changed. Choking the tall pines and stout oaks were twisted vines, black of leaf, and heavy with purple, pendulous fruit, that gave off a cloying odour.

'The vines,' whispered Giano. 'They move.'

Reiner wanted to chide him for his foolish imaginings, but when he looked at the tendrils stretching toward the road he couldn't be sure the Tilean wasn't right.

'Dortman!' came Manfred's voice. 'See if a way can be cut.'

'Yes, my lord.'

Hooves trotted forward and the Blackhearts heard a thwacking of sword on vine. 'It is very thick, my lord. And I can see no end to–'

His words were cut off by a whistling thud, and a crash of armour hitting hard-packed dirt.

'Archers!' cried a knight, and suddenly the air was hissing with arrows. They thudded and rattled off the coach and the Blackhearts jerked back from the windows and dropped to the floor in a frightened pile.

'Fall back!' cried Manfred. 'Back to the castle!'

As the coach lurched around awkwardly, arrow heads splintered through the back wall. They glistened with green putrescence.

Hals hissed. 'Poison.'

THREE KNIGHTS DIED in the ambush, and two more were dying from cuts that barely bled, screaming in agony as poison burned through their veins. The coachman too had died. Klaus had manned the reins in their headlong flight to the castle.

Now Manfred conferred again with Groff in the courtyard while his knights stood by, and the Blackhearts waited with Klaus.

'How many men do you have?' asked Manfred.

'Sixteen knights, my lord,' said Groff. 'And forty foot, most with bows and spears, And I've pressed the staff into service, though they've to make do with pitchforks and fire-irons. Isn't much, I'm afraid.'

Reiner followed Manfred's gaze as the count surveyed the broken walls, where a collection of peasant conscripts, cooks and pot-boys made an inadequate defence. Groff's 'knights' – beardless youths pressed into armour after their older brothers had died in the recent conflict – guarded the widest, most easily breached gaps in the walls. They were spread very thin. Manfred looked grim. Reiner wanted to throw up.

'Pull half those boys off the wall,' Manfred said, 'and set them to tearing apart that scaffolding. Sharpen the ends of the poles and plant them at an angle before the gaps in the walls. Next, use the wood of the stables to make bonfires fifty yards from the walls in all directions so we may see the enemy before they're at our throats. Pour all the lamp oil you have into the moat and be ready to light it when they attempt to cross. It will not be enough. We will die, but at least we will take as many with us as...'

'My lord,' said Reiner. 'Might I make a suggestion?'

'You may not,' snapped Manfred.

'A suggestion that may allow us to win, my lord.'

Manfred turned on him, glaring. 'What is it?'

'The bandits, my lord. They are trained men, armed with bow and sword. If...'

'Absolutely not,' said Manfred. 'They are deserters. We cannot count on their loyalty, or their courage.'

'They are trapped just as we are, my lord. They have little choice but–'

'Silence! I have said no.' Manfred gestured at Klaus. 'Voorman, arm the prisoners and guard the north wall with them. You are their captain.'

Voorman saluted. Reiner snarled under his breath.

'Stiff-necked fool,' said Reiner, furious. 'His righteousness will get us killed.'

The Blackhearts sat on a pile of rubble in a gap in the north wall. The rubble spilled down into the moat, almost creating a bridge to the far side, but there were no blast marks to indicate that the wall had been brought down by artillery. Instead the rocks were cut with great gouges, as if from something impossibly strong had torn them down with its claws. The thought made Reiner shudder.

'Don't know why he cares,' said Hals. 'He don't have a problem using us, and I'll lay odds we're a nastier lot than them bandits.'

'Aye,' said Reiner. 'But he doesn't have the leash around their necks he has around ours.'

'We should just light out for Marienburg and leave him in the lurch,' said Pavel.

'The poison would reach us even there,' said Reiner. 'Even if we could escape the net of vines this sorceress has woven around us.'

'I no want to die,' said Giano. 'Not for foolishnesses.'

'Nor do I,' growled Hals.

'What are you lot jawing about?' said Klaus, from the tower of rubble above them where he stared vigilantly into the night.

'Nothing, sergeant,' said Reiner. 'Only plotting mutiny. That sort of thing.'

'None of your lip, Hetzau.'

Reiner looked below them where Groff's conscripts were wedging sharpened poles into the rubble. Beyond the moat, a wagon full of scrap lumber and brush was crossing the field as more conscripts built bonfires at regular intervals. He sighed. 'I think it's up to us to save ourselves, lads. What do you say we go find those bandits? It's a poor chance, but it's better than sitting here waiting for death.'

The others shot nervous glances up at Klaus, then leaned in.

'I'm in,' whispered Hals. 'If you've a way.'

'Won't Manfred unleash the poison?' asked Franka.

'Not until he knows we're gone,' said Reiner. 'And when the battle begins, he'll be too busy to check on us.'

'Or so you hope,' said Franka.

Reiner shrugged. 'We *might* die if we try. We will *certainly* die if we don't.'

Pavel swallowed. 'I'm in.'

'And I,' said Franka, at last.

'And me too also as well,' said Giano. 'But what we do about...?' He jerked his chin toward Klaus. 'If he tell on us, then...' He drew his finger across his windpipe.

'We'll have to dispose of him,' said Reiner.

'Kill him?' asked Franka uneasily.

Reiner smirked. 'No need to go so far. Plenty of places in all this mess to hide him until we get back.' He looked up. 'Hoy, sergeant. I seem to have cut myself. I don't think I can participate in forthcoming conflict.'

'Hey?' cried Klaus. 'Not participate? Damned if you won't. Let me see this cut of yours.'

Hals grinned and balled his fists as Klaus climbed down to them.

'STAND WHERE YOU are, dead men!'

The Blackhearts raised their arms as a score of spears and five times as many arrows pointed their way.

After binding and gagging Klaus and tucking him behind a fall of rubble, then crossing the moat with the help of a scaffolding ladder, they had stolen one of the wagons which had been building the bonfires, and rode towards the bandit camp. Now, having found it, Reiner was having second thoughts.

A huge, broad-chested villain with matted grey hair and a filthy beard stepped through the outlaws, a scrawny boy at his side who had the swaying gait and roving eye of an idiot.

'Brother,' said Reiner. 'We come...'

'Shut yer gob!' said the giant. He urged the boy forward. 'Sniff 'em out, Ludo. See if they've the taint.'

The boy wove to the Blackhearts' wagon like a dreamer and reached out limp hands. Reiner recoiled. Giano made the sign of Shallya, but they dared not move. The idiot sniffed and fondled them like a dog with hands, then with a whimpering sigh lay his head on Reiner's leg. At this the outlaws relaxed a little.

'Well,' said the giant. 'Yer not touched ones at any rate. What do y'want?'

'We come to ask a boon,' said Reiner, trying not flinch from the idiot's fawning. 'The touched ones, as you call them, mount an attack on Lord Groff's castle, which is grievously undermanned. He and Count Manfred need your help.'

The outlaws roared with laugher.

'Groff needs our help?' asked the leader. 'Groff, who hangs us for hunting the deer of the forest. And another jagger who's no doubt just as bad? Why should we help the likes of them?'

'Because the alternative is worse.'

'Yer mad. I'll dance a jig when Groff is dead.'

'Would you rather the touched ones ruled here in Groff's stead?' asked Reiner. 'Where would you be then?'

The outlaws were silent.

'Groff may hang you now and then,' Reiner continued, 'but at least that death comes quick. How many have you lost to the dark lady's seduction? Good men gone rotten, running naked in the woods, stealing your children to sacrifice to their daemon masters. Is that what you want?'

The outlaws muttered among themselves.

The giant crossed his arms. 'Nobody wants that. But we don't care to walk into a noose either. What's our guarantee that Groff, or this Manfred, won't turn around and hang us after we've saved their worthless hides?'

'I can offer you no guarantee,' said Reiner, 'but I have some sway with Manfred at least, and I will do what I can. Count Manfred is an honourable man. He may even reward you.'

Franka shot him a look at that. Reiner shrugged. He hoped it wasn't a lie, but he had to say something.

After a moment's conversation with his lieutenants, the big man turned back to Reiner. He nodded. 'Alright, silver-tongue, you've convinced us. Lead on.'

A RED GLOW above the trees as the Blackhearts and the bandits approached the castle gave evidence that battle had already been joined. The noise came next. The clash of steel on steel, the cries of men and the screams of horses. When they reached the fields, Manfred's bonfires illuminated a grim scene. The massed cultists – one couldn't call them an army – attacked the ruined castle from all sides, undisciplined but bloodthirsty. They had bridged the moat with tree-trunks, and pressed Groff's meagre forces and Manfred's few knights fiercely at every gap in the walls.

Hals gaped when he saw them. 'The madmen! What're they about?'

Franka giggled.

Reiner grimaced. 'Some things are better covered by darkness.'

The cultists, despite the cold of the spring night, were naked, their only covering swirls of purple and red, which looked more like smeared fruit and blood than paint. But, though naked, they were armed. Men and women, young and old, wielded swords and spears and clubs and bows, and though many seemed unlearned in their use, there were so many of them, and they were so frenzied in their unholy ecstasy, that even alone they might have carried the day.

Unfortunately they were not alone.

Leading them were troops of a different calibre altogether. Fighting at the wall were immense warriors in black and purple armour, while, further out, purple-clad bowmen cut down defenders with impossible accuracy. 'Northmens,' whispered Giano.

'We fought that sort at Brozny,' said Pavel, shuddering. 'Their swords had spikes in the hilts which pierced their own hands as they fought.'

Hals nodded. 'Pain was like drink to them. They loved it.'

'Well,' said Reiner. 'There ain't enough of them to take the castle without their followers. If we can drive them off we'll at least give Groff a fighting chance.'

Loche, the bandit leader, smiled. 'You leave that to me.'

LOCHE BROUGHT HIS men to the wood's edge and spread them out.

'You'll never hit them from here,' said Reiner, priming his handgun.

'No,' said the bandit. 'Groff's cut the woods back two bow shots for that very reason. We'll have to come up to the first hedgerow.'

He signalled his men forward and they and the Blackhearts advanced at a jog. Fortunately, the cultists, expecting no reinforcements, had posted no rear guard. The bandits reached the hedgerow with no alarm raised.

'Ready boys?' asked Loche.

The bandits put arrows to strings and flexed their bows. Franka did as well. Reiner and Giano raised their handguns. Hals and Pavel, pikemen with no skill with a bow, stood by with second guns, ready to reload while Reiner and Giano fired.

'Fire.'

With a thrum like a hundred guitars, the bandits loosed their shafts. Reiner's and Giano's guns cracked like snare drums. The arrows disappeared into the night, but reappeared as if by magic in the bare flesh of the cultists, who screamed and fell by the score.

It took the madmen a moment to understand their plight, and by then, more feathered shafts were cutting them down. A wave of panic overcame them and they ran in all directions, dropping their weapons. Reiner wondered that men so frenzied that they stormed a castle naked would lose courage under fire, but facing an enemy you can see is very different from invisible death speeding from the night.

'Don't waste arrows on the runners, boys,' said Loche. 'Let's circle and strike at another...'

But suddenly it was the bandits who were falling and screaming as feathered death whistled among them. Worse, even those only scratched were falling and writhing in agony, clawing at their wounds as if they were on fire.

Reiner looked at the arrows. They were the same that had riddled the coach on their flight from the ambush.

'The purple archers,' growled Loche, as his men pressed into the hedgerow. 'Concentrate yer fire, boys.'

Reiner sited along his gun barrel as the bandits nocked fresh arrows, but something behind the purple archers caught his eye. Below the north wall, a handful of Northmen, their black armour flashing red in the light of the bonfires, crossed the moat on a plank, and crept toward the postern gate. There were no troops to stop them. Most of the fighting was on the far side of the castle. If this little force could somehow break down the iron-bound door...

Reiner checked as the postern gate swung suddenly open. What treachery was this? Reiner squinted, trying to identify the shadowed figure who let the warriors into the castle. It was impossible. He cursed. The Blackhearts looked around.

Reiner pointed. 'Our efforts may be for naught. Someone lets the Northers in by the back gate.'

Loche looked up. 'Hey?' He peered forward.

Franka groaned. 'We'll have to stop them,' she said. 'Unless we wish to die in this cursed wood.'

Reiner glared at the girl. She was right, but the last thing he wanted to do was hunt through dark corridors after Northern marauders. They'd faced their like before, and nearly died of it. 'It'll take more than the five of us to bring those monsters down. Loche, we...'

'Not to worry,' said the big man. 'I ran from them once, and won my coward's brand for it. I'll not run again. Murgen, Aeloff, pick ten men and come with me.'

'Ten and five.' Hals swallowed, nervous. 'I hope it is enough.'

REINER AND LOCHE and their men entered the open postern gate and peered into the empty kitchen garden. Sounds of the battle echoed around the bulk of the keep, but it was quiet here.

'Where are they?' whispered Pavel.

'Shhh!' hissed Giano, cupping his ear.

They held their breath. From over the garden wall they heard a closing door.

The party started cautiously forward, but Franka slipped quickly ahead. 'I'll keep 'em in sight,' she said.

'Frank... Franz! Wait!' called Reiner, but the girl had already slipped into the garden.

'Come on,' growled Reiner. Damn the girl. He'd had enough of her foolish bravery.

As they entered the kitchen they saw Franka waving them towards the cellar stairs. They followed, and caught up with her at the door to the dungeon.

'What are they doing?' asked Reiner.

'Forcing a cell door,' replied Franka.

'Ah. Udo.'

The sound of steel biting into wood echoed down the narrow hall. Lantern light flickered from a door at the end. Franka started ahead. Reiner stopped her and went forward himself. She gave him a dirty look.

Reiner peered into a low-ceilinged guard room with stout oak doors on each wall. The Northmen had just broken the lock of one and were swinging it open. Udo stepped out and embraced the smallest warrior, who Reiner suddenly realized was the sorceress, dressed in black armour of barbaric splendour. Her six companions wore black and purple as well, and disturbingly, though they were as fiercely bearded as any Northman, were as rouged and painted as Marienberg streetwalkers. Udo's manservant, Stier, stood with them, holding a lantern. It was he, Reiner realized, who had let them in.

After receiving Udo's enthusiastic kiss, the sorceress stepped back. 'It is time, beloved, to seize your destiny. Are you ready?'

The boy nodded, unable to look away from her eyes. 'I am ready.'

The beauty removed a jewelled broach from her cloak. The pin was covered in black crust. 'Then take this and go to your father. A mere scratch and he will fall. When Manfred and his knights turn to assist him, prick as many of them as you can. We will be nearby, ready to protect you from any survivors.'

Udo hesitated, looking at the broach. 'Will it be... painful?'

'Worry not, my sweet,' said the witch, caressing his cheek. 'Your father will not suffer. In fact he will die of an excess of pleasure.'

She turned towards the door with Udo. Her men fell in around her. Reiner backed down the corridor to the waiting bandits.

'Bows out,' he hissed. 'Pin 'em inside the room.'

He and Giano shouldered their guns as the others raised bows. Two warriors filled the door, eclipsing the room behind them with their bulk.

'Fire!'

The warriors bellowed as the barrage battered them. Most of the arrows glanced off the ebony armour, but a few struck home, and Reiner and Giano's shots smashed through brains and bone. The Northmen fell. Behind them, Udo stared at an arrow sticking from his arm.

'I... I am... hit!'

The sorceress snatched him back into the room as one of her warriors leapt forward, sword drawn, and the last three backed up, protecting her.

'Fire!'

Reiner dropped his handgun and fired his pistol as the bandits' bowstrings thrummed in his ears. The massive warrior took the ball and a thicket of arrows full on. He kept coming, eyes blazing with ecstatic fury.

'Fire!'

But the Northman was on them before they could reload. Pavel and Hals shouldered Reiner and Giano aside and jammed their spears into the warrior's chest just as he reached their line.

The force of his charge drove them skidding back, but at last he stopped, blood erupting from his painted mouth as he fell.

'Die hard, don't they?' said Loche, swallowing.

'Aye,' agreed Hals.

The bandits stood with bows flexed, waiting for the rest of the warriors to spill from the room, but they didn't come.

'Don't advance,' said Reiner, reloading his pistol. 'We're in a better position here than fighting them in an open room.'

'No fear, Silvertongue,' said Loche. 'No fear.'

A noise returned their attention to the guard room. Reiner aimed his pistol, but no berserk warriors spewed forth. Instead, stepping into the hall was the sorceress, arms raised... and naked.

'Hold,' she said. 'I would parlay.'

Reiner and the Blackhearts and the bandits stared, open-mouthed, as she paced forward, her ripe curves swaying with every step. 'You wouldn't shoot an unarmed woman, would you?'

Reiner began forming a joke about the woman being better equipped than most armies, but it died in his throat as a delicious scent reached his nose. It wafted from her like musk – vanilla and jasmine – and drifted into his brain like fog.

He tried to tell the others to shoot her before she ensorcelled them all, but found himself unable to speak or raise his gun. The others seemed similarly affected.

The sorceress continued forward, smiling sweetly. 'In fact, you would kill any man who tried to harm me, wouldn't you? You would defend me to the death.'

She stopped in front of them. Reiner fought to free his mind, but her beauty was all-consuming. He couldn't tear his eyes away. He would do anything for her – die for her – if she would only take him into her arms. He heard bows and guns clatter to the floor as they fell from slack hands.

'You, boy,' she said, pointing at Franka. 'Your captain raised his gun to me. Will you protect me? Will you cut his throat?'

Franka nodded and wove towards him, drawing her dagger, glassy-eyed. Reiner raised his chin obligingly. It was true. He had tried to kill the sorceress. He deserved to die.

The woman smiled at Franka. 'Of course you will,' she said. 'No man can resist me.'

Franka stepped to Reiner, raising her dagger. The sorceress licked her lips, her eyes eager.

Suddenly, Franka spun and stabbed the dark beauty in the throat. She stared, open mouthed, more shocked at Franka's disobedience than at the dagger in her neck.

Franka smirked. 'Fortunately, I am no man.'

The woman fell, blood pouring down over her alabaster breasts. The spell was broken. Reiner shook his head. The others did the same, cursing and groaning.

'No! Beloved!'

Reiner looked up. Udo was racing at them, sword above his head. 'Murderers!' he cried. 'Savages!'

Behind him came the three remaining Northmen.

Reiner fired but missed. The bandits were still picking up their dropped weapons and got off only a few shots. Reiner drew frantically, and met Udo sword on sword as Pavel and Hals thrust their spears at the Northmen and the bandits rushed to back them up.

'Foul defiler!' shrieked Udo. 'To kill such a gentle–'

Reiner ran him through. The boy curled in on himself and fell. Reiner felt unexpectedly guilty. There was no glory in killing fools.

Around him, the Blackhearts and the bandits were attacking the Northmen with all their might, but the corridor was too narrow and too crowded to make a good swing, and the warriors' armour was too strong. The men could hardly dent it.

The warriors, on the other hand, swung mailed fists and axes held high on the haft. Reiner saw Pavel reeling back from a fist to the shoulder. An axe sheared off a bandit's arm at the elbow.

'Fall back!' shouted Reiner.

The Blackhearts and the bandits ran up the stairs, leaving their dead and wounded behind, the Northmen hot on their heels. A bandit went down, his skull crushed as he turned to flee.

The men emerged into a corridor and ran across it into the kitchen.

'The table!' cried Reiner. 'Block the door!'

But before they could drag the heavy oak board more than a step, the painted berserks were upon them again, and the bandits, in full rout now, ran out of the kitchen door. Reiner and the Blackhearts followed, inches ahead of the Northmen's blades.

As they burst into the yard, Reiner was momentarily afraid that they had run into more Northmen. The place was full of men in blood-caked armour. But then he recognized Manfred and Groff in the crowd. The knights raised a shout as the Northmen roared out of the kitchen, and a fierce battle erupted as the two sides slammed together.

Reiner was happy to observe from the sidelines, as were the bandits and the Blackhearts, who sucked in deep breaths and mopped at their wounds.

After it became certain that the knights would be victorious, Hals turned to Franka and gave her a curious look.

'What meant ye,' he asked, 'when y'said "fortunately you wasn't a man"?'

'What?' said Franka. Reiner swallowed nervously. The girl was turning bright red. 'I... er, I, well, I merely meant that I am but a boy.'

Hals scowled. 'When I was your age, laddie, I was twice as likely to fall for a woman's wiles.'

But before he could pursue the question further, the last of the Northmen fell and Manfred was striding their way, glaring.

'Hetzau, what is the meaning of this?'

'My lord,' said Reiner as he thought how to answer. 'We are most glad...'

'Never mind that, villain. I...'

Behind the count, Groff suddenly raised a cry. All turned. Servants were carrying Udo's body into the garden. Groff hurried forward and took the boy in his arms. 'Who has done this?' he cried. 'Who has slain my son?'

Manfred glared at Reiner. 'Hetzau?'

'My lord, you wound me.' said Reiner. He crossed to Groff and bowed. 'Lord Groff, the sorceress came to free your son so he might assassinate you, but he refused. They slew him for it.'

Groff looked at him with grateful eyes. 'He resisted then?'

'Yes, my lord. I only regret we were not able to stop them.'

Manfred gave Reiner a cool look. 'Regrettable indeed. And who are these gentlemen with you, who were yet not enough to save Lord Groff's son?'

Reiner swallowed. 'My lord, this is Captain Loche, leader of the noble woodsmen who helped you hold the castle this night.'

Loche touched his forelock to Manfred. 'M'lord.'

'A leader of bandits, you mean,' said Manfred, ignoring Loche. 'Who you recruited against my orders.'

'I thought your lordship might be pleased to find yourself alive at the outcome.'

'I am never pleased to be disobeyed.' He turned to the captain of his retinue. 'Strieger, arrest these outlaws, and all who have remained on the field.'

'What?' said Loche, surprised.

'But, my lord,' cried Reiner as the knights began to surround the surviving bandits. 'They have saved your life. You must admit that. You would be dead if not for their help.'

'That may be,' said Manfred, 'but certainly they aided us not out of any loyalty to the Empire, but only to save their own skins. They are still outlaws. They must still hang.'

'Hang? My lord!' Reiner was sweating now. 'My lord, it took all my gifts to convince these men to come to your aid. I promised them that you would be grateful – that you might even reward them for their service.'

Manfred raised an eyebrow. 'Ah. Then they have no one to blame for their fate but you, who promised things it was beyond your power to grant.' He motioned to Strieger. 'Take them. In these troubled times the laws of the Empire must be firmly upheld.'

As the knights took the bandits in tow, Loche shot a look at Reiner that pierced him to his soul. 'Y'dirty liar,' he rasped. 'I hope y'rot.' He spat on Reiner's boots. The knights jerked him forward and marched the bandits out of the garden.

Reiner hung his head, more ashamed than he'd ever been. He felt like a trained rat who had led his wild brethren into a trap. He wanted to tear Manfred's throat out, but – more shame – he was too much of a coward. He valued his life too much.

Franka put a hand on his arm. It didn't help.

THE NEXT MORNING the Blackhearts were locked back into their coach and Manfred and his knights continued south to Altdorf. As they rode from Groff's castle, Reiner and the others peered back through the slotted windows. Hanging from the battlements were scores of bandits and cultists, mixed together as if the hangmen had made no distinction between them – rotting fruit hanging from a stone tree.

Reiner's heart clenched when he saw Loche's massive body swaying among them. He closed his eyes, then sank back in his seat. 'And that, my lads,' he sighed, 'is fair warning of how Lord Valdenheim will deal with us when he no longer finds us useful.'

Pavel nodded. 'The swine.'

Giano shook his head. 'We dead soldiers, hey?'

'There must be a way out,' said Franka.

'But how?' asked Hals.

And so the endless conversation began again, all the way to Altdorf.

THE BROKEN LANCE

ONE
An Untested Tool

THE HAMMER BRANDS were gone. The shameful scars that had been burnt into their flesh had been removed at last by a sorcery so painful it made the original branding a pleasant memory by comparison. The skin of their hands was clean, unblemished, as if the red iron had never touched it. But the blood beneath that skin, that was another story.

Reiner Hetsau and his convict companions; the pikemen Hals Kiir and Pavel Voss, the Tilean crossbowman Giano Ostini, and Franka Shoentag, the dark-haired archer who only Reiner knew was not the boy she pretended to be, had been given the deserter's brand by Baron Albrecht Valdenheim as a way to force them to help him betray his brother, Count Manfred Valdenheim. He had promised them that when their service to him was done, he would remove the brands. But after they learned that he intended to betray them as well as his brother, they had helped Manfred instead, in hopes that he would make good on Albrecht's promise.

And he had. Manfred had been so impressed by the unorthodox ways in which Reiner and his companions had escaped their predicaments, by their ability to adapt and survive in any situation, and by their utter disregard for what respectable men might call right and wrong, that he had decided to make them agents of the Empire whether they wished it or not. The country, he said, had need of blackhearts who would not flinch at dishonourable duty. So he had ordered his personal sorcerer to remove the brands – which marked them deserters who could be shot on sight, and therefore useless as spies – and instead bound them to him with a much more subtle leash.

He had poisoned their blood.

It was a latent poison, which would lie dormant within them unless they attempted to leave Manfred's service or betray him. Then a spell could be read that would wake the poison and kill them wherever they might run, within the Empire or beyond.

There might be some, Reiner thought, as he folded his compact frame into the bay of a mullioned dormer window and looked out over the moonlit rooftops of Altdorf, who would be happy with the arrangement. Manfred had installed them in his townhouse and given them the run of the place, allowing them to read in the library and practise at swords in the garden, and had provided them with warm beds, fine food and obsequious servants – a soft life in these days of hardship and war, when many in the Empire were maimed and starving and hadn't a roof over their heads to call their own – but Reiner hated it.

The townhouse might be the epitome of comfort, but it was still a prison. Manfred wanted their existence kept a secret, so they were not allowed beyond its walls. It tortured Reiner that Altdorf was just outside and he couldn't reach it. The brothels and gambling halls, the dog-pits and theatres he called home, were within walking distance – on some nights he could hear singing and laughing and perhaps even the rattle of dice. But he couldn't get to them. They might as well have been in Lustria. It was agony.

Not that the others didn't suffer as well. When Manfred had recruited them, he had promised the Blackhearts action – secret missions, assassinations, kidnappings – but for the last two months they had done nothing but sit, waiting for orders that never came, and it was driving them stir crazy. It wasn't that Reiner relished the thought of risking life and limb for the Empire that had falsely branded him sorcerer and traitor, but endlessly waiting to be sent to one's death was a misery all its own – an edgy, endless boredom which set him and his companions at each other's throats. Casual conversations suddenly erupted into shouting matches, or broke off into sullen silences. Though he liked them all, Reiner's companions' tics and mannerisms, which he had once found amusing, now grated like brick on flesh: Hals's incessant barbs and jokes, Pavel's little clearing of the throat before he asked a question, Giano's moaning about how everything was better in Tilea, Franka's...

Well, it was Franka that was the real problem, wasn't it? Reiner had made a terrible mistake falling for the girl. He hadn't thought it would happen. After he had gotten over the shock of learning her true sex he hadn't given her a second thought. She wasn't really his sort – a wiry hoyden with hair shorter than his own – nothing like the laughing, lusty harlots he usually favoured, with painted lips and voluptuous hips. But that day on the crag above Nordbergbusche, when together they had killed Albrecht, they had exchanged a look that had awakened a flame of desire in him he knew could only be quenched in her arms. The trouble was, though she had admitted to him that she shared his passion, had in fact kissed him once with a fervour that had nearly carried them both away, she refused to consummate their lust. She...

The latch in the door behind him clicked. Reiner turned from the window as Franka entered the room, candle in hand. He held his breath. She closed the door, set the candle on a dresser, and began unlacing her jerkin.

'Slowly, beloved,' said Reiner, twirling his moustaches like a stage villain. ''Tis too nice a job to rush.'

Franka gasped, covering herself, then let out an annoyed breath when she realized who was sitting in the window seat. 'Reiner. How did you get in here?'

'Klaus was asleep again, as usual.'

'And so should you be.'

Reiner grinned. 'An excellent idea. Turn down the covers and let's to bed.'

Franka sighed and sat on a divan. 'Must you continue to persist?'

'Must you continue to resist?'

'The year of my vow is not yet up. I still mourn for Yarl.'

Reiner groaned. 'Is it still two months?'

'Three.'

'Three!'

'Only two days have passed since you last asked.'

'It feels like two years.' He stood and began to pace. 'Beloved, we could be dead in three months! Sigmar knows what madness Manfred has in store for us. He could send us to Ulthuan for all we know.'

'A man of honour would not press me on this,' said Franka, tight-lipped.

'Have I ever said I was a man of honour?' He sat on the divan beside her. 'Franka. There is a reason for a soldier's loose morals. He knows every day that he might die tomorrow, and therefore lives each night as if it were his last. You are a soldier now. You know this. You must seize what stands before you before Morr snatches it from your grasp forever.'

Franka rolled her eyes as he opened his arms in invitation. 'You make a compelling argument, captain, but unfortunately I have honour – or at least stubborn pride – enough for the both of us, and so...'

Reiner dropped his arms. 'Very well, very well. I will retire. But could you not at least grant me a kiss to dream on?'

Franka chuckled. 'And have you take advantage as always?'

'On my honour, beloved...'

'Did you not just say you had no honour?'

'I... er, yes, I suppose I did.' Reiner sighed and stood. 'Once again you defeat me, lady. But one day...' He shrugged and stepped to the door.

'Reiner.'

Reiner turned. Franka was beside him. She stretched up on her tiptoes and kissed him lightly on the lips. 'Now go to bed.'

'Torturer,' he said, then turned the latch and left.

UNSURPRISINGLY, REINER FOUND it difficult to sleep, which was unfortunate, for he was woken much too early the next morning. He had been dreaming of Franka unlacing her jerkin and pulling off her shirt, and it was a rude shock to open his eyes to the ugly face of dear old Klaus, the guard in charge of watching over him and his companions, glaring down at him.

'Get yer boots on, y'lazy slug,' Klaus barked, kicking Reiner's four-poster.

'Piss off.' Reiner pulled the covers over his head. 'I was with a lady.'

'None of your sauce!' Klaus kicked the bed again. 'His lordship requests yer presence in the yard, on the double.'

Reiner poked an eye above the blanket. 'Manfred's back?' He yawned and sat up, rubbing the sleep from his eyes. 'Thought he'd forgotten about us.'

'Manfred never forgets nothing,' said Klaus. 'You'd do well to remember it.'

'WHAT HAPPENINGS?' ASKED Giano as the Blackhearts shuffled sleepily down the curving mahogany staircase behind Reiner and Klaus to the townhouse's marble-floored entryway. The curly haired Tilean was still doing up his breeches.

'No idea,' said Reiner. Klaus motioned them through a service door and they entered the kitchen.

'It's something different, though,' said Pavel. He stole a pastry from a tray and stuffed it in his mouth. 'Makes a change,' he said, spitting crumbs.

Reiner chuckled at the sight. The pikeman was as ugly as a wet rat, and utterly unconcerned about it: long necked and scrawny, with a patch over his lost left eye and a scarred mouth that was missing three front teeth.

'Probably just sword drills again,' said Hals, Pavel's bald, burly, red bearded brother-in-arms. 'Or worse, horsemanship.'

Klaus opened the kitchen door and they stepped into the gravelled stable yard. 'Maybe not,' said Franka. 'Look at that.'

Reiner and the others looked ahead. A coach with louvred windows sat just inside the back gate. Two guards stood before it. The Blackhearts groaned.

'Not the coach again,' said Hals.

'We'd all kill each other before we got where we were going,' agreed Pavel.

Klaus stopped in the centre of the yard and called them to attention. They straightened, but only half-heartedly. Months of enforced familiarity with him had bred contempt for his authority. They waited. The morning fog hid the world beyond the stone walls in a pearly embrace, and though it was summer, the sun was not yet high enough in the sky to chase the night's chill away. Reiner shivered and wished he had thought to don his cloak. His stomach growled. He had become used to a regular breakfast.

After a quarter of an hour, the gate to the garden opened and Count Manfred stepped into the yard. Tall and broad, with silver in his hair and beard, the count looked the part of a kind, wise king out of legend, but Reiner knew better. Manfred might be wise, but he was hard as flint. A bright-eyed young corporal in the uniform of a lancer followed in his wake.

Manfred nodded curtly to the Blackhearts. 'Klaus, open the coach, then retire to the gate with Moegen and Valch.'

'M'lord?' said Klaus. 'I wouldn't trust these villains near yer lordship...'

'Obey my orders, Klaus. I am perfectly safe.'

Klaus saluted reluctantly and crossed to the coach. He took a key from one of the guards and unlocked it. Reiner expected Manfred to order them into it, but when Klaus opened the door, four men ducked out and stepped down to the gravel. The Blackhearts exchanged uneasy glances. The men were filthy, unshaved, and half starved, and wore the remains of military uniforms.

'Fall in,' said Manfred.

The four men shambled over and lined up next to the Blackhearts, squaring their shoulders reflexively.

Manfred faced the Blackhearts. 'We have work for you at last,' he said, then sighed. 'There have actually been many jobs on which we would have liked to have used you. There is much turmoil in Altdorf at the moment. Much finger pointing over our losses in the recent conflict, and much clamouring for changes at the top – particularly among the younger barons. It would have been nice to have used you to "calm" some of the more strident voices, but we were hesitant to try an untested tool so close to home where it might fly back into our faces.' He clasped his hands behind his back. 'Now a perfect test has presented itself. Of utmost importance to the well-being of the Empire, but far enough away that you will not embarrass us if you fail.'

'Your confidence in us is inspiring, m'lord,' said Reiner wryly.

'Be thankful I have any at all after your insubordination at Groffholt.'

'Did you not recruit us particularly for our penchant for insubordination, m'lord?' asked Reiner.

'Enough,' said Manfred, and though he didn't raise his voice, Reiner did not feel inclined to push his insolence any further.

'Listen well,' said Manfred. 'For I will not repeat these orders and they will not be written down.' He cleared his throat and looked them all in the eye, then began. 'Deep in the Black Mountains is an Empire fort which guards an isolated pass and protects a nearby gold mine. The mine helps the Empire pay for reconstruction and defence in these troubled times, but in the last few months its output has slowed to a trickle, and we have not received from the fort satisfactory answers to our queries. I sent a courier two months ago. He has not returned. I do not know what has befallen him.' Manfred frowned. 'All that is certain is that the fort is still in Imperial hands, for an agent of mine saw recruitment notices for the fort's regiment going up in Averheim not a week ago.' He looked at Reiner. 'This recruitment is your opportunity. You are to sign on, install yourselves in the fort, discover what is occurring, and if it is treasonous, stop it.'

'You have reason to suspect treason?'

'It is possible,' said Manfred. 'The fort's commander, General Broder Gutzmann, is rumoured to be angry that he was kept in the south when the fate of the Empire was being decided in the north. He may have become angry enough to do something rash.'

'And if he has?'

Manfred hesitated, then spoke. 'If there is a traitor in the fort, he must be "removed", no matter who he is. But know that Gutzmann is an excellent general and loved by his men. They are fiercely loyal. If it is he you must remove, it should look like an accident. If his men discovered that he was the victim of foul play, they would revolt, and the Empire is stretched too thin now to lose an entire garrison.'

'Pardon, m'lord,' said Reiner, 'but I don't understand. If Gutzmann is such an excellent general, why not bring him north and let him hunt Kurgan like he wants? Would that not stop his grumbling?'

Manfred sighed. 'I cannot. There are some in Altdorf who feel that Gutzmann is too good a general, that if he won great victories in the north, he might begin to have ambitions – that, er, he might seek to be more than a leader of soldiers.'

'Ah,' said Reiner. 'So he was kept in the south on purpose. He has reason to be angry.'

Manfred scowled. 'No "reason" can excuse stealing from the Emperor. If he is guilty, he must be stopped. Do you all understand your orders?'

The Blackhearts nodded, as did the newcomers.

Manfred glanced at the new men, then back to the Blackhearts. 'This will be a difficult mission, and it was felt you should be returned to full strength. Therefore we have found you some new recruits. These four men will be under your command, Hetsau. Corporal Karelinus Eberhart,' he indicated the young junior officer who stood to his left, 'will also obey your orders, but is answerable only to me. He is my eyes and ears, and will report to me at the end of this venture on...' He paused, then smirked. 'On how true and useful a tool you and your Blackhearts are. His report will determine whether we will be able to employ you in the future, and consequently, whether we will suffer you to live henceforth. Do you understand me?'

Reiner nodded. 'Yes my lord. Perfectly.' He shot a look at Corporal Eberhart, who was gaping at Manfred with wide blue eyes. Reiner chuckled. The poor lad didn't expect Manfred to be so open about his role in the enterprise. He was unused to the count's bluntness. Reiner was not. Manfred was not accustomed to hiding his cannon behind roses.

'Are these men subject to the same constraints as we, m'lord?' asked Reiner, indicating the four new recruits. 'Have they been...'

'Yes, captain,' said Manfred. 'They have agreed to the same conditions. Their blood bears the same taint as your own.' He laughed. 'They are now your brothers. Blackhearts one and all!'

TWO
We Are All Villains Here

NOT TWO HOURS after Manfred gave them their orders, the Blackhearts left Altdorf for Averheim, largest city of the south-eastern province of Averland, and the closest to the Black Mountains and the pass General Gutzmann's fort guarded. The count, with his customary thoroughness, had arranged everything: fresh clothes and weapons for the new men, horses for those who rode well, a cart for the others. The cart also carried the company's equipment: weapons, armour, cooking kit, tents, blankets and so on. It looked to be a much more comfortable journey than when last they had been recruited into skulduggery, thought Reiner. Then they had crept into enemy territory during a freezing Ostland spring, and packed only what they could carry on their backs. Now they travelled openly through the heart of the Empire, with inns and towns at every stage. Perhaps this was a good omen. Perhaps this foretold an easy duty. This job certainly didn't seem as difficult as the last.

Reiner breathed deep as they took the south road out of Altdorf and began riding though the farms and freeholds that surrounded the city. What a treat to be out of doors again. Just the passing of the scenery was thrilling to him. The simple act of moving was such a wonderful feeling that for a moment he almost felt free.

So enthralled was he by these novel sensations that it wasn't until Altdorf's walls were fading into the morning haze behind them and the dark line of the Drakwald was rising ahead that he noticed that no one had yet spoken. An awkward silence hung about the party, the old Blackhearts and new eyeing each other uneasily. Reiner sighed. This wouldn't do.

'Now, sir,' he said, turning to the new man who rode behind him to his right, a slight fellow with a mushroom cap of mousey brown hair above a sad, sharp face. 'How did you come to be in this sorry fix?'

'Hey?' said the man, startled. 'Why pick on me? What do y'need to know for?'

Reiner chuckled with as much good humour as he could muster. 'Well sir, If I'm to lead you, it would seem advisable to know something of you. And don't worry that you will shock us. We are all villains here, aren't we, lads?' He turned to each of his old companions in turn. 'Pavel and Hals killed their captain when he proved incompetent.'

'We didn't, though,' said Pavel.

'Kurgan killed him,' said Hals.

They both laughed darkly.

'Franz murdered his tent mate for making unwanted advances.'

Franka blushed.

'Giano sold guns to the Kossars.'

'Who know is crime?' asked Giano, turning up his palms.

'And I,' said Reiner, putting his hand to his chest, 'am charged with sorcery and the murder of a clergywoman.' He grinned at the man, who stared around at them all, blinking. 'So you see, you're in good company.'

The man shrugged, suddenly shy. 'I… My name is Abel Halstieg. I am, er, I was, quartermaster for Lord Belhem's Cannon. They claim I bought poor quality powder and pocketed the savings, thereby causing the destruction of the unit.'

'How so?' asked Reiner.

'Er, the guns misfired and our position was overrun. But it rained that day. The powder may have become damp.'

'And since it was cheap powder in the first place…' drawled Pavel from the cart.

'It wasn't cheap powder!' insisted the quartermaster.

'Of course it wasn't,' said Reiner, soothing. 'So, can you aim and fire a field piece then?'

Abel hesitated. 'With help. If pressed. But my talents fall more on the supply side.'

'So it appears,' said Reiner, and turned away before Abel could contest the inference. 'And you, sir?' he asked the other mounted newcomer, a sturdy, stone-faced veteran with long, dark hair pulled back into a braided queue.

The man looked briefly at Reiner, then returned his gaze to his horse's neck, where it had been since the journey's beginning. His brows were so heavy that his eyes remained in shadow despite the brightness of the day. 'I took money to kill a man.'

The man's brevity took Reiner off guard. He laughed. 'What? No protestation of innocence? No extenuating circumstances?'

'I am guilty.'

Reiner blinked. 'Ah. Er. Well. Will you tell me your name, then? And in what capacity you served the Empire?'

There was a long pause, but at last the man spoke. 'Jergen Rohmner. Master-at-arms.'

'An instructor of the sword?' asked Reiner. 'You must be quite the blade.'

Rohmner did not reply.

Reiner shrugged. 'Well, welcome to our company, captain.' He turned to the cart, where the other two new recruits sat amongst the gear. 'And you, laddie,' he said, addressing a smiling, gangly archer with a thatch of red hair and jug ears that stuck from his head like flags. 'How come you here?'

The boy laughed. 'Heh. I killed a man too. Nobody had to pay me for it, though.' He shied a pebble at a passing fence post, startling a pair of crows. 'Me and my mates was posted in some muddy Kiss-leff berg, drinkin' their cow piss liquor, when this fool of an Ostland pike bumps me elbow and spills me drink. So I...'

Reiner rolled his eyes. It was a very old story. 'So you and your mates hit him a little too hard and he had the bad manners to die.'

'Naw, naw,' said the boy, grinning. 'Better'n that. I followed him back to his billet, trussed him up in his bedroll, and set his tent afire.' He laughed, delighted. 'Squealed like a skinned hog afore he died.'

There was silence as the rest of the company stared at the youth, who carried on skimming pebbles into the wheat field on their left, oblivious.

At last Reiner cleared his throat. 'Er, what's your name, lad?'

'Dag,' said the boy. 'Dag Mueller.'

'Well, Dag. Thank you for that illuminating story.'

'Aye, captain. My pleasure.'

Reiner shivered, then turned to the last of the new recruits, a round bellied old veteran with apple cheeks and extravagant moustaches, gone a little grey. 'How about you, sir. What's your tale of woe?'

'Not a patch on the last, I assure you, captain,' said the man with a sidelong glance at Dag. 'My name is Helgertkrug Steingesser, but ye may call me Gert. The brass named me deserter and instigator, and the charge fits well enough, I suppose.' He sighed, but his eyes twinkled. 'Y'see, there was a girl, a big, fine girl. Lived on a farm near where I was billeted in Kislev with the Talabheim City crossbowmen. Her man had died in the war. In fact, all the men of her village had died. It was a village of women. Lonely women. Big, fine women. And it came to me, y'see. The land was fertile, the country beautiful. A man could do worse, I said to myself, than settle down here and raise big, fine children.' He leaned back against their baggage, chuckling. 'And maybe I said it to more than myself, for when I decided to go, a score of my lads came with me, to fill in, so to speak, for the women's dead husbands. Unfortunately, the Empire didn't feel it were done with us. There were a battle the next day and we was missed. When the brass caught us up they accused us of running 'cause we was afraid. I take exception to that. We wasn't afraid. We was... er, eager for companionship.'

The Blackhearts laughed, partly because it was a funny story, but mostly out of relief that it wasn't another horrible one.

Reiner grinned. 'Welcome, Gert. And if y'find another village of lonely women on our way, don't keep it to yourself, hey?'

Franka shot Reiner a sharp look, but the rest laughed. Reiner turned at last to the fresh-faced blond corporal, Karelinus, who rode at his side. 'And you, corporal, how did you come to be minder for such a pack of reprobates? In Manfred's black book, are you?'

'Eh?' said Karel. He had been staring at Dag, and seemed to find it hard to turn away. 'Er. Actually, no. I, er, I volunteered.'

Reiner almost choked. 'You...?'

'Oh yes,' he said, turning on his horse to face the others. 'You see, I am betrothed, or at least I would be betrothed if it were possible, to Count Manfred's daughter, Rowena. But a count's daughter can't very well marry a lowly lance corporal. I must be a knight at least, mustn't I? Unfortunately, my father has had some reverses lately, and wasn't able to pay the tithe to win me a place in one of the knightly orders.' He grimaced. 'I'm afraid I made a bit of an ass of myself when I found I couldn't get in, cursing my fate and vowing to Rowena that I would win my colours on the battlefield or die trying.' He brightened. 'But then m'lord Manfred very helpfully suggested that I take this assignment. He promised me there would be plenty of opportunities to achieve my vow before we returned. That it was just the thing. A real gentleman, Count Manfred. Not every father would do as much for his daughter's betrothed.'

Reiner coughed convulsively, and he could hear Pavel and Hals mumphing with suppressed laughter. Even Franka, who knew well how to hide her thoughts, was having difficulty suppressing a smile.

'I beg your pardon, corporal,' said Reiner when he had recovered. 'A touch of congestion. Very decent indeed of the count to give you such a plum assignment. He must think very highly of you. Very highly indeed.'

They rode on through the rolling farmland, and the ice having been broken, the conversation began to flow at last. Hals, Pavel and Giano traded war stories with the crossbowman Gert, while Reiner and Franka listened with bemused wonder as young Karel prattled on about his close relationship with Count Manfred and how nice everyone was in Altdorf. Abel, the artillery quartermaster, hung at the edge of their conversation, trying to turn it to questions about their arrangement with Manfred and what was expected of them. The swordsman Jergen rode on in silence, his eyes never lifting from his saddle bow, while on the cart, Dag, the lanky archer, out of pebbles, lay on his back and watched the clouds sail by as if he hadn't a care in the world.

* * *

THEY CAMPED IN the woods that night, for though there were inns aplenty along the way, Manfred had forbidden them to sleep under a roof on their journey. He wanted them to appear hungry dogs of war when they arrived in Averheim, desperate to sign on to service as far from the centre of the Empire as possible, and hungry dogs hadn't the gelt to buy a cot by the fire.

The next day passed much as the first, riding at a quick but not punishing pace through league after league of thick oak forest, the gloom of which pressed in on them and stifled their conversation. They passed fewer travellers here; a heavily guarded train of merchants travelling together for protection, a company of knights trotting by double file, pennons flying from their lance tips, a group of Sigmarite fanatics on pilgrimage from Nuln to Altdorf and travelling every inch of the journey on their bare knees. It seemed to Reiner proof of Sigmar's grace that the mad holy men hadn't yet been set upon by the horrors that lurked in the trees.

On the third day, just as the sun was beginning to burn away the morning haze, they at last came out of the Drakwald and into the Reikland, the heartland of the Empire, an endless plain cross-hatched with fields and orchards. After so long in the forest, it was a beautiful verdant sight. But the initial impression of fertile plenty was proved an illusion when they got closer. The fields were green, yes, but as often green with weeds as with crops. The Empire had had a great army to feed these last few years, and fields that in happier times had been allowed to lie fallow to replenish the soil had been exhausted as the farmers tried to meet the demand for fodder. The crops that did grow were meagre and stunted, and the pigsties and cow pastures the Blackhearts passed were nearly unpopulated.

It was all so fragile, thought Reiner. And so precious. For if this died, if the fields withered and the cattle became skin and bones, then the Empire died. The knightly orders might prate about blood and steel and the Drakwald being the hard oaken soul of the Empire, but the knights ate beef and bread and cabbage, not acorns and squirrels, and no one ever fought to defend a forest as fiercely as a farmer defended his farm.

LATE THAT AFTERNOON they travelled along a stretch of road with pear orchards on both sides. The pears weren't quite ripe, it being only the middle of summer, but in the rays of the westering sun their rosy blush was enticing. Reiner felt his stomach growling.

On the cart, Dag sat up, sniffing. 'Pears,' he said. And without another word, he hopped down and started trotting towards the trees.

Reiner grunted, annoyed. 'We've plenty of fodder,' he said. 'No need to forage.'

'I only want one or two.' Dag said, and ducked through the first rank of trees.

Reiner sighed.

'Not much on obeyin' orders,' said Hals.

'Well, he's mad, ain't he?' said Pavel.

Gert harrumphed. 'T'ain't no excuse.'

A few moments later barking erupted from the orchard. The company looked up and saw Dag laughing and running through the trees, arms full of pears, with a big farm dog at his heels. He stumbled over a root and the dog caught him, sinking its teeth into his calf.

Dag fell, crying out and dropping the pears. He rolled onto his back, and before Reiner knew what he meant to do, drew his dagger and jabbed the dog in the belly. It squealed and recoiled, but Dag tackled it and held it down, stabbing it repeatedly in the eyes and neck.

'Sigmar!' choked Karel. 'What's he doing?'

'Mueller!' bellowed Reiner. 'Stop!'

The others cried out too, but before they could dismount, their cries were echoed.

'Hie, ye brigand!' came a voice. 'What do ye to my dog?'

Six farm hands ran out of the trees, armed with pitchforks and clubs, and surrounded the archer. There was a boy with them, who stared blankly at the dead dog. A farmhand clubbed Dag across the back.

Reiner cursed. 'Come on, then.' He dismounted and jogged into the orchard with the others following. 'Hoy!' he shouted.

The combatants didn't heed him. Dag was up, a mad grin splitting his face as he squared up to the farmhand who had struck him. 'And what was that for, yokel?' He held his bloody dagger in a loose grip.

'For? Why, ye killed my dog, ye madman!'

'Then yer in need of killin' as well, for letting him bite.' And before the farmhand could answer, Dag flicked blood at his eyes. The man flinched, and Dag lunged, slashing.

'Stand down, Mueller!' screamed Reiner. 'Stand down!'

The farmhand reeled back, clutching a bleeding shoulder, but as Dag followed, the other farmhands rushed in, swinging their bludgeons. Reiner sprinted forward. Damn the boy! There would be murder done, and Manfred's job botched before it began.

There was a scrape of steel beside him and Jergen blurred past. He hauled Dag out of the ring of farmhands with one hand and swung his sword in a circle with the other. Pitchfork tines and the tips of staves dropped to the grass around him, lopped off like dandelion heads. He ended on guard, Dag hurled behind him, and the point of his longsword touched the wounded farmhand's neck. The man froze, as did his companions, staring at their truncated weapons.

Reiner and the others stared as well, stunned by Jergen's speed, strength and terrifying precision.

'Well... well done, Rohmner,' said Reiner, swallowing. 'Now stand down, all. We'll have no more dramatics if you please. I...'

'Who put his hands on me?' cried Dag, bouncing up. 'No man puts his hands on me and lives!'

'Enough, Mueller!' shouted Reiner, turning on him. 'Shut your fool mouth.'

Dag glared at Reiner, eyes blazing, but Reiner, more by instinct than intent, glared right back, forcing himself not to blink or look away. Dag's anger seemed to surge. He growled in his throat and raised his dagger, but after a long moment, he shrugged and laughed.

'Sorry, captain,' he said. 'Ain't mad at you.' He sneered at the farmhands over his shoulder. ''Tis these gape-gobbed yokels who can't keep their curs to heel that...'

'Ye were stealin' our pears, ye thievin' murderer!' cried the farmhand Dag had wounded – though he didn't move, for Jergen's blade was still at his throat. 'T'ain't bad enough we've to send all our crops north to feed Karl-Franz's army – for starvation prices, too – now ye uniformed bandits come south to snatch the food from our mouths?'

'And kill our dogs,' said another.

'Snatch the food from yer mouth?' retorted Hals. 'Look at all the plenty around ye. Livin' in luxury while we been freezing our fundaments off in a Kislev snow bank, protecting yer worthless hide. There's gratitude for you.'

Reiner's men, who had up to this point sided with the farmhands against Dag, were beginning to range behind Hals.

'And why didn't you pick up a pike?' asked Pavel.

'Aye,' said Abel from behind him. 'Cowards.'

'Because someone had to stay behind and feed ye, y'ass!'

The two sides began to edge forward, drawing daggers and hefting clubs.

'Hold, curse it! Hold! All of you!' cried Reiner. 'Let us not all go mad. There's been enough blood shed already. Adding to it won't solve anything.'

'But he killed my dog,' said the farmhand. 'He cut me!'

'Aye,' growled Hals. 'So take it up with him. It weren't nothing to do with Captain Reiner and...'

'It is to do with me,' said Reiner. 'For, much as I could wish otherwise, I am your captain, and if I cannot control you then I am to blame.'

'Like him and his dog,' said Dag, triumphant. 'If he'd have kept him to heel...'

Reiner spun on him. 'His dog was doing its job. You, you stone skull, were disobeying orders. You were in the wrong, do you understand me?'

Dag frowned for a moment, looking from Reiner to the farmhands and back, then seemingly light dawned. He grinned and gave Reiner a broad wink. 'Oh aye, captain. I understand ye perfectly. I've been bad. Very bad. And I won't do it again.'

Reiner groaned. It was like talking to a post. 'I shall make certain of it.' He turned back to the farmhands. 'So, since I am to blame, I will be the one to make amends. Now, I know no one can put a price on the loyalty of a dog or the pain of a wound, but gold is all I have and not much of that, I'm afraid. So what will you ask in recompense?'

REINER WAS WORRIED that there would be difficulties over who would tent with whom that night, since he was sure no one would want to sleep next to Dag, but surprisingly, Jergen volunteered – with a monosyllabic grunt – and the rest of the company breathed a sigh of relief.

Reiner and Franka tented together; a boon for Franka, who would therefore not have to guard the secret of her sex both night and day, but torture to Reiner, who would have to endure her nearness without being able to touch or kiss her.

As they curled up in their separate bedrolls Franka rose up on her elbow. 'Reiner.'

He looked up when she didn't continue. 'Aye?'

She sighed. 'You know I'm not one to advocate murder in cold blood, but… but this boy is dangerous.'

'Aye,' said Reiner. 'But I cannot.'

'But why not? He's mad. He'll kill someone.'

'Is he mad?' asked Reiner.

Franka raised an eyebrow. 'What do you mean?'

Reiner leaned in and lowered his voice. 'Do you think Manfred is a fool?'

'What has that got to do with it?'

'Manfred admitted as we left that this job was a test, aye?'

'Aye.'

'So, if you were Manfred, and you wanted to know what we did, how I led, if we betrayed you or the Empire, is Karelinus Eberhart the man you would ask to bring you your report?'

Franka frowned for a moment, then a look of comprehension spread over her face. 'You think there is a spy.'

'There must be. Karel can't be anything but a decoy. He's a babe in the woods. One of the others must be working for Manfred as well.'

'And you think it is Dag? You think he only pretends to be mad?'

'No. But I can't be certain. It could be any of them. And if it is him and word gets back to Manfred that I killed him…'

'He'll think you discovered his spy and killed him,' said Franka, then sucked in a sharp breath. 'Any of them? We'll have to watch our tongues.'

'Aye,' said Reiner. 'No talk of running away, or killing Manfred, or flushing the poison from our veins.'

Franka groaned. 'We must find out who it is, and quickly.'

Reiner nodded. 'Aye.'

They stared into the dark corners of the tent for a moment, thinking, then Reiner noticed that their shoulders were touching. He turned and his lips brushed Franka's hair. He nuzzled her neck. 'Let's have a kiss.'

Franka jerked away from him and punched his shoulder. 'Don't be daft. Do you want to be caught?' She rolled over and pulled her blanket up over her shoulders. 'Go to sleep.'

Reiner sighed and lay back. She was right, of course, but that didn't make it any easier to control himself. It was going to be a very long journey.

THREE
The Finest Army in the Empire

THEY REACHED AVERHEIM without further incident. Whether Dag had been cowed by Reiner's scolding, or it was just that there was nothing to tempt him to violence, the boy remained calm and cheerful, watching the clouds and whistling tavern songs.

At twilight on the fourth day they passed close enough to Nuln to see the orange glow of the great furnaces illuminating the undersides of the black smoke that belched from its many hundred forges. There had been a time, thought Reiner, that the city known as Karl-Franz's anvil, the city that made the guns and swords and devastating cannon that protected the Empire, and that housed the College of Engineers and their wondrous weapons of war, had filled him with a sense of pride. Its superior warcraft was what set the Empire above all other lands. Now, however, the place only inspired in him a chill of dread. All the smoke and flame reminded him too much of the last time he had seen such furnaces and such forges. He could almost feel their heat, and the walls of that terrible red cave closing in on him again.

Two further days of dusty roads and sunburned necks, and they saw at last the grey stone walls of Averheim rising behind bare-branched arbours and patchy wheat fields. The spires of the temples of Sigmar and Shallya, and the towers of the elector count's castle, jutted over the walls and glinted in the noon sun.

Reiner stopped the Blackhearts before they came within view of the main gate. 'Right, lads,' he said. 'Here's where we part company. I don't want the recruiters to know we know one another. Too suspicious if we come in as a group. Sign up where you fit. Pavel and Hals as pikemen, Karel as lancer, and so on. Franz will play at being my valet. When we get to the fort, talk to your comrades, listen, and if you hear interesting things – murmurs of mutiny, treason, what have you – you will "befriend" Franz in the mess and tell him what you have heard, and he will relay it to me. Are we clear?'

A chorus of 'Ayes' answered him.

'Then luck be with you. And remember,' he added, 'no matter how tempting it might be to escape with my eye not upon you, Manfred's poison is still in our veins. His leash is still around our necks. It would bring you up short if you ran. It would choke the life out of you.'

The Blackhearts nodded, grim.

Reiner smiled, trying his best to look the brave commander. 'Now be off with you. When next I see you, we will all be honest soldiers again.'

An hour later, Reiner and Franka rode through Averheim's broad city gate and began winding their way through the cobblestone streets to the Dalkenplatz, the great market in the city's centre. There in the shadow of the city jail was spread a sea of bright stalls and tents where one could buy fruits, vegetables, freshly butchered meat, and meat on the hoof. There were knife sharpeners, candle makers, tanners and cloth sellers, farmers, fishmongers, potters and tinsmiths. Bread and pastries were for sale, as well as sweetmeats, cider and beer. Rotund halflings from the Moot rolled wheels of cheese almost as tall as themselves through the crowd. It made Reiner hungry.

'Franz,' he said with a wave of his hand. 'Go and buy us some meat pies and a jug of cider.'

'What's this?' said Franka, looking up sharply. 'Putting on airs?'

Reiner smirked. 'If we are to be master and servant, we should practise a bit, hey?'

Franka rolled her eyes. 'Trust you to take advantage.' She dismounted and bowed flamboyantly. 'As your lordship desires.'

Then she stuck out her tongue and disappeared into the confusion of tents.

After they had finished their snack, the two sought out Gutzmann's recruiters. They were not hard to find. They had taken over a tavern on the side of the square, a sway-roofed two storey building with mullioned windows. Tall banners had been raised on either side of the door – the griffin of the Empire and the white bear on deep blue that was Gutzmann's standard – and a cheerful, bearded fellow in a shining breastplate and blue breeks and doublet stood outside, looking every young man who passed in the eye saying, 'Yer a strapping lad. How'd you like to string yer bow for good old Karl-Franz?' and 'Three squares a day in General Gutzmann's army. And a bonus just for making yer mark.'

There were precious few young men left in the local population, which seemed almost entirely made up of women in widow's grey, children and old men. Still, there was a slow, steady stream of volunteers shuffling through the tavern's doors. Some indeed were young men – some too young by far – but many more were hardened professional soldiers, wearing the colours of every city in the Empire, men with missing eyes and ears and fingers, men with hard-used faces and well-used swords, who wore their leather jacks and their dented helmets and vambraces as if they had been born in them. And there were some of an even rougher sort: gaunt, thick bearded villains in buckskins and rags, with no weapons but bows and daggers, men with the clipped ears and noses of felons and clumsy burns meant to cover the fact that they had been branded murderer, deserter or worse.

As Reiner and Franka rode up to the tavern the friendly sergeant saluted, grinning. 'Welcome, m'lord. Come to lend a hand?'

'Aye, sergeant. That I have.'

'Yer an officer, m'lord?'

'Junior officer,' said Reiner as he and Franka dismounted. 'Corporal Reiner Meyerling. Late of Boecher's pistoliers. Seeking active duty.'

'Very good, m'lord. Right this way.'

Reiner handed the reins of his horse to Franka. 'Wait here, boy.'

'Wait...?' Franka's fists curled, then relaxed as she remembered her role. 'Yes, my lord.'

The sergeant ushered Reiner through the tavern door, elbowing aside the lesser recruits. Reiner saw Pavel and Hals in the line and gave them a wink. They hid their smiles.

The pikemen's line led to a table where more smiling soldiers in polished armour talked to each recruit in turn, asking them where they had fought before and why they had left their previous service. The recruiters didn't seem too picky. A majority of the men were asked to raise their right hands and pledge to serve the Empire 'unto death,' then sign their names in a big, leather-bound book, or at least make an X if they couldn't write. Once pledged and signed, they were given a few coins and a blue and white cockade to pin to their caps. Only a few men were turned away. A few others were taken away in irons, cursing.

The sergeant led Reiner around this scene to a table at the back of the tavern where a lance corporal sat with his spurred boots up, tapping his teeth with a quill pen. At Reiner's approach he abruptly sat up and affixed a big smile to his face.

'Corporal Bohm,' said the sergeant, 'may I present Corporal Reiner Meyerling. A pistolier.'

'Welcome, corporal!' said Bohm, sticking out his hand. 'Matthais Bohm, bugle with General Gutzmann's third lance.' He was a handsome youth with a swoop of brown hair over bright, eager eyes. He had the height and brawn of a knight, but not yet the hardness or gravity that came with experience.

'Well met, sir,' said Reiner, shaking his hand.

Bohm motioned Reiner to a chair, and they sat on opposite sides of the table.

'So,' said the youth, opening a small leather book. 'You wish to sign on with us?'

'I do,' said Reiner. 'Can't have my barking irons rusting, can I?'

Bohm laughed agreeably. 'Well, we can help you there, I think. But if you wouldn't mind telling me of your previous service. And, er, your reasons for coming here.'

'Certainly,' said Reiner, relaxing back into his chair. Manfred had ordered him to assume a false identity for the mission, and Reiner had spent much of the journey thinking of the tale that would be most pleasing to Gutzmann's ears. 'Before Archaon's invasion, I was stationed with Boecher's Pistols at Fort Denkh, and when that monster Haargroth came racing through the

Drakwald on his way to Middenheim, we joined with Leudenhof's army to stop them. Quite a set-to as you can imagine.'

'We've heard stories,' said Bohm, enviously.

Reiner sighed. 'But though I did my part,' he coughed, 'and I think I can modestly say that I pulled more than my weight – I continued to be passed over for promotion.'

'Why so?'

Reiner shrugged. 'I hate to make a charge of nepotism against so august a name as that of Lord Boecher, but it seemed that his sons, and his sons' circle, won the lion's share of honours and commands. And when I was foolish enough to bring a complaint, it only got worse.' He spread his hands. 'The Meyerlings are a small country family. No influence at court. Not enough money to buy what can't be honourably won, and so when I at last realized that there would be no advancement for me under Boecher, I took my leave.'

Bohm shook his head. 'You'd not credit how often I hear that tale. Good men ignored in favour of bad. Well, you've come to the right place. General Gutzmann knows too well the perils of politics and preference, and has made a vow that merit only will be the way of advancement in his army. We welcome all who have felt slighted in other regiments and companies. We are the home of the dispossessed.'

'That is why I sought you out,' said Reiner. 'Lord Gutzmann's fairness is spoken of across the Empire.'

Bohm beamed. 'It is gratifying to hear.'

He turned the little book toward Reiner. 'If you would put your name and rank on this line, and pledge to serve General Gutzmann, Sigmar, and the Empire to the best of your abilities unto death, you will be instated in Gutzmann's army at your full rank, privileges and pay.'

'Excellent.' Reiner raised his right hand and made the pledge, smiling inwardly as he noted that General Gutzmann came before Sigmar and the Empire.

After he had signed Bohm's book, the young corporal shook his hand, smiling broadly. 'Welcome to the finest army in the Empire, Corporal Meyerling. It is a pleasure to have you with us. We leave tomorrow morning from the south gate. Be there at daybreak.'

Reiner saluted. 'A pleasure to find a home, corporal. I will be there without fail.'

As he was leaving, Reiner bumped into Karel coming in. The fool boy grinned at him and almost spoke, but Reiner kicked him in the shin and he yelped instead. A born spy, that one, Reiner thought.

THE NEXT MORNING, Reiner rode, slumped miserably in his saddle, through winding cobbled streets to Averheim's southern gate with Franka at his side. A moist, pre-dawn mist made looming half seen monsters of the brick and timber tenements that leaned their upper storeys over the narrow lanes. The fog without was mirrored by a fog within. Reiner had hoped, since he and Franka were separated from the others, that they would at last be able to get a room together alone, but maddeningly, there had been no private quarters available. With all the recruits in town, and it being market day, the city had been full to bursting. Even with all Manfred's reikmarks, Reiner and Franka had had to settle for sharing a cramped room with four longswords from Talabheim who spent the night singing marching songs. Reiner had drowned his frustrations in too many jars of wine, and now had a throbbing head as thick as army porridge.

He was not alone. Gutzmann's recruitment bonus had been nicely calculated to be just enough to get drunk on but not enough to tempt one to leave town, so the men who formed up before the tall, white stone gate under Gutzmann's banners and amidst supply wagons loaded with sacks of wheat, barrels of cured meat, apples, and cooking oil, as well as bags of oats and bales of hay, were a sad, quiet bunch, clutching heads and puking behind rain barrels. The sergeants, so friendly and cheerful the previous afternoon, were showing new faces now; pulling barely conscious recruits out of doss houses and taverns and bullying and kicking them into line. Other soldiers herded reluctant groups of fellows who, having thought better of joining up, had tried to sneak out through other gates, but hadn't been wise enough to remove the blue and white cockades from their caps.

As they made their way through the crowded square, Reiner saw a few of the other Blackhearts. Giano gave him a wink, and Abel a slight tip of the head. Pavel and Hals were hanging on their pikes like they were all that held them up. Hals had a black eye.

At the head of the line, Reiner joined Matthais and Karel and the other junior officers.

'Good morning, Meyerling!' said Matthais cheerily.

'The only thing good about it,' said Reiner, rubbing his temples, 'is that it will eventually be over.'

'Are you unwell, sir?' asked Karel, concerned.

Reiner gave him a withering look.

'Reiner Meyerling,' said Matthais. 'May I present Captain Karel Ziegler of Altdorf.'

'A pleasure to make your acquaintance for the very first time, sir,' chirped Karel.

Reiner closed his eyes.

After a quarter of an hour in which Reiner stared blankly into space, the sergeants at last chivvied the supply wagons and the new recruits into a rough marching order, Matthais bellowed 'For'ard!' in Reiner's ear, and the column staggered out the gate and into the fog. Reiner wished he were dead.

Reiner recovered considerably after the first meal stop. Whether Matthais's claim that Gutzmann's was the finest army in the Empire was true or no, the general certainly did well by his men as far as rations went. Reiner didn't know what the foot soldiers were being fed, but Franka served him cold ham and cheese and black bread with butter, as well as beer to wash it down with; all of better quality than he'd had in other regiments. The beauty of the day was a restorative as well. They rode through rolling farmland with the buzz of insects all around them and the young wheat rippling in the breeze. A broad blue sky soared above, piled high with fluffy white clouds.

When he at last felt human enough to talk in complete sentences, Reiner urged his horse up to the head of the line, where Matthais was singing the praises of Gutzmann to the new junior officers with the fervour of a fanatic.

'The Empire has yet to use him to his full potential,' said Matthais, 'but rest assured, General Gutzmann is the greatest commander in the field. His victories over the orcs in Ostermark and over Count Durthwald of Sylvania are held up as models of strategy among the knightly orders, and his reduction of the Fortress of Maasenberg in the Grey Mountains when the traitor Brighalter made his rebellion has never been equalled for speed and brilliance.'

'Indeed,' said Karel. 'I have studied it myself. The way he drew Brighalter out from cover was masterful.'

Matthais smiled. 'Consequently, he has won the undying loyalty of his men, for his brilliance keeps losses at a minimum. No one dies unnecessarily in General Gutzmann's battles, and the men love him for it. Also, he shares out the spoils with magnanimity. His men are better paid and better cared for than any others in the Empire.'

'Is there anything this paragon doesn't excel at?' asked Reiner dryly as he swatted at a mosquito on his wrist.

Matthais failed to hear the irony. 'Well, the general is nothing with the bow or the gun, but with sword and lance he is nigh unbeatable. His feats of martial valour on and off the battlefield are legendary. He defeated the orc chieftain Gorslag in single combat and led the charge that broke Stossen's line at Zhufbar.'

Reiner groaned to himself. And this was the man he must kill if it proved that he meant to betray the Empire? To stem the tide of praise, he decided to change subject. 'And what will our duties be when we arrive? What is the situation in the pass?'

Matthais took a sip from his water skin. 'I'm afraid there is presently little chance for glory, though that could change. Our little pass is not of the same strategic importance as the Black Fire. It is much smaller and closed for much of the year by snow and ice. And it is buffered from the dead lands beyond by the small principality of Aulschweig, which has been a good neighbour to the Empire for five hundred years, and is enclosed entirely within one valley. We also protect the gold mine situated at the north end of the pass.'

'There's a gold mine?' asked Reiner, feigning surprise.

Matthais pursed his lips. 'Er, yes. The mine is a primary source for the Empire's treasury.'

Reiner laughed. 'And the officers' retirement fund, no doubt!'

'Sir,' said Matthais stiffening. 'We do not joke about such things. The gold belongs to Karl-Franz.'

Reiner straightened his face. Was the boy pretending, or did he mean it? 'No. No, of course not. My apologies. A poor jest. But if that's all there is to our duties, it sounds a bit sleepy. You promised when I signed on that I'd get some use of my pistols.'

'And you will,' said Matthais, brightening. 'You'll not lose your saddle calluses under General Gutzmann's command, never fear. There are bandits in the hills to be chased down, trading caravans to be escorted across the border, and squabbling among the rulers of Aulschweig to keep an eye on. 'And,' he grinned, 'when there's nothing else to do, we have games.'

Reiner raised an eyebrow. 'Games?'

FOUR
'Tis Always the General

REINER LEARNED WHAT Matthais meant by games four days later, when at last they reached the fort in the pass.

The journey there was uneventful, a dull slog due south from Averheim through farm and dairy land with the Black Mountains rising like a row of rotting teeth beyond them the entire way. Just after noon on the third day they reached the foothills and felt the first chill breezes nosing down from the heights above. By nightfall, when they stopped to make camp in a thick pine forest, summer had fallen away completely and Reiner was pulling his cloak from his pack and wrapping it around his shoulders.

'Why couldn't Manfred send us somewhere warm?' he muttered to Franka as they lay shivering in their tent that night. 'First the Middle Mountains, now the Black. Isn't trouble to be found on the plain?'

It only got colder the next day, as the long column of recruits wound along a torturous path deeper and deeper into the jagged range. At least the sky remained blue and the sun hot, when they weren't in the shadow of some crag.

That afternoon the path tipped down into a small cleared valley and widened into a well-maintained road. Meagre freeholds appeared on the left and right, where stunted cattle grazed on scrubby grass. At the end of the valley the column passed through the mining town of Brunn, which, though small, was still able to support a large, garishly painted brothel. Reiner smiled to himself. That alone proved that there was a garrison nearby.

On the road beyond the village they began to come across parties of men with picks over their shoulders. Those heading south whistled and chatted as they marched. Those coming north were covered in dirt and trudged along in weary silence. Reiner was thus not surprised when, a short time later, Matthais pointed out a branching path, well worn with cart tracks, that he said was the way to the gold mine.

Not a mile beyond that, the steep, thickly wooded hillsides of the ravine opened up, slowly revealing the column's destination. Coming upon it from the north, it was an odd looking fort, for it was one-sided. There were almost no defences on the Empire side, only a low wall and a wide open gate. Beyond that rose various barracks, stables and storehouses, and an imposing inner keep on the right where Matthais said the senior officers had their quarters. Beyond that were the massive southern battlements, a thick, grey stone wall almost as tall as the keep and stretching the whole width of the pass. The top was notched and crenellated with slots for archers and sluices for boiling oil. Squat catapults sat atop four square towers, all pointing south. In the centre was a great gate – a wide tunnel through the thickness of the wall – with massive, iron-bound wooden doors and an iron portcullis at both ends.

As they got closer, the new recruits were startled to hear a great cheer echo through the pass. Reiner's eyes were drawn to the broad, weedy expanse on the Empire side of the fort that stretched between the two walls of the pass. On the right were neat rows of infantry tents – many more than were needed to house the fort's original compliment of troops. To the left, the ground was devoted to horses. There was a fenced off area for them to roam free, a training ring, and a proper tilting yard, with lanes for jousting and straw dummies for practising lance charges. It was from here that the cheer had rung.

Reiner and the other new officers shot questioning looks at Matthias.

He smiled. 'The games. Would you care to see?'

'Certainly,' said Karel.

So, while the veterans began herding the foot soldiers to their new quarters and assuring them that they would be fed and given their new kit in short order, Matthais led the new sergeants and junior officers toward a big crowd of soldiers of every stripe who ringed the tilting field, whistling and shouting.

There was a canopied viewing stand on one side, to which they made their way, turning their horses over to squires and stepping up onto the wooden platform. A handful of men sat on the long benches – infantry captains by their uniforms – but unlike the enlisted men who watched so avidly in the sun, the officers hardly looked at the field, talking instead amongst themselves in low voices.

'Greetings, sirs,' said Matthais, bowing to them. 'I return with the new blood.'

The officers looked around and nodded, but there were no glad cries of welcome.

'Any for us?' asked one.

'Yes, captain.' Matthais indicated three of the new men. 'Two sergeants of pike and a gunnery sergeant.'

'And ten lance corporals,' said another captain dryly.

The captains returned to their conversation.

Matthais grinned sheepishly at the new men and indicated that they should sit along the first bench.

Once seated, Reiner turned to the field and discovered that Matthais's game was 'tent-pegging,' an old parade ground drill where riders took turns trying to pluck brightly painted wooden tent-pegs out of the ground on the tips of their lances while at full gallop. It was a difficult trick, for the pegs were short, and broom stick thin, and it was more dangerous than it first appeared, for if one lowered one's lance just the slightest bit too much, one could catch it in the ground and be catapulted from the saddle.

This happened just as Reiner thought it. A knight flew through the air and landed in a cloud of dust on the hard-packed earth. The crowd of soldiers erupted in cheers and jeers as the knight pulled himself stiffly to his feet. He saluted the soldiers, then walked his horse off the field.

Reiner frowned, puzzled, for the fellow was no youthful lancer, but a hardened knight, in his middle years, long past his training days. He looked around at the other men on the field. There were many young men among them, but just as many looked to be senior officers.

Reiner turned to Matthais. 'Who are the players in this game?'

'Why, all officers corporal and above. The general insists every man be fighting fit.' He sat down next to Reiner. 'We run in sets of five, with all who share the lowest score dropping out before the next heat. Any man unhorsed is out as well. We play until there is only one.' He laughed. 'And 'tis always the general.'

Reiner nearly choked. 'The general plays as well?' He squinted out at the field, the lowering sun harsh in his eyes.

Matthais pointed. 'In the dark blue sleeves. You see him? With the cropped hair and the dented breastplate?'

Reiner stared. The man Matthais had indicated couldn't possibly be a general. He looked hardly older than Reiner himself, a laughing, handsome knight in simple armour, who slapped the backs of those who had made their pegs and joked with those who lost. A captain or obercaptain? Certainly. But a general? He lacked the gravitas.

New pegs were set and a bugle blared. Gutzmann and another knight took their places in their lanes. A soldier dropped a flag and they spurred their mounts into a gallop, lowering their lances as one. As they reached the end of their lanes there was an audible 'tock' and Gutzmann raised his lance high, a bright red peg squarely pinned on his shining lance point, while the other man came up empty. The crowd of soldiers cheered uproariously. It was obvious who their favourite was. Reiner decided that the fellow was a general after all, and one to be reckoned with. These lads would follow him into the maw of Chaos without a qualm. Woe to the fool who brought him low and let his troops discover it. Reiner shivered, hoping fervently that it wasn't Gutzmann who was stealing the gold.

As Gutzmann circled back to the top of the lane, he saw the new men in the stands and trotted over. The infantry officers fell silent as he approached, watching him.

'Well met, Corporal Bohm,' he said, reining up. 'So these are our new companions?'

Matthais bowed. 'Aye, m'lord. And a likely lot they are. Ready for anything.'

'Excellent,' said Gutzmann. He bowed from the saddle to the new recruits, his eyes merry. 'Welcome, gentlemen. We are glad to have you.'

Up close, Reiner could better see the general's age. Though he was as fit as a man half his years, skin drum tight over corded muscles, there were deep lines around his pale grey eyes and silver in his neatly trimmed beard and at his temples.

A knight called from the field and he turned his horse, but then looked back. 'If any of your lads would care to try his luck, he would be more than welcome. We've only recently begun.'

Matthais laughed and held up his hands. 'My lord, we have been riding since before dawn. I think the gentlemen are more interested in rest and a hot meal than tilting at pegs.'

'Of course,' said Gutzmann. 'Foolish of me even to ask.'

'No, no,' said Karel, standing. 'I for one would love to play.'

Reiner and the other new cavalrymen glared murder at the boy. If he had said nothing, there would have been no shame in allowing Matthais's excuse to speak for them, but now that one had volunteered the rest would look weak if they demurred.

'And I,' said Reiner through gritted teeth.

The others followed suit as well, and were quickly brought fresh horses and lances. As Reiner trotted out to the lanes he realized that this had become a test. Whether Gutzmann and Matthais had staged it on purpose or not, they and the other officers would now be watching the new men – to judge their martial skills, of course – but more importantly, Reiner thought, to see how game they were, how much enthusiasm and energy they could muster in the face of an unexpected and unwanted challenge. To see how well they 'played the game.'

It was a game Reiner needed to win. If he wished to learn the fort's intrigues, he would have to become part of the inner circle, and with so horse-mad a garrison, this seemed the best way to do it. Fortunately, though Reiner was only an adequate sword, riding had always come naturally to him, and he had been even more skilled with the lance than the pistol. Only his slight frame had stopped him from becoming a lancer instead of a pistolier. He hoped at least to best Karel. The boy needed a lesson.

Gutzmann's officers watched as the general assigned the new men lanes. They were impressive specimens, tall and broad shouldered to a man, with proud faces and regal bearing. Even though Reiner was of an age with many of them, he felt a boy beside them. And though they called friendly welcomes to the recruits, their expressions remained noncommittal.

Reiner missed his first peg – unsurprising, since neither the horse nor the lance was his own and the ground was unfamiliar, but he made his second, the impact with the peg sending a pleasing shock through his arm and shoulder. Then, after missing on his third and fourth runs, he caught the fifth square in the centre. It was gratifying how quickly the old skills came back. He hadn't couched a lance since before the war, but what his mind had forgotten his body remembered, and soon he was riding just as old master Hoffstetter had instructed him to – rising in the saddle before impact, letting the lance glide along the ground at the correct height, so that instead of stabbing desperately at the peg at the last second, you guided your lance easily into line.

Many of the new officers took only one peg. Some took none at all. So Reiner and Karel, with two apiece, made it into the next round with several of the others. But they would have to improve if they wanted to stay in the game long. Gutzmann's knights all took three or four pegs. Gutzmann took all five.

After three more runs Reiner and Karel were all that were left of the new men. And after another two, Karel was gone as well, having knocked the peg out of the ground that would have tied him with Reiner, but failing to keep it on his lance tip.

Gutzmann gave Reiner an approving nod at the start of the next round, and the other officers began sizing him up. A bearish knight with a bristling black beard pulled up beside him. Reiner had noted him before. A loud, hearty fellow with an ear-splitting laugh and a steady stream of jokes – the sort of man Reiner would have left a tavern to avoid.

'You do well, sir,' said the knight, sticking out a thick-fingered hand. 'Lance Captain Halmer, third company.'

Reiner recognized the name. 'A pleasure, sir. You are the captain of Matthais's company. He spoke highly of you.' Reiner shook the man's hand, then winced in his crushing grip. 'Meyer...ling. Pistolier.'

'Welcome, corporal. It's not often a new man gets this far. Luck to you.'

'And to you.'

Have to watch that one, thought Reiner, wringing the pain from his hand.

Reiner stayed in the running for two more rounds, getting three each time while others got two or less. But the round after that he took only one peg on his first four runs. As he watched the other knights make their fourth runs and bring their tallies to three or four, he knew this would be his last run. Halmer only had two, but he had yet to take less than three and always seemed to come through in the clinch.

Only this time, he didn't. On his fifth run, Halmer's horse stumbled a bit and his point went wide. He had only taken two pegs. Reiner's heart thudded in his chest. His turn was next. If he took his last peg, he would tie Halmer for last, and they would both drop out – petty vengeance for Halmer's crushing handshake – but Reiner had never claimed to be above petty vengeance. He could feel the lance captain's eyes upon him as he circled back to the top of the lanes. He knew the situation as well as Reiner did, and his anger was palpable.

Reiner could barely keep himself from grinning. Suddenly he knew he could take the peg. He had never felt more alive and in command of his abilities. Then he checked himself. He had been commanded to worm his way into the fort and learn its secrets. Making enemies of the officers wouldn't further that aim. He would have to miss the peg and let Halmer win. The temptation to ride his last run with his lance at parade rest had to be fought off too. Halmer would not love him for letting him win, and neither would Gutzmann. The general wasn't the sort of man who would tolerate a man not trying his best. So Reiner must make it look good.

As the soldier dropped the flag, Reiner spurred his horse forward and lowered his lance. It whispered through the sparse weeds of the field like a shark through a shallow sea, homing in on the peg. He knew his aim would be true. He knew he could pink the peg right in its centre. It took every ounce of self control to twitch his lance just a hair to the inside, and he almost played it too close. The peg spun from the ground as he hit its edge.

Reiner reined up, laughing and cursing, then rode back, rueful, to the top of the lanes. 'I had it, my lords,' he said. 'Truly I did. It was the wind from my horse's nostrils blew it aside.'

Gutzmann and the knights laughed, and Halmer joined in, but Reiner felt the captain staring after him, cold eyed and suspicious, as he turned in his lance and rode back to the sidelines.

Franka glared out at the field as she took his reins and helped him from the saddle. 'I wish you'd beaten him. Boasting bully.'

'I wish I could have allowed myself the pleasure.'

Franka turned big eyes on him. 'You let him win?'

'I let Manfred win,' said Reiner, sourly. 'Even from Altdorf he makes me dance.'

FIVE
Paragons of Martial Virtue

After Gutzmann had won the game to the cheers of the soldiers, the officers retired to the fort's keep for dinner in the great dining hall. The new sergeants and corporals were invited to eat with their new comrades, and as the one who had stayed in the game the longest, Reiner was singled out by Gutzmann to join him with his senior staff at the table on the raised dais at the head of the room. The table was long, but even so, it barely had space enough to hold all the officers in attendance. It looked as if Gutzmann had almost doubled the fort's original complement of men – many more than were needed to guard the pass. Both cavalry and infantry captains sat at the table, but Reiner noticed that the cavalrymen sat in the centre seats, nearest Gutzmann, while the infantry were relegated to the wings.

The general made a place for Reiner beside him on his left, forcing a grey-haired, square-bearded knight to shift down. 'Corporal Reiner,' he said as Reiner scooted his chair in and tried to keep his elbows close to his sides, 'May I present Commander Volk Shaeder, my right hand.'

The venerable knight inclined his head. 'Welcome, corporal. You stayed nine rounds I hear. Quite an accomplishment.' He had the soft, grave voice of a scholar, and wore ascetic grey robes over his uniform, but he was as tall and broad as the rest.

A silver hammer of Sigmar hung from his neck by a chain. It looked to Reiner as if it weighed as much as an anchor.

'I would be lost without Volk,' said Gutzmann. 'He sees to the day to day business of the camp and lets me gallivant about playing at soldiers.' He grinned. 'He is also our spiritual navigator, keeping us always pointed toward Sigmar.'

Shaeder inclined his head again. 'I do my humble best, general.'

'To Volk's left,' continued Gutzmann, 'is Cavalry Obercaptain Halkrug Oppenhauer, Knight Templar of the Order of the Black Rose, or Hallie, as we call him.'

A bald, red-faced giant gave Reiner a friendly salute, beaming through a flowing golden beard, his blue eyes twinkling. Reiner recalled that he had been one of the last to drop out of the game. An amazingly nimble rider for a man his size. 'A fine display today, pistolier,' he said. 'Too bad you haven't the weight to make a lance.'

Reiner returned the salute. 'I curse my luck every day, obercaptain.'

'And on my right,' said Gutzmann, motioning with his hand, 'is Infantry Obercaptain Ernst Nuemark, Champion of the Carroburg Greatswords, and hero of the siege of Venner.'

A tanned, clean-shaven man with close-cropped hair so blond as to seem white leaned forward, and nodded solemnly at Reiner. 'A pleasure to make your acquaintance, pistolier,' he said. He didn't seem terribly pleased.

'The pleasure is mine, obercaptain,' said Reiner formally. This was the first time Reiner had seen Obercaptain Nuemark. He hadn't attended the games.

'And where is Vortmunder?' asked Gutzmann, looking around.

'Here, general,' said a captain, standing. He was a wiry, bright-eyed fellow with dark hair and moustaches that had been waxed into jutting points.

'This is your captain, Meyerling,' said Gutzmann. 'Pistolier Captain Daegert Vortmunder. He is a good man. Heed his words.'

'I will, general. Thank you.' Reiner bowed in his seat to Vortmunder. 'Captain.'

'Welcome aboard, corporal. If you can shoot as well as you can ride, we will get along fine.'

'I will endeavour to impress you, captain,' said Reiner.

The first course was served and the officers fell to. The food was excellent.

Gutzmann poured Reiner wine. 'Matthais tells me you fought in the north. With Boecher, was it? Tell me how the end went.'

Something in Gutzmann's voice made Reiner hesitate. Though the general's expression was as friendly and open as ever, there was a hunger in his eyes that made Reiner shiver.

'I'm afraid I was far from the final battle, my lord,' said Reiner. 'I was wounded trying to stop Haargroth's advance, and sat out the end.'

'But you must know more of it than we, stuck as we are on the Empire's hindquarters. Tell me.' It was a command.

Reiner coughed. 'Well, you know the start, I'm sure, my lord: old Huss making dire predictions of invasion from the north, proclaiming his farm boy the reincarnation of Sigmar. Nobody paid any attention until we heard the first news of Erengrad and Praag. Thank Sigmar – or Ulric, I suppose – that Todbringer was quick on the uptake. And von Raukov of Wolfenburg as well. They put enough men in front of Archaon's hordes to slow 'em down for a time and organise a defence.' He sighed. 'That was the hardest part, I think. Getting so many disparate groups to fight alongside one another. Elves from Loren. Dwarfs from the Middle Mountains. Makarev's Kossars. Todbringer practically had to drink from the chalice and swear to the lady to get the Bretonnians in. And still it almost wasn't enough.'

'They had cannon, this time, the northmen,' said Gutzmann.

'Aye, terrible things that seemed almost alive. Their missiles were balls of flame.' Reiner took a sip of wine and went on. 'We had some successes, but there were too many of the devils. It was like trying to stop a river with a gate. And other fiends crept out of the shadows to take advantage of our weakness. Filthy, goat-headed beastmen from the Drakwald, greenskins. They fought amongst themselves as much as they fought us, but it didn't stop the tide.'

'And all the while Karl-Franz and the counts and barons of the south are dithering about who should go and who should stay, and not getting under way,' snapped Gutzmann.

Reiner hemmed noncommittally. 'It may be as you say, my lord. I was at Denkh at the time, preparing for the coming onslaught. The hordes soon took Ostland and then the west of Middenland. That was when I had my moment of glory, such as it was. Took a sword in the leg on my second charge and that was me done, and Haargrath pushed on to Middenheim with the rest of Archaon's horde.' He shrugged. 'I don't mind telling you I'm not sorry to have missed the siege.'

'A bloody business, then?' asked Shaeder.

Reiner nodded. 'Tens of thousands dead by all accounts, commander. Archaon and his henchmen pounded the Ulricsberg for more than a fortnight. Fortunately the Ostland boys had held them off long enough for Todbringer and von Raukov to get their lads in and shore up the defences. Still, it was close for a while, and the northmen were over the walls in places, but then we had a bit of luck with the greenskins. Their chief got it up his snout that he had to be first in, and so went after Archaon. And with the elves and Bretonnians and Kossars harrying the northmen from the forest, they began to lose heart and fell back to Sokh to regroup.' He sat forward. 'Karl-Franz arrived that day and attacked at once, but Archaon held him off, and the battle raged for three days, with Valten and Huss coming in on the second, and engaging Archaon himself in combat on the third.'

'It was there that Valten received his mortal wound, yes?' asked Shaeder.

'Aye,' said Reiner. 'Huss carried him off while Archaon was engaged with the orc chieftain, who had attacked as well.'

Gutzmann snorted at that.

'On the fourth day,' Reiner continued, 'the armies set to again, and it looked grim, for the beastmen attacked Karl-Franz's cannon from the rear, but before either side could win any real advantage, a third force appeared.'

'Von Carstein,' said Gutzmann.

'So my lord has heard,' said Reiner.

'Only rumours. Go on.'

'He raised the dead, my lord. Men of the Empire and of the north alike awoke where they had died and attacked both sides indiscriminately. Archaon's forces fled north while Karl-Franz withdrew his army to Middenheim. The Sylvanians followed, and von Carstein called for the Emperor's surrender and the surrender of the city, but Volkmar stepped out and told him to be on his way, and though I can scarcely credit it, he did. He turned about and buggered off to Sylvania again without another word.'

'And that was it,' said Gutzmann dryly.

'Yes, my lord. Middenheim held, and Archaon's army was dispersed.'

Gutzmann snorted again. 'And Altdorf calls it a great victory.'

'Your pardon, my lord?'

'The Empire was saved not by the reincarnation of Sigmar or the might of Karl-Franz's knights, or the much vaunted Company of Light, but by an orc warboss and an undead sorcerer.'

Reiner coughed. 'Er, they may have been in at the end, my lord, but the brave defensive actions of the men of Ostland and Middenland that kept the hordes at bay cannot be discounted. Middenheim would surely have fallen without them.'

'And if they were well led,' cried Gutzmann, 'the hordes would never have reached Middenheim at all! How many men died unnecessarily because our hide-bound counts continue to think that the only way to defeat an enemy is to fight him head to head, no matter the circumstance? If they hadn't insisted on swinging Sigmar's hammer at targets better slain with a stiletto, it might have been over in weeks, not months.'

'My lord,' said Reiner, annoyed in spite of himself. Gutzmann might well be the tactician he thought himself, but he hadn't faced the hordes. He hadn't stood toe-to-toe with a Kurgan warrior. Reiner had. 'My lord, they were a hundred thousand strong. And the smallest of them as big as two normal men.'

'Exactly!' said Gutzmann. 'A hundred thousand titanic men who must eat pounds of food every single day to keep up their strength.' The general leaned in, eyes gleaming. 'Tell me. You fought them. Did you notice their supply lines? Were they victualled from some northern stockpile?'

Reiner laughed. 'No, my lord. They were barbarians. They had no supply lines. They barely had an order of march. They raped the lands they moved through for their dinner.'

Gutzmann jabbed a finger at Reiner. 'Exactly! So, if one of our noble knights, our paragons of martial virtue, had had the forethought to harvest all the crops and slaughter all the game in Archaon's path, then burned the farms and forests before he reached them?' He banged the table with his palm. 'The northmen would have starved on their feet before they were halfway from Kislev, or more likely fallen to eating each other, the savages. Either way, they would have reduced their numbers considerably with almost no losses on our side. Instead Todbringer and von Raukov sent hastily equipped, unprepared forces against them, which, though they may have slowed them down, also fed their cooking pots and kept them strong.' He laughed bitterly. 'The knights of the Empire so love their tests of arms that they sometimes think that it is better to fight without winning than it is to win without fighting.'

Reiner was no student of military science. He had no idea if Gutzmann's theories would pass muster with other generals, but they sounded sensible.

Gutzmann shook his head. 'It is madness that I should have been sent here while Boecher and Leudenhof and fools of that calibre were sent to defend the Empire in its darkest hour.'

Commander Shaeder leaned forward, eyes anxious. 'But of course we must do as the Emperor bids us, my lord. Certainly he knows better than we how best to defend our homeland.'

'It wasn't Karl-Franz who banished me!' snapped Gutzmann. 'It was that hen-house of Altdorf cowards who were so afraid of my victories in Ostermark that they imagined I would break it from the Empire and crown myself its king. As if I would ever do anything to harm the land I love.'

'Then why,' said a captain of pike from down the table, 'do you turn your back on that land?'

'None of that!' barked Shaeder, glaring at the captain. 'You forget yourself, sir.' A few of the cavalry officers slid nervous glances toward Reiner. Reiner's heart pounded. What was this? This sounded exactly the sort of thing Manfred had asked him to look out for.

'I do not turn my back on the Empire,' said Gutzmann quietly. 'It turns its back on me.' His mouth twisted into a sneer of disgust. 'I wonder sometimes if it would notice if I were gone.'

The table fell silent. Gutzmann looked around, as if only now remembering where he was.

He laughed suddenly, and waved a hand. 'But enough of hypotheticals. This should be a merry occasion.' He turned to Reiner. 'Come, sir. What are the new songs in Altdorf and Talabheim? What do they play on the stage? We are starved for culture here in the hinterlands. Will you sing for us?'

Reiner nearly choked on his wine. 'I'm afraid I am no singer, sir. You would be hungrier for culture when I finished than when I started.'

Gutzmann shrugged. 'Very well.' He turned to the hall. 'Anyone else? Will any of the new men give us a song?'

There was a long pause as the recruits squirmed uncomfortably. But at last Karel stood, knees shaking.

'Er.' He swallowed, then began again. 'Er, if my lords would care to hear a ballad, there is one that the ladies ask for at the moment.'

'By all means, lad,' said Gutzmann. 'We are all ears.'

Karel coughed. 'Very good, my lord. Er, it is called, "When will my Yan come home?"'

Reiner braced himself for the worst, but after a few more hesitations Karel stood straight and began singing in the voice of a Shallyan choir boy; high and pure. The room sat silent and rapt as he sang the story of the farm girl waiting for her lover to come back from the war in the north, only to have him return on the shoulders of six of his friends, dead from a poisoned arrow. It was a heartbreaking song, sung with a heartbreaking sweetness, and when at last the farm girl decided to wed her lover in death by scratching herself with the arrow that killed him, Reiner saw many a knight dabbing his eye.

It only seemed to make Gutzmann angry, though he masked it well. 'A beautiful song, lad. But how about something jolly now. Something to lift our hearts.'

After a moment's thought Karel broke into a song about a rogue brought to ruin by a false nun, which had the whole hall singing along by the second chorus, and after that the atmosphere became relaxed and the conversation turned to light topics and filthy jests.

Towards the end of the meal, when pudding laced with brandy had been served and Gutzmann was involved in a loud conversation with some knights to his right about tent-pegging contests of yore and who had fallen and who had broken an arm or leg, Captain Shaeder leaned toward Reiner.

'You must forgive General Gutzmann,' he murmured. 'He is a passionate man, and the inaction of this posting frustrates him. But we are all loyal men here.' He laughed stiffly. 'If the general had a few more years, he would understand that no post is less important than another. And there are many who would be happy with any post at all.'

'Very true, commander,' said Reiner. 'And I took no offence, fear not.'

Shaeder inclined his head, nearly dipping his beard in his pudding. 'You ease my mind, sir.'

After the meal was done, Matthais volunteered to lead Reiner to his quarters, apologizing that he must bunk in a tent outside the north wall, rather than the pistoliers' barracks within the fort.

'We are too full at the moment,' he said.

'Aye,' said Reiner. 'I noticed. Don't quite understand why. The way you described our situation there doesn't seem the need for so many men.'

'Er, yes, well...' Matthais coughed, suddenly awkward. 'I believe I mentioned before some trouble in Aulschweig?'

'Aye. Infighting amongst the rulers or some such.'

Matthais nodded. 'Exactly. Younger brother wants older brother's throne. The usual Border Princes' nonsense. But there's a danger of it coming to a boil presently. The younger brother is Baron Caspar Tzetchka-Koloman, a blow-by who has a castle just the other side of the border. The older is Prince Leopold Aulslander. Altdorf wants Leopold to remain in power, as he is the more stable and level-headed of the two, so we may have to intervene if Caspar makes his play. Thus, extra troops.'

'Ah,' said Reiner. 'All becomes clear.' Or did it, he wondered. Matthais's explanation made sense, but the angry pike captain's outburst at the dinner table still rang in Reiner's ears.

'At least you'll have a tent to yourself,' said Matthais, 'if that's any consolation.'

Reiner's heart leapt, all thoughts of intrigue gone. Alone with Franka? 'Oh, I think I will manage.'

Matthais had been laughing and merry as they left the hall, but now, as they walked through the fort in the cold night air, the young knight lowered his voice. 'Er, I hope you read no treason in General Gutzmann's words tonight, corporal.'

'Not at all, Matthais,' said Reiner. 'His seems a reasonable enough complaint, considering the circumstances.'

Matthais nodded earnestly. 'Then you understand his frustration?'

'Of course,' Reiner replied, pretending the sort of bluff courage he knew lancers of Matthais's kidney valued. 'Any man would be disappointed to be kept so far from the front.'

'But you see the unfairness of it,' the youth pressed as they exited through the north gate. 'The deliberate slight. The danger into which the Empire was placed because of fear and favouritism.'

Reiner hesitated. Matthais's eyes were shining with almost religious fervour. 'Oh, aye,' he said at last. 'A damned shame. Absolutely.'

The young captain grinned. 'I knew you'd see it. You're a bright fellow, Reiner. Not a stubborn old fool.' He looked up. 'Ah. Here we are, your canvas castle.'

He reached for the tent flap, but it opened from within.

Franka bowed in the opening. 'I have laid out your things, my lord.'

Matthais nodded approvingly. 'You're wise to bring a valet from home. I've had to make do with a local boy. Horrible fellow. Steals my handkerchiefs.' He executed a clipped bow. 'Goodnight, corporal. Good luck with your new duties tomorrow. You'll like Vortmunder. He's a bit of a Kossar, but it's all bluster.'

'Thank you, captain. Goodnight,' said Reiner, returning the bow, then letting the flap drop.

He waited for Matthais's footsteps to fade, then turned to Franka, grinning. 'Ha! Alone at last. I have been waiting the last four months for this moment.'

'And you will wait yet another three, my lord,' she replied tartly. 'For my vow is as strong here as it was in Altdorf.'

Reiner sighed. 'But we have the opportunity now! In three months we might be on the march, or trapped in Manfred's townhouse again, with no chance for privacy.'

'It will only make it the sweeter when the time comes.'

'Bah!' Reiner started unlacing his jerkin. Then he stopped and looked back at Franka. He smirked. 'Unlace me.'

'What?'

'You are my valet, are you not? Unlace me.'

Franka rolled her eyes. 'You wish to continue the charade out of the public eye?'

'And why not. It will keep us from slipping when we are in company.'

Franka scowled. 'My lord, you seek to cozen me.'

'Not at all. I don't ask to unlace you, do I?'

Franka snorted. 'Very well, my lord. As my lord wishes.' She stepped forward and began tugging roughly at his laces.

'Easy, lass,' Reiner laughed, as he fought to stand still. 'You'll scuttle me.'

'"Lass", my lord?' said Franka, ripping open his last stays. 'You call your valet "lass"? My lord's eyes are failing, perhaps.' She grabbed his collar and began yanking it down from his shoulders.

'Franka... Franz... you...' With his arms trapped in his sleeves Reiner couldn't keep his balance. He staggered and fell. Franka tried to catch him, but instead went down with him, tipping the cot over. They ended in a muddle of blankets, the light wood frame on top of them.

Franka flailed a slap at him, laughing. 'You did that a'purpose!'

'I didn't!' Reiner cried. 'You were too rough, sir!'

He caught her wrist to stop another slap and suddenly they were in one another's arms, clinging desperately and kissing deeply. They moaned their desire, their hands moving feverishly. Reiner rolled to pull her on top of him, but Franka broke away with a sob.

Reiner sat up. 'What's this?'

'I am sorry, captain,' she said, hiding her face. 'I do not mean to tease, but I am not as strong as I pretend. This is why I beg you so not to press me. For it would take so little to make me give in, and then I could never forgive myself.'

Reiner sighed and pulled her head to his chest. 'Ah Franka, I...'

There were feet approaching the tent. 'Corporal Meyerling!' came a voice. 'Are you within?' It was Karel.

Reiner and Franka leapt up like guilty schoolboys. Reiner tore off his jerkin and tossed it to Franka. 'Here, take this and put it away. And dry your eyes. Hurry.'

Franka turned to Reiner's travel chest as Reiner righted the cot and piled the blankets on top of it. 'Come in,' he called. Karel ducked through the flap, his saddle-bags and armour over his shoulders.

'Corporal Ziegler?' said Reiner.

'They are overbooked, corporal,' Karel said, smiling. 'Thought they had more tents, but they didn't. I said you wouldn't mind if I bunked with you.'

Behind him Franka made a barking noise that might have been a sneeze, but probably wasn't.

Reiner ground his teeth. 'Not at all, sir. Not at all. Come in. Take the other cot.' He glared at Franka. 'Franz will sleep on the floor.'

FOR OBVIOUS REASONS, Reiner found it difficult to fall asleep that night, and so while Karel snored happily on his cot, and Franka slept curled in her bedroll, Reiner sat outside the tent, wrapped in his blankets, staring at the stars.

Part of him cursed Karel's inopportune interruption. Part of him thanked him. Reiner had no wish to hurt Franka, but whenever he was in her presence, the urge to crush her to him was overwhelming, and he forgot all promises and honour. Three months! Blood of Sigmar, he might explode by then!

A movement to his left caught his eye. He craned his neck. Three figures were slipping through the tents toward the north road. They all wore long cloaks with hoods pulled far forward to hide their faces.

Reiner frowned. The men might of course have a perfectly innocent reason for being abroad at this hour. A patrol, perhaps. And it was cold. They might wear cloaks to keep warm, but something in the furtiveness of their movements spoke of some dark purpose.

So much cheer on the surface of this place, Reiner thought, sitting back. The games, the songs, the love the soldiers had for their commander. But things stirred in the depths. Both Matthais and Shaeder had tried subtly to discover how Reiner felt about

Gutzmann. Was he sympathetic to the general's frustrations, or did he believe the Empire right in all things? Strange – or perhaps not so strange – that Reiner found himself drawn more to Gutzmann's side. The general wanted to escape the suffocating embrace of authority, and so did he.

SIX
Where Does He Lead Us?

THE NEXT MORNING, after entirely too little sleep, Reiner was awakened by Karel, who sprang out of his cot and began donning his new uniform, whistling all the while.

Reiner opened one eye. 'Would you mind very much jumping off a cliff?'

'Did you not hear the bugle?' asked Karel. 'The day has begun.' He took a deep breath. 'I can smell our breakfast cooking in the great hall from here.'

Reiner waved a hand. 'Go on without me, lad. I will follow momentarily.'

Karel grinned as he stepped to the door. 'Don't tarry too long, slug-a-bed, or you shan't get any bacon.'

Reiner groaned, nauseous. Who could think of bacon at this hour?

'I begin to see why Manfred wanted that boy out of his hair,' said Franka, rising from her bedroll.

'Aye.' Reiner sat up, rubbing his face. He sighed. 'Well, Franz, lay out my uniform. Time to go learn my new duties.'

Franka saluted sleepily. 'Aye, sir.' She crossed to his trunk and took out his newly assigned uniform: slashed breeks and jerkin in Gutzmann's deep blue and white. Reiner splashed his face in the bowl of freezing water at his bedside and shivered in the morning chill. He almost longed for the comforts of Manfred's townhouse again. Almost.

'While I'm gone,' he said, as Franka helped him into his jerkin, 'your duties are to nose about and listen to the other valets, cooks and so forth. Rumour flies faster through the kitchen than the parlour, as they say. See what they are saying about Gutzmann and Shaeder and the rest. There's a struggle going on here and I want to know who has the winning hand. If you see any of our comrades, canvass them as well.'

'Aye, captain.'

'And give us a kiss.'

'No, captain.'

'Bah! Insubordination. Intolerable!'

AFTER BREAKFAST, WHICH he found he had a stomach for after all, he presented himself to Captain Vortmunder outside the stables, which were huge – three long wooden buildings – crowded with horses and swarming with knights, lancers and pistoliers.

The captain scowled at him, his moustaches like needles pointing at the sky. 'Sleeping late your first day, Meyerling? An excellent start.'

Reiner clicked his heels. 'Forgive me, captain. I am still a bit unfamiliar with the camp.'

'Then we will remedy that.' Vortmunder looked around at the men walking their horses out of the stables and fitting them with saddle and bridle. 'Hie! Grau! Here!'

A corporal saluted and trotted over. He was a square-jawed bantam-weight, lean and compact, with close-cropped blond hair and a neat beard. Reiner saw that many of the young cavalry officers sported the same look – an army of Gutzmann imitators – or perhaps worshippers. 'Yes, captain,' the corporal said, coming to attention.

'Light duty for you this morning, Grau. You will show Corporal Meyerling around the fort and familiarize him with his duties. Bring him to the parade ground after noon mess, in full kit and ready to ride. That is all.'

Grau saluted, beaming. 'Yes sir!'

Vortmunder turned to Reiner. 'Listen to him well, corporal. I don't care for slow starters. A keen mind is as important as a sharp eye to a pistolier.'

'Yes, sir,' said Reiner. 'Thank you, sir.' He saluted as well, then followed Grau.

When they were out of Vortmunder's earshot, Grau grinned and nudged Reiner in the ribs. 'I'm in your debt, old man. You've got me out of stable duty.'

Reiner raised an eyebrow. 'Pistoliers clean the stables? You have no squires?'

'Gutzmann wishes us to learn discipline. No soft berths here. No buying your way out of duty, no matter who your father is. I hated it at first. But I don't mind so much now. We're the best army in the Empire because of it. There's none to match us.'

'Aye?' said Reiner. 'You're not the only army to claim it.'

'But it's the truth with us. You'll see this afternoon.' He pointed to the big south wall. 'First things first. The great south wall. Thirty feet thick, fifty feet tall. It could probably stop most armies unmanned, but we man it anyway. Gives the foot something to do.' He lowered his hand to the gate. 'Oak doors. Two portcullises. Murder room above, with vents for pouring oil or lead on anyone who manages to get through the first gate. The walls can be reached through the gatehouse guardroom and each of the four towers.'

'And the only army likely to attack is that of a kingdom that has been friendly with the Empire for five hundred years?' said Reiner. 'No wonder you play so many games.'

'Oh, there's fighting, never fear,' said Grau. 'Nests of bandits in the hills. The occasional orc raiding party. You'll know every goat track and rabbit trail for a hundred leagues before you're here a month.' He swung his arm to the keep. 'If an army breaches the south wall – not bloody likely, but if – we fall back to the keep. Armoury and main powder room are in there, as well as quarters for all the top brass and the barracks for their personal guard. The gate is like the south wall's in miniature. Oak doors. Murder room above, which also houses the winches that raise and lower the two portcullises. We've food, water and space to house five hundred men for three weeks.' He coughed. 'Unfortunately, there's two thousand of us at the moment, now that you lot have joined us.'

'Comforting,' said Reiner.

Grau turned to the other half of the fort. 'Stables. Smithy. Feed barn. Infantry drill yard. Barracks for the knights, lancers and pistoliers. Those new ones are for the infantry. Gutzmann built them when he doubled the garrison. And still there ain't enough. Hence the tents north of the fort.'

'Hence I'm sleeping under canvas.'

Grau grinned. 'Invigorating, ain't it?'

'I'll be happy to switch with you.'

Grau laughed. 'No fear.' He started back to the stables. 'Come, let's have a look at your kit. You brought your own horse?'

'Aye.'

'Well, we'll see if he's up to snuff.'

They found Reiner's horse and his gear and Grau looked it over while he explained Reiner's duties and what his days would consist of. Reiner grew tired just hearing it. Rise at daybreak every day, groom one's horse and clean one's tack. Then either drill, drudgery, or duty for the rest of the day. A third of the force was always on patrol, or escorting merchants to and from Aulschweig. A third was drilling on the parade ground, practising turns and wheels, shooting and swordplay from horseback. The last third was cleaning the stables or feeding the horses or mending tack or any of a dozen unpleasant but necessary chores. The more he listened, the more relieved Reiner was that he wasn't actually stationed here. He didn't know how long he would have to maintain his pistolier charade before he learned what Gutzmann was up to, but the sooner he could get away the better. Hard labour had never been his forte.

As Grau and Reiner led Reiner's horse to the smithy to be reshod – apparently Manfred's farrier did inferior work – Reiner heard raised voices coming from the far side of the privy shed, a low, stone building built against the canyon wall behind the stables.

'No man puts hands on me! I'll murder ye, ye clot!'

Reiner groaned. That could only be one man.

And as Reiner and Grau passed the shed, he was proved correct. Dag flew out of the door and fell across their path, his nose streaming red. He bounced back up into the face of a hulking crossbowman, who was cursing and shaking a filthy mop at him.

'Y'filthy little maggot, I'll shove you down the jakes and piss on you.'

'Touch me again and y'won't have nothing to piss from, y'great bullock!' shouted Dag.

'Hoy!' cried Grau. 'Stand down the both of you!'

The men looked up. The crossbowman stepped back, cowed by the presence of junior officers, but Dag, seeing Reiner, held out pleading hands.

'Captain Reiner, help me!' he called. 'This oaf tried to push me in the piss trough.'

Grau looked around at Reiner. 'You know this fellow?'

'Hardly.'

'I only bumped him, sirs,' said the crossbowman. 'The man's mad.'

'Mad!' Dag turned back to the crossbowman. 'Y'call me mad? I'll show ye mad! I'll eat yer liver!'

'Archer!' Reiner barked. 'Come to heel, curse you! What is the meaning of this!' He spun Dag around by the shoulder. Dag's eyes flared, but before he could speak, Reiner jabbed his finger in his face. 'You are mad, you horrible man! Starting fights for no reason! Calling on me as your captain! Do I look an archer? I am a corporal of pistoliers, footman! Your better in every way! And you would do well to remember it! Now stop this foolishness or you'll wind up in stir and be of no use to anyone! Do you understand me, cur?'

Dag hung his head, but Reiner was certain he saw a smile on the archer's lips. 'Aye, captain, er, corporal. I understand. Aye.'

'You will keep your fists, and your insults, and your liver eating to yourself, do you hear?'

'Aye, corporal.'

'Good.' Reiner stood back. 'Now be off, the both of you, and if I hear any more of this I'll string you up myself.'

He turned away with Grau and they continued towards the stables as Dag and the crossbowman slouched sulkily back into the privies, giving each other dirty looks.

Reiner breathed a sigh of relief. The damned madman had almost given the game away. Why had Manfred cursed him with command of such a fool? He shrugged as Grau gave him a questioning look. 'I did the fellow the kindness of letting him fetch me some water in exchange for a few coins one night on the march here, and now he thinks me his master. He's moon touched.'

Grau grinned. 'Well you gave him a proper scolding. You'll make parade corporal with that tongue. Strewth!'

NOON MESS FOR officers was served in the keep's great hall, where Reiner had supped the night before. This time, however, he did not sit on the dais with the captains, but mucked in with the other corporals on the long tables that ran the length of the room. It was a noisy affair, with much banter and horseplay once the oath to Sigmar had been pledged and the bread broken.

But the tensions he had felt elsewhere were here as well. There was very little mixing between the sergeants of the infantry and the corporals of the cavalry. They sat at separate tables and shot suspicious glances at each other. And under the cheery cacophony of insults and jokes he heard darker mutterings.

As he passed a table of sergeants he heard one say, 'We might lead 'em. But it's him and his cursed centaurs they love.'

One of the man's companions came to Gutzmann's defence. 'And why not? He's the best leader you've served under.'

'Aye, but where does he lead us? That's the question, ain't it?'

The question indeed. But though all around Reiner the cavalry officers exchanged sly glances and made veiled references to 'the future,' they were cagey in his presence. It maddened him. Their smug smiles and sly looks spoke of a conspiracy, but Reiner could learn nothing.

He could tell Grau itched to tell him what was afoot. After his lambasting of Dag, the corporal had decided Reiner was a good egg. He spent the whole of their meal cautiously feeling him out, trying to determine his loyalties, but afraid yet to betray himself, just as Matthais had the night before.

'But you've seen it close hand, haven't you, Meyerling?' he asked as they sat with the other pistolier corporals. 'How it is titles that win promotion, not ability. That is the problem with the Emperor's army. Noble lackwits become generals while men with real talent can't rise above captain.' He sighed, perhaps a little too theatrically, 'If only a man like General Gutzmann ran things. We'd have professional soldiers leading us, men with experience in battle instead of politics.'

Reiner nodded sincerely, for he knew that was what Grau wanted him to do. 'Aye. That's how things should be. A modern, professional army, free of patronage. Too bad there's no chance of it happening in our lifetimes.'

Grau's eyes widened. He sat forward. 'You might be surprised, Meyerling. You might be surprised. Things might change quicker than you think. Perhaps not in the…'

The pistolier to Grau's left, a round-faced fellow named Yeoder, elbowed him in the ribs. Grau looked up and followed his gaze. A hush was falling on the cavalry tables as a company of men rose from their table near the dais and walked toward the hall's side door.

They were an impressive sight, twenty tall, stern greatswords, all in black, with snow white shirts showing at their cuffs and through their slashings. Their breastplates were black chased with silver and their kit matched down to the pommels of their swords and the buckles of their shoes. All had the twin comet stitched onto the right shoulders of their jerkins and silver hammers on a chain around their necks, which were smaller twins to the one that Shaeder wore. Their captain was a head shorter than the rest, but as powerfully built, with a magnificent square-cut white beard and eyes as blue and cold as a winter sky.

A circle of silence moved with them as they traversed the room, the conversations at the tables dying off and the cavalry officers turning to look at them over their shoulders after they had passed. Reiner could feel the hate emanating from his companions for the impassive men.

'Who are they?' he asked, when the men had at last left the hall and conversation had resumed.

Grau spit over his left shoulder. 'Shaeder's Hammer, we call 'em,' he said. 'They are Bearers of the Hammer, honour guard from Averheim's Temple of Sigmar, of which Shaeder was once a captain. Now they're his personal guard.'

'Gloomy lot,' Reiner said.

'Bah,' said Yeoder. 'Just stuck up. Think Sigmar is their personal property. Nobody else is good enough.'

'They'll find out,' said another pistol, darkly.

Grau gave him a sharp look and quickly turned the conversation to other things.

* * *

THAT NIGHT REINER stumbled through the flap of his tent and collapsed onto his cot, utterly exhausted.

The afternoon had been one of the most gruelling of his young life. He had thought himself a veteran of the parade ground, having trained under Lord von Stolmen's master of horse, Karl Hoffstetter, considered one of the Empire's finest. But while Captain Vortmunder couldn't teach Reiner anything he hadn't learned already from Hoffstetter, what he did do was drill it into him until his limbs felt like lead and the blisters the constant repetition raised on his fingers, knees and thighs had burst and bled and burst again. No horse master back home had dared ride his pupils so hard. They were the sons of noblemen, used to being waited on and pampered. They would practise for a while and then they would retire to the taproom to boast about their prowess.

Not so with Vortmunder. He had no pity, and no deference to rank. He had his pistoliers ride and fire at targets again and again and again, until the actions became second nature and they hit the bull's-eye ten times in a row. He barked at them for the slightest failure of form. If a pistolier was ahead or behind his fellows as they wheeled, or he took too long to reload on the fly as he circled back from the target, Vortmunder was there, cantering beside him, ram-rod straight in his saddle, pointing out with his riding crop the pistol's offence.

And Reiner had felt the brunt of his attention. He had become the captain's target of choice.

'Let's have Gutzmann's favourite out again,' he would say when he was detailing the next exercise. 'Show us how they do it in the north, Meyerling.' Until Reiner thoroughly regretted his tent-pegging grandstanding the day before.

At the same time, even though by the end of the day he was cursing Vortmunder's guts with a vehemence he usually reserved for loan-sharks and officers of the watch, when the captain pulled up beside him as they were returning their horses to the stables and clapped him on the back with a 'Good work, corporal,' he felt a swelling of pride that almost made him want to do the whole thing over the next day.

Franka laughed at him as she helped him off with his jerkin, for he could barely lift his arms.

'Don't mock me, villain,' he said. 'Shall I tell you how weary I am?'

'Tell me,' said Franka.

Reiner looked over at Karel, who was already fast asleep in his cot, then leaned in to whisper in Franka's ear. 'Even had we the tent to ourselves, you would be as safe as if in a Shallyan convent.'

Franka's eyes widened. 'You are weary indeed, m'lord.'

For five days Reiner's routine continued the same. He was put in charge of ten men, and under Vortmunder's and Grau's guidance, learned the orders to give them, how to lead them in their turns and manoeuvres, and how to work with the other squads of pistols so that the entire company fought as a cohesive unit. It was exhausting, arse breaking work, but though he cursed it every night and every stiff-jointed morning, he found himself enjoying it more and more. He might almost be tempted to make it his life.

He had little time to seek out the other Blackhearts, and when he did they had little to tell him. Pavel and Hals had heard rumblings among the pikemen of some kind of revolt, but no details. Giano and Gert, attached to units of crossbowmen, heard similar whispers, but what shape the revolt would take they couldn't say. Dag had done two days in the brig for fighting and had heard nothing. Abel said he had heard that Gutzmann meant to storm Altdorf, but he said the fellow who had said it was drunk at the time, so he didn't credit it. Jergen said he had nothing to add, and Karel hadn't heard anything. Reiner wasn't surprised. The boy was so wide-eyed and guileless that no conspirator would trust him with a secret.

Of course he had done no better. Several times Grau had seemed to be on the verge of letting him in on the cavalry's secret, but something always made him hesitate at the last moment.

On the morning of the sixth day, as Reiner was saddling his horse outside the stables, Matthais approached on horseback and saluted Vortmunder.

'Begging the captain's pardon,' he said, 'but cavalry Obercaptain Oppenhauer accompanies the trade caravan to Aulschweig and requests an escort of pistoliers.'

'Very good, corporal,' said Vortmunder, and looked around at his men. His eyes lit upon Reiner. 'Ah. Take Meyerling. Time he rode further than the tilt yard and back.' He raised his voice. 'Meyerling, assemble your men and follow Corporal Bohm. He will give you your orders.'

And so, a short while later, Reiner rode out of the north gate at Matthais's side, their respective squads tailing behind them, accompanied by a unit of crossbowmen sitting on the back of an empty cart. The morning sun glanced blindingly off the neat rows of tents beyond the north wall, and glittered the dew on the tilting yard grass.

'Er, isn't Aulschweig south?' Reiner asked Matthais. Matthais grinned as they headed up the north road. 'Aye. But we're to the mine first to pick up some mining supplies before meeting the trade caravan. Every month we bring Empire goods to Baron Caspar at his castle just the other side of the border. In return we get grain, fodder, meat, and cooking oil. All for cheaper than carting it in from Hocksleten or Averheim, and better quality too. Very fertile valley, Aulschweig.'

Reiner raised an eyebrow. 'Aulschweig has a gold mine as well?'

'Er, no,' said Matthais. 'A tin mine. But, er, the tools are the same.'

'Ah, I see. And Obercaptain Oppenhauer comes with us?'

'Aye.'

'What's a cavalry obercaptain doing riding herd on a milk run?'

Matthais shot Reiner a hard glance. 'You are very astute, corporal. Er, well, there is another purpose for our visit. You remember I told you that Caspar has been eyeing his brother's throne?'

'I remember.'

'Well, apparently his grumblings have been getting louder of late, so Gutzmann sends Oppenhauer along to whisper soothing words in his ear. And also to remind him of our might.'

'Sounds a bit of a hothead, this Caspar.'

'You'll see.'

THE MINE WAS only a few hundred yards along a well-trodden path that branched westwards from the pass. Entry to it was guarded by fortifications that mirrored in miniature those of the fort – a thick, crenellated wall that blocked the canyon from wall to wall, with a tower on each side of a deep, portcullised gate.

Inside the wall were barracks, stables, and other outbuildings Reiner couldn't guess the purpose of. A system of pipes ran through one from a small aqueduct. Crowds of dust-caked miners trooped in and out of the mine entrance, a large, square opening in the mountainside framed with tree-trunks, carrying pickaxes and wheeling barrows. Almost as many pikemen and crossbowmen watched over them, patrolling the walls and every inch of the compound.

As Matthais called his party to a halt outside a low, weathered wood building, an overseer bustled out to greet them.

'Morning, corporal. Shipment ain't quite ready. A few minutes yet.'

'Very good.' The lancer turned to Reiner. 'Gives me an opportunity to show you around.'

Reiner sighed to himself. If he never went underground again it would be too soon. 'Certainly, corporal. Lead on.'

Matthais and Reiner dismounted and walked towards the mine. Matthais pointed out different buildings as they went, each of which was as busy as a beehive in the spring. 'That is the sluice room, where the raw ore is separated from the earth by means of a stream and a series of screens. There is the smelter, where the collected nuggets are melted and skimmed of impurities. This is the shakedown room, where the miners must strip and turn out their pockets before they leave the mine, to make sure they aren't absconding with any ore.'

'Very thorough of you.'

'One can't be too careful.'

Reiner shivered as he stepped into the mine. Memories of the last time he'd gone underground flashed through his head, but this cave was very different. It had none of the gloom and despair of the Kurgan mine. Nor the smell. Instead, all was bustle and industry. Two wide tunnels sloped away from the main entrance into the depths, and in and out of them went steady streams of miners, marching away with empty carts and picks on their shoulders, or trudging back with full carts and grime on their faces. Reiner found all this activity very interesting. If the mine was working at such a feverish rate, why was the stream of gold that reached Altdorf the merest trickle? It seemed as if Matthais's tale of difficulties in getting ore from the mine was less than the truth. Reiner didn't feel that now was the time to call him on it.

A third tunnel had no traffic. Its mouth was cluttered with broken equipment and stacks of supplies. Reiner pointed to it. 'Did this one run dry?'

Matthais shook his head. 'Structural problems. Had a cave-in recently. The engineers won't let the miners work it until it is safely shored up again.' He beckoned Reiner towards the left side of the entry chamber. 'This way. I want to show you something.'

As Reiner and Matthais dodged through the streams of miners, Reiner noticed that the men fell into a sullen silence as they passed, and then murmured under their breath behind them. Gutzmann must be driving them hard, Reiner thought. But then he thought there might be more to it than that. For as he looked around, he saw other signs of discontent. The miners had a haunted look, and glanced often over their shoulders. A group of miners had surrounded one of their foremen and were complaining vigorously. Reiner caught the words 'gone missing' and 'ain't doin' nothing about it.'

'Has there been some trouble?' Reiner asked.

Matthais snorted. 'Peasant nonsense. They claim men are disappearing in the mine. Running away, is my guess. There have been a number of village girls "stolen away" as well.' He shrugged. 'It doesn't take a magus to add that up. A few boys manage to steal a nugget of ore or two and off they go with their sweethearts to the flatlands where it doesn't snow eight months of the year.'

'Ah,' said Reiner. 'Like enough.'

They stepped through an open arch into a short hall.

'This is what I wanted to show you,' said Matthais. 'The first owner of this mine was a bit odd. Perhaps he wanted to be closer to his gold. But he decided that he would live in the mine, and so built his house underground. Here.'

He gestured before them to a beautifully carved wooden door that wouldn't have been out of place fronting some noble's Altdorf townhouse. Matthais pushed it open and peeked in, then beckoned Reiner to enter. The illusion continued inside. The entrance hall looked like a townhouse foyer, with a grand stairway curving up to a second floor gallery, and doors leading off to a sitting room on the left and a library on the right. That such a place existed at all so far from civilization was amazing in its own right, but what made it truly incredible was that everything, from the stairway, to the newel posts and banisters, to the statues of buxom virtues tucked into niches, to the moulding on the ceiling, to the oil lamp sconces that lit the place, was carved from the living rock. Even the tables in the library and some of the benches and chairs grew from the floor. And this was no crude cave dwelling. The ornamentation was exquisite, baroque columns wrapped in stylized foliage, heraldic beasts holding the wall sconces, gracefully curved legs on the stone tables and chairs. It took Reiner's breath away.

'It's beautiful,' he said. 'Mad, but beautiful. He must have paid a fortune.'

'Shhh,' said Matthais, as he followed Reiner into the sitting room. 'Not really supposed to be here. The engineers of the mine have taken it for their offices and kip. Gutzmann's had quite a time convincing them not to knock out some of the fixtures to make room for their infernal contraptions. No eye for beauty. If it ain't practical, they don't see it.'

A pair of wooden double doors at the far end of the sitting room opened, pinning them in a bar of yellow light. Shaeder glared out at them.

'What are you men doing here?'

Matthais jumped to attention, saluting. 'Sorry, commander. Just showing Meyerling our local marvel. Didn't mean to intrude.'

Behind Shaeder, Reiner could see a dining room, in the centre of which was a large round table, also carved from the rock. Around it sat a colloquy of engineers: grimy, bearded men in oil blackened leather aprons, many wearing thick spectacles, poring over a parchment spread on the table. Stumps of charcoal and ink quills were tucked behind their ears, and they held little leather-bound journals in their grubby hands.

'Well, now you've seen it,' said Shaeder. 'Be off with you.'

'Yes, sir.' Matthais saluted as Shaeder closed the door again. He shrugged at Reiner like a boy caught stealing apples.

As they tip-toed out through the door again, Reiner looked over his shoulder. 'Is the commander in charge of the mine?'

Matthais shook his head. 'Not officially, but Chief Engineer Holsanger was crushed in the cave-in and the commander has taken over his duties until Altdorf can send a replacement. Stretches him a bit thin. Makes him grumpy.'

'So I see.'

As they came into the mine proper again, Reiner heard raucous laughter and a familiar voice raised in protest. It was Giano, on duty with a squad of crossbowmen who watched the miners as they came and went.

'Is true, I tell you,' Giano was saying. 'I smell with my own eyes!'

'What's the trouble, Tilean?' asked Reiner.

'Ah, corporal!' said Giano. 'Defend for me, hey? They say I am be fool!'

A burly crossbowman chuckled and jerked his thumb at Giano. 'Forget him, corporal. The garlic-eater says there be ratmen in the mine. Ratmen!' He laughed again.

'Is true!' insisted Giano. 'I smell them!'

'And how do you know what a ratman smells like, soldier?' asked Matthais, condescendingly.

'They kill my family. My village. They come up under the grounds and eat all the peoples. I never forget the stinking.'

Matthais glared. 'Ratmen are a myth, Tilean. They don't exist. And if you don't want to spend some time in stir, you'll keep your foolishness to yourself. These peasants are superstitious enough already. We don't need them downing tools every time a rat squeaks in the dark.'

'But they here. I know...'

'It don't matter what you know, soldier,' snapped Reiner. 'Or think you know. The corporal has ordered you to be silent. You will be silent. Am I clear?'

Giano saluted reluctantly. 'Clear as bells, corporal. Yes, sir.'

Matthais and Reiner left the mine.

As THE PARTY rode back toward the fort with the loaded supply wagon, Reiner began to wonder why the armed escort had gone to the mine to pick up its cargo instead of waiting for the cart to come to the fort. Did Obercaptain Oppenhauer really think that a shipment of mining supplies was in danger in the short mile twixt the mine and the fort? Or was Manfred's order to sniff out suspicious activity causing Reiner to read nefarious motives into the most innocent of army procedures?

In any event, they reached the fort without incident. A train of wagons and carts joined them there, piled high with luxury goods from Altdorf, iron skillets from Nuln, wine and cloth and leather goods from Bretonnia, Tilea and beyond. As the party formed into march order, Oppenhauer trotted up on an enormous white charger that still looked small for his gigantic, barrel-chested frame.

'Morning, lads,' he cried in a booming voice. 'Ready for our outing?'

'Yes sir, obercaptain,' said Matthais saluting. 'Beautiful day for it.'

Reiner saluted as well, and they got under way, passing through the main gate into the pass to Aulschweig. The terrain was the same as that to the north of the fort. Steep, pine-covered slopes rising up to rocky, snow-capped peaks. The air was biting cold, but they still found themselves hot in their breastplates as the sun beat down on them.

'So, Meyerling,' said Oppenhauer. 'Getting used to our routine?'

Reiner smiled. 'I am, sir. My arse, however, is still a tenderfoot.'

Oppenhauer laughed. 'Vortmunder running you ragged, is he?'

'Aye, sir.'

They carried on in this merry vein for an hour or so, trading banter, jokes and good-natured insults. Reiner noticed that the lancers and pistoliers were more high-spirited here than in the camp. It was as if they were schoolboys who had run away from their tutor. He wondered if it was only that they weren't drilling and doing chores, or if it was the fact that there were no infantry officers around. He hoped that this relaxation might loosen their tongues, but whenever they started to talk about 'the future' or 'when Gutzmann shows Altdorf his mettle,' Oppenhauer 'harrumphed' and the conversation swung back to the usual barrack room subjects.

After a time one of the lancers began singing a song about a maid from Nuln and a pikeman with a wooden leg, and soon the whole company joined in, traders, draymen and all, inventing filthier and filthier verses as they went on.

But just as they were coming around to the sixth repetition of the chorus, an arrow appeared in the chest of one of the crossbowmen, and he fell off the supply cart. Before Reiner could comprehend what had happened, a swarm of arrows buzzed from the woods, targeting the other crossbowmen. Two more went down.

'Bandits!' shouted Matthais.

'Ambush!' boomed Oppenhauer.

All around Reiner horses were rearing and men were screaming. The surviving crossbowmen were returning fire at their invisible assailants. Reiner's pistoliers were drawing their guns.

'Hold!' Reiner cried. 'Wait for targets!'

A lancer fell, clutching his neck.

Oppenhauer stood in his saddle. An arrow glanced off his breastplate. 'Forward! Ride! Do not stand and fight!'

The crossbowmen hauled their wounded onto the carts and the draymen and traders whipped their carthorses into a lumbering canter. Reiner's and Matthais's squads flanked them. As the party surged ahead, ragged men in tattered buckskin leggings and layers of filthy clothing ran out of the woods after them, spears and swords in hand.

'Now, lads!' called Reiner. He and his squad drew their pistols and fired left and right. Bandits dropped, twisting and screaming. Vortmunder's constant drilling showed in the steadiness of the pistoliers as they used their knees alone to guide their horses, while reloading and firing behind them.

'Meyerling!' bawled Oppenhauer. 'Guard the rear. 'Ware their ponies.'

'Aye, sir. Rein in, lads. Double file behind the last wagon. Fire as you can.'

Reiner looked back as he and his men let the wagons slip ahead. More bandits were bursting from the woods, but these were mounted on wiry hill ponies, half the size of Reiner's warhorse. They raced after the company. The pistoliers could have outdistanced them easily, but the heavily laden carts were too slow. The bandits were gaining.

Reiner reloaded and fired, adding his shots to the ragged volley of his men. Only a few found a mark, but one was a fortunate hit, catching the lead pony in the knee. It screamed, leg buckling, and went down on its neck, throwing its rider. Two more ponies crashed into it from behind and fell. The rest leapt the carnage and kept coming. They closed with every step.

The road jogged sharply around an outcropping of rock. The crossbowmen and traders clung desperately as the carts bumped and fishtailed. Reiner hugged his horse's neck as he leaned into the turn. The cart full of mine supplies hit a stone, bucked, and came to earth again with a bang. One of the smaller crates jumped and slid. A crossbowman made a grab for it, but it was too heavy. It tipped off the back of the cart and bounced a few times before coming to rest on its side. The rest of the carts swerved around it.

'Obercaptain!' cried Matthais, as the box rapidly fell behind them. 'We've lost a crate!'

'Sigmar curse it!' Oppenhauer growled. 'Turn about! Turn about! Defend that crate!'

'Turn about, lads!' Reiner called. He and Matthais reined up and wheeled in tight circles with their men behind them as the traders' carts began lumbering around. Oppenhauer swung around to take the lead. Reiner was baffled. Was the obercaptain so concerned with picks and shovels that he would endanger his men's lives, and his own, to rescue them? What was in that crate?

As Reiner's and Matthais's squads rode back round the bend ahead of the carts, Reiner saw that some of the bandits had stopped. Four of them were trying to carry the crate into the trees. The others were on guard. The four with the crate could barely lift it.

Oppenhauer shouted back to the draymen over the thunder of their hooves. 'Stop your carts left and right of the crate! We shall need their cover while we load.' He pointed at Reiner and Matthais. 'Clear the men at the box, then take cover behind the carts.'

Reiner and Matthais saluted, then raised their arms.

'Pistols ready,' said Reiner.

'Lancers ready,' said Matthais.

The pistoliers held their guns at their cheeks. The lancers pointed their lances at the sky.

'Fire!' cried Reiner.

His men levelled their guns and fired into the cluster of bandits. A few dropped, a few fired back. The rest ran to their ponies, trying to remount.

'Charge!' cried Matthais.

The lancers lowered their lances and spurred their horses into a thundering gallop. Oppenhauer charged with them.

'Sabres!' Reiner called.

His men drew their swords and followed the lancers and Oppenhauer as they ploughed into the bandits, impaling them and running them down. The rest scattered, on foot or on horseback, racing for the woods as the carts pulled up around the crate. More bandits were running up the road, most on foot – stragglers from the ambush – but when they saw the situation they too melted into the woods.

Reiner and Matthais circled back quickly with their squads and dismounted behind the cover of the carts as the crossbowmen began firing bolts into the trees. They were answered by a storm of arrows that thudded into the wagons and cargo.

'Lancers!' bellowed Oppenhauer, jumping off his horse. 'Help me with the crate!'

Matthais and three of his men stepped to the crate and grabbed the edges. Even with Oppenhauer joining them, they strained to lift it. Reiner's questions were becoming suspicions. He saw that the lid had pulled up at one corner and stepped forward.

'Let me give you a hand.'

'We have it, Meyerling,' grunted Oppenhauer, but Reiner ignored him and helped lift. As they edged it up on the cart, next to another just like it, Reiner got a glimpse under the lid. It was filled with small rectangles of yellow metal that shone like...

Gold.

Before he could be sure of what he had seen, Oppenhauer pounded the lid shut with the heel of his hand.

'Now, ride! Ride!' he called.

Reiner glanced at the obercaptain as he hurried back to his horse, but Oppenhauer's face was unreadable. Did he know

Reiner had seen the gold? Had he been hiding it, or just closing the lid?

The carts turned clumsily about as arrows whistled around them. The crossbowmen returned fire, shooting randomly into the woods until they got under way. Oppenhauer, Matthais and Reiner and their squads fell in behind, but the bandits didn't follow, only stole out after the crossbowmen no longer had their range, to collect their arrows and see to their fallen.

The train of wagons continued on toward Aulschweig with four dead and ten wounded. Reiner rode in silence, oblivious to his men's nervous post-battle chatter. He had discovered where Manfred's missing gold was going, though why it was crossing the border he had no idea. More important was its mere existence. The crate he had seen held enough gold to make a man one of the wealthiest in the Empire. And there were two of them, tucked amidst the rest of the cargo. Two fortunes. More than even Karl-Franz himself might spend in a lifetime.

Reiner smiled. He wasn't greedy. He didn't want them both. He needed only one. One would be more than enough to pay a sorcerer to remove the poison from the Blackhearts' blood – to buy their freedom.

The only question now was, how did he get it?

SEVEN
A Man of Vision

THE CASTLE OF Baron Caspar Tzetchka-Koloman sat hunched above the fertile Aulschweig valley like a wolf looking down at a hen-house. It had been built to guard the mouth of the pass from the Empire, when in the wild days of long ago there had been danger of invasion from that quarter – a small, but sturdily built keep that seemed to grow out of the crags that surrounded it. The valley below was like a dream of how the Empire might have been, if not for so many years of war – a bright green jewel of wheat fields not yet ripe and orchards of apple, pear and walnut. Tiny stone and shingle villages nestled in the gentle folds of the land, the spires of their country shrines sticking up above pine spinneys.

Baron Caspar was a restless young man a few years older than Reiner, but a child in temperament. A pale, sharp-faced fellow with jet black hair and dark eyes, he twitched and squirmed in his seat all through the generous dinner he laid before his guests in the high, banner-hung hall of his chilly keep.

'So General Gutzmann is well?' he asked as he mashed peas onto the back of his fork with his dagger. He spoke Imperial with a lilting mountain accent.

'Very well, my lord,' said Oppenhauer between mouthfuls. 'And your brother, Prince Leopold? He is in good health?'

'Oh, fine, fine. Never better, last I heard. Though it's precious little news I get here on the edge of nowhere. From my brother, or General Gutzmann.' He stabbed his meat with more force than necessary.

Oppenhauer spread his hands. 'Are we not here, my lord? Did we not bring the mining supplies you requested? Did I not convey the general's heartfelt greetings?'

'Yes, but no news. No answer.'

Oppenhauer coughed and shot a look at Reiner. 'Let's not spoil a good meal with matters of state, shall we? When we let poor Bohm and Meyerling go back to their men, you and I will speak of other things.'

Caspar pursed his lips. 'Very well. Very well.' But Reiner could see his leg jumping under the table as he bounced his foot nervously up and down.

Reiner waited for Oppenhauer or Matthais to make polite conversation. When they didn't, he cleared his throat. 'So, baron, your mining goes well?'

Oppenhauer and Matthais froze, forks halfway to their mouths.

Caspar looked up at Reiner sharply, then snorted. 'Ha! Yes. My mining goes well, indeed. We have been able to recruit many more men for the work, and with your new shipment of supplies we will be able to expand our operations even more. It is a great cure for my enforced idleness here, mining. I am looking forward to the day that I will be able to show my brother the steel we are bringing from that mine.'

Reiner struggled to keep his face straight. Steel from a tin mine. Interesting.

WHEN THE MEAL came to an end, Matthais invited Reiner to join him and his men in Caspar's guardroom for a game of trumps, but though the temptation to shear these yearling lambs of their golden fleece was strong, Reiner instead pleaded weariness and an upset stomach and retired to his room. He did not, however, stay there long.

Caspar and Oppenhauer had taken their after-dinner schnapps to the library to discuss 'matters of state' by the fire. Reiner wanted to hear that conversation, and so as soon as the footman who had guided him to his room had departed, Reiner stepped back into the corridor and began making his way back to the lower floors. The castle was nearly deserted. Caspar had no wife or children, and only a few knights lived there with him – and those were playing cards with Matthais – so reaching the library meant only avoiding a few servants. Finding a way to hear what went on behind the thick carved-oak door was another matter.

He pressed his ear to the wood, but heard nothing but a low murmur and the roar of the fire. Perhaps there was a balcony window he could listen at if he could get outside. He crept to the next door along the hallway and listened. He thought he could still hear fire, but there were no voices, so he risked opening it.

There was indeed a fire, tightly penned inside an iron grate, and Reiner hesitated momentarily, fearing that the room was occupied after all. But though numerous eyes glittered back at him, they were in the heads of a silent jury of hunting trophies that stared accusingly at him from the walls. Deer, elk, bear, wolf and boar all were represented.

Reiner gave them a mock bow as he closed the door behind him. 'As you were, gentlemen.'

He crossed to tall, velvet-draped windows on the far side of the room and opened one. There was no balcony, only an iron railing to keep one from pitching headlong down the cliffside the castle was built upon. Reiner leaned out and looked to his right, towards the library. There were similar windows there. An agile man, with nerves of steel, might possibly climb over the railing, edge along the narrow ledge that ran between the windows, cling to the library window and listen. But even then he might not hear anything. The windows were tightly closed against the night's chill and the heavy curtains drawn. Still, this was the sort of conversation that Manfred would most want him to overhear. Reiner looked down the cliff, where jagged rocks poked up at him. He swallowed.

With a shrug that hid a shiver, he swung his leg over the railing. A booming laugh erupted behind him. He flinched and almost lost his footing. He looked back. He could have sworn the laugh had come from within the room. Another laugh burst forth, and this time he pin-pointed its source. The fireplace.

Reiner pulled his leg back over the railing and closed the window, then stepped quietly toward the fireplace. Muffled voices came from it. He peered into it, and was surprised to find that beyond the flames, he could see into the library. In fact he could make out Caspar's booted feet tapping nervously as he sat in a high-backed leather chair. Reiner had seen such fireplaces before, cleverly constructed to warm two rooms at once, but in intrigue-riddled Altdorf, where privacy was at a premium, most of them had been bricked up.

'But when?' came Caspar's voice. 'Why won't you tell me when?'

Reiner leaned in as close as he dared. The heat from the fire was intense, and its roar nearly drowned out all other sound, but if he held his breath he could hear Oppenhauer's rumbling reply.

'Soon, my lord,' the obercaptain said. 'We have just recruited the last men we need, but it will take some while to train them, and to discover which are sympathetic to our aims.'

'But curse it, I'm ready now! I tire of this waiting. Rusting here in the wilderness while Leopold sleeps through his reign. To think what could be made of this land if there was a man of vision on the throne!' He slapped the arm of his chair with his palm.

'It will happen,' said Oppenhauer. 'Never fear.'

Reiner leaned in closer as the obercaptain's words got lost in the crackling of the fire. His cheek felt aflame. His left eye was as dry as paper.

'The general is as eager as you, my lord. You know his history. He too has had his ambitions thwarted. Wait only a little longer and you and he will sweep your sleeping brother from his throne and place you upon it instead. Then with you as king and Gutzmann as the commander of your armies, Aulschweig will become all you want it to be. The other border princes will fall before your might, and you will unite the Black Mountains into one great nation. A nation that might one day rival the Empire itself.'

'Yes!' cried Caspar. 'That is my destiny! That is as it will be. But how soon? How soon?'

'Very soon, my lord,' said Oppenhauer. 'Very soon. Two months at the most.'

'Two months! An eternity!'

'Not at all. Not at all. By next month, when I return with more "supplies", I will bring you the general's final plans. And the month after that we will slowly ease our forces into position so that we may spring our trap without losing the element of surprise.'

Reiner stepped back from the fireplace, rubbing his stinging face. So that was the plan. If it were true, then it certainly met Manfred's criteria for 'removing' Gutzmann. Reiner could kill the general and get out of these freezing mountains as soon as they returned to the fort. On the other hand, there were some very good reasons to wait. Some golden reasons.

It was time to have a talk with the old Blackhearts.

EIGHT
Manfred's Noose

IN THE MINING town of Brunn the next night, Reiner strolled into Mother Leibkrug's house of joy like a man coming home. The look of the low ceilinged, dimly lit tap room, with the forms of men and women huddling in its dark corners, the smell of lamp smoke and cheap scent, the sounds of laughing harlots and dice in the cup, were a balm to his soul.

From the time he had left his father's home to attend university in Altdorf, until the day Archaon's invasion had made it impossible for even the least patriotic of Imperial citizens not to answer the call of honour, Reiner had lived his life in brothels such as this. In their salons had he and his friends argued points of philosophy, while bare-bottomed bawds served them beer and fritters. In their boudoirs had he lost his innocence and gained the bittersweet knowledge of lust, love and loss. In their card rooms had he learned and practised his preferred trade, and paid for his lodgings and his tuition with money won from rubes and rustics. He had been away from these hallowed halls so long it nearly brought a tear to his eye to enter them once again.

Franka, however, hesitated on the threshold.

Reiner looked back. 'What's the matter, young Franz? They don't bite unless you ask.'

Franka's eyes darted about the dark room. 'Are you certain you couldn't find a more suitable place to meet?'

'There is none better,' Reiner said. He put an arm around her shoulders. 'A brothel is a place where all soldiers can go, regardless of rank. And a place where one can buy some privacy. Name another place within a hundred leagues that offers as much.'

'I understand. Nevertheless...'

Reiner stopped and turned, a look of amused shock on his face. 'You've never been in a brothel before.'

'Of course not,' said Franka, disgusted. 'I'm a respectable woman.'

'You were. Now you're a soldier. And soldiers and brothels go together like... like swords and sheathes.'

'Don't be vulgar.'

'Beloved, if you removed my vulgarity, there would be precious little left of me.'

As he and Franka crossed to the bar he saw Pavel, Hals and Giano at a table, deep in conversation. He waved, and they rose and joined them.

'Here, barman,' Reiner called. 'I want a private room for me and my lads.'

'Certainly, sir,' said the barman. 'Would you care for company?'

'No, no. Just a bottle of wine for me and beer for the rest. As much as they want.'

'Very good, sir. If you will just follow Gretel.'

A serving girl led the party down a narrow hall and let them into a cramped room with a round table in the centre and grimy tapestries hiding bare-plank walls through which the wind whistled. Two oil lanterns provided more smoke than light and made their eyes water. But there was a brazier for cooking sausages in the middle of the table that kept the room warm. Giano was still arguing with Pavel and Hals as they sat down.

'Is ratmen!' he said. 'I smell their stink!'

Pavel sighed. 'There ain't no ratmen, lad.'

'Something down there,' said Hals. 'That's certain. Plenty of the lads have seen shadows moving where there shouldn't be none. And the boys what pull graveyard duty say the ground shakes under their feet late at night.'

'You see!' said Giano. 'Is ratmen! We must fight!'

'Lads, lads,' said Reiner, holding up his hands. 'It matters not what it is. And with luck we won't have to fight anything. With luck we'll do a quiet month here and be off to Altdorf with enough gold in our kit to win our freedom and be rid of Manfred and his intrigues once and for all.'

All heads turned his way.

'What's this?' asked Hals.

'Is this why you didn't want the others?' asked Pavel.

'Aye,' said Reiner. 'I think I've found our salvation at last.' He leaned forward eagerly. 'Here it is. Gutzmann means to desert to Aulschweig and help Baron Caspar usurp his brother, Prince Leopold, where he will become commander of Caspar's armies.'

'Bold dog,' said Hals, laughing. 'Won't that teach Altdorf to leave its bright sparks at loose ends, hey?'

Pavel nodded. 'Thought it might be some such.'

'What concerns us,' said Reiner, 'is that he helps to fund Caspar's army with regular shipments of gold.' He turned to Pavel. 'I escorted a shipment of it to Aulschweig yesterday, disguised as "mining equipment". And there will be another shipment of "shovels" next month. Which, with some luck, will be ours.'

The others stared at him.

Giano grinned. 'This good plan, hey? I like!'

'Aye,' said Hals. 'I like, too!'

'Free of Manfred's noose at last,' said Pavel.

'But can we do it?' asked Franka.

'Well, it will take some work, that's certain,' said Reiner. 'We can't just cut and run. We'll have to finish the job Manfred's set for us, or he could kill us before we find someone who will take our gold and remove the poison. We'll have to return to Altdorf and pretend...' He paused. Pavel and Hals's faces had fallen. 'What's wrong?'

'We still kill Gutzmann?' asked Pavel slowly.

Reiner nodded. 'Aye. We'll have to.'

Hals grimaced unhappily. 'He's a good man, captain.'

Reiner blinked. 'He's won you over, too? He means to betray the Empire.'

'Ain't that what we mean to do?' asked Pavel.

'We just want to save our own lives. He's leaving our border unguarded and taking his whole garrison with him.'

'Yer starting to sound like Manfred,' grunted Hals.

'None of that.' Reiner sighed. 'Listen, I agree. Gutzmann's better than most. He loves his men, and they love him. But is he worth dying for? For that's your option. If we don't kill Gutzmann, Manfred kills us. It's one or the other.'

Pavel and Hals continued to hesitate. Even Giano was looking glum.

Franka was frowning, thinking it over. 'But what if the poison is a lie? A ruse to keep us tame. What if he never poisoned us at all, only said he did?'

Reiner nodded. 'Aye, I've thought of that as well, and it might be. But since we can't know, we have to act as if it is, don't we?'

'There must be some way we can get away without killing Gutzmann,' said Hals, chewing his lip. 'Yer clever, captain. Cleverest man I know. Y've thunk us out of all sorts of messes, haven't ye?'

'Aye, captain,' said Pavel, brightening. 'Ye'll think of something. Y'always do! There must be some way, hey?'

'Lads, lads, I may be clever, but I'm no sorcerer. I can't just wish it better. I...'

There was a knock on the door. 'Captain Reiner, are you within?'

Reiner and the others froze, hands on their daggers, as the door opened. It was Karel. The new Blackhearts were behind him.

NINE
Is Someone There?

ABEL PEERED OVER Karel's shoulder. 'You see. Didn't I say they'd snuck away together? They hide things from you, corporal.'

Karel stepped into the room, the new men pushing in around him. 'What is this, captain?' he asked. He looked hurt. 'What is the purpose of this meeting?'

Reiner scowled. 'I don't see what business it is of yours, any of you, how we spend our off hours, but if you must know, we were reminiscing, talking over old times.'

'Without us?' asked Abel accusingly.

Reiner gave him a withering look. 'You weren't there for the old times, Halstieg, that I recall.'

There were a few chuckles at that.

Reiner motioned around the table. 'We five have bonds forged in blood and battle. Do you find it strange that we sometimes seek each other's company?'

Dag pushed Abel angrily. 'Told ye ye were a fool! The captain's a good 'un. He'd not play us false.'

'Easy, Mueller,' said Karel. He inclined his head to Reiner. 'Forgive me, captain. Quartermaster Halstieg said he saw you and the others sneaking away and thought you had a suspicious air about you. I see now he was overstating things.'

'It is suspicious,' insisted Abel. 'They told none of us!'

'And they'd no reason to, boy,' said Gert, laying a heavy arm across Abel's shoulder. 'We ain't their minders. Leave it be. Jawing about old battles is the right and privilege of every soldier.'

Abel shrugged and glared at the ground. 'Aye. Fine. Fine.'

'Not to worry, Halstieg,' said Reiner. 'I don't blame you. We none of us like our situation. Death if Gutzmann discovers our purpose. Death if we fail Manfred. New companions and a proven rogue for a commander. It isn't any wonder we're all wary of each other, but if we start fighting amongst ourselves, we're lost before we're begun.' Reiner tipped back in his chair. 'I, for one, want to survive this little job, and the only way to do it is to stick together. Agreed?'

He looked around at the others, questioning.

The men all grunted their ascent, though not all of them wholeheartedly.

Reiner nodded and sat forward. 'Good. Now that's settled, and since we suddenly find ourselves all together, I've a bit of news to share with you all.'

All eyes turned to him.

'Some of you won't like to hear it,' he continued, 'but I've the proof Manfred wanted that Gutzmann is planning to leave the Empire with his men. Which means we must kill him.'

The new men took the news silently, but Reiner saw a few hard looks among them, and Hals stared at the table top, fists clenched.

'I know,' said Reiner. 'He's a fine leader, but he's also a traitor. He plans to help Baron Caspar of Aulschweig snatch the throne from his brother, Prince Leopold, and then accept the post of commander of his armies.'

Karel's jaw dropped. 'By the holy hammer of Sigmar!'

Reiner nodded. 'So we've a job to do.'

'A dirty job,' muttered Hals.

'Yes,' said Reiner, giving him a look. 'A job for blackhearts, to be precise.' He looked up at the others. 'But worry not. Your warm berths are safe for the moment. It will take some time to work out the how and when and where of it. It must look like an accident, and I for one want to be able to walk away if it goes awry. So it will be a month or more before we're ready to begin.'

Reiner pushed back his chair. 'In the meanwhile, I ask you to continue watching and listening. I want to know more of who hates whom, who sides with whom. It may be the key to our puzzle. Report back to me as you can, and be ready to move on the moment. But tonight...' He stood, smirking, and fished in his belt pouch. 'I still have a little of Manfred's travelling money left, and we are in a knocking shop.' He began flipping gold coins at each of them. 'Let us live while we can. Enjoy the night, lads. I know I will.'

The men caught the coins, grinning – at least most of them did. Jergen plucked his out of the air without a change of expression, and turned to the door while the others were still thanking Reiner and making dirty jokes.

As they began filing out into the hall, Reiner put a hand on Franka's shoulder. She looked back. He motioned for her to wait.

When the rest had left, Reiner whispered in her ear. 'We could easily be alone here. Truly alone.'

'For what purpose, besides the obvious?'

'Why, merely to be alone. To enjoy each other's company uninterrupted. To talk, to hold hands...'

'To take advantage of my weak nature,' Franka said, wryly.

'Beloved, I assure you...'

'Don't,' she said sharply. 'Make no promises you cannot keep. I don't want to be disappointed in you.'

Reiner sighed. 'So you won't?'

Franka hesitated, then sighed in turn. 'I know I am a fool, but... I will.'

Reiner pulled her to him for a quick hug.

'Do you start already?' she asked, laughing and holding him away.

'No, no, my love,' said Reiner. 'Mere exuberance.' He looked toward the door, then leaned in to her. 'Now, this is what we will do.'

AFTER DRINKING FOR a short time with the others in the taproom, Reiner approached Mother Leibkrug and hired a girl, as both Hals and Abel had done before him. But unlike them, when he got his girl upstairs, he dismissed her, tipping her lavishly and telling her that he was meeting a secret lover there and only needed the room. Happy to make twice her usual fee, the girl agreed to closet herself above stairs for a while so that all would think she was still with Reiner.

A few minutes later, there was a knock at the door. Reiner opened it cautiously, but when he saw that it was Franka, alone, he pulled her in and held her close. They kissed for a long moment, then Franka pulled away with a sigh.

She straightened her jerkin. 'So,' she coughed, 'conversation?'

'Er, yes, of course. Conversation.' Reiner turned and flopped down on the ridiculously ruffled and beribboned bed. Like all the furniture, it was too big, too elaborate, for the tiny, shabby room – the overstuffed chaise, the wildly curved and carved vanity with the flaking gold paint, the voluminous curtains over rickety windows, the armoire so pregnant with clothes the doors couldn't close.

Franka didn't seem inclined to sit. She paced the room, examining the frilly furnishings and fidgeting. There was a blonde wig on a wig stand. She stroked it absently.

'So what do we talk about?' asked Reiner after a long silence.

Franka shrugged, then chuckled. 'Strange, isn't it? Now that we are free to talk, we're at a loss.'

Reiner tucked a pillow under his head. 'That's because you don't allow me my favourite topic.'

Franka laughed and pulled the wig off the stand. 'Seduction? Are you so limited?' She sat at the vanity. She lowered her head and pulled the wig on, then flipped it back. 'And you claim to be a man of the world.' She turned to him, looking though the blonde tresses. 'Go on. Speak to me of poetry, art. Or, what was your subject at university? Literature?'

Reiner gaped, open-mouthed, at her. 'You're... you're beautiful.'

'Am I?' Franka looked over her shoulder at the mirror, a cracked, poorly silvered glass. She smoothed the wig. 'It looks strange to me now. I have become so used to living as a boy.' She looked up at his reflection. 'Do you like me better like this?'

'Better?' Reiner blinked, transfixed. 'Er, I wouldn't say better. But it makes a change.' He sat up for a closer look. 'A very nice change.'

Franka began searching through the harlot's powders and paints. She found some rouge and smoothed it into her cheeks, then applied a thicker coat to her lips. She looked up at the glass from under her lashes. 'You aren't speaking. I thought you were going to declaim about literature.'

Reiner swallowed. 'You are being disingenuous, you little wench. You tell me we mustn't touch. That you are weak and I mustn't tempt you, but you are tempting me! Deliberately!'

Franka looked down, blushing behind her rouge. 'I suppose I am. And I apologize. It's just that... that it has been so long since I have looked like this. Since I have been able to flirt and be pretty.' She turned to face him. 'It is hard to resist.'

Reiner licked his lips. 'It certainly is. Try on a dress.'

Franka raised an eyebrow. 'And have you accuse me of provocation?'

'I don't care. I want to see it.'

Franka smiled. 'Are you sure it won't act like a red rag to a bull? Are you sure you won't go mad?'

'I... I will be a perfect gentleman.'

Franka laughed and stood. 'That will be interesting. I have never met one before.'

She crossed to the bursting armoire and began sorting through the dresses. She stopped at a deep green one – not as clean as it might have been, and a little frayed at the hem and cuffs, but well cut. She pulled it out and unlaced the stays at the back, then threw the whole thing over her head and tried to tug it down around herself.

'Help me,' she said with a muffled laugh.

Reiner sprung from the bed and began tugging and straightening. 'My lady is used to a lady's maid?'

'My lady is used to doublet and breeks,' said Franka as her head popped out. 'And has forgotten the intricacies.' Her wig was askew. She straightened it, and began pulling the dress into place.

Reiner laughed. 'And I'm afraid I have more experience getting women out of dresses than into them.'

Franka's smile froze, then fell. 'You needn't remind me.'

Reiner's heart lurched. He went down on one knee and took her hand. 'Lady, forgive me. You see I am as confused as you are.

I forget if I speak to Franz or Franka. I will not mention it again.' He kissed her fingers.

Franka laughed and ruffled his hair. 'Forget it, captain. I have no illusions about your past. I don't love you for your virtue. Now stand and tell me how I look.'

Reiner stood and stepped back. The illusion wasn't perfect. Her jerkin and man's shirt stuck up above the low cut collar of the green dress. But in all other respects Franka had become the woman she truly was.

Reiner stepped forward. His arms encircled her waist. 'You are beautiful. Heartbreakingly so. When we are free of our chains, I shall buy you a hundred such dresses, each more lovely than the last.'

Franka giggled and bumped her head against his chest. 'A hundred dresses? Do I want so much trouble and fuss? I think perhaps I've grown used to my breeches.'

Reiner pulled her wig off and kissed the back of her neck. 'As have I. I like knowing there's a woman inside them. I like knowing your secret.'

Franka purred. 'Do you?'

'I do. In fact, it maddens me!' Reiner crushed her to him. Their lips met, then their tongues. Franka's hands ran down his back.

There was a scratching from the window. They leapt apart, afraid they were spied on. Reiner's heart thudded. If they were caught, explanations would be difficult.

'Is someone there?' asked Franka.

Reiner stepped closer, hand on his dagger. 'I see nothing. Just mice, I suppose.' He turned back to Franka. 'Where were we?'

Franka smiled sadly. 'A place we should not have come to, and to which it would be better not to return...'

The window flew open, knocking the curtains to the floor, and figures in dark robes, with burlap sacks over their heads, dived in with inhuman agility. There were at least six of them, though Reiner found it hard to count, they moved so quickly.

'What's this?' Reiner cried, backing away and drawing his sword and dagger.

Franka reached for her weapons as well, but they were trapped beneath the dress. She rucked at her skirts in frustration. The intruders swarmed her, ignoring Reiner in order to grab her arms and legs.

'Reiner!' she screamed.

'Unhand her!' Reiner kicked one and jerked another back by the collar. They were small men, not much taller than Franka, and Reiner was surprised at how easily he booted and threw them across the room. But he was even more surprised by how quickly they sprang up again, seeming to bounce rather than fall, and turning on him with feral snarls.

Franka clubbed one of her captors with the wig stand and kicked another in the head. The man fell back, upsetting the chair, and crashed to the floor. But the other two continued to drag her towards the window.

'Reiner, help me!'

'I'm trying...'

The two Reiner had knocked down attacked him, and another joined them, daggers like curved fangs in their tiny hands. He blocked and parried desperately. They were blindingly fast. And their smell was an attack of its own. The reek was overwhelming. Perhaps it came from the filthy fur shirts they wore under their robes.

Reiner backed away, bleeding from a handful of cuts, and tripped over the chamber pot, left by the door. He kicked it at his attackers. They ducked, and the tin pot smashed the vanity mirror behind them. Glass shards rained to the ground.

One of the robed figures looked back at the noise, and Reiner ran him through. He fell, hissing. The others only pressed Reiner all the harder. Their thrusts rang off his sabre like clanging bells.

'No, you little daemons!' Franka shrieked. 'Let me go!'

Reiner risked a look her way and saw three of the men trying to drag Franka out of the window. She grabbed one by the burlap mask and pulled it askew so that the eye-holes were on the side of his head. The villain let go and fumbled at the sack, blinded.

'Franka!'

Reiner threw his dagger as Franka looked up. It stuck, point first, into the window frame beside her. With a grateful look, she snatched it up and began stabbing indiscriminately at all who held her. They fell away, shrieking thinly.

Suddenly the door slammed open and Hals shouldered in, bare to the waist and dagger drawn. 'What's all the noise?' he bellowed.

Abel and a few other half-dressed brothel patrons stood behind him, harlots peering over their shoulders.

A robed man launched himself at Hals and the pikeman defended himself. Reiner called to the men in the hall as he fought. 'Hurry! Stop them! They're trying to take...' His voice fell off as he remembered who the attackers were trying to take, and how she looked. And as if to confirm his fears, he saw Hals goggling at Franka in her dress. He almost took a curved dagger in the belly before he recovered and returned to the business at hand.

No one else entered the room. Abel backed out, wide-eyed. 'I... I shall protect the women!'

But it seemed the three Blackhearts wouldn't need the help. Hals clubbed his man to the ground with a fist. Reiner kicked his back with a well placed boot, and they were advancing on those grabbing at Franka when one of them looked around, then drew something from its sleeve and threw it at the ground.

Reiner got the briefest glimpse of it before it smashed on the bare floorboards – a small glass ball. But then great billows of smoke erupted from the shards and the room was quickly filled with an impenetrable, acrid cloud that had them choking and their eyes tearing.

Reiner threw an arm over his face. It did no good. He heard scrabbling at the window. 'They're retreating!' he shouted, and stumbled forward, blind.

'Come back, y'wee villains!' coughed Hals.

But at that moment there was a piercing scream from the hallway and Hals stopped so suddenly Reiner bumped into him. 'My girl!' cried the pikeman. 'They're taking Griga!'

He charged back out of the door.

Reiner followed. 'Franz! Hurry!' he called over his shoulders. 'I want to talk to one of these assassins.'

'I'll protect the women,' said Abel again as they ran past him.

Hals and Reiner burst into another dingy boudoir, but they were too late. The window was open, frilly curtains blowing in the breeze, and the rumpled bed was empty. Reiner looked up as he heard feet scritching across the roof above.

'Hals,' he said, turning back to the door, 'you and Abel go up from this window, Franz and I will...' He stopped. Franka wasn't there. He grunted. But of course not. She was still in her dress. She wouldn't have dared join them. Unless...

Reiner swallowed.

He started back down the hall, terror dragging at his guts. 'Franka?' he called. 'Franka?'

Hals followed behind him, and they entered Reiner's room together. The smoke had thinned enough to see that the room was empty, but for the corpse of one of the mysterious attackers. Franka wasn't there.

'Sigmar,' hissed Hals. 'Look at his hands!'

Reiner glanced down at the body as he ran to the window. What he had thought a fur shirt looked now like furry arms, and the hands at the ends of them were scaly, long-fingered claws. But even this unsettling curiosity couldn't distract Reiner from his fear. There was a scrap of deep green velvet caught on a nail in the window sill. He stuck his head out. 'Franka!' There was no response. He climbed out onto the shingled roof, from which rose the second storey, and began pulling himself up the stone wall.

'Who the devil is Franka?' grunted Hals as he ducked out after Reiner.

'Franz, I meant,' said Reiner, and then realized he shouldn't have. He should have said that Franka was the name of his whore, and he was afraid she was taken. Now Hals would associate the names Franka and Franz, and likely draw unfortunate conclusions. But it was too late to call back the words.

He pulled himself up onto the cedar-shingled roof and clambered up the steep slope to the peak. 'Franz!' There was no sign of the robed men, or Franka, or Hals's harlot. He turned in a circle, peering out over the low roofs of Brunn.

'Captain...' said Hals, struggling up the wall.

'There!' said Reiner, pointing. A tangle of shadows slipped around a corner a few blocks away. In the midst of them Reiner had seen a flash of pale flesh. He leapt down to the first floor roof, then slipped and bounced down the shingles on his posterior before pitching over the edge and landing on his ribs on a pyramid of kegs of finest Averheim ale. He slid down this, groaning and wheezing, and ended up sitting in an icy puddle of what he hoped was water.

Hals dropped down beside him in a more controlled fashion. 'Captain…'

Reiner staggered up. 'No time. We can't let them get away.' He ran for the street in a half crouch, clutching his bruised ribs and limping. As they came around the front of the brothel they were met by men and harlots spilling out of the door, including Pavel, Giano, Dag, Abel and Gert. Only Jergen and Karel were absent.

Reiner waved to them. 'Follow us, lads. They've got Fra… Franz!'

Reiner started off as quick as his laboured breathing would allow, Hals at his side, in the direction the robed men had gone.

As they wound through the streets, Hals coughed uncomfortably. 'Er, captain…'

'I know, Hals. I know,' Reiner interrupted, thinking desperately. 'I know what it looked like, but I assure you, nothing could be further from the truth. You see, we… er, we meant to play a trick on Karel. The poor boy. I don't think he's ever had a woman, so Franz and I thought it would be a good joke to rile him up a bit. Franz would dress up like a woman, you see, and… and make advances, then, when Karel got all hot and bothered, Franz would pull off his wig and we'd see what shades of crimson young Karel could turn. Amusing, hey?'

'Aye,' said Hals, flatly. 'And did you mean to dress up as well?'

'What?' said Reiner. 'No, of course not. Who in their right mind would ever mistake me for a woman?'

Hals nodded, his face a blank. 'Then you might want to be wiping yer lips. Y've rouge all over 'em.'

TEN
They Were Not Men!

REINER AND THE Blackhearts found no trace of Franka, Hals's harlot, or the robed men, though they searched Brunn from end to end. The kidnappers and their prey had disappeared utterly. Even eerier, when the search party returned to the brothel to see if anyone else had seen anything, they found that the corpse with the furry arms was gone, vanished when no one was looking, though patrons and whores had been in and out of the room constantly. The only evidence that the whole incident hadn't been some mad fever dream was a small glass ball that Reiner spied under a chair. It looked like the one that had filled the room with smoke, but this one was unbroken, and churned within with a greenish murk. Reiner pocketed it. Combined with the vision of the robed man's clawed hand, it began to stir memories of things he had read in forbidden books while at university.

He stepped out of the brothel and joined the other Blackhearts, who were huddled in a circle before the door.

'We must return to the fort at once,' he said. 'I want to tell Gutzmann of Franz's kidnapping and the new evidence we have about the disappearances.'

It was obvious to Reiner that Abel had told the others all he had seen when he and Hals had burst in on Reiner and Franka, for none of them would meet his eye, and they answered him with surly grunts and mumbles.

Reiner cursed inwardly all the long cold walk back to the fort. Foolishness on top of tragedy. Just when he needed them most, when the life of one of their number was in deadly peril, his men had become suspicious, nearly mutinous. The maddening thing was that if he could tell them the truth all would be well again – at least with him. Things would be much worse for Franka. Only Reiner and Manfred knew the girl's true sex. If it were revealed to anyone else, her usefulness as a soldier would be over, and the count might have her killed. And this didn't take into consideration the reactions of her comrades. Franka loved Hals, Pavel and Giano like brothers. If they turned their backs on her, it would break her heart.

REINER DEMANDED TO see Gutzmann as soon as they returned to the camp, but the general was sleeping, and so Reiner must go up the chain of command, telling his story first to Captain Vortmunder, then to Obercaptain Oppenhauer, both of whom would have dismissed his story out of hand if not for the corroboration of his fellows and the strange glass orb. At last, and very reluctantly, they brought him to Commander Shaeder, who was called from his bed, yawning and cross.

'What is such an emergency that you must wake me at this ungodly hour?' the commander asked as he sat down behind his desk, wrapped in a heavy robe. Vortmunder and Oppenhauer stood on either side of Reiner looking nervous.

'My lord,' said Reiner, bowing. 'Forgive me, but a soldier has been kidnapped, and I fear there are inhuman agents involved that might be a danger to the fort and the Empire.'

Shaeder pinched the bridge of his nose and waved a weary hand. 'Very well, captain, tell your tale.'

Reiner clicked his heels together. 'Thank you, commander. Er, earlier this evening, I and some others, including my valet, Franz, were entertaining ourselves in Brunn....'

'Whoring and drinking, you mean.'

'I was indeed visiting with a young lady, commander,' Said Reiner. 'But before any, er, business, had occurred, the window flew open and we were attacked by men in masks and robes. My valet, Franz, hearing my calls, ran to my aid, and we fought the men. Patrons of the house came at the noise and helped, but just as we were on the brink of victory the men threw some sort of grenade and we were choked by thick smoke.'

Reiner thought he saw Shaeder frown at this, but the tic was gone before he could be sure.

'When the smoke cleared,' Reiner continued, 'the men were gone, as was Franz.' He coughed. 'One of the ladies of the house was taken as well.'

'Most distressing, certainly,' said Shaeder, though he didn't look distressed. 'But in what way is a kidnapping in a brothel a danger to the Empire?'

'I was coming to that, sir,' said Reiner quickly. 'One of the masked men was killed in the fight, and I was shocked to see that his hands weren't hands at all, but claws. Like those of a rat. And his arms...'

'A rat?' Shaeder guffawed. 'A rat did you say? The size of a man?'

'A little smaller, sir. He...'

'Do you mean to suggest that you were attacked by, what do the old women call them? By ratkin? By wives' tales made flesh?' He turned to glare at Oppenhauer and Vortmunder. 'What do you mean bringing this nonsense before me? Are you mad?'

'His story was seconded by several others, commander,' sad Oppenhauer. 'And he has evidence.'

'Evidence?' asked Shaeder. 'What evidence?'

Something in the commander's voice made Reiner reluctant to bring the orb out of his pouch, but there was nothing for it. Shaeder wouldn't be convinced without it. Reiner took out the glass ball and placed it on his desk.

'What is this?' asked the commander, picking it up with reluctant fingers.

'One of the smoke grenades, my lord,' said Reiner. 'The ratmen threw one at the floor and smoke poured out of it when it shattered.'

Shaeder scowled. 'This is a grenade?' He looked up at Oppenhauer. 'You let him convince you this was a grenade? This bauble from a harlot's dress?' He set it on a stack of parchment. 'A paperweight, perhaps.'

'Commander,' said Reiner, getting angry. 'I fought them hand to hand. They were not men!'

'And how do you know? Did you look under their masks? You had a body, did you not? Why are you showing me a marble instead of a body?'

'Er,' Reiner flushed. 'We left the body behind while in pursuit of the others, who were getting away with Franz. When we returned to the brothel again, it... it was gone.'

'Gone?'

'Aye, sir.'

Shaeder paused for a long moment. It seemed almost that he relaxed. Then abruptly he burst out laughing, a loud, derisive bray that had him wiping his eyes. When he had recovered himself he waved a hand at Reiner. 'Go to bed, corporal.'

'Beg pardon?' said Reiner, confused.

'Go to bed, sir. Sleep it off.'

Reiner pulled himself up, indignant. 'You don't believe me sir?'

'I believe that you are one of those remarkable rascals who shows no outward sign of inebriation while being completely pie-eyed drunk.'

'Commander,' Reiner protested. 'I am telling the...'

'I'm sure something happened,' Shaeder interrupted. 'A brawl, perhaps even a kidnapping. Y've wounds enough. But it's just as likely you fought your reflection in some whore's mirror and cut yourself on the glass. Whatever happened, I will not muster the Emperor's might to rescue some Altdorf dandy's valet, no matter how well he polishes your boots. If the boy doesn't show up in the morning, I will assign a detail to look for him in the gutters of Brunn, but until then, I'm for bed, as you should be.'

Reiner balled his fists. 'Commander, I do not think this is a threat that should be ignored. I demand to see General Gutzmann. I demand to put my case before him.'

'You demand, do you?' asked Shaeder. 'The next thing you demand will be a week in the brig for insubordination. Now go to bed, sir. I am through with you.' He turned to Vortmunder and Oppenhauer. 'And in the future, you will think twice before waking me with such foolishness.'

'Aye, commander,' said Oppenhauer, saluting. 'Thank you, sir.'

He and Vortmunder turned with Reiner between them. Oppenhauer gave Reiner a sympathetic shrug as they walked out the door.

'I believed you, lad,' he said.

REINER DIDN'T SLEEP that night. All he wanted to do was ride out in search of Franka, but searching in the dark would have been fruitless, particularly on his own, particularly if Franka had been taken where he suspected she had. When dawn finally came, he reported again to Shaeder, begging to be allowed to join the search detail the commander was sending out, but he had refused, telling Reiner to leave the search to men who better knew the town and the pass.

Reiner couldn't leave it at that. Shaeder's men wouldn't find Franka. They wouldn't look in the right place. And so, though he knew it might compromise Manfred's mission to do so, he had failed to report to Vortmunder for his morning duties, and instead sent word through Hals to the others to meet him behind the parade ground stands where they had watched Gutzmann tent-pegging on the first day. This mass dereliction of duty was sure to arouse comment, but the alternative was to leave Franka to her fate, and that was no alternative at all.

As the men arrived, slouching up in ones and twos, Reiner knew he was in trouble. The suspicion of the previous night hadn't cleared. In fact it seemed to have grown deeper. Their faces were closed and grim. Even Karel looked troubled.

'Here it is,' he said when they'd all gathered in the shadow of the viewing stand. 'I've turned it over in my mind and I believe I know where Franz was taken.' He nodded at Giano. 'As much as we've ribbed our Tilean friend for smelling ratmen under every rock and cellar floor, I think this time he's right. Hals and Abel, you saw the body in the brothel last night. I can find no way to deny its nature. Can you?'

Abel said nothing.

Hals shrugged. 'Not sure what I saw now.'

Reiner groaned. That didn't bode well. 'Well, what of the glass orb? Every fairy tale I've ever heard of ratkin speaks of them using bizarre weapons. What of the stories the miners have been telling about men disappearing? And Giano smelling them in the tunnels?'

Giano's eyes glowed. 'You believe now?'

'I don't know what I believe,' said Reiner. 'But be it ratmen or some other horror, I think something lurks in the mine, and I mean to go down and look for Franz.'

There was a silence. Abel broke it.

'To look for your beloved, you mean.'

Reiner's head snapped up. 'What do you say?'

'Shut yer trap, y'clod,' growled Hals.

'You speakin' ill of the captain?' asked Dag, menacingly.

Karel glared at the man. 'You are out of order, quartermaster.'

Abel looked at them disbelievingly. 'Do you still have loyalty to this... this invert? How can you trust him when he's been hiding his true nature from you all this time?'

The Blackhearts looked at the ground, uncomfortable.

Abel sneered. 'You saw him last night, with red all over his mouth. We all did. He'd been kissing his "boot boy".'

'Enough, Halstieg!' cried Karel. He looked to Reiner pleadingly. 'Captain. Tell them they're mistaken!'

Pavel shifted uncomfortably. 'Captain's a good leader. He ain't led us wrong.'

'Hasn't he?' asked Abel. 'Are you happy to be walking around with poison in your veins? Dancing at the mercy of some cagey jagger. Who led you to that?'

There was a simmering silence.

'Listen...' said Reiner, but Abel cut him off again.

'And he certainly ain't leading you right this time; thinking with his stem instead of his head, asking us to go into some dirty hole that'll most likely cave in on us. For the good of the mission? Because it will get us home quicker? No. It hasn't anything to do with what we came here to do. He's afraid for the life of his precious catamite, and he'll lead us all to our deaths to save him.'

'Enough!' barked Reiner. 'I'll not waste time arguing and explaining. I am afraid for Franz, as I would be for any of you.' He shot a glance at Abel. 'Even you, quartermaster. And I want to try to find him before he comes to harm. As I would with any of you.' He shrugged. 'I won't order you. I never have. But I'm going down there whether or not you accompany me.' He stood and shouldered the pack of pitch torches he'd gathered. 'Who's with me?'

'I!' said Giano immediately. 'I want all my life to be fighting ratmens.' He stepped to Reiner's side.

The rest didn't move. Reiner looked from one to the other. They hung their heads. He sighed. He hadn't expected the new men to come with him. They hadn't fought through the bowels of the Middle Mountains with him. They hadn't faced down Valnir's Bane and Albrecht's mindless army by his side. But when Hals and Pavel wouldn't meet his eyes it felt as if some giant crushed his heart in his hands.

'Sorry, captain,' said Gert.

Dag muttered something under his breath.

Karel hung his head. 'It isn't part of our mission, captain.'

Reiner shrugged, then glared at Abel. 'The poison with which Manfred cursed us is naught compared with that which you wield.' He turned toward the pass road. 'Come, Giano. Let's be off.'

AS REINER AND Giano walked north toward the mine in the cold morning light, Giano jerked a thumb over his shoulder. 'Fella want you job, I thinking.'

And he might get it, thought Reiner, nodding. A tricksy cove, Halstieg. A way with words when he wanted, and a streak of ambition that one might miss at first glance. And no heart at all. Reiner was certain Abel cared not a whit if he loved men, women or goats. He only used the issue to drive a wedge between him and the others, so that he might step in and lead them. The quartermaster was smart enough to know that his survival depended on pleasing Manfred, and if that meant betraying Reiner and proving he was the better man, so be it.

THE MINE WAS as busy as ever, and Reiner and Giano had little trouble in wandering through all the chaos to the closed tunnel. The first hundred feet or so were still open, and were used as a storage area for cartwheels and rail ties and supplies. Reiner and Giano wound around the clutter until they came to the barricade, a wall of planks and cross braces that reached from wall to wall and floor to ceiling. It was dark this far from the entrance. Reiner pulled a torch from his pack and lit it from his tinder box. He and Giano examined the wall. A rough door had been cut in it, locked with an enormous iron padlock.

'Can you pick?' asked Giano.

'I'm afraid not. My burglar's tools are cards and dice.' He began pushing on the planks around the door. 'But I don't think we'll have to.'

'Hey? For why?'

'Well,' said Reiner, as he walked down the wall. 'If the ratmen are in there, and they come out through here, then they wouldn't use a door that locked on this side, you see?'

'Ah! Si. Captain damn smart.'

'Or perhaps not,' grumbled Reiner as he reached the end of the wall without finding a board that gave. He started back along the wall, looking at the boards once again. There had to be something. He couldn't allow himself to believe he was wrong. The ratmen had to be here.

He stopped, frowning. The left edge of one of the boards was grimier than the rest. He reached out and touched the grime. It was oily. He sniffed his finger. It reeked with an animal stench – the same stench the robed men had given off. Reiner's heart jumped. He took another step down the wall. The next plank was clean, but the one after that had corresponding grime on its right edge. He stepped back. Filthy fur pushing through a narrow opening would leave just such marks.

He pointed to the plank between the begrimed planks. 'This one.' He pushed on it. It didn't move. But of course not. It would push from the other side. He looked for some way to pull it. There was no handle, or string. But there was a hole – a knot hole near the floor.

Reiner stuck his finger in the hole. It was greasy as well. He pulled. The board came up easily, revealing utter blackness.

Giano grinned. 'Knock, knock, hey?'

Reiner swallowed. 'Aye. Er, after you.'

Giano ducked eagerly through the gap. Reiner followed more cautiously, sticking his torch through first, then squeezing in afterwards. The board banged down behind him. Inside was a bit of an anticlimax. It looked exactly like the outside – a high, wide tunnel sloping away into darkness.

'No sign of a cave-in,' said Reiner.

'Maybe further down.'

'Or maybe not at all.'

They started down the tunnel, travelling in a small sphere of light through a universe of black. A hundred yards on, they almost tripped over two small crates piled against one wall. Reiner held the torch low. The crates looked familiar.

'What is?' asked Giano.

Reiner snorted. '"Mining tools".'

As they continued on, Reiner's heart thudded with excitement. Now they need not wait for the next shipment to Aulschweig. They could kill Gutzmann whenever they wanted and take the gold from here instead – a much easier proposition than stealing it en route. This was excellent news – at least it would be if Franka still lived.

Shortly after that the tunnel stopped at a rough rock face, and for a moment Reiner's heart sank. But then he saw a small opening in the face. It was a tunnel so narrow that he and Giano had to walk single file. Ten paces in, Giano stopped suddenly and raised his hand.

'Light,' he said.

Reiner put his torch on the ground behind him and they crept forward.

Three yards further the tunnel opened up into a large space, lit with a wan purple light. Giano peeked out then gasped and flinched back. Reiner followed his gaze and jumped back as well, heart thudding. Looming over them was a monstrous insect the size of a house. Huge sabre-like mandibles jutted from its maw. It took a moment of deep breaths to realize that the insect wasn't moving, wasn't alive, wasn't in fact an insect. It was a giant machine. And it wasn't alone.

Giano and Reiner stepped cautiously into the tunnel, looking up at the four massive metal monstrosities that sat on man-high wooden wheels to the left and right of the narrow hole. A thrill of fear ran through Reiner as he divined their purpose. They were digging machines. Mad, skeletal contraptions of iron, wood, leather and brass. The mandibles were giant steel picks meant to chew at the workface. They were attached by a series of axles, gears and belts to an enormous brass tank, green with corrosion, fitted with all manner of valves and levers. Broad leather belts led from beneath the mandibles to the backs of the contraptions, where strings of wooden mine carts were lined up, ready to take the chewed rock away.

The scale of the enterprise made Reiner's head spin. Not even the Empire built machines this large. What were they digging? Did the ratmen mine gold as well? Was there something else of value in the rock? Or...

It came to him with sudden clarity and dread, and his blood turned to ice in his veins. The ratmen were building a road – a road high enough and wide enough to allow an army to march to the surface. And they were only twenty paces from connecting with the mine tunnel, which was just as high and wide. Their work was almost done.

Giano swallowed. 'This bad, hey?'

'Aye,' said Reiner. 'Bad is a word for it.'

As he and Giano crept around the towering machines, weirdly lit by the pulsing purple light that came from glowing stones set high in the walls, Reiner saw movement in the shadows and jerked his dagger out of its scabbard. Rats – of the small, four-footed variety – swarmed over piles of bones and rubbish that cluttered the floor, ample evidence that this wasn't some long abandoned endeavour. Some of the bones looked human. Reiner moaned in his throat. Were the ratmen kidnapping women for food?

There was a small side passage in the left wall, and more dotted the tunnel on both sides as far as they could see. The openings made Reiner nervous. At any moment a ratman could pop out of one, and then where would they be?

He and Giano started forward, looking warily around. A few moments later, distant structures began to emerge from the gloom. At first Reiner thought they were battlements of some kind – the walls and towers of some underground town – but as they got closer, he saw that they were siege towers, mounted on wheels and laid on their sides. They were surrounded by other giant engines of war, catapults, ballisti, and battering rams.

'Blood of Sigmar,' he breathed. 'They mean to take the fort.'

Giano nodded, wide-eyed.

They crept forward at a snail's pace, hugging the wall and keeping low, and at last reached the jumble of machines, Giano sniffing like a bloodhound. As they came around a prone tower, they saw, further on, an encampment of sorts, though to one used to the regimented order of an Empire camp, it was an offence to the eye. Low structures that looked more like piles of blankets than tents hugged the walls of the tunnel and shadows wormed in and out of them like... well, like rats.

Giano stopped, his hand on the hilt of his sword. He was trembling. 'Ratmen!'

'Easy, lad,' said Reiner, as Giano began to draw. 'We ain't here to fight 'em all.'

Giano nodded, but it seemed a supreme act of will for him to return his blade to its scabbard.

As they stepped back behind the tower, an overpowering stench overcame them. They clapped their hands over their noses and looked around. Against one wall was a pile of furred bodies – dead rat men, discarded like old apple cores. There was movement on the pile – the four-legged feeding on the two-legged – and it reeked like a slaughterhouse, an odour equal parts animal filth and diseased death. Some of the bodies were bloated with fat black boils.

Reiner was turning away, nauseous, when he saw a white arm among the mangy limbs. His heart froze, and he stepped, trembling, to the pile, the rats scattering at his approach. Giano followed, covering his mouth with his handkerchief. Reiner reached out toward the arm, then stopped when he saw that it possessed a man's hand, callused and thick. He looked for the rest of the body, and found, half hidden among rotting ratman corpses, and grinning, partially fleshed ratman skulls, the face of a pikeman, his right cheek and temple gnawed away.

'Poor devil,' said Reiner.

Giano made the sign of Shallya.

They returned to their vantage point and surveyed the ratmen's camp. It was not an encouraging sight. The whole place seethed with motion: ratmen darting in and out of the holes in the tunnel walls, ratmen swarming around the tents, rat men crawling over the line of carts in the centre of the tunnel, loading and unloading spears and halberds and strange brass instruments that Reiner feared were weapons as well, ratmen arguing and fighting.

Giano shook his head. 'How we finding boy in all these?'

'I don't know, lad,' said Reiner. His heart was sinking. He wasn't by nature a coward, but neither was he a fool. He wasn't the sort of stage-play hero who charged a horde of Kurgan armed only with a turnip. He was a follower of Ranald, whose commandments stated that one shouldn't go into any situation without the odds clearly in one's favour. Walking into this mess was a sure way to incur the trickster's wrath.

And yet, Franka was in there somewhere, if she wasn't already some ratman's dinner. And he couldn't just turn around and leave without trying to find her.

'Damn the girl,' he growled.

'Hey?' said Giano, puzzled. 'Girl?'

'Never mind.' Reiner pulled himself up onto the prone siege tower. The view was no better. The ratmen were everywhere at once. No area of the camp was ever vacant long. There was no little-used corridor for Reiner and Giano to sneak down – no catwalk high above. They would be discovered at once, and that would be the end.

Unless...

Reiner looked at the tower he clung to. Its timber frame was stretched over with a patchwork of leather and furs. Reiner blanched when he saw that some of the skins had tattoos, but he couldn't be squeamish now.

'Giano,' he said, drawing his dagger. 'Help me cut down some of these skins. They walked robed among us. We shall walk robed among them.'

Giano obediently started cutting but he looked doubtful. 'The rat, he have damn good smelling, hey? He sniffing us even hiding.'

Reiner groaned. 'Curse it, yes. I'd forgotten. They'll smell us for human in an instant.' He sighed deeply, then nearly choked on the stink of the pile of corpses as he inhaled again. An idea brought his head up and he looked at the pile, eyes shining. 'There could be a way...'

Giano followed his gaze, then moaned. 'Oh, captain, please no. Please.'

'I'm afraid so, lad.'

BEHIND HIS POINTED leather mask, and beneath his makeshift leather robes, sewn together with lengths of rawhide unwound from binding that held the siege machines together, Reiner's heart beat as rapidly as a hummingbird's. He and Giano were picking their way through the ratmen's camp, tails cut from the ratmen's corpses tied to their belts and dragging behind them, and with every step, retreat became more impossible and discovery more likely. Though they tried to hug the line of carts, where there were the fewest ratmen, still the beasts were all around them, and a mere skin was all that shielded them from their ravenous fury. If he or Giano revealed their hands or feet they were lost, for the ratmen's appendages looked nothing like theirs. If they were challenged they were lost, for the ratmen's speech was a chittering gabble of hisses, chirps and shrieks that Reiner's throat couldn't possibly have reproduced even if he had understood it. Fortunately, the ratmen hardly gave Reiner and Giano a second look – or to be more accurate, a second sniff – for they were covered in an almost visible reek of rat musk and death, and as such, blended in with the general atmosphere of the tunnel.

Over Giano's piteous protestations, Reiner had ordered the Tilean to follow his example and roll like a pig in mud within the pile of corpses. Reluctantly, they had rubbed themselves and their makeshift robes and masks against the oily fur and decaying flesh and diseased wounds of the bodies, and caked their boots and gloves with their excrement. It had been a foul, gut-churning experience, and was continuing to be. Being trapped inside the hooded mask with the stench was like drinking a sewer. If it hadn't been for the distraction of the wonders and horrors he was seeing through his eye-holes, Reiner would undoubtedly have vomited.

There were so many ratmen, so closely packed together – hundreds, perhaps thousands – within his range of vision, it made his head swim. And the camp continued around the curve of the tunnel with no apparent end. They were loathsome creatures, their long, narrow faces covered in filthy, lice-ridden fur, their mouths slackly open to reveal great, curving front teeth. But it was their eyes that truly repulsed Reiner – vacant black orbs that glittered like glass. They seemed utterly empty of intelligence. If it hadn't been for the scraps of rusty armour that covered their scrawny limbs, and the earrings that dangled from their tattered ears, and of course the weapons that they carried, Reiner would not have believed them thinking beings.

Their filth was indescribable. They seemed not to have separate places to dispose of their refuse and droppings; instead, they appeared to nest in them. Their tents were filled with bones, rags and filth shaped into crater-like depressions in which they slept. Some of the ratkin appeared to be deathly ill, yellow mucus weeping from their eyes and black lesions covering their scaly hands, but the other ratmen made no effort to avoid their diseased fellows. They shared their food and drink and rubbed past them in the narrow byways of the camp without a second thought. Did they wish to get sick? It came to Reiner with a shudder that perhaps they did. Perhaps disease was only another weapon to them.

Some of the weapons Reiner saw them carrying he couldn't even begin to understand: bizarre pistols and long guns that sprouted weird brass piping and glass reservoirs filled with phosphorescent green liquid. On the carts in the centre of the tunnel larger weapons were stored; great spears that hummed as they passed them, handheld cannon connected by leather hoses to large brass reservoirs.

What Reiner did not see was any sign of Franka, or any humans at all. The camp seemed only tents and carts and rats as far as the eye could see. After walking a few hundred yards into it, Reiner's steps began to slow. It was hopeless, pointless. If the myths of the ratmen were correct, their tunnels ran under the whole wide world. Franka might be halfway to Cathay by now. Or he might have passed her bones in one of the piles of garbage that were heaped everywhere. At last he stopped, overcome. He tapped Giano on the shoulder, and motioned him to turn around, but before the Tilean could respond, Reiner heard, very faintly in the distance, an agonized scream – a human scream!

The men froze, listening with their whole beings. The scream came again. It was behind them, back the way they had come – a cry of terror and unbearable pain. Reiner and Giano turned and hurried back through the camp as quickly as they could, listening for further cries. What a bitter irony, Reiner thought. The screams were so pitiful it made him wish the man who uttered them a quick death, and yet, if he was to find their source the man must cry again and again.

They had almost returned to the edge of the camp before the cry came again, and this time it was words. 'Mercy. Mercy, I beg you!'

Reiner turned. The voice came not from before or behind them, but to one side – from one of the branching passages.

'In the name of Sigmar, have you no…' The voice broke off in a bone chilling shriek. Reiner winced, but at least he had pinpointed the passage. He touched Giano's arm and they moved toward it.

The passage was short and opened up at its far end into a room that glowed brightly with the purple light. It was hard to determine the room's dimensions, for it was so cluttered that Reiner couldn't see the walls. Machines from a poppy eater's nightmare loomed on the left: a thing like a casket surrounded by metal spider's legs, each tipped with a scalpel or pipette, a chair with straps to pinion the arms over which dangled a helmet ringed with sharp screws, a rack that seemed to have been constructed to stretch a creature with more than four limbs, a charcoal brazier that glowed with red heat, a contraption of glass bulbs and tubes through which coloured liquids bubbled and dripped.

On the right, piled up like so many children's blocks, was a jumble of small iron cages, none more than four feet high, but all containing at least one, and sometimes three or four, filthy, dung- and blood-smeared humans. Reiner's heart leapt at this sight – foul as it was – for Franka might be among them. He wanted to run forward and check them all, but he daren't. The room wasn't empty.

In the centre was a tableau Reiner had been avoiding looking at directly, for it was from there that the screams came. Now at last he faced it. There was a table, and a man on the table, shackled to it, though so weak now the fetters were no longer necessary. It was extraordinary to Reiner that the man still lived, for his torso had been laid open like a gutted fish, the skin of his belly pinned back with clips so that his organs were exposed. They shone wetly in the purple light. The fellow had the rough hands and hard-lined face of a miner, but he was begging for mercy in the high whimper of a little girl.

Hovering over him like a cook making a pie was a plump, grey-furred ratman, scalpel and forceps held high in gloved hands. He wore a blood-drenched leather apron with a belt full of steel implements slung at his waist, and a leather band circled his brow, attached to which were articulated arms, all fitted with glass lenses of various thicknesses and colours that could be pulled down in front of the creature's beady black eyes. It already wore thick spectacles, which it balanced on its broad furred snout. It was such a caricature of the short-sighted scholar Reiner might have thought it comic, had it not been for the horrible vivisection it was engaged in.

What made the situation even more horrible was that the ratman was speaking to his victim, and not in the chittering gibberish of his kind, but in high-pitched and broken Reiklander. 'Does read Heidel?' it asked, then tsked sadly when the man didn't respond. 'Wasted. Wasted. You Reik-man. Finest books. Finest lib… lib…' It snarled in frustration. 'Book places! And you no read, no think. Just to drink, to mate, to sleep. Shameful.'

The sound of Giano muttering furiously in Tilean beside him snapped Reiner out of his horrified trance. The crossbowman's hand was reaching for his sword. Reiner touched Giano's arm and pulled him out of the doorway behind the bulk of a great black-iron cauldron. Giano patted his shoulder gratefully, recovering himself.

'Here me,' the rat-surgeon continued, sighing. 'Down below. Book come garbage and sewer. But know I more of out world than it.' He severed some membrane in the man's belly. The miner groaned. The ratman ignored him. 'Does know Volman's *Seven Virtue*? History of beer-making in Hochland? Poem of Brother Octavio Durst? I know this. And so more. Many more.'

He set his implements aside, pulled a lens in front of one eye, and began to paw through the man's organs with delicate claws.

'This me confuse. Why man? Why man so big? Why win so many battles? Why so brave?' He shook his head. 'First think, maybe man stupid. Too stupid to be scare. But skaven stupid too, and always scare. Run away, all time run. So not that.' He scooped out his victim's intestines with both hands and set them on the table beside him. 'So now think something new. Fix the moulder way! Pinder say brave in spleen. So I try if man with no spleen will scare. Then, I try if skaven with man-spleen will brave. Ah, here is.' He tugged at an organ with one hand, then cut it from its mooring with his scalpel.

The man convulsed and gasped. Blood welled from the cavity of his belly and his hands began to clutch and grasp. The grey ratman tsked again, then tried to stem the flow with a clamp. He was too slow. Before he had successfully applied it, the table was awash with blood and the man lay still and silent.

The rat-surgeon sighed. 'Another. Too bad. Well, we try again.' He raised his voice and chittered over his shoulder. Two brown rats in leather aprons came out of a further room. The surgeon directed them to remove the body and bring another from the cages.

Reiner and Giano watched queasily as the two ratmen piled the man's intestines on his chest and carried him out of the room by his arms and legs as the surgeon swept miscellaneous body parts off the table. Giano was muttering again. Reiner put a hand on his shoulder. The crossbowman lowered his voice but didn't seem to be able to stop cursing.

The ratmen returned and crossed to the stacked cages. The first opened one at random, with a key from a ring on his belt, and pulled out a small figure.

Franka.

ELEVEN
Black Death Take You

REINER NEARLY SHOUTED out loud. The poor girl was so battered and dirty that, had he not known her so intimately, he wouldn't have recognized her. The dress she had been taken in was gone, as was much of her uniform. Only her breeks and shirt covered her, and they were shredded and caked with filth. Her face was bruised and blank, and streaked with dirt and blood. She looked around dully, as if she had been sleeping, but when she saw where her captors were taking her, she began to scream and fight, kicking at them and trying to wrench her arms from their grasp.

'Unhand me, you vermin!' she cried. 'I'll kill you! I'll cut you to ribbons. I'll...' Her threats dissolved into sobs of fury. The ratmen threw her at the table and she crashed against its metal edge, gasping.

The surgeon chittered angrily at his assistants, motioning for them to hold Franka still while he opened a vial he had taken from a table behind him. 'Quiet, boy. Stop...'

Reiner could take no more, the voice of self-preservation that normally stopped him before he launched himself into deadly danger drowned out by Franka's pitiful moans. He charged forward, screaming inarticulately as he drew his sword. Giano followed, roaring.

The ratmen looked up, startled. Perhaps the hoods Reiner and Giano wore confused them, but for one crucial second they stood frozen, staring. Reiner cut his down before it could pull its cleaver from its belt. Giano evaded the other's wild slash and ran it through the ribs. Franka fell with her dying captors.

The grey-furred surgeon scrabbled backwards, squealing. Reiner leapt after him, but he squirmed behind a giant contraption like one of his four-legged kin. Giano dived to block the back door. The ratman was too swift. He dodged around him and disappeared into the dark hallway beyond. Reiner and Giano gave chase, but the hall quickly split into three curving corridors and they couldn't tell which one he had taken.

Reiner skidded to a stop and turned back. 'Forget him. Let's fly.' He re-entered the room and crossed to Franka, holding out his hand. 'Franz...'

The girl crabbed backward, looking from him to Giano in terror. She snatched up a fallen scalpel and held it before her. 'Back, monsters!'

'Franz?' Then Reiner remembered. He pulled off his mask. 'It's only us.'

Giano pulled his off too. 'See? Nothing to be afraid!'

Franka blinked for a moment, then her face crumpled and she began to sob. The scalpel clattered to the ground. 'I thought... I didn't think... I never...'

'Easy now, easy now,' said Reiner, helping her up and clapping her roughly on the shoulder. 'Be a man, hey? Lad?'

Franka swallowed and sniffed. 'Sorry, captain. Sorry. Forgot myself. You...' she managed a weak grin. 'You certainly took your time.'

'Blame the damned vermin, lad,' said Reiner. What he wanted to do was draw Franka into his arms and hold her, but for Giano's benefit he played at manly heartiness. 'Damned inconsiderate of them, living so far underground. Now...'

'Save us,' said a weak voice.

Reiner, Franka and Giano turned. The men and women in the cages were staring out at them. They were thin, haggard creatures. Some of them had obviously been there for weeks. The skin hung from their bones like wet muslin. Others were hideously deformed, strange growths sprouting from their faces and chests. Still others had extra arms and hands stitched onto them in bizarre places. Reiner groaned. There were at least a dozen of them – probably more. How could he possibly get them all out?

'Please sir,' said a peasant girl with hands like purple mittens. 'We'll die otherwise.'

'You must, captain,' said Franka. 'You've no idea what they do.'

'I saw enough,' said Reiner, swallowing. 'But... but it's impossible. We'd never make it.'

'Y'can't leave us,' said a gaunt miner, gripping the bars. 'Y'can't let 'em have their way with us.'

Faint noises came from the far door: chittering rat-speech and the click of many rat feet.

'They coming,' said Giano.

'Captain,' Franka urged. 'Reiner, please.'

'It's too late. I...' With a growl of frustration, Reiner stepped to one of the dead ratmen and cut a ring of keys from his belt. 'Their weapons,' he said. 'And the scalpels.'

Giano and Franka began stripping the dead ratmen of their cleavers and swords and daggers as Reiner tried a key in a lock. They gathered up all the surgeon's scalpels, chisels and saws as well. The key didn't fit. Reiner tried another. It wouldn't turn.

The rat-voices were getting closer.

Reiner cursed. 'Give them the weapons.' He was sweating.

Franka kept a sword for herself, then helped Giano pass the rest of the blades through the bars to the prisoner's eager hands. Reiner tried another key. Still no luck.

The rat-voices were clear now. Reiner could hear the jingle of weapons and armour.

'Damn damn damn!' He thrust the keys at the man who had spoken first. 'I'm sorry. We must go. Good luck to you.'

'What's this?' said the man, taking the keys by reflex. 'You're leaving?'

Reiner backed to the door, pulling on his mask. 'We must.' He turned to Giano and Franka. 'Hurry.'

'Reiner, you can't...' said Franka.

'Don't be a fool. Do you want to live?'

He pushed her towards the door. She looked like she was going to protest again, then turned on her heel and started into the corridor, her face twisting with emotion. Giano pulled on his mask and followed her.

'Black death take you, you bastards!' cried a woman.

Reiner flinched as he Franka and Giano ran down the narrow corridor to the main tunnel.

'How we take with no face on?' asked Giano, gesturing at Franka.

Reiner closed his eyes. 'Curse me for a fool. Should have made three disguises. Give me a moment to think.'

They stopped just before they reached the tunnel, crouching in the shadow of the opening. They heard cries of rattish dismay behind them as the ratmen found the dead guards.

'No moment left,' said Giano.

'I don't know!'

'Carry me!' said Franka.

'Carry you?' asked Reiner.

'The surgeon sells his mistakes for food. I saw ratmen carry bodies out this way all day.'

'Perfect!' said Reiner. 'Hold tight, lad.' He hoisted Franka over his shoulder like a sack and started into the tunnel. 'And mind you play dead.'

'Or we be dead,' added Giano.

Reiner and Giano crossed quickly to the far side of the tunnel, putting the line of carts between them and the side passage, then hurried for the edge of the camp, hunching low. Before they had got twenty yards they heard their pursuers burst into the tunnel behind them, screeching orders and questions at their brethren. Reiner picked up his pace. Franka bounced slackly on his shoulder. He heard her retch.

'They come,' she whispered. 'Others point the way.'

'Shut up!' Reiner hissed.

He looked back, pulling his mask close with his free hand to see better through his eye-holes. The ratmen were indeed coming; a squad of guards with long spears and steel helms that stretched down their long snouts like horse's barding. They spread out across the width of the tunnel and jogged through the tents and carts, looking high and low – and sniffing.

Reiner pulled Giano around a high mound of garbage, his heart pounding. If the rat-guards had their scent, it didn't matter how well they hid, their sensitive noses would find them.

And just as he thought it, a rat squealed in triumph in the distance. Reiner moaned. The guards had sniffed out their man scent, even under all the rat-filth they had rolled in. It wouldn't be long now. He had to do something to throw them off the trail, to draw their attention. He looked around. The tents and the garbage would make perfect tinder except there was no fire. The rats didn't seem to use it. They ate their meat raw and slept clustered together for warmth, which made sense for a race that lived underground. He considered firing his pistols into one of the wagons loaded with the curious hand cannon and brass tanks, but he had no idea how big a blast they would make, if any.

The ratmen were closing in, following their trail through the camp like dogs after a fox. If Reiner and Giano broke into a run they would be spotted instantly. The sweat was pouring down Reiner's sides. Franka, who had weighed nothing when he picked her up, now felt heavier than an ox. He crossed his fingers and sent a prayer to Ranald. Alright, ye old charlatan, he thought, if ye get me out of this fix I'll trick a thousand men before next I touch wine, and that's a promise.

He dodged around a large tent and tripped over a small, fiercely hot forge, where a ratkin smith was pouring lead into bullet moulds. Reiner swallowed a curse and swerved drastically to avoid crashing into another rat who was busy folding measures of black powder into square gauze packets. Damn fool rats, not enough sense to keep blackpowder away from a...

Reiner stopped dead in his tracks. Giano crashed into him. Franka yelped. Idiot, thought Reiner, cursing himself. His prayer instantaneously answered and he'd nearly dismissed it as an obstacle. He dumped Franka unceremoniously to the ground, whispering, 'Stay dead,' then stepped up to the powder rat. The creature was scooping the powder out of a small wooden cask with what looked like a soup spoon from a nobleman's banquet table. Reiner kicked him off his haunches, caught up the powder keg in both hands, stepped back, and before the rat smith had begun to comprehend what was happening, hurled it at the forge with all his strength.

The cask smashed to pieces on the bricks and the powder caught with a great whump. A huge ball of fire erupted, almost enveloping Reiner in its billows. His mask and robes were smoking as he hurried back to Giano and Franka. The rats around them shrieked. The tent was ablaze. The smith was wreathed in fire and screaming as he scampered in careening circles, setting on fire everything he touched.

'Hurry!' cried Reiner. He scooped Franka up again, then ran on with Giano at his side. The ratmen they passed paid them no mind. They were too busy staring at the spreading fire with blank expressions or pushing forward with blankets and skins of water. The whole tunnel's attention was taken by the fire. Ratmen craned their necks over Reiner and Giano as they ran by. Reiner crossed his fingers again. A thousand men, ye mountebank, he thought. A thousand men.

They reached the edge of the camp and dodged through the jumbled ranks of siege towers and war machines, then stopped with the broad tunnel before them. Reiner set Franka down with a grunt of relief and tore off his mask and robes.

'You take robes off?' asked Giano, worried.

'I don't care,' said Reiner. 'I can't stand another moment.'

'Good.' Giano pulled his off too.

'We'll be sitting ducks,' said Franka looking at the wide open space before them.

'We'll have to risk it,' said Reiner. 'The side tunnels could go nowhere, or double back.'

'So we run, hey?' said Giano.

'Aye,' said Reiner. 'We run.'

RANALD'S GIFT OF luck must have been holding, for they jogged the length of the tunnel without seeing or hearing any signs of pursuit. Reiner hoped their hunters were caught in the fire – or even better, that the whole ratman encampment had gone up in flames. Though even that would not have been enough to ease his mind. The faces of the men and women he had left in the iron cages bobbed in front of him as he ran. Their pleas rang in his ears.

As they neared the end of the tunnel, where the digging machines faced the wall, Franka put a hand on his arm and nodded ahead.

'Torchlight,' she said quietly.

Reiner stopped and peered forward. Beyond the monstrous contraptions, the tunnel's omnipresent purple light was pushed back by a warm yellow glow. Reiner frowned, trying to remember if they had left a torch burning there. No. They had not. They had ground it out.

A shadow appeared on the tunnel wall, grossly distorted, but recognizably the shadow of a ratman.

Reiner froze, his heart pounding. Was it their pursuers? Had they circled around somehow and beaten them there? Were they waiting to kill them?

But then another shadow pushed into the light next to the ratman's. It was human.

'What this?' whispered Giano. 'Rat and man?'

Reiner didn't care to find out. He looked around at the few side passages piercing the tunnel's walls. Was there a way around? He doubted it, and even if there was, which one should he take? They could wander lost down here forever. Had they the luxury of waiting, whoever it was that was blocking their way might go away, but they couldn't wait. Their pursuers might come up behind them at any moment. They had to move.

Reiner put a finger to his lips and motioned Giano and Franka ahead. They crept forward, drawing weapons and keeping the bulk of the massive diggers between them and the torchlight. Reiner began hearing voices, an alternating hissing and rumbling. He paused. He could swear he recognized that rumble. Another few steps and the rumble turned into words.

'But I tell you, you can wait no longer. You must attack as soon as you can. Tomorrow if possible!'

A cold snake of dread began to stir in Reiner's guts. It was Commander Volk Shaeder speaking.

A voice like a knife on slate answered. 'Tomorrow no. Many days cutting from skaven-tunnel to man-tunnel. War machiness not get out unless cutting.'

Reiner almost choked. Giano was growling in his throat. Franka put a hand on his arm to calm him.

'But you don't have days,' continued Shaeder. 'Look. This was left in the brothel. If Gutzmann saw this all would be lost. You must act before your carelessness exposes you!'

The harsh voice hissed, distressed. 'My armies all not here. I half strong only.'

'You needn't worry about that. The fort will be lightly defended. I'll make sure of it.'

There was pause, then the rat-voice spoke again. 'This trick?'

'Why would I trick you when we want the same thing? You want Aulschweig for a grain farm. I want the gold we've shipped to Caspar. All that stands in our way is Gutzmann and the fort. Then I will be away to Tilea with more gold than the richest man in Altdorf, and you will have food for your people for all time.'

The ratman practically crooned his answer. 'Yes. Yes. Grain farm, man-slaves to work, and make strong us with they flesh. No more we eat you garbage. Now we grow strong.'

Reiner could almost hear Shaeder biting his tongue. 'A grand dream, to be sure.'

'This you do,' said the ratman. 'Close mine. Say no safe. We dig all day and night and day again. Ready tomorrow moon-rise.'

'Excellent,' said Shaeder. 'I will...

Giano spat, drowning out the rest. 'Traitor! Traitor to man! He die! I must–'

Reiner clapped a hand over the Tilean's mouth, but it was too late. There was silence from beyond the digger. And then a harsh slither of syllables from the ratman.

Clawed feet skittered toward them and Reiner could hear swords scraping from sheaths. He backed away, pulling Franka with him.

'Sorry, captain,' said Giano. 'I carry away myself...'

'Shut up and move, you fool,' Reiner growled. 'Out from under these things.'

They ran out of the shadow of the diggers, and not a moment too soon. Black shapes swarmed around the big machines, slipping under them, over them and through their skeletal structures like eels.

'Against the wall,' said Reiner. 'Don't let 'em encircle us.'

They ran to the left wall and turned, swords at the ready. Reiner drew his pistol. From the diggers came ten of the biggest ratmen Reiner had yet seen: tall, lean warriors with glossy black fur and gleaming bronze armour. Their swords were rapiers, long and thin. They flickered like heat lightning in the purple gloom.

TWELVE
The Honour of Knights

As the ratmen closed in, Reiner saw, behind them, Shaeder running into a side passage, and a tall black-furred ratman in burnished armour watching from a safe distance. Then there was no time to pay attention to anything but the blades slashing toward him. Reiner fired his pistol into the eyes of the closest ratman, and it flew back, its face a red crater. Another lunged at him savagely, though its shiny black eyes betrayed no emotion. Reiner threw his pistol at it and blocked with his sword while drawing his dagger.

Beside him, Franka and Giano were parrying and dodging like mad. Nine blades poked and chopped at them, and the ratkin were no mean swordsmen. Though not a match for Reiner or Giano in strength, they more than made up for this deficit with their terrifying speed. The three humans had no chance to counter-attack. They were too busy keeping the ratmen's blades at bay – or at least trying to. They were failing miserably.

Reiner barked as a ratman cut him across the forearm. He heard Franka and Giano gasp as they too were pinked. Another ratman sliced Reiner's forehead, and blood trickled into his left eye, half blinding him. A third blade slid across his ribs.

A ball of rage and despair welled up in him. The scriptures of Sigmar told one that dying in battle against the enemies of mankind was the noblest destiny a man of the Empire might attain. Well, it was a lot of bunk. Reiner wanted to die of his excesses at a ripe old age, surrounded by fabulous riches. Instead he was going to die here in a filthy tunnel, pointlessly, shoved through the gate of Morr with his whole life ahead of him.

Any notion that dying beside his beloved was in some way romantic was bunk as well. It was the cruellest of jokes. There was so much they hadn't done. They hadn't danced together or lived together. They hadn't made love together. And worst of all, they hadn't been free together. For the entire time Reiner had known her, he and Franka had been prisoners, under the thumb of the Empire or Manfred or his brother. Reiner had never been able to take her where he liked, show her his old haunts, explore new places with her, or even stay in and forget the world with her.

He could feel his arms growing heavier as he fanned them this way and that to catch all the steel stabbing his way. A blade pierced his leg. Another nicked his ear.

'Franka. I–'

The girl flicked a look his way between ducking and blocking. Her eyes shared his sadness. She grinned crookedly. 'Should have broken my vow, hey?'

Reiner laughed. 'Well yes, damn ye, y'should have. But–' A blade nicked his shoulder. 'Curse it! What I wanted to say–'

'Hoy!' came a cry, and one of the ratmen Reiner was facing suddenly had a crossbow bolt sprouting from his neck. It fell, choking and screeching.

Both the ratmen and the humans looked around. Running through the giant diggers and drawing their weapons were Karel and Hals and Pavel, as well as Dag, Jergen and Gert. Only Abel was missing.

Despite what the rat-surgeon had said about his kind having no spleen, the ratmen did not break, but met the new threat in good order. Three locked up with Pavel and Hals, one forced Gert back, besting the reach of his short-hafted axe with its long blade. Their leader, who had previously hung back, lunged at Karel, pressing him strongly. Dag windmilled wildly at another with a short sword and dagger, screaming his head off but doing little. Reiner, Franka and Giano, freed to fight one ratman apiece, continued on the defensive while they recovered their strength.

Jergen, as silent as ever, once again made all the other Blackhearts look like children waving sticks. He cut down the first ratman he faced with a single stroke, and before it had collapsed, had stepped past another and beheaded it with a backstroke. A third, seeing him with his sword arm stretched behind him, lunged at his exposed chest. Jergen swayed slightly to the left, allowing its sword to pass by his ribs, then trapped the blade under his arm and chopped down through the ratman's clavicle to the heart.

'Would you look at him work,' breathed Franka.

This sudden butchery at last unnerved the other ratmen. Their attacks faltered as their comrades screamed and spouted blood. Their leader sprang back from Karel and cried the retreat.

The ratmen scampered away towards their encampment, so quick that not even Jergen got in a last lick as they disengaged. Their wounded cried after them piteously, but they never looked back.

Franka stepped forwards to dispatch these with her dagger as the others started after the retreating rats.

'No!' said Reiner. 'There's a whole army down there.'

And just as he said it, he noticed shadows moving on the tunnel walls beyond the retreating rats. Their pursuers had finally resumed the chase.

'We must fly,' he said. 'There's more coming.'

The men reluctantly turned back, wiping down their weapons and sheathing them.

'Walking vermin,' said Gert wonderingly. 'Just as y'said.'

As the men started to crowd into the hole, Dag made a face. 'That you what stinks, captain? Thought it was the rats.'

'We had to disguise our scent.'

'Ye did that well enough,' said Pavel covering his nose.

Reiner looked around for Franka. 'Franz?'

She was sitting on the chest of one of the fallen ratmen, mechanically plunging her dagger into its chest over and over again, her eyes streaming tears.

'Franz.'

She didn't respond.

He crossed to her. 'Franz!'

He caught her wrist.

She looked up, snarling. Then blinked. Her face relaxed. 'I... I'm sorry. You didn't see...'

Reiner swallowed. 'No need to explain. But they're coming.'

She nodded and stood, and they followed the others into the hole.

As they emerged into the mine tunnel, Reiner caught Hals's eye. 'Changed your mind, did you?'

Hals scowled and looked away. 'We... we couldn't let y'die. But yer safe now, so, uh, we'll be on our way.'

'Fair enough,' Reiner said.

Pavel and Hals and the others turned and started hurrying up the slope. Reiner snorted as he pressed his kerchief against the cut above his eye. It was ridiculous. They were all travelling the same way, but Reiner allowed them to pull ahead for appearance's sake.

Franka shot him a questioning look.

'Hals and Abel saw you in your dress,' Reiner said softly.

Franka groaned. 'So they know my secret?'

Reiner chuckled. 'No, no. They think I have one.'

'They...?' Franka's eyes widened. 'Oh, no!'

The divided party continued on in uneasy silence, but after a while, Pavel looked over his shoulder. 'So, what do ye know of these rat-things.'

Reiner cocked an eyebrow at him. 'You're speaking to me?'

'We only ask as it concerns the safety of the garrison,' said Gert.

'Ah.' Reiner hid a smirk. 'Well, they mean to take the fort, and Aulschweig after that. Shaeder's in with them, betraying Gutzmann for the gold in the mine.'

Hals stopped and turned. 'Is this the truth?'

'Ask Giano. He heard him too, talking to their leader.'

Pavel looked at Giano. 'Tilean?'

'Aye. Is true. He tell them attack tomorrow.'

Pavel gaped. 'Tomorrow!'

Hals spat. 'Chaos take Shaeder. Jagger's more rat than these vermin.'

'Worse than Gutzmann,' said Pavel. 'That's certain.'

'Aye,' said Gert. 'Filthy turncoat. Ought to be fed his own guts.'

Karel shook his head. 'I can't believe that a knight of the Empire would do this. Is honour dead?'

The Blackhearts laughed. Karel looked baffled.

'You forget the company you keep,' said Reiner. 'We are all too well acquainted with the honour of knights.'

'This is bad,' said Hals. 'We've to warn the fort.'

Gert laughed. 'And will you be the one to tell 'em ratmen are coming to kill 'em? They'll lock you up.'

'Why warn 'em at all?' asked Dag. 'They be no mates of ours. Let's put these cursed mountains behind us and find someplace warm to hole up.'

'Forgotten the poison in our blood, lad?' asked Pavel. 'We've still a job to do, ratmen or no. And it may take longer than a day to finish it. We have to warn 'em.'

'Someone does,' said Hals.

The pikemen slid another glance toward Reiner.

Hals coughed. 'Er, captain...'

'Is it captain now?' Reiner drawled.

'You think you can trust him?' asked Gert.

'I trust him to save his own skin,' said Pavel, cold. 'He always looks after that.'

Reiner grunted. 'All right. I'll speak to Gutzmann. But it would serve you right if I lit out on my own.'

'But... but we're to kill Gutzmann,' said Karel, frowning. 'Gutzmann is a traitor to the Empire.'

'Who else would you have us tell?' asked Franka. 'Shaeder?'

'Shaeder's a traitor to mankind,' said Gert.

Karel was upset. 'So we ask Gutzmann to save us one moment, and then kill him the next?'

'It ain't all roses is it, laddie?' said Hals.

'Blame your future father-in-law if you don't find it to yer liking,' said Pavel.

'Manfred couldn't have known what we would find here,' said Karel defensively.

'There is a way Gutzmann might be spared,' said Gert. 'We're to kill him only as a last resort, aye? Maybe he gets a chance to fight for the Empire for once, he might think twice about leaving.'

'Aye,' said Pavel, brightening. 'That's true. He might.'

Hals nodded at Reiner. 'All right, captain. You tell him. Let's go.'

'As you wish.'

IN THE MAIN entry chamber of the mine all was chaos. The Blackhearts heard it before they saw it: bells ringing, horns braying, guards bellowing orders. As they crept out of the closed tunnel, they saw miners streaming from the two open ones, picks on their shoulders and worried expressions on their faces. The guards herded them towards the exit with shouts and shoves.

'What's all this?' asked Reiner of a guard as they joined the crush.

'Commander Shaeder's orders. Engineers say the lower tunnels could collapse at any moment. Mine's to be closed until further notice.'

'Shaeder ordered this? When?'

'A few minutes ago, sir. Now on your way.'

Reiner frowned. The last he had seen of Shaeder he had disappeared down a side passage in the ratmen's tunnel. It must come out somewhere up here. He wondered where.

IT WAS DUSK when they at last reached the fort, wheezing and gasping from the long run.

The gate guard saluted Reiner and stepped in his way. 'Pardon, sir,' he said, covering his nose. 'But Captain Vortmunder asks that you see him immediately about absenting yer duties all day.'

Reiner dodged around the man. 'My regards to Captain Vortmunder, and tell him I will see him as soon as I am able.'

'Ye might have a bath first!' the guard called after him.

Reiner made directly for Gutzmann's quarters, the rest of the Blackhearts trailing behind him. Reiner kept a weather eye out for Shaeder or his guards, the Hammer Bearers, but they didn't appear.

Two of Gutzmann's personal guard stood outside his door, chatting together. They came to attention as Reiner and the rest rumbled down the hall.

'Easy now, sirs,' said the first, holding up a hand. 'What's all this?'

Reiner saluted, breathing heavily. 'Corporal Meyerling reporting, sir. I wish to speak to General Gutzmann about danger within the mine and treachery within the camp.'

The guard stepped back, hand over his nose. His mate gagged. 'You must take it through the proper channels, corporal.'

'This is an emergency, sir,' said Reiner, drawing himself up. 'It cannot wait to go through channels.'

'Sorry, corporal. I got my orders...'

The door opened behind him and Matthais looked out. 'What's the trouble, Neihoff...?' He broke off as he saw Reiner. He sniffed, frowning. 'Meyerling. What are you doing here? And what's that horrible stink?'

'Never mind the stink. I've something to tell the general. What are you doing here?'

'Er, a fellow made a disturbing report to me. I brought him to Gutzmann.'

'Well, what I've to say is disturbing as well. Can you ask him if he'll see me?'

'I, er, yes. I will. Wait here.'

Matthais closed the door, and there was a wait, during which Reiner and the others caught their breath, and the guards held theirs. Reiner wondered what was troubling Matthais. He was far from his sunny self.

After a minute he reappeared and held the door open.

'All right, he'll see you,' he said. 'The rest are to wait in here.' He indicated the general's ante-room.

Reiner and the Blackhearts filed in as Matthais spoke to the guards. He then beckoned Reiner into Gutzmann's inner office and followed him in.

Gutzmann sat in a deep chair by the fire with his booted feet up on the fender. He waved as Reiner saluted. 'Ah, Hetsau. You wished to see me?'

'Yes, sir. I...' Reiner froze as he realized that Gutzmann had called him by his real name. 'Er...'

'I believe you know my guest?'

There was another chair at the fire, which faced away from Reiner. Its occupant leaned forward and looked around.

It was Abel.

Reiner cursed inwardly. A damned neat trick. He would have applauded if it hadn't been directed at him.

'My lord, I don't understand.' He spoke automatically, his mind racing. What was Abel's game? Why betray him when he was betraying himself as well? He would hang from Gutzmann's battlements right beside Reiner.

Gutzmann snorted. 'Don't be tiresome, Hetsau. You understand perfectly well. Quartermaster Halstieg has told me everything. How you were commanded by Count Valdenheim to assassinate me. How you joined my army under false pretences to do so. How you spied on my officers to discover my plans. How you attempted to recruit Halstieg and others to help you in your plot.'

'I beg your pardon, my lord?' Reiner's heart thudded in his chest. Now he was beginning to see. He'd underestimated Halstieg. The quartermaster was cleverer than he looked. He had found a way to at once betray Reiner and clear himself. This way he could remove Reiner, take Manfred's job for himself, and win his way into Gutzmann's confidences all at the same time.

Gutzmann scowled at him. 'Do you deny the charges?'

Reiner hesitated. He might try to brass it out and deny everything; try to use his powers of persuasion to convince Gutzmann that Halstieg had made it up out of the whole cloth, but there was little chance of success that way. Reiner had already condemned himself out of his own mouth. He cleared his throat. 'I do not deny that I was sent by Valdenheim, but not as an assassin. Halstieg and I and the others of my group were ordered by my lord Valdenheim to travel here and discover who was taking the Emperor's gold, and then to stop those responsible. Execution of the culprit was not beyond the purview of our brief, this is true, but neither was it our only option. We might have found a way to convince you...'

'We? Our?' cried Abel. 'Don't try to tar me with the brush of your guilt, deceiver. I had nothing to do with it.'

Reiner looked at Gutzmann. 'Is that what he has told you, my lord?'

'Hetsau came to me here, my lord!' said Abel. 'The first day he arrived! He approached a number of us, trying to turn us against you.'

'My lord,' said Reiner. 'Halsteig has been with us from the beginning. There are ten of us. We came, all of us, from Altdorf. We...'

'And the others wait in my ante-room?' asked Gutzmann. 'Have you decided that I am your culprit? Did you come to kill me?'

Reiner pursed his lips. 'My lord may accuse me of treachery, but I hope he doesn't think me unsubtle.'

Gutzmann laughed. 'Then why did you come? Other than to foul my offices with your odour. Sigmar, Matthais, you warned me, but I had no idea.'

Reiner paused. Caught flatfooted by Abel's betrayal he had almost forgotten why he had come. But now...

He sighed. He had been close to convincing Gutzmann that he was a more honest villain than Abel; and given time, he might have found a way to salvage the situation, but now, now he must mention the ratmen, and all his credibility would wither away in a storm of laughter.

Unfortunately, ridiculous as it sounded, the danger was real. The camp would be overrun, the garrison slain, Aulschweig enslaved – and most distressing of all, he and Franka and the other Blackhearts might be caught in the middle of it. Someone had to do something. He only regretted that that someone appeared to be him.

He licked his lips. 'Know, my lord...'

Muffled cursing and shouting came from the anteroom. Reiner could hear the sounds of a scuffle. He looked at the door.

'Pay it no mind, corporal,' said Gutzmann. 'It is merely your men being arrested. Pray go on.'

Reiner groaned. He was beginning to think that, poison or no poison, Manfred or no Manfred, he and the Blackhearts should have turned north when they ran out of the mine, and just kept running. 'Yes, my lord.' He took a deep breath. 'Know that when I speak you will call me mad. But if you are wise, you will see that its very lunacy is proof of the truth of my warning. For only a terrible danger would cause me to squander what little goodwill you feel toward me at such a delicate moment.'

'What are you babbling about?' said Gutzmann, confused.

Abel laughed, a high nervous giggle. 'He's about to tell you about the ratmen!'

'The...?' Gutzmann looked at Abel.

'The ratmen,' Abel repeated, still chuckling. 'It was the tale he meant to tell to lure you away. Ratmen in the mine. He would, er, lure you there and then bury you in a rock fall, claiming an accident.'

Gutzmann frowned. 'You said nothing of this before.'

Abel shrugged. 'Can you blame me, my lord?'

Gutzmann turned to Reiner, an eyebrow raised. 'Is this true? Is this the ruse you meant to use?'

Reiner cursed inwardly. Abel had twisted his words before he had even said them. But he had no choice but to go on. 'Except that it is no ruse, my lord. There are ratmen mustering in tunnels below the mines. And they mean to attack the fort.'

Gutzmann laughed and looked at Abel wonderingly. 'You were right. He prates the stuff of fairy tales. It is beyond understanding.' He turned to Reiner. 'Come sir, why do you persist? Ratmen? Could you think of nothing better?'

'They exist, sir. I have today seen them with my own eyes. We fought them. I have their blood on my clothes. The odour that offends you is theirs.'

Gutzmann stared at him with his bright blue eyes, as if trying to see into his soul. 'You don't seem mad...'

'There is worse to come, sir. But still I must tell it.' Reiner coughed and continued. 'While returning from their tunnels, we came upon a party of these ratmen talking to a man. We crept forward and discovered that it was Commander Shaeder.'

'What!' Gutzmann banged his hand on the arm of his chair. 'Sir, your foolishness goes too far. How dare you malign the commander's name?'

'He betrays you, my lord. It seems that the ratmen mean to take Aulschweig for a grain farm, and Shaeder has promised them an easy victory over you so they might cross over the pass. In exchange, they promised him all the gold from the mine. The reason...'

Gutzmann laughed uproariously. 'Now I know you are mad.' He raised his voice and called through the door. 'Neihoff!'

After a moment, the guard poked his head in the door. 'General?'

'Fetch Commander Shaeder here. He must hear this.'

The guard ducked his head and disappeared again.

Gutzmann tipped back in his chair. 'You've betrayed yourself, for you don't know Shaeder. There isn't enough gold in the world for that old Sigmarite to turn his back on the Empire. He loves it more than life itself. If he were to betray me, it wouldn't be for gold, it would be to stop me from leaving.'

'I only repeat what I heard, sir,' said Reiner. 'The cave-ins are a lie. The reason he shuts the mine is so that the ratmen may use their digging machines, which they have heretofore used only at night, all this day and night to widen their tunnel to the mine in order to bring up their siege engines and attack the fort tomorrow after dark.'

Gutzmann was red in the face. 'Enough sir, enough. Digging machines? Siege engines? It is already madness to believe in ratmen, but to credit them with the ability to build machines of such complexity?'

'My lord, please!' Reiner held out his hands. 'Think for a moment. Why would I put myself at such great risk to tell you a foolish lie? I have found already the proof Manfred asked me to seek out. I know you intend to desert the Empire and help Caspar usurp his brother's throne. I know of the shipments of gold.'

'You...!' Gutzmann's eyes bulged. 'Quiet, you fool!'

Reiner ignored him. 'If I had wanted to betray you, I would have found a way to kill you and escaped north with the gold you hide in the crates in the third tunnel.'

Reiner saw Abel's head come up at that.

Veins were throbbing in Gutzmann's temples. 'You know all this?'

'And yet,' said Reiner. 'Still I came here to warn you, when a fortune and Manfred's favour were within easy reach.'

'But...' said Gutzmann. 'But, ratmen?'

There was a knock at the door and Shaeder entered. 'You wished to see me, general?'

'Shaeder, come in,' said Gutzmann. He wiped his brow and composed himself. 'I... I thought you should face your accuser.'

Reiner thought he saw Shaeder pale a little as he turned and saw him. The commander had recognized him in the tunnel then – and undoubtedly thought him killed by the black rats.

He recovered instantly, however. 'Corporal Meyerling? Of what does he accuse me?' His nose wrinkled. 'And why does he smell so?'

'He says that you conspire with ratmen who live in tunnels below the mine to overrun the fort and make of Aulschweig a, what was it you said, sir? A grain farm? And that you did all this for the gold in the mine.'

Shaeder laughed, long and loud. But stopped when he realized that Gutzmann hadn't joined him.

He frowned. 'I'm sorry, general. It is no laughing matter. For whether the man is mad, or has some more sinister purpose in spouting this nonsense, he is dangerous, and should be locked up before he tries to do you injury. You can't possibly believe him?'

Gutzmann shrugged. 'I don't know what to believe now.'

Reiner swallowed. 'My lord, I don't ask you to believe me. Only go to the end of the closed tunnel and see what you find. If after that you find nothing, you may do with me what you will.'

'You see, general,' said Abel, 'he seeks to lure you to a cave-in. Hang him.'

Reiner thought he saw a sly smile flick across Shaeder's lips as he turned to Gutzmann, chuckling. 'No no, my lord. I could not live with your suspicion hovering over me. I insist that you come to the mine and see for yourself the falseness of Meyerling's story. Merely allow the engineers tomorrow morning to make sure that he hasn't planted some vile trap and I will have them escort you down to the cave-in that blocks the tunnel.'

Gutzmann nodded. 'I will. I have meant to see it for myself anyway.' He turned to Reiner, his face sad and hard. 'I can pity a madman, sir, but I do not care for liars. As you will discover.'

Reiner cursed himself as Gutzmann motioned for Matthais to take him away. What a fool he was. He had played directly into Shaeder's hands. He had given him the perfect excuse to deliver Gutzmann to his doom. He didn't resist when Matthais took his arm, or notice when he gave him a hurt look. He didn't even spit at Abel as he passed. He was too absorbed in flagellating himself.

THIRTEEN
Do You Still Say I Lie?

THE REST OF the Blackhearts were sitting in sullen silence when Matthias and two guards threw Reiner into a dank, straw-strewn stone cell deep beneath the keep. He could barely see them as they raised their heads, just their eyes glinting in the dim torchlight that found its way through the oak door's heavily barred window. Franka nodded to him, but said nothing. She sat apart from the others.

Only Karel brightened at the sight of him. 'Captain, you're here! The others thought you might have betrayed us.'

Reiner shot a look at Hals and Pavel. 'The others will think anything of me, it seems.' There was little room left to sit. Much of the floor was studded with heavy iron bolts from which the chains had rusted long ago. No one seemed inclined to make room for him. He sighed, then crossed deliberately to Franka and sat down beside her. No one spoke. 'It wasn't I who betrayed us,' he said at last. 'It was Abel. He named us assassins.'

'Hey?' said Giano. 'For why?'

Gert snorted. 'So he can get us out of the way and claim the credit of killing Gutzmann for himself. Always thought that boy was a mite too smart.'

'Aye,' said Reiner, pointedly. 'There's a fellow who truly cares only for his own skin.'

There was an uncomfortable silence after that. In the darkness, Reiner could see Pavel nudging Hals. Hals shoved back, angry, but after a moment he sighed.

'All right, all right.' He looked up at Reiner, his mouth pulled down into a bulldog frown. 'Captain, I'll ask ye plain what we all been wondering. What went on in the room in the brothel before the ratmen attacked?'

Reiner shook his head. 'We are locked in a cell, with our true purpose exposed and the noose getting nearer by the second, and this is what concerns you?'

'I no care,' said Giano. 'Is they who is caring. Love is love, hey?'

'That weren't an answer,' said Gert.

'Then I'll give you one,' Reiner snapped. 'What happened in that room is no business of yours. Now, have any of you any ideas for escaping this pit?'

'But it is our business! How are we to follow ye when ye keep secrets from us?' asked Pavel. 'How can we trust ye when y've lied?'

Reiner snorted. 'Don't be ridiculous. We're all of us liars. We've every one of us secrets. You and Hals still haven't told what really happened with your captain, to name an instance.'

'We have, though,' said Hals.

'And t'ain't the same anyway,' Pavel said, shaking his head. 'The secrets we keep don't make us unfit to lead.'

'Nor does mine.'

'Captain,' said Karel, pleadingly. 'Just deny it plainly and have an end to it.'

Pavel sneered. 'Being a lover of men may not matter in Altdorf gambling houses, but t'ain't right in the army, where we all live, er, cheek by jowl, so to speak...'

'Captain ain't an invert, curse you!' cried Dag. 'And I'll kill the man who says so!'

'Then y'll be killing all of us, I think,' said Gert.

Reiner sighed. 'And that's what it comes down to, isn't it? It's not the secrets. It's not the lies. Well, let me set your minds at ease. Dag is right. I am not a lover of men.'

'You see!' cried Dag. 'You see.'

'Though if I was,' continued Reiner, 'I wouldn't be the first or the last to lead men...'

He stopped when he saw Hals's and Pavel's faces. They were almost comically downcast.

'What now?'

'We hoped at least that ye wouldn't lie,' said Pavel.

Hals clenched his fists. 'Captain, I saw ye!'

'What you saw wasn't what you thought it was,' said Reiner. 'You were mistaken.'

'Then what was it?' asked Pavel.

Reiner's eyes slid to Franka, then away. 'I cannot say.'

'T'ain't good enough,' said Hals.

'Pikeman,' said Karel, angry. 'You have no right to harass a superior officer this way. Captain...'

Reiner waved a hand at Karel. 'Forget it, lad, forget it.' He sighed and looked back to Hals. 'And if I were to say I am, would you trust me again? Would you follow me?'

There was a long pause. Everybody looked at the floor.

At last Reiner chuckled. 'You see, I was right. The lies and secrets don't matter. It's only who I bunk with that concerns you. Something that matters not the slightest...'

'So you admit it?' said Hals.

'No, I do not,' said Reiner scornfully. 'You put words in my mouth.'

Gert sneered. 'Better than what you put in your mouth, captain.'

Dag shot to his feet, fists balled. 'Y'filthy dog. Y'll die for that!' He leapt at Gert, swinging blindly. Gert lurched aside, absorbing most of the punches with his bulk, then grabbed the archer's legs and pulled him down. They rolled about on the floor in a chaos of flailing arms and legs. Everyone but Reiner and Jergen shouted at them and tried to pull them apart.

Franka jumped up, furious. 'Stop it, you fools! Stop it! You're all mad! Captain Hetsau isn't a lover of men!' she cried. 'And I should know better than any of you!'

Reiner's heart banged against his ribs. 'Frank – Franz! Don't be a fool!' He tried to pull her back down.

She wrenched her arm away. 'The reason I was wearing woman's clothes, and the reason Captain Reiner was kissing me...'

'Franka! Stop!'

'…is because I am a woman!'

Reiner groaned. The secret was out. Franka would be a soldier no more. Manfred would send her away from him. The other Blackhearts would shun her.

The other Blackhearts hadn't heard her. They were too busy trying to separate Gert and Dag. She grabbed Pavel and shook him by the shirt-front.

'Listen to me, curse you! I'm a woman!'

'Hey?' Hals blinked. 'What d'ye say, lad?'

'I'm not a lad,' Franka screamed. 'Are you deaf?'

The others were turning now. Even Dag and Gert were slowing their punches.

'Not a lad?' said Pavel, confused.

'No,' said Franka, struggling for patience. 'I am a woman. I disguised myself as a boy so I could fight for the Empire.'

The men stared at her. Dag and Gert gaped at her from the floor.

'Is true?' asked Giano.

'Of course it ain't,' said Hals. He shook his head sadly. 'Lad. I know why y'do this. Ye wish to protect the captain, and 'tis a noble thought. But it won't wash. We've seen y'fight. Lasses don't fight.'

'I do,' said Franka. 'Come, have you never wondered why I've never bathed with you? Why I always tented alone? Why I said I'd kill any man who touched me?'

'Y'might have been afraid of, er, temptation,' said Pavel.

Franka laughed. 'Do you think yourself so irresistible,' pikeman?'

'Why don't y'ask her to show ye proof,' said Gert.

Dag laughed. 'Aye. Aye, give us a show.'

'No!' cried Reiner. 'I forbid it. Get away, you filthy jackals!'

Franka shrugged. 'I think I must, captain. There seems no other way to convince them. But not to all of you, curse you!' she shouted, catching their looks.

She turned from one to the other, then at last came to a decision. 'Hals, stand in the corner.'

She pointed to the far end of the cell. Hals looked embarrassed. The others chuckled.

'Come on, come on,' said Franka. 'Let's be done with it.'

With dragging feet, Hals trudged to the corner and faced out. Franka stood in front of him and began unlacing her jerkin.

The company waited in silence. Dag's eyes gleamed. Reiner wanted to kill them all for forcing Franka to this indignity. How dare they not take her at her word? Then he recalled that she had had to do the same for him in order to convince him.

Hals shifted uncomfortably as Franka opened her jerkin and began undoing her buttons. He didn't seem to know where to look. At last Franka pulled aside her shirt and tugged down the bandages with which she bound her chest. 'There,' she said, glaring. 'Do you still say I lie?'

Reiner and the others couldn't see Franka's nakedness, but the look on Hals's face told them all they needed to know. Reiner laughed in spite of himself. The veteran pikeman was gaping like a gaffed trout. He looked like the cuckolded husband from an innyard farce.

'Yer... yer a lass!' he said, blinking.

Franka pulled up her bandages and closed her shirt. 'Aye,' she said dryly. 'So now you've no reason to distrust the captain, yes?'

'But this is no better!' cried Pavel, stepping forward. 'We, we've cursed in front of you. Told barracks stories in front of you.'

'We've pissed in front of you, for Sigmar's sake!' roared Hals, outraged. 'Y've seen us naked.'

'Not to worry,' said Franka. 'I took no pleasure in it.'

Gert laughed. 'The lass has wit, at least.'

Karel turned to Reiner, very stiff. 'Captain, you have known this girl's secret for some time?'

'Since the caves of the Middle Mountains,' said Reiner.

'And you have allowed her to fight, to put herself in danger?'

'Aye.'

'And you still call yourself a gentleman?' The boy was red in the face.

Reiner sighed. 'First, lad, I have never called myself a gentleman. Second, you try stopping her. She won't listen to me.'

'But this won't do,' said Hals. 'A lass can't fight. It ain't right. We've to tell Manfred. Send her back to her husband.'

Franka shuddered.

Reiner put his hand on her shoulder. 'You can be sure Manfred already knows. His surgeons had their way with her as they did with us.'

Karel choked. 'Count Manfred lets her fight?'

Reiner smiled. 'After all this time you still find yourself shocked by your future father-in-law's behaviour? To him Franka is only another criminal, whose imposture is another sword he holds over her head to force her to do his bidding.'

'Well, damn Manfred and damn you,' said Hals. 'I won't have it! Never let it be said that an Ostlandman stood by and let a lass fight while there was still life in his limbs!'

'Hear hear!' said Pavel. And Gert and Dag echoed him.

A sudden sob from Franka stopped them. They looked at her.

'I knew it would be like this!' she moaned. 'I knew it!' She balled her fists at her sides. 'Is this one thing enough that you turn against me? Am I not your friend?'

'We don't turn against you, lass,' said Pavel softly. 'We want to keep you safe from harm.'

'But it's not what I want! I want to be with you! I want to be a soldier!'

'But y'can't be,' said Hals. 'Yer a lass now.'

'As I always have been! All that has changed is that you know it.'

Hals shook his head. 'And I can't unknow it. I'm sorry, girl.'

Gert shrugged. 'What matters it one way or t'other? Likely we die swinging before we've a chance to fight again anyway. Either Gutzmann hangs us for spies, or Shaeder feeds us to his furry friends.'

The others sighed, returned by this unwelcome reminder to the reality of their situation.

'True enough,' said Pavel. 'But still, she shouldn't be here, should she?'

'Nor should any of us,' said Reiner. He straightened up. 'And if we turn our minds to getting free, we might be able to continue this fascinating debate later in more pleasant surroundings. Like the Griffin in Altdorf. What say you?'

After some sullen reluctance, the others agreed to try to think of some way out of their predicament, but the day had been long and filled with running and fighting and uncertainty, and once they had returned to their places against the walls and wrapped their arms around their knees, the talk quickly devolved into mumbles and grunts, until at last, one by one their heads nodded and dropped.

Just as he was drifting off, Reiner felt Franka slump against him. He put his arm around her and pulled her close. At least there is that, he thought. At least there is that.

THEY HAD NO idea how long they had slept or what time it was when they woke. Neither noise nor light penetrated this far underground, so they couldn't tell if it was morning or afternoon or still the middle of the night, or what might be happening in the fort above. Frustrated, Reiner tried to puzzle it out from what he had learned the previous night, but it was so cold that he found it hard to concentrate. Would Gutzmann discover Shaeder's treachery and come down to free them with profuse apologies and praise, or would a flood of ratmen pour down the stairs and tear them to bloody shreds? After a while his thoughts became a muddle and he could do no more than lean against Franka and stare at the opposite wall, numb with boredom and despair. The others were no better. They had tried at first to invent an escape plan, but all started, 'Once we get out of this cell...'

Reiner had thought he might be able to accomplish something by engaging their guards in conversation. For if he could make friends with them he might trick them into relaxing their guard, but they must have been warned of his powers of persuasion. He could get nothing out of them but grunts and curses.

Sometime later he woke panting from a nightmare of pleading voices and twisted hands reaching from iron cages to tug at his clothes, to find that Franka was shaking him.

'What's the...'

She shushed him, pointing to her ear. There were voices outside the cell. He sat up and listened. Karel was crouched at the door.

'But we're not to be relieved until evening mess,' said one of their guards.

'You're relieved now,' said a new voice. 'Commander Shaeder's orders.'

The Blackhearts looked around at each other.

'That's us done then,' whispered Hals.

Reiner cursed. 'How many are there?'

Karel rose up to peek through the window then dropped back down again. He held up four fingers. His eyes were wide. 'Shaeder's greatswords!'

The light increased as boot heels clopped closer to the door. Reiner slapped at his belt, but of course his sword wasn't there. They had all been disarmed. 'On your feet!' he hissed. 'Be ready.' He wished he knew for what.

The Blackhearts pulled themselves up, stiff and groaning, trying to shake feeling into their numb limbs. Karel shifted away from the door.

The key turned in the lock.

FOURTEEN
May Sigmar Speed You

REINER'S MIND RACED, trying to think of some way to overcome the greatswords. It was impossible. They were proven veterans. They had seen everything. They were ready for any trick, and they were armed to the teeth. What could he possibly do to throw them off their stride, to shock them?

The door was swinging open. He could see the four Hammer Bearers standing beyond it, swords out. The leader held a lantern at his side. They had the look of witchfinders on the hunt, seeing sin in everything.

His heart banged against his chest. He had it!

'Franka!'

He grabbed the girl's wrist and dragged her before the door just as the four greatswords stepped in, raising their swords.

'Your time has come, villains,' said the leader.

Reiner pulled Franka into his arms, crying, 'Kiss me, beloved!' Then put action to his words and mashed his lips against hers with all the passion he could muster.

The greatswords gaped, paralyzed with shock. The tip of the leader's sword hit the stone floor with a clank. 'What abomination is this? Inverted degenerates...'

As quick as an eel, Jergen darted forward and kicked the lantern from the leader's hand, then ripped his sword from his slack fingers as the cell was plunged into darkness.

'Rush 'em!' Reiner shouted.

He dived at the second man's knees as Franka headbutted him in the chest. The fellow hit the floor. Around him, Reiner could hear, but not see, swords clanging as the others charged forward, screaming battle cries. Fists smacked into skin. Men grunted and yelped. There was a sharp gasp, and the unmistakable sound of steel chunking into flesh.

Reiner flailed for his greatsword's sword arm, trying to catch it before the man could swing. He caught the sword instead and razored open the base of his thumb. Reiner wrapped the blade in his arms and hugged it as the man tried to pull it away.

'Sit on him!'

'I am!' came Franka's voice.

Reiner fought the man's hands and kneed for his groin as shouts and thumps and clanks came from all over the cell. There was a sickening crack nearby. His man convulsed. A second crack and all the strength went out of the fellow's limbs. Another and he let go of his sword.

'Franka! Enough.'

'Oh.'

Reiner grabbed the Hammer's sword and stood, but the sounds of the other conflicts were trailing off except for one last thrashing fight in the centre.

'Is me you have!' came Giano's voice. 'Get he...!'

Reiner groped around in the darkness and found the lantern. He righted it and fumbled in his belt pouch for flint and steel, but the flame had not gone out, only guttered, and now came to life again.

Reiner looked around. Giano was fighting a disarmed greatsword, and Dag was fighting Giano, trying to punch him in the kidneys. Around them the other Blackhearts were rising to their feet. Their opponents remained motionless.

'Dag!' Reiner called. 'Leave off! Get the greatsword! I want to...'

Dag sprang up as he saw the greatsword was still alive. As the others stepped forward to help, he jumped on the man's chest, snatched his dagger from its scabbard and plunged it into his eye up to the hilt. He laughed like a child with a pin-wheel as the man spasmed and jerked, then lay still.

'Got him, captain,' he said, looking up. 'What'd ye want?'

Reiner balled his fists. He had never in his life come across a fellow who was in more need of killing. He forced himself to speak slowly. 'I wanted... to speak... to him. To find out if Shaeder had put his plan into action yet.'

Dag looked at him blankly. 'Oh. Well, too late for that now, hey?' He giggled.

'Aye,' said Reiner. 'Too late.'

The rest of the greatswords were dead as well. Gert had crushed the windpipe of one with his thumbs while Pavel and Hals held his arms and legs. Jergen had accounted for another, with the help of Karel, who had held the man by the ankles. The life poured out of his neck in a red flood. Franka sat on the chest of the last. The back of his head was a crimson crater, and hair and brains slicked one of the iron rings that stuck up out of the floor. Franka held clumps of the man's beard and hair in her clenched fists. She shivered with revulsion when she saw what she had done, and flung the tufts away.

'Well done, lads,' said Reiner, wrapping his cut thumb with his handkerchief. 'Rohmner, check the guardroom.'

Jergen stepped to the door and looked out. He gave the all's well sign.

Gert laughed as he stood up. 'What in Sigmar's name inspired you to kiss the lass?'

Reiner shot a chagrined look at Franka. 'It worked, did it not?'

'Almost didn't,' said Hals, scowling. 'Ye surprised me near as much as ye surprised them.'

'Aye,' said Pavel. 'I nearly pissed m'self.' He blushed and looked at Franka. 'Beggin' yer pardon, lass.'

'Stop that!' Franka barked.

The others laughed.

Reiner took the sword belt, keys and gloves from his man and gave Franka his dagger. The others looted the rest, sharing out swords and daggers as best they could.

'So,' said Gert. 'What's yer plan, captain?'

Reiner smirked. 'Captain again, is it? Well, I...' He hesitated. He knew what he wanted to do. He wanted to get Gutzmann's gold out of the mine and scurry off back to civilization before the ratmen poured out of their hole. But he couldn't do that until he knew Gutzmann was dead. The fact that Shaeder's greatswords had come to kill them suggested he was, but Reiner couldn't be sure. He sighed. 'Well, I suppose we should go up and see what's in the wind first.' He glared at Dag. 'Since we've no one to ask.'

He stepped out of the cell with the others behind him. A stairway ascended into darkness on the far side of the square guardroom. They took it, swords at the ready. As they turned up the last flight they saw at the top a guard with his back to them, standing on the far side of a locked gate.

Reiner motioned them back down around the corner. 'Any of you recognize that fellow? Or recall his name?'

Gert frowned. 'I need another look.' He crept up to the landing, peeked around, then came back down. 'Herlachen, I think,' he said. 'Or Herlacher. Some such. His tent's by mine. We did wall duty together t'other day.'

Reiner shrugged. 'It will have to do. Now back down a bit, then come up marching.' He looked to Jergen. 'When he opens the door, you run up and pull him in. You understand?'

Jergen nodded.

The Blackhearts backed down another flight, then Reiner dropped his hand and they began marching up, kicking the stairs with their boot heels.

Just before they reached the last flight again, Reiner called out, gruff and loud. 'Herlachener! Open the gate!'

The guard's voice echoed down to them. 'Yessir! Right away, sir.'

Reiner listened to the jingle and clank of the guard putting key to lock. He held up his hand and the Blackhearts marched in place. It wouldn't do to come around the corner before the fellow had opened the door. At last he heard the scrape of the key and the squeal of the door swinging open.

'Now, Jergen!'

Jergen darted around the corner as Reiner and the rest resumed marching.

They mounted the last flight just in time to see him springing up at the surprised guard. Jergen punched him in the nose as he tried to draw, then caught him around the back of the neck and flung him down the stairs, where Reiner and Giano caught him and clamped hands over his mouth. Reiner held his breath as the swordmaster took the keys from the lock, pulled the gate closed and slipped back down the stairs. He expected shouts and challenges, but none came. He exhaled.

'Right,' he whispered. 'Tie him up and leave him downstairs.'

'Better to kill him, hey?' said Dag.

'We ain't at war with the army, lad,' growled Reiner.

As Hals and Pavel tied the guard's wrists and ankles with the laces of his jerkin, Reiner craned his neck to look through the gate. The soldiers who wandered through the hallway beyond it seemed calm, which told Reiner that the ratmen had not yet attacked, and Gutzmann had not been reported dead or missing. Daylight streamed into the hall from the courtyard door. It looked to be late afternoon.

He waited for the hall to empty, but it never did. The armoury was the first door on the right, the barracks where Gutzmann's retinue of knights slept the second. On the left were the tall doors that led to the main hall – usually locked – and beyond them, the door to the courtyard. The hall was in constant use.

'We'll have to brass it out, lads,' Reiner said. 'With luck, our fall from grace isn't common knowledge. We'll just stroll out like naught's the matter.'

'You forgetting you and Ostini and the lass smell like a latrine, captain?' asked Gert.

'And look like ye fell in one,' added Pavel.

Reiner sighed. 'Curse it, I had. Well, I'll think of something.' He hoped he wasn't lying. 'If anyone challenges us, let me do the talking. If they call guards, run for the north gate.' He took a deep breath. 'Right. Off we go.'

Reiner mounted the steps and pushed open the gate with the others behind him. He tried to keep his breath steady, but every soldier who stepped into the hall made him jump. They all wrinkled their noses as the Blackhearts passed.

At last a knight stopped, scowling. 'Sigmar's oxter! What happened to you, corporal?'

Reiner saluted. 'Sorry for the smell, sir. Floor of the guardroom latrine caved in. Some of us got banged up a bit. Going to clean off now.'

The captain made a face. 'Well be quick about it.'

Reiner saluted again and they continued to the courtyard door. Reiner looked out, then pulled back, heart thudding. Shaeder was on the steps before the keep's main door, talking with Obercaptain Nuemark.

'Shaeder,' said Reiner over his shoulder. 'Curse the luck. We'll have to wait a moment...'

Before he could finish there was a commotion at the gate, and a lance corporal galloped into the courtyard on a lathered horse. 'General Gutzmann,' he called, reining up. 'I have urgent news for General Gutzmann.'

Shaeder stepped to the lancer as he dismounted. 'General Gutzmann is called away to the mines, corporal,' he said. 'Tell me your news.'

Everyone in the courtyard turned to listen as the lancer saluted. 'Yes commander. My lads and I were patrolling the southern pass, bandit hunting, when we saw a column coming from Aulschweig.'

'A column?' asked Shaeder, frowning. 'What do you mean, man?'

'Commander, it was Baron Caspar at the head of an army. We crept forward to observe and counted six company of horse, eight hundred pike and musket, and siege engines.'

'Siege engines?' Shaeder sounded shocked. 'What is he about? Does he mean to take the fort?'

'My lord,' said the corporal. 'I believe that is exactly what he means to do.'

There was uproar in the courtyard as everyone within earshot began talking at once. Lancers began pushing past Reiner and the Blackhearts into the courtyard. It was a perfect opportunity. No one, not even the guards at the gate, would look at them now.

'Around the edge, lads,' Reiner murmured. 'And keep your heads down.'

They shuffled out in the midst of a crowd of lancers. Shaeder had mounted the steps and was issuing orders to the assembled troops. 'Daggert, ride to the mine and ask General Gutzmann to return at once. I will take command until he can be found.' He turned to Nuemark. 'Obercaptain, assemble a force of three hundred pike and a company each of pistoliers, knights, lancers, swords and handguns, then march south to Lessner's Narrows and hold it for as long as you are able so that we may have time to prepare. In the meantime, all other captains are to have their troops make the fort ready to receive an attack. And someone find Obercaptain Oppenhauer and ask him to see me in my offices at his earliest convenience. Now go, all of you, and may Sigmar speed you.'

The courtyard erupted into confusion as men ran hither and thither while officers shouted questions and bellowed for horses.

Above it all, Infantry Obercaptain Nuemark called out his orders in a clear, calm voice. 'I will have Knight Captain Venk, Lance Captain Halmer and Pistolier Captain Krugholt report to me as well as Pike Captain...'

The rest was lost as Reiner and the Blackhearts dove into a stream of men rushing out of the gate. No one stopped them as they passed into the fort. In fact, they gave them a wide berth.

'Aulschweig attacks now?' cried Karel as they hurried along. 'What rotten luck!'

'Don't be a fool,' said Reiner. 'Couldn't you see? That little scene was more staged than one of Detlef Sierck's murder plays.'

'Staged?' queried Karel. 'What do you mean?'

'It's a trick,' said Franka, answering before Reiner could reply. 'There is no attack from Aulschweig. Shaeder only pretends there is to draw the fort's attention south while the ratmen attack from the north.'

'And he sends away half the fort to make it even easier for them,' said Gert. 'By the time Nuemark's forces return from their wild goose chase they will be locked out, and at the mercy of our cannon in the hands of the rats.'

Reiner motioned to the others, and they pushed out of the flow of men into a narrow alley between two cavalry barracks.

'But... but it can't be,' said Karel, catching his breath. 'The man who gave the warning was a lancer. The lancers are loyal to Gutzmann.'

'I'm sorry to be the one to break it to you, lad,' said Reiner. 'But even a cavalry man can be bought.' He sighed and leaned against the wall. 'Lads, I've a feeling there's nothing left for us to do here. If Shaeder makes his move, then Gutzmann must be dead. I think our best play is to head home and report the commander's treachery to Manfred.'

'And leave the fort to the mercy of the ratmen?' asked Karel, aghast.

'What would you have us do, lad?' asked Reiner. 'We nine can't stop an army of monsters, and we've tried warning the brass already. Twice.' He looked around at the others. 'I am, of course, open to suggestions.'

The Blackhearts looked unhappy, but said nothing.

'Right then.' Reiner pushed away from the wall. 'We go. I want to return to the mine to be sure Gutzmann is dead first. Then we head north.'

The others nodded, glum. Franka shot Reiner a sharp look.

FIFTEEN
They Knew

The Blackhearts split up briefly to return to their various tents and barracks and arm themselves. Though time was of the essence, Reiner took a moment to strip out of his befouled uniform, rinse himself off, and put on fresh clothes. There really was no other option.

His pistols had been taken by his jailers and he hadn't a second pair, so for weapons he had to make do with the sword he had taken off Shaeder's man – a greatsword much too big for him. When he was ready, he borrowed a spare horse and pulled Franka up behind him. Her bow was slung across her back. They met the others again at the edge of the tent camp. They had commandeered a hay cart. Reiner was relieved to see that Giano had taken the time to clean himself as well.

There was no one to stop them leaving. The camp was nearly empty, as captains and sergeants bullied their troops into their armour and then herded them into the fort. As they rode into the pass, a bitter wind whipped up and clouds began to race across the sky. Their fat shadows slid across the jagged sunset peaks above the treeline like slugs across rough gold. Reiner cursed as he looked north. An armada of clouds was bearing down on them. The weather would be less than ideal for travelling, and he wanted to be far away before they stopped for the night.

Franka hugged Reiner's waist and leaned into his back. 'What are you up to, my lord?' she whispered. 'It isn't like you to ride into danger. You know Gutzmann's dead. There's no reason to go back to the mine.'

Reiner whispered in turn. 'Gutzmann's gold.'

She cocked an eyebrow. 'You intend to mine it yourself?'

He shook his head. 'On our way to rescuing you I discovered where the general holds it for shipment to Aulschweig. There are two crates in the closed tunnel.'

'So why lie to the others?'

'You forget the spy?'

'Isn't Abel the spy?'

Reiner shrugged. 'And if he ain't?'

'Then how do you intend to get it out without the others knowing what you do? Will the boxes fit in your pockets?'

Reiner laughed. 'I'm still working on that.'

THE WIND MOANED through the ravine as the Blackhearts approached the mine's defensive wall. The light had faded to a bruised purple as the sun dropped behind the mountains and the clouds spread across the sky. Reiner's nerves were so on edge that he was seeing ratmen in every murky shadow and patch of scrub. The vicious vermin could pour out of the mine at any moment and slaughter them all. And he was leading his companions closer to them with every step.

Reiner shivered as they entered the compound. What a contrast to the bustling industry of yesterday. The place felt as if it had been deserted for decades. The mine's heavy iron gates hung open and squealed like doomed souls as the wind pushed at them. The shutters of the outbuildings banged open and shut. Dust devils fought in the alleys and pebbles rattled down the piles of waste rock, making the Blackhearts jump and turn.

The square black entrance of the mine looked like the maw of some great fish, a leviathan of legend, into which they were being inexorably drawn. The wind moaning across it sounded like the beast's mournful cry. Reiner and Franka dismounted as the others stepped down from their cart. Though there was no threat apparent, they all drew their weapons. Franka, Giano and Gert set arrows and bolts to their strings.

'Come on, then,' said Reiner.

Inside, the wind's moan became a roar. Reiner couldn't hear his own footsteps. The entry chamber was lit by a single flickering lantern hung from an iron hook to the right of the entrance. Its light was not enough to touch the far walls, but the mine was not entirely dark. As Reiner's eyes grew accustomed, he could see a faint glow of torchlight coming from the mouth of the third tunnel.

Pavel noticed it too. 'Is it the rats?' he asked nervously.

Reiner shook his head. 'It's torchlight. The rat light is purple.' That the source of the light was human was to some extent comforting, but it was also frustrating. Who was it? What were they doing down there? Why were they in his way? The gold was down that tunnel. Was someone else after it? 'Let's find some torches and have a look.'

But as the men stepped further in, a clash of steel and a hoarse cry cut through the wind. They froze in their tracks and looked around, weapons at the ready. It had come from within the mine, but where was hard to tell.

'A fight,' said Giano.

'That was Gutzmann's voice,' said Hals. 'I swear it.'

Karel nodded. 'I heard it too.'

The cry came again, and more clang and clatter. This time the direction was clear. The sounds were coming from the engineers' quarters – the strange subterranean townhouse.

Reiner snatched the lantern off its hook and ran for the passage that led to the house. The others pounded after him. It took a few strides for Reiner to realize that he wasn't sure what exactly he meant to do. Was he hurrying to save Gutzmann or to kill him?

As they entered the passage the sounds of fighting became clearer – grunts and cries and the clash and slither of swordplay. The beautifully carved door was half open, and the lamps within threw a hard-edged bar of light into the hall. Reiner skidded to a stop and held up his hand. The others peeked over his shoulders as he tilted his head around the door.

The beautiful stone foyer was lit with a massive marble chandelier. The parlour to the left was dark, but the dining room beyond it glowed with lamplight, and Reiner gaped at the scene revealed there. It was like a painting done by a poppy fiend in his madness. The table was set as if for a state dinner, with fine porcelain plates and goblets and flatware of silver glinting in the mellow light. Bottles of wine were open, and rich platters of meat, fish and game surrounded a central candelabrum. Each plate was filled with a half-eaten meal.

As strange as the dinner was, in the light of current events, the diners were stranger. Seated around the table was a number of ratmen, all dressed in armour and holding bloody daggers in their gnarled claws. Each of them was stone dead, hacked and pierced with horrible wounds. But what tipped the scene into lunacy was the sight of General Gutzmann, bleeding and exhausted, fighting a handful of Shaeder's Hammer Bearer greatswords around and across the table. The greatswords were comically hampered by a strange disinclination to disturb any of the particulars of the scene. They checked their swings so as not to smash any of the plates or goblets, and straightened the dead ratmen in their chairs when they bumped into them. It was this, more than any dazzling feats of swordsmanship, that was allowing Gutzmann to hold his own in such an unequal contest.

'Sigmar's beard!' whispered Karel. 'What madness is this?'

Reiner shook his head. 'I've never seen the like.' He slipped into the entryway for a better look. The others eased in behind him, hiding behind the massive granite urns and ornate stone furniture. It was hard to turn away from the scene. What did it mean, Reiner wondered? What was Shaeder up to?

'At least we haven't to sweat killing him ourselves,' chuckled Dag. 'Those lads'll do for him.'

'Are y'mad?' said Hals. 'We have to help him. Gutzmann's the only one who can save the fort!'

Pavel turned to Reiner. 'We help him, captain. Don't we?'

'We...' Reiner hesitated. What did he do? Here indeed was the salvation of the fort, but also the best opportunity yet to fulfil Manfred's orders and kill the man who was stealing the Emperor's gold, or at least see him dead. Of course, if they saved Gutzmann now, they might kill him later once he had beaten the ratmen. But the general knew their orders now. He would protect himself. Such a chance wouldn't come again. 'We...'

He looked at Franka. Her soft brown eyes had somehow grown sharp as daggers. They lanced his soul. 'We...'

There was a clatter of boots in the passage behind them. The Blackhearts turned as the front door flew open and six engineers burst in, faces flushed.

'They're coming!' cried the first, slamming the door behind him. 'Hurry! Let's be...' He stopped short as he saw who he faced.

Reiner glanced back to the dining room. Gutzmann and Shaeder's greatswords were looking into the foyer as well. For a long moment the tableau held, as each side sorted out who was who and what was what.

It was Gutzmann who broke it, by leaping up and running across the table, sending plates and goblets flying, then charging through the parlour to skid to a stop at Reiner's side.

'Kill them!' called one of the Hammers. 'They mustn't expose the plan!'

Gutzmann grinned, though it was obvious he was in pain from a dozen wounds. 'So, Hetsau. Right in all particulars. I owe you an apology.'

Reiner was embarrassed by the general's trust, for he had been thinking that he could stab him in the neck and fulfil Manfred's orders then and there. But the engineers were drawing swords and hammers and axes and advancing on them on one side, and Shaeder's greatswords were coming through the parlour on the other. Reiner needed Gutzmann's sword more than he needed him dead. And more than that, he didn't *want* him dead. He felt a kinship with him. They were both bright men. They shared a wry humour. And they had both been manipulated and betrayed by Altdorf. Perhaps he wouldn't have to kill him after all. Gert's foolish notion that if the Empire was threatened here, Gutzmann would reconsider deserting, suddenly became very attractive.

'Back the way we came, lads,' said Reiner. 'Jergen, Karel. Help me hold the swordsmen. The rest, break through these ditch diggers.'

The men shifted around so that Reiner, Karel and Jergen faced the Hammer Bearers while the others jabbed at the engineers with spears, swords and axes.

Gutzmann stood shoulder to shoulder with Reiner as the Hammers closed with them. There were six of the black-clad giants. Reiner's wrist nearly snapped as he parried a cut from one. Gutzmann blocked another and riposted with ease. Wounded as he was, he looked like he could fight all night.

'I never thought I'd be glad to see anyone break out of my brig,' he said.

'Four of this lot came to kill us,' said Reiner. 'We turned the tables on them.' He ducked a slashing blade and pinked his opponent in the leg. 'We thought they'd done for you.'

Gutzmann grinned. 'They meant to. But when they took me down into the mine I started to suspect, and ran away. We've been playing hide and seek in the tunnels since.'

The engineers were falling back. Though armed and schooled as soldiers, they were not used to hand to hand combat. Hals stabbed one in the arm and he dropped his mallet. Gert brained him with his axe. Franka ducked a hammer, and was about to run her man through when Pavel pulled her back.

'Behind me, lass,' he said.

'What!' Franka shoved him. 'Don't be an ass!' She tried to squirm back around him, but he and Hals closed ranks.

Gutzmann blinked. 'Lass?'

'I'll explain later,' said Reiner.

The Blackhearts forced the engineers back while Gutzmann, Jergen, Karel and Reiner protected their rear. They could do little more than block and retire, for even Jergen was reduced to playing a defensive game against so many skilled blades. At last the engineers broke and fled out of the door. Pavel, Gert, Franka and Giano ran after them.

Hals stopped at the door. 'Clear, captain. Disengage.'

'Fall back!' shouted Reiner.

Jergen, Karel and Gutzmann jumped back from the Hammers with Reiner, and ran for the door. The greatswords lunged forward, stabbing at them as they darted through. Hals slammed the door in the Hammers' faces.

As they ran down the short hall Reiner frowned, for at the end, the rest of the Blackhearts and the last few engineers stood together, not fighting, but instead staring into the entry chamber.

'Go! Go!' called Reiner. He pushed through them, dragging at Franka, then froze as he saw why they had stopped.

'Sigmar's balls,' said Gutzmann, beside him.

The greatswords came roaring down the passage, swinging at the Blackhearts' backs.

Gutzmann spun on them, hissing. 'Quiet, you fools, or we're all dead!'

And such was his aura of command that they skidded to a stop before him.

Gutzmann pointed. 'Look.'

They looked.

It seemed, in the dark, a muddy river, flowing through the mine – a river at full flood that carried branches and trees and wagons with it. It was ratmen – so many, so densely packed, and so fleet of foot that it was difficult to see them as separate bodies. They poured out of the third tunnel in an unending tide, spears and halberds bobbing above their heads, and disappeared out of the mine entrance without break or pause. They didn't march as men. They kept to no formations. There were no ranks and files, no order, just a pulsing, fevered rush. The carts, overloaded with odd brass contraptions and strange weapons, careened through it all, pulled by scrawny, filthy rat-slaves that were harnessed to them like oxen. More frightening than the weapons were hulking, half-seen shapes, taller and more massive than men, that lurched along, roaring, as ratmen in grey robes guided them with whips and sticks.

Reiner could feel the vibration of the army's passage through his feet, like an avalanche that never stopped. And the smell was overwhelming. They seemed to push it out of the tunnel before them. It filled the entry chamber like a solid thing – a reeking, animal stink mixed with the stench of illness and death. Reiner covered his mouth. The others did the same.

Fortunately, the ratmen seemed so intent on their purpose that they looked neither left nor right, and so hadn't yet seen the men at the side of the chamber, but there were outrunners – sergeants perhaps – who loped along beside the river of rat-flesh, and it was inevitable that one of them would eventually look their way.

'Back into the house,' whispered Gutzmann. 'Quietly.'

The men backed away, Blackhearts and engineers and greatswords together, too awed by the horror before them to remember to fight each other.

As they tiptoed back into the stone house, Gutzmann turned on the Hammer Bearers, who looked sick with shock. 'You disgust me! To deliver your fellows into the hands of such monsters! How can you stand to live?'

'You have it wrong, general,' said their sergeant. 'Commander Shaeder has a plan.'

'A plan?' Gutzmann sputtered. 'What kind of plan allows these vermin to take the fort unawares?' He pointed his sword at the sergeant, then hissed and pressed his elbow to his side 'You, Krieder. You will... You will escort me. We will take the hill track back to the fort as quickly as we may.' Below his breastplate his jerkin was red and damp. He was more wounded than he had let on.

'We cannot allow that, general,' said Krieder.

The greatswords raised their swords.

Gutzmann, Reiner and the Blackhearts went on guard as the Hammer Bearers began to close with them again. The engineers hefted their weapons again as well, but seemed reluctant to return to the melee.

A greatsword lunged at Reiner, slashing at his head. Reiner parried and dodged away, but before he could counter, a bang and a muffled shriek from the parlour made everyone jump. Reiner looked beyond the Hammers, who had stepped back again. The parlour fireplace was moving, the mantle splitting in the middle and opening out with a grinding of stone on stone, revealing a secret door.

Out of the black opening staggered an engineer, his face bloody and his clothes shredded. He dragged another, whose arm was over his shoulder, but the man was obviously beyond help. Half his skull had been blown away and his brains were spilling down his neck.

The living engineer threw out a hand to the Hammer Bearers, his eyes wild. 'Save us. We are lost. They knew!' He tripped over his friend's slack legs and fell.

Krieder ran to him and pulled him up. 'What do you say, man?' He shook him. 'Speak, damn you!'

The Hammer Bearers joined him. Gutzmann, Reiner and the rest followed them into the parlour.

The engineer's lower lip trembled. 'They knew! They swarmed the cart before we could loose it! The tunnel remains open!'

'Bones of Sigmar,' breathed the greatsword sergeant. 'This is...'

Before he could finish, a crowd of ratmen swarmed out of the secret door, looking around with darting black eyes. They stopped when they saw the men and snarled, brandishing curved swords and halberds.

'So Shaeder had a plan, did he?' said Gutzmann as the men edged back from the rats.

Sergeant Krieder dropped the dying engineer and joined his fellows. 'It wasn't to be like this.'

'I'm sure it wasn't.'

The ratmen charged, flowing around the Hammers, the Blackhearts and the engineers in a brown flood. The men slashed at them in a terrified frenzy. One of the greatswords went down immediately, a halberd in his neck. The others closed ranks. An engineer fell, screaming, pierced by two blades. Gutzmann killed a ratman, then grunted and stumbled into Reiner, his leg bleeding. Before Reiner could help him he stood again, and renewed his attack on the squirming wave of fur that surrounded them. These were not the tall black-furred killers Reiner and the others had faced before. They were of the smaller brown variety, but there were more of them.

'Protect the general!' cried Krieder, the Hammer sergeant.

His men pressed forward to form a wall around Gutzmann. They hacked down the front line of ratmen like so much underbrush.

'Bit of an... an about face hey, Krieder?' said Gutzmann. He was having trouble breathing.

'My lord,' said the Hammer sergeant, without looking around, 'we have doomed the fort through our intrigues. If we must die so that you can save it, so be it.' He decapitated a ratman. Its head spun across the room. Two more took its place.

Though the Hammer Bearers were in the thick of it, there were plenty of ratmen to go around, a seething jumble of slashing, screeching monsters. Reiner fought three, and all around him he could see the Blackhearts and the engineers kicking and hacking and stabbing. An engineer threw down his hatchet and tried to run away. The ratmen chopped him to pieces.

Franka's voice raised above the fray. 'Let me fight, curse you!'

Reiner looked around. Franka was shoving Hals and trying to dodge around him. The butt of a ratman's spear caught her in the temple. She fell.

'Franka!' Reiner cried. He fought to her and stood over her, blocking a spear that stabbed down at her.

'Sorry, captain,' said Hals. 'She won't stay back.'

'And will you let her die to keep her from fighting?'

Franka staggered to her feet as Reiner held off the rats. 'I'm all right, captain,' she said. But her hands shook as she lifted her sword.

Reiner stepped back as he parried a halberd. His calf touched an obstacle. He looked back. A stone bench.

'Draw your bow, lass,' he said. 'Get up. Gert, Dag, Giano. You too.' The four eased back and stepped onto the bench as Reiner, Gutzmann, Karel and the Hammer Bearers protected them, then wound their crossbows and nocked arrows. Pavel, Hals and Jergen took up positions behind the bench and guarded their backs. There were no engineers left standing. The bowmen fired over their protector's heads into the crowd of ratmen and loaded again.

Another Hammer Bearer went down. Only three remained, but each fallen greatsword had accounted for a handful of ratmen. The vermin lay in mounds around the survivors, but more rats stood on their dead to fight them.

Gutzmann stumbled into Reiner again, and narrowly missed being spitted by a ratman's spear. Reiner pulled him out of the way.

'My thanks,' Gutzmann said, gasping. 'Just need to catch my breath.'

'Yes, general.' But Reiner was afraid it was more than that. Gutzmann was pale and shaking.

The tide was turning. The fire of bow and crossbow was thinning the back ranks of the remaining ratmen as the Blackhearts and the Hammers cut down their front lines. But just as Reiner thought the worst might be over, Gutzmann collapsed entirely, and this time sprawled across the floor before the ratmen, utterly exposed. A rat halberdier raised his heavy weapon to stab down at him.

'No!' Krieder leapt forward and gutted the ratman, but two more ratmen gored him with swords. The Hammer sergeant vomited blood and fell across Gutzmann's body.

With a roar of anger, the last two greatswords charged into the thick of the ratmen, swinging their swords with an utter disregard for defence. One took a sword in the groin, but their opponents fell back in pieces, arms, legs and heads severed. It was too much. The ratmen broke in terror, filling the room with a horrible sweaty musk as they tried to flee back to the secret passage. They didn't make it. Franka, Gert, Giano and Dag shot them down, while Jergen, Karel, Pavel and Hals caught the ones they missed.

As the last rat fell, everyone stopped where they were, sucking air and staring around at the heaps of brown-furred bodies. Reiner felt numb, as if he had been battered by a hurricane. He wasn't yet recovered from the surprise of the ratmen's initial attack and already it was over.

'Sigmar,' said Hals, snatching up an unbroken wine bottle from the floor. 'What a dust-up!' He took a drink and held the bottle out to Reiner. 'Captain.'

Reiner reached for the bottle, then stopped. He'd almost forgotten his vow to Ranald. He let his hand drop. 'No. No thank ye.'

Hals shrugged and passed the bottle to Pavel.

As his head stopped swimming, Reiner felt again the steady throbbing vibration of the ratmen on the march. He cursed and looked for a living engineer. There were none. Only one Hammer Bearer still lived. He was rolling Krieder's body off Gutzmann. Gutzmann was wheezing wetly. The greatsword's eyes glistened with tears.

Reiner squatted beside them. 'Pardon, general,' he said, nodding to Gutzmann, then put a hand on the Hammer's shoulder. 'What was that about closing the tunnel? What was your plan?'

The Hammer Bearer looked up at him blankly.

Reiner shook him. 'Quickly, damn you!

'The–' the man swallowed. 'The engineers filled a mine cart with explosives and hid it in the secret passage where it slopes down to the ratmen's tunnel. All they had to do was light the fuse and cut the rope, and it would roll down into the tunnel and explode, bringing down the roof and trapping the ratmen inside. But they…'

'Yes. They knew. This passage?' Reiner pointed to the open fire place.

The greatsword nodded. 'At the bottom.'

Reiner looked at Gutzmann. He was very pale. 'General, can you travel?'

'I'll have to, won't I?' He said it through gritted teeth.

Reiner stood and looked around. The Blackhearts were looking a bit worse for wear. Franka had a cut on her leg, as did Hals. Dag had a bump the size of a goose egg over his temple and was weaving slightly. Jergen was wrapping his hand in strips torn from the tablecloth, and Pavel had apparently lost most of his left ear. He was wrapping his head with a strip cut from the dining room tablecloth.

Reiner sighed. 'Bind up your wounds, lads. We're not done yet. Karel. Stay here with the general. Make him ready to move.' He glared at the Hammer Bearer. 'You'll show us the way to the cart.'

SIXTEEN
Shallya Receive You

REINER AND THE Blackhearts raced with the Hammer Bearer down the winding, always descending passage, torches in hand. Every second counted, for the longer they left the tunnel open the more ratmen would attack the unsuspecting fort. As they ran, the Hammer Bearer told Reiner what Shaeder had intended.

'The commander never meant to betray the Empire. He only wanted to discredit Gutzmann and prove himself to Altdorf by winning a great victory over a terrible enemy.'

'So he did all this out of jealousy?' asked Reiner, incredulous.

'Not jealousy,' said the greatsword stiffly. 'Duty. Gutzmann meant to desert. Shaeder had to stop him, but unless the general was made to look a traitor to his troops, they would have revolted, and the border would have been undefended. Shaeder didn't know how to proceed until the engineers discovered the rats.'

Reiner frowned. 'So he set up that charade with the dead ratmen and the dinner table to make it look like Gutzmann was conspiring with them?'

'Aye,' said the Hammer.

Reiner nodded. 'And he planned to bring down the tunnel after only half the rat army had come out, so the men would see the threat, and yet would have an easy victory?'

The greatsword nodded. 'Aye. You have it. Brilliant, was it not?'

'Except it didn't work,' growled Hals.

'The ratmen betrayed us,' said the Hammer Bearer, angry.

Reiner rolled his eyes. 'You shock me!'

The Hammer held up his hand and they slowed to a stop. 'Around the next bend,' he said, catching his breath.

Reiner nodded. 'Right. Giano?'

Giano handed his torch to Gert and crept forward into the darkness. After a short wait, he returned, eyes bright and eager.

'They making to be moving it. Six, seven soldier-rat, and ten maybe slave-rat,' he said. 'They putting rope on back to let down slow.' He grinned. 'We take 'em easy, hey?'

'Have they started?'

Giano shook his head.

'Good,' said Reiner. 'And the cart. It's still full of powder kegs?'

'Aye.'

Reiner grunted, satisfied. 'Right. Then we leave our torches here, and go in swift and silent. Gert, Giano, Dag and Franka, bolts and arrows on the string. The rest, stay low. The moment they see us coming, you four let fly, and we run in swinging. We want to take 'em all in the first charge, aye?'

The others nodded.

'Good, then off we go.'

The men laid their torches in a line on the floor and drew their weapons. Gert and Giano set bolts in grooves as Franka and Dag nocked arrows.

Hals glanced at Franka. 'Shouldn't the lass stay back here?'

Reiner's jaw tensed. 'We need all the cover we can muster.'

'But...'

'This isn't the time, pikeman.'

Hals grunted and looked at his boots.

'Don't worry, Hals,' said Franka. 'I'll do my best not to shoot you in the back.'

'She can put a rabbit's eye out at fifty paces,' said Pavel.

Hals glared at him.

The men started down the passage, hunched low, with Dag, Giano, Gert and Franka at the rear. Reiner, Pavel and Hals shared the front with Jergen and the greatsword. As they rounded the bend the darkness was absolute for a moment, and then a faint purple glow lit the walls ahead. A few more steps and the cart and the rats were revealed. It was as Giano had said. Seven rat soldiers stood around the cart, directing a crowd of starved and stunted rat-slaves who were tying ropes to the back of the cart, which was almost as wide as the tunnel itself. There was another rope, stouter, that was lashed to a ring set in the tunnel floor. This held the cart in place at the top of the rails that disappeared down the steep slope into darkness.

Reiner quickened his pace, but stayed on his toes, holding his sword behind him so the blade wouldn't reflect the purple light. The others sped up as well. Twenty paces to go. Fifteen.

A ratman lifted his nose, then twitched his head toward them. He squealed a warning.

'Now!' cried Reiner, and pounded forward with the others, silence forgotten.

Bolts and arrows sprouted from two ratmen's chests as they drew their swords. Then Reiner and the Hammer Bearer and the Blackhearts were among the rest. Slashing and chopping. Two more went down immediately, but the slave-rats were running every which way in a panic and got in the way. Reiner and the others kicked and shoved through a swamp of furry, filthy bodies as the last three rat soldiers retreated around the cart.

Franka, Giano, Dag and Gert leapt up onto the back of the cart. Franka and Dag fired over it at the retreating rats as Giano and Gert reloaded their crossbows. Franka hit a slave-rat.

Jergen and Reiner forced their way down the left side of the cart as the Hammer Bearer went down the right, chopping through the slave-rats like dense undergrowth. Hals and Pavel followed the Hammer, gutting the fallen, and spearing the slave-rats who tried to swarm the greatsword.

Giano and Gert fired again as Franka and Dag got off their third shots. One of the rat warriors fell with an arrow and a bolt in his back, but before the archers could load again, slave-rats crowded onto the cart, trying to escape the three swordsmen, and got in their way.

Reiner and Jergen stumbled out on the far side of the cart and lunged at the last two rat soldiers. The greatsword staggered out as well, throwing and kicking slave-rats in every direction, but one swung by his jaws from the man's neck like a pit-dog hanging from a bull. With a cry, the greatsword thrust it away and it fell to the ground, but it had a bloody chunk of his neck in its teeth. The Hammer dropped to his knees, his gloves shiny red as he tried to stop the fountain of blood that pumped from his jugular.

One of the rat soldiers hurled a dagger at Reiner. He flinched, and it spun by his ear. A slave-rat screamed behind him. Jergen ran the knife-rat through as Reiner angled for the other. It threw a glass globe at the ground and the tunnel filled with smoke. Reiner slashed where he thought the rat was, covering his nose and mouth with the crook of his arm. He hit nothing.

'Fire!' he cried. 'Fire!'

He heard bolts and arrows thrum past him into the smoke, and a rattish squeal, but couldn't tell if it had been a fatal shot.

Jergen charged into the smoke, his sword spinning in a figure eight, but Reiner heard no cries or impacts. He ran in after him, heart thudding – fighting blind was for fools. After a few steps he was beyond the smoke, but the clouds blocked the light and the tunnel was pitch black. He heard Jergen returning.

'Get him?'

'No.'

Reiner sighed and turned, stumbling over the rails. 'Then they will be coming.'

'Yes.'

The others were finishing off the last of the slave-rats as he and Jergen stepped out of the dissipating cloud.

'Clear the rails,' said Reiner. 'We must light the fuses and cut the anchor. One got away. They'll be coming back.'

The Blackhearts kicked and rolled slave-rat bodies off the rails. On the cart, Gert began checking the powder kegs. After a second, he groaned.

'Captain,' he said. 'They've pulled the match cord.'

'The what?'

'The fuses. They've taken them from the powder. And I don't see 'em.'

Reiner cursed. 'Check the bodies.'

The Blackhearts frisked all the rat-corpses, both slave and soldier, but none had the match cord.

'Captain,' said Pavel. 'They're coming.'

Reiner looked up. Far down the slanting passage a purple light was moving along the walls. 'Ranald's loaded dice!'

'Can y'just stuff bits of rag in and light them?' asked Pavel.

Reiner shook his head. 'The engineers would have timed it to a nicety. Too short and the cart blows before it reaches the tunnel. Too long and the rats snuff 'em when the cart hits the bottom.'

'Somebody would have to ride down with it, torch in hand,' said Franka. 'But that would be suicide.'

Reiner nodded. Someone would have to light the powder by hand just as the cart reached the ratmen's tunnel, but whoever did it... Reiner looked around, trying to decide who he could most afford to lose. His eyes fell upon Dag. The boy had been trouble from the beginning – a loose cannon who had done more harm than good, and whom no one in the company could trust. And he was fiercely – foolishly – loyal to Reiner. He would do it if Reiner asked. On the other hand, the boy was so scatterbrained and unreliable that it was better than even odds he would muck it up. He cursed. There was no time to think. He had to make a choice now. He...

'I do,' said Giano.

Everyone looked up.

'What?' said Reiner.

The Tilean was white faced. He swallowed. 'I do. This I want whole my life. I vow revenging on ratmans ever they kill my family. How I can kill more ratmans than here? With sword and bow, I kill ten, twenty, fifty? This I do, I kill hundred, thousand.'

'But, lad, you'll die,' said Hals.

Franka looked horrified. 'You can't.'

'We need you,' said Reiner. He could pick out the faces of the advancing ratmen now. There were thirty or more, all warriors.

'You need me do this,' said Giano. 'I get torch.' He turned and ran back up the corridor out of sight.

The others looked at each other blankly.

'Will you let him do this?' asked Franka.

'Someone has to,' said Reiner.

'Aye,' said Pavel, his eyes sliding toward Dag like Reiner's had done. 'But...'

'Someone who can do it,' said Reiner. He turned. 'Gert, chop open the kegs. As many as you can.'

Gert nodded and climbed on the cart, drawing his hand axe. He began staving in the tops of the kegs.

Giano reappeared carrying two torches. He hopped onto the back of the cart and swung his legs in. Jergen stepped to the anchor rope and raised his sword.

Giano faced Reiner. He swallowed again. 'Captain, you good man. I happy to fight for you. Grazie.'

'You are a good man too, Ostini. Giano.' There was a lump in Reiner's throat. He forced it down. 'Shallya receive you.'

The ratmen were a hundred paces away. They were sprinting.

Gert jumped down off the cart. 'Ready.'

Giano raised a torch in salute. 'Cut rope.'

Reiner tried to think of something noble to say, but Jergen didn't hesitate. He chopped through the heavy hawser with a single stroke and the cart began rolling down the sloping rails. Giano threw his arms wide and opened his mouth. At first Reiner thought he was screaming, but his cry became a word, and Reiner realized he was singing some wild Tilean song.

'Damned fool,' said Hals thickly.

Franka turned away, hand over her eyes. Reiner heard her sob.

The cart rapidly picked up speed. The approaching ratmen saw it coming and threw themselves to the left and right, but there were too many of them. They couldn't get out of the way. As the cart blasted through them, they were thrown up like a bow wave, pin-wheeling and smashing against the walls. Some were cut in half under the iron wheels. A few got caught on the sides and were dragged, heads bouncing and cracking as they hit each successive tie.

And then the cart was gone, vanishing into the black of the passage beyond the ratmen's purple light. Reiner stared after it for a moment, but the surviving ratmen were picking themselves up and finding their weapons.

'Right then,' he said hollowly. 'Let's be off.'

He started up the passage with the others following, their faces grim.

'But how do we know it worked?' asked Hals, as they ran. 'How do we know the poor lad didn't kill his fool self for naught?'

'We don't' said Reiner. They reached their line of torches, now two fewer. He picked one up. 'We'll just have to pray.' He looked back down the tunnel. 'Come on now, hurry. We don't want those rats catching us up. And all that powder might shake things up down–'

Before he could finish there was a huge boom, and a blast of hot air hit them like a ram. Reiner clapped his hands to his ears, which felt like they might explode from the pressure. The shock came a second later. It knocked them all off their feet. Before they hit the floor another thunderclap deafened them, and then another, each bigger than the one before. The concussions pushed them up the passage like a giant hand shoving at them. Then twin shocks shook the passage so hard that Reiner was lifted off the ground and slammed into the wall. He landed on top of Pavel, who was screaming and holding his ears. Reiner couldn't hear him.

The walls, ceiling and floor cracked, pebbles and dust sifting down on them like snow. A chunk of stone the size of Reiner's head landed next to his foot. Then all was still. Reiner stayed where he was, waiting for more explosions and working his jaw to try and pop his ears. When no blasts came, he sat up. The tunnel spun around him.

'Come on, lads,' he said, staggering to his feet. 'The place might come down any minute.'

'Hey?' said Hals, putting a hand to his ear.

'Say again?' said Gert.

'What?' said Franka.

Reiner could barely hear them. He pointed up the tunnel. 'Run!' he shouted. 'We must run!'

The others nodded and tried to stand, weaving and staggering like drunks. Reiner clung to the wall, dizzier than if he had spun in circles. They started up the hall at a zigzagging trot, stumbling over their own feet. Before they had gone twenty paces a rushing wall of smoke caught them, billowing up out of the passage. At first it had the sharp battlefield tang of blackpowder, but behind that came an eye watering alchemical stink that had them all retching and gagging. Through his tearing eyes Reiner swore that the smoke that buffeted them glowed a faint green.

'Hurry!' he choked.

They ran as hard as they could, covering their faces with their shirts and jerkins as they went.

'Must have hit one of their weird weapons,' rasped Franka beside him.

'Or a whole wagon full,' said Reiner.

THEY RAN OUT of the fireplace into the parlour of the stone house to find Gutzmann lying still and alone on the floor, surrounded by mounds of dead ratmen. The room was filled with a smoky haze.

Reiner stepped to him uneasily. 'General, do you live? Where is Karel?'

Gutzmann raised his head weakly. He smiled. 'Success, then? We... felt it.'

'Aye, but...'

Karel ran in from the foyer. He saluted. 'Captain, I am glad to see you. The ratmen have stopped. After the explosion some turned back, but no more come from the tunnel.'

'Praise Sigmar,' grunted Pavel. 'Maybe Ostini didn't die for nothing.'

Karel turned to him. 'The Tilean is dead?'

'And the Hammer Bearer,' said Reiner.

Karel made the sign of the Hammer and bowed his head.

'I hope it weren't for nothing,' said Hals bitterly. 'So many got out before he blew it. Might not make a difference.'

'They were only beginning to bring their siege engines out,' said Karel. 'So we are saved that.'

'We must return to the fort... immediately,' said Gutzmann. 'But first, cut off a ratman's head and... and give it to me.'

Reiner made a face. 'Whatever for?'

'I shall show it... to the men.' Gutzmann raised an eyebrow. 'As you should have done, when... when you came to me.'

RETURNING TO THE fort was easier said than done, for though no more ratmen poured out of the tunnel, many still milled about in the entry chamber, though whether they meant to dig out their brethren or were just unwilling to continue toward the fort without the full might of their army, Reiner couldn't decide. Either way, it made exit that way an impossibility.

'The hill track,' said Gutzmann from the stretcher Pavel and Hals had made of their two spears and a red brocade drapery. A bundle of blankets shielded him against the cold. He cradled the severed head of a rat in his arms like a baby. 'The chief engineer told me once. They cut a... a hidden staircase behind an upstairs closet. It leads... to the mountainside above the... the mine, and from there to the fort.' He chuckled. 'In case of cave-in, he said. But I begin to think it had... another purpose.'

'We'll look for it,' Reiner said, wincing. Gutzmann's words bubbled in his throat and he had to take two breaths for each sentence. He was not long for the world.

After a mad search through the upstairs rooms – a series of beautiful, stonework suites that the engineers had turned into a fetid dormitory hung with grimy clothes and littered with papers, books, and the strange tools of their trade – they found the stairs at last behind a door in the back of a closet in what had once been a grand boudoir. The secret panel was opened by pressing in the eyes of a bas-relief griffin that stood rampant above the closet door. Behind it, a crude, narrow spiral staircase had been cut into the rock. It was too tight, and the angle too steep, to manoeuvre Gutzmann's stretcher, so Jergen, the sturdiest of the men, carried him on his back.

After a hundred steps, the stairway ended at a stone door. When they pressed a lever, the door swung in smoothly, revealing a small cave.

Reiner stepped into it cautiously. Some animal made the cave its home, but it was not here now. He crept to the jagged mouth and peeked out. The cave opened onto a narrow goat path high up on a sharply sloping mountainside. Below were the outbuildings and the fortifications of the mine, almost invisible in the cloud cloaked night.

Reiner beckoned the others forward and he stepped onto the path. The wind that had blown them into the mines was still whipping around the crags. He shivered as the others filed out, Hals and Pavel once again carrying Gutzmann on his stretcher.

The general pointed south. 'Follow the path. It leads to the... the hills above the fort. You will find a branch that... brings you beyond. To the Aulschweig side. As long as we still hold... the south wall...'

Reiner motioned the Blackhearts forward, then walked beside the general. 'This path allows one to circumvent the fort?'

Gutzmann grinned. 'This and others. The bandits... They go where they please. But not... not worth defending. No army could navigate... this.'

Reiner caught his balance as the wind nearly blew him off the mountain. He swallowed. 'No. I suppose not.'

They hurried on as quickly as they could, but it was difficult going, particularly for Pavel and Hals, carrying Gutzmann. There were places where the path went straight up a rock face and the general had to be passed up it from hand to hand. In other places it was barely a lip of stone on the edge of a cliff and his weight threatened to pull them into space. At one point the path went under a jutting rock and everyone had to crawl. Pavel and Hals pushed and pulled Gutzmann along on their hands and knees.

But though they bumped and jarred him, and twisted him into undignified and uncomfortable positions, not once did the general complain, only urged them to go faster.

'If those vermin have hurt my men,' he said more than once, 'I shall slaughter all of them, above and... and below ground. They shall be... wiped from the earth.'

It took the company twice as long to reach the latitude of the fort as it would have if they had walked the pass, but at last they came over the spine of a pine covered hill and saw it below them. The battle had not yet begun. The rats were still forming up in the darkness of the pass, keeping out of sight of the tent camp. They needn't have bothered. No one manned the north walls. No one was in the camp. The entire force of the fort was on the great south wall, crossbows loaded, handguns primed, cannon ready, all waiting for the Army of Aulschweig to march up the southern pass. Shaeder's ruse was a complete success.

Reiner wished he could reach out an unimaginably long arm and tap the defenders on their collective shoulder, make them turn about and take notice of the menace to their rear. But a warning was impossible. Even if he shouted at the top of his lungs no one would hear him.

'Skirmishers!' said Franka, pointing.

Reiner looked. Furtive figures were snaking through the empty camp. The first of them were already at the north wall, peeking through the undefended gate.

He turned to Gutzmann in his stretcher. 'It begins, general. We must hurry. Tell us where the path to the far side is.'

The general didn't respond.

Reiner stepped closer. 'Sir?'

Gutzmann was staring up at the stars.

Reiner knelt beside him. His hand was halfway to his mouth, which gaped open. It looked like he had paused in the middle of a cough.

'General.'

Reiner shook him. He was stiff and cold. Hals and Pavel moaned and lowered the stretcher to the ground. The others gathered around.

Reiner grunted and hung his head. 'What a bastard Sigmar is,' he said under his breath.

'Hey?' said Hals. 'Blasphemy?'

'Sigmar says he wants his champions to die fighting, and here's one of his best, and what does he do?' Reiner swallowed. 'He pinches out his flame right before the fight of his life.' Reiner looked up at the sky. 'You can kiss my arse, you great hairy ape.'

Pavel, Hals and Karel shied away from him, as if afraid they might get caught by the thunderbolt that would shortly stab out of the sky and burn Reiner to a crisp. The others shifted uncomfortably.

'We must still warn them,' said Karel at last.

'To what purpose?' said Reiner, standing. 'They'll know soon enough. Look.'

The others followed his gaze. The ratmen were on the move, a living carpet that filled the pass from wall to wall. Dotted among them were a few weird artillery pieces, but not, at least, any siege towers. Those hadn't made it out. As the rat army exited the pass it spread out like molasses spilling from a jar, and flowed through the neat ranks of tents. No alarm had yet sounded. If there had been any guards on the wall, the skirmishers had silenced them.

'But we could warn the men Shaeder sent south,' said Franka. 'If we reached them quickly enough they might make the difference.'

'Aye,' said Reiner. 'They might, but they're led by Nuemark, who is undoubtedly in on Shaeder's scheme. He'll kill us before he listens to us.'

Karel frowned. 'I think we must still try.'

Reiner nodded unhappily. 'Aye, lad. I'm afraid we must.'

'There is some cavalry there,' said Franka. 'I heard Nuemark calling the captains. They can't be in on it, can they?'

'No,' said Reiner. 'I doubt it.' He frowned, thinking. 'Matthais will be there, under Halmer. Maybe we can convince them to stage a mutiny.'

Hals cursed and looked down at Gutzmann. 'Why'd y'have to die, y'mad jagger. If it was ye coming to 'em, the whole lot'd follow you to the Chaos Wastes themselves.'

Pavel nodded. 'That they would. And I'd join 'em.'

'We'd best bring him with us,' said Reiner. 'Him and his rat head are the best evidence we have of Shaeder's treachery.'

Pavel and Hals lifted Gutzmann on their spear stretcher again, and the party started south.

SEVENTEEN
To Betray a Traitor!

THE BLACKHEARTS CONTINUED along the ridge, doing their best to find the path among the black shadows of the thick pine forest. A half league beyond the fort, they found Gutzmann's split and followed it down to the floor of the pass. Hals and Pavel continued to carry Gutzmann, but they were no longer so gentle.

Just as Reiner and the others stepped onto the road, an eerie echo of a thousand voices rose behind them. Everyone stopped and looked back towards the fort. The roar continued, punctuated with faint crashes and explosions.

Gert cursed. 'It's begun.'

Reiner nodded, a shiver running up his spine.

Hals made the sign of the hammer. 'Sigmar protect ye, lads.'

They turned and jogged quickly south, but less than a league later they slowed again. There were torches ahead. They drew their weapons. Reiner pulled Gutzmann's blankets over his face.

Four silhouettes stood before them. One held up his hand. Reiner could see he was a sergeant of pike. 'Halt! Who comes?' he said. 'Stand where you are.'

Reiner saluted and stepped into the light. 'Sergeant, we come from the fort with desperate news. The invasion from Aulschweig was a trick. We are attacked from the north instead. The detachment must return immediately.'

But the man didn't appear to be listening. He peered behind Reiner. 'Who's that behind you? How many are you?'

The others came up around Reiner.

'We are eight,' he said, continuing to walk forward. 'Now let us pass. We must deliver our message.'

'Er.' The sergeant stepped back. He shot a glance towards the trees. 'Can't allow that. We've orders to... to stop anyone who might be...' He looked at the trees again. 'Er, be an Aulschweig spy.'

Without warning Reiner leapt ahead and put his sword to the sergeant's throat. The man's companions stepped forward, crying out, but then stopped, not daring to move. The Blackhearts spread out to encircle them.

'Call 'em out,' Reiner said. 'Call 'em out or you're dead.'

The sergeant swallowed, his adam's apple pressing against the tip of Reiner's blade as he did. 'I... I don't know what you mean.'

Reiner extended his arm a little, pricking the man's skin. 'Don't you? Shall I tell you, since you've forgotten?'

The sergeant was too frightened to respond.

'You are here to stop anyone from the fort from warning Nuemark's force,' said Reiner, then stopped, holding up a hand. 'No. I am wrong. You are to let one man through. A messenger from Shaeder, who will make sure that Nuemark arrives just in the nick, and not a moment before.' He raised the sergeant's chin with his blade. 'Do I have the right of it?'

The man sighed, and waved a defeated hand towards the woods. 'Come out, Grint. Lannich. He has us.'

After a moment, there was a snapping of twigs on either side of the road and two sullen handgunners stepped out of the brush.

'We should kill you for this,' said Reiner. 'But there will be enough Empire blood spilled this day.'

'We was only following Shaeder's orders,' said the sergeant.

'To betray your general. Very nice.'

'To betray a traitor!' the sergeant said.

Reiner laughed unpleasantly. 'Well, ease your mind. Gutzmann is betrayed and Shaeder commands. But he needs your help in the fort's defence. Leave your weapons here and return. With luck, the men on the walls won't mistake you for Aulschweigers.'

'But how are we to help in the defence if you take our weapons?' the sergeant pleaded.

Reiner sneered. 'You will find plenty of weapons in the hands of the comrades who are dead by your treachery.'

The sergeant reluctantly began unbuckling his sword belt. His men followed his example.

AFTER SUPPLEMENTING THEIR kit with the guns, swords and spears of the sergeant's men, and sending them scurrying for the fort, Reiner and the Blackhearts continued south through the pass. After a quarter of an hour, the mountains began to draw in and grow steeper.

'There they are,' said Pavel, pointing forward.

The road twisted behind a screen of trees as it entered Lessner's Narrows, and the armour and helmets of soldiers glinted yellow and orange through the branches in the light of an orderly row of small campfires.

'And there.' Dag pointed towards the highest, narrowest part of the trail. Against the cloudy grey of the night sky, Reiner and the others could see the outlines of mounted scouts watching for the army that wasn't coming.

Reiner called a halt and squatted down in the road, thinking. 'There will be a picket, and it will be Nuemark's greatswords. He doesn't want any messenger to come except the one he expects. We'll need to draw 'em off.' He raised his head suddenly. 'Dag. How would you like to make a little trouble?'

Dag grinned. 'Ye want me to kill 'em for ye?'

'No, no,' said Reiner hastily. 'Only start a fight. I want you to run down the road like a madman, screaming about ratmen attacking the fort, aye?'

Dag chuckled. 'Aye.'

'Be loud. Act drunk. And when the picket comes, punch as many of them in the nose as you can, aye?'

Dag smacked his fist into his palm eagerly. 'Oh, aye. Oh, aye. Thank'ee, sir.'

Reiner looked around to be sure the rest were ready to move, then nodded at Dag. 'Right then, off you go.'

Dag giggled as he stood, and began trotting off down the road that curved around the stand of trees.

The others looked at Reiner, eyes wide.

Hals voiced what they all were thinking. 'They'll kill the boy.'

Reiner nodded. 'Oh, aye.' He stood. 'When the shouting starts, we cut through the woods. Got it?' He hoped none of them could see the flush that rose on his cheeks. As much as the lad deserved it, Reiner still felt ashamed. It was like kicking a dog who'd done wrong. The dog wouldn't understand why you hurt it.

Franka looked up at him, eyes unreadable, as the company moved towards the woods.

Reiner swallowed a growl. 'Don't tell me you're disappointed in me?'

Franka shook her head. 'No. On this I am with you.' She shuddered and squeezed his hand.

From a way off came a cry. 'Ratmen! Save us! Save us, brothers! Ratmen attack the fort! Get up ye sluggards! Ride! Ride!'

Reiner could see movement in the camp, soldiers turning their heads and standing. There were more furtive movements as well. Men in the trees closed in on the road, quietly drawing weapons.

'That's our cue,' said Reiner.

The Blackhearts started through the woods, angling away from Dag's shouting. Other voices soon joined him, shouting challenges and questions.

'Take me to Nuemark,' shouted Dag. 'I wan' tell him about the ratmen!'

The Blackhearts reached the far edge of the trees. The makeshift camp spread out before them. The infantry sat in formation on the road, looking towards Dag's shouts. The lancers waited in a slanting meadow off to the left, their horses tethered in neat lines. A small command tent had been set up between the two forces. Nuemark's Carroburg greatswords stood on guard before it.

Dag's shouts ended in a yelp of pain as Reiner peered through the trees beside the meadow, searching for Matthais among the lancers who stood or squatted by little fires, rubbing their hands and stamping their feet in the cold wind that swooped down from the mountain. At last Reiner saw him, sitting on a flat rock, talking to Captain Halmer.

Reiner groaned. Halmer had disliked him from the moment he rode out onto the parade ground that first day. Reiner didn't want to have to tell his story in front of him. He'd call for his arrest before he got out two words. But there wasn't time to wait for him to leave. The battle at the fort was raging. Every second meant more Empire men dead.

Matthais and Halmer were three ranks in. Reiner was trying to think of a way to reach them without being taken for an interloper, when the answer nearly stumbled on him. A lancer strode into the woods and began relieving himself against a tree not ten paces from the Blackhearts. They held their breath, but he didn't look their way.

When he had gone, Reiner turned and took the wrapped rat-head from Gutzmann's dead hands. He tucked it under his arm. 'Wish me luck,' he said.

The Blackhearts murmured their replies, and he started for the edge of the woods, undoing his flies. As he stepped into the meadow he began doing them up again, as if returning from a piss. No one remarked his passage. He walking as nonchalantly as he could manage to Matthais and Halmer and squatted down beside them.

'Evening, Matthais,' he said.

'Evening, lancer,' said Matthais, turning. 'What can I...' He stopped dead, his jaw hanging open. 'Rein...'

'Don't shout, lad. I beg you.'

'But you're meant to be in the brig!'

Halmer turned at that. 'Who? Isn't this...? You're Meyerling. Gutzmann put you in stir.'

Reiner nodded. 'Yes, captain. I escaped. But I have...'

'Sigmar, sir!' choked Halmer. 'You've some nerve. Where are Nuemark's guard. I'll have you...

'Please, captain, I beg you to hear me out.'

'Hear you out? I'll be damned if...'

'Sir, please. I won't fight. You can take me to Nuemark and be done with me. But I beg you to listen first.' He looked at Matthais. 'Matthais. Won't you speak for me?'

Matthais sneered. 'Why should I? You came here to assassinate the general. You lied to me.'

Halmer stood, drawing his sword. 'Enough of this. Give me your sword, villain.'

'This is not a lie,' said Reiner, angrily, and flipped open his bloody parcel. The rat-head's death filmed eyes stared blindly up at them. Matthais and Halmer gasped. Reiner closed it again.

'Now will you listen?' he asked.

Halmer sat down on the rock with a thump. He stared at the bundle. 'What... what was that.'

'A ratman,' said Matthais, wonderingly. 'So all that was true? The ratmen in the mine? Attacking the fort?'

'Ratmen don't exist,' said Halmer, angrily. 'It must be something else.'

'Would you like another look?' asked Reiner. He opened the bundle again. Halmer and Matthais stared.

Halmer shook his head, amazed. 'It seems incredible, but I must believe my own eyes.'

'Thank you, captain,' said Reiner. 'Now, believing that, will you also believe what I told Gutzmann about Shaeder? That he is in league with these horrors?'

Matthais made a face. 'But Gutzmann proved you wrong about that. Shaeder would never betray the Empire, and certainly not for gold.'

Reiner nodded. 'I was wrong about him betraying the Empire. He was betraying Gutzmann because Gutzmann was betraying the Empire. He is jealous of the general, as you may know, and so meant to ruin his name and take his position in one sly move.'

Halmer and Matthais stared at him, agog.

'Shaeder meant to allow the ratmen to attack the fort, and make it seem that Gutzmann was in league with them. Then by defeating the vermin, he would prove to Altdorf that he was the man to replace the traitor.'

Halmer closed his mouth. His lips pressed into a thin line. 'That sounds like Shaeder.'

'Unfortunately,' continued Reiner, 'he has been too clever for his own good. He planned to blow up the ratmen's tunnel before their full strength emerged, but they discovered his black powder and stopped him.'

'What!' barked Halmer.

'They...?' Matthais jumped up. 'You mean this happens now? The rats attack the fort now?'

Reiner hauled him down. 'Be quiet you fool!' He lowered his voice as nearby lancers looked around. 'Yes. The rats are attacking as we speak. Shaeder intended to call you back to make a last minute rescue, and so increase his glory, but he has many more ratmen to deal with than he expected.'

'I don't understand,' said Halmer. 'Where is the general? Is he not in command of the fort?'

'No,' said Matthais, his face falling. 'Shaeder drew him away to the mines. I remember now. He invited him to see the tunnel. The devious...'

'Gutzmann is dead,' said Reiner.

The two lancers gasped, staring.

Reiner nodded. 'He died fighting Shaeder's Hammers in the mine.' He looked toward the woods. 'My men carry him.'

Halmer and Matthais made the sign of the hammer and bowed their heads. Then Halmer stood. 'We must return at once. We must tell Nuemark.'

'But he is Shaeder's creature,' said Reiner. 'He already knows.'

'Not all. Surely when he learns that Shaeder's trick has failed...'

'If he believes it.'

There was a sudden clatter of hooves on the road. Reiner, Matthais and Halmer turned. A rider was pulling up before Nuemark's tent.

The obercaptain stepped out as if on cue. 'What news?' he asked in a loud voice. 'Is something amiss at the fort?'

Reiner rolled his eyes at this display. The man would never make an actor.

Nuemark frowned, confused, as the rider got off his horse and whispered in his ear instead of crying his news to the heavens. Reiner didn't need to read the rider's lips to know what the message was, for even in the uncertain flicker of the torches, he could see the obercaptain pale as he took it in. He looked around, then motioned to his infantry captains, and dragged the rider into his tent.

'What does he do?' asked Matthais. 'Why isn't he calling us to order? Why aren't we getting under way?'

They waited a moment, thinking the obercaptain would come out again and make his announcement, but he did not.

'He's bunking it,' said Reiner. 'He's going to cut and run.'

'Impossible,' said Halmer. 'Leaving the fort in enemy hands would be treason.'

Reiner shook his head. 'You saw the fear in him. He's in there now, looking for an excuse. I'll lay odds on it.'

'But we must go back!' Matthais insisted. He turned to Halmer. 'We can't leave when there's a chance!'

'Unfortunately I am not the obercaptain,' Halmer growled. 'I cannot give the order.' He glared at the company of greatswords standing before Nuemark's tent. 'And I wouldn't care to fight through his Carroburgers to usurp him.'

Reiner's head lifted slowly and he turned to look at the captain, eyes wide.

Halmer drew back, uneasy. 'What?'

Reiner grinned at him. 'Captain, you have given me an idea. Will you allow me?'

Halmer nodded. 'Speak.'

Reiner leaned in. 'We will need a horse, armour, a lance, and as much rope as we can gather.'

EIGHTEEN
Shoulder Your Weapons

A SHORT WHILE later, Infantry Obercaptain Nuemark stepped from his tent with his four infantry captains behind him. He was sweating despite the cold night. The messenger he had brought in with him was conspicuously absent.

He spoke to the cavalry captains, then mounted his horse and waited while they sent their corporals to bring the lancers and knights down to stand alongside the foot soldiers who were rising and turning to face him at their sergeants' urging.

When all were assembled, Nuemark saluted the troops and cleared his throat. 'Friends.' He tried again, raising his voice. 'Friends. Comrades. We have been betrayed by one whom we held dear. Our removal here was a trick perpetrated by General Gutzmann. There is no army coming from Aulschweig. The general has turned against us and sided with an army of monsters. The fort is overrun.'

A low, questioning murmur came from the troops, and quickly became a roar of disbelief and anger.

'Yer off yer head, Nuemark,' cried a handgunner.

The obercaptain waved his hands for silence. 'It is true! I have just received word from the fort. General Gutzmann attacked the fort at the head of an inhuman army. Lord Shaeder defended it as best he could, but at half strength he could not hold it. It is lost.'

The roar became a howl, and the troops, both infantry and cavalry surged forward. Only the curses and punches of their sergeants and corporals held them back.

'Believe me,' cried Nuemark, his hands shaking. 'I am as grieved and outraged as you are. But we cannot prevail. We must retire to Aulschweig and help Baron Caspar defend the border until word can be sent to Altdorf and reinforcements can be brought.'

'If General Gutzmann has taken the fort,' shouted a knight, 'then we are with General Gutzmann, whoever he sides with.'

'Fools! You don't understand! General Gutzmann is dead!' bellowed Nuemark. 'Killed by his vile compatriots!'

The howl dropped to a murmur as the troops took this in. They were stunned. They asked each other if such an impossible thing could be true.

Into this lull came a new voice, calling, 'General Gutzmann is not dead! The fort is not lost!'

The troops turned. Nuemark and his captains looked up.

Down the road that curved around the stand of trees came a knight on horseback, holding aloft a lance tied with pennons of blue and white. He was led by two men, and followed by a ragged company. As they walked into the light, the troops erupted in cheers, for the knight was General Gutzmann.

Reiner, holding the general's bridle, raised his voice again. 'Your general is here, lads! To lead you against the vermin who storm the fort! And against the coward Shaeder, who betrayed us all.'

The cheers echoed off the mountains. Reiner saw Captain Halmer and Matthais and their company at the front of the troops, doing as he had bidden them and crying loudly for Shaeder's head. Good men.

Nuemark was staring, his jaw unhinged. The infantry captains were the same. Reiner beamed. Was ever an entrance so perfectly timed? Had even the great Sierck ever written so stirring a scene? It was perfect. A masterpiece, worth every moment of sweat and furious, grisly effort. For it hadn't been easy. Gutzmann had been frozen with rigor mortis and they had had to break his limbs to get him into Matthais's armour. They had had to clean his face and cut off his eyelids so his eyes would stay open. Matthais had wept. Karel had vomited.

Tying the general to Halmer's second horse had been more difficult than expected as well. He weighed a ton, and tended to hang to one side. Fortunately, Matthais's cloak was made for winter weather, long and heavy, and hid a multitude of ropes, straps and stays. Unfortunately, the youth's head was smaller than Gutzmann's and they had had to force his helmet down over the general's brow most cruelly. It had been essential however. The ruse wouldn't work in full light. Not even in the flickering light of a torch. They needed the shadows of a helmet to hide the stillness of Gutzmann's face.

'Command us, general!' cried a lancer. 'Lead us to the fort.'

Reiner swallowed. Now came the hard part. He raised his voice. 'The general was terribly wounded defending the fort and cannot speak nor fight, but he can yet ride. He will lead you! He will command you! Mount up, knights and lancers. Mount up, pistoliers! Shoulder your weapons, ye pike and sword and gun! We've a battle to win!'

The troops cheered.

'Wait!' cried Nuemark, desperately trying to shout them down. He seemed totally undone by the situation. 'We dare not... we... This is madness! The fort is taken, I tell you! Even with the general at our head we cannot hope to prevail. We must retire!'

'Don't listen to him,' shouted Matthais. 'He is Shaeder's creature! He betrays us as well.'

'A lie!' yelped Nuemark. 'I only urge caution!'

'And look what he betrays us to,' said Reiner. He nodded to Franka, who stood in the shadows behind Gutzmann's horse. She stepped back, pulling surreptitiously on a rope that ran up under the general's cloak. Gutzmann's arm raised – somewhat mechanically – but at least it raised, thought Reiner, exhaling with relief. Hanging from the general's hand was the bloody head of the ratman.

'Look what foul monsters kill our brothers as we speak!'

The troops stared, repulsed, at the long-nosed, long-toothed head, with its mangy brown fur. Its black eyes glittered evilly in the torchlight, looking strangely more alive than Gutzmann's.

'The ratmen!' Reiner cried. 'The ratmen are real! They are slaying our comrades!'

The troops bellowed their fear and rage. Captain Halmer and Matthais mounted their horses and clattered to Gutzmann's side as Reiner turned Gutzmann's horse and Franka lowered his arm.

'Form up!' Halmer yelled. 'Form up behind your general, lads! We march for the fort, and victory!' He winked down at Reiner as the men cheered and began lining up in their ranks. 'Nice work, pistol. You've a talent for mummery. I'll handle him now.'

Reiner bowed, hiding a smile. The captain wasn't about to allow Reiner to be Gutzmann's voice for a second longer than necessary. He turned away as Halmer began barking at one of Matthais's lances. 'Skelditz, ride to Aulschweig and remind Baron Caspar of his sworn duty to help the Empire defend this border. Ask him to bring as many men as he can, as swiftly as he can.'

Wandering through the column in search of the Blackhearts, Reiner saw Nuemark before his tent, sitting slack on his horse. He stared at the ground while, one by one, his captains deserted him to take up command of their companies.

The Blackhearts were forming up in the last rank of the first company of pike. Reiner joined them.

'Not riding with the pistols, captain?' asked Hals.

'No fear,' said Reiner. 'I've no wish to be first in. If I thought we could get away with it, I'd wait here until it was all over. We've done our part.'

'No thank'ee,' said Pavel, grinning as he touched his missing ear. 'I owe them ratties a few lopped ears. I want at 'em.'

'Aye,' said Karel. 'Me as well.'

'And me,' said Gert.

Jergen nodded.

'Hoy, captain!' came a voice.

The company looked around. Dag was stumbling towards them, waving and grinning. He had a black eye and a missing tooth.

'I did good, hey?' he said, falling in with them.

Reiner flushed. 'Aye, it worked. Er, sorry you were ill used.'

Dag shrugged. 'Had worse.' He pointed to his purple eye. 'And I broke three of this one's fingers, so I got mine in.'

'Well, that's a comfort at least.' Reiner turned away, exchanging uncomfortable glances with the others. The boy seemed to have no inkling that Reiner had hung him out to dry.

At the head of the column, Matthais raised his bugle and blew 'forward,' and the men got under way. Reiner groaned as the foot soldiers fell into a brisk trot behind the cavalry. He couldn't remember the last time he had rested. It felt a decade since they had escaped the cell under the keep, and not a single break from running, fighting and sneaking since. Oh, for the quiet life of a gambler.

The pikemen on the other hand were well rested and eager for action, inspired by the presence of General Gutzmann at their head. They made the trip back to the fort in half the time the Blackhearts had taken, and Reiner and Gert and some of the others were gasping when Halmer slowed a half a league from the fort.

Reiner looked ahead. A trio of men, wounded and ragged, had waved down the column and were now jogging beside the captain and talking to him in urgent tones. Halmer nodded and saluted, and the men stepped to the side and watched the column pass.

Reiner called out to them. 'What news, lads?

'Bad, sir,' said one, a lanky fellow with a wounded arm. 'Very bad. The rat-things have all the fort but the keep and the main gatehouse. Even the great south wall is theirs. And there are many dead.'

Reiner saluted the man. 'Thank'ee for the warning.'

'Sigmar!' moaned Karel. 'Are we too late then?'

'They won't have an easy time breaching the keep,' said Reiner. 'There may still be hope.'

As the black battlements of the great south wall rose in the distance, Halmer stood and turned in his saddle, calling back to his captains. Reiner could only just hear him. 'Pass back General Gutzmann's commands! Cavalry will enter the fort at the charge! Infantry will follow and hold our position! Do not allow the enemy behind you!'

Halmer's captains repeated the orders to the men behind them and the command echoed down the column.

Two hundred yards out, Matthais raised his bugle again and began blowing 'rally,' a three note tantara, as loud and as often as he could.

Reiner and the others craned their necks, trying to see around the horses before them. Reiner found his teeth were grinding with tension. If the ratmen had since taken the gatehouse, then this attack was over before it began. They would be locked out of their own fort, a besieging army with no ladders, siege engines or cannon.

At last Pavel breathed. 'It opens.'

Reiner leaned to one side and saw it through pumping horse legs – the iron portcullis rising, the massive oak doors behind it swinging in. He sighed with relief.

Matthais's bugle blew 'charge', and the horsemen before the Blackhearts' adopted company of pikemen began to pull away. Reiner fought down a surge of regret as he watched the lancers and pistoliers move through the familiar rising rhythms of trot, canter, and gallop. What a thrill to be sprinting in, pistols at his shoulders, closing with the enemy. But then he saw a lancer fall, and another, and heard the reports of the ratmen's jezzails firing from the walls. He shivered. Better not to be a gunner's first target.

Led by Gutzmann, who held aloft the borrowed lance in his dead hand, Halmer, Matthais and the lancers plunged into the black hole of the gate four abreast, howling fierce battle-cries. The knights and pistoliers charged in behind them without pause.

Pikemen fell, screaming, to Reiner's left and right in a rain of bullets as the company ran after the horsemen. The bullets seemed to explode on impact, ripping through breastplates as if they were muslin. At last they reached the gate and ran out of the deadly hail. The thunder of hundreds of boot heels ricocheted off the walls of the arched tunnel, almost drowning out the roar of battle that came from within. Reiner drew his pistols. Franka, Dag and Gert readied their bows and crossbows. The others drew their swords.

And then they were in.

Directly ahead, the lancers and knights hit the back of a solid mass of ratmen with an impact Reiner could feel through his feet. Rat soldiers flew through the air, blood spraying, as the first rank of knights raised them on their lances. More were crushed under the charge. Reiner saw an iron shod hoof pop a ratman's skull like an egg. The ratmen recoiled from the unexpected attack, screeching and terrified.

In the centre of the line, Gutzmann's horse reared and kicked while the general sat bolt upright, the pennons of his lance waving bravely. And it seemed that nature – or perhaps Sigmar – conspired with Reiner to help him with his grand illusion, for just as the charge hit, the clouds above the fort broke and the light of Mannslieb shot through, haloing Gutzmann in an unearthly blue-white glow. His armour gleamed, the rat head he held shone silver and black.

Rat gunners, drawing a bead on the beacon of the general's breastplate, raised their jezzails and fired. Bullets punched hole after hole in his armour, but Gutzmann remained ram-rod straight, not even flinching. The ratmen before him fell back, awed, at this miracle.

Inspired by their general's superhuman fortitude, the lancers and knights pressed forward, their ardour for battle redoubled. They left their lances in the backs of the first rank of rats, then drew their swords and hammers and laid about them in a fury. The pistoliers swung left and right, emptying their pieces into the ratmen, then wheeling in to meet them sabre to sword. The infantry captains screamed at their troops to block the sides, and the four companies of pike spread out in a long curving line as the force's lone company of handgunners fired into the ratmen's right wing. Reiner and the Blackhearts ran in the last rank of their adopted pikes to close with the rats on the left.

They had to chase them, however, for already the ratmen were retreating. Panicked by the sudden shock to their rear, and as unnerved by Gutzmann's invulnerability as his troops were inspired by it, they fell back in confusion, leaving a putrid animal musk in their wake.

'By Sigmar,' said Hals. 'We've done it. They've broken.'

'To the keep! cried Halmer.

The knights and lancers surged forward, but were not able to overtake the ratmen's scampering retreat. The rest of the troops followed at a run, and found themselves stumbling over the bodies of fallen men and horses, lying on the blood slicked flagstones. They had been hacked to pieces.

Karel choked as he tripped over a gilded helm. 'Captain, look! Cavalry Obercaptain Oppenhauer! Was he caught unawares?'

Reiner looked back. Oppenhauer's round, rosy-cheeked face was gazing at the sky, an expression of horror frozen upon it. It was missing an eye, and his beard was matted with clotting blood. His breastplate was pierced with the heads of three halberds. The jolly old fellow didn't look right without a grin on his face. Reiner swallowed as he ran on. 'They're in full kit. They tried a sortie.'

'A sortie? But that is madness! A single company?'

Reiner looked darkly at the keep. 'Maybe they were ordered to.'

Karel goggled at him. 'But... but why?'

Reiner shrugged. 'Shaeder continues to remove all who might challenge him.'

Ahead of them, the sea of ratmen surrounded the keep, and lapped halfway up it like drifts of dirty brown snow. Some mounted ladders, but just as many were climbing the great piles of their dead that hugged the walls. The defenders fired down into them from the battlements, killing many, but never enough. The keep's gate burned with a weird green fire.

To the right, the stables and some of the other outbuildings were aflame as well, painting the scene a garish orange. From above, cannons roared, and stones and masonry exploded from the walls of the keep. Reiner could see ratkin crews silhouetted on the main battlements as they worked the fort's great guns.

'Our own cannon, turned against us,' said Gert, bitterly.

As they ran through their fellows, the fleeing ratkin alerted their besieging brethren to the threat at their back, and they turned, rat commanders laying about them with whips and staves and squealing orders. In seconds, what had been the ratmen's unprotected flank bristled with spears and swords.

The cavalry slammed into them first, but armed only with swords now, and facing a prepared enemy, the charge was not as successful. Reiner saw men and horses go down, impaled on the ratmen's polearms.

Next came the pikes and swords. As the Blackhearts raced toward the ratmen with their pike company, Reiner fired into the seething mass with both pistols, then holstered them and drew his sword. Gert shot his crossbow before tossing it aside to pull his axe. There would be no time to reload. Pavel and Hals began pushing up with their spears to the first rank.

Reiner cursed. 'Stay back, fools! Let the pikes make the charge!'

They ignored him.

The company hit the rat-wall as one, pikes punching their first line back into their second, but there were more behind them, and more behind those. The vermin swarmed forward, trying to overwhelm the men's line with sheer numbers.

'Don't let 'em through!' cried Reiner.

Reiner and the Blackhearts slashed and thrust from the third rank, stabbing at the vermin who attempted to get behind the front line. It mattered not where they struck, there was a furred body there to receive their blades. The ratmen went down like wheat before the reaper, but there were always more – an endless tide of monsters: yellow teeth snapping, curved swords slashing, gashing arms, biting fingers, clawing eyes. Reiner was almost instantly bleeding from a dozen wounds, and pikemen fell all around him. Hals and Pavel were stabbing and thrusting like machines. Jergen spun his sword around him with deadly grace. Gert cleft rat skulls with his axe. Dag flailed like a drunk with a fire iron. Franka lost her dagger in a ratman's ribs and was punching rats with her off hand as she blocked attacks with her short sword.

All along the line, the men of the Empire slowly brought the ratmen to a standstill, and then started to press them back. The gate of the keep was coming into reach. But just as Reiner thought they might break through, men and rats began dropping all around him, screaming and writhing, as exploding bullets ripped through them. The jezzail-rats who held the great south wall had found them. Worse, they had turned the fort's artillery away from the keep. A cannon boomed and a horse reared, its head missing. Another collapsed, legs gone. Another cannon fired and ploughed a trench through the front lines, dismembering man and ratman alike.

'Do they not care about their own troops?' asked Franka, horrified.

Reiner shrugged. 'Would even a ratman like another ratman?'

The knights and lancers redoubled their efforts to reach the keep's gate, in a frenzy now to get out of range of the gunners on the great south wall. They hacked a bloody path through the carpet of ratmen as more and more men fell under the deadly barrage. And the ratmen were flowing around the ends of the men's lines now, trying to surround them. To protect their flanks, the pike companies folded back like two wings, at last meeting behind the cavalry to form a rough square, pressed on all sides by ratmen.

Matthais's bugle blew the rally again and again as Halmer bellowed up at the keep. 'Open up! Open the gates!'

Reiner wondered if that was even possible, for behind the portcullis, the huge wooden doors were a roaring green inferno. Teams of ratmen stood before them, aiming weapons that Reiner recognized from his adventure in their tunnels. A brass tank carried by one rat, connected by a leather hose to a gun aimed by the other that painted the door with flames that stuck like syrup. The great oak beams were being eaten away, and Reiner realized with horror that the ratmen might be thin enough to fit through the iron bars of the portcullis.

'Pistoliers! Handgunners!' came Halmer's cry, and the gunners fired into the flame-crews. Four of the rats jerked and twitched as the bullets smashed into them. A flame gunner dropped his gun as he fell, and it sprayed fire all around, catching his tank-carrying comrade on fire. The burning rat danced and screeched, trying desperately to unbuckle the straps of his unwieldy canister.

The flames spread to his back, and with a blinding explosion, he was no longer there. A boiling ball of flame erupted where he had stood, and knocked the other ratmen in the vicinity flat, catching them on fire.

The first rank of knights were pushed back into the second by the blast, shrieking in pain, bits of red hot brass sticking out of their breastplates and faces. Their horses screamed as well, similarly wounded.

The way to the gate was clear, though it was still aflame. Matthais blew the rally blast again, as Halmer's force pushed forward. Halmer and the other cavalry men screamed up at the keep. 'Open the gate! Open the gate!'

The portcullis didn't move.

Matthais blew his bugle again, then shook his fist at the keep's walls. 'Let us in, curse you!' he cried. His forehead exploded in gore, and he sagged back in his saddle.

Halmer cried out. Reiner looked up. The shot had come from the keep. Someone in the murder room above the gate was shooting at the knights. Another shot fired, and another. Two hit Gutzmann, one in the head, one in the chest. The general never wavered. Matthais, however, toppled slowly off his horse and crashed to the ground, face first, his bugle rattling across the flagstones. Reiner swallowed. The poor lad. A shame for one so faithful to be so faithlessly cut down.

Another shot took Halmer in the shoulder. He gripped his arm and spurred his horse into the lee of the gate. 'What are playing at, y'madmen?' he cried. 'We come to your aid!'

Reiner groaned. He had a fair idea of who was firing on them.

More shots came, but the target was still Gutzmann. The worse problem was that if the portcullis stayed closed Halmer's force would remain completely exposed to the guns on the great south wall, which were picking them off in twos and threes. Halmer rose in his saddle and bellowed at the square of troops. 'Around the keep! Put it between you and the walls!'

The square began to shift around obediently, pressing against the wall so the pikemen only had three sides to defend. Reiner swallowed as he saw one of the giant rat-monsters wading toward them through the rat army.

'Hetsau!'

Reiner turned. Halmer was waving at him.

Reiner hurried to the captain, hunching low, though what protection that was from bullets from above he didn't know.

Halmer was in a heated discussion with the other captains as Reiner stepped up to his horse. 'It's the only way!' he barked, then turned to Reiner. 'Hetsau, you broke out of our keep. How would you like to try breaking in?'

'Er, if it's all the same to you, captain...'

'It wasn't a request, Sigmar take you! Someone must enter the keep to stop those guns and open the cursed gates, someone who ain't afraid to disobey Shaeder.'

'Yes, sir,' said Reiner. 'But how am I...?'

'There's an underground passage from the gatehouse in the great south wall to the keep dungeon.'

Reiner looked back to the gatehouse in the southern wall – the distance they had just come. There was a roiling mass of ratmen in the way. 'Sir…'

'Yes, I know,' snapped Halmer. 'We are discussing that. Someone must get you to the gatehouse, then try to retake the south wall's battlements.'

'Captain,' said a voice behind Reiner. Everyone turned. It was Nuemark. He was almost as pale as his hair. His greatswords were behind him. He swallowed and squared his shoulders. 'Captain. I… I have much to make up for. Let me and my Carroburgers do this thing.'

Halmer looked taken aback. 'Er, you… you outrank me, Obercaptain. I will not command you. But if it is your wish….'

'It is my duty.'

'Very well.' Halmer turned to Reiner. 'Gather your men. The obercaptain will escort you.'

Reiner saluted, and returned to the Blackhearts, still fighting in the last rank of their adopted pike company. His stomach sank as if it had been loaded with rocks. Charging across the battlefield under heavy fire from the walls was certain death. On the other hand, staying here outside the fort was certain death as well. Better perhaps to be moving.

'Blackhearts!' he called. 'To me. General's orders.'

The Blackhearts backed out of their rank, allowing their pikeman comrades to fill their gaps, then joined him. The square had now tucked in behind the keep, out of the great south wall's line of fire, and the shooting from the keep had stopped as soon as they had moved away from the gatehouse. In fact, here, handgun and crossbow fire from the keep was supporting them, dropping rats all around Halmer's force.

'What's the job?' asked Hals.

'There's a passage into the keep dungeon from under the main gatehouse. We're to go in and open the gates.' He looked up at the walls. 'And discover who's shooting at the general.'

'A passage into…' Pavel cursed. 'Would've been nice to know that when we was trying to break out, hey?'

Reiner led them to where Nuemark was forming up his twenty greatswords. He looked even more scared than before, his face grey and slick.

Reiner saluted. 'Ready, obercaptain.'

Nuemark nodded. 'Very good.' He turned to his men. 'Swords of Carroburg, I have dishonoured your name with my cowardice today, and you should not die that I may make amends. Do not make this sacrifice for me, but to save the lives of your comrades, the men I helped betray to these foul vermin.'

The greatswords drew their weapons, their faces grim. Their sergeant saluted. 'We are ready, obercaptain.' They fell into two rows, one on either side of the Blackhearts, shields on their outer arms. One of them growled in Reiner's ear.

'Y'better be worth it, boy.'

Nuemark turned. 'Gunner captain! When you are ready.'

The captain of the handgunners nodded and signalled his men to advance to the southernmost edge of the square. Nuemark's greatswords and the Blackhearts fell in behind them. The handgunners stopped directly behind a triple rank of pikemen. Every other man knelt. 'Pikemen!' called the gunner captain. 'Make a hole!'

The pikemen looked behind them, then parted ranks. Ratmen tried to flood the hole, but they were not quick enough.

'Fire!' called the gunner captain, and his men unloaded their shot directly into the narrow gap, slaughtering four ranks of ratmen in one volley.

'In!' cried Nuemark. 'Carroburgmen charge!'

The greatswords ran into the opening made by the dying ratmen, swords high, roaring the name of their city. Reiner and the Blackhearts ran with them, hunched down to hide behind their massive, armoured bodies and their round shields. The greatswords hit the massed ratmen like a boulder smashing into a mud lake. The sound of steel chopping rat-flesh and rat-bone was music to Reiner's ears.

The party rounded the corner of the keep, a tiny raft of humanity in a swamp of vermin. The greatsword who had growled at Reiner went down beside him, a rat-spear thrust through his groin. He held his killer's severed head in his shield hand. Another Carroburger went down on the other side. The others closed ranks.

A third dropped, shrieking, as a bullet ripped through his breastplate. The metal of the breastplate seemed to melt away from the bullet, and the flesh beneath it boiled. The rats on the walls had found them. The Carroburgers raised their shields over their heads. Reiner wondered if that would help.

A rat spear darted through between two greatswords and stabbed Reiner through the thigh. He stumbled as his leg gave out, but Gert caught him and hauled him up again.

'Steady, captain.'

Reiner looked down. The wound was deep. Blood was crimsoning his leggings. 'Bollocks!' He couldn't feel it, at least. And then he could, and he grunted. It hurt like fire. He almost fell from the pain. Gert caught him again.

'Can you walk, captain?'

'I'll manage.'

Reiner limped on, his leg jolting agony with every step. Fortunately, the ratmen thinned out the closer they got to the gatehouse, for their attentions were on the keep. But in a way this was also unfortunate, for it made the men clearer targets for the gunners on the wall. Two more greatswords fell, and Dag screamed and shook his left hand. It was missing two fingers. Blood poured from the stumps.

At last they ran under the shadow of the main gate, a thick crowd of rats still harassing them. Nuemark beat on the thick gatehouse door with the pommel of his sword. 'Let us in! Let us in!'

A voice came through the studded wood. 'Commander Shaeder's orders. No one to come though this door.'

'We are on General Gutzmann's orders, curse you!' cried Nuemark. 'Let us in.'

There was a short pause, then Reiner and the others heard bolts being drawn and crossbars raised. Reiner's leg was making him feel nauseous. The gatehouse door swam before him. He gripped the wall and steadied himself.

'All right, captain?' asked Franka.

'Not in the least,' he said. 'But there's nothing for it now.'

The door opened to reveal a few terrified guardsmen. Nuemark shoved Reiner through. 'Skirmishers. In. Hurry.'

The Blackhearts pushed in behind Reiner and turned. It was a tiny room, already crowded with guardsmen, who had to press into the corners to make room for the new arrivals. There was a table and chairs in the centre, racks of weapons on the walls, and a spiral staircase in one corner that led to the battlements. The left wall was filled with the machinery that raised and lowered the portcullises.

The greatswords made to follow the Blackhearts in, but the rats, seeing an opportunity to take the room, attacked furiously. Another greatsword went down. The rest faced out, chopping into the mass of rats.

'In, curse you!' roared Nuemark. His knees were shaking. He nearly lost his grip on his sword.

One by one the greatswords backed into the door as Pavel and Hals stabbed at the rats over their shoulders with their spears. But with each one through the door, those left outside were pressed all the harder. Another went down, and another. At last there was only Nuemark and one other, and the rats were beginning to slip around them.

Nuemark pushed his last man through the door. 'Close it! Close it, you fools,' he cried. He was weeping with fear, but he never stopped slashing with his sword.

The greatsword sergeant slammed the door shut and the gatehouse guards dropped the heavy bar.

Through the thick oak, Nuemark's voice rose to a wail. 'Sigmar forgive me! Sigmar forgive...' His words were cut short as the sound of halberds cutting through armour and into human flesh made every man in the cramped room shudder.

Nuemark's sergeant made the sign of the hammer as he finished his captain's plea. 'Sigmar forgive him.'

'We could have had him in,' said Hals.

'He didn't wish it,' said the greatsword sergeant.

Reiner collapsed on the stone stairs and cut at his leggings, exposing his wound. A ragged trench had been dug in his left thigh by the spear. The very sight of it made the pain worse. Franka hissed when she saw it.

With more than twenty men in it, the room was terribly cramped. A few of the greatswords were seeing to wounds of their own. Dag was giggling hysterically as he tied his kerchief over the stumps of his missing third and fourth fingers.

'All right, archer?' asked Reiner as he stripped out of his jacket and tore the sleeve from his shirt.

Dag grinned glassily and held up his ruined hand, waggling his first and middle finger. 'Fine, captain. Still have my shooting fingers.'

Reiner ripped his sleeve into strips. He glanced up at the guardsmen. 'Have any of you some water? Or better yet, kirschwasser?'

A guard pulled a flask from a cupboard and handed it to him. Reiner uncapped it, and had it halfway to his lips before he remembered his vow. He cursed. Damn Ranald anyway, another nine hundred and ninety-six men at least before he could drink again. What had he been thinking? He poured the liquor on the wound. It stung like wet ice. Reiner hissed. Franka tied the strips of cloth tight around the wound. Reiner's vision eclipsed at the pain, and he turned quickly away to avoid vomiting on her. He vomited on Pavel instead.

'Thank you very much,' said the pikeman, recoiling.

'Sorry lad. Surprised me, too.' He pushed himself up and faced the guard room sergeant. His leg screamed but held. 'Where is this trap?' he asked through clenched teeth.

The sergeant pointed to a rack of spears built into the wall. 'Lundt. Corbin. Open the bolt hole.'

Two guardsmen tugged four heavy pegs from the frame of the rack then lifted it away from the wall, revealing a narrow staircase that descended into darkness.

'So Gutzmann's alive?' asked the guard sergeant.

'Aye,' said Reiner as he helped Gert to his feet. 'And he commands you hold this door at all costs. Let no rat in.'

'Aye, sir. No fear of that.'

The Blackhearts and Nuemark's greatswords stood and made themselves ready. Reiner saluted their sergeant. 'Thank you for the escort,' he said. 'Sigmar watch you.'

'And you as well,' said the greatsword. He turned and led his men up the stairs.

Jergen stood and faced Reiner. 'Captain.'

Reiner nearly jumped out of his skin. He wasn't sure the swordsman had ever addressed him voluntarily before. 'Aye, Rohmner?'

Jergen nodded at the greatswords. 'I will be best used with them.'

Reiner looked at the greatsword sergeant. 'Will you have him?'

'Can he fight?'

'Like several tigers.'

The greatsword chuckled. 'Then fall in, bravo.'

Jergen joined the men climbing the stairs.

Reiner turned to the Blackhearts. 'Ready lads?'

They nodded. Reiner took a torch from the gatehouse wall, then ducked through the secret door and they all went down into the dark.

The passage was narrow and direct. At the end, there was a second staircase and a door in the ceiling. Reiner found the catch and shot it back, then pressed his back against the door. It didn't budge.

'Steingesser. Kiir,' he called, limping down. Gert and Hals squeezed around the others and stepped up to the trap. They pushed with hands and shoulders.

A muffled 'Hoy!' came from above, and they heard a confusion of steps.

The trap slammed open, and a ring of handgunners aimed down at them, fingers on their triggers. Gert and Hals threw up their hands.

Reiner did too. 'Hold, brothers. We are men.'

The handgunners eased back, but continued to look at them warily. 'What men are ye?' asked a sergeant.

'I bring a message for Commander Shaeder,' said Reiner as he and his companions stepped slowly up the stairs. They were coming up in the guardroom just outside the cell Gutzmann had imprisoned them in the night before. The room was packed with a company of handgunners, sitting in rows with their guns across their laps. Gert and Hals had apparently lifted a few of them along with the trap. Their sergeants were their only commanders.

'Is the battle over?' asked a redheaded sergeant.

'What?' said Reiner. 'Hardly. What are you doing down here? Where is your captain?'

'We was told to bide here 'til the order came to retake the walls, sir,' said the sergeant, saluting. 'But it never come. Captain Baer went to ask, but he ain't come back.' He coughed, nervous. 'Er, is it true the general's returned, sir?'

'Aye, sergeant,' said Reiner, smiling as big as he could manage. 'Returned to lead us, and he commands you to take the great south wall. There's a company of greatswords clearing the way for you now. Away with you. And Sigmar guide your aim!'

'But our captains...'

'There's no time. I'll send 'em after you. Go. Go!'

'Aye, sir!' said the sergeant, grinning. 'This way, lads! Action at last!'

The handgunners jumped up, relieved to be doing something, and began clattering into the trap after him.

Reiner and the others hurried for stairs.

Franka shook her head. 'I don't understand. I know Shaeder wished to kill Gutzmann. But at the cost of killing himself as well?'

Reiner shrugged. He had no answer for her.

The gate at the top of the stairs was open and there was no guard. The boom of guns and a buzz of voices echoed from outside, but the hallway was empty. Reiner held up his hand, then crept forward. The door into the dining hall was open. They looked in. The room was packed with pikemen, all staring glumly towards the main entrance.

The fort shuddered as a cannon ball struck it.

'The ratmen still control the guns, then,' said Karel.

'Jergen'll see to them,' said Hals, then spat to be sure he hadn't cursed the swordsman by speaking too quickly.

The Blackhearts passed on to the courtyard door and looked out. A crowd of lancers and pistoliers filled it, waiting on their horses in full kit, but like the handgunners in the dungeon, they had no captains. They were rigid with tension, every fibre ready to charge out, but instead only their eyes moved, darting from a knot of men banging on the north door of the murder room, to the burning doors of the gate, which looked about to collapse, to the clamour of desperate battle coming from over the north wall, where Halmer's force fought the rat army. Reiner could see that the thud and clash of weapons, the screams of men and horses, the high chittering of rats, were driving the cavalry men insane. Their fellows were dying not twenty yards away, and they could do nothing but sit and listen.

Reiner's pistolier company was near the door, arguing amongst themselves as they watched the walls.

'Hist!' Reiner called, stepping out. 'Grau!'

The corporal turned. Reiner beckoned him over. He dismounted and hurried to the door. Two of his men came with him.

'Where have you been, Meyerling?' asked Grau. 'Vortmunder's been calling for your head.'

'Never mind that. What's all this? Gutzmann's getting chopped to bits outside. Why do you not ride out?'

'We want to,' said Grau, angrily. 'But Shaeder's lads have barricaded themselves in the murder room and that is where the winches are. He's locked us in, the traitor.'

'Shaeder ain't a traitor,' said Yoeder. 'It's a trap, like he said. Aulschweig men, dressed up as Reiksmen to lure us out to our doom.'

'Yer mad,' said the third, a stout fair-haired man Reiner didn't know. 'That's Gutzmann out there. I saw his face.'

'It ain't!' said Yeoder. 'Gutzmann couldn't ride so poor if he tried. Damned imposter sits a horse like he's made of sticks.'

'It is Gutzmann,' said Reiner. 'I've just come from him. He's grievously wounded, but he wouldn't stay away while you were trapped here.'

Yeoder stared at him. 'It's Gutzmann? Truly?'

'Truly.'

Grau cursed. 'Some of the captains are up trying to break down the door. The rest are in arguing with Shaeder in Gutzmann's quarters.'

Reiner pushed a hand through his hair. 'This is madness. You must ride out.'

'Too bad old Urquart ain't still with us,' said Pavel. 'He'd knock them doors down with one swing.'

'If only we had one of them glass balls the ratties got,' said Hals. 'We could smoke 'em out.'

Reiner looked at him, eyebrows raising, 'Amazing. A pikeman with a brain.' He turned, looking around the courtyard intently. 'Franka, a feedbag from the stables. And fill it with hay. Oh, and a good length of rope. Karel, a keg of powder from the armoury if you please. Pavel and Hals, lamp oil and bacon fat from the kitchen. As much as you can carry. And a big pot. Hurry. Meet us on the wall at the south door. Aye?'

As they ran off, the gate's wooden doors finally collapsed with a great roaring and eruption of sparks. Through the smoking rubble Reiner saw the forms of ratmen trying to eel through the bars of the portcullis.

'And pray we are not too late.'

NINETEEN
All Must Die!

REINER, DAG AND Gert ran up the stairs to the murder room as sergeants called squads of handgunners and swordsmen to defend the gate below it. The gunners fired through the inner portcullis at the ratmen that squirmed through the outer one. The murder room had two heavy, banded doors that opened onto the battlements to its left and right. Narrow arrow slot windows pierced the inner and outer walls. There were no other openings. Reiner listened at the south door when they reached it. He could hear the captains pounding uselessly on the north door and demanding that the men inside let them in. There was an iron ladder bolted to the wall. He looked up it then turned to the others.

'Dag, I'll have you here. Gert, can you make it onto the roof?'

Gert scowled. 'Ain't that fat, captain.' He started up the ladder.

Franka was first to return to them, a coil of rope slung over her shoulder and a leather feedbag stuffed with hay dangling from one hand.

'Good, lad. Er, lass,' said Reiner. 'Now get that rope around your waist.'

'What?' Franka looked alarmed.

'Not afraid of heights, are you?'

'No, but...'

'Once knew a topside monkey with a second storey mob. Made his living this way. Here, let me tie you off.'

Karel came back next, holding a keg of powder like a baby.

'Now pour as much of that as you can down into the hay,' said Reiner. 'But don't pack it.'

Pavel and Hals ran up just as Karel was finishing. Hals had two jugs of lamp oil. Pavel carried a big iron pot with a jar of drippings in it.

Reiner grinned. 'Excellent. Pavel, smear some fat on the bag. Hals, pour the lamp oil in the pot.'

Pavel made a face, but dug some of the fat out with his dagger and scraped it off onto the bag as Hals filled the big pot. When he was done, Reiner took the bag and lowered it into the pot of oil, pushing it down with the butt end of Pavel's spear until the hay and the leather were well saturated with the volatile oil.

As Reiner was lifting the bag out, Pavel raised his head. 'The cannon have stopped.'

Reiner cocked his head. It was true. The guns on the great south wall had gone silent.

Hals grinned. 'That's our Jergen. Lets his sword do his talking.'

Reiner hung the dripping bag from the point of the spear. The fumes made his eyes water. He stood. 'Hals, Pavel, Karel, stay here with Dag, ready to run in when the villains run out. Franka, up the ladder. I'll hand your weapon to you.'

Franka looked at him askance as she climbed the ladder. 'I begin to like this less and less.'

Reiner handed the spear up to her, then climbed up himself, carrying his torch. He stepped to the courtyard edge and looked over. Franka joined him. She swallowed. It was a long way down.

'Sorry, beloved,' he said. 'You are the lightest.'

He handed the end of her rope to Gert. 'Keep it taut, and pay it out slowly when I tell you.'

Gert gathered up the slack. 'Aye, captain.'

Reiner turned to Franka. 'Ready?'

Franka made Myrmidia's sign, then stepped up onto the wall, her back to the courtyard, and held the spear out to her side. 'Ready.'

Reiner crossed his fingers to Ranald and held the torch under the feed bag. The oil caught with a *whump* and a ball of fire boiled up from the bag, followed by oily black smoke.

'Lower away.'

Franka stepped backward off the wall as Gert let out the rope, and as Reiner watched, walked slowly down the wall, the bag roaring and smoking at the end of the spear like a filthy comet. The entire courtyard was watching as well, the pale, upturned faces of the lancers and pistoliers frowning in confusion.

A few more steps and Franka was at the level of the window slots.

'Now lass! Now!'

Franka jammed the spear point into the window on the left. For a moment Reiner thought all was lost, for the flaming bag became caught between the bars, but Franka pulled the spear back and stuffed the burning mess through like a handgunner jamming wadding into his barrel.

The violence of her action caused Franka to lose her footing, and she banged against the wall, dropping the spear.

'Up!' Reiner called over his shoulder. 'Pull her up!'

Gert hauled away. Reiner held down his hand and caught Franka's wrist as she bumped up the rough wall.

'Did it work?' asked Gert, when Franka had tumbled over onto the roof.

Reiner looked over. Black smoke was beginning to curl out of the murder room windows, and he could hear shouts and choking from below. He grinned. 'I believe it did. Ware the doors!' He cried.

He helped Franka up, and they stepped with Gert to the ladder and looked down. With a frantic turning of bolts and scraping of bars, the door flew open and three Hammer Bearers flew out, gasping and retching, accompanied by a great cloud of greasy black smoke. They were in no mood to fight, and Karel, Pavel and Hals just pushed through them as they stumbled past, coughing and weeping sooty tears.

Reiner heard the south door crashing open as well, and a cheer going up from the men outside it. He clambered down the ladder and snatched Hals's spear, then dashed into the room, ducking low and covering his mouth and nose. The burning bag was under the courtyard-side windows. He stuck it with the spear and hurried back to the door, his eyes streaming, and flipped it out over the battlements.

'In lads!' he coughed, beckoning them. 'Man the winches!'

The Blackhearts ran in, stepping to the great spoked wheels that raised the two portcullises. They fell to with a will, pulling on the spokes with all their might, and a great cheer came from the troops in the courtyard below.

More men ran into the room from the south door – the captains. Vortmunder was at their head.

'Meyerling!' he cried. 'You surface at last! Good work! I'll take a day off your stable duty for this.'

Reiner saluted. 'Thank you, captain! May I suggest you return to your company. Your way will be clear momentarily.'

'Very good! Carry on.'

Just then the cheers in the courtyard turned to shouts of alarm. Reiner, Vortmunder and the other captains ran out and looked down. Squirming under the slowly raising portcullis was a spreading tide of ratmen. The handgunners were falling back as a company of swordsmen ran in to meet the invasion. Steel clashed on steel.

Vortmunder turned to Reiner. 'Raise it as fast as you can, corporal, so that we may charge.' He ran off with the other captains.

Reiner ran into the murder room. 'Put your backs into it, lads. We...'

'What is this!' cried a voice. 'Who disobeys my orders?'

Reiner looked up. Standing in the south door was a crazed figure. It took a moment for Reiner to realize it was Shaeder. His grey hair was disordered, his eyes wild. He looked like he had aged ten years in a night. He stepped into the room, drawing his sword. The Hammer Bearers who had held the murder room came in behind him, as did their glowering, white-bearded captain.

'Lower those portcullis, curse you!' shouted Shaeder, and lunged at Dag, who was hauling one-handed on the left-hand wheel with Gert and Franka.

'Sod off, y'berk!' said Dag, and punched him in the nose with his ruined hand as the others turned, drawing their weapons. The wheels stopped.

Shaeder stepped back, cursing, blood running over his lips. 'You... you dare? You peasant.' He ran Dag through the chest. A bright spike of steel sprouted from the archer's back. He convulsed, vomiting blood, then raised his head and sneered through bloody teeth. 'Get stuffed.' He poked Shaeder in the eyes with his two remaining fingers.

Shaeder howled and jerked back, clutching his face. Dag dropped off Shaeder's sword and flopped bonelessly to the floor, dead. An unexpected pang of sadness struck Reiner at the sight. He had spent all the time that he had known Dag trying to be rid of him. The boy had been a dangerous madman, but dead, Reiner felt a strange fondness for him. He chuckled sadly to himself. That was the best way, really. Better for Dag to be dead and miss him, than have him running around wreaking havoc.

Shaeder and his Hammer Bearers attacked the Blackhearts on the wheels. Shaeder flailed wildly, half-blind. The Blackhearts defended themselves. A cry of dismay came from the courtyard as the wheels started to spin backwards.

'Damn you, Shaeder!' Reiner ran forward, swinging his sword. He caught Shaeder's blade before it came down on Pavel's head. 'Gert! Hals! Franka! Stay on the wheels. The rest, defend them!' The Blackhearts turned to their tasks as Reiner thrust savagely at Shaeder, 'What ails you? We must attack!'

Shaeder riposted, forcing Reiner back. The whites of his eyes were blood red. 'No! We must die! All must die!'

'You're mad. We might still win.' Reiner parried desperately. Mad or not, Shaeder was still the better swordsman, and his frenzy gave him strength.

'And have Altdorf learn of this?' Spittle flew from Shaeder's lips with each word. 'No one must survive to get word back. They won't understand. They won't see that it was Gutzmann who was the traitor, and I the patriot! We will stay here until the rats overwhelm us!'

The Hammer Bearers shot uneasy glances at him. Their swords faltered. 'Do we not wait for Gutzmann to be defeated?' asked the white-bearded captain. 'You said Aulschweig came to reinforce us.'

'I said what was necessary.'

Reiner sneered. 'So you kill an entire garrison to hide your foolish manipulations? You are worse than a traitor. You are a bad general.'

Shaeder's eyes went wide. 'Villain! Take back that slander!' He rushed forward, swinging wildly. Reiner caught Shaeder's blade on his hilt, and his shoulder on his chest. The commander clawed for his dagger.

Reiner got his boot up between them and kicked with all his might. Shaeder flew back, flailing for balance. He stopped in the door – or rather, something stopped him. The doorway was filled with dark, hunched figures.

Shaeder looked around as clawed hands gripped his arms and legs. 'Who…?'

Reiner and the Blackhearts and the Hammer Bearers stared as a jagged bronze blade reached from behind the commander and sawed his neck open from ear to ear. Ratmen poured into the room over his body before his blood began to flow.

There was a cry from the courtyard. 'They're over the walls!'

The Hammer Bearers stood shoulder to shoulder with the Blackhearts to meet the ratmen's charge. Hals, Franka and Gert left the wheels to help.

'No!' Reiner ran forward. 'Keep turning! We'll hold 'em back!'

Hals cursed. 'But, captain…'

'You've the strongest back, laddie.' Reiner cleft a ratman's skull to its curved front teeth as he joined the line. 'Push 'em out! Franka! Close the other door!'

Franka ran to the north door. She slammed and locked it as Hals and Gert hauled on their wheels. With only one man turning each, they raised by inches instead of feet at a pull.

Reiner found himself fighting beside the captain of the Hammer Bearers.

'I swear to you,' the captain said, 'I swear we didn't know.'

The ratmen swarmed around them, trying to reach the wheels and cut at the ropes. Reiner cut one down and kicked a second back. Karel blocked a bronze halberd and gutted its owner. Pavel wielded his spear like a quarterstaff, knocking heads left and right. The Hammer Bearers stabbed and sliced around them like men possessed. One went down, impaled on a hooked spear. Reiner feared it was all in vain. More and more ratmen were squeezing through the door.

An arrow sprouted from the eye of a rat swinging a cutlass at Reiner. It fell, shrieking.

'Franz,' Reiner called over his shoulder. 'Get back to your wheel!'

'No, captain,' said Franka.

Another arrow appeared in a rat's throat.

Reiner grunted. Even with her arrows they were certain to be overwhelmed. But just as he thought it, the ratmen who still filled the door began turning and squealing. Battle cries echoed into the room from the battlements.

'For Gutzmann!'

'For the Empire!'

Reiner's heart leapt. The keep's sword company! He raised his voice in answer. 'For the Empire! For Gutzmann!'

The others joined him. 'For Gutzmann! For the Empire!'

Outside, the swordsmen cheered.

Reiner could see a wave of panic ripple through the ratmen as they realized they were caught between two forces. They began slashing about themselves in a frenzy, striking at their comrades as often as their foes. Reiner caught a wild slash in the forearm. He dodged back.

'Press forward as one!' cried the leader of the Hammer Bearers. They and the Blackhearts walked forward, jabbing at the ratmen in unison until the vermin fought each other to get out of the door and collided with those who were fighting to get in. Through the doorway, Reiner saw the swordsmen on the battlements, holding off a wave of ratmen that were pouring over the wall.

'Franz! The door!'

'Aye, captain.'

As Reiner and the others backed the ratmen into the doorway, Franka edged around and squeezed behind the door. She began pushing it closed. Reiner stood at its edge, defending her and adding his shoulder to her weight, but there were too many ratmen in the way.

Reiner waved at the Blackhearts and the Hammers. 'Jump back! All at once!'

Pavel scowled at him. 'Hey?'

'Trust me, curse you! Jump back! Now!'

The Blackhearts jumped back. Shaeder's Hammers were only a step slower. The ratmen in the door, suddenly without resistance before them, stumbled forward into the room, off balance.

'Now!'

Reiner and Franka pushed at the door as one and got it nearly closed before it hit the crowd of ratmen beyond it. It started opening again. The Hammers waded into the ratmen in the centre of the room. Pavel and Hals dodged around them and charged into the door, slamming it closed. Outside, a ratman shrieked. Reiner looked down. A naked pink tail lay on the floor, severed from its owner.

Reiner turned the lock. Franka dropped the bar. They ran back with Pavel and Hals to the wheels as the Hammer Bearers finished off the remaining ratmen. The Blackhearts threw down their weapons and pulled on the spokes for all they were worth. After a moment the Hammers joined them.

A roar of triumph rose from the courtyard as the wheels jarred to a stop. The portcullises were open at last. A horn blew 'charge,' and hooves thundered below them.

Reiner locked his wheel and breathed a sigh of relief. Gert did the same at the other wheel. The Blackhearts ran to the arrow slots, but could see nothing. Franka darted to the south door and threw it open. The Blackhearts and the Hammer Bearers ran out and looked over the parapet, craning their necks to see the scene below. The lancers were already through the gate, wheeling left toward the thick ring of ratmen that surrounded the ragged remains of Halmer's square. The pistoliers were right behind them, arcing wide to broadside the ratmen as they raced past. Next came a stream of pikemen, ten wide, running at full charge. The Blackhearts and the Hammer Bearers joined the swordsmen cheering them from the walls.

The companies hit the rats' flank with a devastating triple impact, all their enforced inaction and pent up rage exploding in bloodthirsty fury. The rats fell before them like trampled grass, crushed under the hooves of the lancers, riddled with bullets from the pistoliers, and impaled by rank after rank of pike.

It was too much. The ratmen had expected the battle to be over almost as soon as it had begun. Instead they had fought Halmer's troops to a standstill for more than a quarter of an hour, all the while taking heavy crossbow fire from the walls of the keep, and now fresh troops were crashing into their rear. The ratmen turned and fled before the charge. Seeing them flee, their brethren fled too, and soon the entire rat army was scrambling away, some on all fours, in full rout, with the lancers and pistoliers chasing them down.

Reiner would have wagered that Halmer's men would have called it a day and let their comrades finish the job, but to his surprise, they joined the pikemen and trotted north after the cavalry. At least those still standing did. At Reiner's guess, more than half the men who had ridden into the fort with Halmer lay dead or wounded below the wall of the keep. Others were too tired to move and sat down unheeding among the broken bodies and spilled viscera of their enemies and friends.

Hals let out a huge sigh. 'So we did it, then.'

Reiner nodded and closed his eyes. He leaned against the battlement. 'Aye. Well done, lads. Well done.'

'Manfred damned well better thank us for this one,' said Pavel.

'Aye,' agreed Franka.

'It weren't the job he sent us on, that's certain,' said Gert.

'Oh, Sigmar,' said Karel. Reiner thought he was about to kneel in prayer, but the boy sobbed and retched. 'Oh, Sigmar, they're eating them.'

'What's the matter?' Reiner opened his eyes. 'Who's eating who?'

Karel was looking over the wall. 'The rats. They're eating the dead.'

'The rats?' asked Reiner, turning with the others to look. 'The ratmen?'

'No. Rats. Big rats.'

Franka choked. 'They're eating Matthais!'

TWENTY
Heroic Deeds

The Blackhearts ran down to the courtyard and out of the keep. The grounds of the fort were strewn with the dead and dying. Men and ratmen lay in long heaps of bodies that defined where the lines of battle had been, highest where the fighting had been the fiercest. To the left of the gate was the place Halmer had called to the keep to open the portcullis.

Reiner peered at the bodies there. Things were moving among them, but he didn't wish to believe they were rats. They were the size of pit dogs, and as muscular. They scurried over the bodies, gnawing and clawing at them. And they didn't just prey on the dead. Reiner saw a wounded man try to push away a rat with feeble strength. The rat sat on his chest and chewed through his throat.

'It's horrible,' muttered Franka. 'Horrible.'

'Begone, beasts!' cried Karel, stamping his feet and waving his sword.

The rats looked up, but failed to run at his advance. Their eyes glowed red in the light from the keep's gate.

Reiner grunted and waved the others ahead. 'We get Matthais, but no more. There are too many. We'll tell someone once we're back inside.'

As they started moving through the bodies, Reiner saw Jergen crossing towards them. He saluted as he approached.

'Rohmner,' Reiner said, nodding. 'How went the battle for the walls?'

'Well.'

Reiner snorted. 'A veritable fountain of words, aren't you, Rohmner?'

Jergen nodded, then fell in with the others. Reiner sighed. The man was unreachable.

After a moment, Reiner saw the body of Matthais's horse. They picked their way to it, keeping wary eyes and weapons on the huge rats. Matthais lay behind it, almost lost in shadow but for the bright, straight line of his sword. Two huge rats hunched over him, one chewing on a leg, the other on an arm.

'Shoo!' called Karel. 'Go away, you horrible things!'

'Ware, laddie,' said Reiner.

He hurried after him, stepping on bodies as he went. One squealed and squirmed. Reiner stopped and turned. The squeal had not been human. A plump ratman in long robes knelt among the bodies, a scalpel in its hands, a handgunner neatly laid open before it. It blinked up at Reiner through thick spectacles. Reiner frowned. He knew this creature.

'The surgeon!' cried Franka. She started forward, her teeth bared. 'I want his spleen!'

The ratman snarled in anger, and started to crab backwards.

Franka lunged at it, slashing with dagger and short sword. The rat scrambled away with surprising speed, chittering in his own tongue and pointing at the Blackhearts. The giant rats looked up like dogs hearing their master's voice, then leapt to the attack.

Reiner sprang back, slashing at three rats that snapped at his legs. The others were similarly infested.

'Ahoy the keep!' Reiner cried. 'Help us!' No one responded. He cursed. 'Back to the fort!'

But it was difficult to disengage. Hals pinned a rat to the ground but another had him by the boot. Pavel flung one over his shoulder on the point of his spear. A second jumped on his back. Franka kicked one back and stabbed another as she tried to reach the surgeon. Gert hacked one with his axe and stomped another flat. Two more leapt at his chest. Jergen decapitated one and cut another in two. He stepped toward Pavel to help him with his. Karel cut at two, backing away from their claws and teeth. A huge shadow loomed out of the darkness behind him. He didn't see it.

'Lad!' called Reiner. 'Behind you!'

Karel turned, and ducked a great, chisel-shaped claw. The monster slashed at him again. The thing was the size of an ogre, rippling with fur-covered muscles. Karel dodged back, then lunged at it, slashing it across the arm. It roared and attacked.

Reiner rushed in with Franka and Jergen, but before they could reach the beast, the surgeon skittered ahead of them. 'Such brave,' it cried. 'Such courage! Take! Take!' It gibbered an order at the rat-ogre, and the thing curled its fist and clubbed Karel to the ground instead of gutting him. The boy's sword clattered to the flagstones.

Reiner tripped on a pile of bodies trying to reach the monster. He fell. Jergen leapt the pile and swung at the beast, gashing its shoulder. It backhanded him, knocking him into Pavel and Franka.

Before they could regain their feet, the rat-ogre caught up Karel's limp form with one claw while the surgeon clambered up on its shoulders. The ratman rapped his monstrous mount on the head with his bony knuckles and pointed to the north wall, squeaking all the while. The beast vaulted over a dead horse and disappeared into the shadows, Karel tucked under one arm. The giant rats ran behind it in a bounding carpet.

Reiner clenched his fists. 'Curse the boy! The battle's won! The day is saved! Why does he have to go and get himself taken now?' He looked around at the Blackhearts. They were waiting, expectant. He sighed. 'All right. Come on.'

They ran for the north gate, Reiner's wounded leg screaming with each step, as stiff as a tree branch.

THE PASS WAS strewn with dead ratmen. Their panic had apparently not abated, for they had all been cut down from behind. Reiner and the Blackhearts jogged through it, peering ahead anxiously into the darkness. Only occasionally did the clouds part to allow them to see their quarry bounding before them. They were gaining on the rat-monster, but slowly. Reiner's breath was like knives in his throat. He couldn't remember when he had run more in one night.

They veered into the branching ravine that led to the mine. The dead rats were thicker here where the narrowing walls had slowed their retreat, and the Blackhearts stumbled over bodies and were forced to weave around abandoned flame guns and other strange equipment.

Soon they saw the outer walls of the mine before them, and a moment later the weird silhouette of the ogre-mounted surgeon lurching through the gate, followed by its boiling shadow of rats. Reiner expected to hear echoes of battle from within the compound and see the light of torches, but it was silent and empty.

As they ran in they saw at last evidence that the ratmen and the soldiers had come this way. A crowd of armoured horses milled about in front of the mine entrance, waiting for their riders to return. The soldiers have chased the rats to their hole, thought Reiner. He prayed the vermin the explosion had trapped hadn't dug themselves out.

'There,' said Hals, pointing.

In the centre of the compound, the rat-ogre was shambling wearily on, its burdens at last slowing it down. Franka stopped and nocked an arrow, then pulled her bowstring back to her ear. She let fly. The rat-surgeon squeaked and toppled off his mount's shoulders, arms flailing. The rat-ogre stopped and turned.

The Blackhearts sprinted forward while Gert and Franka stayed back and fired at the beast. Jergen shot out ahead, holding his sword out to his side. The rat-ogre saw them coming and dropped Karel to step over the surgeon, roaring defiance. The giant rats surrounded it, hissing and snarling.

Jergen leapt over them, sword high. The rat-ogre raised an arm instinctively. A clawed hand spun away, severed cleanly by Jergen's flashing blade. The beast bellowed its pain and knocked Jergen sideways. The swordmaster landed shoulder-first among the rats and rolled. They snapped and clawed at him.

Reiner kicked left and right at the rats and aimed a thrust at the monster. His blade slid off its ribs, opening a crimson gash in its dark fur. It clubbed him aside with its bloody stump. Reiner staggered, his vision blurring from the impact, his bad leg buckling.

Pavel and Hals tried to reach the rat-ogre as well, but found themselves fending off the rats instead. The monster surged forward, swinging at Pavel. Franka and Gert peppered it with arrows and bolts, but it kept coming.

Reiner limped forward again, but as he waded into the rats, chopping in all directions, Karel stood up behind the rat-ogre, weaving and drawing his dagger.

'Get away, laddie!' Reiner shouted.

But the boy leapt on the beast's back, stabbing it in the neck. It howled and clawed behind it in agony, catching Karel by the arm. Reiner lunged in at its exposed side and plunged his sword into its guts. It roared and smashed Karel down on top of him, flattening him to the cobbles. The boy's elbow cracked him in the cheekbone. Reiner gasped, trying to suck air into his collapsed lungs. Karel's weight lifted off again and he rolled away, slashing blindly to keep the rats away.

He looked up. The rat-ogre towered above him, its hideous face contorted in a snarl. It had Karel by the leg now and was swinging him around like a club. Pavel and Hals were flying back, knocked off their feet. Franka and Gert were holding fire, afraid to hit Karel.

Reiner tried to rise, tried to get his sword in front of him. The rat-ogre glared down at him and raised Karel over its head. Reiner threw himself aside. The beast brought the boy down like an axe. Karel smashed onto the cobbles with a sick smack Reiner felt through his hands.

Pavel and Hals staggered up, shaking off rats and wading towards the beast. Franka and Gert fired.

Reiner rolled to dislodge a rat and saw the rat-ogre raising its human weapon again. Reiner flailed, but he couldn't get out of the way. He was covered in rats. One bit his arm, another his side, another his foot. He felt none of it. His whole world was the rat-ogre.

Motion flickered in the corner of his eye. Jergen. The swordsman ran up the monster's back, blade high. He chopped down like an executioner. The ugly head split in two, gushing blood, Jergen's steel lodging between its two front teeth. The beast fell like a tree, face first, right beside Reiner. Karel flopped flat to his right.

Jergen sprang off the monster and laid into the rats around Reiner.

Reiner killed the one on his chest and flung it at two more. He rolled to his knees, slashing in a circle, then staggered to his feet and joined Pavel and Hals, who stabbed and kicked and chopped at the vermin in a frenzy. Franka and Gert shot arrows and bolts into them as fast as they could. After a red blind moment, Reiner stopped and looked around, breathing heavily. The others were doing the same. They had run out of targets.

'All dead?' Reiner asked.

'Aye,' said Hals.

'There's one moving,' said Gert.

The Blackhearts turned. The rat-surgeon was writhing about in agony, Franka's arrow still lodged in his back. He had lost his spectacles.

Franka approached him, sword out, her face blank and hard. The surgeon squinted up at her, trying to back away. 'Mercy... Mercy please!'

Franka sneered. 'This is mercy, torturer!' She chopped at his neck. The first cut failed to decapitate him, and he shrieked as she hacked at him a second time and cut his head off. The headless corpse flopped and spasmed.

Franka collapsed to her knees.

Hals nodded. 'Well struck, lass.'

There was a moan behind them. They spun around, swords at the ready.

It was Karel. The boy's hands were moving weakly, but he was not long for the world. Reiner knelt stiffly at his side. The others gathered round. Franka retched and sobbed. Karel's chest was an odd shape. A red rib jutted up though his jerkin. He had a gash in his scalp Reiner could see his skull through. It was cracked. The boy lay in a lake of his own blood.

'Lad. Are you...' Reiner swallowed. 'Are you still with us?'

'Row...' Karel was trying to beckon to Reiner, but he hadn't much control of his hands. His breath whistled through his teeth in short gasps.

Reiner leaned close. 'What is it, lad?'

'Rowena.' Karel clutched Reiner's arm. His grip was painfully strong. 'Tell her I died... thinking of her.'

Reiner nodded. 'Certainly I will.' The poor fool, he thought. The girl had likely forgotten him as soon he had left her sight.

'But,' Karel pulled him closer. 'But... invent a better death.' He grinned up at Reiner, though his eyes gazed past him. 'You're good at that, aye?'

Reiner smiled sadly. 'Aye, laddie. That I am.'

Karel relaxed his grip and sank back. 'Thank you. You aren't... what Manfred said.' His eyes closed.

'Poor foolish boy,' said Hals.

Pavel made the sign of the hammer. Franka murmured a prayer to Myrmidia.

'He'd no business being mixed up in all this,' said Gert.

Reiner snorted. 'None of us did.'

A noise brought their heads up. They looked around. The sound came from outside the compound – the slow hoof steps of a single horse, echoing hollowly off the walls of the ravine. As they watched, it wandered through the gate, unguided by its rider, who was revealed slowly as it moved out of the shadow of the wall. The knight hung sideways from the saddle at an unnatural angle. A broken lance drooped from his mailed hand, blue and white pennons smeared with blood and dirt. His eyes stared vacantly beyond them.

'Sigmar!' hissed Pavel. 'It's Gutzmann!'

They all stood and turned to face the dead general, but no one seemed eager to approach him. They were transfixed. A chill ran up Reiner's spine as Mannslieb cut through the clouds and haloed the dead rider. Where had he come from? Had he got lost in the army's pursuit of the ratmen? Had he followed the Blackhearts?

The horse stopped in the centre of the compound, its head low, as noises began to come from the mine – the thud of boots, the creak and jingle of armour and sword, and above it all, loud laughter and exuberant banter – the voices of a victorious army returning from battle. Reiner stole a look behind him. Lancers, swordsmen and pikemen were swaggering out of the mine, boasting to each other of their exploits. Others came limping, or carrying fallen comrades, but even these seemed to be in an ebullient mood. The enemy was vanquished. The Empire – or their little corner of it – was saved.

Their merry chatter faltered and fell silent however, as one by one they noticed the lone knight sagging gracelessly from his saddle in the moon glow. They came forward in small groups to stand with the Blackhearts, until at last the entire garrison – or what was left of it – stood in a half circle, looking at their leader, who in life had nearly led them to folly, but in death had led them to victory.

They watched thus for many minutes, no one wanting to end the unearthly eerieness of the moment. But then, with a loud snap, one of Gutzmann's ropes broke and he crashed to the ground.

The garrison gasped and cried out. Then Captain Halmer, who had been standing with his men, stepped forward. 'Make a bier. Carry him back to the fort.' He raised his hands. 'May Sigmar bless our fallen general!'

The garrison raised their voices in unison. 'Hail Gutzmann! Praise Sigmar! Long live the Empire!'

The crowd of soldiers began to break up as some of Halmer's lancers went forward and started making a makeshift stretcher of their lances. Riders found their horses, pikemen and swordsmen formed up in their shattered companies.

Halmer saw the Blackhearts and saluted. He crossed to Reiner and clasped his hand, then leaned in. 'The garrison and the whole of the Empire owe you. I owe you. Unfortunately, for the morale of the men, I think it might be best if they were allowed to continue to believe that Gutzmann died here, now, after the battle was won, rather than before it began.'

Reiner exchanged wry looks with his comrades. 'That's all right, captain,' he said. 'We're used to it. Heroic deeds play best when it's heroes that perform them. Nobody wants to hear a ballad about the blackhearts that propped a would-be deserter on his horse and sent him off to save the day.'

Halmer scowled at that. 'Good. Then you would do well to keep it to yourself.' He turned on his heel and began calling the troops to order.

Franka rolled her eyes. 'The soul of diplomacy as always.'

Reiner shrugged, grinning. 'The truth is never diplomatic.'

THE SUN ROSE on a cold, bright morning as General Gutzmann led his army for the last time. Four knights carried him back to the fort on crossed lances as their comrades marched silently behind them, heads uncovered, and swords, lances and pikes held at the shoulder. The ceremonial mood was marred however, when it was discovered that another army occupied the fort. A thousand fresh Aulschweig knights, spearmen, swordsmen, and crossbowmen held the great south wall and the keep. An Aulschweig captain at the head of a company of swordsmen held up a hand as the column entered.

'Baron Caspar Tzetchka-Koloman's regards,' he said, 'and would you be so kind as to ask your captains to meet him in the great hall?'

Halmer stiffened. 'A foreigner gives orders in an Empire fort?'

'It is a request only,' said the Aulschweiger, bowing.

'Very well,' Halmer said. He dispatched a corporal to summon the other captains.

Reiner didn't like the look of things. He motioned his comrades off to one side. 'I think, lads, that it is time for us to go. Collect your things and meet me back here as soon as you can. We'll want to be away before...'

'Hetsau!' came Halmer's voice.

Reiner cringed. He turned and saluted. 'Captain?'

Halmer dismounted and stepped close to him. 'I may have need of your guile just now. You will attend me as my assistant. Come.'

Reiner sighed. 'Right ho.' He looked back at the Blackhearts as Halmer led him towards the keep. 'Get ready,' he mouthed.

BARON CASPAR WAITED for the garrison's captains on the steps of the great hall. He looked every inch the dashing hero, dressed in armour of silvered plate, with a cloak and surcoat of blazing white over it.

'Welcome, gentlemen,' he said. 'Pray come in.'

He turned and led them into the great hall, which was still in great disarray after being used to house pike and sword companies the night before. Caspar pushed through the clutter of benches and tables and stepped up onto the raised dais, extending a gracious hand. 'Take your seats, gentlemen.' He circled the table and dropped into Gutzmann's chair.

The captains froze where they were.

'My lord,' said Halmer. 'That is the general's chair.'

Caspar shrugged. 'I am a general, yes?'

'Yes, but not...'

The hall's great double doors boomed closed behind them. Reiner looked around with the others. Armed men filed through the side door and surrounded them.

'What is the meaning of this?' asked Captain Vortmunder.

Caspar smiled. 'It means I now have the right to sit in this chair.'

Vortmunder stepped forward. 'But you were the general's friend. He was helping you...'

'And the general is dead,' Caspar cut him off. He sighed. 'I was becoming tired, anyway, of all the delays. All the shilly-shallying. Of having to beg for Gutzmann's gold and make extravagant promises to get it.' He sat forward. 'Now I no longer have need of such compromises. Now I no longer have to buy the golden eggs, since as of this moment, I own the goose that lays them.' He laughed. 'This is the best of all worlds! With the mine and the fort in my possession, my brother will not long stand against me. I will rule Aulschweig, and soon all the principalities!'

'You swine!' cried a knight captain. 'You break treaty!'

'The Empire will destroy you!' said Vortmunder.

'You won't get away with this!' said Halmer.

'The Empire will never know,' said Caspar. 'For no one will leave here. Besides, as long as I continue to send Altdorf a few meagre shipments of gold they won't bother to ask who sends it to them.' He smiled. 'And if they do someday learn who holds the pass, it will be too late, for I will have built my own empire by then.'

'You madman,' cried Vortmunder. 'You are a mere tick on the backside of the Empire. You...'

Caspar shot to his feet. 'I will not be insulted in my own keep!' He shouted. 'Speak to me that way again and you will be shot.' He sat back down, composed again. 'Now. You will be held hostage against the good behaviour of your men until I decide how to dispose of them.'

Reiner watched the captains seething with impotent rage as Caspar outlined his commands and conditions. Their hands clenched. Their eyes bulged with fury. They were too angry to think, too outraged by this grievous insult to the Empire to examine the situation. At any moment one of them might explode and say something that would get them all killed. Reiner didn't wish to die. Something had to be done. He leaned in and whispered in Halmer's ear. After a moment, the lance captain nodded.

'My lord,' he said, stepping forward. 'I regret to inform you that you are too late. Altdorf will be sending a force to reinforce this garrison within a month.'

'What do you say?' asked Caspar, sitting up. 'What's that?'

'A messenger was dispatched before we left the mine, my lord,' replied Halmer. 'Informing Karl-Franz of our battle with the ratmen and requesting reinforcements. There will be a full garrison on its way as soon as he reaches Altdorf. And though you may well hold the fort against that force, you won't hold it against the force that will come after the first. The Empire is relentless against its enemies, as you know. It will not stop until you have been wiped from the face of the earth.'

Caspar turned red. He turned to one of his captains. 'Send a squad to hunt down this messenger. I will kill him before he leaves the mountains.'

'You might, my lord,' said Halmer levelly. 'And you might not. He has quite a lead.' He coughed. 'I have another suggestion that you might find palatable.'

Caspar glared at him. 'You think to make terms with me? You are my prisoners!'

'It is only a suggestion my lord. You may do with it as you will.'

'Speak,' snapped Caspar.

'You might, my lord, allow a second messenger to be sent after the first, informing Altdorf that you hold the fort for them. That after Commander Shaeder's betrayal of General Gutzmann to the ratmen and the subsequent loss of the fort, you rode in and saved us.'

Vortmunder turned on Halmer, eyes wild. 'What horrible lie is this! We needed no help! We defeated the ratmen! We held the fort!'

'But we don't now, captain,' said Halmer. 'Would you rather lose the fort to assuage your pride, or serve the Empire with your humility?' He turned back to Caspar. 'My apologies, my lord. As I was saying, you could send a message to Altdorf that you have saved us, and that you hold the fort for Karl-Franz until reinforcements can be brought up, thereby keeping the Empire's southern border safe.'

Caspar sneered. 'And why should I do that? Why should I kiss Karl-Franz's spotty behind?'

The captains bridled at that, but Halmer only smiled. 'Because, my lord, just as the Empire's vengeance is relentless, so is its benevolence limitless. In return for your help in this matter, the gracious Empire would support you against your brother and very likely back you in your ambitions against the other princes of the region. Altdorf has for centuries longed for more stability on its southern border.'

Caspar sat back in his seat, brow furrowed. Reiner could see his suspicious nature fighting with his greed and ambition. He smiled. He knew which of those combatants always won out with a man like Caspar. He exchanged a look with Halmer and nodded. The captain had done a masterful job. He hadn't made any demands, any threats. He had laid it out as Reiner whispered it to him. A reasonable plan presented by a reasonable man.

After a long moment Caspar nodded. 'Very well, send your messenger. But you will be held as hostages in Aulschweig. If Altdorf betrays me, you will all die. You understand me?'

Halmer and the others nodded, their heads held high. They knew that, in reality, the Empire would come for Caspar's head, and Caspar would kill them for betraying him, but they were knights of the Empire. They were ready to make this sacrifice.

Reiner, on the other hand, was not. 'Er, captain,' he said to Halmer. 'I would be honoured to be allowed to convey this message to Altdorf.'

TWENTY-ONE
Freedom

REINER CHIVVIED HIS comrades out of the fort as quickly as he could. His shoulders remained tense as they waited while horses were found and they were outfitted and provisioned. At any moment Caspar might change his mind and lock down the fort, or Halmer might decide he had too much need of Reiner's guile to let him go. But at last they were all kitted out and mounted up, with a little pony cart following them to carry their supplies. Reiner had insisted on the cart.

Hals spat over his left shoulder as they got under way, riding into the pass out of the shattered remains of the tent encampment outside the fort's north wall. 'Ain't sorry to be showing that place my backside.'

'Didn't think I'd get out with mine intact,' said Gert.

Pavel laughed. 'Ye've enough. Y'could've left some of it behind.'

Franka shivered. 'The sooner we're out of these accursed mountains the better.'

Jergen nodded.

Reiner spurred his horse. 'I agree. But we have a stop to make first.'

THE MINE'S THIRD tunnel was choked with the bodies of ratmen, piles of them, their limbs and torsos broken and cut to ribbons.

At the end of the tunnel where the explosion had closed it off the bodies were packed to the ceiling, and it appeared that these had torn each other apart in their frenzy to return to their underground world. The wounds that had killed them weren't the straight cuts of swords, but the ragged shredding of claws and teeth.

But though the stench of blood, bile and filth was unbearable, Reiner had searched every foot of it, for he couldn't find Gutzmann's gold. Reiner had led the Blackhearts to the spot where he had discovered the crates, but they were no longer there. At least he was almost sure they weren't. He couldn't be certain he hadn't missed them somehow.

He cursed. 'We'll search again as we go up,' he said.

Hals made a face. 'But what do we look for?'

'Is it really worth all this stink?' asked Pavel.

Reiner shot a look at Gert and Jergen. They were all that was left of Manfred's new men. Either one could be his spy. And at the same time, neither could be. The spy might have been... Dag? It hardly seemed possible. More likely Abel. But if that was the case, he had decided early on to switch from observer to leader. And what had become of him anyway? Reiner hadn't seen the quartermaster since he had betrayed him to Gutzmann.

'Aye, it's worth it,' Reiner said at last. 'It's evidence. For Manfred. Something that'll impress him. That we might be able to use to convince him to free us. Now come. Pavel and Hals, look on the left. Gert and Jergen on the right. Franka, stay with me in the centre. Don't miss an inch.'

The Blackhearts groaned and began trudging back up the tunnel.

HALF AN HOUR later Reiner had to admit defeat. The crates were nowhere in the tunnel. The Blackhearts returned to their horses and the cart, and at last got on the road for Averheim and Altdorf.

Reiner was glum, his shoulders slumped. The gold had been their chance at freedom, and now it was gone. They were back were they were before Manfred had sent them on this fool mission – firmly in his clutches with no way that Reiner could see to get out. It was maddening.

As they passed out of Brunn and started up the next rise Franka patted his arm.

'Don't feel so bad,' she said. 'Didn't we survive?'

'Aye, but for what? More servitude?'

Franka looked at him. 'Don't you feel any pride in what you've done? If you hadn't put Gutzmann on his horse and tricked all his men into following him, the day would have been lost. The ratmen would hold the fort, and everyone would be dead. You...'

'A thousand men!' said Reiner suddenly.

'What?' Franka frowned. 'Where?

Reiner laughed, loud and long. 'Pavel,' he cried. 'Open a bottle of wine.'

'Hey,' said the pikeman. 'Now?'

'Yes now. I need a drink. We all do. A celebration.'

Pavel shrugged and dug through the supplies on the cart.

Franka scowled at him quizzically. 'What are you on about?'

Reiner wiped his eyes and shook his head. 'When I was in the ratmen's tunnels trying to free you, and it looked like we wouldn't make it, I made a pledge to Ranald that if he saved me, I would not touch drink again until I had tricked a thousand men.' He grinned. 'Well, he saved me.'

Franka smiled. 'And you tricked a thousand men.'

'And now I need a drink.'

Pavel handed Reiner a bottle and he raised it. 'Here's to luck and the brains to use it.' He took a long drink and passed it to Franka.

'Here's to those that didn't make it, and to us that did. Sigmar bless us all,' she said, and tilted the bottle up for a few swallows. 'And Myrmidia.' She passed it to Pavel.

'Here's to home and hearth,' he said. 'May we see them again at last.' He drank and passed the bottle to Hals.

'Here's to Gutzmann,' he said. 'May he sup with Sigmar tonight.' He drank deep and handed the bottle to Gert.

'Here's to new friends,' he said. 'May we drink again in better circumstances.' He gulped down two big swallows, then passed it to Jergen.

The swordsman raised the bottle, but not his eyes. 'Freedom.' He drank and returned it to Reiner.

The others nodded, and echoed him. 'Freedom.'

Reiner finished the bottle, then tossed it at the rocky wall of the pass. It smashed into a hundred pieces. Red drops spattered the rocks.

A FEW MILES later, the companions came around a bend in the path and saw a cart up ahead. It was in a ditch, and the horses and driver nowhere in sight. As they got closer, Reiner noticed crates on the back of the cart, and his heart jumped. He recognized them. He spurred his horse forward. He was shaking. Could it be?

The crates had been opened, the tops pried off. Reiner stepped off his horse onto the cart, and looked inside them. They were empty. His fists clenched. Empty!

He kicked one to the ground. There was a single gold ingot beneath it, missed by whoever had looted them. He snatched it up. Hardly enough to buy an hour of a sorcerer's time, let alone pay him to remove whatever poisonous curse Manfred had put on them. He hurled it into the brush.

'Reiner,' said Franka, as the others caught up to him. 'Look.'

Reiner turned to where she was pointing. On the far side of the cart was a body. He jumped down and turned it over, then recoiled. The Blackhearts gathered around him, staring and gagging.

It was Abel. He was dead, but not from any weapon of steel. Reiner was almost certain he had been dead before those who had robbed the cart had struck. His face was stretched in a hideous rictus grin, as if something inhumanly strong had grabbed the flesh at the back of his head and pulled it tight. His tongue was thick and black and protruded from his mouth like a sausage. His hands were so flexed that the bones of his fingers had snapped, and his arms and legs were as rigid and hard as iron.

''Tis the poison,' breathed Pavel. 'Manfred knew he betrayed us and he set it loose.'

Reiner swallowed. 'So it isn't a ruse after all.'

'He can see us all,' moaned Hals. 'He knows what we're thinking.'

'But how can that be?' asked Franka, shivering. 'It's impossible.'

It was impossible, thought Reiner. But that left an even more unpalatable option – that Manfred's spy still lived. That he was one of them. Reiner looked around. Gert or Jergen – which was it? Then an even more horrible possibility struck him. What if Manfred had reached one of the original group? The spy could be any of them. Any of them.

Reiner and the others mounted up again and continued north, but the mood of camaraderie that had united them mere moments ago was lost, replaced by an uneasy silence.

A cold wind began to blow. Franka urged her horse up beside Reiner's and rubbed her leg against his. He instinctively returned the sweet pressure, but then stopped. What if it was she who...?

He edged away from her, hating himself. Suspicion was a poison that would kill them all. She looked up at him, confused.

He pulled his cloak tighter around him and rode alone.

TAINTED BLOOD

ONE
The Tide of Chaos

ABEL HALSTIEG'S BODY lay at Reiner Hetsau's feet, his face frozen in a rictus grin, eyes wide, bloated tongue sticking through bared teeth. Abel's limbs were twisted to the breaking point by the poison that filled his veins. Reiner's companions – Pavel and Hals, Franka, the girl who disguised herself as a bowman, Gert and Jergen – stared at the corpse as well. Reiner looked at them, knowing one of them had poisoned Abel, and had the power to poison the others with a word. But which one? Who was the spy?

They raised their eyes to him. Hals and Pavel grinned, as if sharing a secret. Gert's eyes twinkled with malicious glee. Jergen glared. Franka smirked. Dread dragged at Reiner's heart. Were they *all* spies? Was he alone? Was there no one he could...?

Reiner jerked awake, heart thudding. He blinked around the moon-rimmed darkness. He was in his bed in Count Manfred Valdenheim's Altdorf townhouse. Only a nightmare. Then he chuckled bitterly. What did one do when one's nightmares were nothing more than the truth?

Someone tapped at the door. Reiner rolled over and stared. That must have been what had wakened him. He wished he had a dagger, but Count Manfred allowed the Blackhearts no weapons in his house. 'Who is it?' he cried out.

The door opened. A slight figure eased in, candle in hand. It was Franka, still in her boyish kit, though the other Blackhearts now knew her secret. 'Only your valet, m'lord,' she whispered, closing the door and tip-toeing to the bed. 'Come to polish your... sword.'

'Eh?' said Reiner. His head was still clouded with the nightmare.

Franka smiled. 'Come, now. Surely a man as worldly wise as his lordship can't be so obtuse?'

Reiner stared at her blankly. She sighed and sat on the eiderdown, setting the candle on his bedside table. 'Very well, I will spell it out. Yarl has been dead a year. My mourning is over. Indeed, I waited a year and a week, so as not to appear in an unseemly hurry. But now...' She paused, suddenly shy. 'Now, I am my lord's to command.'

Reiner blinked. Since the Blackhearts' return from the fort in the Black Mountains, he had been so trapped in his tortuous thoughts that the subject that had once filled his waking moments – and his sleeping ones as well – had gone completely from his head. He remembered counting the days – the hours – until he could be with Franka, but now, though his lust for her was more enflamed than ever, now...

'Perhaps,' he said. 'Perhaps we should wait yet a little.'

'Perhaps...?' Franka burst out laughing. 'Reiner! What a joker you are! You almost...' She paused. Reiner wasn't smiling. 'You aren't joking?'

He shook his head.

'But why?' Franka asked, baffled.

Reiner couldn't look at her. If she was only one of the legion of doxies and camp followers he had dallied with over the years they would already be hard at it, but Franka wasn't the sort of girl you used and threw away. 'We... we aren't free. It would ruin it. I don't want to be with you when we have to hide what we do.'

Franka scowled. 'Is this the same man who wanted to have at me in a tent surrounded by our unwitting companions? Weren't your arguments exactly to the contrary, saying we would be stealing moments of freedom? What has got into you?'

'Poison!' said Reiner. It exploded from him before he could stop it. '*Poison* has got into me.'

Franka shrugged. 'But, it has been these many months. And you made no bones about it before.'

'That isn't the poison I mean,' said Reiner. 'I mean the poison of mistrust that has plagued us since–'

'Since we found Abel.'

Reiner nodded. 'One of us is a spy for Manfred. One of us cast the spell that poisoned Halstieg. You've seen how it has hurt us. I'll wager our companions spoke not ten words to each other on our return to Altdorf.'

'*You* certainly didn't,' said Franka. 'But I understand. Gert and Jergen are good companions. I'm as reluctant as you to think that one of them might be Manfred's creature.'

'Who's to say it must be Gert or Jergen?' snapped Reiner, then cursed and clamped his mouth shut. Too late...

Franka looked up at him, blankly. 'What do you mean?'

'Nothing. Forget I spoke.'

'Reiner. What do you mean?'

Reiner looked at the floor. 'I know I am a fool, but I haven't been able to get it out of my head since that day. Manfred might have turned one of us – one of the first lot – made some promise, offered freedom, gold, what-have-you, in exchange for spying on the rest.'

'But, Reiner,' said Franka. 'All that's left of us is Hals, Pavel, you, and myself. Surely you can't suspect–' She froze as a thought came to her, then stood abruptly, trembling. 'This is why you don't want to be with me.'

'No, I...'

Franka stalked to the door. Reiner threw off his blankets and charged after her. 'Franka, listen to me!'

She opened the door. 'What is there for you to say? Do you truly think I am a spy for Manfred?'

'No! Of course not!' Reiner couldn't meet her gaze. 'But... I can't be sure.'

There was a pause. Reiner could feel Franka's eyes burning into him. 'You're mad,' she said. 'You've gone mad.' She stepped into the corridor and slammed the door.

'Yes,' he said to the closed door. 'Yes, I believe I have.'

THE BLACKHEARTS WERE fed in the servants' hall to keep them out of sight of Manfred's frequent visitors. These days the companions, who had once bantered and argued like Altdorf fishwives, ate like grim automatons, as they had since returning from the Black Mountains. Franka kept her eyes on her plate. Hals and Pavel muttered in each other's ears, heads together. The brawny sword master Jergen stared into space as he chewed. Gert shot sad glances at the others. The barrel-chested crossbowman was a born teller of tales, and it seemed to physically hurt him not to have anyone to talk to.

It was a relief therefore, when, the next day at dinner, just as Reiner was swabbing his plate with his bread, boot heels sounded on the stairs and Manfred entered the kitchen, ducking his silver, leonine head under the blackened beams. The cooks and footmen vanished at a wave of his hand, and he sat down at their table with a sigh. Reiner saw that he was tired and worried, though he kept his face as placid as ever.

'I go to Talabheim tomorrow,' he said, 'accompanying the elf mage Teclis on a diplomatic mission. You will accompany me, as my servants.' He smiled as they reacted to this. 'It would defeat your purpose if I called you my spies, wouldn't it? And I am adding four to your number, who you will meet tomorrow.'

The others tensed at this news. Things were strained enough without adding strangers to the stew.

'You believe you will have need of spies in Talabheim?' asked Reiner. 'It is not a foreign land.'

Manfred looked down and toyed with a table knife. 'This is not to be spoken of, you understand, but something has happened in Talabheim – an eruption in the energies of Chaos so strong it woke the great Teclis from his sleep last night here in Altdorf. He fears that if it is not stopped, Talabheim will fall to Chaos, if it hasn't already.' He jabbed the table with the knife. 'And when the tide of Chaos rises, it is my job to suspect agents of the Ruinous Powers. This is where you come in.' Manfred looked up. 'I head a Reikland embassy which will offer aid to our Talabec brothers in their hour of need. But while we are there, making speeches of mutual support, you will be hunting for the cultists and criminals and conspirators that I feel certain will be found to be the cause of the trouble.'

He sighed and stood. 'We leave tomorrow before dawn. Sleep well.' With a heavy tread, he walked up the stairs again.

Reiner and the others sat silently.

'A tide of Chaos rising in Talabheim?' said Pavel, at last, scratching under the patch that hid his empty eye-socket. 'And we're riding straight for it? That's fine, that is.'

'At least it ain't the cursed mountains again,' growled Hals.

'Maybe we'll all die this time and get it over with,' said Franka, staring at her plate.

Her sadness stabbed Reiner in the heart.

TWO
An Honorable Profession

REINER SAT IN Manfred's opulent coach, waiting for the count's train to get underway. It was still as dark as pitch, and the coach yard flickered with yellow torchlight. Reiner was dressed in a plain grey clerk's doublet, which still smelled faintly of clerk. An inkwell hung from his belt, and a beautiful parchment case rested on his knees. Through the coach's windows he caught glimpses of Pavel, Hals and Gert filling their new positions – Pavel whistling on the buckboard of a provisioning wagon, Gert huffing as he loaded cured hams and sacks of flour onto it, Hals securing chests and baggage on a second wagon, his bald head shining with sweat.

Other men also assisted in the preparations. Reiner eyed them closely. They were not servants of Manfred's household. Were they the new Blackhearts? There was a swaggering, barrel-chested fellow with a bristling red beard seeing to the horses. A meek youth of about the same size, but with a slow, moping gait, followed red-beard around, helping him and laughing obsequiously at his constant jokes. Standing by a mule loaded with leather satchels was a thin young man in the grey robes of the College of Surgeons who blinked around him in a daze. Beside him was a tall, wiry villain with darting eyes who looked utterly unconvincing in the smock and leggings of a surgeon's assistant.

Manfred climbed into the coach, accompanied by Jergen, in the uniform of the count's guard, and Franka, in page's livery emblazoned with Manfred's gold lion. Jergen sat next to Reiner, trying vainly to keep his broad shoulders from crowding him. Franka sat beside Manfred. She wouldn't meet Reiner's eye.

Manfred smiled as he saw Reiner's costume. 'I believe you have found your calling at last, Hetsau. You look every inch a clerk. Perhaps one of those fellows who write letters for the unlearned at a pfennig a sheet.'

'Thank you, m'lord,' said Reiner. 'It is at least an honourable profession.'

Manfred scowled. 'There is no more honourable profession than defending one's homeland. It pains me that a noble son of the Empire must be forced to the task.'

'If I recall, m'lord,' said Reiner, 'we were not asked.'

'That is because I am an astute reader of men.' Manfred rapped on the ceiling. 'Kluger! Let's be off. We're late as it is!'

The coachman's whip cracked and the coach rolled forwards. Reiner saw Hans and Pavel out of the window wheeling their wagons around to follow Manfred out of the gate.

THE PROCESSION WOUND through Altdorf's cobbled streets in the pre-dawn grey. The grand palace of Emperor Karl Franz loomed in the mist like a gigantic griffin guarding its nest, the buildings of the Imperial government clustering around it like its brood. After passing through the merchant quarter, they came to the river and the Emperor's private docks, a gated enclosure hemmed in on three sides by barracks, stables and warehouses and on the fourth by the river.

As they entered, Reiner began to understand the importance of their mission. He had assumed Manfred would travel with, at the most, an escort of knights and swordsmen, but the yard was crammed to bursting with the men-at-arms of half a dozen different nobles, all trying simultaneously to load their horses, wagons and equipment on four large, flat riverboats.

Torchlight glinted off the helms of Count Manfred's ten knights and those of the twenty spearmen and twenty archers from his Altdorf retinue, but these were a mere fraction of the assembled force. Here were the greatswords of Lord Schott, a captain of Karl Franz's honour guard, arguing with the knights of Lord Raichskell, Master of the Order of the Winged Helm. Behind them, the handgunners of Lord Boellengen, undersecretary to Baroness Lotte Hochsvoll, Chancellor of the Imperial Fisc, were engaged in a heated shouting match with the Hammer Bearers of Father Olin Totkrieg, representative of the Grand Theogonist, Esmer the Third, while the hooded initiates who accompanied Magus Nichtladen of the Imperial Colleges of Magic watched impassively.

Each lord also had an entourage of secretaries, valets, cooks and grooms that rivalled Manfred's own, as well as wagons full of chests, strong boxes, and provisions. Reiner had seen whole armies set out with smaller trains.

In the centre of this mad jumble was a white island of stillness that made Reiner and Franka catch their breath. Elves. Though Reiner considered himself a well-travelled, well-educated man, he had never seen an elf before. The fair did not leave their homeland often, and when they did, they didn't mix in at the Three Feathers or the Griffin. They met with heads of state, were feted with official banquets, and sailed home laden with fine gifts. So, try as Reiner might to remain cool and aloof, he stared along with everyone else at the six statuesque warriors in silver breastplates and white surcoats who stood motionless before the gangplank of the lead boat.

The elves' faces were as set as carved ivory: sharp, proud and cruelly handsome. Long, thin swords hung at their sides, and curved bows rose from leather scabbards on their backs. It was hard at first for Reiner to tell one from the other. They seemed cast from a single mould. But as he looked, he began to notice subtle differences – a beaked nose on this one, fuller lips on that one. He hoped, however, that he wouldn't be required to remember which was which.

'Wait here,' said Manfred. He stepped from the carriage and crossed to a half-timbered building. Reiner and Franka's gaze remained fixed on the elves, who looked neither right nor left, nor spoke among themselves.

'I thought,' said Franka softly, 'that they would only be men with pointed ears, but… they aren't men.'

'No,' said Reiner. 'No more than we are apes.'

He and Franka exchanged a glance, then looked away.

To hide his discomfort, Reiner turned instead to Jergen, who looked down as if daydreaming. 'You seem unimpressed by our fair cousins, Rohmner.'

'I am impressed,' said Jergen. 'They have great control.'

'Control?' Reiner asked. It was rare for the taciturn swordsman to volunteer an observation.

'They are aware of everything, and distracted by nothing. It is a trait to emulate.'

Reiner chuckled. 'You're well on your way, laddie.'

The clamour of the courtyard abated. All heads turned. Reiner leaned over Jergen to see out of the other window. From the half-timbered building came Manfred and a cluster of officials, in the centre of which was an elf in snow-white robes and a high, mitred cap. He walked with a slight limp and steadied himself with an intricately worked white staff, but there was nothing weak about him. His demeanour commanded attention – majestic and terrifying at the same time. Reiner couldn't take his eyes off him. Though the elf's face was as smooth and unlined as those of his guard, there was an impression of impossible age about him, a depth of wisdom and pain and terrible knowledge in his opal eyes that could be seen even across the dark quay. The men babbled at his heels, all trying to catch his eye.

'But, Lord Teclis,' cried Lord Boellengen. 'We must come. The exchequer must assess the damages!' He was scrawny and chinless, with a bowl of grey hair, and looked, in his parade armour, like a turtle in too big a shell.

'The Emperor has asked me to survey the situation personally,' barked Lord Schott, a squat soldier with a trim black beard. 'I cannot disobey him.'

'The Grand Theogonist must know the extent of this plague of Chaos!' bellowed Father Totkrieg, a white bearded warrior-priest in black robes over polished armour. 'We will not be left behind.'

'If there is Chaos to be fought,' said the towering Lord Raichskell fiercely, 'the Order of the Winged Helm will not be denied the fighting of it. It is not honourable to stay in Altdorf while daemons stalk Talabheim.' His blond beard hung down over his enamelled green plate in two thick braids.

'The investigation of arcane threats is the responsibility of the colleges of magic!' said Magus Nichtladen, a sunken cheeked grey-beard in a rich burgundy robe. 'We must be allowed to do our duty!'

Teclis was deaf to them all. Accompanied by his guard, he walked up the gangplank onto the river boat, spoke briefly to Manfred, then disappeared below the deck.

Manfred stalked back to his coach and slammed in, furious. 'Self-important fools,' he said, dropping into his seat. The coach began to roll forward, manoeuvring to ascend a ramp onto the back of the first riverboat. 'It was to be Teclis's guard and mine. A legation, not an army. Now we are more than two hundred. But if any of them are left behind the Emperor will never hear the end of it. Sometimes I don't blame the fair ones for sneering at the pettiness of men.'

THEY SAILED NORTH and east up the wide grey Talabec, winding slowly through farmland toward Talabheim, the City of Gardens, an independent city-state buried deep within the dark forests of Talabecland. Reiner looked forward to seeing it, for it was one of the Empire's marvels, a city built entirely inside an enormous crater, the walls of which were said to be impenetrable.

The riverboats passed green pastures and brown fields in which gaunt peasants ploughed under the stalks of this year's crop to make mulch for next spring's planting. The earth was fresh in many a country graveyard as well, for it had been a hard year in the Empire. Many farmers' sons had come home from Archaon's invasion in coffins if they came home at all. And there had been famine even while the wheat ripened on the stalk, for much of last year's grain had been sent north to feed the armies, and the farmers of the north whose farms had been burned by the invaders had come south and turned to banditry, stealing the rest.

Reiner, Franka and Jergen were kept busy all day, acting as Manfred's servants, while the count held council with Teclis and the other members of the legation in his stateroom. Late in the afternoon, at the point the river entered the Great Forest, Manfred ordered the boats to land and the servants to make camp. No one thought less of him for this caution. Greater armies had disappeared without a trace under the thick canopy of the old forest, and even the river was not safe as it wound between the looming trees. As it was they would be within it for five days and nights before they reached Talabheim. There was no need to press their luck by passing a sixth night in its shadows.

Manfred had a great tent erected in a fallow field, and dined with the other leaders. Reiner and Jergen were dismissed and joined their comrades around a campfire, where Reiner was at last able to meet the new recruits. Only Franka, who was kept busy serving Manfred pheasant and wine, was not in attendance.

Pavel and Hals had already become friends – or at least amiable sparring partners – with the big redheaded groom, exchanging cheery insults with him as they spooned stew out of the pot as Gert chuckled appreciatively beside them.

'One Talabecman is worth ten Ostlandmen,' the redbeard was saying.

'In a pissing contest mayhap,' said Hals. 'The only thing the Talabecland pike ever successfully defended was a brewery, and they surrendered after the beer ran out.'

'Ha!' countered redbeard. 'The only thing Ostland pikemen defend is their sheep, and only if they're faithful.'

Reiner laughed. 'Hals, who is this fiery fellow you war with?'

Hals looked around, and it hurt Reiner to see the mistrust that crossed the pikeman's face when he saw who addressed him. 'Er, aye, captain,' he said. 'This is Augustus Kolbein, of Talabheim. He's one of us. Kolbein, this is Captain Hetsau, our leader.'

Augustus nodded and touched his forelock with a hand like a ham. 'A pleasure I'm sure, captain,' he said. 'Though I can't say I'm happy with the terms of service.'

'Nor are any of us, pike,' said Reiner. 'And while I'm pleased to have so strong a soldier with us, I am sorry you had the misfortune to be pressed into our cursed company. But, come, tell us how you fell foul of the Empire.'

Augustus grinned, making his beard bristle even more. 'Ah well, it's entirely my own fault, captain. Y'see I have a temper fiery as my hair, and there was a Reiklander captain of sword at a tavern in Altdorf, some nose-in-the-air jagger – er, beggin' yer pardon, m'lord,' he said, colouring suddenly.

'Never mind,' said Reiner. 'Don't care for the type myself. Go on.'

'Aye, sir. Well, he were badmouthing Talabecland something terrible, saying we was all drunks and yokels and that we, er, performed unnatural acts with trees and the like, and I was taking it well enough. We Talabeclanders have thick skins about that nonsense. But then he had to go and say things about the countess, calling her a Taalist whore who rutted with filthy woodsmen and I don't know what else. Well, I saw red and the next thing I know I'm in the brig and the latchkey is telling me I broke the delicate little thing's neck and spooned out one of his eyes with me thumb.' Augustus shrugged. 'I've no doubt I did, but spit me if I recall it.'

Reiner nodded. 'Maiming a superior officer. Aye, there's no doubt you belong with us. Though again, I am sorry you've come to such a pass.'

The pikeman shrugged. 'Better this than the noose.'

Reiner grunted. 'You may come to change your mind about that.'

The others looked away.

Reiner turned to the big, moonfaced youth who sat next to Augustus. 'And you, lad,' Reiner said. 'What's your tale? Are you a killer of men, an eater of children? We've had all kinds with us over time, so fear not that you will shock us.'

'Thank you, captain sir,' said the boy in a high, nasal voice, 'Thank you. My name is Rumpolt Hafner, and it's an honour to serve under you, m'lord.' He ducked his head. 'Er I, I'm sorry to say I'm not much of a villain, though I will try my best not to disappoint you. And, er, I would certainly do murder if I met again the rotten blackguards who brought me to this.'

'You cannot disappoint me if you do your best and put your trust in me as I put my trust in you,' said Reiner. It sounded false as he said it, and Hals and Pavel shot him sharp looks over the fire as it sank in. He was glad Franka wasn't there. 'But tell your tale and we shall judge how much a villain you are.'

Rumpolt's lower lip stuck out. 'I still don't know why mine was a hanging offence. All I've done is steal a banner. It was a dare. I'd just joined Lord Loefler's handgunners in Stockhausen. There was another company there who were Loefler's rivals, Lord Gruenstad's Men, and my sergeant and his comrades said if I truly wished to be one of their company, I must perform a brave deed against them.'

Hals and Pavel smirked.

Rumpolt clenched his fists. 'They told me I must steal Lord Gruenstad's banner and stand it in the camp privy! How was I to know taking a banner is considered stealing the Emperor's property?'

'It ain't just that, lad,' said Gert, his hands crossed over his heavy belly. ''Tis a company's honour. They defend it with their lives on the battlefield. You think they'd take kindly to some wet-behind-the-ears booby sticking it in a midden?'

'But I didn't know!' moaned Rumpolt. 'And when I was caught, and told the captain that the sergeant and his fellows had put me up to it, the villains denied knowing anything about it.' His looked around at them pleadingly. 'Surely you can see I've been wronged?'

Pavel, Hals and Augustus looked away, disgusted. Reiner heard Augustus mumble, 'How could he not know?' and Pavel reply, 'It ain't a question of knowing.' Jergen as usual said nothing, and the other two new Blackhearts, the shy 'surgeon' and his hawk-faced assistant didn't seem to care.

'Well lad,' said Reiner, soothingly, 'never mind. There's more than one of us who claims he's innocent, so you're in good company. Welcome to you.'

'Thank you, captain,' said Rumpolt. 'I'll do my best. I swear it.'

Reiner turned next to the wispy-haired young man in the surgeon's robes. 'And you, physician, what is your name?'

The fellow jumped at being spoken to. 'Er, my name is Darius Balthus-Rossen. Of Nuln, originally.'

'You haven't the look of a soldier,' said Reiner. 'Surely Manfred didn't recruit you from the brig.'

'No, m'lord. He found me in the Altdorf city jail.' He shivered. 'An hour before my hanging.'

'And why were you to be hanged?' asked Reiner.

The young man hesitated, glancing around uncertainly.

Reiner sighed. 'We are a company of convicts and lost men, lad. You cannot be more evil than some we have called comrade.'

The scholar shrugged, splaying his hands. 'I am nothing, a student of plants and the mysteries of life's natural processes. I haven't killed or maimed anyone, or stolen anything, or betrayed the Empire. I'm not a villain at all, really.'

'You must have done something,' said Reiner, dryly. 'They were going to hang you, after all.'

Darius hesitated for so long Reiner thought he wasn't going to speak at all. 'I... I was found in possession of a forbidden book.'

'What sort of book?' asked Reiner, though he already had an idea.

'Er, ah, it was nothing. Nothing. A treatise on the medical uses of certain, er, unusual plants.'

'Then why was it forbidden?'

'Because,' said the scholar, suddenly angry, 'my learned professors are blind, hidebound, incurious demagogues who have no interest in learning anything they don't already know. How can the world's knowledge expand if one is forbidden to try new things?' He clutched his thin hands into fists. 'An experiment isn't an experiment if it's been done before. We know so little of how the world works, why plants and animals grow, how the winds of magic twist that growth, how they twist us. The "wise men" are too afraid of the unknown. How–'

'Magic,' said Reiner, interrupting him. 'So, you are a witch then?'

Darius looked up and saw the others staring at him uneasily. 'No,' he said. 'No, I am a scholar.'

'A scholar of magic,' Reiner pressed.

The young man sighed. 'You see? Fear of the unknown. Had I been a baby eater, you would have shrugged and welcomed me, but because I have studied the arcane, no matter how academically, I am a pariah.'

'But are ye a witch?' asked Hals, menacingly.

Darius's shoulders slumped. 'No. No, I am not. Though of course you won't believe me now. I am a man of theory. I have less practical knowledge of the art than a village wise woman. I certainly can't hex you, if that is what concerns you.'

Hals and Pavel made the sign of the hammer, Gert spat over his shoulder.

Reiner coughed. 'Then why are you here? Manfred certainly didn't take you out of the Altdorf jail for your knowledge of plants.'

Darius shrugged again. 'The count told me that I was to see to your wounds. I have some small knowledge of physicking. My father was a surgeon. I can set a bone and patch a wound.' He looked down at his surgeon's robes with a weak smile. 'I seem the only man here whose garments are not a disguise.'

There was silence around the fire. It was clear the others didn't believe him.

Reiner didn't either. If Manfred had wanted a surgeon, he could easily have found one in a military brig who had battlefield experience. Darius had clearly been chosen for another reason. 'Well,' he said at last, 'it seems you have shocked us after all. But give me your word that you will keep your witching to yourself and I will welcome you. And I ask the rest of you,' he said, glancing around, 'to let the lad prove himself by his actions, like you have with all our other comrades.'

Darius sighed. 'I am not a witch. But nevertheless I give my word.'

'Can you magic the poison from our blood?' asked Rumpolt.

Reiner's heart lurched. Out of the mouths of babes! He hadn't thought of that. By Sigmar, if it was true!

Darius laughed. 'If I could, would I be here, enduring this interrogation?'

Reiner sighed. How foolish a thing hope was. Manfred would never choose a witch with so much skill. He turned to Darius's hawk-faced assistant, who was throwing twigs into the fire.

'And you, friend,' Reiner said with as much cheer as he could muster. 'Have you any dark secrets to share? Or at least a name?'

The man looked up with weary contempt. 'I ain't your friend, jagger. Nor friend to any of ye,' he said, his eyes darting to the others. 'Dieter Neff's my name. I'm here because 'twas a less certain death than the noose. And I'll be gone soon as I sort beating this poison, so there's no reason for how-de-dos and telling tales.'

'Dieter Neff!' said Reiner, with a laugh. 'I know of you. You're the "Shadow of Elgrinstrasse," the "Prince of Murder," with a hundred notches on your belt. I saw you once in Stossi's Place when I used to skin the marks there.'

'A hundred and seventeen notches,' said Dieter.

'So they caught you at last,' said Reiner.

'Never,' Dieter sneered. 'I was sold out by an employer who didn't care to pay when I done the job.' He threw another twig on the fire. 'He'll get his...'

Reiner waited for Neff to elaborate, but the man just stared into the fire. Reiner sighed. 'Well, if Master Neff won't speak, I can certainly tell you what I know. He is the best thief and assassin in Altdorf, known for getting into and out of places other men cannot. He once stabbed a man to death in the middle of Lord von Toelinger's annual banquet in full view of ten score armed knights and got out unscathed.'

Dieter barked a laugh, though he didn't look up. 'Y'don't know the half of it, jagger. The burgher I killed was the man who hired me. And I didn't kill him.'

'Eh?' said Rumpolt. 'What do you mean?'

Dieter paused, and Reiner could see he was weighing his contempt for his audience against his desire to brag. 'Berk was a wool merchant named Echert,' he said at last. 'Owed a lot of dangerous people money, so he decides the best thing to do is die. So he hires me to fake killing him and make it look good.' He shrugged. 'Not my usual line, but I like a challenge, so I worked it out. Told him to go to that banquet, then jumped him during the fish course. Cut him up something horrid, but no stab wounds. Screamed very life-like too, 'cause I hadn't said I was going to bleed him. Then I tells him to lie still, and his servants run in and drag him out before anyone gets a close eye on him. Worked like a charm. He was off to

Marienburg in a closed coach before they'd given up searching for me.'

Darius snorted. 'This Echert better hope we all die then, for you've betrayed his secret to us.'

Dieter's eyes blazed. 'I ain't never betrayed a client. Echert's dead. Died of the lover's pox two months after he ran, stupid berk. All that money he paid me, wasted.'

Pavel, Hals and Augustus laughed. Darius shrugged. Jergen stared off into the darkness beyond the fire.

'Well,' said Reiner. 'While you may not intend to stay with us long, Master Neff, you may find the riddle of Manfred's poison harder to crack than you expect, so welcome. We are glad to have a man of your skills with us.'

'I take care of my own skin,' said Dieter. 'The rest of ye can fend for yourselves.'

Reiner sighed. 'Then you likely *will* be taking care of your own skin, for no one else will be eager to do it. Carry on, lads. I've done my bit.' He sat back and took a mouthful of stew, then swallowed hastily as he had a thought. 'Er, one last thing.'

The others looked up.

'I tell you now so there's no trouble later,' Reiner said. 'One of our number is a woman.'

'What?' said Rumpolt, looking around at the others.

Reiner laughed. 'Not these ruffians. Our archer, who plays page to Manfred at the moment. We have kept her secret, and so shall you.'

'An archer?' asked Augustus, dismayed. 'She's a soldier?'

'Aye. A better one than some men I've known,' said Reiner. 'But hear me. If you get any ideas, forget them. The man who hurts her answers to me.'

'And me,' said Hals and Pavel in unison.

'And me,' said Jergen.

The new men looked at the others curiously, but nodded.

As Reiner returned to his stew he heard Augustus murmuring unhappily to Hals and Pavel.

'I know it ain't right,' said Hals. 'But she won't listen.'

'And she can shoot,' added Pavel.

Jergen spoke in Reiner's ear. 'Someone watches us.'

Reiner looked around. 'Who? Where?'

'I know not,' said Jergen. He nodded toward the river, in the blackness beyond Manfred's camp. 'But they are there.'

Reiner stared in the direction the swordsman had indicated. He could see nothing. He shivered.

THREE
The City of Gardens

AFTER FIVE DAYS' sailing up the river, while every eye swept the banks for furtive shadows, Manfred's boats, on the morning of the sixth day, rounded a bend and Reiner saw the towering crater that was Talabheim's impregnable natural defence. It was an awe-inspiring sight, rising hundreds of feet above the carpet of trees, and of so wide a circumference that the wall didn't appear to curve. It stretched like an endless cliff into the distance in both directions.

Augustus beamed from the rail. 'Taal's fortress.'

'Taal's drinking cup, more like,' said Hals, laughing.

Augustus chuckled good-naturedly.

An hour later, oar-boats guided them to slips among the docks of Taalagad, Talabheim's port, a weathered little town huddled in the shadow of the crater wall. It was a damp, dingy place that seemed to consist of nothing but warehouses and taverns. The taverns were crowded, but the warehouses were deserted, for trade appeared to have come to a standstill. Piles of crates and barrels and burlap sacks sat under tarpaulins on docks and around the tariff houses, unclaimed.

The lords and their retinues disembarked and made themselves presentable while word of the legation's arrival was sent into Talabheim. Reiner looked up at the crater, which filled nearly all his vision. A road zigzagged a third of the way up it to a huge fortified gate, the entrance to Talabheim's fabled Wizard's Way, so called for the rumour that it had been cut by sorcery, not human labour.

After a long wait, a company in the red and white of the Talabheim City Guard made their way down the road, pikes glinting, to the docks. They looked tired and haggard, like men too long at the front of some great war. With them was a long-bearded ancient in rich robes and a velvet cap. He bowed low to Manfred.

'Greetings, Count Valdenheim,' he said. 'I am Lord Dalvern Neubalten, the countess's herald. I welcome you to Talabheim on behalf of her Excellency and her court.'

'You are most gracious, Lord Neubalten,' said Manfred, bowing in turn. 'We thank her for her courtesy on behalf of her emperor, Karl Franz.'

'Thank you, count,' said Neubalten. 'The countess has been informed of the reason for your visit, and grants Lord Teclis and your legation leave to enter the city. She asks, however, that you instruct your companies to hold here in Taalagad until you have met with her. I will escort you to her when you are ready.'

'Certainly,' said Manfred, bowing again. He withdrew to speak with Lord Schott and the others.

'Leave our companies outside?' asked Lord Schott. 'In this flea pit? Does she mistrust us?'

'She insults us if so,' said Grand Master Raichskell. 'We are sent by Karl Franz himself.'

'Merely caution, I think,' said Manfred. 'It is a foolish leader who lets two hundred armed men into her city without parley.'

'But did not Lord Teclis say it was dangerous within?' said Lord Boellengen, looking nervously up toward the gate. 'Will we be safe?'

'Sigmar is with us,' snorted Father Totkrieg. 'There is nothing to fear.'

Half an hour later, the companies quartered by the river, the emissaries gathered in their carriages, their servants and luggage in a train behind them, ready to travel.

'You'll walk, Hetsau,' said Manfred, returning to his carriage with the herald. 'Lord Neubalten will ride with me.'

'Very good, m'lord,' said Reiner. He bowed Neubalten into the coach.

Manfred pulled Reiner a few paces away and lowered his voice. 'Your duties begin now,' he said. 'You will be at my shoulder, quill in hand, when we are presented to the countess, but your true purpose will be to observe her court, noting names and temperaments. Whatever occurs within Talabheim, you can be sure the members of her Excellency's parliament will be trying to gain advantage over their fellows by it. We will use these rivalries to foil the Talabheimers' attempts to save themselves from their predicament.'

Reiner frowned. 'You don't want to save Talabheim? Then why have we come?'

'You misunderstand me,' said Manfred, impatient. 'That is precisely what I want. I want Teclis and the forces of the Reikland to be the ones to save Talabheim. You are here to make sure that Talabheim finds it impossible to save itself.' He nodded at the city guards, lined up to escort them into the city. 'These woodsmen have become a deal too independent of late. They must learn that they are better off within the Empire than without it.'

'I shall do my best, m'lord,' said Reiner. He smiled as Manfred returned to his coach. Ever the manipulator, Manfred. He undoubtedly calculated the political effect of what he had for breakfast every morning.

Reiner joined the baggage train with the rest of the Blackhearts, sitting with Augustus and Gert on a provision wagon as the procession got under way, climbing the zigzag road to the immense fortified gate known as the High Watch. They passed under its cannon emplacements and the sharp points of its portcullis, then disappeared into the darkness of its wide mouth, as if marching down the gullet of some legendary behemoth.

TALABHEIM HAD GONE mad.

Even from the exit of the Wizard's Way, high on the interior wall of the crater, Reiner knew it. Columns of smoke rose all over the city, which stretched out below him, rising to a pall of murk that hid the crater's far edge, thirty miles away. Strange colours glowed within the cap of smoke like occluded lightning, but there was no accompanying thunder. Reiner had seen the like once before, over a Kislev battle field, when his pistol company had faced a horde of northmen. He shivered. Hals and Augustus spat and made the sign of the hammer. Darius cringed away from the clouds.

The city climbed the inside of the crater almost to the Wizard's Way, tumble-down hovels and primitive dwellings cut into the very rock lapped up the slope like filthy debris left by a retreating flood. Below these, growing larger and more prosperous away from the wall, were houses and buildings and manor houses, and everywhere, parks and gardens and open spaces. It was the greenest city Reiner had ever seen. At the edge of his smoke-hampered vision it dwindled away entirely into forest and wild land – the Taalgrunhaar, Taal's sacred forest, that featured so prominently in jokes about Talabecmen and their wild revels.

As the legation wound down a switch-back road that matched that on the outside of the crater, Reiner saw narrow paths leading off into the nearly vertical slum. Furtive figures haunted these alleys, ducking behind precariously perched shacks as the procession passed. The air reeked of death and rotting vegetation and stranger things, and Reiner's ears were assaulted by wailing cries and distant crashes. The wall of the crater loomed over his shoulder menacingly. He felt hemmed in, trapped inside a madhouse.

Things only got worse as they reached level ground. The tree-lined street their escort led them down had once been handsome and well kept. Now many of its buildings were nothing but charred skeletons. Others had all their windows smashed. Furtive faces peered from them, watching the passing legation with empty eyes. A pile of naked bodies burned in a square – men, women and children – all ablaze. One body had a fang-toothed face where his stomach should have been. Corpses hung from a gibbet erected before a livery stable.

Reiner heard a choking sob beside him. Augustus was staring around, tears running into his red beard. 'What has become of it?' he moaned. 'What has become of it?'

Reiner nodded. 'Aye, terrible.'

'What do you know of it?' the pikeman snarled. 'This is my home! And it's–' A sob cut off his words. 'It's murdered. Murdered!'

A man in rags broke from a house and bolted for an alley. His head was a sack of loose flesh that bobbled with each step.

Peasants armed with clubs chased him down and beat him mercilessly as he screeched and wept. The Talabheim guards marched on impassively.

Augustus turned away. 'This cannot be. Talabheim is the fairest city in the Empire. The city of gardens. The–' He stopped suddenly. Across the street was a gutted tavern. Only the front door and the placard above it, blackened beyond reading, still stood. 'The Stag and Garland!' Augustus cried. 'And is old Hans the barman dead then?' His fists clenched. 'Someone must pay for this. Someone must die for this.'

Closer to the city centre the streets became more populated. Priests of Morr, their faces covered in burlap, threw bodies onto pyres. Brazen thieves carried paintings and silver out of houses. A man with tin charms in the shape of hammers cried that they were 'blessed by the Grand Theogonist himself,' and guaranteed to protect against madness and mutation. He did a brisk business. Gaunt peasants crowded around a wild-eyed priest of Taal, who shook a wooden staff wrapped in holly leaves.

'Are not the waking of the trees and the destruction of the Sigmarite temple signs of Taal's displeasure?' he cried. 'Taal is angry with us for allowing the upstart Sigmar to be worshipped in his land. This is Taal's land, and we have betrayed him by kissing the feet of the foreign tyrant Karl Franz. Repent, ye faithless ones! Repent!'

Before his words faded out behind Manfred's train, the bellowing of a priest of Sigmar haranguing another mob reached Reiner's ears.

'Is not the waking of the trees proof that Taal is a daemon?' he roared. 'What but a daemon would set its servants upon its worshippers? What but a daemon would drive men mad and twist their bodies with foul mutations? What but a daemon would raze Sigmar's new temple? We must bring torches to the forests, brave Sigmarites, and destroy their hidden temples as they have destroyed ours!'

'Sigmarite scum!' growled Augustus under his breath.

'You speak against Sigmar?' asked Gert, moustache bristling. 'You seek a black eye?'

'That's enough,' said Reiner sharply.

'But captain, did y'not hear–?' said Gert.

Reiner cut him off. 'I heard a pair of ranting fools. And you are a pair of fools if you listen to them. Now have done.'

Both Gert and Augustus opened their mouths to protest, but a sudden movement to their right distracted them. Hollow cheeked men, women and children spilled from an abandoned building, hands outstretched.

'Food, sirs!' bleated one.

'A pfennig, for your pity,' called another.

'Help us,' wept a woman.

The guards shoved and kicked them back, knocking them to the cobbles. The beggars lay where they fell, clutching their bloody heads and wailing. They hadn't been beggars long. Their clothes were dirty, but still whole, but already hope was gone from their eyes.

'Can these truly be men of Talabheim?' asked Augustus, dismayed. 'Talabheimers don't beg. They don't back down from a fight. What ails them? They should be robbing us blind. Or trying to.'

'They've seen too much, I'll warrant, and it's broken them,' said Gert. 'I've seen it before. An entire company of Ostermark sword. They'd fought some... thing, in the defence of Hergig, and though they beat it, afterwards it was as if the thing had torn out their hearts and left the rest of them whole. Worse than death, to my mind.'

Augustus shivered, then nodded. The two men seemed to have forgotten their argument.

In the centre of a weedy park, a jeering crowd surrounded a naked girl tied to a stake. They threw cobbles and clods of dirt at her as she wailed and begged for mercy. There were bundles of tinder at her feet and a fellow in a pointed red hood danced around her with a torch. She was very beautiful, though her face and body were bruised, but her legs were furred and hoofed like a goat's, and she had a hairless purple tail. Her high thin voice penetrated through the howls of the mob.

'Please! I ain't done nothing,' she whined. ''Tisn't my fault. It just happened.'

The hooded man touched his torch to the hay and it went up in a rush. The girl began to scream. Reiner turned his head, but the sound stayed with him.

All along their route were barricaded streets manned by weary guards, some wearing the red and white of the city watch, others in the livery of this lord or that, or in no uniform at all, protecting streets or neighbourhoods from invasion. At some streets it seemed the guards and barricades were there to keep the inhabitants in. Beyond these was wholesale destruction, and slinking shapes that might once have been men.

Further on, they passed between the great grey stone edifice of the Grand Courthouse of Edicts, where the Talabheim parliament convened, and the Hollows, in the bowels of which those convicted in the courts served out their sentences. The gibbets and punishment cages in the forecourt of the courthouse were so thickly hung with corpses that it looked like a butcher's window.

Rising over the low, dormered buildings of the Law district, Reiner could see the buildings of the temple quarter, known as the City of the Gods – golden Myrmidia brandishing a spear at the top of a granite column, Shallya's slender white steeple, Taal's upthrusting rowans, and high above them all, Sigmar's stern stone bell-towers. It looked a calm, serene place, until Reiner noticed the pillars of smoke rising among the spires.

Soon after, the procession came to a high stone wall with a large, well-defended gate. Knights on horseback sat at parade rest before it, and trebuchets were mounted on turrets to either side. Over the wall Reiner could see the gables of fine houses and the tops of tall trees. A procession of priests of Morr was exiting the gate. They carried a handsome coffin. Reiner smirked. The rich, it seemed, were not burned like tinder in city squares.

The captain of their escort exchanged words with the gate captain, and Manfred's train passed once again into another world. The horror and clamour of the merchant district fell away instantly, replaced by quiet calm and stately beauty. Large, elegant manor houses surrounded by extravagant gardens lined the empty street. Everywhere upon the houses were swirling designs of oak leaves, vines and acorns, and ornate beam ends shaped like the heads of stags, boars, and bears. There was no one abroad in the neighborhood, and Reiner began to realise that what he had mistaken for calm was actually paralysis. The nobles hid in their homes, waiting for the storm to pass.

The procession came to a stop before another high stone wall, even more well defended than the previous one, and after more challenges and conferring, they were admitted. Inside was a grand estate, with extensive grounds, gardens, groves and out-buildings and, in the centre, a sprawling, ivy-covered old manor house, as big as any five of the noble houses they had just passed stuck together. And indeed, that was exactly what it looked like. Reiner could count at least seven distinct architectural styles in the portions he could see, representing additions made in as many centuries.

'This is the countess's residence?' he asked, turning to Augustus, confused.

The pikeman nodded. 'Aye, the Grand Manor.'

'But, but she doesn't live in a castle?'

''Course she does,' said Augustus. 'Look around you.' He swept his hand around toward the walls of the crater, now miles away, but still visible through the trees in all directions. 'The greatest castle in the Empire.'

'Ah, of course,' said Reiner.

'Was a castle once,' said Augustus. 'Back in Talgris's time, when the crater wasn't fully tamed. You can still see the old keep there.' He pointed toward the centre of the manor, where a fat, rough-hewn barrel keep reared its ugly, crenellated head over the civilized gables and dormers of the later additions. 'Still use it for the dungeon and the treasure vaults, and kitchens and the like too, but nobody quarters there any more. Cold and drafty.'

Their escort led them up a tree-lined avenue past barracks buildings and fortified sentry posts, and came to a halt in a gravelled forecourt on the west side of the Grand Manor where a company of the countess's greatswords waited for them.

Manfred stepped out of his carriage with Lord Neubalten, and Reiner took up his place three paces behind them. The courtyard grew hushed as Teclis joined them. It seemed Talabecmen were no more immune to the awe elves inspired than their Reikland cousins.

The legation crossed to tall double doors, where the greatswords waited for them, all dressed in green and buff, with brightly polished steel breastplates. Their captain, a tall man with a narrow head of close-cropped blond hair and the grim eyes of a veteran, stepped forward and saluted.

'Lord Teclis, Count Valdenheim,' said Neubalten, 'May I present Heinrich von Pfaltzen, captain of Countess Elise's personal guard.'

The captain clicked his heels and bowed, doing his best to remain unmoved by Teclis's presence. 'M'lords,' he said. 'The countess awaits you.'

The legation, escorted by the greatswords, followed von Pfaltzen through a series of broad carpeted corridors. Rich tapestries of woodland scenes were hung at regular intervals, and archways opened into richly appointed sitting rooms, libraries and galleries. It was magnificent, as befitted the seat of a countess, yet it maintained a slightly rustic ambiance, like that of some royal hunting lodge.

At a pair of tall, intricately-carved wooden doors, von Pfaltzen was challenged by two halberdiers in elaborate green and buff livery. He announced that Lord Teclis of Ulthuan and Count Manfred of Emperor Karl Franz's court in Altdorf and their retinue begged the countess's permission to enter.

The halberdiers saluted, and said that the countess granted her guests leave to enter, then swung open the heavy doors.

Lord Neubalten bowed Teclis, Manfred and the party into a high, handsome throne room. A green and yellow stained-glass clerestory painted the long room with mellow golden light. Rows of wood-clad pillars carved to resemble tree trunks rose up to spreading branches that supported a patterned green ceiling so that the room looked like a sun-dappled forest glade.

The herald led the party down between the pillars to a raised dais under a green velvet canopy, while von Pfaltzen and his men took up positions to either side of it.

Upon the dais, sitting on an ornate oak throne, was Countess Elise Krieglitz-Untern, ruler of the free city of Talabheim. After all the beauty of the Grand Manor she was a bit of a disappointment. Squat and broad and dowdy, even in a green and gold dress of exquisite workmanship, with lumpy features in a round, red face, she looked more like a fish-wife than a countess.

No wonder the common folk were reputed to love her, thought Reiner. They could claim her for their own. The one evidence of her nobility was her bearing. She carried herself with enough regal hauteur for three countesses – her posture ramrod straight, her bulbous nose high and proud, her eyes hard and flashing.

Noble courtiers stood in clusters around the dais. Everyone was staring at Teclis, who seemed to glow with his own inner light in the shadowy green room. Even the countess stared.

Lord Neubalten stepped forward and began announcing the names of those who came before the countess, giving all their titles and honours. Bored, Reiner glanced around the room, doing as Manfred had ordered, trying to judge the character and importance of the lords and ladies of the countess's court by their dress and manner. That one with the neatly trimmed beard was undoubtedly a pompous ass. And that one, with the slouching shoulders, a born rogue if ever there was. And the woman standing behind the pillar with the young lord at her side was...

Reiner's heart stopped. The woman was Lady Magda Bandauer, the devious witch who, when he had last been in her presence, had tried to kill him with the power of the cursed banner, Valnir's Bane. Reiner's hand went to the hilt of his sword, but then he released it. The bitch certainly deserved to be hacked to pieces, but perhaps this was not the place. What was she doing here, he wondered? Did these poor fools know the evil they had welcomed into their court?

Magda turned, as if she felt Reiner's eye upon her. Her gaze swept past him at first, then jerked back, and the look of fear that sprang to her face was gratifying, even if her discovery of him was unfortunate. They eyed each other silently across the throne room before the voice of the countess brought Reiner back to the business at hand.

'Lord Teclis,' she was saying. 'Wisest of the fair, most benevolent counsellor of men, we welcome you to our humble court and to the free city of Talabheim, jewel of Talabecland.'

Teclis inclined his head. 'I thank you, countess.' His voice was soft, but carried with unnatural resonance.

'And welcome also to you, Count Valdenheim,' she said in a much colder tone. 'Though we admit bafflement at your presence here with so great a force and with no prior notice of your coming.'

Manfred bowed low. 'Thank you, countess, and I beg you to accept my apology for this unheralded visit. We come at the great Teclis's request, and with the most peaceful of intentions. The fair one warned Karl Franz that some great evil had befallen Talabheim, and in a spirit of brotherly concern, the Emperor has sent this humble embassy to give you what assistance we can.'

The countess's face remained impassive, but Reiner could see that she was taking Manfred's diplomatic hyperbole for what it was worth. 'We are moved by the Emperor's concern, but there was no need for him to trouble himself. While we would welcome the wisdom of Lord Teclis at any time, we have the situation well in hand. We expect to divine the cause of this disturbance shortly, and are fully capable of defending our city until that hour comes.'

'You do not have the situation in hand,' said Teclis, as softly as before. 'The currents of Chaos in Talabheim daily grow stronger, your subjects die in the streets, and you haven't the manpower to stop this, only to protect the less affected neighbourhoods and the homes of the wealthy. And if the cause is what I believe it to be, not even your greatest scholars can put it right.'

Reiner saw the countess's eyes flare at this bald statement of fact, but there was little she could say. Teclis was an elf. He had no need to trade in courtesies, for his status was unaffected by political manoeuvring. He had seen many emperors come and go, and would likely see three more ascend the throne in Altdorf. 'We welcome any aid you can give us, great one,' she said through tight lips. 'But if, as you say, there is nothing human efforts can do, would it not have been just as well for you to come alone?'

Manfred spoke up before Teclis could reply. 'The Emperor would not allow so noble a guest to travel alone within his domain. Nor would he allow the niceties of courtesy to delay aid for our fair sister Talabheim if it were necessary. We came in force, but with the hope that we would not be needed. And while your soldiers may indeed have the situation well in hand, there is no reason to turn away reserves when they are here to help.'

'To interfere, you mean,' said the countess. 'To take credit for Talabheim's victory over this trouble.'

'Countess,' said Manfred. 'I assure you...'

'And I assure you that your help is not needed. You have delivered the great Teclis to us, and we thank you for that. You may now retire, certain that we will keep him safe and will bring no shame upon the Empire while he is our guest. Thank you.'

It was an unmistakable dismissal, but Manfred only bowed and drew a rolled parchment from his doublet. 'Countess, it grieves me that I must remind you that, while Talabheim is a free city, it still resides within Talabecland, and that Talabecland is a state of the Empire, subject to its laws and to the commands of its Emperor.' He held up the parchment. 'Though gently worded, this document is not an offer of aid, but a command from Karl Franz, signed by his own hand, ordering your government to allow his representatives to assist you until they have determined that the danger to Talabheim, and the Empire, has passed.'

Manfred passed the parchment to Neubalten, who took it to the countess. She passed it to a scribe that scurried forward from behind the dais. He read it quickly, then whispered in her ear while her knuckles grew white upon the arms of her throne.

'This is an outrage,' she said at last. 'The Emperor oversteps Imperial law. The duchies have the ruling of their own lands, and need brook no interference from the Emperor unless it is a matter that affects the whole of the Empire. This is clearly Talabheim's problem, and–'

'Forgive me, countess,' said Teclis. 'I take no sides in the affairs of men, but you are incorrect. Though this disturbance happens in Talabheim, if unchecked it will affect not only Talabecland and the Empire, but also the stability of the whole world. I would not be here else.'

The countess paled. 'Is it truly so serious?'

Teclis nodded gravely. 'It is.'

'Then,' she said, flashing a sharp look at Manfred, 'on your authority, fair one, and your authority alone, do I submit to this unwished-for interference by these foreign lords.'

'Thank you, countess,' said Teclis. 'I would meet with those of your court most concerned with this affair at your earliest convenience, to learn what they have learned of it.'

'Certainly,' said the countess. 'I will call an emergency meeting of the parliament tonight. We will make enlightening you and the Emperor's embassy our business. Until then, if you will follow Lord Neubalten, he will make all arrangements for your lodging.'

Teclis and Manfred and the rest of the Reiklanders bowed and stepped back.

'Thank you, countess,' said Teclis.

'Most gracious, your eminence,' said Manfred.

As the party followed Neubalten out of the throne room, Reiner leaned into Manfred. 'M'lord, do you recall Lady Magda Bandauer?'

'How could I not?' said Manfred, frowning. 'The woman brought my brother to war against me. Why?'

'She is here,' said Reiner. 'With the young man in blue and burgundy to the left of the dais.'

Manfred looked discretely over his shoulder, then nodded, his face grim. 'I see.'

'M'lord,' said Reiner. 'It would give me great pleasure if you were to order me to remove her.'

'And it would give me great pleasure to so order you,' said Manfred. 'Unfortunately, the young man is Baron Rodick Untern and Lady Magda wears his colours. As much as I might wish to destroy my brother's corrupter, it would be impolitic at this moment to murder the wife of the countess's cousin.'

FOUR
A Great Opportunity

THAT EVENING, THE Parliament of Talabheim met in a large wood-panelled chamber within the Grand Courthouse of Edicts. Countess Elise sat at the northernmost seat of a large U-shaped table. The members of her parliament – representatives of Talabheim's noble families, the merchant guilds, the city's temples, the colleges of magic, the countess's exchequer, as well as the three generals of the Hunters' council, Christoph Stallmaier, commander of the Taalbaston, Detlef Kienholt, commander of the city guard, and Joerg Hafner, commander of the militia, her minister of trade, and her minister of public works, filled the other seats. Extra seats had been added to accommodate Teclis and Manfred, and more were set along the walls for the other Reiklanders. Reiner sat with them, trying to put names, faces and titles together.

Arch Lector Farador, the voice of Sigmar in Talabheim, was speaking. 'The brothers of the Order of the Cleansing Flame have wrung many confessions from captured mutants, but little have come of them. It appears some lied, even under torture, and though the confessions of others led us to new nests of mutants and heretics, we have yet to find the villain who has set this curse upon us.'

'The brothers of Taal have not been idle either,' chimed in Heinrich Geltwasser, the temple of Taal's representative. 'Though we scorn the uncivilised methods of the Sigmarites, we have prayed to Father Taal unceasingly, and performed ceremonies to quiet the trees. We have admittedly had little success.' He shot a dark look at Farador. 'Too many of our faithful are being drawn away to other religions, and our prayers haven't the strength they once did.'

'Prayer cannot take the place of action,' said Farador. 'If you had been hunting mutants instead of dancing naked in the forest, this crisis might already be over.'

'Do you mock the mysteries of Taal?' cried Geltwasser.

'If the exchequer weren't so tight-fisted,' said Lord Otto Scharnholt, a thick-jowled dandy with rings on every finger, who was Talabheim's minister of trade, 'we would have more troops in the streets and they would be better outfitted.'

M'lord has grown rich from the office, thought Reiner, eyeing his broad belly. Takes a cut from every cargo that comes through Taalagad, no doubt.

'And where does the minister of trade expect these monies to come from?' asked Lord Klaus Danziger, the Countess's exchequer, a sober, long-faced fellow in a black doublet of the plainest cut. 'The treasury is empty, m'lord. Empty!'

'Fathers, lords, please.' Teclis's soft voice easily cut through their barking. 'Your attempts to quell the disturbance are to be commended, but the madness and mutations are not the result of a lack of faith, and cannot be defeated by soldiers. A great eruption of Chaos energy has occurred somewhere in the city. Only when the eruption is found and... capped, will the mutations cease and the madness fade.' He looked around the table with his penetrating stare. 'Here is what I must know. In what area of the city are the mutations most prevalent? Have any ancient ruins or strange artefacts been uncovered within the limits of the city? Have any weapons or artefacts of great power been stolen? Any of these may point to the source of the disturbance.'

All the parliament members began speaking at once.

'Pfaffenstrasse crawls with mutants,' said the master of the wool merchants' guild.

'Pfaffenstrasse has nothing on Girlaedenplatz,' said the master of the union of coopers and wainwrights. 'They are thickest there.'

'It's those filthy peasants in the Tallows,' said Scharnholt. 'My tenants there have gone mad. They've burned down my property. The trees...'

'There are none in the Manor district,' said Danziger primly. 'They wouldn't dare.'

'It comes from the woods,' said a Sigmarite.

'It comes on the wind,' said a Taalist.

'It comes from the wells,' said the master of the bakers' guild.

'Gentlemen, please!' The countess rapped her mace of office on the table. 'You will all be given a chance to speak. Now–'

'Your pardon, countess,' said Teclis, holding up his hand.

The room quieted and turned to him. Teclis pointed a long finger at a haughty mage in green and gold robes. The man swallowed nervously.

'Your name, magus?' asked Teclis.

'I, lord? Er, I am Magister Lord Dieter Vogt, representative of Talabheim's College of Jade Magic.'

'You said something just now, magister lord,' said Teclis. 'Please repeat it.'

'Er, well, I, I said some members of our college found a large stone recently. But nothing came of it,' he added hurriedly. 'It had no power at all.'

Teclis placed his hands flat on the table. 'I see.' There was the faintest tremor in his voice. 'And where did you find this stone?'

Magister Lord Vogt coughed, acutely aware that Teclis was displeased. 'Er, well, when the Temple of Sigmar collapsed...'

'The temple did not collapse!' cried Arch Lector Farador. 'It was destroyed by cultists!'

'It wasn't,' said the minister of public works. 'You built it over a sink hole. It fell in, then smashed through into the caves.'

'A sign,' said Taalfather Geltwasser, 'as if any were needed, that the Sigmarites' faith is founded on unsound doctrine.'

'What caves are these?' Teclis asked the minister of public works.

'Er, well, yer lordship,' said the minister, ducking his head. 'We didn't know about 'em until the temple opened 'em up, but there are caves under the city. Haven't yet had a chance to look about much, what with all this madness.'

'The caves are where we found the stone, m'lord,' said Magister Lord Vogt. 'When men were sent into them to look for survivors, it was discovered that the stones of the temple had smashed open an ancient crypt set into the floor of the cave. Our college was asked to determine if the crypt was an arcane threat.'

'It was elven,' said Teclis.

Lord Vogt looked up in surprise. 'Er, yes. It was. How...'

'And it contained a rune-covered stone the height of a man.'

'Indeed, fair one,' said the mage. 'Much of the crypt was destroyed by the falling temple, and the runestone was dislodged from its pedestal, but miraculously it was intact.'

Teclis breathed a sigh of relief at that. 'So you have the stone then.'

Vogt nodded. 'Yes, lord. Our scholars thought it might have some magical properties, and so brought it back to our lodge to examine it, but it had no magic and seemed to serve no higher purpose.'

'No higher purpose than maintaining the stability of the world,' said Teclis. He sat back, pressing his chest with his hand as if he were in pain, then looked up. 'What your scholars uncovered is a waystone. It appears magically inert because its purpose is to draw away magic. It absorbs emanations of magical energy – Chaos energy – and shunts it into... another place. Its removal is the cause of Talabheim's trouble. Without it, the source of the Chaos energy under your city spreads unchecked.'

'But, Lord Teclis,' said Magister Lord Vogt. 'Talabheim is one of the least magical places in the Empire. It takes a great deal of concentration to cast even the simplest spell here. At least that was true until... ah. I see.'

'Yes,' said Teclis. 'Since the plague of madness, you have found your powers greatly increased. But the risk of spell work has increased as well, and many mages have gone mad. Is this not the case?'

Vogt looked reluctant to speak. The countess spoke for him. 'Ten mages have been put to death in the past week, having succumbed to madness. I have ordered a moratorium on the practice of the art until the crisis has passed.'

Teclis nodded. 'This crater, in which Krugar, chief of the Talabec tribe, founded your city thousands of years ago, was formed thousands of years before that, when a great meteor of pure warpstone struck the earth. My forefathers, whose land this was at that time, placed the waystone above the shattered fragments of the meteor in order to make the land habitable again. There are many such waystones buried around the world, capping similar loci of Chaos energies. The danger when one of these waystones is removed is not just to the land around it, but to the world as a whole. For just as the removal of one link in a shirt of mail weakens it, so the loss of one waystone weakens all others and causes the weave of protection they knit around the world to unravel. If left uncapped, the emanations which poison your city will spread like ripples in a pond, unseating other nearby waystones, which will in turn unseat further waystones until the earth becomes the endless nightmare of madness that it was when the rifts of Chaos first opened, eons ago.' Teclis coughed and touched his chest again. 'And this time, the elves could not contain it, for we are not what we once were.'

The countess and the parliament paled at this vision of apocalypse.

'You are fortunate,' Teclis continued. 'I was near enough to feel the eruption when the stone was dislodged, for only an elf mage with a knowledge of the old lore can reseat the stone. If you had had to send to Ulthuan for assistance I might have come too late.' He turned to the countess. 'I will take the waystone and prepare it. In the meantime, the crypt that held it should be cleared of rubble, and preparations made to seal it once I have reset the stone. Too much time has been wasted already. Men die needlessly as we speak.'

'Yes, Lord Teclis,' said the countess, inclining her head. 'It shall be done. Magister Lord Vogt, escort our guest to your lodge.'

Vogt stood and bowed. 'Yes, countess. Right away.'

'THEY'VE LOST IT!' laughed Manfred as he slammed into the coach and fell back into his seat. 'Half a tonne and as tall as a man and they've lost it!'

Reiner had been sitting in Manfred's coach for the past hour outside the tree shrouded compound of the college of jade magic, waiting while Manfred, Teclis, Magus Nichtladen, and the countess – the only persons the secretive mages would allow in – went with Magister Lord Vogt to retrieve the stone.

'Lost it?' he asked.

'Aye!' chuckled Manfred. 'Mages scurrying around like housemaids looking in cupboards and attics. But it's gone. Stolen most likely.' He rubbed his hands together.

'And you are pleased?'

'Eh?' said Manfred. 'Don't be a fool! Of course I'm pleased. If Vogt had produced it, the Jade college would have got the credit, but now we have as much chance as any to find it. This is a great opportunity.'

'Your concern for the citizens of Talabheim is admirable, m'lord,' said Reiner dryly.

'My concern,' said Manfred, 'is for the Empire as a whole, and if a few must die to ensure its stability over the long term, then I am prepared to take their deaths upon my conscience.'

Reiner smirked. 'Most noble of you.'

WHEN THEY RETURNED to the Law Quarter townhouse the countess had provided for the Reikland legation, they found Lord Danziger, the prim, black-clad exchequer, waiting for Manfred in the drawing room.

'If I might have a word with you in private, lord count?' he asked. His manner was as stiff as his high collar, and his posture as rigid.

'Certainly, Lord Danziger,' said Manfred. 'Hetsau, show his excellency to my quarters.'

When they were settled in Manfred's private rooms and Reiner had served Reikland wine, Danziger spoke.

'As the countess's treasurer,' he said, 'it pains me to see all the funds wasted so far attacking this problem from the wrong end. As you have seen, the parliament is a fractious group, too concerned with casting blame to take decisive action, and though I am loath to say it, I believe some members hope to profit by this trouble. That is why I come to you. You are a confidant of Karl Franz and of the great Teclis. I know you must hold the Empire's interests uppermost, and wish to bring an end to this unpleasantness as quickly as possible.'

'Indeed,' said Manfred, with every appearance of sincerity. 'And if you have some information that may help us to that end, I would be extremely pleased to hear it.'

'I believe I have, sir,' said Danziger. 'I, like most men of means in the city, have volunteered my house guard to assist in the protecting of those neighbourhoods that remain whole. When Teclis spoke of this "waystone" just now, I remembered an incident my captain, Gerde, related to me recently. It seemed nothing at the time. But now...'

'Please go on, m'lord,' said Manfred. Reiner could see him trying to mask his eagerness.

'Gerde was manning the Schwartz Hold barricades,' said Danziger. 'And just after midnight, he saw a group of men carrying a heavy burden into an old granary that had been burned down when the madness began. Gerde dispatched one of his men to follow them and see what they were about.'

'And what did this man discover?' asked Manfred.

'He returned after an hour, saying the thieves had carried their burden through a hole in the granary's cellar to the sewer below it. He trailed them through the sewers and catacombs below Talabheim, until they reached at last a place guarded by well-armed men, and he could follow no further.'

Manfred leaned in. 'This incident was not reported to the city guard?'

'I do not believe so,' said Danziger.

'Then only we know of this?'

'Aye, m'lord. And it would be wise to keep it so.' said Danziger. 'Talabheim is a city of intrigues, and telling one man a confidence is the same as telling a hundred. If we wish to strike swiftly we must remain covert.'

Manfred nodded. 'Very good. Then I will strike tomorrow morning, before sunrise. Send your man to me that he may guide us. Thank you for this information, Lord Danziger.'

'Er, by your leave, sir, if I added my men to yours, I think we would be assured of success.'

Manfred smiled wryly. 'Certainly. Be here tomorrow at the fifth hour and we will see if we can find the stone.'

'Excellent,' said Danziger. 'Tomorrow morning then,' He stood and bowed crisply. Reiner escorted him to the door.

'You don't trust him, m'lord?' he asked, returning.

'As far as I can throw a horse,' said Manfred. 'That is why I ensured that he would accompany us.'

'By implying that you would rather he didn't.'

Manfred nodded. 'He could have meant to send us to our deaths. And had he allowed us to go alone I would have known that was what he intended. Now I know he plays another game.'

'He intends to use us to help capture the stone, and then take it and the credit for himself,' said Reiner. 'Just as you mean to use him for the same purpose.'

'You learn the craft well, Hetsau,' said Manfred.

'But what's to stop him from doing as he intends?' asked Reiner.

Manfred smiled. 'I shall bring Teclis.'

'Ah,' said Reiner. 'And Danziger dare not take the stone from the elf, while you may claim the credit of its recovery for Altdorf and yourself because it was you who brought the fair one here.'

'That is the hoped for outcome, yes,' said Manfred. 'But, just in case, I will have you and your Blackhearts along to make it a certainty.'

Reiner sighed as he collected the wine glasses. 'And you brand *me* rogue,' he said under his breath.

Manfred shot him a sharp look.

FIVE
Will a Fire Unmake It?

'ENJOYING THE HIGH life, captain?' asked Hals, sneering. 'Poncing about with counts and countesses and elves.'

'While we see to the luggage,' said Pavel.

'And the horses,' added Gert.

'And polish the boots,' said Franka.

'You needn't blame me for it,' said Reiner. 'It was Manfred's plan. Not mine.'

Reiner sighed. What would have been jovial banter in the days before Abel Halstieg's death was now in earnest. The poison of suspicion had curdled the Blackhearts' comradeship. He wished he could think of something to say that would make it as it had been, but when he knew one of them was a spy, and would report anything he said to Manfred, he was at a loss for words.

The Blackhearts stood shivering and rubbing their hands in the carriage yard behind the Reiklanders' Law Quarter townhouse. The sun had not yet risen and the morning mist swirling in the torchlight was bitter cold. They were dressed in the livery of Manfred's house guard – black doublet and breastplate painted with his white and gold lion – and armed with swords and daggers in addition to their preferred weapons. Augustus and Rumpolt were stealing curious glances at Franka in her soldier's kit, but said nothing. Darius and Dieter looked more ridiculous as soldiers than they had as surgeons.

Ten of Manfred's Nordbergbruche spearmen stood by them in two neat lines before their captain, a brawny youth named Baerich. They shot dirty looks at the Blackhearts, who slouched and yawned in utter disregard for military discipline.

There was a rap at the back gate and Captain Baerich opened it to admit Danziger and ten swordsmen, all in kit as plain and black as his own.

'We go rabbit hunting with this army?' muttered Hals. 'They'll hear us coming miles away.'

A few minutes later Manfred and Teclis stepped out of the house, followed by Teclis's guard. The elves had exchanged their snow white garb for dark blue surcoats worn over their gleaming armour. Teclis too was dressed for war, with a long, thin sword strapped to his back, though he still walked with his white staff.

Danziger gaped when he saw him. 'Lord… Lord Teclis comes?' he asked Manfred.

Manfred nodded gravely. 'Certainly. The thieves may have magic of their own. It would be foolish to attempt to wrest the waystone from them without a mage.'

Danziger licked his lips. 'Of course, of course.' But he looked suddenly much less enthusiastic about their venture.

Manfred smirked behind his back.

As Captain Baerich's men were opening the gate so that the party could get underway, there came a rumble of running boots from the alley, and the men in the yard went on guard.

Men in green and buff uniforms stopped in the gate, a smaller squad in blue and burgundy behind them. Reiner peered at them in the darkness and recognised Captain von Pfaltzen with fifteen of the countess's personal guard, and behind them Lord Rodick Untern, the countess's cousin – and Lady Magda's husband – with eight men of his own.

'What is this assembly?' demanded von Pfaltzen, panting from running. 'Where do you go so armed?'

Manfred sighed, annoyed. 'We go, captain, to recover the waystone.'

'You have learned its whereabouts?' von Pfaltzen asked, shocked.

'We follow a rumour.'

'And you neglected to inform the countess?' said Rodick. 'I find that very strange.' He had a high, piercing voice.

'We thought,' said Manfred, 'that the fewer persons party to the secret, the less the chance that those who hold the stone would learn of our coming. Apparently we were not covert enough.' He looked to Teclis for support, but the elf was glaring at them all with equal disgust.

'I think I see more reluctance to include Talabheim in the recovery of the stone,' said von Pfaltzen, 'than any concern for secrecy.'

'Yes,' said Rodick. 'You seek to cheat us of our share of the glory.'

'Am I invisible, sirs?' said Danziger, indignant. 'I am a Talabheim man. The city is represented.'

'Are you, m'lord?' asked Rodick sharply. 'Would not a true Talabheim man have informed his countess had he news of the city's salvation?'

'I must insist this venture not continue unless I and my men are part of it,' said von Pfaltzen.

'And as kin to the countess, I must come as well, in order to represent her interests.'

Manfred frowned. 'This is folly, gentlemen. You impede the great Teclis in his work. The thing requires stealth and swiftness. We are already too many. If your men are added, we will surprise no one.' He turned to Teclis. 'Fair one, can you not say something to make them understand that...'

'I care not who stays or who goes,' said Teclis coldly. 'As long as we go quickly. Too much time has been wasted already.'

'Very well,' said Manfred, reluctantly. 'All may come.'

As the companies began organising themselves into marching order, Reiner saw Danziger biting his lip, his eyes darting from one commander to the other, then to the man who was to guide them to the waystone.

Reiner stepped quickly to Manfred and whispered in his ear. 'M'lord, Danziger is not pleased. I don't believe he wishes to recover the stone under these circumstances. Given the chance, he will tell his man to lead us astray.'

'Then he cannot be given the chance,' said Manfred. He crossed to Danziger, speaking loudly. 'So, m'lord. Who is the fellow who will lead us? I would like to meet him.'

He put an arm around Danziger's shoulders, ignoring the exchequer's discomfort, and remained at his side as they, Teclis, von Pfaltzen and Rodick Untern, and the sixty-one men of their combined companies, marched from the townhouse, following the guide through the city under the strangely glowing clouds that capped the crater and hid the dawn.

The Blackhearts marched behind Reiner in surly silence, all but Augustus. 'Glad to see von Pfaltzen with us,' he said cheerfully. 'Didn't seem right, going behind the countess's back. A Talabheim man should lead in Talabheim.'

Danziger did not share Augustus's pleasure at von Pfaltzen's company. 'That's the trouble with men of this city,' Reiner heard him whisper in Manfred's ear. 'They think of nothing but their own advancement!'

'Aye,' agreed Manfred, without a hint of sarcasm. 'It makes it that much harder for honest men such as ourselves to get things done.'

Manfred beckoned to Reiner as Danziger and von Pfaltzen spoke to the chief guard at the Schwartz Hold barricade. 'In the unlikely event this bloated company manages to recover the waystone,' he whispered, 'you are to make sure that only Teclis or your Blackhearts or my Nordbergbruchers comes away with it.'

'Yes, m'lord,' said Reiner. 'Er, are we permitted to use force?'

'Eh? No!' said Manfred. 'We are unwelcome here as it is. Just be in the right place at the right time.'

'Very good, m'lord,' said Reiner, pleased that he managed to keep a straight face.

Manfred returned to Danziger's side before von Pfaltzen left him alone.

The further into the blighted neighbourhood the company went, the more oppressive the clouds above them seemed. A damp wind whimpered around them with an almost human voice. Just as the black curve of Talabheim's crater began to stand out against the grey sky behind it, the men reached the gutted granary. As the Blackhearts waited for the other companies to pick their way down into the wreckage, Reiner saw Dieter squinting over his shoulder.

'What is it?' he asked.

Dieter shot him a sullen look. 'Nothing, jagger.'

'Nothing? Or nothing you care to tell me?'

Dieter glared at him, then shrugged. 'We're being tailed.'

Reiner started to turn.

Dieter stopped him. 'Damn fool! Don't let on! Nothing to see anyway.'

Reiner looked sceptically at the thief. 'You can hear a tail in the midst of this army?'

'Can feel it,' said Dieter. 'Like an itch on the back of my neck.'

'So who is it, then?'

Dieter shrugged. 'Ain't shown himself. Canny cove, and no mistake.'

Reiner shivered and thought back to Jergen on the road to Talabheim, looking out into the night. He had said the same thing.

IT TOOK A quarter of an hour, but eventually all the soldiers descended into the burned-out cellar and through the black hole into the sewers. The companies lined up in single file on the narrow ledges that flanked the reeking channel, which ran down the centre of the low, barrel-vaulted brick tunnel. In the channel ran a sluggish brown stream, thick with bobbing lumps that Reiner didn't care to identify. It was bridged at regular intervals by granite slabs, and fed by pipes that ran down the walls. Rusting rungs set into the walls disappeared up into chimneys, which led to iron storm grates in the streets above.

Manfred lined up the Blackhearts and his Nordbergbruchers on the left side of the channel behind the elves, while Danziger's men and von Pfaltzen, with the countess's guard, lined up on the right. Rodick's men were somewhere in the darkness at the back. When all were in position, the companies marched forward behind Danziger's guide, who trotted ahead of them like a hound.

Rats scurried away before them, pushed into drainpipes and holes by the light of their torches. And there were other vermin. Fleeing human shadows disappeared down cross tunnels and skulking shapes peered at them from behind fallen rubble. Hunched forms huddled around meagre fires far down long corridors. Some were not quite human. Reiner got fleeting glimpses of twisted limbs, and misshapen heads, and heard distant subhuman growls. None seemed inclined to attack so large and well armed a force.

There were places where holes had been broken through the walls. These opened onto dirt, or shadowed cellars or flooded chambers. From one came a reek of rat so strong that it overpowered the omnipresent stink of the sewer. Reiner and the other Blackhearts exchanged uneasy looks, but said nothing. Some things were better not speculated upon.

At an intersection, above which were painted faded street names, Danziger's guide paused, frowning, as he looked left and right.

Reiner saw Danziger's eyes light up and he stepped forward. 'Er, Elger, did you not tell me you had made a left at Turringstrasse?'

The man blinked back at Danziger. 'Er, no, m'lord. Now that you say it, I believe it was a right.'

'Are you *certain?*' said Danziger, through clenched teeth.

Elger didn't take the hint. 'Yes, m'lord. A right at Turringstrasse. It's come back to me now.' He led the party right as Danziger tried to keep his face calm.

Reiner chuckled. Elger would be receiving a hiding later on, that was certain.

A short while later, they came to another rubble littered hole, and Danziger's swordsman entered it. The companies followed. It opened high in the wall of the cold cellar of an old warehouse. Smashed barrels and terracotta jars littered the floor. Wooden shelves had been propped against the wall under the hole as a ladder, and two of Danziger's men held it steady while the rest climbed gingerly down two at a time.

The storeroom was the first in an odd maze of interconnected basements, corridors, sections of unused sewer, earthen tunnels, crawlways and foundations, all with shattered walls and slumping ceilings propped up with bits of lumber. The company tramped up and down stairways and through knee-deep pools. Some passages were so low the soldiers must bend double, and some so narrow they must turn sideways. Reiner cringed at these choke points. Not the place to be caught if things went wrong.

The black circles of old fires were everywhere, as were broken bottles, half gnawed bones, and piles of stinking waste. Graffiti in several languages was scrawled on the walls. Reiner read, 'The countess is a whore!' and 'Peder, where are you?' and 'Rise and burn!' There were worse things too – evil-looking runes and smeared drawings of unmentionable acts and screaming faces. Withered corpses lay in the shadows, eyeless skulls staring at the soldiers as they passed.

At last, Danziger's guide stopped in an ancient corridor and pointed ahead to a pair of rotten wooden doors that hung off their hinges on the left-hand wall. 'Through them doors,' he said, 'is a big room with a hole in the far wall. Some guards are watching it. That's where they took the stone.'

'We must remove the guards before they raise an alarm,' said Danziger. 'Perhaps two of my–'

'I have a lad who can shoot a pigeon's eye out at fifty paces,' said Manfred, interrupting him. 'He–'

'There is no need,' said Teclis. He signalled two of his elves forward. They strode silently to the doors, nocking arrows on their bowstrings. They peered in, then, so swiftly it was hard to believe they had time to find their targets, they pulled and fired. Then they entered, fresh arrows ready. A moment later, they reappeared in the door and beckoned.

'We may proceed,' said Teclis, starting forward.

The companies followed. Reiner saw a flicker of motion further down the ancient corridor as he stepped through the doors, but there had been timid movements in the shadows all along the way. He ignored it.

The room inside was wide and deep, and reeked like stale beer. The left wall was hidden behind a row of enormous wooden vats. On the right, pyramids of giant hogsheads rose out of the darkness. Not one of them was still whole. Their faces had all been staved in, and dried, sticky puddles of evaporated beer pooled around them.

By the far wall was a small fire, illuminating two bodies which lay beside it, white arrows sticking from their necks. Behind the bodies, the thick stone wall was pierced, like a block of lard that had been impaled by a red-hot poker, with a perfectly circular man-high hole, its curves as shiny as glass. Frozen ripples of rock spread below it like melted wax. Reiner shuddered at the implications of the hole. Who or what had the power to do such a thing? And was the thing that had done it in the next room?

Reiner saw the same thoughts were going though Manfred's mind. Danziger, however, seemed to have no fear. He was urging his men forward eagerly.

'Come along,' he said. 'Before they know we are here.'

Manfred hesitated. 'Er, fair one? Is it–'

'Fear not,' said the elf. 'It is centuries old. The portal and halls beyond it are crudely warded, but I will clear them as we go. Proceed.'

Manfred nodded and signalled the Blackhearts to catch up to Danziger. Von Pfaltzen and Rodick moved their men up as well.

The weird hole opened into an old prison. The air inside smelled of smoke and made hazy halos around the torches. The elves led the way down a cell-lined corridor, Teclis moving his hands and whispering under his breath constantly. The air before him would occasionally shimmer like a soap bubble before popping with a relaxation of pressure Reiner could feel in his chest.

Three times men appeared far down the hall, then turned to run, and three times the elven archers cut them down before they could take a step.

'Might as well have left us at home,' grumbled Hals.

Teclis turned one of the dead men over with a pointed boot and pulled aside his shirt with the tip of his sword. A strange rune had been branded over the man's heart.

'A cultist,' said Teclis. 'This is the mark of the Changer of the Ways.'

Reiner swallowed, and though he was not by nature pious, he made the sign of the hammer. The men around him did the same. Teclis stepped over the corpse and moved on.

The hall ended in a stairwell. The smoke that filled the prison came from the stairs. Teclis and his elves crossed the room and began to descend them. The companies followed, coughing. To Reiner's annoyance, the elves seemed unaffected.

At the bottom was an arched doorway that glowed like the red mouth of hell. The Blackhearts and Danziger's men followed Teclis hesitantly through the door and onto a balcony that overlooked a deep, square pit. The other companies tried to crowd in behind them, but there was no room. The balcony was enclosed in a cage of iron bars. Left and right stairs led down to the pit. These had once had gates, but they had been ripped from their hinges. The smoke was so thick in the pit that at first all Reiner could make out was that an enormous fire blazed in its centre, but as he wiped his eyes he could see men surrounding the fire. They were raising their hands and chanting. A man in blue robes led them.

'The stone!' hissed Franka, pointing. 'They're destroying it!'

Reiner squinted. In the heart of the blaze was a roughly cut oblong menhir, black with soot.

Teclis smiled faintly. 'They may try,' he said. 'But it took a falling temple to unseat it. Will a fire unmake it?'

There was a hoarse shout from below as a chanter noticed the intruders. One of Teclis's elves shot him in the back and he crashed through the men and landed with his head in the blaze. The men at the fire leapt up, grabbing weapons and turning toward the balcony. The robed man began chanting and making elaborate motions with his arms.

The elves fired at him. Their arrows bent away as if pushed by a wind. The cultists charged, roaring, for the two stairways. There were at least fifty of them.

'Nordbergbruchers!' called Captain Baerich, drawing his sword. 'Hold the left!'

'No!' cried Manfred. 'My guard goes first!' He pushed Reiner forward as Baerich glared. 'You must get in ahead,' Manfred whispered. 'Go!'

Reiner grunted and drew his sword. 'Right lads, let's get stuck in.'

'And about time too,' growled Hals.

The Blackhearts charged down the left-hand stair with Manfred and the Nordbergbruchers behind them, as Danziger and his men ran down the right. The cultists met the companies at the bottom, a frenzied mob of frothing degenerates, armed with daggers and clubs, and bare of armour.

Pavel and Hals gutted two with their spears immediately. Reiner hacked at a fellow with purple boils covering his face, then kicked him back into his comrades. Jergen, the swordmaster, impaled one, then another, and cleaved the skull of a third. Augustus stabbed with his spear from the second row while Rumpolt, having fired his gun, now waved his sword around to no effect. Franka and Gert shot over their shoulders, burying shafts and bolts in unprotected chests and necks.

Behind them, Darius and Dieter did nothing but try to stay out of the way. There was little they could have done anyway, or any room for them to do it. The Blackhearts were in a tactically perfect position; they held the high ground in a narrow, easily defended choke point. All they had to do was hold here and...

Manfred prodded Reiner from behind. 'Go out!' he shouted. 'Get the stone! The spears will hold the stair.'

Reiner groaned. He didn't want to die because of Manfred's political rivalries, but the count's displeasure meant certain death, while wading into a crowd of crazed fanatics was only nearly certain.

'Blackhearts forward!' he called, and pushed into the mob with Jergen on his left and Pavel and Hals on his right. Gert and Augustus faced out on the flanks. Franka, Dieter and Rumpolt walked backwards, forming the back wall of their small square with the scholar Darius in the centre, eyes wide with fright.

'This is madness,' stuttered the scholar.

'Get used to it,' said Gert as cultists fell all around them. He shot a dirty look back at Manfred, who was calling encouragement from behind his Nordbergbruchers. 'Puttin' his pride before his duty, I'm thinkin'.'

'Seems we might die in a prison after all,' grumbled Hals.

Jergen decapitated two cultists with a single blow and they were through the throng. Some followed them, but most continued to press for the stairs. Von Pfaltzen's men were pushing onto the balcony from the stairwell and trying to get to the fight. Rodick and his house guards had somehow got in front of them and were fighting down the right-hand stair beside Danziger's swordsmen. Teclis stood at the bars, one fist clenched before him, while his elves shot shaft after shaft into the pit. As Teclis raised his arm the Tzeentch sorcerer jerked into the air above the fire, clawing at his throat as if the high elf's hand was throttling it. Then he dropped and bounced off the waystone into the flames. The way to the waystone was clear.

'Hals, Pavel, Augustus!' called Reiner, as the Blackhearts hurried forwards. 'Get your spearheads under the stone and lever it out of the blaze.'

While Reiner, Jergen and the others protected them, Hals, Pavel and Augustus thrust their spears into the fire and jammed them under the waystone, then pushed down, using the burning logs as fulcrums.

'All together, lads!' cried Hals.

It was hot work. The waystone was in the centre of the fire, and the spears were only just long enough to reach. The pikemen were instantly drenched in sweat, and Augustus's wild eyebrows were smoking at the ends. It was hot work defending them as well, for the cultists were leaving the stairs to stop them. Reiner, Jergen, Rumpolt and Dieter stood in a half-circle around Hals, Pavel and Augustus, protecting their backs from the seething mob, while Franka and Gert shot around them and Darius crouched behind, hiding his head and whimpering.

The cultists' numbers thinned quickly, however, for their retreat from the stairs had allowed the companies to enter the pit, and a sea of colourful uniforms and steel breastplates spilled across the floor to plough into their flanks.

Manfred was just pushing through the press to Reiner and crying, 'Well done, boys' when, with a final unison grunt, Hals, Pavel and Augustus at last levered the waystone off the burning lumber. The blackened menhir rolled to the floor on the opposite side of the fire, and rocked to a stop directly in front of the exquisite gold-trimmed boots of Lord Rodick Untern.

The young lord immediately put a foot upon it as if it was a dragon he had just slain and turned to Teclis, who was crossing to them. 'Fair one,' he said, bowing. 'We have the waystone. Please allow the house of Untern, family of our great countess, protector of Talabheim, the honour of carrying it to your quarters.'

Reiner cursed. The boy was quick.

Manfred, Danziger and von Pfaltzen all raised their voices in protest, but Teclis held up a hand. 'To forestall argument,' he said, 'Yes. Carry the stone. Now, let us be gone.'

'Thank you, fair one,' said Rodick as one of his men unstrapped a bundle he carried on his back. It contained four long, sturdy poles and several coils of rope. Rodick had come prepared.

'Bungling fool,' Manfred whispered in Reiner's ear. 'Look what you've done.'

'Yes, m'lord,' said Reiner. 'Very sorry, m'lord.'

Manfred turned away in disgust. 'What sort of Blackheart are you?'

Not a patch on you, you villain, thought Reiner.

Rodick's men were trying to roll the waystone onto the four poles using spears and lengths of lumber.

'You may use your hands,' said Teclis. 'It will be cool to the touch.'

The soldiers didn't appear to believe him. One reached out warily and brushed the stone with his fingers.

'He's right,' he gasped. 'It ain't hot at all.'

The soldiers were not reassured by this unnatural phenomenon, but none-the-less manhandled the stone onto the four poles and lashed it in place with the ropes. Each then took a pole-end and, grunting, lifted it up like a sedan chair.

'So we're done, then?' asked Augustus, as the companies began marching up the stairs and out of the room. 'Weren't as hard as the count made out it would be.'

'Aye,' said Pavel. 'Not really worth getting us out, was it?'

'Beats sitting about in Altdorf on our arses,' said Hals.

The companies wound through the abandoned prison with Rodick's men in the centre, and Danziger, seeming petulant and out of sorts, bringing up the rear.

They had passed out of the prison through the melted portal and were halfway across the vast vat room when Teclis stopped, looking into the shadows. His elves went instantly on guard.

'There are men here,' he said, loud but calm. 'Hidden by magic. We are ambushed.'

Before the words were out of his mouth, a hundred dark forms were swarming from behind the huge vats, waving swords and shrieking, 'The stone! Get the stone!'

Teclis uttered a short phrase and, with a bang, a ball of sun-bright light popped into being above his head, throwing every object in the room into sharp relief. The soldiers of the companies were shocked by this sudden illumination, but their ambushers must have seen something more than light in the ball's radiance, for they cringed away from it, and some turned and fled.

'Blackhearts! Nordbergbruchers!' called Manfred. 'Protect Teclis! Protect the stone!'

Reiner and the others formed a rough square around Teclis and Rodick just as the first wave of attackers hit. Von Pfaltzen and his men encircled them too, but Lord Danziger, caught just coming through the melted hole, fell back to it.

Reiner's mind raced as he fought. Whoever they were, these madmen hadn't been here when the companies first came through the room. Teclis would have sensed them. That meant they had known the companies were coming here to take the stone from the Tzeentchists. And they couldn't have followed them from the granary. Even without Teclis, the companies would have noticed so great a force behind them. Which meant that they had known where the stone was being held. Which meant that someone had eyes in more than one camp.

These attackers were as frenzied as the Tzeentchists, but, unlike them, these men looked not enraged, but enraptured. Their eyes were rolled back in their heads and beatific smiles split their faces as they hacked at the companies. When Reiner slashed one across the arm, he moaned in ecstasy. Nor were these ill-equipped acolytes, caught unawares. These men were well armed and clad in leather and steel.

'Who are these?' cried Rodick, slashing wildly at two slavering men.

'Cultists of the Lord of Pleasure,' said Teclis, then began mouthing another incantation. His elves sent a torrent of white shafts into the attackers. Every one found a mark.

Rumpolt reeled back, clutching his forehead. Reiner's knuckles were shredded from punching a fellow in the teeth. He saw a Nordbergbrucher go down with a hatchet buried in his back, and further down the line, one of the countess's guards toppled, lifeless. But now that their initial confusion at the sudden attack had passed, the discipline of the companies began to show, and more cultists began to fall.

'Forwards, you layabouts!' Manfred cried.

Reiner looked back to see the count pushing Rodick and his men toward the front line. 'You wanted the honour of carrying the stone, then you should welcome the honour of defending it!'

Reiner shook his head in wonder as he parried a sword stroke. Even in the midst of an ambush that they might not survive, Manfred jockeyed for the stone.

Teclis's voice grew louder, and the air around him vibrated with contained energies. He raised his arms and glared out at the ravening horde. Glowing tendrils began to boil from his hands. But just as he began to declaim the last thunderous words of his incantation, a black arrow sped from the darkness and impaled his chest.

SIX
Touch Not The Stone

TECLIS COLLAPSED BACKWARD, falling across the waystone. His guards turned, shocked, but recovered instantly, and flew into action. As five of the elves fired white shafts in the direction from which the black shaft had come, their captain snapped the black arrow nearly flush with Teclis's chest, then picked up the fallen mage in his arms as if he weighed nothing. The others clustered tightly around them, facing out, two with arrows nocked, the others holding swords. Without a word to their human companions they hurried for the exit, cutting down the cultists who got in their way.

'Does he live?' called Manfred after them. 'Does Teclis live?'

The elves did not answer.

As they reached the vat room's broken doors, a flood of deformed mutants poured through them, waving clubs and rusted swords. The elves laid about them furiously, but the mutants seemed uninterested in them, and instead ran directly at the men defending the stone.

'Cowards!' shouted Rodick, shaking his fist as the elves disappeared out the door. 'They've left us to die!'

The horde of mutants broke upon the companies and the Slaaneshi cultists alike, clawing and flailing with misshapen limbs, their eyes glazed. 'The stone,' they moaned. 'Get the stone.'

'We're done for,' whimpered Rumpolt as the Blackhearts fought a swirling chaos of cultists and mutants. 'This is death.'

'Shut yer hole, infant,' growled Hals.

The Slaaneshi attacked the mutants as fiercely as they fought the men, screaming 'Back, foul vermin!' and 'The stone is ours!' The soldiers struck at anything that didn't wear a uniform.

Manfred edged to Reiner, stabbing a cultist in the throat. 'Take up the stone,' he said. 'While our enemies fight each other.'

Reiner nodded, happy to leave the front line. 'Fall back, Blackhearts!'

The Blackhearts disengaged carefully, allowing the other companies to close ranks around them.

'Take up the stone!' Reiner shouted. He stooped to grab a pole-end as the others found their places and did the same.

'What's this?' cried Rodick, turning and ducking a sword as the Blackhearts lifted the waystone by the poles. 'We were told to carry the stone!'

'And you shall again,' said Manfred. 'But my men already have it up. To the corridor! We are too exposed here.'

'This is underhanded, sir,' said Rodick, as the Blackhearts started forward. 'I protest!'

'Protest if we live,' said Manfred.

The waystone was lighter than Reiner expected, and the Blackhearts made good time to the door, walking it in the centre of a moving island of soldiers, who were in turn surrounded by a boiling surf of screeching mutants and cultists. The floor underfoot was slick with blood. Seeing that his colleagues were leaving him behind, Lord Danziger and his men left the safety of the melted portal and fought across the room after them. The mutants in particular seemed to offend Danziger's sense of propriety. 'Disgusting perversions!' he bellowed. 'Unclean vermin! Touch not the stone!'

Reiner, freed from the fight, at last had time to wonder at the black arrow that had felled Teclis. Who had shot it, and why? And what dread power must he have to pierce Teclis's wards and armour as if they were nothing? Close on those questions came another. Why had the mutants, who had before cowered away from the companies, suddenly attacked so savagely, and with such singleness of purpose? And how did they also know of the stone?

The island of men reached the door, and the Blackhearts squeezed through, surrounded by Manfred's spearmen and Rodick's house guard. Danziger's men pushed in behind them as von Pfaltzen's troops stayed in the door, penning in the majority of the mutants and cultists.

'Go,' cried von Pfaltzen, waving a hand. 'We will hold them. Get the stone to the countess!'

Manfred saluted him. 'Courage, captain,' he called, then motioned the Blackhearts down the hall with the Nordbergbruchers and Rodick's and Danziger's men guarding them.

Reiner looked back at von Pfaltzen. It was possible, he thought, that the captain was the only man in this whole enterprise who cared more for the security of Talabheim than his personal advancement.

Danziger's men took the rear as the companies ran through the maze of cellars and catacombs, while Rodick's men scouted the way ahead. The Blackhearts sloshed across flooded chambers and ducked through stifling crawlways. The waystone soon felt twice as heavy as when they had picked it up, and they sweated through their shirts.

As they trotted through a series of looted crypts and mausoleums, Rodick dropped back to Manfred.

'You have held the waystone long enough,' he said. 'We will take it again.'

Manfred sneered. 'Your ambition is showing, Untern. No matter who carries it, it goes to Teclis in the end.'

'And what of your ambition?' asked Rodick.

'I have no ambition but to serve the Empire and my Emperor,' huffed Manfred.

Their argument was interrupted by a shrieking swarm of mutants that poured from another corridor. They crashed into Danziger's men, tearing at them with bare hands and bashing them with bricks and stones. The swordsmen hacked and kicked at them, shouting with anger and surprise. Mutants died by the score, but more came behind them.

Reiner looked back, baffled. 'Where do they all come from? How do they find us?'

Manfred smirked. 'Don't look a gift horse in the mouth.' He waved the Blackhearts on. 'Hurry. While they're engaged.'

'But Lord Danziger will be left behind,' said Augustus.

'Precisely.' said Manfred. 'Hold them, Danziger!' he called. 'And fear not. We will get the waystone to Teclis!'

'Curse you, Valdenheim!' shouted Danziger. 'Come back!'

Manfred sighed as the Blackhearts followed Rodick's men and the Nordberbruchers around a corner. 'What has become of the spirit of noble sacrifice that made this Empire great?'

Rodick giggled. Reiner held his tongue.

More mutants followed them, pacing the party like wolves. They kept their distance, but Reiner could hear them murmuring, 'Get the stone. Get the stone,' in monotonous unison.

The Blackhearts gasped and stumbled under the weight of the thing. Gert's round face was as red as a steak. Franka's eyes were glassy. Reiner's legs ached and his arms shook. The carrying pole was slipping in his sweaty grip. He cursed Manfred for denying Rodick's men their turn to carry it. He would have been happy to give it up.

At last they reached the abandoned cold cellar that led up to the sewers. The Blackhearts staggered wearily to the tilted shelves that served as a ladder to the hole, Rodick's men and Manfred's Nordbergbruchers trotting around them.

'Down! Put it down!' choked Reiner.

The Blackhearts gratefully eased the stone to the ground as the party looked back. Lurching and shambling across the floor came the mutants. There were scores of them, some already bloody and limping from the earlier melees. Reiner didn't understand what drove them. Many cried out in pain at every step, yet they came on, still mumbling their endless refrain, 'Get the stone. Get the stone.'

Reiner took stock of Manfred and Rodick's forces. Baerich and five spears were all that survived of the Nordbergbruchers. Rodick had lost only one man – proof they had indeed hung back in the fighting. The Blackhearts had all their number, though they were neither whole nor hearty. Reiner could barely lift his arms.

'Up, men,' said Rodick, and clambered up the tilted shelves and over the rubble that littered the lip of the hole with his men behind him. 'Hurry,' he called from the top. 'Before they reach us. Pass up the stone!'

'Come down, curse you,' barked Manfred. 'Take the defence. Your men are untouched.'

'But my men are already up, and there is no time to change,' said Rodick, mimicking Manfred.

'Do you mock me, sir?' Manfred looked back. The mutants were nearly upon them. He grunted with frustration. 'Death of Sigmar! Spearmen, hold them off! Blackhearts, pass up the stone.'

'Aye, m'lord,' said Reiner. 'Lift away, lads. Frank... Franz, guide us up.'

As Baerich and the remaining Nordbergbruchers spread out in a meagre half circle, Reiner and the Blackhearts took up their poles and lifted the stone. Behind him, Reiner heard the mutants hit the thin line of spears. He cringed. He could feel daggers and swords striking for his back. He could feel foetid breath on his neck.

The shelves creaked ominously as Hals and Pavel stepped up onto them with the stone carried between them. Two of Rodick's men stepped through the hole and put feet on the top shelf to brace it. One of the men had his back foot on a heavy chunk of granite. It rocked and he nearly fell.

'Careful,' called Rodick.

Reiner heard a scream of agony behind him, and Manfred cursing.

'Hurry, you sluggards!' bellowed the count. 'They overwhelm us!'

The Blackhearts took another step. The shelves flexed beneath them. The howling of the mutants and the cursing of the spearmen filled Reiner's ears.

'Step!' he called.

The shelves groaned as they took more weight. The sides bowed. The stone slid back alarmingly, and the ropes that tied it to the poles creaked. Rodick's men reached down toward them. Rodick had joined them, stretching out his hands.

'Now pass it up,' said Reiner.

With grunts of effort, the Blackhearts passed the four stone-laden poles hand to hand up the shelves. At the top, Pavel and Hals handed the first pole to Rodick's men and took the second from Dieter and Rumpolt. Jergen and Augustus, having passed the last to Reiner and Gert, stepped to the sides of the shelves and pushed against them, trying to hold them together.

Rodick's men took each of the poles in turn, and the shelves groaned in relief as they were relieved of the weight. Finally, Rodick took the fourth pole from Pavel, bracing his foot on the unsteady granite boulder. As he lifted, his foot slipped and the boulder toppled down, smashing through the shelves and glancing off Jergen's right shoulder, knocking him to the floor. The other Blackhearts crashed down in a rain of splintering wood as the shelves disintegrated.

Rodick gasped. 'Count! Forgive me! What an unfortunate accident.'

'Accident my arse,' growled Hals, picking himself up. A horned mutant threw itself at him. Hals elbowed him in the eye, groping for his spear. Reiner drew his sword and stepped between two of the spearmen, cutting and thrusting. There were only three Nordbergbruchers left, and they were sorely pressed. Manfred was bleeding from a dozen small wounds.

'Blackhearts, hold the line!' Reiner shouted.

The others caught up their weapons and faced out, limping – all but Darius, who cowered against the wall as usual, and Jergen, who sat dazed, his right arm limp at his side.

The count snarled up at Rodick. 'You did that deliberately.'

Rodick saluted him as he lifted the stone with his men. 'Hold them, Valdenheim! And fear not. We will get the waystone to Teclis!'

'Curse you, Untern!' shouted Manfred, as the young lord and his men disappeared into the sewer with the stone. A mutant gashed Manfred's arm with its claws and he turned back to the fight, hacking left and right. 'Hetsau,' he said. 'We must get after him. Get us out of this hole.'

'Aye, m'lord.' Reiner backed out of the line and looked around. One of the side panels from the shelves was still whole. He propped it against the wall under the hole, next to where Darius was examining Jergen's useless sword arm.

'Up you go,' said Reiner. 'Both of you.'

Darius tottered up first as Reiner braced the plank with his shoulder, then Jergen. Reiner grunted under his weight.

'Ready to retire, m'lord!' he called.

Manfred glanced back. 'Very good, Hetsau. Bows and guns back to cover the rest.'

Franka, Gert and Rumpolt dropped out of the line and clambered up the plank. When they reached the hole. Gert and Franka turned and fired down into the mutants while Rumpolt loaded his gun.

'Baerich, Nordbergbruchers!' said Manfred. 'Fall back.'

The captain and his last two spearmen stepped back from the fight, grateful, and pulled themselves wearily up the plank.

Now only Pavel, Hals, Augustus, Dieter and Manfred stood against the horde, and the mutants were beginning to edge around them toward Reiner.

'The rest will have to run back all at once, m'lord,' called Reiner. He hacked down a mutant who pawed at the plank.

'On your command, then,' said the count.

Reiner cut down another mutant, then waved up at the others, watching anxiously from the hole. 'Pull up the plank and hold down your hands!'

Darius hauled up the plank, then got on his belly with Jergen, Rumpolt, Baerich and the Nordbergbruchers, and stretched down his arms, while Franka and Gert continued to fire at the mutants.

'Now, m'lord!' said Reiner.

'Fall back!' shouted Manfred.

Reiner had to give Manfred credit. Conniving manipulator he might be, but coward he was not. He was last to turn from the mutants, slashing about wildly to protect the others while they disengaged, then running and springing for the wall like a man half his age.

The men in the hole caught the hands of the men on the ground and pulled for all they were worth, and Hals, Pavel and Augustus scrabbled with their toes. Dieter needed no help. He flew up the wall like a cat, then turned and added his arm to Darius's and dragged Manfred into the sewer tunnel.

Reiner had caught Jergen's left hand and he could see the swordsman's grim face turn white with agony as he braced himself with his wounded arm. Franka dropped her bow and grabbed Reiner's other hand. The fear for him that he saw in her eyes sent a thrill through him. Maybe he hadn't lost her after all.

Claws grabbed Reiner's ankles. He screamed, thrashing and kicking his leg. 'Pull, curse you!'

Jergen and Franka redoubled their efforts and Reiner inched up, then came up all at once as he caught the mutant who held him in the teeth and it let go. Reiner landed face first on the rubble-strewn sewer ledge and rolled away, panting as Pavel, Rumpolt and Dieter hurled stones down at the leaping mass of mutants and stomped on their fingers.

Manfred brushed himself off and looked in the direction Rodick had gone. 'Enough. We must catch Untern,' he said. 'The pup needs a lesson.'

The Blackhearts and the Nordbergbruchers backed away from the hole, then lit fresh torches and followed Manfred down the hall, limping and groaning.

Reiner fell in beside Franka. 'Franka...'

Her face hardened as she caught the look in his eyes. 'Yes, captain?' she said, loud. 'You wish to speak with me, captain?'

Reiner cringed. 'Never mind, never mind.' Damn the girl.

They reached an intersection of tunnels. There was no torchlight in any direction.

Manfred cursed. 'Where has he got to? Did he fly?'

Dieter took a torch and examined the floor and walls around each of the four corners. 'This way,' he said at last, pointing to a scrape on the bricks of the right-hand passage. 'They touched the wall with the stone.'

'Excellent work,' said Manfred. 'Lead on. Is this the way we came?'

'Aye,' said Dieter, and started down the tunnel, eyes on the ground. But as the others followed, Jergen looked behind them.

'Captain,' he said to Reiner. 'They come again.'

Manfred heard and cursed. 'Double time, trailbreaker.'

Dieter grunted, but picked up his pace. After a bend, the tunnel straightened out.

Manfred shook his head when he saw no torchlight before them. 'How could they have got so far ahead?'

Fifty yards along, Dieter stopped abruptly. 'Hang on,' he said. He turned back, looking at the floor, then paused at an iron ladder bolted into the brick wall. He examined the rungs, then looked up into a dark chimney. 'They went up.'

'Up?' asked Manfred, incredulous. 'With the stone?'

'Aye,' said Dieter, pointing. 'Scrapes on the rungs. Rope strands. Footprints.'

'Then we must go after them,' said Manfred. 'Come.' He mounted the ladder and began to climb. A black arrow whistled out of the dark and glanced off the wall next to his face. Manfred flinched back with a cry.

'Climb another rung and the next will find your heart,' said a voice.

Everyone turned. Limping out of the shadows, surrounded by a crowd of blank-eyed mutants, was a tall, pale-skinned elf, a black longbow in his left hand, an arrow on the string.

Reiner heard shuffling behind him and looked around. More mutants were pushing into the torchlight from that direction as well. They were surrounded.

SEVEN
The Hand of Malekith

AT FIRST REINER thought the elf was one of Teclis's guard, for he had the same proud, cold features and regal bearing, but he wore no armour, and his beautifully made doublet and leggings were black, not blue. It was in his glittering dark eyes, however, that the difference was most evident. Though they were as distant and alien as those of Teclis and his guard, there was a malevolence there that went beyond mere uncaring indifference to the fates of lesser beings.

'I am grieved to hear,' he said in a pleasant voice, 'that the stone has eluded me. But at least I have you, and that may yet win me the stone. Surrender your weapons to my slaves and come with me.'

Manfred sneered. 'We have beat back your "slaves" before, sir. We can again.'

A black shaft sprouted from Captain Baerich's chest and he collapsed at Manfred's feet. The arrow pierced his breastplate and stuck out his back. Reiner hadn't seen the elf move, and yet he was laying another arrow on his string. The other Nordbergbruchers cried out and started forward, spears lowered. They were dead before they had taken a step.

'It isn't my slaves you should fear.' the elf said, coolly. 'They are only to keep you from running. Now, need more die?'

Manfred looked down at the corpses of Baerich and his men, his face pale. At last he licked his lips and looked up. 'Surrender your weapons,' he said.

'M'lord!' protested Augustus.

'Obey my orders,' barked Manfred.

The Blackhearts reluctantly handed their swords and spears and bows to the drooling mutants, who then hemmed in their prisoners in a stinking wall of diseased flesh. Reiner was in full agreement with Manfred. Surrender was the only option, but to give in to such pitiful foes felt wrong, even to a Blackheart.

'Now, my slaves,' said the elf to the mutants, 'Take me to your deepest, most fortified hole. I require a residence.'

He limped forward with a wince, and Reiner noted for the first time that the elf had the broken-off shaft of a white arrow sticking out of his jerkin, a handbreadth above his left hip-bone.

'We will move slowly,' he said. 'For while Teclis's guard are poor archers, they are extremely lucky.'

THE MUTANTS LED them down into the earth by means of abandoned cellars, airshafts, and what appeared to be an ancient tin mine, until they reached natural caverns, the walls of which glittered in the torchlight as if they were embedded with glass. There was a faint roaring in Reiner's head as they entered, which he first thought was air moving through the caves, but when he focussed on it he wasn't sure it was a sound after all, more a babble of random thoughts bubbling beneath the surface of his consciousness, like a fly buzzing inside his skull. He fought the urge to swat it. He could see that the others were affected as well, shaking their heads and twitching. Darius had his hands to his temples, moaning.

'All right, scholar?' asked Reiner.

'Fine. I'm fine,' Darius snapped.

Reiner wasn't so sure.

They came at last to an enormous, roughly circular cave, its walls encrusted with pitiful rag-and-stick tents, out of which crawled more mutants, even more twisted than those who held them. It soon became obvious, however, that the mutants were not the first visitors to this underworld. A massive arch was carved into the wall to the left of the main entrance, and straight ahead, where a deep chasm cut through the floor, a stone bridge had been built, beyond which Reiner could see more tunnels in the far wall. Both arch and bridge were aeons old, their geometric designs nearly worn away by time.

The elf limped through the stone arch, the mutants following with the captives. Inside was a high, round chamber, in the centre of which was a circle of black stones, twice the height of a man, surrounding a flat, round altar. Cut into the walls around the stone circle were a score of iron-barred cells.

The elf nodded approvingly. 'An aspect of Khaine was worshipped here. A more fitting home for a son of Naggaroth than a sewer.'

Manfred's eyes went wide. 'You are a dark elf?'

'I am Druchii,' said the elf, raising his chin. 'That other name is a slander invented by our treacherous cousins. Now listen well. Today is a great day. The despised Teclis is dead, and one of Ulthuan's precious waystones is within my–'

'How can you be certain Teclis is dead?' interrupted Manfred.

The elf turned cold eyes on the count. 'Because,' he hissed. 'I struck him with an arrow poisoned, diseased, and enchanted with magics created just for his murder. My dear mother may have named me Valaris, but I am nothing but Teclis's death. I have trained since my birth, seven hundred years ago, to do one thing and one thing only – kill the great mage of Ulthuan. It was said that no assassin could defeat Teclis's magics, and no mage could penetrate his defences, so I was made to be both. I learned the ways of the slayer at the knee of the master of shadows, and spent a hundred years in servitude to the sisterhood of Khaine to be allowed to study their mysteries, all that I might defeat the "fair one".' He snorted. 'And so that he is dead, I care not whether I survive. I am but the hand of Malekith. My death – my pain – means nothing.'

Reiner stared at the elf. He had been told that Teclis was thousands of years old, but the knowledge had the quality of myth about it, and was hard to think of as a reality. Here was a being who had lived fourteen human generations in the pursuit of a single goal.

Valaris eased his weight to his unwounded side. 'However,' he said, 'with a chance to destroy a waystone and undermine the foundations of our treacherous cousins' stranglehold on the world within my reach, I am thankful I was spared, though I am frustrated that my wound makes it impossible for me to accomplish the task myself.' He sighed. 'At least I have a tool that will do what I cannot.'

'You speak of us?' asked Manfred. 'We are not your slaves.'

'And I am glad of it,' said Valaris, looking around at the mutants. 'They would be unsuited to the task. The warpstone taint has destroyed their minds, making it possible for me to control them. But it also makes them unable to think for themselves. And I have no doubt it will take cunning to win the stone.'

'And what makes ye think we'll do what ye want, y'chalk-faced twig?' said Hals.

Valaris raised an eyebrow. 'Hark, hark. The dogs do bark.'

A mutant behind Hals raised a cudgel and bashed the pikeman on the back of the head. Hals clutched his head and cursed.

'You will do what I want,' continued the elf as if nothing had happened, 'because I will hold the count hostage, and will kill him if you fail to bring the stone to me in three days.'

Reiner's heart jumped. By Ranald! Was this the chance for which the Blackhearts had waited so long? The dark elf might be able to control the minds of the mutants, but it was clear he couldn't read thoughts. He had no idea that Reiner and the others would leave Manfred to die in a heartbeat – all but the spy, of course. Reiner grunted. Always it was the spy who ruined every chance. But if they could discover and kill him while Manfred was still Valaris's prisoner, they might escape the count's insidious poison at last.

Reiner saw Manfred had come to the same realisation. His face was nearly as white as the elf's. 'Sir,' he cried, trying to look noble, though his brow was wet with sweat. 'If you think such a scheme will work, then you do not know the men of the Empire. The restoration of the stone is the salvation of our land, and my men know that I would gladly sacrifice my worthless life to that end. If you send them on this errand, they will not return, and I will applaud them for it.'

The elf smiled. 'I believe I know the men of the Empire well enough. Did I not just see them leaving each other to die in order to appear the hero that rescued the stone? I believe, count, that you try to trick me into letting you go. You are too fond of your life, and your position, and your wealth, to make so noble a sacrifice, and your men are no doubt greedy animals like all their kind, and will bring the stone back to me for the rewards you will heap upon them for your salvation.'

Reiner rejoiced in silence. The dark elf's prejudices were going to free them. They would walk out of the catacombs and, once they found the traitor, they would walk out of Talabheim and disappear into the world with no one left alive to order the poison loosed into their veins.

Manfred pursed his lips. 'Then send them and you will see. But I ask a small mercy of you. That if they do not return, you grant me a few moments to pray.' The count said, turning cunning eyes on Reiner. 'Blessings for the brave men who join me in sacrificing their lives for the good of the Empire.'

The elf looked up, his eyes darting from Manfred to Reiner. 'Blessings you say?'

He frowned, then stepped to Reiner and took his wrist, circling his left hand over it. A throbbing pain pulsed through Reiner's arm and he tried to jerk away.

Valaris held him in an iron grip, then let him go laughing. 'I have underestimated the cunning of men,' he said. 'This is almost Druchii. Bound by poison.' He smiled at Manfred. 'You shall be allowed your prayers. Now,' Valaris waved a hand at the mutants and they herded the men toward the cages in the wall. 'I have gifts I must prepare for you. I will return.'

He turned away and limped out of the room as the mutants pushed the men into one cramped cage.

As the mutants locked them in, Reiner turned to Manfred. 'So, m'lord. It is your wish that we do not return for you, and do not bring the stone to the dark elf? Your sacrifice is truly worthy of the great heroes of the Empire's golden age.'

'Don't be an ass, Hetsau,' said the count. 'If you fail to bring the stone here in three days, you will not see a fourth.'

Reiner gasped, feigning shock. 'But m'lord. Do you mean that you lied? That you are not willing to sacrifice your life for the good of the land? Do you fear death?'

'I fear nothing,' spat Manfred. 'And if it would save the land, I would welcome death, but the Empire needs me, Hetsau, as much as it needs the waystone. Even more, now that Teclis is dead. For with him gone, the waystone is useless until another elven mage can be brought from Ulthuan to reseat it. I will be needed to keep order and negotiate with the elves. I must stay alive, you see?'

Reiner saw that Manfred *was* afraid. Strange that a man who showed no fear in battle would prove such a coward in captivity. Perhaps it was that a man with a sword in his hand always felt there was a chance, while a caged man felt powerless. Whatever the reason, Reiner had seen mercenaries and engineers face their fates with more heart.

'I see, m'lord,' Reiner said. He didn't bother to hide his sneer. 'But your humble servants have many fewer reasons to live. In fact they grow weary of life under the yoke, and might feel that the Empire would be better off keeping the waystone and getting rid of you, and would be willing to sacrifice their lives to that end.'

Franka's eyes went wide as Reiner's words sank in, and the others stared at him.

Manfred went pale. 'What are you suggesting?'

'Nothing, m'lord,' said Reiner. 'Except that the threat of death begins to lose its force if one's life isn't worth living. So, if you truly wish us to steal the waystone from the Empire, and bring it to a sworn enemy of mankind at the risk of our lives, and against all natural inclinations, perhaps you would consider adding an incentive in addition to the usual intimidation.'

'And what would that be?' asked Manfred, sneering in his turn. 'Gold? Better quarters? Harlots at your beck and call?'

'Freedom.'

The Blackhearts looked at Reiner, hope glittering in their eyes.

'Let this be the Blackhearts' last mission,' Reiner continued. 'Promise us that if we free you, you will free us. A simple trade.'

Manfred raised a sceptical eyebrow. 'And you say you are willing to die if I do not agree to this?'

Reiner looked around at the others questioningly. He hoped he had gauged their temper correctly.

'Aye,' said Hals, nodding. 'This is no life.'

'Might as well kill us now and save us the trouble,' said Pavel.

Franka stuck out her chin. 'I am ready.'

'And I,' said Jergen without looking up.

Gert just glared at Manfred, arms crossed.

The newer men didn't look so certain, but they didn't disagree.

Manfred hesitated, looking around at them all, then sighed. 'Very well. You have given me good service, and though it saddens me that brave men would turn away from their duty to protect their homeland, I will release you if you succeed in getting me to safety.'

The Blackhearts let out tense breaths.

'We have your word?' asked Reiner.

'You have my word as a gentleman and a representative of the Empire of Karl Franz.'

Being born of the gentle class himself, Reiner knew what the word of a gentleman was worth, but he was in no position to force any other guarantee from the count. 'Very well,' he said. 'Then we will recover the stone and free you.'

'In three days,' said Manfred.

'Three days,' agreed Reiner.

There was a disturbance among the mutants and the men looked up. Valaris was returning.

'I have a gift for each of you,' he said, looking at them through the bars. 'And another for the leader of the men who will go.' He opened a small square of cloth, revealing what appeared to slivers of blue glass. 'While Teclis lived, you were protected by his spells against the effects of Talabheim's warpstone. Now he is dead, that protection is removed. I care nothing for your welfare, but you must be sane to be useful, so I have chipped shards from a crystal I wear. Placed under your skin, they will ward off the emanations.'

'Under the skin?' asked Manfred.

'Yes,' the elf grabbed Rumpolt through the bars and pulled him close with casual strength. 'Like so.' He rucked Rumpolt's sleeve up and, selecting one of the crystal slivers, he pushed it under the boy's skin so that it lay like a cyst just beneath the surface. Rumpolt squealed and jerked his arm away. Blood ran freely from the wound.

Valaris curled his lip. 'Do you flinch from your salvation? Pathetic.' He held the cloth out. 'Come, take them. I do not care to touch more of you.'

Manfred, Reiner and the others stepped forward and took slivers from the box. Reiner jabbed his shard in swiftly, so he didn't have time to think about it. The murmuring that had cluttered the back of his brain since he had entered the glittering caves receded almost to nothing. The others slid their crystals in too, grunting or hissing. Darius sighed, seemingly relieved. Only Franka hesitated.

Reiner stepped to her. 'Do you want me to do it?'

She looked up at him and her face hardened. 'No. You have cut me once already.' She shoved the splinter vehemently into her arm and stifled a cry as it went too deep.

'Franka!' Reiner hissed.

She turned away from him, wiping her eyes with the back of her hand.

'Now,' said Valaris. 'Who leads the rescuers?'

Reiner reluctantly turned to the elf. 'I do.'

'Then come, and bare your chest.'

Reiner stepped to the bars, unbuckling his breastplate, then pulling open his doublet and shirt. Valaris drew a black-bladed dagger and, eyes closed, chanted under his breath in his own tongue. Faint curls of smoke rose off the blade and Reiner could smell the scent of hot iron. The tip of the dagger glowed a dull red.

Reiner wanted to run and hide from the smouldering knife, but the prospect of being dragged from the cage by filthy mutants and held down while Valaris did what he intended anyway made him decide that gripping the bars and holding still was the better option.

The elf finished his incantation and opened his eyes. 'Hold steady,' he said. 'If I mar it, I will have to start again in a new place.'

He pressed the blade into Reiner's flesh, just below his right collar bone, and began cutting a curving line. The pain was indescribable, a bright line of agony that seemed to grow worse after the blade tip had passed. Reiner flushed with a cold sweat. His palms slipped on the bars, slick. His knees shook.

'Steady, fool.' said Valaris. He moved to Reiner's left side, sketching quickly but precisely with the smoking blade. Reiner's hands squeezed the bars so tightly he felt he might bend them. He closed his eyes. Explosions of colour burst across his eyelids. His head spun and he thought he might be falling. He opened his eyes again, terrified that he had moved and that Valaris would repeat the torture from the beginning. He couldn't do it twice.

'Done,' said the elf, stepping back.

Reiner sank to his knees, moaning. Through swimming eyes he looked down at himself. High on his chest were bubbling red lines in the shape of a complex elf rune.

'I am no fool,' said the elf. 'I know you will seek to betray me. The younger races have no honour. This is my safeguard. While these wounds are fresh, what you see and hear, I will see and hear. So if you intend to bring the countess's army with you when you return the stone, or if you conceive some other treachery, I will know it, and the count will die.' He smirked. 'After, of course, he has said his prayers.'

He turned to the mutants. 'Now, come slaves, return to these noble warriors their weapons and let them be on their way. And may the blessings of Sigmar be upon them.' He laughed darkly.

Reiner groaned and got to his feet as the mutants opened the cage door. Franka was looking at him, biting her lip, but she turned away when he tried to meet her eyes.

EIGHT
The Countess Demands An Explanation

After a long, weary walk back up through the catacombs to the sewers, then across the mad city under blood-red late afternoon clouds, Reiner stopped the Blackhearts just before they reached the back gate of the Reiklander legation's town house.

'Hold a moment,' he said, groaning. The sweat seeping into Valaris's knife work made it burn like it was still on fire. 'It just came to me. Without Manfred, we are in a difficult position. If we return without him, we will be questioned about his disappearance, and quite possibly arrested.'

'So we don't go in?' asked Pavel.

'How are we to get the stone if we don't?' Reiner asked. 'A gang of masterless ruffians will not be allowed to get anywhere near the stone. We need Manfred's influence to reach it.'

'So we're sunk before we begin,' said Hals.

'No,' said Reiner, thinking. 'No, we take Manfred in with us.'

'Eh?' said Rumpolt. 'But Count Manfred is in the cave with–'

'Not at all,' said Reiner, grinning suddenly. He looked around, sizing up the Blackhearts. 'Darius, give Jergen your cloak. Jergen, pull the hood well forward and keep your head down. Good. Now, an arm over my shoulder and one over

Dieter's, and see if you can manage a limp. Excellent.' He looked at the others. 'When we go in, we will disperse and don our servant's garb again. See to your wounds as best you can. I will send Franka with word when I learn where the stone is held and contrive a plan for its recovery. Now, onward.'

'Open the gate,' Reiner cried as they reached it. 'Open the gate for Count Manfred!'

A Nordbergbruche bowman looked out, then threw open the back gate when he saw them.

'Is the count hurt?' he asked, concerned.

'Yes, he's hurt, blast you,' said Reiner. 'Now go before us and clear the way!'

'Where is Captain Baerich?'

'Dead. Now go.'

The bowman paled, but led Reiner, Dieter and Jergen toward the house as servants ran before them, crying the news. The other Blackhearts turned toward the servants' quarters. Reiner, Dieter, Jergen and Franka followed the bowman through the stableyard and the kitchen unmolested, but as they reached Manfred's second floor suite, the other members of the Reikland legation spilled into the hall, all calling to Manfred and demanding to know where he had been.

'Darius,' said Reiner, slipping out from under Jergen's arm. 'Take him inside. Bowman, return to your post.'

Reiner threw open Manfred's door, then stepped toward the jabbering lords and clerics, as the others hurried Jergen into the count's room.

'M'lords, please!' called Reiner. 'Quiet yourselves! Count Valdenheim is grievously wounded and must take to his bed. He is too hurt to speak.'

'But he must!' cried Lord Boellengen, looking like a flustered goose. 'He has embarrassed us all with this skullduggery! The countess demands an explanation!'

'As do we,' puffed Grand Master Raichskell. 'Why were we not informed of this morning's undertaking? It is outrageous that Knights of the Order were not included.'

'Nor were my Hammer Bearers!' cried Father Totkrieg.

'There is some mystery here,' said Magus Nichtladen.

'If Valdenheim has done something to dishonour the Emperor's name,' said Lord Schott, 'he will answer to me!'

'My lords,' said Reiner. 'I cannot speak for the count, but I will communicate your questions to him and bring you his answers. Now, if you will excuse me.'

'We do not excuse you,' piped Lord Boellengen imperiously. 'We must speak to Count Valdenheim regardless of his condition. Countess Elise has called an emergency meeting of the parliament. He must attend.'

Reiner sighed and opened Manfred's door. 'Enter if you must, m'lords. But Count Valdenheim is incapable of speech. He was cut with an unclean blade, and his mouth and throat are choked with boils. His physician fears they may be infectious. Some sort of Chaos pox, it might be.'

The lords recoiled, hands going instinctively to their mouths.

'He... he is ill?' asked Raichskell.

'So it seems, m'lord,' said Reiner.

'But he must attend,' said Boellengen, backing away. 'The countess will expel the legation if she is not given an explanation of the morning's occurrence.'

Reiner paused, pretending to think. 'Perhaps it would be permissible for me to appear in the count's place, and give his explanation?'

'You?' sneered Boellengen. 'A clerk?'

'The countess may find my presence more palatable than Count Manfred's, m'lord,' said Reiner. 'He is a bit... unpleasant to behold.'

The lords grimaced, then muttered together for a long moment. At last Boellengen turned back to Reiner. 'Very well. The parliament meets in an hour. Make yourself presentable.'

'Certainly, m'lord.' Reiner bowed, then slipped through the door and locked it behind him, breathing a sigh of relief. Darius had his physician's kit unrolled and was tending to Dieter, Jergen and Franka, who sat on Manfred's enormous canopied bed.

'Will we live, scholar?' asked Reiner.

Darius shrugged. 'Nothing appears mortal, sir, but I have limited skills as a physician.'

'How's your arm, Rohmner?'

The swordmaster had his shirt off, massaging his thickly muscled shoulder. It was black and blue. 'Numb and stiff, captain. But it will pass, I think.'

'That's a mercy.' Reiner turned to Manfred's wardrobe. 'While I'm gone all of you must keep the door locked and let no one in, no matter what they say or who they are. Is that clear?'

'Aye, captain,' said Franka.

The others nodded.

'I,' he said, taking a fresh shirt from the wardrobe, 'must go speak to the countess and her parliament.' He sighed. 'I'd sooner face the mutants again.'

'WHEN THE REIKLAND legation came to us yesterday,' said Countess Elise from her chair at the northernmost point of the parliament's U-shaped table, 'we were cautious. But Count Manfred promised co-operation. He promised the help of the great mage Teclis. Yet, not ten hours after he speaks these words, he attempts to recover the waystone without informing any official of Talabheim, and–'

'I was there, countess,' piped up Danziger.

His face was mottled with bruises, and his left hand thickly bandaged. Von Pfaltzen was in attendance as well, a cut over his left eye. Reiner was surprised to see them. When he had left them, their situations had seemed desperate.

'Without my authority!' the countess snapped at Danziger. 'And with knowledge you should have shared with the parliament. And what comes of this unsanctioned undertaking? The stone lost as soon as it is found. Nearly thirty men dead. Count Manfred and Lord Teclis wounded near unto death…'

Reiner choked, and then was caught with a fit of coughing. The stone lost? Teclis alive? Was this good news or bad? He patted his chest and nearly screamed in agony. He had forgotten Valaris's knife cuts. Valaris! He groaned. Now the dark elf knew Teclis lived. At least he hadn't cut a mouth into Reiner's chest. He couldn't order him to kill the high elf.

Reiner looked up to see the countess and the parliament glaring at him. He ducked his head. 'Forgive me, countess, members of the assembly, but the count sent me immediately from his side to be with you. We had heard no news, of Teclis or the waystone.'

'Then let me inform you,' said the countess dryly, 'so that you may inform the count. The noble Teclis lives, though barely. At his request we house him in a secret location, so he may tend to his healing without fear of further attempts on his life. And our cousin Rodick has informed us that he was robbed of the stone by cultists as he left the sewers. It is therefore with great anticipation,' she said, turning cold eyes on Reiner, 'that we wait to hear Count Valdenheim's mouthpiece explain his master's reasons for attempting the action.'

Reiner stood and bowed. 'Countess, the count thanks you for your courtesy, and answers that he moved in secret in order to catch those that held the stone unawares. He further says that, though he made his plans known only to Teclis and his own men, Lord Rodick and Captain von Pfaltzen knew of it by morning. He is wounded to think that his noble hosts might have had him under surveillance.'

'And did he not prove the necessity of our caution by his actions?' asked von Pfaltzen.

'Count Valdenheim also finds it disturbing that agents of the ruinous powers knew of the mission almost as soon as Captain von Pfaltzen and Lord Untern did,' continued Reiner. 'He will undoubtedly be more displeased when he learns of the theft of the stone after he took such great personal risks in order to recover it.'

'Does he suggest,' cried the countess, 'that the parliament of Talabheim colludes with cultists?'

'I do not know what he suggests, countess,' said Reiner. 'Only what he says.'

'It appears that Talabheim has more spies and informers than it has trees,' sniffed Lord Boellengen, who sat with the rest of the Reikland legation along the wall.

The parliament erupted at this, with every member shouting at the Reiklanders and the Reiklanders shouting back, turning the chamber into an echoing cacophony of insults.

In the midst of this tumult, a page came in and whispered in the countess's ear. She listened at first with confusion and then with surprise, then called for order. When this failed to quiet the room, she pounded the table with her mace of office, and at last the members of parliament and the representatives from the Reikland turned and fell silent.

'Noble visitors and learned colleagues,' she said with unconcealed sarcasm. 'It may be that all our recriminations are for naught, for I have been told that one waits without who has knowledge of the stone's whereabouts and wishes to speak to this assembly. Do you wish to hear her?'

A few voices questioned who 'her' might be, but most said 'aye,' and the countess signalled for the chamber's doors to be opened. Reiner and the others craned their necks to see who the visitor might be. Reiner's heart jolted as he saw that it was Lady Magda Bandauer – or rather Lady Untern now – who entered, wearing a tightly ruffed satin dress in her husband's colours of blue and burgundy. Her face was as composed and serene as a statue's. She looked as if she ruled here instead of the countess. And if she has her way, thought Reiner, she will.

The lords eyed Magda solemnly as she curtsied deeply to the countess, then stood demurely, waiting to be spoken to.

'Lady Magda,' said the countess. 'Wife of my dear cousin, Rodick. Welcome. We are told you have some new knowledge of the waystone?'

'I do, countess,' said Magda. 'And I thank you for allowing me entry to these hallowed halls. It is a great honour.' She curtsied again and continued. 'As you know, my husband, your cousin, has not rested since the masked villains robbed him of the stone earlier today. He has hunted them high and low, and offered bounties for information, and sent men of our house into the most dangerous, unsavoury quarters of Talabheim looking for news of it, and at last he has had some success. He believes he knows, almost to a certainty, where the stone is, and who possesses it.'

'Yes?' said the countess. 'And who is this person? Where do they hold it?'

Lady Magda lowered her eyes. 'That I do not know, countess, for Rodick would not tell me.'

The countess's eyes flared. 'Then... then why are you here? Have you come to tease us? I do not understand.'

'I apologise, countess,' said Magda. 'I did not mean to appear coy.' She raised her head, jaw set. 'The difficulty is that Rodick believes that the person who holds the waystone is so highly placed, and so powerful, that he dare not reveal his name until he has irrefutable proof of his guilt. Unfortunately, Rodick's ability to gather this proof is hampered by his powerlessness and his lack of men.'

The countess raised an eyebrow as the parliament began to rumble with whispers. She sat back in her chair. 'Rodick is hardly powerless, lady,' she said. 'He is a knight of the realm, and if he has need of men he has only to ask. I am his cousin after all.'

'And he is grateful for your charity, countess,' said Magda. 'But Rodick fears retaliations even you may not be able to protect him from. What if my husband recovers the stone without succeeding in gathering enough evidence against he who holds it? That person could strike back at him, and without a more prominent position and a force of men to call his own, Rodick might be murdered for his bravery. This should not be the reward of the man who saves Talabheim and the Empire.'

The countess smiled, as if a question had been answered. 'And what measures does my dear cousin feel will ensure his safety?'

'Countess,' said Magda. 'In order to further his investigations, and to ensure that he has an official voice to counter any accusations after he has recovered the stone, Rodick asks that he be made Hunter Lord Commander of the Talabheim city guard, and be given the seat in Parliament that comes with the position.'

The parliament erupted, the voice of Detlef Keinholtz, the current commander of the city guard, louder than all the others. 'It's nothing but blackmail!' he shouted.

'Rodick has recovered the stone already!' said Lord Scharnholt. 'There is no highly placed villain.'

'Recovered it?' cried the bakers' guild master. 'Don't be a fool! He never lost it!'

'It's all a ruse!' said Arch Lector Farador. 'A play for a seat in the parliament. And he risks the safety of the city to do it!'

The countess banged her mace for order and the hubbub slowly subsided. She turned a pleasant smile on Magda. Only the sparkle of her eyes revealed her fury. 'So, if we grant him this appointment, Rodick will guarantee the recovery of the stone?'

Magda nodded. 'There are no guarantees in life, countess. But it will certainly make his task much easier.'

'No doubt,' said the countess. 'Particularly if he already has the waystone in his possession.'

'My lady,' said Magda, looking hurt. 'I cannot say how deeply it pains me to find such distrust in the hearts of such noble men and women. If you must search my lord's house in order to satisfy your suspicions...'

'We would certainly find nothing, of course,' said the countess, dryly. 'And the reason that my cousin does not make his case in person has nothing to do with the fact that, if he were here, I could order him to turn over the stone and imprison him if he did not, but only because he is even now on the trail of the waystone and cannot break away from the hunt.'

'Why yes,' said Lady Magda. 'That is exactly the reason, countess.'

There was more uproar at this. The countess leaned forward and conferred with those beside her. Reiner stared at Magda. What a woman! What aplomb! He was torn between wanting to bow to her mastery, and wanting to strangle her with his bare hands.

The countess raised her hand. 'Lady Magda, we thank you for bringing this news to our attention and for making our cousin's wishes known to us. We require a little time to consider his terms and ask that you return to us in three days' time to hear our answer.'

'Thank you, countess,' said Magda. 'We await your pleasure. Though I remind you that the plague of madness grows daily worse, and much tragedy may befall in three days.'

'Thank you, lady,' said the countess, drawing herself up haughtily. 'We need no reminders of the city's troubles. You are dismissed.'

Lady Magda curtsied low, then turned and walked to the exit with unhurried grace. Reiner looked around at the members of the parliament. If looks could kill, Lady Magda would have been a red smear on the chamber's polished floor.

NINE
In My Heart I Know It

It was near midnight before Reiner returned to the Reikland legation's residence and climbed the stairs to Manfred's suite of rooms. He knocked on the door.

'Can't come in,' came Franka's sleepy voice.

'It's Reiner.'

There was a clacking of locks and the door opened. Franka blinked out at him, rubbing her face. He stepped past her and she locked them in.

'At least you are unaccompanied by bailiffs,' she said, yawning.

'No,' said Reiner. 'We are not arrested. The parliament was distracted from our villainy by greater villainy.'

'Oh?'

'Magda.'

'Ah.'

'She and Rodick hold the waystone hostage with the job of chief constable and a seat in the parliament as ransom,' said Reiner, sitting wearily on the bed and pulling off his boots. 'Where are Jergen and Dieter and Darius?'

Franka jerked a thumb at the adjoining valet's quarters. 'Sleeping.'

'Any trouble?'

'No.'

Reiner nodded, then looked shyly at Franka. He opened his mouth, then shut it again. Valaris was eavesdropping. He would hear everything Reiner wanted to say to Franka. Reiner flushed. It was like being on stage. Then he shrugged. What did Valaris care about their lives? He only wanted the stone. He couldn't wait to speak until after the dark elf had freed them. They might be dead before then.

'Er... er, Franka.'

'Captain?'

Reiner sighed. 'Less of the "captain" if you don't mind. It's Reiner to you and you know it.'

'Do you order me to call you that?' asked Franka, stiffly.

Reiner kicked his boots across the room. 'Curse it, girl,' he said. 'I know I am a fool, but can you not forgive it? Can you not understand?'

Franka shrugged. 'I can understand the reasons you think I might be a spy, but can I forgive it? No.'

Reiner flopped back angrily on the bed and hissed as he jolted his inflamed chest.

Franka looked down at him, pain creasing her forehead. 'Reiner, only say it. Say that you know I am not the spy.'

'But I do know you are not the spy!' he cried. 'In my heart I know it.'

'But only in your heart?' asked Franka, fixing him with shining eyes.

Reiner held her gaze for a long moment, trying to will himself to say what she wanted him to say, to lie to her as he had lied to so many in his life. It would be so easy. But...

He looked away, ashamed, and heard a sob in her throat. He threw himself off the bed and stood, straightening his doublet. 'Summon the others, archer. Get them all up.'

'Now?' asked Franka, sniffing.

'Now.'

THE BLACKHEARTS STUMBLED, sleepy and surly, into Manfred's rooms, and sprawled on the available furniture, scratching and yawning. Reiner stood in the centre of them, arms crossed, feeling hard as stone, and hoping he looked that way.

'I have good news,' he said, when they had all settled themselves.

'Manfred's died of the gout and we're all free men?' asked Hals.

'Stow it, pikeman,' snapped Reiner. 'I'm not in the mood.'

Hals's eyes widened. 'Beg pardon, captain.'

'The first bit of good news,' Reiner said, starting again, 'is that Teclis lives.'

The Blackhearts brightened at this.

'Good old chalkie,' said Gert. 'Tougher than he looks.'

'The second piece is that Rodick and Magda hold the waystone ransom and refuse to give it up to the countess unless Rodick is made chief constable.'

'This is good news?' asked Pavel.

'It gives us an even chance,' said Reiner. 'Had Rodick given the stone to the countess, it would be locked away in her manor behind ten score guards and Sigmar knows what locks and wards. Clever as they are, Magda and Rodick haven't those resources. So it is only a matter of finding where they've hidden it.'

'We'll have some company there, I'm guessing,' said Hals.

'Aye,' said Reiner. 'The countess asked Magda for three days to consider her offer, and you can be certain it wasn't so she might confer with her cabinet. If she hasn't already sent von Pfaltzen and his men and the whole of the Talabheim city guard out sniffing for the stone I'll be very surprised.'

'Magda must know this,' said Franka.

Reiner nodded. 'She practically dared the countess to search her house, so she's hidden it well. Fortunately,' he said smirking, 'being thieves, tricksters and villains, I hold out some hope for our success.' He sighed. 'Only remember this. If we fail, and the waystone is returned to the countess, our job becomes that much harder.'

The Blackhearts nodded and began to rise.

Reiner held up his hand. 'There... there is one other thing.'

The Blackhearts settled back again, but Reiner only chewed his lip, staring at the Araby carpet.

At last he looked up. 'This should have been spoken of long ago, and it has hurt us that it hasn't.' He laughed bitterly. 'It might hurt me to say it now. Might kill me. But I can stand it no longer.' He looked around at them all. 'One of us is a spy for Manfred.'

They looked back at him levelly, but said nothing.

'I see this comes as no surprise to you,' he said. 'I didn't think it would. Ever since Abel's poisoning, we have been treating each other like lepers, and I have been the worst of all. I have suspected even those I... I have known longest.' Reiner forced himself not to look at Franka. 'I don't blame Manfred for wishing to spy on us. We are Blackhearts after all. I might have done the same.' He sighed. 'Unfortunately, since Abel's death, the presence of the spy has had an unexpected consequence. It has destroyed the camaraderie and the trust that are essential to a fighting company. We have been lucky so far, but if we can't depend upon one another, it will eventually kill us, and I don't know about the rest of you, but I want to live to see my freedom.'

The Blackhearts still said nothing, but Reiner could see them thinking it through.

'So here it is,' Reiner continued, letting out a shaky breath. 'Now that Manfred has agreed to free us if we can free him, we are all on the same side. There is no longer any need for secrets. In fact there is more need for us all to be honest and above board with each other so that we can better work together for Manfred's salvation.' He swallowed. 'Therefore, I ask the spy to reveal himself, so that the poison of suspicion will stop eating away at us and we can rely upon one another again.'

The Blackhearts looked around expectantly, waiting for someone to speak up. Reiner's heart thudded. His nails bit into his palms. No one spoke. No one stood. No one raised their hand or attacked them. They only continued to glance around, waiting for someone else to do something.

Reiner's fists clenched. 'No?' he asked. 'You haven't the courage? My arguments did not convince you?'

'Maybe there isn't a spy,' said Gert.

'Of course there is a spy!' spat Reiner. 'Beard of Sigmar! There may be two! A new one among our new recruits to keep an eye on the old one! Or maybe three! Manfred could have turned one of us first four to watch the others! Maybe you are *all* spies! Or maybe I am the spy! Maybe...' He caught himself – a little too late perhaps, for the others were looking at him warily – and dropped his arms abruptly to his sides.

'Get out,' he said through clenched teeth. 'Go. Assemble at dawn in the coach yard. Dress to hunt.'

The Blackhearts stood and filed out silently, keeping their eyes fixed on the floor. Reiner watched after Franka as she turned into the hall. Her face was drawn and pale, her eyes troubled. She didn't look back.

Reiner lay awake in Manfred's luxurious bed. He couldn't sleep. Thoughts of Franka and her stubbornness rattled unceasingly in his head like dice in a cup. The cuts in his chest kept him awake too, their dull throb spiking to agony every time he turned. He needed something to kill the pain, both pains. He needed... he needed to get drunk. He didn't want to leave the room and hunt for the pantry. Boellengen or one the others might corner him with questions. Maybe Manfred had a bottle.

He got out of bed and opened the armoire, pushing Manfred's clothes aside, and opened a valise, burrowing through shirts and ruffs and combs and perfumes. Nothing drinkable. He tried another. At the bottom, under Hern's *Histories and Families of Talabec*, was a small leather-bound book. Reiner flipped it open idly then stopped. It was a journal, written in Manfred's hand. The entry he had opened to was from two years previous. It read, 'The Emperor has learned of Holgrin's "treachery" through a third party. He will be hanged tomorrow. All goes as planned.'

Reiner's blood ran cold. Sigmar's balls! What had he stumbled upon? He flipped forward to the last entry, dated only two days ago.

'Our recovery of the waystone is paramount. It must be proved that Talabheim cannot rescue itself. And if "evidence" could be found that the countess was behind the stone's disappearance, so much the better. (Put Reiner's lot to work on this?) The Emperor has expressed a wish that Talabecland develop closer ties to the Reikland, and what better way to achieve that than have a Reiklander rule Talabecland's greatest city, and then soon the duchy itself. With Elector Count Feuerbach missing, there is no better time to strike. I have languished too long in the shadows. It is time to step into the sun.'

Reiner stared slack-jawed at the words. He had known Manfred to be manipulative and unscrupulous in his dealings with his underlings and those he considered traitors, but this ambition was something Reiner hadn't noted before. And his willingness to destroy the innocent as well as the guilty if they stood in his way was, well, criminal. Reiner forgot about drinking and returned to bed. He turned up the lamp and read long into the morning.

'WE'RE NOT ALONE, that's certain,' said Gert, poking a spyglass through the curtains in the chilly second storey room of an abanadoned manor house across the Avenue of Heroes from Lord Rodick Untern's palatial residence where Reiner was attempting to spy on Lady Magda's movements.

It had been surprisingly easy to find a deserted house nearby. Many noble families had fled the crisis in Talabheim for the less affected areas of Crater Lake and Dankerood. They had had their pick of three.

Reiner peeked from the room's other window, surveying the street. 'No,' he said. 'Those three on the corner, dressed as Taalist brethren. Isn't the heavy fellow one of von Pfaltzen's lieutenants?'

'Aye,' chuckled Gert. 'I can see his breastplate under his robes.' He pointed to the left. 'And the young knight who has been fussing with his horse's bridle for the last hour. He was one of Lord Danziger's men, who fought beside us in the sewers.'

'So he is,' said Reiner. 'See, he has a bandage on the fingers of his right hand.'

'And the two dandies walking past Magda's door?' asked Gert. 'They are certainly someone's spies.'

'In the mustard and violet?' asked Reiner. 'Aye, I've seen those colours before. Lord Scharnholt's I believe. These Talabheimers do not seem to care to work together.'

'Aye,' said Gert. 'Just like yesterday. None of 'em wants to share the glory.'

'A seven-legged beetle,' muttered Darius from the far corner of the room. He held up something that squirmed in the tweezers from his surgeon's kit. 'Even the insects are affected.'

Reiner looked around. 'Put it down, scholar,' he said. 'Sigmar knows what it might do to you.'

Darius sighed and tossed the thing away. 'What is my reason for being here?' he said glumly. 'You don't need a scholar. I am of no use in a fight. I have no skills helpful in espionage. I am not the witch you think me. I cannot make light or fire with a word. If you wanted me to deduce the genus of a plant from its leaves or root structure I could do it in an eye blink, but somehow I doubt it will come up.'

'Would you rather be back in prison, with the noose waiting for you at dawn?' asked Reiner.

Darius shrugged. 'As you said to m'lord Valdenheim yesterday, the threat of death loses its force if one's life isn't worth living.'

There were footsteps in the hall and Hals pushed in, dressed in a peasant's smock and straw hat. Reiner raised a questioning eyebrow.

Hals shook his head. 'Nothing, captain. I took that barrow of leeks and squash we stole around to the kitchen gate like ye asked, and chatted up the cook when she come out, but she don't know nothing.' He tossed the hat on a chair and wiped the sweat from his bald head. 'The mistress ain't at home. The master is out fighting the madmen. Ain't cook's business to ask their business.' He fished a silver coin from his pouch, grinning. 'Sold her six leeks and two squash at least, so we've some profit from it.'

'Hmmm,' said Reiner. 'That's something, though. She doesn't feed a company of men with six leeks and two squash, so Magda didn't lie about Rodick being away. Magda's home however, no matter what the cook says. We've seen her in the upper windows.'

The door opened again and Franka, Pavel and Dieter came in.

'Well?' Reiner asked.

Pavel shrugged. 'I followed that footman to the boot maker, the draper, a bookseller, and the houses of three different lords. Two of 'em he gave letters at the front door. At the third he sneaks around back and plays kissing games with the chambermaid.'

'What were the names of the lords to whom he delivered notes?' asked Reiner.

'I didn't hear the names, but I can lead you back,' said Pavel.

'Good,' said Reiner. 'Franka?'

'The scullery maid and lady's maid went together to the market, to a dressmaker, a chandler and a sweetmeat shop, then returned. They spoke to no one but tradesmen.'

Reiner laughed. 'The rest of the city may be in flames, but m'lady must have her sweets.' He turned to Dieter. 'And you, master shadow?'

Dieter put his feet up on a decorative table. 'I got in. Climbed up to the roof, then jimmied a dormer. Cased the shack from attic to cellar.' He smirked. 'Tiptoed behind the lady's back three times. The stone ain't there. Nor is Rodick or his men. She's alone but for the servants and the guards.' He made a face. 'And rats. Needs to set some traps in her cellar.'

'Captain,' said Hals, eyes glowing. 'What a chance! We can–'

Reiner shook his head. 'No. We daren't. Not until the stone's found.'

'We could twist it out of her,' said Franka coldly. 'And then kill her. She deserves that and more.'

'Aye, we could,' said Reiner. 'But this close to freedom, I don't care to be torturing and killing the wives of cousins of countesses. It would be just like Manfred to free us from his poison only to turn us over to the hangman for crimes done in his service.'

'But, captain–' said Pavel, but he was interrupted by voices coming from the hall.

'Stand downwind, curse you,' came Augustus's bellow. 'Y'reek like a beggar's kip.'

'And so might you,' Rumpolt whined. 'If I'd pushed you.'

The door opened and Jergen ducked in, a pained expression on his usually stolid features. He was followed by Augustus and Rumpolt. The young handgunner was covered in wet brown slime, and the room was filled with an overpowering faecal stench. The Blackhearts retched and covered their faces.

'What in Sigmar's name?' asked Reiner, coughing.

'The clumsy infant fell in the sewer,' said Augustus, laughing.

'You pushed me!' bleated Rumpolt.

'I tried to catch you, fool!'

'Shut up, the both of you,' cried Reiner, standing. 'Rumpolt, go wash yourself in the trough! Curse you, why did you come up here in the first place?'

'Because I knew he was going to lie about–'

'Never mind! Just go!' shouted Reiner. 'Run.'

Rumpolt pouted, but turned and hurried back out the door.

Gert made a face. 'Augh! Sigmar's death. He's left footprints!'

'Come on,' said Reiner. 'Let's adjourn to the dining room. I'm not cleaning that up.'

When they had resettled themselves around an oval dining table two floors down, Reiner turned to Augustus. 'So, anything below?'

Augustus shook his head. 'Nothing. No secret ways into the house. No holes. No hidden vaults or crypts. We even fished in the channel, which was when moon-cow fell in. He didn't find anything.'

The others chuckled.

'I found no hidden doors inside either,' said Dieter.

Reiner sighed. 'Curse the woman. Where has she hidden it? We'll have to check the lords she sent notes to, though I doubt she'd be so incautious.'

'You blame her and not her husband?' asked Darius. 'He seemed a devious little brat.'

Reiner smiled. 'You don't know the Lady Magda as some of us do. She is more devious than ten Rodicks. In fact, it is she more than anyone who's to blame for us being under Manfred's thumb. If she hadn't filled Manfred's younger brother Albrecht with evil ambition, he wouldn't have recruited us to fetch that cursed banner for him, and we wouldn't have run to Manfred asking for protection.'

'And Manfred wouldn't have done his brother one better by poisoning us,' said Franka bitterly.

Hals spat over his shoulder. 'I knew she was a bad'un, even before she turned on us at the convent.'

'You didn't!' said Pavel. 'Or we would have heard you go on about it all the way there. You were as fooled as the rest–'

'The convent!' cried Reiner, interrupting him. 'Sigmar bless you, pikeman. The Shallyan convent!'

Everyone turned and looked at him, confused.

Reiner tipped back in his chair. 'Lady Magda doesn't appear to have told anyone in Talabheim that she was once a sister of Shallya. She no longer wears the robes – not even a dove-wing necklace. None would think she had any connection to the faith. None but us.' He turned to Augustus. 'Kolbein, this is your city. Where is the temple of Shallya?'

Augustus frowned. 'Er, there's the sanitarium and the big temple in the City of the Gods, and some kind of mission down in the Tallows. Don't know any other.'

Reiner nodded. 'Well, the Tallows are overrun, yes? It would have to be the big temple then.' He stood. 'Come. Let us go speak to the sisters before the walls pass along our words and all of Talabheim joins us.'

The others rose with a scraping of chairs and turned towards the door, but just then Rumpolt appeared in it, panting. He was dripping wet, his boots leaking streams of water.

'Why did you move? Were you hiding from me?' he asked accusingly.

'Don't be an ass, Rumpolt,' said Reiner. 'Now turn about. We're going.'

Rumpolt sidled aside to let the others through. 'You needn't be mean about it,' he muttered.

THE BLACKHEARTS HURRIED through the broad, deserted avenues of the City of the Gods, passing temples and shrines to Taal, Sigmar, Myrmidia and Ulric, and then up the wide marble steps of the Shallyan temple, a low, modest building of white stone almost hidden in the looming shadow of the gleaming marble sanatorium attached to it. They ran under the carving of outstretched dove's wings above the lintel, and into the cool stone interior. But the usual air of soothing calm one expected in the Lady of Mercy's temple was distinctly absent. Grey-robed sisters ran this way and that, and cries and moans came from the corridors beyond the main chapel.

The temple's abbess ran toward them, wimple trembling in agitation. 'Thank Shallya you've come!' she said. 'They have overwhelmed our guards and are breaking into...' She paused. 'But you are not the city guard. I sent Sister Kirsten...'

'We are not the guard, Mother,' said Reiner. 'But we will help. Who is attacking you?'

'Hooded men,' said the abbess, pointing to a door in the left wall. 'They came up through a hole in the floor of the catacombs. They break into the vault as we speak.'

'Wait here for the guard,' said Reiner. 'We will see what we can do.'

'Shallya bless you, my son,' said the abbess as they raced across the chapel.

The door led to a stairway that wound down to the catacombs. Screams and crashes echoed up to them as they clattered down it.

'Someone's got in ahead of us,' growled Hals.

'But how did they know?' asked Reiner, taking a torch from a bracket and starting down the stairs. 'I don't understand it.'

Reiner tripped over the corpse of a sister at the base of the stairs. More dead sisters were strewn about the corridor, as well as three dead guards, swords clutched tight in their bloody hands. The Blackhearts leapt the bodies as they hurried forward. Rats scurried into the shadows at their approach.

A heavy door lay torn from its hinges. The Blackhearts looked through it into the temple's vault. Statues and paintings and piles of books and scroll tubes cluttered it. A sister wept in a corner, her grey cassock spattered with red. Blood made interesting patterns as it flowed across the decorative tile floor away from three bodies. Two were guards. The third was a hooded figure in brown robes with a burlap bag covering his face. Reiner shivered as he saw it, and prayed it wasn't what he thought it was.

The wounded sister groaned and pointed behind the Blackhearts. 'Stop them! They've stolen Lady Magda's gift!'

'Eh?' said Reiner. 'What gift?'

'A beautiful statue of Shallya, taller than a man. She only bequeathed it to us yesterday and already it's gone!'

Reiner exchanged looks with Pavel and Hals. 'Poor Lady Magda,' he said.

'There!' called Franka, pointing to a cross-corridor.

The Blackhearts ran to the intersection. Down the right corridor, a cluster of hooded figures was manoeuvring a heavy object through a door.

'Come on, lads,' said Reiner.

They charged down the corridor, swords out. The hooded men redoubled their speed. Jergen sprinted ahead, but before he could reach them, the thieves had squeezed the white statue through the door and slammed it in his face. Reiner heard bolts slide home as he skidded to a stop.

'Bash it in!' he cried.

Gert drew his hatchet and started chopping at the sturdy panels while Jergen stabbed it with the tip of his sword and began prying away splinters.

'Silly fools,' said Dieter. 'Let me.'

He pushed forward and knelt by the keyhole, taking a ring of strangely shaped tools from his pouch. Gert and Jergen watched as he pushed his picks into the hole and twisted. Almost before he had begun he had finished, and pulled the door open. 'There,' he said.

The Blackhearts rushed into the room. Rats skittered into the shadows. It was a store room, filled with medical supplies and trundle beds. A rough hole yawned in the floor, surrounded by heaps of cracked flagstones and moist earth. A length of heavy hawser dropped down into it. Reiner and the others ran to it and looked down. The sluggish flow of the sewer channel glimmered in the light of Reiner's torch. The reek of sewage was mixed with a rank animal musk.

Franka recoiled at the smell, trembling. 'Myrmidia's shield, no. Not again.'

The others cursed and wrinkled their noses.

'Maybe it's only rats,' said Pavel, but it didn't sound like he believed it.

'Aye. Like Magda had in her cellar,' said Reiner grimly. 'Come on. Down we go.'

They took more torches from the hall, then climbed down the rope one at a time, Jergen first, and looked up and down the dark, curving tunnel. The waystone thieves were out of sight.

'This way,' said Dieter, examining the floor.

They ran in the direction he indicated and after a short while saw flutters of movement far ahead of them as the thieves ran under a sunlit grate.

'How fast they move,' said Rumpolt, panting. 'We couldn't carry it half that fast.'

'They are twice as many,' said Augustus.

The Blackhearts hurried on, trying to keep up with the fleeing figures, but the thieves carried no torches so it was hard to tell how far ahead they were.

'How do they see?' asked Darius. 'It's black as pitch down here.'

Reiner kept his theories to himself.

After a long stretch where they saw no sign of the robed men, Dieter skidded to a stop.

'Wait!' he barked, turning and studying the ground. 'They've turned.'

The rest watched him as he trotted back along the ledge, frowning. He stopped at one of the granite slabs that bridged the channel. 'Crossed over.'

The Blackhearts followed as he stepped across and turned down a side corridor, then paused a dozen yards in, scratching his head. 'Tracks stop here. They... ah!' He began to examine the wall closely, running his hands lightly over the crumbling bricks. 'There must be...' he mumbled to himself, then, 'Aye, here's the... So where...? Ha!'

With a grin of triumph Dieter pulled a brick from its place high on the wall and reached into the gap, digging about with his fingers. A muted clatter of gears came from under their feet, and a section of the wall sank inward a few inches. Dieter pushed on the wall. It swung in, revealing a cobweb-choked corridor that sloped away from them into darkness. The dust on the floor had been lately disturbed by many feet. Reiner didn't care for the smallness of the prints, nor their unusual outline.

The Blackhearts hurried on, following Dieter's lead through another confusing maze of cellars, forgotten catacombs, collapsed tunnels and buried temples. From time to time Reiner thought he heard the scurrying of feet in front of them, but it was difficult to be certain above all their own gasping and creaking. He continued to look ahead, though it was impossible to see beyond the light of their torches.

After half an hour, they entered the strangest place Reiner had yet seen in Talabheim's underground. It appeared to be a city street, complete with tall tenements and shops on either side and cobbles underfoot, except that the ground was tilted at such a drastic angle that it was difficult to walk, and that the third floors of all the buildings disappeared into a hard-packed earth ceiling above. It looked as if the street had been dug out after some great avalanche of mud had buried it. Slanting shafts of weak sunlight shot down from narrow chimneys bored in the roof. Burning torches jammed into broken brick walls and the smell of meat smoke spoke of current habitation, but the

Blackhearts saw no one as Dieter led them around corners and down side streets, his head down like a wolfhound on the hunt.

As Dieter turned down an alley, Reiner put a hand on his shoulder, for there was movement in the darkness at the end of it. The thieves were lowering the statue of Shallya into a gaping rift in the alley floor. Shallya's shoulders disappeared as they watched. It looked like the goddess was sinking in a sea of earth.

'Now's our chance, lads,' said Reiner. 'On them!'

As the Blackhearts raced forwards, Franka hopped onto a pile of rubble and loosed a shaft at the thieves. One squealed and fell with an arrow in its chest. The rest looked up and the statue dropped abruptly through the rift. Reiner felt a thud of impact through his feet. The thieves crowded into the ragged hole after her, their long robes flapping.

Jergen caught the last few and slashed left and right. They pitched into the hole, their severed limbs spinning down after them. Reiner looked down into the rift. It was as black as the void. The Blackhearts gathered around him, staring down warily.

'Captain,' said Franka, behind them.

Reiner and the others turned. Franka crouched over the thief she had slain with her arrow. She held its burlap leper's mask in her hand.

The thief had the head of a rat.

TEN
This is Not My Home

'A RATMAN!' SAID Pavel.

Hals spit over his shoulder.

'Not again,' said Gert.

Reiner groaned. He had known it in his heart since he had smelled the rat stench in the cellar of the Shallyan temple, but having his fears confirmed made him sick.

'Don't be daft,' said Augustus. 'Ratmen are a myth. They don't exist.'

'Well, this one don't,' said Hals. 'Not any more. Nice shooting lass.'

Rumpolt backed away, making the sign of the hammer. Dieter crossed his fingers. Darius stepped closer, eyes glittering.

'Vindication!' he said. 'The professors said the outlawed books I read were wrong, the scribblings of a warped brain. Another example of their close-minded, reactionary ignorance.' He looked up at Reiner. 'Can we take it with us?'

'We've other things to worry about at the moment, scholar,' said Reiner, looking down into the hole.

'You're not going down there?' wailed Rumpolt. 'There were twenty of the things at least.'

'Oh, there'll be more than that, laddie,' said Hals. 'Hundreds.'

'Thousands,' said Pavel.

'But have we a choice?' asked Augustus. 'We have to recover the stone. The elf will kill us if we don't.'

'And the ratmen will kill us if we do,' said Franka.

'The executioner's joke,' laughed Gert, and put on a highbrow accent. 'Will you have the noose or the axe, m'lord?'

A rattle of pebbles made them look up. Creeping into the alley from both ends was a throng of mutants. Reiner grimaced. These were more deformed than the poor broken men they had fought yesterday. There were many with extra limbs or eyes. Some were only barely recognisable as human. One walked on stork-like legs that sprouted from his back, while his human legs dangled, shrivelled and useless below him. A little girl with an angelic face had tree-stump arms and legs, crusted in rocky scabs. A woman whose face had no features groped forward with hands that had eyes on each fingertip. A man limped forward on stubs of legs that ended in ever-bleeding orifices. He wore the remains of a Talabheim guardsman's uniform.

But no matter how pathetic the mutants appeared, their eyes shone with hunger and hatred, and they clutched bones, stones, clubs and swords in their twisted hands.

'Kill them!' said a gaunt giant with translucent skin. 'Kill them before they bring soldiers and kill us all.' Reiner could see the man's tongue working through his glassine teeth.

The mutants howled and charged. The Blackhearts turned out to face them, slashing wildly. Reiner chopped through the stork-man's spindly bird-shanks like they were matchwood and he fell. Hals buried his spear in a man whose entire body seemed one giant boil. He popped, splashing pus everywhere.

'Into the hole!' shrieked Rumpolt. 'Into the hole! It's our only chance!'

'No!' bellowed Reiner. 'And be trapped twixt these fiends and the rats? Are you mad?' He looked around, then pointed to the back of a looming tenement. 'Through that door!'

Gert threw his bulk against a rotten wood door, caving it in, and the Blackhearts backed through, keeping the horrors at bay with swift spear and sword work.

Inside was a filthy, plaster-walled hall, knee-deep in rubbish, which opened out into a small central court – little more than an air shaft – ringed at each floor by balconies that accessed the apartments. An open stairwell rose into the earth ceiling on the far side, a door to the street beyond it. More mutants goggled down at them from the upper floors before flinching back out of sight.

'Dieter,' called Reiner. 'Can you lead us back out of this hell hole?'

'Aye,' said the thief. 'If we can get through these... things.'

'Wait, captain,' said Franka. 'There's a wind coming down. Fresh air.'

Reiner raised his head and sniffed. Blowing down from the stairwell was a faint breeze with a distinct hint of outdoors on it.

'Up then!' he said.

They struggled across the court, elbowing through mounds of smashed furniture, broken crockery, rotting vegetables, rotting corpses, and pig bones. As the Blackhearts left the hallway the mutants spread out, clambering over the rubbish and trying to surround them. Reiner drove his sword through the neck – at least he thought it was its neck – of a thing whose entire skin was a carpet of writhing pink tendrils. Augustus speared a boy with batwing membranes between arms and ribs. Rumpolt tripped over the corpse of an old woman as he swung his handgun wildly by the barrel. Franka stabbed the transparent man in the groin and he fell back wailing and gushing blood that looked like water.

'Now up!' shouted Reiner. 'But 'ware above!'

He pushed Jergen forward and the swordsman took the lead, two steps at a time. The others ran up after him, Hals, Pavel and Augustus coming last and walking backwards, spears levelled.

A man with veins on the outside of his skin shouted up to the storeys above. 'Don't let 'em get away! They'll bring the guards! Stop them!'

Mutated hands reached through the rails to grab legs and ankles. Reiner and the others stomped and slashed, leaving severed hands and tentacles twitching in their wake. A cresting wave of horrors clambered and leaped over the banister. Gert caught one in mid air and hurled it down into his fellows, a length of railing crashing to the floor below in a rain of tinder and falling mutants. More came from above, but only in ones and twos, and Jergen's flashing sword quickly dispatched them.

When they had reached the second flight and the mutants were thinning around them, Reiner shoved Rumpolt's face into the wall.

The handgunner looked around, eyes wide, a smear of dust on one cheek. 'What was that for?'

'I give the orders,' said Reiner, pushing him up the stairs as he spoke. 'No, "Into the hole", or "Retreat" from you, you understand?'

'But–'

'I'm a reluctant leader,' Reiner carried on, ignoring him, 'as the lads will tell you. But in battle, there's one voice. And it certainly ain't yours!'

'But I was only...'

Reiner shoved him again. 'You aren't listening! One voice, you hear me, gunner? One!'

'Aye, captain,' said Rumpolt, thrusting out his lower lip.

Reiner turned away from him, disgusted, and the company continued up the stairs.

Three storeys up, the stairway rose up into the earth ceiling. The chill wind the Blackhearts were following whistled down from the darkness. There were no more mutants above them, but the mob that swarmed up the stairs had swelled to a hundred or more. The stairs ended at an open door, black as night. Reiner stopped and thrust his torch in, revealing a peak-roofed attic, low and cramped. The Blackhearts halted behind him.

'Are y'certain there's a way out?' asked Gert, uneasy.

'There must be,' said Reiner. 'Or they wouldn't be trying to stop us.'

The first rank of mutants were being pressed into the pikemen's spears as the rest pushed up behind them. The stairs creaked ominously.

'They'll be climbin' over us soon, captain!' called Hals, over his shoulder. An axe blade missed him by a hair's breadth.

Franka stabbed between them and opened up a gash in a mutant's belly. Rumpolt picked up a loose brick and hurled it, and hit Pavel in the back of the head.

'Rumpolt!' Reiner roared.

Pavel stumbled forward, grunting, and a sword blade skidded across his breastplate and plunged into his arm. He thrust back reflexively and spat at the mutant who had struck him, but he was unsteady on his feet. 'Who threw that paver?' he shouted, furious.

Rumpolt ducked his head guiltily, but Pavel saw him. 'I'll be having words with you, laddie!'

'Less of it, pikeman,' shouted Reiner. 'Hold the door 'til we find the way out.'

'No trouble, captain,' Pavel said. 'If the infant doesn't kill us first.' He kicked a mutant in one of its faces and gutted another. Three more thrust at him.

Reiner entered the attic. 'Hafner, with me. Take this torch. And don't throw anything.' Reiner hurried forward with Rumpolt, Gert and Jergen, crouching low beneath the slanting roof. Franka, Dieter and Darius filed in behind them. Pavel, Hals and Augustus stayed in the door and set their spears.

Filthy blankets and piles of straw were tucked under the eaves where the roof touched the floor. Scraps of food and bits of candle littered the planks, and roaches scuttled everywhere. Something marginally human backed away from their torchlight, its eyes glowing like a cat's. The low room bent at a right angle. The cold breeze blew in Reiner's face as he turned into it.

'There,' said Jergen, pointing ahead.

Reiner followed his gaze. Ten paces on, the planks and slates of the roof had been torn out, leaving a ragged hole a yard high and just as wide. A rough tunnel slanted up from it. Reiner stepped forward and looked in. Only a few yards above, bars of golden light shone down through a grate.

'Franka,' said Reiner. 'Up there and have a look.'

'Aye, captain.' She clambered up on fingers and toes and peered up through the grate.

'All I can see is sky, captain.' she called back.

'Sky,' said Gert. 'Thought I'd never see it again.'

'We'll have to risk it,' said Reiner. 'Up you go Gert, and be ready to raise the grate on my command.' He turned to the others. 'The rest of you in behind him.'

Dieter, Jergen, Rumpolt and Darius began ducking into the hole as Reiner ran back to the corner. In the doorway, Hals, Pavel and Augustus were bathed in sweat and blood. Dead mutants were piled at the top of the stairs as high as Pavel's belt, and more clawed over them, stabbing madly at the three pikemen with swords and staffs.

'Now, Gert!' called Reiner to his left, then, 'Fall back, pikes! Run!' to his right.

There was a second's pause, then Reiner heard a muffled clang from the tunnel, and Darius, who stood outside the hole staring at Rumpolt's backside, followed the handgunner in and disappeared.

The three pikemen jumped back from the door and turned, running in a crouch. The mutants tumbled through the door behind them, crawling over the pile of their dead.

Reiner pointed the pikemen at the hole. 'In boys, in!'

Hals dived in head-first and Pavel and Augustus followed. Reiner took one look back at the swarming mutants, then shot in after them, his skin crawling, but though he heard the things scrabbling and slobbering behind him, he reached the grate unscathed and was lifted out bodily by Hals and Augustus, who set him on his feet. They were in a burned out cellar, open to the sky. The blackened beams of the upper floors lay like dragon bones across the ash covered flags of the floor.

'The grate, quick!'

Jergen and Gert muscled it to the hole, and dropped it with a clang, smashing heads and crushing forearms as the mutants surged up. But there were too many behind the first wave and the grate began to rise. Gert and Jergen jumped on it, trying to hold it down with their weight, but they rocked and teetered like men standing in a shallow boat.

Reiner looked around. One end of a massive roof beam rested precariously at the very end of a crumbling brick wall next to the grate.

'Lads! The beam!'

All the Blackhearts but Jergen and Gert ran to it and began pushing at its side. It wouldn't budge. They grunted and strained to no effect as Jergen and Gert stabbed down through the bucking grate.

'Not the beam!' said Pavel. 'The wall!' And to illustrate, he began jabbing at the powdery bricks below the beam.

'Good thinking!' said Reiner. 'Everybody at it!'

The Blackhearts began hacking and chopping at the end of the wall with their spears and swords. Reiner stepped to Gert and took his hatchet from his belt, then hammered on the wall with the back of it. Bricks smashed and fell out of the dry mortar like hail until it looked like a giant had taken a bite from the wall.

Suddenly, with a groan and a popping of exploding bricks, the beam's weight finished the job, crushing the unsupported bricks below it and sliding toward the edge.

'Gert! Jergen!'

The swordsman and the crossbowman leapt clear of the grate as the beam crashed to the flags with a deafening boom. The grate lifted, the mutants welling up under it, but the beam bounced once and mashed it back down, pinning their arms and fingers and necks beneath it. Horrible muffled screams came from below it.

Reiner slapped Pavel on the back while the others caught their breath. 'Well done, lad. Now let's away.'

Reiner led them up a stone stairway and they spilled through a door onto the street, and froze in shock. The neighbourhood had become a jungle.

The Blackhearts stood at the base of the crater wall, the street rising rapidly to their right into the cluttered vertical slum of shacks that clung to its inner curve. But though there were buildings all around them, it hardly seemed they were in a city at all.

Talabheim had been long known throughout the Empire as the city of gardens. Its parks were famed for their beauty. Trees lined most streets, and even the poorest hovels had flowers at every window, but now the trees and flowers had consumed everything. Mutant ivy poured down the crater wall like a green waterfall. Once stately oaks and beeches had grown into twisted monstrosities, sprouting gnarled, questing branches that had smashed through walls and pushed down buildings. To the left was a hulking, black-leafed giant that might once have been a larch. Fat purple fruit hung from its branches. The fruit screamed through gaping sphincters.

The structures that still stood were wreathed in matted vegetation. Some were choked by pale, pulsing lianas that sprouted wet pink flowers. Others were hung with torso-thick black vines that bristled with thorns as long as daggers. Burned tenements rose out of this underbrush like tottering matchstick giants. The vines that covered the lower storeys of one were hung all over with bodies. Reiner cringed as he saw that the vines had grown through the corpses like curved spears. Blood-red grass grew between the cobbles, coarse and sharp.

Hideous mutants crept through this jungle like wild beasts, travelling in packs for safety and eyeing each other warily. Reiner watched a man with a parrot beak for a mouth lead what might have been his family across the street and into a shattered bakery. Before they were all in, the branch of an oak tree twitched down and snatched up one of his children.

The parrot man turned and beat the branch savagely with his staff, until with a rustle of leaves, it dropped the boy to the ground. The man grabbed him and ran inside with his four-armed wife.

'Shade of Sigmar,' said Reiner softly. 'Where are we?'

'Hell,' said Gert hollowly. 'This is hell.'

'It is the Tallows,' said Augustus. 'At least... Oh, Father Taal! What have we done to you?' he cried suddenly, turning away and covering his eyes. 'This is not my home,' he mumbled. 'This is not my home.'

Franka too was moved. Tears streamed down her cheeks. 'Captain,' she said, choking. 'Reiner, this cannot be the fate of the Empire! We cannot allow this to happen! Look at them, the poor horrible things! They could be my mother and father. They could be...' She firmed her jaw. 'We cannot give the stone to that... elf. I care not what he does to us! We must bring it back to Teclis. We must put everything right!'

'Quiet, you little fool,' said Reiner, tapping his chest meaningfully though it was agony to do it. 'Of course we will bring the stone to the Druchii. We made a bargain with him and we will honour it.'

The others looked at him sullenly. He ignored them and turned to Augustus. 'Right, Kolbein. You know this place. Lead us back to civilization.'

'Aye, captain,' Augustus said dully. He looked around at the horizon. 'The Street of the Emperor's Grace is... this way.' He pointed left down the street, then started marching stolidly through the long red grass. The others fell in behind him, weapons out.

The journey was quite literally a nightmare. Here they saw a man hacking off his fur-covered left hand with an axe. There was a thing with a head like a bobbing bouquet of eyeballs. Here was a dog dragging itself by its front paws, its back half a scaly fish tail. There walked a naked woman with fangs down to her chin trying to nurse her dead baby at her breast.

Fortunately, most of the denizens seemed too concerned with their own affairs to bother with the well-armed Blackhearts. Reiner hoped they reached their destination soon, however, for the sun was setting quickly and the thought of travelling though this place at night made his blood run cold.

As they walked, Hals examined the blood matted hair at the back of Pavel's head while Pavel wrapped the gash in his arm with linen from Darius's kit.

'Not to worry, lad,' said Hals. 'He ain't knocked yer brains out. Ain't even a hole.'

'I'd knock his brains out,' said Pavel, giving Rumpolt a dirty look. 'If he had any.'

'It was an accident!' cried Rumpolt. 'I meant to throw it at the mutants.'

'And if y'hadn't thrown it at all,' said Hals, 'there'd ha' been no accident.'

'Y'owe Voss a pint of blood, infant,' said Augustus.

'I was only trying to help.'

'Aye,' said Pavel. 'Help. It's no wonder the lads of yer company sent ye to the gallows. They were trying to save their lives.'

'Have ye no common sense?' asked Hals. 'Were ye not trained?'

'Trained?' laughed Augustus. 'He's hardly weaned!'

The pikemen laughed, as did Dieter and Gert.

Rumpolt looked close to tears. 'Captain, will you let them mock me so?'

'I'm waiting for them to say something that isn't the truth,' said Reiner dryly.

'You side with them?' said Rumpolt, disbelieving. 'When they abuse me for a mistake?'

'I side with them because they are proven men,' he said. 'You'll have to prove yourself their equal before I think of siding with you. And you've a long way to go, laddie. A long way.' Of course one of the others is a spy, Reiner added gloomily to himself, but at least they could handle themselves in a fight.

Rumpolt lowered his head. His hands gripped his gun barrel as if he were trying to choke it.

Reiner grunted. Curse the boy. He seemed to invite insult by his mere presence. He was trying to think of something encouraging to say when a yelp from behind made them all turn.

Thirty paces back, Darius was being dragged into an alley by an obese, toad-like woman with a mouth that opened to her navel. The scholar had a knife in one hand and a clump of writhing vines in the other.

'Hie!' cried Reiner. 'Leave off!'

The Blackhearts ran back, shouting and waving their weapons. The toad-woman dropped Darius, terrified, and bounded with surprising speed into the shadows.

Reiner pulled Darius up roughly by the arm. 'Are you mad? What are you doing falling back?'

'I... I'm sorry,' said Darius. 'I was taking cuttings.'

'Cuttings?'

'Aye. Look.' Darius held up the wriggling plants. 'The mutations are fascinating. I want to plant the seeds and see if they breed true away from the influence of the warpstone. Imagine what might be learned from–'

Reiner dashed the stalks from his hands. 'Fool! They're diseased. Do you want to spread this madness?'

Darius glared at him. 'I am a man of method. I would not let that occur.'

'You certainly won't,' said Reiner. 'Because you're leaving them behind.' He shoved Darius forward and the Blackhearts marched on.

As THEY PASSED through the barricades at the border of Old Market and the company began to march wearily through the only marginally less lunatic merchant quarter, a crushing depression settled upon Reiner. With every step, the futility of continuing their quest was more apparent. The ratmen had the waystone. And by tomorrow morning, if the fables of the beasts' globe-spanning tunnels were true, it might be anywhere in the world. The Blackhearts' chances of recovering it were worse than a mark's chance of winning at dice in a rigged game.

Giving up would be such a relief. All he had to do was lie down and do nothing for three days and then Manfred would kill them before the dark elf killed him. It would all be over – all the struggle, all the confusion with Franka. Nothing but blissful oblivion.

But the faint, flickering hope of freedom floated ahead of him like a will-o-the-wisp drifting across a swamp, and try as he might, he couldn't let it go. It was so tantalisingly close. Only an army of vermin stood in the way.

'Right, lads,' he said as they reached the townhouse's back gate. 'We'll carry on as before, and make another try for the stone tomorrow, after I have thought of a way to get it away from the ratmen.'

That none of them laughed at that foolish statement was proof of their weariness. They only nodded and wandered off to their various quarters. Reiner, Jergen, Darius and Franka climbed the stairs to the second floor, then stopped as they saw the nobles of the Reikland legation in full armour milling around Count Manfred's quarters, all talking at once. Manfred's door was open.

'Hetsau,' called Lord Boellengen, his chinless face livid with outrage. 'What is the meaning of this? Where is Count Manfred?'

ELEVEN
Beasts and Vermin

REINER GROANED. HE was not ready to be clever. All he wanted to do was close his eyes. He took a deep breath and stepped forwards, looking as earnest and concerned as he could manage.

'M'lords, I apologise if we have caused you any concern. I would have informed you of events earlier but, as you can see, we have had a trying day ourselves and are only just returning from the most desperate adventure.'

'Do not try to oil your way out of this, rogue,' said Lord Schott, sneering. 'Where is Count Manfred?'

'I am endeavouring to tell you, m'lords,' said Reiner. 'There was an attempt on the count's life early this morning, in this very house. Strange assassins breached the locks of his room by unknown means, and only the skill of Jergen here held them off. Afterwards, for his safety, the count felt he should be moved, like Teclis, to an undisclosed location, and this we have done.'

'What nonsense is this?' rumbled Grand Master Raichskell. 'We heard no attack. We did not see the count leave.'

'The assassins were very silent m'lord,' said Reiner. 'And we removed Manfred as quietly as possible, so as not to alert any spies among the household staff.'

'I see,' said Boellengen, sceptically. 'And where is the count now?'

'Er, forgive me, m'lords,' said Reiner. 'But the count has asked that I keep his new quarters a secret, even from his allies. He has reason not to trust the walls of Talabheim with the knowledge.'

Boellengen and Schott and the others exchanged looks. Boellengen said something to an attendant, who hurried away, then he turned back to Reiner. 'We begin to suspect, Hetsau,' he sniffed, 'that you have abducted Count Manfred. You and these others will turn over your weapons and surrender to our custody.'

'M'lord,' said Reiner. 'I assure you, we have done nothing to Lord Manfred. We are, in fact, entirely concerned with his safety.'

'Be that as it may,' said Boellengen, 'we will hold you until you agree to bring us to Count Manfred and he tells us that all these peculiarities were by his command.'

'But, m'lord…' said Reiner, desperately. Sigmar! If they were locked up, it was over. The dark elf's deadline would pass and they would be found in their cells twisted and dead by Manfred's poison. His foolish wish to end it all would come true.

Boellengen interrupted him. 'I am disappointed that we cannot question you immediately, but a crisis has arisen that requires our immediate action, and we must go.'

Men in Boellengen's colours appeared at his shoulder. More men came up behind them on the back stairs. Jergen put his hand on his hilt.

Reiner shook his head. 'Save it, lad. We'll end up fighting the whole Empire.'

'Shaffer, Lock them and the rest of Manfred's "servants" in the cellar,' said Boellengen. 'And place a guard, for these are cunning men. Then join us at the Shallyan temple. We must go.'

Reiner's heart jumped. 'The Shallyan temple, m'lord?' he said as a soldier laid a hand on his shoulder. 'So you discovered Lady Magda's trick too? And know that the waystone has been stolen again?'

Boellengen turned back sharply. 'What do you know of this?'

'We saw the thieves take the stone, m'lord,' said Reiner. 'We pursued them.'

Lord Schott stepped forward. 'You are the men the sisters spoke of? Who came before the city guard? You know of the… creatures?'

'The ratmen, m'lord?' said Reiner. 'Aye. We had learned of Lady Magda's treacherous attempt to hide the stone, and went to recover it, but the vermin were there before us. We tried to stop them, but alas–'

'Never mind your excuses,' said Boellengen. 'Did you pursue them to their lair? Do you know where it lies?'

'We followed them to its entrance, m'lord,' said Reiner. 'But were attacked by mutants and were forced to retire. I could lead you to the spot.'

'Lord Boellengen,' said Raichskell, aghast. 'You would trust this villain?'

'With a rope around his neck and a sword at his back?' said Boellengen. 'Aye.' He gestured to his captain. 'Collect the rest of his companions and make them ready to depart. I want them before us, to spring any traps they might lead us into.'

As he waited with the Blackhearts in the courtyard of the barracks of the Talabheim city guard while the Reikland and Talabheim companies assembled for a massive expedition into the ratmen's domain, Reiner pieced together from scraps of overheard conversation the events that had led to it. Shortly after the Blackhearts had followed the ratmen out of the Shallyan temple, the city guard had arrived. They had lost the trail, but found the bodies of ratmen in the vault. These bodies and the story of the theft of Lady Magda's 'gift' were eventually brought to the countess, who quickly added two and two together and ordered a full scale search for the waystone in Talabheim's underground.

Five hours had passed while the various parties had wrangled over who should go and who should stay, but the grand coalition was now nearly ready to get under way. Seven hundred armed men stood in ordered rows waiting for the signal to march, each company carrying coils of stout rope, lanterns and ladders. In addition, Magus Nichtladen had provided each company with a mage, charged with keeping the emanations of the warpstone from affecting its men.

From the Reikland came Lord Schott's greatswords and Lord Boellengen's handgunners, as well as Grand Master Raichskell's Templars, augmented with Manfred's Nordbergbruche Knights, and Father Totkrieg's Hammerbearers. From Talabheim came

Hunter Lord Detlef Keinholtz, leading four hundred Talabheim city guard, von Pfaltzen with forty of the countess's personal guard, as well as companies of swordsmen from both Lord Danziger and Lord Scharnholt. They filled the barracks courtyard from wall to wall, waiting for their masters to finish arguing.

'I fail to see,' Lord Scharnholt was saying, 'why m'lord Danziger is allowed to join us.' The minister of trade was outfitted in a brilliantly polished breastplate that might once have fit him, but now could barely contain his overflowing figure. Reiner wondered if he could even reach across his belly to draw his sword.

'It was not I who stole the stone, but Lord Untern,' said Lord Danziger, haughtily. 'I wonder why the Minister of Trade, who hasn't seen fit to step onto the field of battle in fifteen years, decides to join us. Not even the invasion of the Kurgan was enough to stir him from the dinner table.'

'Battles are won not only on the field, Danziger,' said Scharnholt. 'I stayed behind to ensure the provisioning of the troops.'

'Ha!' barked Danziger. 'Perhaps that is why half of them starved on the return from Kislev.'

'And where is Lord Untern?' asked Lord Boellengen, his skinny neck sprouting from his breastplate like an asparagus from a flowerpot. 'And Lady Magda, his wife? Have they been apprehended?'

'We intend to find them directly after the waystone has been recovered,' said von Pfaltzen, then shot a cold glance at Reiner. 'Now, if m'lord's terrier is ready to lead us to the rat hole, we will get underway.'

'He is ready,' said Boellengen. 'Wither away, ratter?'

Reiner bowed his head, hiding fury behind a mask of servility. 'To the Tallows gate, m'lord. I will direct you from there.'

Von Pfaltzen signalled, and the companies got underway.

Despite Boellengen's threat, Reiner hadn't a rope around his neck, but his breastplate had been removed, and his wrists were securely bound together and two of Boellengen's men walked behind him with drawn swords. The other Blackhearts hadn't been bound, but their weapons and armour had been taken, and each had a minder watching their every move.

Reiner felt less like a ratter than a piece of cheese before a rat-hole.

The small army marched through the dark streets of the city, the weird twisting aurora in the sky above the crater casting odd highlights on their weapons and helms. Reiner shuffled forwards in a fog of fatigue. The other Blackhearts were no better. They had been up before dawn, and chasing ratmen and fighting mutants ever since.

When they reached the Tallows barricade, the massive logs were walked aside, and the army streamed through. Reiner shivered as he stepped once again into that nightmare realm. He almost wished Boellengen had blindfolded him as well as bound his wrists, so he wouldn't have to see it again. Mercifully, he was spared. Though fires flickered in the broken windows of some of the tree-tangled tenements, and shadows shambled in the distance, the denizens of the lunatic quarter had enough sense still to stay well away from so large a force of men. The army met no one on its way to the collapsed building under the lee of the crater wall.

Reiner led Boellengen and von Pfaltzen and the other lords into the blackened cellar and pointed to the beam that lay over the grate in the floor. 'There is a narrow tunnel leading down from here to the attic of a buried tenement. There are several blocks of buried streets down there, m'lord. Dug out like tunnels. The rift the ratmen went into is in an alley.'

'Buried streets?' Boellengen scoffed. 'What tale is this?'

'He speaks true, m'lord,' said von Pfaltzen. 'A century ago there was a mudslide after a heavy rain. A portion of the crater wall broke away and an entire neighbourhood disappeared. Thousands died. It was decided that it would be too expensive to dig out, so it was built over.'

'It was only tenements,' said Scharnholt.

'A callous thing to say, sir,' said Danziger, drawing himself up. 'My grandfather owned those tenements. He lost five years' rent to that disaster. Not to mention the expense of building new structures.'

After a detail of thirty men had lifted away the beam and cleared the bodies of the trapped mutants, Reiner led the way into the slanting tunnel to the attic, then down the tenement's spiralling stair, stumbling and falling against the walls because Boellengen refused to untie his wrists. Reiner saw nothing but fleeing shadows as they descended.

It took more than an hour for all seven hundred troops to march down the stairs and then form up in the buried street, then Reiner took Boellengen and the other lords into the alley behind the tenement and showed them the rift in the ground. 'They went down there m'lord, but we were attacked by the mutants and could not follow. I know nothing beyond here.'

Boellengen took a torch and dropped it into the dark hole. It bounced down a vertical chimney for a few yards then spun through open space to land a way below that. 'Then you shall explore,' he said. He turned to Reiner's minders. 'Put a rope down there, and another around his neck.' He smiled smugly at Reiner. 'If all is clear, give one tug. If you are in trouble, give two, and we'll pull you out.'

'By the neck, m'lord?' asked Reiner. 'That will end my troubles indeed.'

'Oh, we'll free your hands. You look strong enough to hold yourself up.'

'Your confidence in my abilities is inspiring, m'lord.'

Reiner's minders secured two lengths of rope to a gate post. One threw one coil down the hole, while the other, who must have been a hangman in his spare time, made a very competent noose with the second.

He grinned as he snugged it around Reiner's neck. 'Don't let yerself down too fast. Y'might come up short.'

He untied Reiner's hands. Reiner took up the first rope and began to back down into the hole, bracing himself with his feet against the rough walls. Two body-lengths down, the chimney ended in open space and he had to lower himself hand under hand. He looked down, half-expecting to see a sea of ratmen looking up at him, fangs gleaming, but the area illuminated by the torch was empty – a narrow, sandy-floored tunnel with dark, glittering walls.

When his feet touched he picked up the torch. The shattered remains of the statue of Shallya lay around them. It had been hollow, as he suspected. The ratmen's footprints led left into darkness. Reiner walked a little way in each direction, making sure there were no hidden dangers, then tugged the rope once.

Three more ropes dropped down, but the rope around his neck began to pull taut and he went up on his toes to keep from choking.

'All clear, curse you!' he shouted. 'All clear!'

'Aye, we heard,' came Boellengen's voice from above. 'Just don't want you getting any ideas about slipping your leash.' He giggled.

Reiner cursed silently as his toes cramped and his throat constricted – arrogant coward. Did he truly think Reiner would run in this labyrinth of horrors?

Boellengen's captain and three of his men slid down and faced the darkness, swords out.

'Come ahead,' called the captain, then turned grinning to Reiner. 'Practising yer hangman's hornpipe, villain?'

'I'm practising dancing on your grave, whore-son.'

The captain kicked him in the stomach and Reiner swung, gagging and clutching at the rope, before his toes found the floor again.

'That'll learn ye,' said the captain, chuckling, and undid the noose, but not before he had retied Reiner's hands.

Reiner added him to the list.

The Blackhearts followed Boellengen's men down the ropes, and then came all the other companies, four men at a time. They lined up three abreast down the tunnel in the direction the ratmen had taken. It took another hour and a half. If there were any ratmen in the vicinity they would have decamped long ago, thought Reiner, or attacked.

At last they got underway, the long snake of men twisting away into darkness. The tunnel was a long-dry riverbed, at some points so narrow the company had to go single file, at others so steep they had to use ropes to descend.

After a time it levelled off, and the walls showed signs of having been widened.

Shortly after this, Franka shivered. 'The light,' she said.

Reiner looked around him. It was almost invisible in the blaze of the company's torches but he could see it in the shadows; the weird purple light that lit the ratmen's world. Reiner shivered too, memories of the ratmen's filthy encampment under the gold mine, their terrifying weapons, the vivisectionist ratman in his surgery where Reiner and Giano had found Franka caged and lost to all hope. It must strike Franka even worse than he, he thought, and reached out unconsciously and squeezed her hand.

She squeezed back, then, realising what she was doing, took her hand away.

They rounded a curve in the tunnel and came upon the source of the light, a glowing purple globe set high in the wall. More lit the tunnel into the distance.

'What is that?' asked Scharnholt, pointing.

'A rat-lantern,' said Reiner.

'Eh? They make them?' asked Lord Schott.

'Aye, m'lord.'

'Impossible,' said Danziger. 'They are beasts. Vermin. It must be some natural phenomenon.'

'These are the least of their marvels, m'lord,' said Reiner.

'And you know everything about them, do you, mountebank?' sneered Raichskell.

Reiner shrugged. 'I have fought them before.'

Boellengen brayed a laugh. 'Ha! Myths are but mundanities to him. He is a teller of tales, friends. Pay him no mind.'

A distant clashing and screeching made them look ahead. A cluster of hunching figures dressed in scab-brown jerkins ran across the tunnel from a passage fifty yards away. Long furred snouts poked from brass helmets and curved swords dangled from scaly claws. A shot boomed and one fell sprawling as his fellows raced on. Another mob of ratmen, these in jerkins of greyish green, were hot on their heels. Two knelt and fired long-barrelled guns after the first group, then hopped up and ran on, reloading on the fly.

'Beasts and vermin, m'lords?' said Reiner as Boellengen and the others gaped at the disappearing ratmen.

'But... but...' Boellengen stuttered.

'They seem to me to have all the trappings of civilization,' Reiner said dryly. 'Weapons, uniforms, they fight amongst themselves.'

A little further on Reiner began to hear a sound rising over the tramp and jingle of the companies. At first he couldn't make out what it was – just an echoing cacophony like people shouting over the roar of a waterfall. Then he began to make out individual clashes and screams and bangs. It was a battle, and not a small one, and it was nearby.

Reiner looked at Boellengen and Schott. They had heard it too, and their eyes darted around, searching for the source.

Von Pfaltzen pushed up to the lords. 'What is that?' he asked. 'Is that a battle? Where is it?'

Lord Boellengen licked his lips. 'Ahead of us, I think.'

Von Pfaltzen sent scouts forward and they came back white-faced and shaking. Reiner couldn't hear what they told von Pfaltzen, but the captain paled as well. He and the Talabheim and Reikland commanders clustered together, arguing over strategy. Reiner caught only scraps of it.

'...thousands of them...' from von Pfaltzen.

'...protect the rear...' from Scharnholt.

'...this blasphemy cannot be allowed...' from Father Totkrieg.

'...return with more men...' from Boellengen.

At last a strategy was agreed upon, and the companies edged around each other in the cramped tunnel, rearranging their order of march, then started forwards again. Reiner and the Blackhearts travelled with Boellengen's men, now nearly at the rear. Only a hundred paces on, the tunnel made a right turn and opened out into a vast chamber from which the sounds of battle rang sharp and clear.

The companies edged out onto a broad plateau that looked down into a wide, fan-shaped valley over which soared a stalactite studded ceiling. But as big as the cavern was, it seemed hardly large enough to contain the swirling mass of ratmen that warred within it.

TWELVE
Great Magic is Done Here

TWO GREAT ARMIES fought each other in the cavern valley, though the action was so fierce it was difficult to tell them apart. There seemed no order to the conflict, just hordes of spearmen – spear-rats, Reiner corrected himself – fighting hordes of sword-rats, while teams of rats from both armies wandered through the mayhem, shooting flame from brass hand cannons. Explosions of green smoke erupted from all parts of the field, causing all the ratmen near them to collapse, choking. An enormous rat-ogre, like the one Reiner and the Blackhearts had fought at Gutzmann's fort, waded through a cluster of spear-rats, swinging an axe with a blade as large as a knight's shield. It left broken bodies and rivers of blood in his wake.

Just below the Talabheimers and Reiklanders, on the slope that descended from the plateau to the valley – so close Reiner could pick out their scars – ranks of brown-clad rat-long gunners fired into the melee. On the far side of the chamber, gunners in green did the same. Ratmen by the score died on every part of the battlefield, but more poured from half a dozen tunnels and passages to join both sides.

Most of the chamber was made from the same glittering stone as the rest of the caves, but the right wall was different. It was glossy black, with a greenish sheen, and when Reiner looked at it, it seemed the mind-whispers that Valaris's crystal slivers had dampened grew louder again. Darius trembled as he stared at it. Rickety scaffolding covered it, from which hung wooden ladders and ropes and pulleys and buckets. On the floor before it mine carts sat upon iron rails that disappeared into tunnels and further chambers. Neither the green army or the brown army was using the scaffolding to fire from, nor were they damaging it.

'Hoped I'd never see them nasty little buggers again,' said Gert, wrinkling his nose. 'Why do they fight, d'y'suppose?'

Reiner chuckled. 'For the waystone? Cursed thing seems to sow discord wherever it goes.'

'But why?' asked Franka.

Reiner shrugged.

Lord Boellengen cowered behind von Pfaltzen, staring at the sea of ratmen. 'Sigmar! We are outnumbered ten to one.'

Von Pfaltzen trembled with righteous indignation. 'This cannot be allowed. They must be exterminated. This cannot happen under the streets of Talabheim.'

'Nor anywhere in the Empire!' said Father Totkrieg.

'But perhaps we should return with more troops,' said Danziger, chewing his lip.

'And artillery,' said Scharnholt.

'You overestimate them,' said Schott. 'Look how easily they die. We will drive them before us.'

A huge rat-ogre lumbered out of a side tunnel onto the plateau, its handlers whipping it toward the rear of the rat-handgunners on the slope. Boellengen's handgunners fired at it in a panic. It roared, then crushed one of its handlers as it fell, riddled with bullets. The other handlers ran back into the tunnel.

Von Pfaltzen and Schott cursed.

Schott turned on Boellengen. 'M'lord, control your troops.'

The damage was done. The rat-gunners had heard the firing and were looking up the slope. They saw the companies and pointed, squealing. Some fired, dropping a few of the Talabheim guard, but most ran toward the battle, chittering warnings.

'Lord Keinholtz,' von Pfaltzen called. 'Form your spears in a triple line four paces back from the crest of the slope. Be sure you cannot be seen from below. Place your bowmen to the right. Lord Boellengen, you will take your handgunners to the left. Bows and guns will catch the enemy in an enfilade as they top the rise. Lord Schott, you will protect Boellengen's gunners on the left. I will protect those on the right. Father Totkrieg's hammers will flank the enemy's left once they are engaged. Master Raichskell's knights will do the same on the right. Lord Danziger, hold your men behind the Talabheimers and fill in as necessary. Lord Scharnholt, watch the tunnel mouth behind us for an attack from the rear.'

The companies scrambled to obey his orders, running this way and that, as below, the rats did the same, both green and brown armies shifting to address this new threat, their own squabble temporarily forgotten. They advanced on the hill as one, squealing for human blood.

Reiner looked around. No one was paying any attention to the Blackhearts. Lord Boellengen and his company were getting into position and priming their guns, their duty as the Blackhearts' minders forgotten.

'This is our chance, lads,' said Reiner softly. 'Back up to the tunnel the rat-monster came from, as if you were defending it.'

They edged away and pretended to stand on-guard at the side tunnel even though they had no weapons. Jergen crossed to where the crushed handler was still struggling to crawl out from under the rat-ogre. It snapped at him. Jergen kicked it unconscious, then took its dagger and cut its throat.

He returned to Reiner. 'Your hands, captain.'

Reiner held out his wrists and Jergen cut his ropes with a single stroke. 'Thankee, swordmaster.' He looked around. Scharnholt's men were to the right, guarding the mouth of the wide tunnel. They were still being ignored. All the other companies faced the slope, bracing themselves for the ratmen's charge.

'Right then,' said Reiner. 'Let's find this blasted rock.'

As they stepped into the narrow passage Reiner heard a shout behind him and froze, thinking they had been seen, but it was only a command to fire, quickly followed by a rattle of gunfire and the squeal of dying ratmen. Reiner let out a breath and motioned the others on. A few yards along, the passage split, one branch curving left toward the main tunnel, the other becoming a hairpin ramp that looped sharply down and back. They took the ramp and saw, as they reached the bottom, a triangular opening at the end through which they could see the big chamber. Before the opening were drifts of furred corpses – the remains of some side conflict.

'Arm yourselves, lads,' said Reiner.

The Blackhearts picked through the corpses reluctantly. The ratmen's weapons were strangely shaped, and sticky with slime and filth.

Hals and Pavel sneered as they tested spears with serrated tips.

'Flimsy twigs,' said Hals. 'Snap if y'look at 'em hard.'

Franka and Gert sought in vain for bows, but the ratmen didn't seem to use them. Franka settled for a curved short sword, Gert a longsword. Dieter found a pair of saw-toothed daggers.

As Reiner fixed a sword and dagger to his belt, he noticed a handful of egg-sized glass spheres spilling from a ratman's satchel. The ratmen's smoke grenades! He had been victim of one the last time the Blackhearts had encountered the walking vermin. They had kidnapped Franka out from under his nose in a cloud of smoke. He scooped up three and stuffed them in his belt pouch. Jergen selected the biggest sword he could find. Rumpolt pulled a long-barrelled gun from the bottom of the pile.

Reiner shook his head. 'No, lad. Take a sword.'

Rumpolt looked insulted. 'You don't trust me with a gun now?'

Reiner suppressed a growl. 'It ain't that. It's too dangerous. The bullets are poison.'

'Fine.' Rumpolt threw down the gun.

It fired with a deafening bang and the bullet ricocheted off the walls. Everyone jumped, then turned on the boy.

'Idiot!' snapped Hals.

'What d'ye think yer doing?' shouted Pavel.

'Y'mad infant!' said Augustus. 'D'ye mean to kill us?'

Reiner hissed. 'Quiet!' He looked around at the others. 'Anyone hit? No? Then carry on.'

They continued to the triangular opening and looked out into the chamber. The horde of ratmen was surging up the slope, squealing and shaking their weapons in fanatical rage. At the crest, Boellengen's handgunners disappeared in white smoke as they fired their third volley. The lead ratmen flew back, twisting and screaming. Their comrades leapt over their bodies, uncaring, and charged, crashing ten-deep into the Talabheim front line.

The spearmen held, though they were pushed back several steps, and began stabbing into the wall of fur before them. Totkrieg and Raichskell's companies swept into the rat army's flanks, swords and hammers rising and falling like threshers.

'Good lads,' said Augustus approvingly.

'They can't last, though,' said Pavel, surveying the seething mass of rats on the slope. 'Look at 'em all.'

'Ain't there ever an end to 'em?' snarled Hals.

'At least they won't be looking our way,' said Reiner. 'Edge round to that wide tunnel there.' He pointed to a dark mouth, near the scaffolded black wall.

The Blackhearts crept out, hugging the cavern wall, keeping as much as possible behind stalagmites and jutting boulders.

As they got closer to the black wall, the whispering in Reiner's brain got louder, and his skin began to tingle as if he stood too close to a fire. He noticed the others were twitching and frowning as well. Hals waggled a finger in his ear. Darius winced like he was in pain.

'Warpstone,' Reiner said, looking at the wall amazed. 'The vermin are mining warpstone.'

'How do they stand it?' said Darius.

Dieter looked at his arm, rubbing the lump caused by the dark elf's shard of crystal. 'Ain't this supposed to protect us? I can hear the buzzing again.'

'It's too much, perhaps,' said Darius. 'The shards can only do so much.'

'Then let's find the stone and get out,' said Hals. 'I've all the arms and legs I need, thankee.'

'I could use another eye,' said Pavel, touching his eye-patch as they continued on.

Gert grunted. 'Not in the middle of yer forehead.'

An outcropping of towering boulders stuck out from the wall. They began slipping around it when Franka, who had taken point, pulled up short.

'Hold,' she said. 'More rats, guarding a tunnel.'

Reiner and Hals edged forward and looked beyond a big rock. There were twelve tall, black-furred ratmen in gleaming bronze armour standing on their toes in front of a low opening, trying to see over the boulders to the battle. A flickering purple glow came from the tunnel behind them. Reiner and Hals eased back.

'The black'uns,' said Hals grimly. 'I remember them. Hard villains. Not like the rest of these scrawny runts.'

Reiner nodded, remembering the ten vicious vermin in Gutzmann's gold mine who had nearly been his death, as well as Franka's. 'Nonetheless, I've the feeling what we seek is behind them. They must guard something important, or they would be in the battle.' He looked around at the Blackhearts. 'We'll need to take 'em out all at once, so they can't raise any alarm. Can we do it?'

'Wish I had a bow,' said Franka.

'Or armour,' said Augustus.

Rumpolt muttered, 'Or that gun.'

The others nodded.

'Right then,' Reiner said. 'We'll wait for the next handgun volley. The noise will mask our bootsteps. Weapons ready.'

The Blackhearts held their weapons at their shoulders and gathered behind the rock, listening to the clashing and cries of battle behind them.

Boellengen's quavering voice rose above the clamour. 'Fire!'

'Now!' whispered Reiner.

The Blackhearts surged around the rock as stuttering gunfire echoed through the chamber. For an instant the vermin didn't see them coming, and it was their undoing. The Blackhearts were upon them before they could draw, Jergen in the lead. He clove through the leader's skull as it cleared its sword, then spun and cut another's arm off before facing two others. If the swordmaster was thrown off by the short length and light weight of his stolen weapon he didn't show it. He still fought like any three of the others.

Pavel, Hals and Augustus fought in a line like the pikemen they were, and forced back three ratmen. One of them screamed, Hals's spear in his ribs, but the spearhead snapped off as the ratman fell.

Hals cursed. 'Y'see?' He began laying about him with the butt end.

Gert hacked at one, but he was no swordsman, and made little headway. Rumpolt fought another, flinching away from the ratman's attacks and making none of his own. Darius hid and did nothing, but by now, no one expected him to. Dieter seemed to have disappeared.

Reiner fenced two vermin, the curved rat-sword twisting awkwardly in his hand. Franka hovered at his shoulder, and as one of the ratmen lunged at Reiner's chest, she darted in and gashed its wrist. It barked, surprised, and Reiner impaled it, then dodged a thrust from his second opponent.

A second rat fell before Pavel, Hals and Augustus and they pressed the third, who leapt back, squealing. Rumpolt echoed that squeal and fell, rolling, as his rat slashed down at him. Jergen, two more black ratmen falling away from his crimson blade, turned at Rumpolt's cry and leapt to knock his attacker's blade aside.

Dieter appeared behind the ratman Gert fought and stabbed him in both sides with his serrated daggers. The ratman screeched and tried to turn, and Gert ran it through the heart.

Reiner and Franka cut down Reiner's second opponent, and looked around. The others stood over the dead ratmen, panting and wiping their blades.

Rumpolt rolled on the ground, holding his foot. 'I'm murdered,' he moaned. 'Murdered.'

Reiner motioned to Darius, who was coming out from behind a rock. 'See to him, scholar.'

Jergen picked up one of the black vermin's longswords and tested it, then nodded.

'Better?' asked Reiner, taking one for himself.

'A little,' said Jergen.

The others followed Jergen's example.

Hals stayed with his broken spear. 'Never got the hang of them toothpicks,' he said.

'I haven't my kit,' said Darius, looking at Rumpolt's foot. 'Fortunately, it isn't much of a cut.'

'But it hurts!' Rumpolt whined.

The melee had not been noticed. The battle on the slope raged on behind them, and the purple light flickered unabated from the tunnel.

'Right,' said Reiner, starting toward it. 'On your guard. Get up, Rumpolt.'

'But I'm hurt,' said Rumpolt.

'Up!'

Rumpolt pouted, but pulled himself up and hobbled after the others as they entered the tunnel.

Darius flinched back, hissing.

'What is it, scholar?' asked Reiner.

'Great magic is done here,' Darius said. His eyes were wide. 'Dangerous magic.'

The Blackhearts slowed, uneasy. Hals and Pavel made the sign of the hammer. Augustus touched his legs, chest and arms in the Taalist 'roots, trunk and branches' gesture. Gert spat. They continued on at a crawl, wary as cats, the purple light growing brighter with every step.

As they rounded a curve the end of the tunnel came into view – a glowing purple gash in the gloom, flickering with lightning flashes. Reiner could feel the hair rising on his head and his forearms. A rushing, like that of a wind storm, filled their ears, and under it, a weird, sibilant chanting.

'We shouldn't be here,' said Rumpolt. His sword shook in his hand.

'Aye,' said Hals. 'We should all be in a taproom somewhere, having a pint, but we ain't.'

'If ye want to go,' said Augustus, 'we won't miss you.'

'That's enough, pikeman,' said Reiner. 'Come on.'

They pressed on, though it felt to Reiner like they were chest deep in a river and pushing against the current, and at last reached the glowing opening. Within was a roughly oval chamber that tapered to a point far above like an enormous tent. The walls were pierced by several entrances. The floor was a shallow bowl polished smooth by water.

In the centre of the bowl was the waystone, set upon an eldritch symbol inscribed in the floor in blood. Glowing purple rocks pulsed in six bronze braziers placed at regular intervals around it. Lavender mist rose from these. Between each brazier a snow-white ratman in long grey robes faced into the circle, shaking and clawing at the air as it chanted hissing syllables. It seemed to Reiner that the vermin were pulling the purple mist from the air and pushing it with great effort toward the centre of the circle, where it whirled like a tornado around the waystone.

Purple lightning flickered in the mist and danced around the white rat-mages, who shook as they fought to contain the power they manipulated. Their fur ruffled and their robes whipped around them. Reiner shivered. For despite all the whirling motion and noise, there was no wind, only a strange, still pressure that pushed on his chest and made him want to pop his ears.

'What are they doing?' he whispered. 'Do they seek to destroy it?'

'I... I think not,' said Darius, hesitantly.

'Then what?' asked Reiner.

The scholar frowned, squinting at the lightning. 'I think... I think they mean to reset it.'

THIRTEEN
I Am Not An Infant

'Reset it?' asked Reiner. 'You mean, er, make it work again?'

'Aye, I think so,' said Darius.

Reiner looked back at the chamber, where the rat-mages' chanting was rising in pitch and the shaking of their bodies grew more violent. 'How can you tell?'

'Er, well, their ceremony seems to mimic a ritual of binding, and the symbol on the floor looks like an elf rune.'

Everyone turned to stare at him.

'So, you are a mage,' said Reiner.

'No, no!' Darius shook his head. 'I've told you. These are things I've studied in books. I cannot make use of them.'

The others looked sceptical.

'But why would they want to fix it?' asked Reiner at last.

Darius shrugged.

Reiner turned back to the oval chamber, chewing his lip. 'Have you any idea how to stop them?'

'Stop them?' said Darius, alarmed. 'That would be very dangerous.'

Suddenly, the pressure got much worse. It felt like a giant was crushing Reiner's chest. Darius cried out and staggered, clutching his head. The rat-mages began screeching their litany while the vortex of mist whirled faster and lightning kissed the walls. The roaring was deafening. The Blackhearts backed away.

Reiner shook Darius. 'What's happening?' he shouted.

'I think they are losing control of the energies they have summoned,' said Darius, his face contorted. 'We must run!'

'Run?'

'If the energies escape...' Darius struggled to find words. 'Anything might happen!'

'Fall back!' Reiner cried.

The Blackhearts didn't have to be told twice. They bolted down the passage as the arcane wind rose to a scream and the desperate chanting of the rat-mages dissolved into frenzied chittering. Lightning chased them, licking down the tunnel. They leapt over the bodies of the black-furred vermin.

'Behind the rocks!' cried Darius.

The Blackhearts sprinted for the outcropping and dived behind it.

There was a deafening thunder crack and a blinding purple flash that knocked them flat. Dust and rocks rained down upon them. The great chamber glowed so brightly it seemed a purple sun had appeared in it. The shadow of the Blackhearts' rocky refuge was as sharply defined as an ink spill on white paper. Lightning played across the ceiling and shot into the warpstone wall as if drawn to it like a magnet. Reiner's brain felt like it was being collapsed to the size of an acorn. Strange voices screamed in his ears and his skin felt on fire. Though he could feel the ground under him, it seemed as if he was falling.

Through half-blinded eyes he could see ratmen running everywhere, clawing at their eyes and ears. Many lay dead, long faces twisted in agony. Many more were falling. Their putrid animal musk filled the chamber. Their squealing was pitiful.

Then the light faded and the lightning ceased, leaving the cavern in almost total darkness. The ratmen's purple lights had gone out. Only the Blackhearts' torches and those of the men upon the plateau remained. There wasn't a living ratman left in the chamber.

The Blackhearts writhed on the ground, clutching their forearms and crying out. Reiner frowned at this strange phenomenon, then suddenly he was doing it himself. His arm burned as if it had been touched with a brand. He looked down and saw a bright blue glow coming from beneath his skin. Valaris's crystal shard! It was hot as an ember.

'Make it stop!' cried Rumpolt. 'Cut it out! It burns!'

The boy drew his dagger, but before he could slit his skin the shards began to dim and cool.

Reiner sat up, head swimming, his hair dusted with dirt and pebbles. The others did the same. Only Darius remained on his back, his head buried in his arms, whispering under his breath.

'All whole?' asked Reiner. 'All in our right minds?'

'Ain't been in my right mind since I took Albrecht's brand,' grumbled Hals as the rest nodded.

Reiner shook Darius. 'Scholar?'

Darius slowly unfolded. His nose was bleeding. 'Is... is it over?'

'You would know better than I.'

Darius blinked around, shivering. 'The... the energies have dissipated, but there is still much residue.'

'Is it safe to go back?'

Darius shrugged. 'As safe as it is here.'

'Go back?' barked Augustus. 'Are you mad? I'll fight any man, beast or monster alive, but what can a spear do against that?'

'But not going back will *certainly* be our death,' said Franka.

'Maybe it's better to die by Manfred's poison,' said Augustus.

'No,' said Reiner, remembering Abel Halstieg's twisted body and rictus grimace. 'No, it isn't.' He got to his feet and looked up to the plateau where the Talabheim guard and the other companies were dazedly recovering themselves. The rats on the slope below them had fled. The rats on the floor of the cavern had died. It was strewn with their carcasses. 'Come. We haven't much time.'

The Blackhearts picked up their weapons and their torches and followed him around the boulders – and stopped again, staring. The side of the outcropping facing the tunnel to the invocation chamber reflected their torches like glass. Indeed, every surface on that side of the cavern looked like it had been polished in a furnace. Once jagged rocks were as smooth as beach pebbles. The sandy, rubble-strewn floor had fused into a slick lumpy slab. The tunnel had melted like hot wax, and shone with a faint internal luminescence.

'Sigmar!' said Pavel. 'Had we been caught in that…'

Jergen pointed silently to the dead black ratmen. They were but bones, and the bones glowed purple.

Though Reiner was as reluctant as any of them, he pushed ahead. If it was still intact, the waystone was only twenty paces away. He couldn't hesitate now.

The tunnel walls were as smooth and phosphorescent as the intestine of some deep sea leviathan. Purple light pulsed down them, turning the Blackhearts' skin an unhealthy grey. Reiner could hear hissing and popping as if from cooling rock, though the tunnel was as cold as the rest of the caves.

The walls of the invocation chamber were melted to a glowing, glassine sheen. Of the blood daubed rune on the shallow bowl-like floor there was no sign, but the copper braziers were now copper puddles. The rat-mages had been vaporised, but their shadows remained – long grey silhouettes that stretched away from the centre to the walls. Reiner scuffed one with the toe of his boot. It was burned into the rock.

The stone pedestal on which the ratmen had placed the waystone slumped to one side like a collapsed layer cake, but the waystone itself, though it had fallen on its side, was entirely untouched, as white and clean as a tooth.

'The thing's uncanny,' breathed Gert.

'Well,' said Darius. 'Precisely.'

'Come on,' said Reiner. 'Let's get it up.'

'Wait,' said Dieter. 'Company.' He pointed to a tunnel on the far side of the chamber.

The Blackhearts listened. There were voices – human voices – coming from it.

Reiner cursed. 'Douse torches. Quick.'

The company ground their torches out on the floor and backed out of the chamber. There was still light to see by. The walls radiated purple.

As Reiner watched, men stepped cautiously into the chamber – Lord Scharnholt and his house guard.

Scharnholt's eyes lit up when he saw the waystone. 'Ha!' he cried. 'Excellent.' He strode forward, puffing a little, with his men trailing more cautiously behind him. 'Come, all of you. Before the others come. They'll have been put off by that blast, but not for long.'

'Another opportunist,' muttered Franka, disgusted. 'Only out for himself.'

'This will be a great victory for our master Tzeentch!' said Scharnholt as his men began laying poles next to the waystone. 'All praise the Changer of the Ways for returning the stone to us!'

'All praise Tzeentch!' murmured his men.

'Father Taal, preserve us,' murmured Augustus.

The others made warding signs and spat over their shoulders.

'At least,' said Reiner dryly, 'he isn't thinking only of himself.'

Hals glared at him. 'Y'cannot joke about this, captain. We cannot let this daemon lover live.'

'No.' Reiner drew his vermin sword. The others readied themselves. 'Particularly not when he has our stone. But wait until they've lifted it before we attack. We don't–'

'Ah!' came a voice behind him.

Rumpolt was hopping on one foot and glaring at Augustus. 'You oaf! You've trod on my hurt foot!' he hissed.

'What was that?' said Scharnholt, looking up.

Reiner turned back to the chamber, and locked eyes with the lord.

'Valdenheim's villains,' Scharnholt cried. 'Kill them!'

'Curse it!' said Reiner. 'Right, lads, in we go.'

'Now look what you've done! Y'damned infant!' spat Augustus. He shoved Rumpolt to the floor, then turned and raced after the others as they charged forward to meet Scharnholt's men.

'I am not an infant!'

The two sides slammed together. Reiner angled for Scharnholt, but the podgy lord backed behind two of his men, muttering and waving his bejewelled fingers. Reiner parried the thrust of the first and ducked the second's swing, then slashed him across his forward leg. His sword sliced open the man's breeks, but didn't even scratch his skin. Reiner frowned. Augustus thrust his spear between his opponent's breastplate and shoulder guard, stopping him short, but the man only grunted and knocked it away, and Augustus had to spring back desperately to avoid his counter-thrust. Jergen brought his sword down on his man's unprotected forearm so hard that the man dropped his blade, but the blow made not a mark in his flesh.

Hals stepped back, blood leaking from a shallow cut on his neck, his broken spear hacked and splintered. 'Die, ye filth! Why won't ye bleed?'

Reiner looked at Scharnholt. His fingers inscribed a cage in the air. 'Rohmner. On Scharnholt. It's his doing.'

Jergen nodded and began hacking and shoving his way toward the lord. Before he got far, Reiner saw movement behind them.

It was Rumpolt, charging Augustus's back, tears in his eyes. 'I am not an infant!' he shrieked.

Augustus fought two men, and didn't hear. Rumpolt slashed him across the back, blooding him. Augustus yelped and stumbled forward. The pommel of his right-hand opponent's sword cracked him in the temple. He dropped like a sack of flour.

'Rumpolt!' Reiner cried, trying to back out of his fight.

Jergen jumped in front of Augustus to protect him from the Tzeentchists, his sword everywhere at once. Hals, Pavel and Gert spread out instinctively to hold the rest at bay.

Franka screamed at Rumpolt over her shoulder. 'What are you doing, you fool!'

'Stop shouting at me!' screeched Rumpolt. He swiped a backhand at her.

Franka ducked sideways, nearly stepping into her opponent's thrust. She twisted desperately. Rumpolt raised his sword at her back.

'No!' Reiner leapt away from his two adversaries, taking a cut on the calf, and blocked Rumpolt's strike. 'Calm yourself, you madman, or we'll all die!'

Rumpolt was beyond reason. 'Why does everyone shout at me?' He swung clumsily at Reiner, weeping. Reiner parried easily and ran the boy through the heart.

Rumpolt's eyes went wide with surprise. 'It... it isn't my fault.' He clutched at Reiner as he slid off his sword, tearing open his doublet.

Reiner kicked him away and turned to block his opponents, who had followed him. There was no time for anger or remorse. Scharnholt's men had taken advantage of the confusion and pressed the Blackhearts on all sides as they stood over Augustus. They laughed as the Blackhearts' blades glanced off them. Pavel took a gash in the shoulder. Even Jergen bled – a cut across his left palm. He tried to push for Scharnholt again, but the Tzeentchists knew his goal now, and blocked him.

'Darius,' said Reiner. 'Can you counter his magic?'

'Why won't you listen to me?' wailed Darius. 'I am not a witch. I am a scholar.'

'Sod magic,' said Hals, and spun his broken spear-end at Scharnholt.

It caught Scharnholt on the ear and he cried out, his fingers pausing in their pattern.

Three of his men went down instantly, surprised as their invulnerability vanished.

'Ha!' barked Hals, snatching up Rumpolt's sword. 'Come, ye cowards! Now we'll see!'

But before another blow could be struck, a loud voice bellowed behind them. 'What is this? Cease this melee at once!'

Reiner looked back. Boellengen, Danziger and von Pfaltzen were entering with their companies and fifty Talabheimers. Reiner heard Scharnholt curse, and Reiner echoed him. A few moments more and they might have been away with the stone.

'M'lords,' cried Reiner, springing back from the fight. 'Thank Sigmar you've come! We have just found Lord Scharnholt stealing the stone and claiming it for his master, Tzeentch!'

'Madness!' shouted Scharnholt. 'He lies!'

The two sides backed apart, eyeing each other warily.

'He used magic against us, m'lords!' continued Reiner. 'Our swords could not cut the flesh of his men! Arrest him as a traitor to Talabheim and the Empire!'

'What madness is this?' asked von Pfaltzen. 'You accuse a lord and member of the parliament of Talabheim of such a heinous crime? Have you any evidence?'

'There can be no doubt he is marked, captain,' said Reiner. 'No follower of the Ruinous Powers so adept as Lord Scharnholt could remain unblemished by his master's touch. If you were to remove his breastplate and...'

'Don't be ridiculous!' said Scharnholt. 'How can you listen to this proven rascal, m'lords?'

'So you claim his story false, m'lord?' asked von Pfaltzen. He actually seemed to be weighing the case.

'No,' said Scharnholt, causing gasps from the lords. 'It is true in every particular, except that it was *he* who *I* came upon trying to steal the stone. And he who used foul sorcery to protect his men.' He pointed to his dead men. 'Look at my poor fellows. His men are barely scratched, but for the brave fellow who refused his evil orders and was killed for it. Naught but sorcery could allow such rabble to prevail over my trained troops.'

'Ye want another go?' growled Hals.

Reiner shot him a sharp look. 'M'lords, please,' he said. 'Did I not bring you to this place as promised? Have you not found everything I said you would find? Is the stone not at your feet? Why would I lie now?'

'Because you hoped to take it for your evil ends while we fought the vermin,' said Boellengen.

'M'lord,' Reiner pled, inwardly cursing Boellengen for hitting upon the truth. 'You know not who you aid with this argument. If you would only ask him–'

'I will not open my...' interrupted Scharnholt.

Lord Boellengen held up his hand and turned on Reiner. 'Hetsau, there is one way to prove yourself credible and make us take seriously your accusations against Lord Scharnholt.'

'Anything, m'lord,' said Reiner. 'Only name it.'

'Bring us to Count Manfred,' said Boellengen. 'Show us that he is safe and we will listen to you.'

Reiner balled his fists, his stomach sinking. He couldn't do it. He couldn't even lie and say he would, for the dark elf would be listening. 'M'lord, I have made a vow to Count Manfred not to reveal his whereabouts under any circumstances. I will not break that vow, though I die for it.'

Scharnholt laughed. 'Just the sort of thing he would say had he killed the count.'

Boellengen sneered. 'If that is your answer, then you *will* die, but slowly, on the rack, having told us long before what we wish to know.'

Snakes of fear crawled up Reiner's spine. He was terrified of torture, but he was equally terrified of Manfred's poison, and the hope, faint though it might be, that he might yet escape before they brought him to the rack, refused to die. He swallowed. 'I will not betray Count Manfred,' he said.

Boellengen sighed. 'Very well.' He waved at hand at von Pfaltzen. 'Captain, I ask you to arrest this man and his cohorts for attempting to steal the waystone and dooming the city of Talabheim to madness and Chaos.'

Von Pfaltzen nodded. 'With pleasure.'

'Wait!' said Scharnholt, pointing at Reiner. 'What is that on his chest?'

Reiner looked down. His torn doublet had fallen open, revealing a part of Valaris's knife work. He put a hand up to close it, but Danziger stepped forward and ripped it open, revealing the symbol the dark elf had carved in his chest.

Boellengen recoiled, horrified. 'A mark of Chaos!'

The lords and their men made the sign of the hammer and muttered prayers under their breath.

Von Pfaltzen drew his sword, his face cold and set. 'Cultists are not arrested. They are executed.'

FOURTEEN
All We Must Do Is Nothing

REINER CHOKED. 'MY lords… I can explain.'

Von Pfaltzen turned to the Talabheim Guard. 'Take their weapons and have them kneel. My men will take their heads.'

The Blackhearts backed up, pressing into a wary clump as a score of Talabheim archers aimed at them.

'Ye daft fools!' said Gert. 'We ain't daemon lovers! Y'have it wrong!'

'Y've a plan, captain?' whispered Pavel hopefully.

Reiner shook his head, lost. His hands dropped to his sides. He froze. His left was touching his belt pouch. There were three hard lumps within it. His heart leapt. He looked behind him. Only a few Talabheimers stood between them and the tunnel Scharnholt had entered from.

'Lay down your weapons, dogs,' said the Talabheimer captain.

'Do as he says,' murmured Reiner. 'Then join hands and be ready for smoke.'

'Smoke?' said Darius.

As the Blackhearts threw their swords and daggers to the ground, Reiner slipped his right hand into his pouch and raised his voice. 'Join hands, brothers! We will face this martyrdom together, as we have faced all other wrongs prosecuted against us!' He took Franka's hand with his left and raised his right as the others grasped hands.

Von Pfaltzen and the others stared, puzzled at this strange outburst.

'We'll show it our heels,' said Reiner, and smashed the two glass orbs he had palmed on the ground. Instantly great clouds of thick black smoke billowed up and enveloped them.

'To the back tunnel!' Reiner hissed, and ran, dragging Franka with him.

'What in Taal's name!' choked Augustus, but he ran with the others.

Shouts echoed through the murk. An arrow thrummed past Reiner's ear. He flinched and continued running. His eyes were burning and he couldn't stop coughing. The Blackhearts hacked and wheezed around him, bumping into each other and stumbling over their feet in the spreading cloud. Reiner's outstretched hand touched the glassy wall and he felt left and right in a panic. If they didn't find the tunnel this would all be a black joke. There! He pushed forward into shadow and the smoke dissipated. He looked back. The Blackhearts stumbled into the tunnel behind him, coming out of the oily smoke with eyes shut and tears on their cheeks.

'Now run!' he said. 'We haven't bought much time.'

They ran. Though they had no torches, the residue of the rat-mages' magical blast still lit the tunnel in a dim purple glow, so they were not entirely blind. Sounds of pursuit came from behind them – running boots, men shouting orders. They sped up, but almost immediately they heard noises ahead of them as well.

'The rats!' said Franka. 'They're coming back!'

Reiner looked around. The purple glow was fading as they travelled beyond the radius of the explosion. In the darkness Reiner saw a blacker darkness, low on the right wall. Beyond it, a steady purple light was bobbing closer.

'In there!' Reiner hissed.

The Blackhearts dived into the low hole, pushing down it as fast as they could.

Then Pavel jerked to a stop. 'Waugh!' he said. 'What is that stink?'

A horrific death stench overwhelmed them. All the Blackhearts choked and retched and swore.

Reiner covered his mouth. He had only smelled something so foul once before – the last time he had travelled in the ratmen's domain. 'It's... it's a vermin rubbish tip.'

'Back out!' said Darius. 'Find another place!'

'Ah!' cried Franka. 'What did I put my hand in?'

'We can't stay here, captain,' said Augustus. 'It's foul!'

'Shhh, curse you!'

The ratmen were right outside the hole, passing by, squeaking excitedly. The Blackhearts held their breath. Suddenly the vermin's voices rose and Reiner thought they had been discovered, but then, beyond the chittering, they heard the shouting of men.

'Fall back! There's too many!' came one voice.

'Ratties must have got 'em,' came another. 'Back to Boellengen.'

Though Reiner couldn't understand their gibbering, it sounded to him as if the vermin were similarly reluctant to engage. They backed past the rubbish hole again, squealing, then turned and ran. The passage fell silent, though they could hear shouting and movement in the distance.

'They've gone,' said Pavel. 'Let's get out of this midden.'

No,' said Reiner. 'We'll wait here until things have settled a bit.'

'But, captain!' said Augustus. 'The smell–'

'The smell will keep anyone from looking here, won't it?' said Reiner. 'When it's quiet, we'll follow the army back out, and see if we can make a try for the stone along the way.'

'You think you can take it from five hundred men?' asked Darius.

'Easier than stealing it from the countess's manor house.'

They sat silent for a moment, the buzzing of flies and the skittering of roaches growing loud in their ears. Reiner's fatigue, which he had kept at bay while moving, caught up to him, and his limbs felt like lead.

'What was that smoke?' asked Dieter at last.

'An invention of the ratmen,' said Reiner. 'A grenade of sorts, but it makes only smoke.'

'Great trick,' said Dieter. 'Come in handy in my line of work.'

A party of men went by the hole and they froze. The party's reflected torchlight illuminated the Blackhearts' surroundings. Reiner wished it hadn't. They sat hunched against a mound of rat-corpses, rotting grain, gnawed bones, offal, and broken machinery. The place crawled with rats and roaches. The Blackhearts grimaced, then the party passed and darkness fell again.

'Nice work with Rumpolt, captain,' said Hals after a moment. 'Only wish it had happened sooner.'

Reiner swallowed. He'd nearly forgotten. The boy's shocked, dying face flashed before his eyes.

'A minute sooner would have suited me,' said Augustus. 'Mad infant cut me worse than them daemon-lovers did.'

Reiner sighed. 'Damned fool boy. He left me no choice.'

'I've no pity for him,' said Pavel. 'We might have the stone but for him. Trouble from the beginning, he was.' He snorted.

'Aye,' said Gert. 'Manfred made a mistake with that one, certain.'

'He had no business being a soldier,' said Franka. 'Let alone a spy.'

There was another silence, then Hals chuckled. 'The look on Pavel's face when he bashed 'im with that brick.'

Pavel laughed. 'Woulda' gutted him there and then if my hands hadn't been full.'

'And when he fell in the sewers?' guffawed Augustus.

'What a reek!' said Gert.

'We shouldn't mock the dead,' said Franka, but she giggled too.

They fell silent again.

Reiner put his head down on his knees, just to rest his eyes. 'We'll go in a moment,' he mumbled. 'Once we catch our breath.'

REINER'S HEAD SNAPPED up and he opened his eyes. Or had he? It was as dark with them open as closed.

Where was he? His hand went to his sword. It scraped on the ground. The noise was greeted by grunts and snorts.

'Who's there?' mumbled Pavel.

'Are we ready to go?' Franka yawned.

A horrid odour assaulted Reiner's nose and he remembered where he was – and what he was meant to be doing.

'The companies!' He leapt up and cracked his head on the midden's low ceiling. 'Ow! Curse it! We've... Ow! We've slept! They've gone!' He crouched again, rubbing the top of his head. 'Let's have a light, someone.'

'Aye, captain,' said Pavel. 'Hang on.'

There followed a stretch of grunting and cursing and scrabbling, then a flare of tinder and finally the orange, brightening glow of a torch. The Blackhearts were sitting up and yawning and rubbing their eyes.

Franka shrieked. She was covered with roaches. They all were. They brushed at them furiously.

'Out! Out!' said Reiner.

The Blackhearts scrambled out of the hole, cursing and choking, then recovered themselves in the passage. Reiner looked down it in both directions. There was no sound or light.

'How long have we slept?' asked Franka.

'I'll tell you next time I see the sun,' growled Augustus.

'I think a good while, curse it,' said Reiner. 'The companies must have removed the waystone long ago.'

'Y'don't think the ratties got it back?' asked Hals.

Reiner shook his head. 'I doubt it. Too scattered. Which means that the cursed stone is... is in the countess's manor house.'

As the enormity of that truth hit him, Reiner groaned and slumped against the wall, then slid down to squat on the ground. The waystone was in the manor, guarded by thick walls and iron gates and a hundred guards. How could they get it out? They couldn't. It was impossible. 'Curse it,' he muttered. 'Curse everything. I'm too tired. I don't care anymore.' He looked down at his chest and pulled open his shirt, revealing the dark elf's raw red cuts. 'Valaris, you corpse-skinned sneak, do you hear me? I'm finished. Let Manfred say his prayers and put us out of our misery. I'm done with this poxy life. There's not a thing in the world worth living...'

He stopped as he saw Franka gaping at him. They locked eyes. His heart thudded. She was furious. He knew her expressions well enough to see that – angry that he was giving up, angry that he was selfishly killing them all because he felt he couldn't go on. But suddenly her angry face was the most beautiful thing in the world. He would gladly take a scolding from her. Happy or sad, mischievous or sullen or sulky, he loved her, and realising this – that he did have something worth living for – he knew he had to go on. He had no idea how he was going to do it, but as long as Franka lived and cared enough about him to be angry with him, he would keep trying to find his way to the end of this nightmare.

'Er,' he said, then forced a light-hearted laugh which sounded, to his ears, like somebody strangling a cat. 'A joke, Lord Valaris. A joke, born of weariness. But I do not give up. I do not wish to die, and we will recover the stone if every knight in the Empire stands in our way, never fear.'

The Blackhearts stood motionless, eyes darting around as if expecting Manfred's doom to come winging out of the darkness. When nothing happened they relaxed.

'Captain,' said Hals, exhaling. 'Captain–'

Reiner held up a hand. 'I know, and I apologise. I'd no right to include you in my little... joke. I'll... we'll have a vote next time, eh?'

Hals stared at him for a long moment, then guffawed and turned away, shaking his head. 'Mad. He's mad.'

Pavel snorted. 'And what does that make us?'

The others chuckled nervously – all but Jergen, and Franka who looked at Reiner with big, baffled eyes.

'Well,' said Reiner, tearing his eyes from her with difficulty. 'We better go back and see what they've done with it. Then we'll see what we can do about getting it back.'

'Er, captain,' said Augustus as the others began to gather themselves together. 'Being a good Talabheim man, I'm wondering...' He paused, uncomfortable. 'If it might not be the right thing to do... to do what you meant to just now.'

'Eh?' said Reiner, confused. 'What do you say, pikeman?'

'Well, everything's as we'd want it, ain't it?' said Augustus, slowly. 'Er, if it weren't for the count and the poison and all. The countess has the stone and Teclis will fix it. All we must do is nothing and all will be put right, aye?'

Reiner's stomach turned. 'Are you suggesting that we should sacrifice our lives for the good of the Empire? That we should betray Lord Valaris and die so that others might live?'

Augustus nodded. 'Aye, I suppose that's what I mean. Aye.'

Reiner sighed. From the moment Manfred had made his bargain with Valaris, Reiner had been trying to discover a way to defeat it – to deliver the stone to the dark elf, free Manfred, then bring the might of Teclis and the Empire down on the dark elf before he destroyed it. But with Valaris eavesdropping on every word anyone said in Reiner's presence, he couldn't tell the others his plans. He hoped his old comrades knew him well enough to guess what he had in mind, but there was no way for Reiner to reassure Augustus of his intentions. Instead he had to reassure Valaris that Augustus's wishes were not his own.

'Pikeman,' Reiner said, 'there is a reason that Count Manfred has named us his Blackhearts. It is because we have no honour. We are criminals over whose heads he holds a noose. We do his bidding because we value our lives more than we value any friendships or loyalties to country, race or family. I don't like what happens to Talabheim, but if I must choose between Talabheim and my own skin, I will choose my skin, and drink to Talabheim's memory when once again we return to Altdorf. Do you understand me?'

Augustus blinked at him for a moment, blank faced, then lowered his head, his jaw clenching. 'Aye, I begin to. I guess I thought ye might have more honour than that backstabbing jagger.'

'More honour than a count of the Empire? Don't be ridiculous,' laughed Reiner. 'We're gallows birds. Now,' he said, turning to the others, 'enough of this. Let's be off.'

The others were looking at him with the same sullen stares Augustus had turned on him.

He snarled. 'What? Does it pain you to hear it put so baldly? We are villains! Now, onward.'

THE BLACKHEARTS SKIRTED the mine chamber, taking side tunnels and hiding from the ratmen patrols, until they found their way back to the top of the plateau where the army of men had formed their line. They stayed low and well back from the slope, for below them, in the fan-shaped valley, the ratmen were regrouping and returning to work. Soldiers of the green army were shackling their brown rivals into long coffles, then turning them over to whip-wielding overseers, who put them to work digging at the warpstone workface and carrying the stuff to the waiting carts.

The army of men must have retreated with the waystone in a hurry, for they had left their dead where they had fallen and the plateau was thick with them – men of every company, staring through sightless eyes, blood staining their colourful uniforms.

The Blackhearts robbed the corpses of their gear and their gold, happy to strap on human weapons and armour again, as well as stuffing themselves with the scraps of food they found in the dead men's belt pouches and taking tinderboxes and torches. Reiner wolfed down a half-eaten chicken leg and some mouldy bread. He was so hungry he didn't care.

Hals ground the butt of a tall oak-shafted spear and pushed against it. It hardly flexed. 'That's more like it,' he said. 'That'll take a knight's charge.'

Franka found a bow and Gert a crossbow and they filled their quivers with arrows and bolts plucked from the bodies of dead ratmen.

Once they were all kitted out, Reiner signalled them again, and they began the long walk up through the sandy tunnels.

IT WAS MID-MORNING when they at last returned to the surface and began making their way again through the Tallows. Again, the denizens of the corrupted ward seemed more interested in fighting each other than preying on the Blackhearts, and they passed through it, unmolested, the roiling clouds and strange glowing aurora churning unceasingly above them.

As they made their wary way, Reiner motioned for Franka to fall back a bit.

'Yes, captain?' she said, stiff.

'Aye,' said Reiner quietly. 'I know you're none too pleased with me at the moment. My little tantrum was uncalled for, and I apologise. But I want to tell you what it was that called me back from the brink. For I think I might have gone through with it – killed us all out of peevish misery, but when I saw your face...' He blushed. It sounded mawkish and juvenile to him now, but it was the truth. 'Well, I no longer cared to die.'

Franka looked at the ground. She held the pommel of her sword very tightly. 'I see.'

'I've been an idiot,' Reiner continued. 'Not trusting you, I mean. I've let my suspicious nature rule me. I know one of us is Manfred's spy. But I also know – I've always known, really – that it isn't you. I just haven't let my head trust my heart. They... they are now of one accord.'

'And so you expect me to forgive you?' she asked.

Reiner's heart sank. 'No, I suppose not. I should never have mistrusted you in the first place. The original crime cannot be undone, and I would not blame you if you never forgave me, no matter how much that would grieve me.'

'Ask me again,' she said coolly, 'when once again we return to Altdorf and drink a toast to Talabheim's memory.'

Reiner stared at her. 'You, er... When...? Do you mean that...?'

She turned and poked him in the chest, directly on top of one of Valaris's cuts. Reiner hissed in pain.

'You'll have no further answer from me until then, captain,' she said, and turned away.

Reiner rubbed his chest, wincing. His heart pounded in excitement and confusion. What had she said? Did she mean that she forgave him? Or did she mean she believed him the villain he had told Augustus he was? She couldn't believe that, could she? Surely she knew him better than that? Surely... He caught himself. The little witch! She had turned the tables on him and no mistake. She was showing him how she had felt when he hadn't trusted her. Unless she truly didn't trust him. Could she be so blind?

All the long way back to the Tallows barricade his mind turned in tight circles of worry, and at the end he was no more reassured than when he started.

FIFTEEN
We Have Tonight

REINER TURNED A sausage over the small fire Jergen had made in the cellar of an abandoned cooperage in the merchant district. Bloody light filtered down through the caved-in floor above. Reiner, Franka, Jergen, Augustus and Darius sat in the fire's red glow, making a meal of sausages, black bread and beer, for which they had paid ten times the normal fare. Reiner didn't mind the price. He'd paid for it with dead men's gold. At least they had found food to buy. That was getting harder as the farmers outside the city were staying away out of fear of the madness, and the looting and robbery in the neighbourhoods got worse.

Reiner looked around at his companions and chuckled mirthlessly. This was the band of brave adventurers who were going to storm the countess's manor and steal the waystone out from under the noses of a hundred guards? Franka stared into the fire with glazed eyes. The fingers of Jergen's cut left hand were so swollen he could barely make a fist. Dieter rotated his head around like he had a kink in his neck. Augustus was as silent as Jergen. Darius muttered under his breath. No one seemed inclined to conversation.

Unsteady boot steps clunked on the floorboards above. They looked up. Hals's voice reached them.

'Izzis the one?' he slurred. 'All look alike t'me.'

'Think so,' came Pavel's voice. 'I 'member the barrels.'

The boots moved to the stairs.

'Don't matter if it ain't,' said Gert loudly. 'We can lick any beasties might be hiding in th' shadows. We're 'ard men, we are.'

The three pikemen stumbled down the stairs and cheered loudly as they saw the others.

'Here we are, lads!' cried Gert.

'Told ye it were the place,' said Pavel.

'Long live the Blackhearts!' crowed Hals.

'Quiet you pie-eyed fools!' whispered Reiner. 'Have you drunk the city dry?'

Hals put his finger to his lips and the other two giggled. They found places around the fire.

'Shorry, captain,' said Hals. 'Took a bit of drinking to get mouths moving. These Talabheimers can put it away a bit.'

'Hope they told ye nothing,' muttered Augustus.

'No no, they tol' us,' said Pavel. 'But izz bad news.'

'Aye, very bad,' said Gert. 'Very bad.'

'How bad?' asked Reiner, grimly.

'Well,' said Hals, sticking a sausage on a stick and holding it over the fire. 'Met a few of von Pfaltzen's lads at the Oak and Acorn. Just come from eight hours in the deeps under the countess's manor, guarding they didn't know what in her treasury vault.'

'Secret ain't out to the common soldiers,' said Pavel. 'But they knew something was up. All the jaggers been grinning ear to ear and patting themselves on the back about some great victory.'

'An' we know what that is, don't we?' said Gert, winking.

'So it's locked in a treasure vault?' asked Reiner.

'Aye,' said Hals. 'Vault's three floors down under the old barrel keep, below the kitchens and the store rooms, by the dungeons. Guard's been doubled at the vault, and at the gate up the head of the dungeon stairs.'

'That ain't th' bad part,' said Pavel. 'Th' bad part is that the vault has three locks. And the three keys for the three locks are held by three different captains on three different watches.'

Reiner held up four fingers. 'So, we've the Manor district gate, the gate to the countess's manor, the gate to the dungeon, and the door of the vault to get through, and out of, carrying a half tonne block of stone. Lovely.'

'And ye can't just waltz through the house, neither,' said Pavel. 'There are guards and servants everywhere. Someone would be sure to notice.'

'Do you know the names of the captains who hold the keys?' asked Reiner.

Hals, Pavel and Gert looked at each other, frowning.

'Wasn't one of them Lossberg or Lassenhoff or…?' asked Gert.

'Bromelhoff?' asked Hals. 'Bramenhalt?'

'It was Lundhauer,' said Pavel definitively. 'Or… Loefler? Lannenger?'

'So we don't know their names,' said Reiner, sighing. 'We'll have to speak to more guards.'

'Captain,' said Hals, looking queasy. 'Ye'd have to carry us back if we was to drink answers out of more guards tonight.'

'And I doubt we'd remember the names even if we got 'em,' mumbled Pavel.

'I'll go,' said Reiner. 'You lads haven't learned the gambler's trick of only *seeming* to drink.'

'Bad news,' said Dieter's voice behind them.

The Blackhearts jumped. The thief stood at the bottom of the stair. No one had heard him approach.

'How unexpected,' said Reiner dryly.

Dieter crossed to the fire and dipped a cup into the open cask of beer. He took a swallow, then sat. 'I looked in on Scharnholt like you asked,' he said. 'Found a place outside his library window where I could listen to his comings and goings without being seen.' He grinned, showing sharp teeth. 'Not a happy jagger, Scharnholt. Someone he called his "master" ain't very pleased with him. Had a few messengers come by to tell him that.'

'That's bad news?' asked Gert. 'Trouble for Scharnholt ain't bad news to us.'

'I ain't got to the bad news,' said Dieter, annoyed. 'The bad news is that Teclis is recovered, or so says Scharnholt. And he means to work his magic on the stone tomorrow. It's to be locked somewhere deep down in the earth with wards and curses and spells so thick no one'll ever find it, let alone steal it.'

'So,' said Reiner, his heart sinking. 'We have tonight.'

'Tonight?' said Hals, dismayed. 'Captain, is that possible?'

'There's worse yet,' said Dieter.

Everybody turned to look at him.

'If we try for the stone tonight,' he said, 'we'll have company. This "master" has ordered Scharnholt to get it. He's called a meeting an hour past sundown to make their plans.'

There were groans from the Blackhearts, but Reiner smiled. 'Ha!' he said. 'That's better news than we've had.'

'Eh?' said Pavel. 'Why so?'

'Another gambler's maxim,' said Reiner. 'Out of confusion comes opportunity.' He looked at Dieter. 'We must attend this meeting. Do you know where it is?'

Dieter shook his head. 'No, but it won't be any trouble following Scharnholt to it.'

'Even with me along?'

Dieter gave him a contemptuous once over. 'We'll manage.'

Reiner had expected Scharnholt to sneak out of his house by the back way, cloaked and masked and furtive, and consequently, they watched the back gate and almost missed Scharnholt when he left openly, in his coach, and made his way through the Manor district by the main streets.

Dieter and Reiner followed him to an old stone building built at the edge of a large green park called the Darkrook Downs. There were many such buildings around the edge of the park that bordered the Manor district, all with a banner hanging above their door. These were the chapter halls of Talabheim's knightly orders. Some were local chapters of orders that had knights all over the Empire. Some were orders founded by noble Talabec families or by bands of knights who had come together here for some great purpose in times past.

Reiner and Dieter watched from the shadow of a high yew hedge as Scharnholt entered the hall of the Knights of the Willing Heart, whose device was a crowned heart held in two red hands. More coaches arrived, as well as men on horseback and some on foot.

'Can it be here?' asked Reiner. 'Perhaps he just stops here on his way.'

'This is the hour,' said Dieter.

'A corrupted order?' wondered Reiner aloud. 'Or do they not know what is done under their roof?'

Dieter shrugged. 'Better have a look.'

Reiner looked sceptically at the hall. It had the proportions of a townhouse, but was built like a castle, with a courtyard behind a fortified gate and little more than arrow slots for windows. 'Are you certain you can get us in?'

'Always a way in,' said Dieter as he started down the street, away from the chapter hall. 'Although sometimes it's murder.'

He led Reiner half a block before crossing the street and slipping between two tall houses. Like all the chapter halls, they had large stable yards behind them, the gates of which opened onto the park. This was divided into common-held riding rings, tilting yards, racing ovals and archery lanes, all deserted at this hour. Reiner and Dieter crept along hedges back to the Order of the Willing Heart.

'Hold here,' said Dieter. 'Might be a patrol.'

And there was. Moments later two guards in the colours of the house rounded the right corner of the stable yard, then turned into the grassy alley between the chapter and its left-hand neighbour. Jutting from the left wall was a small chapel of Sigmar. There was a faint glow behind its stained-glass windows.

'In there, maybe,' said Dieter.

'In a chapel of Sigmar?' said Reiner. 'There's cheek for you.'

Dieter sized up the chapel. The stained glass windows rose up two storeys with griffin-capped buttresses between them. 'An easy climb,' he said. 'I'll go up and lower the rope. Tie it to your belt when you climb up, so it comes with you, aye? Don't want it dangling where they can see it.'

'Aye,' said Reiner.

When the guards had turned down the green alley again, Dieter set off low and silent, then spidered up one of the buttresses with no apparent effort. At the top he took a rope from his sack and tied it around a gargoyle.

Reiner was about to start forwards when Dieter held up a hand. Reiner hid until the guards once again appeared and disappeared, then Dieter dropped the rope and beckoned him on. He hurried forward, trying to be as noiseless as Dieter, but his shoes thumped on the grass and his elbows scraped noisily through the bushes. He felt as quiet as an orc warband on the march.

Reiner reached the buttress and tucked the rope into his belt, then began pulling himself up. For all his recent running and fighting and climbing, this was not easy. His arms shook before he was halfway up. His foot rasped across the masonry as he braced himself, and he heard a disgusted grunt from above. At last, Dieter hauled him onto the buttress by his belt and he lay over it like a sack of flour, wheezing.

'Ye'll never make a second storey man, jagger,' Dieter whispered.

'Never wanted to,' answered Reiner. 'It's Manfred puts me in these undignified positions.'

'Hush.' Dieter drew up the rest of the rope as Reiner held his breath. The guards appeared below them, muttering to each other, then passed on without looking up.

'Now,' said Dieter. 'Let's see what we can see.'

He took a tiny stoppered jar from his pouch and pulled out a ball of putty, which he pressed against a square of stained glass. Next he drew a glazier's tool around the putty in a rough circle, then, holding the putty with one hand, he tapped the glass very gently. There was a click, Reiner froze. Dieter wiggled the putty and a disk of glass came out with it.

'Try your eye, jagger,' he said, edging behind Reiner on the narrow buttress.

Reiner braced his shoulder against the chapel wall, and leaned in toward the hole. A low mutter of voices reached him, but at first he could see nothing but crossbeams and pews. However, with a little shifting he found the altar – and nearly fell off the buttress.

It might have once been a chapel of Sigmar, but it was no longer. The plain altar had been covered by rich velvet of the deepest blue, embroidered in gold with eldritch symbols that seemed to twist before Reiner's eyes. Three shallow gold bowls sat on the cloth, coals of incense glowing in them. The hammer of Sigmar that should have hung above the altar had been replaced by what appeared to be a child's skeleton, hung by one ankle, and covered entirely in gold leaf and swirling lapis traceries – and it was this that had made Reiner's heart jump, for there were eyes in the skull and they seemed to look directly at him.

When the thing didn't stretch out a skeletal arm and point at him, Reiner steadied his breathing and continued perusing the room. A cluster of silhouetted men sat in the pews near the altar, facing another man who stood. All were dressed in robes, most of blue and gold, but a few in purple and black. The man who stood wore the richest robe of all, more gold than blue, and wore a mask as well. Though his face and every inch of him was covered in heavy cloth, he had a presence about him that was tangible even from Reiner's perch.

Reiner put his ear to the hole and the muttered words became clearer. He held his breath and listened as hard as he could.

'Master,' came Scharnholt's voice, whining. 'Master, in all humility I object to this alliance with the followers of the purple one. Did they not, only a few days ago, lead the forces of the accursed Hammer God to our secret invocation chamber and disrupt the ritual of unmaking?'

'They did,' said the master in a whispery hiss. 'And that is precisely why we invite them to this colloquy. The goals of the Changer of Ways and the Lord of Pleasure do not always coincide, but here our paths run parallel. It is foolish to fight one another when the return of Talabheim to Chaos honours both our patrons.'

'These are pretty words,' said another man whose face Reiner couldn't make out. 'But how can we trust you? It is not for nothing that Tzeentch is known as the God of Many Faces. This one shows a smile, but what of the others?'

Reiner's jaw dropped. It was Danziger's voice. The tight-laced little bookkeeper was a follower of Slaanesh?

'Have we not trusted you with the location of our secret headquarters?' asked the master. 'Could you not betray us to the countess with a word? Surely that is proof enough of our intentions.'

Danziger was silent for a moment, then said, 'Very well. And have you a plan to take the stone?'

'We do not take the stone,' said the master.

The hooded men looked up, surprised.

'Why risk having it taken from us again when there is a better alternative?' he continued. 'Unfettered by the unseating of the waystone, the warpstone beneath the city gives the spells of our sorcerers more potency than they have ever had. Where once it took a hundred initiates to call forth even the most minor inhabitant of the void, now ten may raise a daemon lord. And that is what we will do. Once we open the vault, we will summon an infernal one within the manor, and beg him to take the waystone into the void with him, removing it from Teclis's reach forever.'

'A brilliant plan, master,' said Scharnholt obsequiously.

'But the vault is heavily protected,' said Danziger. 'Could the lord not break it open and take the stone for us?'

The master sighed. 'That is the trouble with the followers of the Lord of Pleasure. They dislike work. Unfortunately, only in the deepest levels, far below the dungeon beneath the countess's manor, will the emanations of the warpstone be strong enough to allow our magi to call forth a great one of sufficient power. We must bring the stone there or fail. Fortunately,' he said, 'our patrons have blessed you both with position and power that allows you to walk your men though the gates of the Taalist bitch's castle without question. We must therefore only find a way to pass through the door to the dungeons and open the vault.'

'We will easily defeat the men who guard the dungeon gate,' said Scharnholt. 'And if my men then hold it and say that the guards were killed by cultists who we chased away, we will divert the attention of von Pfaltzen's fools.'

'One of the captains who hold the keys to the vault is ours,' said Danziger, 'and will surrender it for the cause.'

'Then there are only two to steal, and the men at the vault to defeat,' said the master.

'We will take Captain Lossenberg's key,' said Scharnholt.

'And we will take Captain Niedorf's,' said Danziger.

'And together you will defeat the men at the vault,' said the master. 'And then descend to the nether depths. Our goal will at last be attained. All glory to Tzeentch!'

'And Slaanesh,' said Danziger.

'Of course,' said the master.

Reiner pushed back from the hole, deep in thought, then turned to Dieter. 'We must find a place to watch them leave.'

* * *

'LORD DANZIGER!' REINER called. 'A moment of your time!'

Reiner and Dieter had followed Danziger's coach, which, like Scharnholt's, had travelled openly to and from the Order of the Willing Heart, until its path had diverged from those of the other conspirators. Then Reiner had told Dieter to hang back out of sight, and ran after the lord, seemingly alone.

Danziger looked back, and his two guards, who sat with his coachman, stood with their hands on their hilts.

Danziger's eyes bulged when he saw who approached him. 'You!' he cried. 'You dare show your face, you dirty cultist? Horst! Orringer! Cut him down!'

Reiner stopped as the coach drew up and the swordsmen hopped from their perch. 'I am indeed a cultist, m'lord,' he said without raising his voice. 'Indeed, we attended a meeting of cultists just now, you and I.'

'What?' yelped Danziger. 'I a cultist? Preposterous!' The whites showed all around the lord's pupils. 'Kill him.'

'Kill me if you will, m'lord,' Reiner said, backing away from the guards. 'But you should know that Scharnholt means to betray you.'

'Eh? Betray...?' He waved his hand. 'Desist, Horst! Bring the villain to me. But take his sword and pin his arms.'

Reiner surrendered his sword belt and stepped into the coach. The two guards crushed him between them on the narrow bench opposite Danziger.

'Are you mad?' said the exchequer in a fierce whisper. 'Speaking such things in the street?'

'My apologies, m'lord,' said Reiner. 'But I was desperate to warn you of Scharnholt's treachery.'

Danziger looked Reiner up and down. 'Who are you, sir? It seems I have seen you on every side of this game. How do you know Scharnholt's business? The last I saw, you fought each other tooth and nail.'

Reiner inclined his head. 'M'lord, you are right to be cautious. And I admit that my actions may appear, from the outside, strange. Please, allow me to explain.'

'By all means,' said Danziger. 'And explain well, or you leave this coach with your throat cut.'

'Thank you, m'lord,' said Reiner, swallowing. 'Earlier this year, my master, the Changer of Ways, saw fit to allow me to place myself and my compatriots in the service of Count Valdenheim, one of the most influential men in the Empire. As his secretary, I was privy to the Emperor's most secret dealings, and I have used this knowledge to advance the glory of Tzeentch.'

'Go on,' said Danziger, sceptically.

'When the Reikland legation arrived in Talabheim, I intended to contact Lord Scharnholt and offer him what help I could, but before I was able, you approached Valdenheim, betraying your Tzeentchist rivals to him so that you might try for the stone for yourself.'

'It is only what he would have done to me,' huffed Danziger.

'Indeed, m'lord,' said Reiner. 'Unfortunately, this meant that I was forced, so as not to expose myself, to fight the very men I meant to help.' He sighed. 'Naturally, Lord Scharnholt, when we did at last meet, thought me a false Tzeentchist, saying that I should have turned on Manfred in the sewers and helped those who held the stone. I explained to him that this would have been suicide, which, because of my unique position, would be displeasing to Tzeentch. But he refused to see it,' Reiner sniffed. 'And would not include me in his plans for recovering the stone.'

'That does indeed sound like Scharnholt,' muttered Danziger. 'The pompous ass.'

'As you know, I then tricked von Pfaltzen and the others into the caves so that I might steal the stone while they were engaged with the ratmen, only to have Scharnholt attack me from behind and try to take it for himself. After that, I... well, I had had enough.'

Reiner sighed. 'Perhaps I am a poor student, but I had always thought the followers of the Great Betrayer were meant to betray unbelievers, not one another.' He looked sadly at Danziger. 'That is why I have come to you. I wish to learn more of Slaanesh, to whom treachery is not a sacrament, and to warn you that Scharnholt may once again endanger the cause of Chaos by trying to take all the glory for himself.'

The exchequer leaned forward. 'What does he intend?'

Reiner lowered his voice. 'He means, m'lord, to bring von Pfaltzen down upon you once the ceremony in the manor depths is done. He will help von Pfaltzen kill you, denouncing you as a cultist and making himself out a hero for discovering your plot.'

Danziger sneered. 'Always he has cared more for his worldly position than for the good of Chaos. He wants to both destroy the Empire and to rule it. But,' he bit his lip. 'But how will he do this?'

'You recall how he said that his men would guard the entrance to the lower levels?' asked Reiner. 'That is so they can let him out and trap you within, while he calls von Pfaltzen.'

Danziger paled. 'But... but how am I to keep this from occurring. We must destroy the stone, and yet–'

'It is simple,' said Reiner.

'Simple?' Danziger asked hopefully.

'Indeed.' Reiner spread his hands. 'Never let Scharnholt's men hold any position on their own. Say that you wish to share the honour of holding the stairs to the dungeon. If he says his men must go do such and such, you send your men too. Warn your men to be wary of a dagger in the back, and return any such attack tenfold, and swiftly, so no alarm is raised by your fighting.'

Danziger nodded. 'Yes. Yes, of course.'

'I will help you, if you wish,' said Reiner demurely. 'My men would welcome a chance to help Slaanesh, and get back a bit of our own.'

Danziger frowned. 'Surely Scharnholt will recognise you and know something is afoot?'

'He will not see our faces,' said Reiner. 'We have our own way into the manor, and will be masked when we meet you inside. You may tell Scharnholt that we are servants from the manor that dare not show our faces.'

Danziger nodded. 'Very well. Slaanesh is a welcoming god, and rewards loyalty and bravery. Help me bring down Talabheim and destroy Scharnholt, and you will find me generous. Betray me...' He looked into Reiner's eyes and Reiner flinched from his cold, lizard stare, 'and nothing you learned at the clawed feet of Tzeentch will prepare you for the exquisite agony a follower of Slaanesh can bestow with a single touch.' He sat back and waved a hand. 'Now go. We enter the manor at midnight.'

Reiner stood and bowed as the guards let go of his arms and returned his sword. 'Very good, m'lord.'

He nearly sank to his knees as he stepped down from the coach. His heart was pounding like an orc wardrum. He had done it. He had tricked Danziger into allowing him to ride his coat-tails through the dungeon gate, and hopefully into the vault as well. Now all he had to do was work out a way to sneak into the castle and back out again carrying a half-tonne rock. He laughed bitterly. Was that all?

SIXTEEN
I Will Not Betray My City

'BROTHERS!' CRIED REINER, stepping out of an alley and falling in with seven priests of Morr who walked a plain casket through the rubble of the merchant district toward the Manor district gate. 'Do your labours take you to the Grand Manor this night?' He was dressed in black robes too, the Blackhearts having just relieved a Morrist corpse-burning detail of them not an hour ago.

'Aye, we do, brother,' said the lead priest. 'A sergeant of the guard has succumbed to the plague and his superiors wish him removed without anyone seeing his, er malformations.'

'Naturally,' said Reiner, his heart surging. At last! This was the fourth such procession he had asked this question, and the midnight hour was fast approaching. He signalled surreptitiously behind him.

'Why do you ask?' asked the priest.

'Er, we go the same way,' said Reiner. 'We thought we might travel together for safety.'

'We?' said the priest looking around. He shrieked as eight looming figures surged out of the alley and descended upon his fellows.

'ONE MOMENT, FATHER,' said a guard at the Hardtgelt gate. 'Where are you bound?'

'For the Grand Manor, my son,' Reiner said as the black-robed Blackhearts came to a halt, their stolen casket held between them. 'A sergeant of the guard awaits Morr's gate.'

'You have the order of removal?' asked the guard. He didn't seem eager to stand too close to the casket.

'One moment,' said Reiner. He withdrew a rolled parchment from his voluminous sleeve. He held it out, but the guard didn't take it.

'Open it, father. No offence meant,' he said.

'None taken,' said Reiner, and unrolled the scroll, pleased. The more disinclined the guards were to approach servants of Morr the better the Blackhearts' chances.

The guard gave the order a cursory glance. 'And the casket.'

'Certainly,' said Reiner. He lifted the lid so the guard could see in.

The guard stood on tip-toe so he didn't have to step nearer the casket, then waved them in. 'Carry on, father.'

'Bless you, my son,' said Reiner.

The Blackhearts started into the Manor district, Gert and Pavel and Hals moaning and weaving in the throes of savage hangovers. Behind them Reiner heard the guard mutter, 'They even stink of death.'

Reiner smiled, for there was a reason for the smell.

As they approached the Grand Manor, Reiner saw Scharnholt and his men entering through the gate. The gate guards saluted them. Reiner held back until they had entered, then approached. There was no sign of Danziger. Reiner hoped he was already within. It was almost midnight.

The scene at the Manor district gate was repeated with minor variations here, though the inspection was more thorough, and rather than passing them through, the chief guard assigned them an escort to take them where they were to go – a storeroom near a guardroom in the lower levels of the old barrel keep. Their escort was a sturdy young guard who seemed less than happy with his duty and hurried ahead of the Blackhearts as if he were trying to lose them.

Reiner did his best to memorise their route, and looked for stairs leading down. Their guide took them away from public areas of the manor, where the nobles might be offended by their presence, and into a maze of service corridors and back stairs.

After a while the hallways became tight passages of undressed stone, and Reiner knew they had entered the old keep. At the bottom of a twisting stair they passed a guardroom full of guards, talking and playing cards, then stopped just around a corner at a bolted wooden door with a sleepy guard before it.

'Jaffenberg,' said their guide. 'You're dismissed. They've come.'

'About time,' said the guard as he took a key from his pouch. 'Never done a duller watch.' He handed the key to the guide and saluted. 'See you at Elsa's later?'

'Aye, I suppose.'

Jaffenberg hurried off as their guide turned the key in the lock and pushed open the door, revealing a narrow storeroom filed with blankets and cakes of soap and jars of lamp oil. Lying on the floor was a dead guard with a second head, small as a baby's fist, peeking out of his collar next to the first.

The guide shivered at the sight. 'Poor beggar. Treat him well. He was a good man.'

'Better than we'll treat you,' said Reiner.

'Eh?' The boy turned and flinched as Reiner put his dagger against his jugular. 'What are you...?'

Gert covered the boy's mouth from behind with one big hand and pinned his sword arm with the other. He walked him backwards into the store room as Reiner kept the blade at his throat.

The others pushed in behind them. Ten people and a casket made it very crowded inside. Franka could barely close the door.

'Now, lad,' said Reiner, flashing the dagger in their guide's frightened eyes. 'Where are the stairs to the lower levels? And know that if you try to scream, you will die as you draw your breath.' He nodded to Gert. 'Let him speak.'

The boy took a breath. He was trembling. 'I... I won't tell you. I'd rather die.'

Reiner smiled kindly. 'Very brave, lad. But are you brave enough to not die?'

'To... to not die?' asked the boy, confused.

'Aye,' said Reiner. 'Dying is easy. It is over in a second. But Gert can break a man's neck so that he loses all movement in his limbs and yet doesn't die. Can you imagine it? Alive in the limp sack of your body, unable to move, or feed yourself, or wipe your own arse, or make love to your sweetheart, for the next fifty years? Are you brave enough to face that?'

'I will not betray the countess!' gabbled the boy. 'I will not betray my city–'

Gert twisted the boy's head, steadily increasing the pressure.

'Are you certain?' asked Reiner.

The boy's eyes were rimmed with white. His face was bright red. Gert twisted harder.

'To the right!' squeaked the boy. Gert relaxed the pressure. 'To the right until you pass the laundry, then left past the kitchens and down. It's below the store rooms, may Sigmar forgive me.'

'And may you forgive me,' said Reiner, and cracked the boy in the temple with the pommel of his dagger. He sagged in Gert's arms.

'Right,' Reiner said. 'Tie him up and give me his key. Then get out of these robes.'

Gert chuckled. 'Break his neck so he can't move?' He bent to bind the boy's wrists. 'How do you invent these things, captain?'

Reiner shrugged. 'Desperation.'

'Bad business,' Augustus growled. 'Hurting an innocent boy.'

'He stood in our way,' said Reiner, coldly. 'We had no choice.'

'No choice but to die,' said Augustus.

'That isn't a choice.'

There followed a few moments of bumping elbows and muffled curses as the Blackhearts struggled out of their robes in the tight space.

'Put 'em in the casket,' said Reiner. 'The arm too. And leave the masks off for now. We'll look more suspicious with 'em on than off.'

Darius, looking queasy, took a long, lumpy, triple-wrapped parcel from a deep pocket in his robe, and dropped it with a thud into the casket.

'Good riddance,' he said.

When they were ready, Reiner squeezed to the door. A mask like a crow's beak hung from a ribbon around his belt. The others had similar masks. Reiner had bought them from a huckster who claimed they would protect them from the madness.

'Right,' he said, grinding out his torch. 'Dieter, on point. Jergen, at the rear. To the right.' He opened the door a crack and looked out as Dieter joined him. A clatter of boots made him close it right back up. He waited until the sounds had faded away, then cracked the door again. Raised voices and reflected torchlight came from the guardroom around the left-hand corner, but the hall to the right was clear.

'Off we go.'

The Blackhearts followed Dieter into the unlit hall as quietly as they could. Reiner locked the door behind them and took up the rear. After a moment of feeling bindly along the stone walls, Dieter's silhouette became visible again and they heard women's voices and sloshing water ahead. On the left-hand wall an open door glowed with yellow light. There was a smell of steam and soap.

'He ain't my sweetheart,' said a shrill voice.

'Now don't lie, Gerdie,' cackled another. 'We saw ye makin' eyes at him. And he do look quite fetching in 'is uniform, don't he?'

Dieter edged forward until he could see into the door. He held up a palm. The others waited.

'So you fancy him, yerself, do ye?' said the first voice. 'Well, he don't like fat old… oh now look, this will never come out. That's blood, that is.'

Dieter beckoned Reiner across, and he tip-toed past the door, catching a glimpse of a handful of women stirring dirty clothes into boiling iron cauldrons with long wooden paddles. Another darned stockings in a corner.

Dieter pointed to the rest of the Blackhearts in turn, and they slipped across the opening one by one. The women never looked up from their gossiping.

Just beyond the laundry was the kitchen corridor. Dieter and Reiner looked down it. It was well lit, and voices came from it, rising over the clatter and hiss of a busy kitchen. As they watched, five footmen with large trays on their shoulders walked from a right-hand door and hurried toward a shadowy stair at the far end. A scullery maid crossed the hall, struggling with a huge skillet.

Dieter frowned, rubbing his chin. 'Bit more difficult, this. If we had one of them ratty smoke grenades…'

Reiner shook his head. 'I think this calls for brass, not stealth.'

'Brass?' asked Dieter.

'Aye.' Reiner turned to the others. 'Right lads, two abreast, weapons on shoulders. Dieter, Darius, er... do your best.'

The Blackhearts formed up, Hals and Pavel in front.

'Now,' said Reiner. 'Like you belong here. March.'

He plucked a torch from the wall and started forward with a brisk step. The Blackhearts tramped in unison behind him as if they were on an important duty.

Reiner waved back a footman carrying a platter. 'Stand clear, fellow.'

The man let them by with a look of surly patience, then followed after them. Cooks and kitchen assistants glanced up as they passed, but didn't give them a second look. When they reached the stairwell, Reiner led the Blackhearts down while the footman went up. Reiner breathed a sigh of relief. No one had sensed anything amiss.

As the noises of the kitchen faded behind them faint sounds came from below, growing louder with each step.

'That's a fight,' said Hals.

'Aye,' said Pavel. 'I hear it.'

'On your guard,' said Reiner, drawing his sword. 'But no need to hurry. Let Danziger and Scharnholt do the dirty work.'

They continued down the stairs, listening to the melee below as they descended past the storeroom level. Turning down the last flight, they saw shadows fighting in the light cast from a wide archway.

Reiner raised a hand, and the Blackhearts halted.

'Masks on,' he whispered.

The Blackhearts slipped their black crow-beaks on. Reiner hoped they wouldn't have to fight in them. He had no peripheral vision through the eyeholes.

As they started down again, a body flew backwards through the archway, spilling blood. A man in a black breastplate followed him in and stabbed him in the chest, finishing him off. The killer looked up, and jumped as he saw the men on the stairs. It was Danziger.

'Who?' he gasped, then relaxed. 'Ah, it's you. You're late. Come. We're in.'

They followed him into a low, square room with a stout, iron bound door in one wall. The place was crowded with Danziger's and Scharnholt's men, busy killing the twelve guards who manned the door. Scharnholt stood in the centre, directing with a casual hand and mopping his round face with a white linen handkerchief. Reiner noticed that men in both Scharnholt's and Danziger's companies had short poles strapped to their backs for carrying the waystone.

'Pedermann, the door,' Scharnholt said. 'Dortig, cut every throat. These men know us. We can have no survivors.' He frowned as Danziger approached him with the Blackhearts. 'Who are these?'

'More of ours,' said Danziger. 'Servants who dare not show their faces.'

Reiner smiled to himself. Danziger was repeating his words to the letter.

'I see,' said Scharnholt, curling his lip. 'I hope they can fight as well as serve.'

'I assure you, m'lord,' said Danziger. 'They are most capable.'

'I will leave ten men here,' said Scharnholt as his men opened the door. 'With the story that they came upon some cultists slaughtering the guards and chased them off, then took it upon themselves to guard the door until more guards could be summoned.'

Danziger paused, shooting a knowing look at Reiner before smiling at Scharnholt. 'An admirable plan, brother. But let our men share this dangerous duty. I would feel remiss if you took the risk entirely upon yourself.'

Scharnholt raised an eyebrow. 'Do I sense mistrust, brother? Are we not united as one in this?'

'Indeed we are united,' said Danziger, indignant. 'It is why I offered to share the dangers with you. Perhaps it is you who are mistrustful. Or do you mistake concern for mistrust because you plan some treachery?'

'He speaks of treachery who betrayed my followers to Valdenheim and Teclis when we already had the stone?' asked Scharnholt, putting a hand on his hilt.

Danziger did the same.

Reiner stepped forward. 'M'lords,' he said, aping a slurring Talabheim accent to disguise his voice. 'Please. Remember our purpose here.' He wanted the two lords fighting, but not yet. Not before they opened the vault for him.

Scharnholt let go of his sword. 'Your man speaks wisdom. This is not the place to argue. Very well, we will share the duty.' He turned to the door. 'The dungeon is on the same level as the vault, and has its own guards. I will make it so that the noise of our battle does not carry, but you must not let the men we fight escape to warn the dungeon guards. Now let us go.'

SEVENTEEN
Kill Them

As the companies lined up to enter the door, Reiner heard Augustus mutter 'Only doing their job,' under his breath as he looked around at the dead guards. His fists were balled at his sides, knuckles white.

Scharnholt and Danziger both left ten men behind to hold the door and led the rest down the steps. The Blackhearts marched in behind them, and started into the depths. The big door boomed closed above them. Reiner swallowed. No turning back now.

At the second landing, Scharnholt began muttering and waving his podgy fingers. The air around Reiner seemed to thicken and there was a pressure on his eardrums as if he had dived into deep water. The cultists and the Blackhearts were opening their mouths and wiggling their fingers in their ears, trying to clear the pressure, but it wouldn't go.

'What is it?' asked Franka, wincing.

Reiner could barely hear her. It sounded like she spoke from behind a thick pane of glass. All the noise around him was damped. The jingle and creak of the men around him was almost inaudible. The men followed. Their marching made as much noise as a cat walking through grass. It was as if the air had become a jelly and the sounds caught in it.

Three flights down, the stairs ended at a wide corridor that stretched away into darkness, other passages intersecting it at wide intervals. Were they still within the walls of the barrel keep, Reiner wondered? Surely the corridor carried on further than that. He shook his head. It was a wonder all of Talabheim didn't cave in, considering how much of it was riddled with tunnels.

Danziger pointed to a right-hand passage and the men filed in. It ended in an iron gate, through which they could see torchlight.

Scharnholt handed the key ring to Danziger without missing a beat in his mumbling. Danziger turned to the company and gave an order no one could hear. He rolled his eyes in annoyance and brandished his sword with an exaggerated motion.

The cultists and the Blackhearts drew their weapons as Danziger turned the key in the lock. It made no noise. Nor did the swinging of the gate. Danziger waved forward, and the men rushed into the room, as silent as a breeze.

Reiner took in the room as he ran. It was a vaulted rectangular chamber, longer than it was wide, with archways to the left and right, and ten guards standing in a line against a massive stone door at the far end, which was bound with iron bands.

The guards shouted in surprise as they saw the cultists. Their voices barely sounded in Scharnholt's bubble. They drew their weapons and met the charge valiantly, but they were too few. Danziger's and Scharnholt's men quickly chopped them to pieces in a horrible, silent bloodbath. Reiner and the Blackhearts hung back and took no part. Reiner felt ashamed nonetheless. Was standing aside to let good men be killed less villainous than swinging the sword oneself? Augustus was swearing out loud. Fortunately none could hear him.

'The keys!' said Danziger, shouting to be heard.

One of Danziger's men handed him two keys. One of Scharnholt's had another. But as he turned to the door, more than a score of guards poured out of the two archways, charging the cultists' rear.

'Kill them all!' cried Danziger, though it came out a whisper. 'Let none escape!'

Scharnholt stepped back to the door as the cultists turned to face their foes. He could give no orders, for he had to maintain his incantation. The two sides clashed together with almost no sound, mouths open like mummers miming shouts and screams.

Augustus glared at the backs of the cultists as they fought the guard, his hands gripping his spear as if he were about to attack. Reiner put a hand on his shoulder. The pikeman snarled and pulled away. The others looked nearly as mutinous. Reiner didn't blame them. But there was nothing for it. They had to get the waystone.

He stepped to Danziger and shouted almost inaudibly in his ear. 'M'lord. Give us the keys and defend us, and my men will open the vault so that we may be away all the quicker.'

'Aye,' said Danziger. 'Good. And make the stone ready to carry as well.'

'Of course, m'lord,' said Reiner. His heart leapt. The fool gave him more than he'd asked.

Reiner collected the keys and the poles from the men who carried them and motioned the Blackhearts to the door as Danziger's and Scharnholt's men formed a protective semi-circle around them, hacking and thrusting at the maddened guards. He gave keys to Franka, Darius and Dieter, then yelled to the others. 'Watch their backs,'

They nodded and faced out toward the melee, standing behind Danziger's men – all but Augustus, who only glared, spear at his side, at the carnage. Though they weren't invulnerable, as Scharnholt's men had been in the ratmen's caves, many of the cultists wore amulets written over with vile runes. Reiner saw a guardsman's sword veer away from a cultist's head as if pushed aside by an invisible hand.

The key plate was set into the floor before the vault door, an oblong steel plaque decorated with geometric patterns. Franka, Darius and Dieter knelt over it. The designs that framed each keyhole were different. One was a square, one a circle, and one a diamond, which corresponded to the backs of the three keys.

Dieter shook his head as they inserted them into the locks. 'Dwarf work,' he shouted to Reiner. 'Glad y'haven't asked me to pick it.' He looked at the others. 'Now all together, or we'll have to go again.'

Franka, Darius and Dieter slowly turned their keys, and they hit home together. Reiner felt a heavy clunk under the floor.

Dieter smiled. 'Prettiest sound in the world.'

Reiner checked the battle. The guards were surrounded now, and falling fast. He slapped the backs of Hals, Pavel, Gert, Augustus and Jergen. 'Here! Push!'

They turned and pushed on one of the massive stone doors. At first it didn't move and Reiner momentarily feared they hadn't unlocked it after all, then slowly it swung in.

When the gap widened enough to walk through, Reiner waved a halt. Pavel and Hals gathered up the poles and rope and the Blackhearts filed into the vault. The faint sounds of battle faded entirely beyond the door. They stopped and gaped in wonder. Augustus's torch glittered upon a thousand golden treasures. There were twenty gilded chairs and jewelled silver armour with a dragon helm. Swords with gold-chased scabbards and gemstone pommels sprouted like flowers from a Cathay vase. Beautiful paintings and statues and tapestries were piled everywhere. Caskets and chests lined each wall. The waystone stood among a grove of beautiful marble statues, looking out of place among them.

'Strewth,' said Pavel. But they were still within Scharnholt's circle of silence, so Reiner could barely hear him.

'Nice haul,' shouted Dieter. 'Like to have a peek in them chests.'

'We aren't here for that,' said Reiner. 'Unfortunately.' He pointed to the waystone. 'Get it ready. Once Scharnholt and Danziger defeat the guards, I will try to turn them against each other, and then we will kill the survivors.'

'Sigmar be praised,' said Hals.

'About damned time!' said Augustus.

The others nodded in agreement. They moved to the waystone and began to tip it down on the poles.

'Wait,' called Franka, suddenly. 'Wait! I have a better idea!'

'Eh?' said Augustus. 'There ain't a better idea than killing them cursed daemon-lovers.'

'It'll be better if we survive and escape, aye?' snapped Franka.

'What's the idea, lass?' bellowed Reiner.

Franka started to explain. Reiner couldn't hear her.

'What? You have to shout!'

Frustrated, Franka pointed to a statue of a buxom nymph next to the waystone, which was roughly the same height and circumference, then to a rolled rug.

Reiner laughed. It was a brilliant plan. They could get out without a fight. 'Yes! Good!' He waved to the others, shouting. 'Hide the stone and wrap that instead. Quickly. Jergen, let no one in.'

Reiner helped Hals, Pavel, Augustus and Gert carry the waystone behind the stand of statues, as Franka and Darius unrolled a rug and draped it over the statue.

'Will it work?' shouted Gert as they lowered the wrapped statue onto the poles.

Reiner shrugged. 'If it doesn't, you'll get your fight.'

Gert grinned. They bound the statue to the poles, making sure that the ropes made it impossible to pull back the rug and see underneath.

'Good,' said Reiner when it was secured. 'Get it up. If all goes wrong, kill Scharnholt and Danziger first.'

He looked out as the others raised the wrapped statue. They were just in time. The cultists were killing the last of the guards and wiping their blades. Scharnholt ceased his incantation and turned toward the vault with Danziger. Reiner's ears popped and sound rushed into his head, battering his eardrums. Boot heels on flags, the laughter of the cultists, the moans of the dying, were suddenly unbearably loud.

Reiner beckoned the Blackhearts forward, then stepped out, waved at Danziger and Scharnholt. 'M'lords! We have it.'

The Blackhearts edged the covered statue through the partially open stone door. Reiner's palms were sweating. This was a dangerous moment. If the lords asked to see the stone they were in trouble. If they asked the Blackhearts to carry it, that was trouble as well.

'Lead on, m'lords,' he said with a wave of his hand. 'We will carry the stone.'

'Eh?' said Danziger, suddenly suspicious. '*You* will carry the stone?'

'What does he say?' said Scharnholt. 'Does your servant order us?'

'Your men have been fighting,' said Reiner. 'We are fresh and strong. Do not trouble yourselves. We have it well in hand.'

Danziger and Scharnholt exchanged a look, then turned back to Reiner.

'No, brother,' Danziger said. 'We will carry the stone. Since your fellows are fresh and unhurt, you will guard our backs in case we are followed.'

Reiner shrugged and bowed, hiding a smile. 'As your lordship wishes it.' He motioned for the Blackhearts to put down the stone.

After some argument, Scharnholt and Danziger agreed that their men would carry the stone together, and the party got underway, travelling without torches. As they neared the passage to the dungeons, Scharnholt resumed his muttering and silence again closed around them. Reiner looked down the corridor as they passed it. Not far down he saw the shadows of bars and of moving men in a square of light cast across the floor.

The main corridor dimmed into darkness beyond the dungeon passage. Scharnholt changed incantations and led the way with a faint blue light that flickered above his outstretched palm. The back of the column was in total darkness. Reiner motioned the Blackhearts to slow their steps, and by the time they reached the stairs to the bowels of the manor, they lagged twenty paces behind. They descended two flights in darkness, then Reiner stopped, listening. When no query came from below, he whispered, 'Back. To the stone. Quietly.'

The Blackhearts padded back up the steps, then along the corridor toward the torchlight. They slowed at the hall to the dungeons and crept past it. He waved them by. Augustus scraped his spear butt on the flagstones as he passed and it made a horrendous noise to their oversensitive ears. Reiner wondered if he had done it on purpose.

When no reaction came from the dungeon corridor, they pressed on to the vault room. It was as they had left it, the vault door ajar, the bodies of the dead guards lying in spreading pools of blood. They hurried across the chamber, taking off their stifling beak masks and snatching up four spears with which to carry the stone.

They entered the vault, and Hals, Pavel, Gert and Jergen covered the stone with another rug and lashed it to the spears while the others watched, nervous, and Dieter wandered the room, examining the treasures. But just as they lifted it, they heard movement from the guard chamber.

'Sigmar! What's this!' cried a voice. 'Captain! The Vault!'

'Blast it!' said Reiner, and rushed into the chamber, sword out.

But the guard was already in the hall, screaming at the top of his lungs. Reiner was about to race after him, when he stopped. He darted back into the vault and gestured at the Blackhearts. 'Set it down and stay hidden!'

He returned to the guard chamber. Voices and boot steps were approaching from the hall. He dropped and rolled in a puddle of blood, smearing it on his face, then flopped back as if dead just as a captain and ten dungeon guards ran in.

The captain stared. 'Sigmar! This... this is impossible! How did we not hear?'

'And the vault is open, captain,' said the first guard. 'Maybe they who did this are...'

Reiner spasmed up, groaning artistically. 'The thieves...' he said. 'They...' He looked around blindly for a moment as the guards turned to look at him, then flung out his hand. 'Captain! Cultists! They've stolen something! They took it to the basement and mean to do some strange magic with it! If you hurry, you might stop them!'

Reiner had hoped – prayed in fact, with fingers crossed to Ranald – that the captain would run off after the thieves in a screaming panic, but the cursed stoic barely raised an eyebrow.

'Yeager!' he said. 'Take two men into the cellar and see what's what! Krieghelm! Tell the boys up top the vault's been breached! Tell 'em von Pfaltzen's wanted. The rest stay with me. The vault cannot remain unguarded.'

The men raced off.

Reiner groaned. 'But, captain,' he said. 'There are more than thirty of 'em! Three men will not be enough!'

'Nor will fifteen, sir,' said the captain. 'Which is all I have.' He turned to the vault, motioning to his remaining men. 'Three of you with me.'

Reiner watched in horror as the captain and his three men started for the open vault. 'No! Beware!' he cried. 'They used some terrible magic to open the door. It is too dangerous!'

The captain ignored him and entered the vault, torch high. Reiner cursed, knowing what was coming. He got to his feet, still pretending to be hurt, and edged anxiously toward the door.

'Ho!' came the captain's voice. 'Stand forward, you!'

Something heavy smashed.

The guards in the chamber looked around, surprised. Reiner ran into the vault and came upon a frozen tableau. The captain and his three men were on guard, a toppled suit of armour at their feet, facing the Blackhearts who stood in a dark corner beyond the waystone, swords out.

'Captain, wait!' said Reiner, though what he meant to say after he had no idea.

'Guards! To me!' called the captain. 'The thieves are here!'

Reiner cursed. 'Kill them!' he said.

'Reiner, no!' cried Franka.

But when the captain lunged for Reiner, she came forwards with the rest. Only Augustus and Darius hung back, Darius hiding behind a stack of paintings, Augustus staring, mouth agape.

Reiner parried the captain's thrust and the man died with Jergen's longsword in his back. His three men went down an instant later, impaled by Pavel and Hals's spears and butchered by the others' swords. But as they fell, nine more rushed into the vault. They cried out as they saw their captain dead and ran around the statues at the Blackhearts, who spread out to meet them.

'No!' cried Augustus. 'No, you damned traitor! I won't stand for it!' He lowered his spear and charged straight at Reiner.

EIGHTEEN
We Fight On The Wrong Side

Reiner yelped and leapt aside, then fell sprawling across the waystone as Augustus's spear and the swords of two guardsmen passed above him. He rolled away, slashing about wildly. All around him the Blackhearts were crossing swords with the guards.

'Ye daft pike!' shouted Gert, and clubbed Augustus over the head with his heavy crossbow.

Augustus stumbled, grunting, and turned to stab Gert, but the crossbowman kicked him in the chest and he fell backward into a Cathay urn as big as a hogshead of ale. His arms and legs waved ridiculously as he struggled to get out.

Reiner staggered to his feet, parrying the guards' questing swords, and recovered himself. It was an awkward and horrible fight. The vault was so cluttered that there was hardly room to move and none to swing. Marble statues and suits of armour toppled and smashed, and priceless paintings were cut to ribbons.

The Blackhearts fought with a grim resignation Reiner had never seen in them before. They hated what they did. Franka wept as she fought. Gert cursed Manfred with each swing. Pavel and Hals were tight-lipped with fury. Jergen's face had even less expression than usual. Only Dieter seemed unaffected, stabbing men from behind with a superior smirk on his face.

Reiner backed into the thicket of statues to protect his flanks from his two opponents. Their swords skipped off marble shoulders and breasts. Reiner kicked a statue into one man and ran him through as he dodged. The other pressed forward, and he and Reiner fenced through the forest of frozen figures.

Jergen fought like a machine, gutting one man with a down stoke, then backhanding another's head off before turning to face a third. None could touch him. Franka dumped a fortune in Reikmarks before her opponent and opened him up from knee to groin as he slipped on them. Gert had a jewel-encrusted ceremonial mace in one hand and his hatchet in the other. Both ran with blood, as did his chest.

Reiner ducked under a slash and cracked his head on the stone elbow of a former Elector Count of Talabecland. His eyes dimmed and he sat down suddenly. He threw his sword arm up, more to cover his head than to attack, and gutted his man by accident. He fell across him, vomiting blood. Reiner pushed him off, fearing another guard would take advantage, but none came. It appeared the battle was over. The Blackhearts stood panting over their kills. Franka's sobs were the only other sound.

Reiner looked at the guard he had killed. He was only a boy, his first beard just coming in, his dead eyes gazing sightlessly at the ceiling. Reiner stood, trying to clear the tightness in his throat. It wouldn't go.

'Are we all well?' He asked. He saw Jergen kneeling in the middle of four bodies, his head down. 'Are you hurt, Rohmner?'

Jergen looked up, and Reiner had never seen anything sadder than his scarred, solemn face. 'I am praying, captain.'

'Well?' growled Hals. 'We ain't well by a long stretch. This…' He spread his hands helplessly at the carnage.

Pavel shook so hard that he had to sit down. He glared at Reiner. 'Captain, we done some bad things before, but…' He made the sign of the hammer. 'Sigmar, forgive us.'

The others followed his example. Franka made Myrmidia's spear.

Reiner licked his lips. 'You heard me try,' he said. 'I tried to send them away. I didn't–' He choked and looked back at the boy he had killed, then away.

There was a smash and Augustus rose from the shards of the Cathay urn, shaking with rage. 'You'll die for this!' he said, his voice trembling. 'I'll bring the whole city down on you!' He started edging for the vault door.

'Don't be a fool, lad,' said Gert, as the others spread out. 'It's a bad thing we've done. But we had to do it. Manfred–'

'Damn Manfred! Damn the whole lot of you!' roared Augustus. 'We fight on the wrong side! He's made villains of us all!'

The others tried to calm him, but Reiner's heart was pounding. This was it! Or half of it at any rate. If Augustus ran, he could warn the authorities and they would come for Valaris. But no, Valaris would know the warning had been sent, and lower the boom. If only there were some way to make the dark elf think Augustus had been killed...

Reiner froze as inspiration suddenly flooded into him. By the gods! He had it! It was perfect, as long as the others played along.

'Do you think you can get by us?' Reiner shouted. 'Do you think we will just let you walk out and warn the countess of what we do and where we go?' Reiner laughed. 'You selfish little suicide! You may wish to sacrifice your life for the greater good, but as I told you before, we are blackhearts. We look out for our own skin. The rest of the world can go hang. Do you think I'll let some sentimental fool stop me when our salvation is at hand? We have the stone. All we must do is bring it to Valaris and we are free!'

'Then come ahead,' said Augustus, lowering his head like a bull. 'Least I'll die on the right side.'

He stooped to grab his spear, but Reiner was quicker. He snatched up a small bust of Magnus the Pious and leapt at the pikeman, bashing him in the head with it. Augustus fell back and Reiner kicked him in the groin. The pikeman moaned and squirmed like a beetle on its back, clutching himself.

The Blackhearts stared. Reiner laughed and tossed the bust aside, turning away nonchalantly. 'Kill him, Neff. Kill him as you killed that traitor Echert.'

'Eh?' said Dieter, and for a second Reiner thought he was going to give the game away. But then the thief smirked and drew his dagger. 'Oh aye. And my pleasure!' He motioned to Hals and Pavel. 'Hold him, lads. Let an artist work.'

The light slowly dawned in Hals's eyes. He grinned and nudged Pavel. 'Come on, lad. Just like Echert.'

'Oh,' said Pavel, getting it at last. 'Oh, right. Like Echert.'

They pinned August's arms as Dieter knelt on him and raised his knife.

'What are you doing?' screamed Franka, jumping in to grab his hand. 'Have you all gone mad? This isn't our way!'

Jergen caught her and held her tight, clapping a hand over her mouth.

Reiner groaned. Franka had been serving Manfred dinner. She hadn't heard Dieter tell his story of faking the death of the merchant Echert. She didn't know it was a trick. She struggled in Jergen's grip as Dieter's dagger rose and fell and rose above Augustus, blood spattering everywhere. Her eyes bored into Reiner's over Jergen's thick fingers. Reiner's heart sunk to see the hate and despair there.

Reiner watched from a distance. He didn't want to be too close for fear of ruining the illusion. If they were smart, Hals and Pavel would be telling Augustus to play dead, and it was imperative that Reiner didn't hear their whispers or all was lost. It certainly looked savage enough from where he stood. In fact, it looked so real, Reiner had a sudden fear that Dieter had misread his command and was really killing the pikeman.

After a moment, Dieter stood, dagger and hands dripping blood. He grinned at Reiner. 'It's done, jagger.'

Reiner stepped forward, and still couldn't be sure Dieter hadn't killed Augustus. The Talabheimer lay motionless, his shirt shredded, and terrible, bloody gashes all over his breast. Reiner curled his lip and turned away quickly in case Augustus took a breath. 'And no more than he deserved, the swine,' he said. 'Come, let's finish this business.'

Franka stood slack in Jergen's arms, staring at Augustus's body. There were tears in her eyes.

Reiner jabbed a finger at her. 'And not a word out of you, *boy*, or you'll be next! You understand me?' He took her from Jergen, then motioned to the others. 'Pick it up.'

With Augustus 'dead', there were only six to carry the waystone, Pavel, Jergen and Darius on one side; Hals, Gert and Dieter on the other. They grunted it up and walked it out of the vault. Franka stumbled along in a daze, Reiner guiding her with a hand on her shoulder.

Halfway across the guardroom they heard footsteps running in the hallway, and the guard the captain had sent upstairs burst in.

'Captain!' he said. 'Something's amiss. The men above wouldn't let me...' He froze as he saw the Blackhearts. He was another boy.

Jergen let go of his spear-end and drew his sword. Reiner waved him back and faced the boy.

'Your captain is dying in the vault,' he said. 'Go to him.'

The boy hesitated. 'I don't...'

'Go to him, or die here!' shouted Reiner.

The boy flinched and ran for the vault, skirting wide around the Blackhearts.

Reiner took Dieter's place carrying the waystone. 'Lock him in.'

Dieter nodded, and when they had walked the stone through the guardroom gate, he knelt with his tools and locked it up.

They carried the waystone up the stairs to the last landing before the oaken door. It was already piled with the bodies of the guards Danziger's and Scharnholt's men had killed and replaced. Reiner motioned the Blackhearts to set it down.

'Here will be a fight more to our taste,' he whispered. 'Stay out of sight until I call.'

He slipped his beak mask on again and began crawling up the stairs as they drew their swords. When he reached the door he beat on it with his fist.

'Brothers!' he cried. 'Brothers! Open in the name of Lord Danziger! Open in the name of Slaanesh!'

There was a brief mumble of argument and then the key turned in the lock. Reiner hoped his dramatics here would be more successful than his last.

'Brothers!' he cried to Danziger's men as the door swung open. 'We are betrayed! Lord Scharnholt has slain Lord Danziger and stolen the stone! Kill the traitors!'

The Slaaneshi and the Tzeentchists looked at each other alarmed, hands on their hilts.

'Murderers!' cried one of Danziger's men.

'It is a lie.' shouted one of Scharnholt's men. 'A Slaaneshi lie. Show us the body!'

Reiner cursed. They were going to argue rather than fight! He surged up, charging the nearest Tzeentchist. 'I'll show you a body! To me, Slaaneshi!'

He hacked the man across the chest. The cultist was wearing a breastplate, so the strike did little damage, but it had the desired effect. The man slashed at Reiner, as did two of his comrades. Danziger's men bellowed, outraged, and leapt to Reiner's defence. The two sides came together, sword on sword, screaming curses and accusations.

Reiner parried his opponent's attack and fell back behind his Slaaneshi 'fellows.' No one paid him any attention. They were too intent on killing each other. He edged through the door, then hurried down to the Blackhearts, who looked up at him, concerned.

'Now we wait for a victor,' he said.

'And kill them,' said Gert.

'Aye.'

They listened as the sounds of battle rose and fell above them. Swords clashed. Men screeched. Bodies thudded to the ground. Then the sounds ceased.

'Lubeck, can you stand?' asked a voice. 'How many are we?'

'Is it true?' asked another. 'Did our lord mean to betray Danziger?'

'We must go below and see,' said the first.

'Now!' whispered Reiner.

The Blackhearts rushed up into the square room. Only Franka stayed behind, staring at nothing. The fight was over almost before it was begun. Only four of Scharnholt's men still stood, and not one of them was unwounded. Jergen cut down two with one stroke, and Pavel and Hals ran the other two through with their spears. Dieter made sure they were dead.

'Now the most dangerous part of all,' said Reiner, as the others returned to the stone and he collected Franka. 'For if we are discovered before we reach the storeroom, no amount of murder will save us.'

They carried the waystone up the steps past the storeroom level to the kitchens. Reiner called a halt in the dark stairwell and looked down the long kitchen corridor, which had just as much traffic as before.

'We'll brass it out again,' said Reiner. 'Make out it's a dying man. Ready?'

But just then Danziger and Scharnholt's voices echoed up the stairs from below. Reiner could only hear snatches of words.

'...killed these too?' Scharnholt was shouting.

'...Hetsau must be...' Danziger was screaming.

'Curse it!' said Reiner. 'They've found our trick too soon. Hurry.'

They hurried down the kitchen passage, Reiner shouting, 'Make way! This man is dying! Stand aside!'

The cooks and serving maids scurried out of their way. Reiner thought he heard a rumble of running boots behind them, but it might have been his imagination. They turned right and passed the laundry, not bothering now to be silent, and Reiner saw the women look up disinterestedly. They had to tiptoe the last twenty yards to the store room, because the guardroom was just around the corner.

They were almost at the door when Reiner heard running boots again, and this time he was certain it wasn't his imagination. He let go of Franka and hurried ahead, fishing in his pouch for the storeroom key. He unlocked the door as quietly as he could and opened it.

'Did some men pass here?' came Scharnholt's voice. 'Carrying something?'

'Oh aye, m'lord,' a laundress replied. 'Just now.'

As the boot steps resumed, the Blackhearts angled around to walk the waystone through the door. They stopped short. The carrying spears were wider than the door.

Reiner cursed. 'Tip it!' he whispered. 'Pavel's side down! Hals's side up!'

Darius, Jergen and Darius lowered their spear-ends almost to the floor, while Dieter, Gert and Hals struggled to raise theirs over their heads. Reiner helped Darius, who looked about to drop his end. In this awkward arrangement they walked forward again. Pavel's spear butt just caught the edge of the door.

'Left!' he hissed.

The party waddled a few inches left. Reiner thought his back would break. The boots were closing in. Reiner could see torch-light reflecting from the right.

'Now ahead.'

They started forward again, and this time just cleared the jam. The end of Reiner's spear juddered noisily along the ground and he strained to hold it up.

'On! On!' he breathed.

They continued forward, tripping over the casket. The bound guard gave a muffled cry as someone stepped on him. The Black-hearts set the stone down, grunting and hissing, and Reiner spun to close the door behind them. He fumbled his fingers under the door handle in the dark, but found no keyhole. It couldn't be locked from inside.

'Jergen. Gert. Here!'

Reiner heard Jergen and Gert feeling their way forward. The boots passed by outside. Reiner held his breath.

'You men,' came Scharnholt's voice. 'Have any men passed here, carrying a heavy burden?'

'No, m'lord,' said a voice from the guardroom.

Scharnholt cursed. 'Have we lost them? We must go back. Cultists have stolen a valuable relic from the vault!' he called to the guards. 'Let none pass unquestioned!'

'Aye, m'lord!'

Sounds of commotion came from the guardroom as the boots turned in the hall.

Reiner leaned in to Jergen and Gert. 'Push on the door.'

Jergen and Gert pressed their shoulders against the door with Reiner. Reiner felt pressure on the door as someone shook the handle.

'Locked,' said a voice, and the boots moved on.

Reiner waited until they had faded completely and the men in the guardroom had run off before he relaxed his pressure on the door.

'Right,' he said. 'Let's have a light.'

Hals lit Reiner's long-handled priest torch and they got to work – untying the covered waystone and putting it in the casket, then struggling once again into the black priest's robes while the gagged guard glared balefully at them from where he lay beside the dead, mutated sergeant.

'Where's the arm?' asked Reiner.

Darius held out the long, lumpy packet, wrinkling his nose. Reiner took it and stepped to the casket. He threaded a length of rope around the waystone at shoulder height then unrolled the packet, revealing a decaying, mutated arm with seven long sucker-tipped fingers. The stench of death rolled up from it in a solid wave, making them all gag. Reiner's eyes watered.

Wrapping his hands in a blanket from the storeroom shelves, he tied the arm to the waystone, so it looked like it had sprouted one greenish limb. The others draped more blankets over the carpet-wrapped waystone, making sure all of it was hidden, but leaving the arm exposed.

'There,' he said, standing. 'Now the final touch.'

He picked up the blanket with which he had handled the arm as Dieter continued fussing with the blankets. He stepped to Gert. The crossbowman shied away.

'What are you doing?' he cried.

'Shhh! You fool!' said Reiner. 'Hold still.'

As Gert cringed, Reiner wiped the blanket's slimy residue on his robe. He repeated the process with each of them and finished with himself. The reek was inescapable. 'Now we're ready. Lift it up.'

He listened at the door as Dieter closed the casket and the Blackhearts raised it. There were sounds of excitement and alarm coming from all over the manor, but none directly outside the door. He opened it and edged around the corner. The barracks room was deserted.

He hurried back and took up his torch. 'Right, ready.'

The Blackhearts walked out, the casket between them. Reiner locked the door behind them. 'Slow and dignified,' he said. 'The best way to be caught is to look like we're running.'

THEY WERE STOPPED as soon as they left the barrel keep and entered the modern part of the manor again. A sergeant of the guard with ten men at his back saw them coming out of a stairwell and raised his palm.

'Halt!' he said, striding forward, then stopped as if he had run into a wall. He backed off, covering his mouth and making the sign of the hammer. 'Death of Sigmar, what a reek!' he choked.

Reiner bowed. 'My apologies, sergeant. The corpse was in an advanced state of decay. It was being eaten by its own mutations.'

'Never mind that,' said the sergeant, as his men edged back unhappily. 'Where is your escort?'

'Er, he ran off, sir,' said Reiner. 'There was some uproar while we were fetching the body. He went to see what it was and never came back. Would you provide us with another? We seem to be lost.'

'Let me see your order of removal,' said the sergeant.

Reiner pulled it from his sleeve and stepped to the sergeant.

'Stay where you are!' The sergeant cried. He snatched the paper from Reiner's fingers and backed away to read it. He glanced unhappily at the casket. 'Er, I'll have to look inside. There's been a theft.'

'It's not a pretty sight sir,' said Reiner. 'He is much changed.'

'Open it, curse you.'

Reiner shrugged. 'Very well.'

He lifted the lid. The smell of death poured from it in a cloud. The sergeant retreated, gagging, then inched forward again. The suckered fingers of the rotting arm stuck up over the lip of the casket. They crawled with flies.

The sergeant retched. 'Sigmar preserve us!'

'Shall I pull back the blanket so you may see the face?' asked Reiner.

'Don't you dare!' The sergeant was furious. 'What is the matter with you, priest! Why did you wait so long to come! You endanger the whole manor! We might all catch the madness! Take it out! Hurry!'

'But sergeant,' whined Reiner. 'We have no escort. How are we to hurry when we will be stopped and asked to expose the body at every step?'

The sergeant's jaw clenched and unclenched. At last he growled. 'Right. Follow us. But stay far back, you hear me? Far back!'

'Of course, sergeant.'

The Blackhearts fell in behind the guards and followed them through the manor. Reiner crossed his fingers. With Ranald's luck, this was the last hurdle. The sergeant would walk them out and they would be free. But as they stepped out into the forecourt and approached the gate, Reiner saw von Pfaltzen and Danziger standing by it, talking with the chief gate guard.

'Heads down, lads,' Reiner whispered, and pulled his hood down over his eyes. The Blackhearts looked at their feet.

'No one is to leave the grounds,' von Pfaltzen was saying. 'No one, you understand. The thieves are still within. You will hold all visitors here until they are found.'

The chief gate guard saluted. 'Aye, sir.'

'I volunteer my men to help watch the gate,' said Danziger. 'The thieves may try to make a break.'

Reiner cursed. Five minutes earlier and they would have been through and gone.

The gate guard turned as the Blackhearts' escort approached the gate. 'Wait! No one is to go out, sergeant. The priests must bide.'

'But, captain, the corpse is diseased. It–'

'No exceptions, sergeant,' said the gate captain. 'Von Pfaltzen's ord–' He stopped as the Blackhearts' smell hit him. 'By Sigmar!'

'You see,' said the sergeant. 'It isn't safe.'

'Just a moment,' said von Pfaltzen, stepping forward with Danziger behind him. 'Open the casket.'

NINETEEN
There Is Blood To Be Spilled

THE SERGEANT SPREAD his hands. 'Sir, I have already seen in. I vouch for the contents. It would not be wise...'

'Open it.'

Reiner's hands shook as he lifted the lid. Flies buzzed up from within. Here was where he died. There was no escape. Curse Ranald. The old fraud had let him down again. Reiner held his torch high so the lid cast a shadow across the casket's interior and hung his head. Von Pfaltzen grimaced and covered his nose and mouth, but he kept coming, looking steadily into the casket. The torchlight glistened on the slimy arm.

'You see, captain,' said the sergeant.

Von Pfaltzen ignored him and reached his sword into the casket. Reiner groaned. It was all over. They were dead. They would be chopped to pieces. Von Pfaltzen prodded the blankets. Reiner expected a hard clink as his sword touched the stone, but the tip sunk in as if into a pillow. Reiner nearly yelped. He was glad for his cowl, for he was gaping like a peasant at a magic show. He heard Darius whimper with relief. Von Pfaltzen prodded again, then coughed and stepped back.

'Let them out,' he said, waving at the gate captain. 'They cannot stay.'

The gate captain nodded, relieved, and signalled his men to stand aside and let the Blackhearts out. Reiner led them forward in a daze. He was baffled. What had happened? Had Ranald sent a miracle after all? Had the stone softened? Had some hidden sorcerer caused von Pfaltzen to see what Reiner wanted him to see?

Reiner did not like the unexplained. And he was almost as frightened by their escape as he was thankful.

When they were out of earshot of the gate, everyone sighed and cursed.

'What was that?' said Hals. 'We should be dead.'

'It was a miracle,' said Pavel.

'Sorcery,' said Gert. 'Did ye cast a spell, witch?'

'I am not a witch,' said Darius.

'It was Sigmar's grace,' said Hals.

'Or Ranald's,' said Reiner.

'I only hope the filth didn't damage 'em,' muttered Dieter.

'Damage what?' asked Reiner.

Dieter said nothing. Reiner looked back, they were out of sight of the gate. There was a side street just ahead. 'Turn in there,' he said. 'And set it down.'

The Blackhearts angled into the side street and set the heavy casket down with groans of relief.

'Don't get any ideas I'll share,' said Dieter. 'I stole 'em fair and square.'

Reiner threw open the casket and flipped aside the blanket where von Pfaltzen had poked. Rolls of stiff canvas had been tucked down next to the stone. Reiner pulled them out.

'Easy, easy!' said Dieter, sharp.

Reiner uncurled the rolls and found that they were four paintings by famous masters, cut from their frames, which had been stacked with the others in the vault. There was a hole at the same spot on each painting.

'There!' said Dieter, disgusted. 'Cursed jagger ruined them with his poking. That was a fortune that was. Now they're worthless!'

'They saved our lives,' said Darius. 'I don't call that worthless.'

Dieter snorted.

Reiner re-rolled the paintings and stuffed them back under the blanket. 'Right,' he said. 'One more gate and we're free. Off we go.'

* * *

THE BLACKHEARTS PASSED through the Manor district gate with no difficulties, and made their way to the sewers and then the catacombs below them. It was a slow, silent trip. Slow because Reiner wanted to give Augustus as much time to get to the authorities as he could. It was quiet because, except for participating in the occasional argument about which was the right path, Reiner didn't care to speak for fear of saying something which might give away their ruse.

It seemed the others felt the same. Franka stumbled along like a sleepwalker, staring blankly ahead. It broke Reiner's heart to see her. He wanted more than anything to let her in on the trick, but he couldn't. His greatest fear was that she would run, but she seemed too stunned. His second greatest fear – after they had made several wrong turnings and had had to double back – was that Augustus would not remember the way either and lead their rescuers in circles in the catacombs while the dark elf destroyed the stone.

At last they came to the huge, glittering cave with the bridge over the chasm at one end, and the cyclopean arch at the other. The mutants came out of their hovels to surround them, even more deformed than before, and carried them, like a sea carries a bottle, into the chamber with the cages and the stone circle.

Valaris was waiting for them. In the days since they had left him he had built a home for himself. Beautiful if mismatched tables and chairs, vases and tapestries, all scavenged by his twisted slaves, were arranged against one wall. He had even managed to find a magnificent canopied bed in which to sleep.

To the right of this was a grand oak throne, and from this he rose to greet them, a wry smile on his cruel lips as they set down the casket.

'My friends,' he said. 'Your adventures have provided me with more amusement than a year's worth of blood sport. And had the success of your enterprise not meant so much to me, and the news that I had failed to kill Teclis not angered me, I would have laughed all the harder.'

He looked at Reiner with something akin to fondness. 'You in particular, captain, twisted more prettily than a snake pinned by a spear. So many times did I give up on you, so many times did I come within a hair's breadth of allowing your master to murder you before murdering him in turn, when suddenly you would pull an escape out of thin air and I would relent in order to see what fresh comedy was in store.' He chuckled. 'Never have I seen a man more torn between following his conscience or saving his own skin. For though you protest otherwise, I know you are not entirely the rogue you play, and your internal struggle was as entertaining as your fight with the Imperials. Thankfully your venality has won out at last, as I knew it would, and I was treated to the high drama and low farce that was the murder of your comrade. Beautiful. I almost wish...' He looked wistfully at them, then shrugged. 'But no, it is impossible. Khaine needs strong, pure blood in order to unmake the waystone.'

'Khaine needs... blood?' said Reiner, the brief flash of triumph in the knowledge that he had fooled the elf dying as he realised the elf had tricked him too. '*Our* blood?'

'Yes,' said Valaris. 'The mutants are too diseased. Their blood would be an insult.'

'But, Lord Valaris,' said Reiner, though he knew it was hopeless. 'You promised us our lives. You promised that we would go free with Count Manfred if we procured you the stone. It is the only reason we agreed to do it.'

'Naturally, I promised,' said Valaris, shrugging. 'Would you concern yourself with a promise made to a dog, no matter how clever its tricks?' He motioned to his slaves. 'Bring out the prisoner and tie them all to the stones. We will proceed at once.'

'Ye fish-belly cozener,' snarled Hals. 'Ye twist-tongued cheat!'

'Coward!' shouted Pavel. 'Tell yer dirty pets to stand off and face me sword to spear. I'll gut ye where ye stand.'

'But, lord,' said Reiner desperately. 'Our blood is tainted as well. Will Khaine accept poisoned blood?'

Valaris smiled. 'Khaine's sacrifices often die by poison.'

Manfred was led, blinking, out of one of the cages. He was gaunt and wild looking, his hair and beard matted and his clothes bedraggled and grimy.

His miserable expression changed to one of joy as he saw Reiner. 'By Sigmar,' he said, amazed. 'Have you done it? Have you freed me at last?'

Reiner laughed as the mutants dragged the Blackhearts to the tall basalt stones. 'No, m'lord. You have doomed us. The elf does not honour his bargain.' He wanted to add 'unless Augustus brings our rescue,' but even now he didn't dare speak, for fear of giving the dark elf warning.

'What!' cried Manfred, looking at Valaris. 'You devious deceiver! How dare you! I am a count of the Empire!'

Valaris was directing his slaves as they took the waystone from the casket, and ignored Manfred.

'Come, m'lord,' said Reiner. 'You of all people should not be surprised by treachery.'

The mutants began to tie the Blackhearts tightly, if inexpertly, at chest and waist in coils of filthy rope, trapping their hands. Manfred was tied to the stone to Reiner's right. Franka was tied to his left.

'Franka,' Reiner whispered, but she only stared ahead.

When his slaves had raised the waystone on the central altar and withdrawn to the walls of the chamber, Valaris drew his dagger and approached Reiner. Reiner tensed, thinking this was the end, but instead of plunging the knife into his chest, instead Valaris gripped his wrist and cut out the sliver of crystal, flicking it carelessly to the ground. Instantly, the whispering warpstone buzz filled Reiner's mind again.

The dark elf moved around the circle, removing the crystals from each of them. When he had finished, he stripped to the waist, revealing a dead white, whipcord torso, and a blue crystal – mother to their slivers – on a chain around his neck. He began a chant, harsh and sibilant, while cutting himself at seven well-scarred points on his chest. He touched a finger to each of the wounds, then began to daub strange symbols across his chest and down his arms.

As he wrote the last symbol, Valaris's chant became a song, high and beautiful and terrifying. He moved around the waystone in a slow, sinuous dance, and with each move, it felt as if all Reiner's blood was being pulled to the front of his body. His pulse pounded behind his eyes and in his ears. His heart pounded as if he had run a ten mile race. His fingers and toes throbbed.

The song grew wilder, as did Valaris's movements, and the pressure increased inexorably. Dieter and Gert cried out. Darius vomited. Spatters of blood appeared on Valaris's chest and back, partially obscuring the symbols. Reiner thought at first that they came from the dark elf's seven wounds, but as he looked down at himself, he saw that the blood from his wounded wrist was dripping, not to the floor, but sideways toward Valaris. Drops flew at the elf from all the Blackhearts, as if he had become the centre of gravity.

That gravity was getting stronger. Reiner's whole body was being pulled forward. The ropes cut into his flesh cruelly. It felt as if his heart would burst from his chest, and it came to him with a nauseous shudder that this was exactly what was meant to happen – a tenfold coronary explosion that would bathe Valaris in heart-blood and give him the power to crack the waystone. Reiner suddenly knew he was going to die. Augustus would not arrive in time. This was the end.

He turned his head to Manfred. 'Valdenheim! For your pity, who was the spy?'

But Manfred had lost consciousness, his head bobbling at the end of his neck.

Reiner turned to Franka. 'Franka!'

She looked up. Her mouth drooled red and the whites of her eyes were flooded with blood.

'Franka!' he called. 'I beg you, beloved, before we die! Forgive me! Say you forgive me!

Franka's face twisted in disgust. 'Before we die?' she choked. 'I am already dead. You killed me when you killed Augustus.'

'No, listen!' He opened his mouth to tell her the truth, but with a jerk, the pressure increased violently. Blood streamed from his nose and mouth to splash on Valaris's torso. He couldn't breathe. Couldn't speak. The pain was incredible, but the agony of his mind was greater. He wanted to weep. It was so unfair. How could he die with Franka thinking him a cold-blooded murderer?

His head began to fill with screams and shrieks. At first he thought it was the others dying, or the mad whispers in his head calling to him, but then he heard the ring of steel above the shouting. Was Valaris striking the waystone with his knife?

He forced his eyes open. Valaris was looking over his shoulder. The pressure eased. The roaring in Reiner's brain faded.

As Valaris stopped altogether, Reiner and the others sagged in their ropes, sucking in great ragged breaths. Now Reiner could hear it – the clamour and clash of battle. The mutants were running into the huge cavern, waving their makeshift weapons.

Valaris stared after them, then turned burning eyes on Reiner, knife raised. 'You... you deceived me!' Reiner flinched and twisted in his ropes, but the dark elf paused as he drew back the knife, and raised his head like a wolf scenting blood on the wind. 'Teclis!' A leering smile spread across his face. 'You have brought me my prey, captain. For that, you shall die correctly.'

He crossed to his strange bedchamber and snatched up his sword and bow, then called to the few mutants that remained in the chamber. 'Come, slaves. There is blood to be spilled!' He strode into the big cavern at their head.

Hals laughed wearily. Blood ran in rivulets from his eyes, nose and mouth. 'So Augustus comes through at last.'

'And not before time,' said Pavel, spitting crimson.

'Au... Augustus?' said Franka, looking up, wide-eyed.

Reiner coughed blood. 'It was a trick. Dieter only pretended to kill him.' He swallowed. 'I couldn't tell you without telling Valaris. I'm sorry.'

Franka gaped at him, then looked away with a sob, trying to bury her face in her shoulder.

'You mean,' said Manfred groggily, 'you mean we are saved?'

'If Augustus brought enough troops,' said Reiner.

At that moment, Danziger came through the arch with his men. He smiled as he saw the Blackhearts' predicament. 'How convenient,' he said. 'We will be rid of your meddling once and for all.'

TWENTY
Spears To The Front

DANZIGER ENTERED AND motioned his men towards the waystone. 'Put it in the casket and hide it. We'll return for it when the others have gone.' He turned toward Reiner, grinning evilly. 'I reserve this pleasure for myself.'

'Lord Danziger,' said Manfred. 'What is the meaning of this?'

Danziger turned sharply, seeing Manfred for the first time. 'Count Manfred! We... we believed you dead.'

For a moment, Reiner thought Danziger would try to dissemble his earlier words, but then a cunning smile curled his lips and he looked back at the door.

'And why shouldn't you be?' He turned from Reiner to Danziger. 'What a coup this will be for Slaanesh! A count of the Empire.'

'You filthy cultist,' spat Manfred. 'You reveal yourself at last. You will burn for this.'

Danziger put his dagger to Manfred's chest and cut through the top button of his doublet as, behind him, his men waddled the waystone to the coffin. 'And who will know it was I? I will run out weeping that the elf has slain you, and–'

'Spears ready!' roared a voice from the door. 'Talabheimers, attack!'

Danziger and his men spun, groping for their swords. The waystone crashed down, smashing the coffin and crushing the legs of two of the men. Out of the shadows ran, not a company of spearmen, but a single man, his spear levelled. Augustus!

The pikeman ran past Danziger and the confused cultists, straight for Reiner. For a terrifying second, Reiner thought Augustus was coming to kill him, but then he saw the mad laughter in his eyes a realised he meant to cut him free.

'Not me, you fool!' Reiner shouted. 'Jergen!'

Augustus veered right and chopped at Jergen's ropes. The spear was an awkward tool for the job, but fortunately the ropes were rotten and Jergen's strength immense. He heaved mightily at the partially cut cords and they popped and hung slack.

'Behind you!' shouted Reiner.

Augustus whirled about, swinging his spear like a sword and fanning back Danziger's men, who had run up behind him.

Jergen drew his dagger and slashed at the ropes around his chest.

Augustus took a sword across the back of his breastplate and dodged behind Jergen's stone. The cultists followed him.

'You imbeciles!' shrieked Danziger. 'Don't kill the free one! Kill the trapped ones before they're freed!'

And putting action to his words, he started toward Manfred again as his men tried to get around Augustus to the bound Blackhearts. Haggard as Manfred was, there was some fight in him. He kicked Danziger in the stomach.

Danziger cursed, and dodged aside to cut Manfred's throat from behind, but he was too late. Jergen was free and leapt at him, sword drawn. Danziger shied away and Jergen slashed through Manfred's bonds with a single stroke, then spun and did the same for Reiner before running to defend Pavel and Hals from three cultists. Augustus jumped before Dieter and Gert, fending off two others.

Reiner staggered forwards and fumbled out his sword, his arms numb and weak. His mouth and nose were still filled with blood and it was hard to breathe. On his right, Manfred wrestled Danziger for possession of a dagger. On his left, two cultists were approaching Franka's stone.

'No!' Reiner shouted. He lunged at them, but as they turned, he found he had little strength to fight them. Valaris's ceremony had left him trembling and sore. He managed to parry the left one's thrust, but the other nearly took his ear off.

Elsewhere, however, the tide was turning. Jergen had freed Hals and felled another cultist, and Hals was freeing Pavel. Now in possession of Danziger's dagger, Manfred circled the cult leader, who jabbed at him with his sword.

Reiner wiped his nose and flicked the blood in the eyes of his left-hand opponent, then drove the one on the right back toward Franka. She raised both feet and kicked him in the spine. He stumbled forward, yelping, right into Reiner's out-thrust blade, and then Reiner faced only one.

As he saw Jergen cut down another of his men, Danziger finally had enough. He sprang back from Manfred shouting, 'Fall back! This is foolishness. We will win another way!'

His men danced out of their engagements and raced with him for the door. Hals and Pavel gave chase.

'No! Regroup!' Reiner shouted over the battle beyond the door.

Pavel and Hals stopped and turned back, then helped Reiner and Augustus cut down Franka and the others as Dieter slit the throats of the men crushed by the waystone.

'Thankee, lad,' said Reiner to Augustus. 'Wasn't sure you'd come back.'

Augustus's face darkened. 'I came for the stone.'

'Could ha' done that without cutting us down,' said Hals. 'We're obliged.'

Augustus snorted and glared at Reiner. 'Couldn't let the captain die. I owe 'im a kick in the eggs.'

'You have all done well,' said Manfred as they bound their wounds and gathered their weapons. 'If we survive this adventure, you shall all be richly rewarded.'

'Never mind that, jagger,' said Hals. 'Just free us like ye promised. That's all we ask.'

Manfred smiled. 'You need have no fear about that. Now, are we ready?'

Reiner frowned as the Blackhearts fell in behind Manfred. What had he meant, exactly? Gert also seemed to be wondering, for he was staring hard at Manfred's back.

Blinding flashes of blue and white light illuminated the door, and through it they could see the battle only in brief silhouetted flickers of seething bodies and glinting blades. The mutants surged around a square of men in a thick, undisciplined horde, more pouring into the cavern from the tunnels.

At the fore fought von Pfaltzen and the countess's guard, blood and black fluids staining their green and buff uniforms. On the far side of the battle Boellengen shouted orders at his handgunners as they emptied a volley into the churning mass. Scharnholt's men and Totkrieg's Hammers supported the handgunners, cutting down the mutants who survived their fusillades. A hundred Talabheimers under Hunter Lord Keinholtz defended the near side of the formation, spears in front, bowmen firing over their heads. Danziger, now returned to the main body of his men, encouraged them from the rear, shouting and waving his sword. Nearer the main entrance, Lord Schott's greatswords and Raichskell's Templars were doing butcher's work among the madmen. They were red to the elbows and mutants lay in waist high drifts around them.

But though the mutants died in droves, having only the crudest armour and weapons, they also fought with suicidal abandon, throwing themselves at the men without any regard for safety, and many a throat was torn out and gut ripped with their dying breath. They impaled themselves on swords and spears solely to drag them down so their brothers and sisters could rush over them and overwhelm their slayers.

In the centre of the conflict was the source of the blinding light. Like dark and light stars circling each other in a swirling celestial vortex, Teclis, in shining armour and Valaris, naked to the waist, attacked each other with spell and sword. Their blades glanced off each other's wards in showers of sparks, and their spells and counter spells met and burst against each other like colliding waves. Neither was making any headway against the other. It seemed the loser would be he who tired first, and Teclis, though no longer at death's door, looked feeble and exhausted.

Reiner was surprised to see Teclis without his guard, but then he saw them, lying at Valaris's feet, black bowshafts sprouting from their chests and throats.

'M'lord,' said Reiner to Manfred. 'The mutants only fight at the dark elf's bidding. Once he is killed, they will lose heart.'

Manfred nodded. 'Then you know your duty, captain. Kill him. I will join Boellengen and direct his men to cover your attack.'

'But... but m'lord,' said Reiner. 'He is warded by dark magics. We haven't a hope...'

'Then distract him and allow Teclis to prevail.'

Reiner saluted to keep himself from punching the count. 'Yes, m'lord. As you command, m'lord.' He turned to his companions. 'Blackhearts! Spears to the front! Forward!'

'Spiteful jagger,' grunted Hals. 'Wants to kill us before he has to let us go.'

Teclis and Valaris fought behind the mutants' line, the biggest, most monstrous mutants defending the dark elf from the spears of the Talabheim guard. Valaris's back was, however, entirely unprotected, and the Blackhearts charged for him across empty ground, Hals, Pavel and Augustus at the fore, Reiner, Dieter and Jergen on the flanks with Franka and Gert at the back, nocking arrows. Darius stumbled along behind, whimpering as usual.

Jergen, Reiner, Dieter and the spearmen stabbed and slashed at Valaris's naked back as one. Blinding sparks cracked, and their weapons bounced away as if they had swung them at granite. Reiner's hand stung like he had grabbed a thorn bush.

Valaris glanced back, and in that brief second Teclis pounced, battering him with a barrage of spells and sword strikes. The dark elf spun back, parrying and muttering madly to protect himself. At last he recovered and their stalemate resumed.

'Again!' called Reiner.

The Blackhearts struck another blow at Valaris, but this time his attention didn't leave Teclis. Instead, five of the massive mutants, each taller than Augustus and broader than Jergen, turned like automatons from the battle line and attacked, swinging huge clubs and claws and rusty greatswords.

Pavel and Hals squared off against a towering thing with a horse-skull head and bones that grew through its skin in a lattice of armoured ridges, ducking its bony, hammer-like fists. Jergen closed with a red, woolly-haired beast with four arms and four swords. Augustus plunged his spear into an obese doughy thing. It stuck like glue and the monster clawed the spearman as he tried to yank it out again. Dieter hacked at a walking flower.

It had long legs and useless, shrivelled arms that flopped at its sides, but a head like a sea anemone with long ropy tentacles and a snapping beak at the centre. Gert and Franka stood back and peppered the things with bolts and arrows.

Reiner hacked at a broad, leather-skinned thing with a mouth that split its pumpkin head from ear to ear. It laughed at his attacks. One of Franka's arrows dangled harmlessly from its thick hide. Reiner cursed as he ducked the thing's claws. If the Blackhearts could reach Valaris again it might be enough. They had proved that a single distraction could be his undoing. But would they get a chance? Teclis was weaker than before. He had put too much into his last attack, hoping to end the fight, and was flagging. Valaris sensed this and pressed him hard, eyes shining. His crystal glowed like a star on his chest. Beyond the Talabheimers' line, Reiner saw Manfred directing Boellengen and Schott toward them. They would undoubtedly be too late.

Reiner blinked. The crystal. The crystal!

'Reiner! Look out!' screamed Franka.

Reiner flinched back and leather-skin's claws slashed his shoulder, knocking him to the ground. It raised its arms, roaring, then stumbled back, yelping, an arrow jutting from the roof of its mouth. Pavel and Hals gored it simultaneously, and it fell, spraying blood. Horse-head lay dead behind them, bloody spear wounds between its external ribs.

'Thankee, lads,' said Reiner as he picked himself up. His shoulder was shredded and bloody, but he couldn't take his eyes from Valaris. The crystal must help the dark elf absorb Teclis's magical attacks. If Reiner could take it... But that was impossible. A sword couldn't penetrate the assassin's defences, how could a hand?

Then he noticed something curious. As Jergen pressed the four-armed thing, it stepped back into Valaris's sphere of protection and was not repulsed, though the wild swings of its four swords still bounced away.

Augustus, Hals and Dieter killed the sticky, blubbery thing. Hals and Augustus held it at arm's length with their spears and Dieter knifed it under the ear. They had to abandon their weapons though, for they could not withdraw them. They found shoddy replacements among the dead mutants and helped the others. Gert shot the flower thing through the heart and it died lashing its tentacles in violent spasms. Jergen cut four-arms' legs out from under it, and pinned it to the ground as it fell on its face.

'All on Valaris!' said Reiner. 'And don't mind that you can't hit him.'

The Blackhearts attacked the dark elf's back and the flanks, though all their strikes rang on shimmering air long before they touched him.

'Back away!' called Teclis, angrily, before returning to his mumbling.

'No! Keep at it!' said Reiner, and stepped behind the dark elf, praying the others held his attention. He reached forward. It felt like he pushed his hand into a hot wind. The air glistened around his fingers. He moved slower and the wind lessened, but as he reached further, his hand began to prickle, and then to sizzle with pain. It felt as if he was reaching into boiling water. He expected to see his flesh blistering, but it looked no different.

The pain made him try to push harder, and he lost three inches as the barrier shoved his hand back. He forced himself to creep ahead, though he trembled with agony and sweat poured into his eyes. Another inch. He had to shift as Valaris and Teclis circled and the Blackhearts kept up their futile attacks. Another inch. He could almost touch the dark elf's back. His arm was on fire to his shoulder. The pain made him dizzy. His knees shook. Another inch. His fingers rose toward the silver chain. Now his face was within the sphere. It felt as if the skin was peeling from his cheeks. His fingers closed on the silver chain. He shoved forward and was thrust back violently by the barrier. The chain snapped and came with him. He landed in a heap three yards away, spasming and dizzy.

'No!' screamed Valaris, spinning around. 'What have you…?'

Teclis's eyes flashed. He thrust his palms forward. The air around Valaris warped and his chest collapsed, his ribs snapping and jutting through his white skin. Air hissed from his slack mouth. He flopped to the ground, dead and staring, blood pooling around him.

Teclis fell to the ground too, utterly spent, and the Blackhearts made a protective ring around him. There was no need. With

Valaris's death, the mutants' fury dissipated, and they fled from the assembled companies.

Teclis looked up at Reiner, breathing hoarsely. 'My thanks.' He took a vial from his pouch and drank it down. A shudder passed through him and he closed his eyes, then recovered somewhat. 'Now, where is the stone?'

Across the room, amid the weary soldiers, Manfred raised a bloody sword. 'Well done, men of Talabheim! Well done, Reiklanders!' he cried. 'But there is further work to be done.' He turned toward Danziger. 'We have traitors in our–'

'Followers of Tzeentch!' cried Scharnholt, interrupting. 'Kill the unbelievers! The stone will be ours!' He turned to von Pfaltzen, who stood beside him, and cut his throat from ear to ear.

TWENTY-ONE
The Gate Is Open

VON PFALTZEN TURNED uncomprehending eyes on Scharnholt, then crumpled, crimson jetting from his neck. At this signal, all of Scharnholt's followers, and some men of the other companies, turned on those next to them. Cries of shock and pain came from all over the chamber. Then, while the men of the companies tried desperately to defend themselves from those they had thought their fellows, Danziger, too, raised his voice.

'Followers of Slaanesh! Do thou likewise!' he cried. 'Take the stone and Talabheim falls! All glory to our delicious master!'

His men fell on those already fighting the Tzeentchists. As Reiner and the Blackhearts and Teclis watched, stunned, a quarter of the combined companies were murdered before they recovered enough to group together and defend themselves. Many cultists died as well, but as they fell, bloodthirsty cries echoed through the chamber and from the main tunnel burst a mob of masked figures waving swords and axes and spears. Half wore robes of blue and gold, while the others wore purple and red.

Teclis sighed as he stood. 'If it were not a matter of the stability of the world, I would let this city die.'

The companies fell back from the flood of cultists and clustered to the right of the main entrance. Scharnholt and Danziger and their men ran to join their masked comrades.

'Help me to Valdenheim,' said Teclis.

'Yes, lord.'

Reiner and the others carried him through the chaos to where Manfred stood with Boellengen, Schott, Raichskell and Hunter Lord Keinholtz, conferring with Magus Nichtladen. Father Totkrieg was dead. Their troops were close to panic. Their companions had turned on them. The battle they had thought won must now be fought all over again, against more dangerous enemies.

And it only got worse. As the cultists charged the companies, behind their lines, sorcerers commenced chanting. The air around them began to warp and shimmer.

'Magus!' called Manfred to Nichtladen. 'Protect us!'

The magus called orders to his few remaining initiates, and they began intoning warding spells. They appeared to be having difficulty. They stuttered their invocations. Their hands jerked and twitched. All at once one screamed. His eyes exploded, and he dropped, blood pouring from his mouth. Another began tearing the flesh from his face with his fingers. The air was tingling. Flames flickered around the feet of Boellengen's handgunners. They cried out in fear and fell back. The cultists advanced.

Teclis shook as he summoned his strength. 'The warpstone amplifies the cultists' powers,' he said, then spoke a single word and swept his hands apart.

At once the flames winked out around the handgunners' feet. The remaining magi recovered themselves.

Teclis was near to collapse. 'Your men and magi must slay the sorcerers,' he said wearily. 'I have only enough strength to keep them at bay.' He touched his chest where Valaris's arrow had pierced it. 'Naggaroth may have slain me after all.'

'Yes, Lord Teclis,' said Manfred. But even as he turned to order the men, columns of smoke began to rise within the circles of the Slaanesh and Tzeentch sorcerers.

'Quickly,' croaked Teclis. 'Attack them! Disrupt their ceremony!'

The troops pressed forward and the magi wove their spells, but they were too late. Things were moving within the columns of smoke, and the chamber filled with strange choking odours.

From the Tzeentch side came a smell like sour milk, and from the Slaanesh side, an intoxicating perfume. Then things came out of the smoke. Reiner's eyes were repelled by the one and drawn by the other.

The Tzeentchists' conjuration literally hurt to look at. It was a shapeless, constantly changing pink mass. Horns and limbs and slavering mouths pushed out of its skin and sank away again like fish-heads bubbling to the top of a stew. It sweated pus, and moved by extruding a new leg before it and retracting an old one. Reiner wanted to run from it, to tear his eyes out.

The Slaaneshis' summoning, on the other hand, was so alluring Reiner found himself uncomfortably aroused – a lavender-skinned beauty with lush red lips and graceful horns. Her perfect, naked breasts swayed hypnotically with each sultry step and her almond eyes seemed to look at no one but Reiner. He took a step toward her, unlacing his doublet.

'He's beautiful,' said Franka. She too was stepping forward, her eyes glazed with lust.

'He?' said Reiner, dully. For the briefest second, Reiner saw something else where the purple wanton stood – still purple, but hard and chitinous. What he had thought were red lips was a mouth like a remora's. The almond eyes were black holes. Then the vision of beauty reasserted itself, but he could fight it now.

The companies were reacting as he had, backing away from the Tzeentch nightmare, and stepping toward the Slaaneshi temptress. The cultists cut down both the terrified and the mesmerised in droves.

Teclis groaned, then redoubled his chanting. The influence of the daemons lessened at once. Recovering, Manfred stepped forward, raising his sword.

'Hold fast, my Reiklanders! Hold fast, men of Talabheim!' he shouted. 'Steel your minds! Have we not faced these creatures before, and prevailed? Did we not push them and their filthy kind back to the Chaos Wastes? Fear not! The mighty Teclis will protect us! Kill the men and the horrors will fly! Now fight!'

The men fought.

On the left, Keinholtz and the Talabheimers charged into the Slaaneshi with renewed vigour, roaring, 'For von Pfaltzen and the countess!' While on the right Schott and Boellengen and Raichskell led their men against the Tzeentchists crying, 'Karl Franz! Karl Franz!' Even Reiner, who knew that Manfred had less honour than a common pimp, was stirred by his words. Whatever else he is, he thought, the old scoundrel is a leader.

But inspired as the men were, they were pitifully few, and they had just fought a pitched battle. The cultists were fresh. And the daemons, though their mental influence was diminished by Teclis's wards, slew all who stood before them with their claws and teeth and tentacles.

'I cannot protect them for long,' wheezed Teclis. 'If you cannot slay the sorcerers, we are finished.'

Manfred turned to Reiner. 'Hetsau! Add your men to the line. Cut through to the circles!'

'No, m'lord,' said Reiner. 'I've a better idea. This way, lads.'

As Manfred squawked, Reiner led the Blackhearts left to the cluster of shacks that ran around the chamber's wall. He gripped Darius's elbow.

'Listen, scholar,' he said as they ran. 'This is your moment. This is where you prove your worth.'

Darius gulped. 'What... what do you want me to do?'

The Blackhearts crept through the shacks, circling the Slaaneshi flank.

'Cast a spell at the fellows who called up the thing with the mouths,' said Reiner. 'It matters not what, so long as they know they are being attacked. Something with lots of flashes and smoke.'

'I am not a witch, curse you!' whined Darius. 'I've told you a thousand times.'

'And a thousand times I haven't believed you,' said Reiner.

They were behind both the Slaanesh and Tzeentch armies now, looking out from the hovels. The cultists had tightened their ring, and the companies' numbers were shrinking fast. The purple beauty raised a man on the tip of her sabre-like claw and flung him into Schott's greatswords. Two fell, and the cultists cut them to pieces before they could rise. The pink horror was gulping down three bodies with three different mouths.

'But it is true,' said Darius. 'I am a scholar. I know only theory. Not practice.'

Reiner shook him. 'Liar! Manfred chose you for a reason. He could have found a better surgeon anywhere. You're just too much a coward to do what he bade you. Is that it?'

'I... No, I cannot! I dare not!'

'So you do know something!' Reiner cried, triumphant. 'I knew it! Use it! Hurry!'

'No! I can't!'

'Damn you! Speak!' Reiner hissed. 'What is it? What can you do?'

'Nothing! It's useless. A way to make plants grow faster. I told him, but he wouldn't listen...'

'And you have plants in your pouch, I shouldn't wonder, though I told you to throw them away,' said Reiner. 'Make them grow.'

'I daren't!'

'Fool! Are you still afraid of our scorn? We need your skill!'

'It isn't that!' said Darius miserably. 'I am afraid of it! I... I nearly lost myself the last time. That is how I was caught. I was found by my landlady unconscious amongst my circles and braziers, and–'

'So you are afraid of death?' asked Reiner.

Darius wailed. 'Of course I–'

'Good.' Reiner put dagger to his throat. 'For I will kill you if you do not obey this order. And this is no game as with Augustus. You can risk death and save a city, or you can die now. Which will it be?'

Darius cringed from the blade. 'I– I will do it.' There were tears in his eyes. 'I wish Manfred had never found me.'

'Then you would have swung weeks ago,' said Hals. 'And saved us all a lot of whining.'

'Hush, pikeman,' said Reiner. 'Now listen. This is what we will do.'

MOMENTS LATER, REINER and Darius crept on their bellies as close to the Slaaneshi rear as they dared. The Tzeentchists were to their left. Reiner looked beyond them and saw Franka and Gert getting into position in the shadows. Reiner prayed his gambit wasn't too late. It seemed the Reikland and Talabheim lines must break any second.

'Ready?' he whispered.

Darius shrugged. His face was blank.

'Then go!'

Darius sat up and took a handful of plant cuttings from his pouch. He muttered over them, moving his hands in complicated patterns. At first nothing happened, but then Reiner heard a tiny pop, and watched amazed as the cuttings began lengthening and sprouting tendrils. Darius's words grew more guttural and the plants blackened and twisted. He swayed as if dizzy. The words came hard and harsh.

'Now?' asked Reiner.

Darius nodded and staggered up, hurling the rapidly growing plants at the Tzeentchists with all his might.

'Come, plants!' cried Reiner at the top of his lungs. 'Do the bidding of thy master Slaanesh. Strike down these treacherous Tzeentchist heretics!'

Of course, thought Reiner, as he pulled Darius down and hid, the whole plan would collapse if the cuttings grew into daffodils and cabbages. He needn't have worried. The shoots had been cut from the mad plants of the Tallows, and under the influence of Darius's spell and the presence of so much warpstone, they exploded in rocketing spurts of mutated growth. Creepers undulated across the floor like serpents toward the Tzeentchists, sprouting questing tendrils and dagger thorns. Roots thrust into the hard ground and shot up like trees, branches bursting from their trunks and bearing unwholesome fruit in the wink of an eye.

Panting flowers drooled sap as they sniffed toward the cultists. Vines wrapped around ankles. Men were crushed in verdant embraces and impaled by foot-long thorns. Men who fell were instantly swarmed by the breathing flowers, which sucked at them like leeches.

The Tzeentchists chopped at the vines and looked for the culprits. Those who had heard Reiner's invocation pointed angry fingers at the Slaaneshi. Then an arrow shot from behind the Tzeentchists and buried itself in a Slaaneshi's neck.

'Slay the Slaaneshi scum!' bellowed a voice that sounded suspiciously like Gert's. 'See how they turn on us? Betrayers!'

Another Slaaneshi fell, clutching an arrow in his arm. His companions turned, looking toward the Tzeentchists, who were running toward them shaking their weapons. Cultists fell upon one another and the brawl began to spread. Reiner watched, gratified, as they turned from fighting the companies to fight their rivals. A Tzeentchist with an axe charged the circle of Slaaneshi sorcerers. He could not pierce their wards, but the sorcerers looked around at the confusion. The Tzeentchist sorcerers were turning as well, and the thing they had summoned began to pale. A rope of fire shot from the Slaaneshi to the Tzeentchists, burning all it touched. The Tzeentchists retaliated with a yellow cloud that caused men to choke and fall. The summoning circles broke in confusion, and with a thunderclap of displaced air, the pink horror and the purple beauty winked out of existence.

The Talabheimers and the Reiklanders cheered and renewed their attacks on the squabbling cultists.

'Well done, scholar!' cried Reiner. 'We've done it. Let's away.'

Darius lay whimpering on the ground, staring at his hands as if he'd never seen them before. Blood seeped from his nose and his tear ducts.

'Lad?'

Darius didn't respond. Reiner caught him under the arm. The scholar came up like a sleepwalker. Reiner led him back toward the shacks, joining Gert and Franka, who were creeping back as well.

'Good work!' he said.

'Hetsau!' cried a voice behind them. 'I might have known!'

Reiner turned. Danziger glared at him from behind a pile of rubbish where he and his men had taken refuge. He called toward the battle. 'Stop! Stop fighting! Manfred's dogs have duped us!'

No one heard. There was too much noise, and the cultists were fighting the plants and each other too fiercely.

Danziger cursed. 'Well, at least I shall have my revenge! At them!' He charged at Reiner, his men behind him.

Reiner turned to run with Franka and Gert, but Darius was on his knees, looking at his hands again.

'Damn you, lad! Up!' He grabbed the scholar's arm.

Darius shoved him, screeching.

Reiner fell, surprised, his sword skittering away. Danziger and his men were nearly on top of him.

'Reiner!' shouted Franka.

She turned back to cover him. Gert followed, cursing. Reiner scrabbled for his sword and grabbed the blade, cutting his palm. The rest of the Blackhearts were sprinting toward him from the shacks, but they were much too far away.

Franka lunged for Danziger, but one of his men swung at her head and she dived to the ground. Reiner fumbled for the right end of his sword. Danziger lunged at him. He couldn't twist away in time.

'Captain!' shouted Gert.

Gert jumped before Reiner, slashing at Danziger with his hatchet. The lord ducked and stabbed through Gert's groin. Another cultist gored him in the side. Gert collapsed against Reiner, clutching himself. Reiner thrust over the big man's shoulder and ran Danziger through the throat. The lord squealed and jerked his head, trying to escape the blade, and it tore out the side of his neck. He toppled, fountaining blood.

Gert fell as Franka sprang up, and she and Reiner stood over him, back to back in the centre of Danziger's six remaining men. Swords thrust at them from all directions. Reiner parried two and turned so another took him in his wounded shoulder instead of the heart. Franka dodged one blade, beat aside another, and raked a man's chest with a lunge, but took his riposte in the forearm.

But then the cultists were turning at the Blackhearts' thundering boot steps and they went down like straw before Jergen's sword and the spears of Pavel, Hals and Augustus.

Reiner glanced to the battle to be sure no one else was coming for them, then squatted beside Gert. The crossbowman's breeks were crimson to his boots, and stuck wetly to his legs. 'All right, lad?' he asked, though he knew the answer.

'It's bad, I think,' said Gert. His face was paper-white. 'Captain, I–'

'Not here,' said Reiner. 'Too open. Jergen. Augustus. Get him to the shacks.'

Augustus and Jergen hauled Gert to his feet and put their shoulders under his arms. The big crossbowman looked like the stuffing had been pulled out of him. His face sagged. He moaned with each step.

Reiner touched Darius on the shoulder. He was still staring at his hands. 'Scholar.' Darius didn't look up, but allowed himself to be led away.

They had just reached the shacks when Scharnholt screamed behind them.

'Stop them!'

Reiner turned, cursing, but amazingly, Scharnholt wasn't pointing at them, but at a cluster of grey-robed figures who were creeping around the edge of the chamber toward the bridge that crossed the chasm. Two in front led the way. The others carried the waystone casket.

'Oh, now who are these?' Reiner groaned.

The thieves stepped onto the bridge. Franka fired an arrow after them. It hit the shorter of the two leaders in the upper arm. The figure stumbled and cried out in a voice Reiner thought he recognised. But the procession didn't slow.

Scharnholt's voice was rising, crying strange words. He thrust his hands forward and a column of fire shot from them and exploded on the bridge. The thieves were enveloped in a blossoming ball of fire.

As it dissipated Reiner and the others saw the casket bearers, mangled and on fire, tumbling into the chasm as their leaders ran into a dark tunnel on the far side, their cloaks smoking. The casket was aflame too, and teetered on the edge of the bridge.

The entire cavern gasped in horror. Tzeentchists, Slaaneshi and Empire men all rushed forward, but before any had taken five steps, the flaming casket tipped up like a sinking ship and slid off the bridge. There was utter silence among the combatants, as the object of the battle disappeared into the depths.

'Sigmar bugger a troll,' said Hals softly.

The tableau broke as a white light shot from the Empire ranks and Scharnholt screamed. He was held in a flickering penumbra of light, his back arched in agony. His skeleton glowed through his skin like phosphorus, brighter and brighter, and then with a blinding flash and thunderclap, he was gone. The Empire troops roared in triumph and fell upon the disheartened cultists.

Augustus and Jergen laid Gert down among the shacks. He was barely conscious. His boots spilled blood. The others gathered around him.

'Scholar!' barked Reiner. 'Darius! Patch him up!'

'I know no spells,' Darius mumbled.

'I'm not asking for spells,' said Reiner. 'Doctor him, curse you!'

'I know no spells,' Darius repeated.

'Forget it, captain,' croaked Gert. 'Too late. Listen...'

'None of that,' said Reiner, kneeling and unbuckling his sword belt. 'We must tie off that leg. Help me.'

The others knelt as well, but Gert waved a feeble hand. 'No! Listen, damn you, Hetsau!' His eyes flashed. 'Let me speak!'

Reiner turned, surprised at the use of his proper name from a common soldier.

Gert glared up at him, grey and sweating. 'You were right. Manfred had a... spy.' He tapped his chest. 'He didn't trust you. 'Spected you would try some... trickery.'

Reiner's heart was pounding, shaken by a score of simultaneous emotions. The Blackhearts exchanged glances.

'Thought I was minding a villain.' Gert shook his head weakly. 'Yer less a villain than he, though we was comrades once.' He tapped his chest again. 'Captain Steingesser. Time was I would'a died for him, but he's changed. Now I...' He chuckled and looked up at Reiner. 'Well, seems I died for you, eh?'

Reiner's throat constricted. 'Gert, if you'd just shut up, you might not...'

'How did you kill Halsteig?' asked Hals, bluntly. 'Yer no sorcerer. You never said no spell.'

'Hush,' said Augustus. 'Let the man die in peace.'

'Ye weren't there,' said Pavel. 'Ye didn't see. We might have all died like that.'

Gert grimaced. His gums were white. 'Phylacteries,' he said. 'Made by Manfred's magus. Carry 'em in my pouch. Throw one in a fire and...' He made to snap his fingers but could barely raise his hand.

Reiner's blood chilled at the thought of the risks Gert had taken while wearing that pouch. But he said nothing, only clasped his hand. 'Thank you, captain. Sigmar welcome you. You've... eased our minds.'

When he let go, Gert's hand sank to his side. The crossbowman, or captain, or spy, or whatever he had been, was dead. Reiner wasn't sure when he had gone.

Hals and Pavel made the sign of the hammer. Augustus muttered a prayer to Taal. Franka made Myrmidia's spear. Reiner closed Gert's eyes and took his pouch. He opened it. At the bottom he found a rolled length of leather, sewn with nine little pockets. Inside each was a glass vial labelled in florid script. Reiner pulled out the one with his name as the others watched. Inside a lock of hair floated in a red liquid. Around the hair was a strip of parchment inscribed with arcane symbols. He shivered and slipped the vial back into its sheath, then put the roll in his pouch.

'Be careful with that, captain,' said Pavel.

'Indeed,' said Reiner. He looked beyond the shacks. The battle was over. The companies were chasing down the last cultists and cutting the throats of their wounded. 'Right, we'll take the old fellow back to Manfred. But we don't let on we know what's what, aye?'

The others nodded in agreement, but as Hals and Pavel began making a litter, Darius tugged on Reiner's sleeve.

'Captain,' he said. 'Captain.' He spoke with a feverish intensity.

'Have you returned to us, scholar?' asked Reiner.

'The gate lets in as well as out,' Darius said.

'Eh?'

'I cannot close it. I cannot close the gate. The wind.' His voice rose. 'It howls in me. It whispers through my skull. Whispers. Captain, the whispers. The whispers, captain.' There were tears in his staring eyes. The others watched him, uncomfortable.

'I'm here, lad.'

Darius crushed Reiner's wrist. 'Kill me, captain. I beg you. Kill me before I listen.'

'Come, lad,' said Reiner, his heart sinking. 'Is it that bad?' He didn't want to believe Darius had gone mad – didn't want to believe it was his fault.

'Captain, please,' said Darius. He held out his hands in supplication.

Reiner stepped back involuntarily. In the centre of each of Darius's palms was a mouth like a vertical slit, filled with sharp little fish teeth. It was 'that bad.' Reiner moaned and cursed himself for ever thinking he could be a leader of men. He'd forced the boy. Forced him.

'Please, captain,' said all three mouths. 'The gate is open. I cannot close it. I cannot.'

'Captain,' said Jergen, drawing his long sword. 'Let me.'

Reiner shook his head, though he wanted more than anything to pass the responsibility. 'No. I caused this.' He drew his sword. 'Bow your head, scholar. I'll stop the wind.'

The mouths in Darius's hands were jabbering at him, telling him to run, to attack, to drink Reiner's blood, but with a great effort, Darius clenched his fists and lowered his head, exposing his neck.

Reiner raised his sword over his head with both hands, praying he would make a clean job of it. Franka turned her head. Reiner chopped down, felt the jar as his sword hit Darius's spine, and then he was through, and Darius's body fell forward onto his head.

'Well struck,' said Jergen.

Reiner turned away, hiding his face. 'Right. Leave him. The priests won't bury him with those hands. Let's go.'

As Hals, Pavel, Jergen and Augustus walked Gert's body back to the companies, Hals tried to catch Reiner's eye.

'Ye did what y'had to, captain.'

'Did I?' asked Reiner angrily. 'Was there a need for the spell? We might have accomplished the same thing with arrows and shouting.'

'And we might have not,' said Hals.

Reiner stepped ahead. He didn't want to speak of it.

There were less than fifty Talabheimers and Reiklanders left. In their centre Manfred, Boellengen, and Schott and Keinholtz stood around Teclis, who leaned against the cave wall as if he could not have stood without it. They were the only commanders left.

'We could lower men into the chasm,' Keinholtz was saying as the Blackhearts approached. 'Then fix ropes to the waystone and raise it.'

'If it isn't shattered,' said Boellengen.

Teclis raised his head. 'The waystone would not shatter.'

'But we know nothing of the chasm's depth, or what might be down there,' said Schott. 'It might be a river, or a lake of fire.'

'Then we will have to mount another expedition,' said Manfred with a weary sigh.

'We must return to the surface before any new venture,' said Teclis. 'I must restore myself.'

Manfred groaned. 'Days if not weeks.' He saw the Blackhearts setting Gert's body down and turned to them. 'Is... is he dead?'

'Aye,' said Reiner casually. 'As is your witch.' He smiled to himself as he saw Manfred looking for Gert's pouch.

'Did he have...' Manfred started, then thought better of it. 'Well, I'm sorry to hear it.'

'As am I,' said Reiner. 'He stopped a blade meant for me.'

'Did he?' Manfred looked uncomfortable. 'Well–'

'Quiet!' said Teclis. He looked around sharply. 'Listen.'

Manfred, Reiner and the others listened. At first Reiner heard nothing. Then came a vibration in the ground and a sound like far off rain. It grew steadily closer until Reiner recognised it as the rumble of an army on the march.

Manfred and Schott and Boellengen shouted to their troops to form up. The Blackhearts went on guard with the rest, looking from tunnel to tunnel, waiting to see from which this fresh menace would come.

It came from all of them – three endless columns of ratmen in green-grey jerkins armed with spears, swords, and long guns, spilling out in a silent flood that filled the enormous cavern from wall to wall. There were thousands of them. The fifty men huddled together, all facing out. The ratmen surrounded them entirely, staring at them with glossy black eyes.

TWENTY-TWO
The Hero Of The Hour

'WELL, LADS,' SAID Hals. 'Nice to know ye.'

'See ye in Sigmar's hall,' said Pavel.

'Lord Teclis?' said Manfred nervously.

'I am at the end of my strength, count,' said Teclis. 'I can kill many, but not all.'

Manfred firmed his jaw. 'Then we will sell our lives as dearly as we may.'

The other commanders nodded and their men dressed their lines, but still the ratmen stood motionless.

'Why don't they attack?' asked Franka.

A disturbance began at the rear of the vermin army, and out of the tunnel beyond the chasm came a cluster of ratmen. They crossed the bridge and pushed slowly toward the front. There were at least twenty of them, led by a tall, snow-white ratman who carried a long, verdigrised staff. The front line parted and the knot of ratmen stepped forward. The companies gasped. The vermin carried the waystone.

The white-furred ratman pointed imperiously at Teclis. 'You, sharp-ear,' he said with a voice like a knife on a plate. 'Fix elf-thing. Make good. Seer Hissith say!'

Manfred, Schott and Boellengen exchanged baffled glances.

Teclis frowned at the rat-mage. 'You wish me to reset the waystone?'

'I command!'

'Why?'

'No why!' spat Hissith. 'Do!'

'Why?' asked Teclis, calmly.

The rat-mage trembled with rage, and Reiner expected him to order his troops to attack, but at last he spoke. 'We Greenfang clan! Warpstone only for us! Then elf-thing break. Other clan smell warpstone. Come stealing. Crippletail Clan. Deadeater clan. We fight.' He pointed to Teclis. 'You fix elf-stone. They smell no more. Warpstone only for us again!'

Reiner exhaled, relieved and amazed. They weren't going to die. As insane as it sounded, the ratmen needed them.

'Lord Teclis,' said Schott, aghast. 'You cannot do this. The Empire does not treat with evil! We must fight them!' He looked to Manfred. 'Is it not what the Emperor would wish, count?'

'Er...' said Manfred. He looked like he wished to smash Schott in the face.

'Fortunately,' said Teclis. 'Your emperor does not rule me.' He nodded to the rat-mage. 'I will do this.'

'M'lord!' cried Schott, outraged.

'Silence, Schott!' hissed Manfred. 'Would you lose Talabheim and the stone for a point of honour?'

The rat-slaves set down the waystone and backed away as the rat-mage pointed at Teclis. 'You trick, you die! We come! Kill all! Hissith say it so!'

'He threatens us, lord count!' said Schott, eyes blazing.

'Let him,' said Manfred, and bowed, smiling, as the rat-mage returned to his troops.

Without a word, the horde of vermin withdrew into the tunnels again like an ebbing brown tide. The men looked around at each other as if they couldn't believe they were still alive.

'Don't stand there!' snapped Manfred at Reiner. 'Pick it up and let's be off before we lose it again!'

The Blackhearts picked up the waystone and, surrounded by the shattered remnants of the Talabheimers and Reiklanders, walked it wearily back to the surface.

* * *

FOUR DAYS LATER, deep under Talabheim, Teclis reset the waystone, binding it with powerful wards, then burying its crypt below thousands of tonnes of rock. He then cast a spell of forgetting upon all the labourers who had built the new vault so that they could tell none where it was, and a similar spell upon the vault itself, which would make any who came looking for it forget what they had come for.

Instantly upon the setting of the stone, the mad plants of the Tallows began to wilt, the clouds and strange aurora over the city dissipated, and the madness that had plagued Talabheim faded. There was still much to be put right – neighbourhoods to be rebuilt, mutants to be hunted down, cultists to be hung, but no new cases of mutation were reported and Taalagad was reopened to trade.

To celebrate, the countess threw a grand ball, to which Manfred and the Reikland legation were invited. Reiner did not expect to be invited. He thought Manfred would shove him into the shadows and take all the glory for himself, but to his surprise the count ordered him to attend, while Lord Schott was sent back to Altdorf early to inform the Emperor of their success.

'Damn stubborn bull wouldn't play the game,' Manfred said as they rode to the Grand Manor. 'In order to save the countess embarrassment and keep relations with Talabheim smooth, we must pretend that Scharnholt and Danziger died heroes' deaths fighting the mutants. There can be no suggestion that her court was plagued with cultists. Schott refused to cooperate in the deception, so I've sent him home.' Manfred glared at Reiner. 'Instead, you will be the hero of the hour – the noble secretary who led Scharnholt, Danziger, and von Pfaltzen to the lair of the evil elf. And if you don't play it just as I've said, and praise Scharnholt and Danziger to the heavens, I'll have your head, you understand?'

'Your lordship always makes himself perfectly clear,' said Reiner, bowing.

AFTER TELLING HIS story – or rather, Manfred's story – a dozen times, Reiner saw, across the countess's grand ballroom, Lord Rodick and Lady Magda, talking and laughing with the countess herself. Reiner broke off in the middle of a humourous anecdote. The cursed woman landed on her feet like a cat. How were the traitors back in the countess's good graces? Lack of evidence? Or did the countess not want one of her own family to be accused of treason?

Reiner had no such qualms. He excused himself from his audience and crossed to Manfred, who was talking to Talabheim's high priest of Taal.

'M'lord,' he whispered in his ear. 'If I might speak with you?'

Manfred finished his conversation then turned to Reiner. 'Yes? Why aren't you telling your tale?'

'M'lord, if you are still interested in destroying your brother's corrupter, I believe I have a way. Only invite me to tell our adventure before Magda, Rodick and the countess.'

Manfred nodded. 'Come.'

Magda and Rodick attempted to excuse themselves when Manfred approached the countess, but Manfred begged them to stay and hear the tale of his rescue and the waystone's retrieval. 'Reiner was the discoverer of the plot, and tells it so much better than I.'

And so they listened, fidgeting, while Reiner told how he had seen mutants dressed as priests of Morr sneaking from the Grand Manor and warned Danziger, Scharnholt and von Pfaltzen of the theft, then led them to the dark elf's lair. When he began to tell of the hooded thieves who had tried to steal the waystone in the middle of the battle he noticed that Magda's upper lip was sweating.

'My man Franz is a dead shot,' Reiner said. 'And when Scharnholt cried that thieves were taking the stone, Franz loosed an arrow after them. Unfortunately, the range was long and his shot only hit one of the leaders – a little fellow – in the arm, and he and the other escaped before the dark elf blasted the others off the bridge.' Reiner frowned, disappointed. 'I am mortally sorry those men got away. It would be a great service to Talabheim to learn what traitors had designs on that stone. Unfortunately, it is beyond practicality to ask every man in Talabheim if he had been shot in the arm just "here".'

As he said 'here,' he squeezed Magda's arm hard, just above the elbow. Magda shrieked. Her knees buckled.

Reiner gasped, as if shocked. 'Lady, I am terribly sorry! Are you wounded there? What an unfortunate coincidence!'

'Take your hands from her, you oaf!' cried Rodick angrily. 'You've crushed her arm.'

'M'lord, I swear I only touched her!' Reiner said. 'I meant no harm.'

'An unfortunate coincidence indeed,' said the countess, looking levelly at Magda. 'Come with me, lady. I will have my royal physician look at you.'

'There is no need,' said Magda, smiling though she was white as a sheet. 'He only surprised me. I am fine.'

'I insist,' said the countess, and there was no mistaking the threat in her voice. She turned and signalled her guards, who stood nearby. 'This way. Cousin Rodick, won't you join us?'

Magda shot a look of pure venom at Reiner as she was lead away.

Reiner bowed deeply. 'Goodbye, lady. The pleasure was all mine.'

AND SO, ON the morning that the Reikland legation left for Altdorf, Reiner and the other Blackhearts watched with satisfaction as Lady Magda Bandauer was hung from the gallows before the Grand Courthouse of Edicts. Lord Rodick, being cousin to the countess, had been allowed to take poison. Magda had then been charged with his murder – all neat and tidy with no awkward questions about waystones and statues of Shallya asked.

Magda carried herself with great poise on the gallows, and might have gone to her death with all dignity intact had she not, when the executioner offered her a chance to speak, begun to denounce the countess and the Talabheim parliament for covering up Scharnholt and Danziger's corruption and the threat of the ratmen who lived under the city.

Reiner chuckled as she was gagged and hooded and the noose snugged around her neck. Spiteful to the end, the bitch. He'd have done the same, of course.

'And that's for Captain Veirt,' said Pavel, as Magda dropped and jerked at the end of the rope.

'And poor Oskar,' said Franka.

'And Ulf,' said Reiner.

'Too bad she's that sack over her head,' said Hals. 'I want to see her face now she's tasted death herself.'

'And yet,' said Reiner. 'We have her to thank for our lives. Without her scheming we would have all been hung long ago in the Smallhof garrison.'

'This is a life?' asked Pavel.

The others, who hadn't known the men Magda had caused to die, watched silently as she twitched and fought under the gibbet.

Manfred seemed distracted throughout the proceedings. Reiner smiled, for he knew why. The night before, after Reiner had helped pack Teclis's belongings – for with his guard dead the elf had no servants – he had done the same for Manfred. The count made Reiner go through every case and box three times looking for a small leather-bound journal. When it couldn't be found, he had accused Reiner of stealing it, and searched his belongings as thoroughly as he had searched his own, but when he found nothing he had finally dismissed Reiner, furious. Reiner had heard him rummaging all night long.

TWENTY-THREE
Unfinished Business

THEY REACHED ALTDORF seven days later, and the Blackhearts were once again installed in Manfred's townhouse while the count closeted himself with the Emperor and his cabinet, explaining what had occurred in Talabheim.

The Blackhearts fidgeted and fumed, for nothing had been said of their release, and Manfred was never there to question. But at last, on the evening of the third day, Reiner was told the count would see him in the library.

Manfred sat in a high-backed chair by the fire when Reiner entered, flipping through official papers. Reiner stood at attention until, after a few moments, Manfred looked up, pretending he hadn't noticed him before.

'Ah, Hetsau,' he said. 'Sit. You wished to see me?'

Reiner cursed inwardly, for he knew then and there that Manfred did not intend to honour his promise. Still, he must ask. 'Yes, m'lord. Thank you.' He sat. 'I have come on behalf of the others, m'lord, about your promise. That if we freed you from the dark elf, you would free us.'

'Ah yes,' said Manfred. 'In the press of events I had nearly forgotten.'

'We have not, m'lord,' said Reiner.

Manfred paused for a long moment, then sighed. 'I'm afraid your success has defeated you, Hetsau.' He looked up at Reiner with a curious expression. 'What you did in Talabheim was impossible. The odds you overcame are not to be calculated. And because of this I... I find I cannot let you go. You are too valuable.'

Reiner nodded, resigned. 'I was afraid you would say that, m'lord. I have given up expecting honour from the nobility.'

Manfred stiffened. 'My position doesn't allow me honour, just as yours does not. If I am to keep the Emperor and the Empire safe, I must do what must be done.'

'And get a little of your own in as well, m'lord?' Reiner winked.

'Eh?' Manfred scowled. 'What's this impertinence?'

Reiner cleared his throat. '"It must be proved that Talabheim cannot rescue itself. And if 'evidence' could be found that the countess was behind the stone's disappearance, so much the better".'

'What did you say?' Manfred gripped the arms of his chair.

'"The Emperor wishes that Talabecland develop closer ties to the Reikland. How better than to have a Reiklander rule Talabheim? I have languished too long in the shadows. It is time to step into the sun".' Reiner shrugged. 'Forgive me, m'lord, if I have misquoted you, but I speak from memory.'

'So you *do* have the book,' said Manfred. 'Well, valuable as you are, you will die for its theft.'

'No m'lord, we will be released for its return.'

Manfred laughed. 'Blackmail? You are in no position. All your belongings are in my house. I will find the book and kill you all.'

'Fortunately,' said Reiner. 'I had the foresight to hide it outside the house before we returned here. It is in a place where your rivals will find it if we die.'

'And if I torture the location out of you?' asked Manfred.

Reiner shrugged. 'You may well, but looking for it where it is hidden may bring it unwanted scrutiny. You may lose it even as you retrieve it.'

'What have you done, you blackheart?'

'Merely taken precautions, m'lord, as one blackheart must when dealing with another.'

Manfred fumed silently. He looked like he wished to strangle Reiner where he sat.

'All you need do, m'lord,' said Reiner, 'is remove our poison and the book will be returned. I have no wish to destroy you, nor stand in the way of your ambitions. We only want you to honour your promise. We only want our freedom.'

Manfred glared at him, then chuckled. 'I think I am fortunate that you seem to have no ambitions of your own. Very well, Hetsau, the poison will be removed. I will speak to Magus Handfort in the morning. But know this,' he added. 'If you think to trick me on this. If you haven't the book, or you do not mean to return it, your freedom will be very short indeed.'

'Of course, m'lord.' Reiner stood and walked out.

MAGUS HANDFORT'S EXTRACTION of the poison was the most painful thing Reiner had ever endured, more excruciating even than reaching for Valaris's necklace. Indeed, at times Reiner wondered if Manfred had betrayed them after all, for it felt as if his blood were burning through his veins and his kidneys ached as if they had been battered with clubs. But at last it was over and the Blackhearts were returned, barely conscious, to Manfred's carriages.

'Now,' said the count, as he signalled his driver to return them to his townhouse. 'Where is the book?'

Reiner felt in no condition to carry on a conversation. He could barely open his eyes. 'Not yet, m'lord.'

'What! You promised me!' Manfred kicked Reiner in the leg. 'Wake up, curse you! I have done as you asked. Where is the book?'

Reiner flinched. His entire body felt as tender as a raw wound. 'I said I would give you the book when the poison was removed,' said Reiner. 'But is it? You may have tricked us.'

'Are you mad?' Manfred cried. 'Do you think I would go to such lengths to fool you?'

'I have read your journal, m'lord,' said Reiner. 'You have gone further to gain less. I want proof.'

'And what proof can I give you? Do you want me to swear by Sigmar? Do you want Magus Handfort to take an oath.'

'I want Lord Teclis to examine us,' said Reiner.

'Dog!' said Manfred. 'You cannot disturb so great a person for so paltry a reason. I refuse!'

Reiner shrugged. 'Then kill us and be prepared to hang when the book is found.'

Manfred glared at him, then with a vicious curse rapped on the ceiling of the coach. 'Kluger, turn about. Take us to Lord Teclis's residence.'

'AND HOW DID this poisoning occur?' asked Teclis. The high elf lay propped up in bed, in a white, sunlit room in the house Karl Franz had provided for him in Altdorf. He was still weak, but looked better than when Reiner had packed his trunks.

'It was the dark elf, m'lord,' said Reiner, smirking at Manfred. They sat at the mage's side while the Blackhearts stood uncomfortably at the door. 'He used it to force us to do his bidding.' Reiner pulled open his shirt, revealing Valaris's knife-work, still pink and raw. 'He said that with this he would know if we betrayed him, and would poison us from afar. He promised to provide an antidote when we brought him the stone, but he lied.'

'My magus, Handfort, attempted to remove the poison,' said Manfred. 'But such is my love for my men that I came to ask if you might confirm it.'

Teclis ignored him, looking at Reiner's scars. 'I am sorry I am too weak at the moment to remove it. Perhaps another day. Your arm.'

Reiner held out his arm. The elf took it and made a circular motion over it with his left hand. Reiner tensed, but there was no pain.

After a moment, Teclis looked up. 'There is no poison here. Bring the others.'

One by one the Blackhearts approached Teclis and offered their arms. At last he lay back, drained. 'They are free of poison.'

Manfred looked at Reiner. 'Are you satisfied?'

'Thank you, m'lord. I am.'

Manfred stood. 'Then take me to the book.'

'A moment, m'lord.' He turned to Teclis. 'Lord Teclis, your pardon.'

Manfred put a hand to his dagger, afraid of some treachery.

Teclis opened his eyes. 'I am tired, man. What is it?'

Reiner bowed. 'Forgive me, lord, but when I saw to your luggage in Talabheim, I inadvertently packed one of Lord Manfred's books among yours. May I retrieve it?'

'Of course,' said Teclis, closing his eyes. 'Then leave me, please.'

Reiner turned to Teclis's bookshelves. Two stacks of books, still tied with twine, sat before them. Reiner cut the twine from one and removed a slim, leather-bound volume.

'Here you are, m'lord.' He handed it to Manfred, who gaped like a fish.

'But... But, it might have been found. It...'

'It might have, m'lord. But it wasn't. Shall we go?'

WALKING OUT OF a door is an everyday act, but when he walked out of Manfred's front door with Franka, Pavel, Hals, Jergen, Augustus and Dieter, it felt to Reiner a greater occasion than the coronation of a new emperor. He had been trying to walk out of that door for more than a year. His heart pounded like a drum. He wanted to leap for joy. He inhaled the smell of Altdorf, of cooking fires and piss, of rotting vegetation, cheap scent and sausages, and thought he had never smelled a more intoxicating perfume in all his life. He grinned from ear to ear. They had no minder. They had no mission. They had no leash. They were free. They could go where they pleased. And Reiner knew exactly where that was.

'To the Griffin, lads! And the drinks are on me!'

The others cheered. Even Jergen smiled. They turned down the cobbled street, their packs over their shoulders and an unaccustomed swing in their step.

Half an hour later they were tucked into a corner table by the fireplace under the Griffin's smoke blackened beams. There were mugs of beer in their hands and a crispy brown goose lay on a platter before them.

Pavel raised his mug. 'A toast!' he said, but Reiner waved his hands.

'Wait!' he said. 'There is one last thing we must do.'

The others watched as he reached into his pouch and pulled out the rolled length of leather. He unrolled it and removed the phylactery with his name on it, then handed each of the others theirs. 'I am certain Teclis did not lie,' he said. 'All the same, I'd like to be sure.'

He turned to the fire, and though he knew there was no risk, it still took a fair amount of courage to throw the vial into the flames. There was a pop and a hiss, and then, nothing. Reiner let out a sigh. The others did too, then one by one, they solemnly threw their vials into the fire.

'Now the toast, pikeman!' said Reiner.

Pavel grinned and stood. 'There ain't no toast better than what our mumchance brother once gave,' he said, nodding to Jergen. He raised his mug. 'To freedom!'

'To freedom!' The others cried as one, then downed their mugs in a single long draught.

'Barkeep!' roared Hals over their heads. 'Y'better bring the keg! We've been working up this thirst for a year!'

A FEW HOURS later, when Pavel and Hals and Augustus had reached the stage where they were singing marching songs and challenging everyone in the tavern to arm-wrestle, Reiner whispered in Franka's ear. 'We have unfinished business. Will you join me upstairs?'

Franka gave him a shy look, then nodded.

They slipped away during the seventh chorus of 'The Pikeman's Shaft.'

'WELL,' SAID REINER as he closed the door of the small, plain room and faced Franka awkwardly. 'You asked me to ask you if you forgave me once we had returned to Altdorf and drank to Talabheim's memory. And, well, I'm certain we did that a few times just now, so...' He coughed. 'Do you forgive me for not trusting you?'

Franka looked at her boots. 'Do you forgive me for not trusting *you*?'

Reiner frowned. 'It added a nice bit of drama when you tried to stop Dieter killing Augustus, but it did hurt to think you didn't know me well enough to see it was a trick.'

'Well, good,' said Franka, sticking her chin out. 'Now you know how it felt.'

'Aye, aye, tit for tat,' he said. 'But did you truly believe I had turned murderer? Could you really think that of me?'

Franka looked at him, eyes glinting. 'In my heart I knew you were not, but...'

Reiner laughed. 'But only in your heart!' She had turned his own words against him. 'You, lass, are much too clever for your own good. It is one of the reasons that I...' He faltered as he realised what he was going to say. He had said the words many times when he didn't mean them, why were they so hard to say now? 'That I... I....'

Franka put a finger to his lips. 'Shhh. You don't have to say it.' She smirked up at him. 'I trust you.'

Reiner's throat closed up. His eyes glistened. 'Damn you, girl!'

He crushed her to him. They kissed. And this time there was no breaking away.

Reiner and Franka stumbled down to the Griffin's common room very late the next morning, for though they had awoken hungry, they had also been so delighted with their newfound freedom that they'd had to partake of it all over again. The others were already there, clutching their heads and trying to eat their eggs and trout as quietly as possible.

'Morning,' said Reiner cheerily.

Hals glared up at him. 'You two look very pleased with yerselves.'

'We're certainly very pleased with each other,' said Reiner.

Franka elbowed him in the ribs, blushing furiously, as the landlord brought more plates. They tucked in, and Reiner looked at Franka as if for the first time. He smiled. I will be having breakfast with this beauty for the rest of my life, he thought. But then he began to wonder what that life would be like. What would they do? How were they to support themselves? Reiner was a gambler by trade. Would Franka stand for that? For the late hours? The life of cheating rubes? He supposed he could take her back home to his father and become a gentleman farmer. But he had run from that life as fast as he could. Altdorf was his home. The question was, could he make it hers as well?

It seemed the others were having similar thoughts.

'Wonder if me dad's farm's still there.' Hals said. 'And Breka, who lived toward Ferlangen. Fine girl, Breka.'

'Weren't much there when we went through last year,' said Pavel glumly. 'Our people all dead most likely. Could go up and start again, I suppose.'

Hals frowned. 'Lot of work, that.'

'The Talabheim I knew is gone,' said Augustus. 'And they'd lock me up again if I went back to my company.'

'And ye, swordsman?' asked Hals looking up at Jergen. 'Y'have a girl somewhere? A farm?'

Jergen stared at his plate. 'I... cannot go home.'

There was an awkward silence, then Dieter stood.

'I can,' he said. 'And I will.' He wiped his mouth. 'My old digs ain't a stone's throw from here, and the watch thinks I'm dead. Time I pay them what sold me out a visit.' He picked up his pack and made a smirking bow. 'A pleasure making yer acquaintances, I'm sure, but I'm for home.' And with that he walked out.

The Blackhearts watched him go, then returned to their food.

'Wish I was certain as that fellow,' said Pavel.

'Aye,' said Augustus. 'Nice to know what ye want.'

Franka and Reiner looked at each other uneasily. Reiner could see that some of the things he had been worrying about were occurring to her too.

He grunted annoyed. 'There's a whole world out there,' he said. 'Surely we can all find something to do.'

But at the moment he couldn't think of anything, and apparently neither could the others, for they just carried on eating in silence.

At last Hals snorted. 'Maybe Manfred is hiring.'

The others laughed. Reiner nearly spat trout across the table. Then the laughter died away and they all fell silent again.

Nathan Long was a struggling screenwriter for fifteen years, during which time he had three movies made and a handful of live-action and animated TV episodes produced. Now he is a novelist, and is enjoying it much more. For Black Library he has written three Warhammer novels featuring the Blackhearts, and has taken over the Gotrek and Felix series, starting with the eighth installment, *Orcslayer*. He lives in Hollywood.